The LION and the JACKAL

W. T. Tyler

THE LINDEN PRESS ▪ SIMON AND SCHUSTER

New York   London   Toronto   Sydney   Tokyo

Copyright © 1988 by W. T. Tyler
All rights reserved
including the right of reproduction
in whole or in part in any form.
Published by The Linden Press/Simon and Schuster
A Division of Simon & Schuster Inc.
Published by Simon & Schuster Inc.
Simon & Schuster Building
Rockefeller Center
1230 Avenue of the Americas
New York, NY 10020
THE LINDEN PRESS/Simon and Schuster and colophon are
registered trademarks of Simon & Schuster Inc.
Designed by Levavi & Levavi
Manufactured in the United States of America
10 9 8 7 6 5 4 3 2 1
Library of Congress Cataloging-in-Publication Data
Tyler, W. T.
    The lion and the jackal.
    I. Title.
PS3570.Y53L5   1988   813'.54   87-34254
ISBN 0-671-64003-8

The lyrics to "Goin' Back" by Neil Young
© 1978 Silver Fiddle .
Used by permission. All rights reserved.

THE LION AND THE JACKAL

CHAPTER ONE

The Bush Soldier

Logan Talbot spent the last days before his return to Africa visiting Eric and Grace Bowser in Manhattan. Eric, his old Princeton roommate, was now an investment banker. His green-eyed wife Grace was a psychiatrist. Both were in their early thirties, a year older than Talbot, but he wouldn't have known that from their eighth-floor apartment overlooking Central Park West. Their success was everywhere visible: the gilded Louis XVI fauteuils in the guest room, the rose du Barry damask on the library walls, the faux marble cornices, moldings, and pediments in the salon; his had dropped into obscurity since he'd left Europe for the African camel shag. He no longer got Christmas cards or unexpected letters from old friends and forgotten classmates, asking about car rentals, boat trips up the Rhine, and quiet little pensions for their upcoming spring or summer holidays in Rome, Germany, or the Low Countries, when they hoped to buy him a drink, maybe even drop in for bed and breakfast afterwards if that was convenient.

In New York again after those years abroad, he felt very much the odd man out. Walking along Fifth Avenue on a gusty March day with Grace Bowser settled comfortably on his arm—her admonitory green eyes had troubled him at first, but after three days he'd relaxed; she and Eric were very much satisfied with their lives and he envied them—he discovered his suits and ties were eccentrically out of fashion, his shirt collars a little threadbare. Skiing at Stowe or visiting his parents in Wilmington, he hadn't noticed his obsolescence so much. Grace didn't agree. She said he looked stylishly unfashionable, even intriguing, the look Manhattanites so identical in every way tried to buy but couldn't; his was genuine, honestly earned. He took it as a compliment but even so thought he should do a little shopping those last days. He never got around to it. He didn't get his hair cut either but did manage to have his squash racquet restrung.

The Bowsers gave a small dinner the night before his departure. No one among the guests quite knew where Jubba was and had never heard of Benaadir, its capital: a Trucial State on the Arabian Peninsula, a sultanate in the Persian Gulf, an Indian Ocean archipelago?

"A nasty little state of mind," he might have said but didn't, looking suavely up to date in his host's borrowed dinner jacket. The wife of a Manhattan banker who lived in Westchester, privy only to enough of the conversation to learn that Talbot was with the State Department, brought her chair close to his near the library's *faux bois* fireplace he was admiring and inquired sweetly about life in Albany these days.

So much for Chase Manhattan's debt-chasing dollar merchants and the Third World.

It was snowing in New York the night he left Kennedy. A cold rain was falling in London during his day there. He tramped about most of the afternoon, despite the rain, trying to walk himself into a stupor before his late-evening departure from Heathrow. He visited the Tate, picked up the shirts he had ordered, bought some paintbrushes for Ambassador Harcourt, three tins of tennis balls for Julia Harcourt, and spent the last hours of the dimming winter afternoon in a large bookstore on Oxford Street. In a dusty corner

on the third floor he found a book on nomadic pastoralism in East
Africa recommended by his friend Dr. George Greevy, the British
parasitologist. He should have read it two years ago, when he
made this same trek, but he bought it now, together with a secondhand copy of Sir Richard Burton's *First Footsteps in East Africa*.

His plane left Heathrow a little after nine. He arrived early and
had a few Double Diamond pints, hoping they'd help him sleep.
They didn't. He sat up instead reading Dr. Greevy's introduction
to nomadic pastoralism. Bored senseless, he finally dropped it aside
and browsed instead through Burckhardt's selected letters. The
book was from his undergraduate library, forgotten for over ten
years. Grace Bowser had discovered it on her own bookshelves
while packing to move into their new apartment and had found his
youthful signature on the inside cover.

In it he found vaguely familiar sentences, phrases, even entire
paragraphs; fragments from his past, vaults from a buried Troy, the
unexcavated Talbot. Had he written all those cryptic comments in
the margin? His handwriting was an affected undergraduate scrawl.
For a few hours, rereading the book, he had the uneasy feeling
every word he'd written in the past ten years was copied from a
State Department correspondence crib.

Beyond the window a rose and purple dawn was beginning to
dissolve the star-filled night sky as it lifted from the wasteland between Cairo and Khartoum. As the light slowly percolated through
the cabin, he watched the dun-colored wasteland below and consoled himself by remembering Eric Bowser had inherited a little
money from an aunt in Rochester as an undergraduate, when he'd
begun reading the *Wall Street Journal* and accumulating a penny-
stock portfolio. The investment world had never interested Talbot,
who'd accumulated secondhand books at the Firestone Library's
withdrawal sales instead. He'd intended to go on to graduate school
in European history but was drawn into the diplomatic service by
some quixotic notion, inspired by the Kennedy years, that men of
action more than men of reflection shaped the history of their times.
He had thought, foolishly enough at the time, that he might be
among them.

He arrived in Nairobi too late to find a hotel for a few hours'
sleep and too early for his ongoing flight, scheduled for an eleven

o'clock departure. He spent two hours in the terminal and was lucky he did. His flight had been overbooked. At the check-in counter he found himself elbowed about by a flotsam of nationalities before he stubbornly anchored his place in the queue. There were Arab traders from the Gulf who looked Persian en route to Sanaa, a North Korean delegation in dark blue tunics, a half-dozen Cubans, a sleepy-eyed little South Yemen vice president with a Zouave beard returning to Aden, a blind mullah in a white robe led by a small woman in chador, and the usual cargo of blustering African and Arab businessmen.

He checked his luggage through, was assigned a seat, and moved on to the departure lounge. Looking up a few minutes later, he caught sight of a familiar face across the crowded lounge and recognized Pete Ryan, the Nairobi-based journalist who'd stayed with him during the Muzaffar missile imbroglio. He was about to leave his seat and say hello when Ryan disappeared into the crowd at the heels of an airline hostess. A Lufthansa flight to Johannesburg was waiting on the tarmac and he supposed Ryan had come in the wrong gate.

Fifteen minutes later Talbot's flight was called. As he made his way out across the tarmac, he was surprised to see Ryan ahead of him, red-faced, arguing angrily with a steward at the foot of the steps.

Talbot called out; Ryan turned.

"Logan, for Christ's sake."

"What's happening?"

"The bastards said I could get an airport visa, now they've reneged. What the hell are you doing here?"

"On my way back."

Ryan followed along the tarmac as Talbot climbed the stairs, moved along by an impatient stewardess. "You're kidding. On your way back?"

"Afraid so. I'll tell you about it."

"Can you do something about my visa?"

"I'll try."

"Talk to the foreign ministry. Then send me a cable."

Talbot waved and disappeared inside.

Every seat on the 727 was occupied. The plane was twenty min-

utes late taking off and unbearably hot. Only after they were twenty
minutes airborne did a cool scented breeze begin to circulate
through the cabin.

His seat companion was an emaciated Asian who smoked constantly during the flight. One of those tubercular little refugees
from the international underclass, Talbot supposed, conscious of
his bitter Gitanes or Gauloises, sent from the bidonvilles of Paris
to recruit revolutionaries in the African scrub. From the badly
printed newspaper he was reading he guessed he was Cambodian.
Not until he'd seen his embarkation card did he realize the little
bastard was from Hanoi.

Across the aisle sat a dapper Brazilian World Bank official in a
black shantung suit with his nose buried in a German skin magazine.
It would be confiscated at customs, where the officials would give
him a long and humiliating harangue on the evils of Western por
nography. If the Brazilian hadn't been so preoccupied, Talbot
might have warned him.

They were over the coast, banking out over the Indian Ocean
as they began their approach.

Watching the sprawling seaside capital swim into view, bone-
white in the midday sun, he remembered his arrival two years
earlier. When he'd first learned he'd been proposed for assignment
to the obscure little capital on the littoral below, he'd telephoned
his career counselor in personnel to protest. His ambition had
nothing to do with chivalric service in Africa or the Third World.
For him, Europe was the heart and soul of the diplomatic service;
it had never occurred to him there might be another. What he knew
of those more remote places had been learned from his European
colleagues in Bonn, Rome, and The Hague who'd served in the
antipodes and had told him their outrageous stories. He'd been
amused but never tempted. None of his European colleagues believed themselves improved by their experiences in the hinterlands;
most resented the time wasted.

Over the next week his counselor in personnel pointed out the
advantages of the assignment. If the European bureau was the
heart and soul of the career service, the apprenticeship was longer,
the layers of officialdom denser, and opportunities for individual
distinction or heroism rare. How often had a European embassy

or consulate been sacked by local street mobs chanting "Ya Arafat!" or "Death to American-Zionist imperialism!" So were the hazards of bureaucratic oblivion. At thirty he couldn't hope for a European posting of similar responsibility for another four or five years. In Paris, the assignment he'd been dickering for, he would be another second secretary in the political section. East Africa promised something more. The massive Soviet presence had transformed the small somnolent backwater nation on the Indian Ocean littoral into a sinister challenge to U.S. and European security interests.

"A virtual Soviet satellite," the middle-aged INR and DIA analysts insisted as they proudly showed him their satellite imagery of Soviet missile deployments at Muzaffar and Benaadir, some of which had been in the CIA's daily brief for the president that week.

In addition there was the title. The position carried with it the rank of counselor for political affairs.

So in the tradition of those restless young subalterns who escaped their duties as aides-de-camp or staff officers in the basements of Whitehall or the war office to earn their reputations in the Ha'jaz, the Hindu Kush, or the Transvaal, he'd stupidly agreed.

What he didn't expect was the ugly paranoia of the host government, the parching isolation of the post, and the mediocrity of its staff, bureaucratic dotards flung up on this remote shore by the tides of career misfortune, clownish facsimiles of the diplomats he'd known in Europe. It amounted to a betrayal of sorts—a kind of Botany Bay, he'd decided following his first country team meeting after listening to thirty-five minutes of debate about the equity of the diplomatic liquor ration and whether the fox terrier belonging to the embassy nurse should be permitted in the compound pool area. What surprised him was that he would come to dislike it so quickly.

He'd survived disappointment before. His first overseas posting to Rome as vice consul was just as depressing. While his peers were burning draft cards, laying siege to the Pentagon, and in other ways frustrating White House policy, he was matching wits with wily southern Italians and Sicilians trying to evade U.S. immigration laws, or bickering with the consul general, a creaking overaged nonentity who'd blown a nose valve somewhere along the way, either drink or apoplexy, maybe both. There was nothing in the old

impostor's head except visa law and the *Foreign Affairs* hand-
book, about which they argued almost daily in Talbot's small high-
ceilinged office, shrouded in perennial Roman twilight. A man with a
proboscis like that couldn't be taken seriously, and Talbot's contempt was carelessly disguised. His Italian consular assistants
weren't much better; they knew more than he about visa regulations and often reminded him of it. His long hours in the consular
section interviewing visa applicants, examining documents, and
drafting refusal memos were as monotonous as those of a Wilmington mail sorter, a prospect his father, a Delaware corporation lawyer
with two years' experience in Washington during World War II, had
cautioned him about.

But a year after his posting, he attracted the attention of the
deputy chief of mission by his handling of the visit of two cur-
mudgeonous U.S. senators and was moved to the executive section,
responsible for the care and feeding of those troublesome American
officials and dignitaries who descended on Rome every spring and
summer. He was an equerry, nothing more, an Osric at the ambassadorial court, a role he disliked, but his career prospects improved.

He was posted to The Hague and Bonn as a political officer and
then to Brussels on the staff of the U.S. mission to NATO. The year
following he was rewarded with a year at the NATO Defense College in Rome. His dissertation, *The Politics of Bipolarity,* later appeared in a condensed version in a little security review published
at MIT.

In Jubba, however, there was no escape, not into scholarship,
not to the mountains or veld, only into a discreet affair or two. His
travel was limited to a forty-kilometer zone around the capital, his
phone was tapped, he was kept under constant surveillance. During his first six weeks he was the victim of two crude disinformation
efforts, one of which spread quickly in the Arab diplomatic community. It was said he was Jewish, a Sabra, born in Tel Aviv, a
rumor he first learned of when the Egyptian counselor questioned
him about it. He refused to deny it.

The ambassador at the time, Harcourt's predecessor, was bewildered. "You refused to deny it! My God, man, this is the Arab
world! It's not true! Of course you'll deny it. If you're to have any
kind of success with the Arab diplomats here, you'll have to deny

it." Talbot stubbornly refused. To his pleasant surprise the incident
had awakened memories of a Jewish girl from Wilmington he'd
once been in love with. Her name was Lisa Lerner. She was studying ballet in New York during his first two years at Princeton, as
troubled and uncertain of her talent as he'd been. He didn't know
what had become of her, he hadn't thought about her in ten years,
but during those first confusing weeks at the embassy she seemed
the only friend he had, his memory of her as fresh and sustaining as
it had been during those lonely Sunday night train rides back to
Princeton after a weekend at her Greenwich Village apartment, his
shirt and skin still fragrant with her mystery, his wrinkled flannels
still covered with cat hairs from her couch.

The other story was that he was a graduate of the NATO spy college in Rome, a report which surfaced repeatedly during the first
months and was more difficult to put to rest. Twice that first week
he'd received late-night telephone calls from anonymous informants
offering unspecified military information "of great interest to your
government and its NATO allies." His callers proposed to arrange a
meeting downtown; Talbot told them to come to the embassy, under
twenty-four-hour surveillance. The provocations gradually ceased.

He was also disappointed at his reception by the embassy staff.
Later, he heard the tales:

"A prig, a stuffed shirt, an EUR carpetbagger, what else?" an
embassy secretary had told a few loungers around the embassy pool
as she'd circulated photocopies of his letter to the ambassador announcing his arrival. The salutation had been in a fine stubby script
rather than typewritten, and resembled those Whitehall-style notes
received from the British ambassador, enclosing some memento on
the Horn of Africa from *The Observer* or *The Times* of London. It
was signed "T. Logan Talbot."

"What's the 'T' stand for?" someone had asked.

"Theodore," she had informed them, reconfirming those cynical
impressions that would later circulate after his arrival at the airport, looking then very much as he did now, dressed like a middle-
aged counselor of embassy in a gray pinstripe with a twin-vented
jacket, his lank blond hair sleekly combed, carrying a raincoat and
an umbrella. Sticking from his calfskin briefcase was the handle of
a new squash racquet. He might have just stepped from the door of

the New York Athletic Club, a visiting journalist from *Time* arriving on the same plane told the USIS public affairs officer, who repeated the story to the amusement of the country team the following morning while Talbot was still sleeping off jet lag in his lonely seaside villa.

The stories had rankled at first, but after a few months he ignored them. They were all silly people, he decided, but their silliness gave him a certain advantage. In a competitive career service, an advantage was something to be cultivated, not denied. Who among them wasn't an impostor?

The suit was a little thin in the seat and knees, a little baggy, too, as Grace Bowser had said, his shirt collar a little threadbare, but it was the same suit. He hadn't had his hair cut, but his squash racquet had been restrung, positioned now as it had been on that arrival day two years ago, the handle obtruding even more cavalierly from his briefcase.

□ □ □

He was the last to disembark, kept prisoner in his window seat by the crush of noisy passengers crowding the aisles even before the turbines whined to a stop. It was a little before one o'clock as he stepped from the cabin into the staggering heat of the midday sun.

The hot breeze blowing inland from the Indian Ocean east of the runway brought the tang of brine to his lips, as palpable as sea spray. The fiery heat lay on the tarmac like gases from a hearth furnace. A small protocol officer hurried through the gate reserved for dignitaries to intercept the Koreans, Cubans, and the Vietnamese and lead them back to the *salon d'honneur* in the western wing of the terminal. Two Russian couriers separated themselves from the other passengers to move toward the protocol gate, where their dragomen were waiting. Talbot followed, keeping a discreet distance behind the official delegation come to meet the South Yemen vice president. It was led by his old nemesis Dr. Mohammed Hussein, the director of protocol at the foreign ministry.

Peterson, the middle-aged embassy general services officer, was standing just inside the open gate.

"Not waiting long, I hope," Talbot said cheerfully.

"Not too long. How was home leave?" Peterson was short and plump, dressed in Nairobi suntans, the kind favored by game park guides and tourists. His balding head was hidden beneath a white golf hat with a logo from an Oklahoma City driving range. From the square chin hung a small billygoat beard, neatly trimmed, as white as combed flax. Pressed close to him by the delegation of Jubba ministers to the rear stood Abucar, the embassy customs expeditor.

"Not long enough. Hello, Abucar. Thanks for coming out. How are things at the Bug House?"

"About the same. Before I forget, the ambassador said to say he couldn't come, says he'll see you tonight. Cocktails and a buffet. The invitation's in the car."

"Cocktails and buffet, righto." A government photographer moving through the gate jostled him from behind as Talbot produced a small leather *Economist* pocket diary from his jacket and fluttered through the pages. "Sorry. What time?"

"Seven, I think, maybe seven thirty. Abucar needs your passport and ticket. Here, lemme take that."

He reached for Talbot's briefcase, the same battered briefcase that accompanied him up the embassy stairs each morning and down again each afternoon.

"Thanks, I can manage. Hold these, would you?" He handed Peterson his raincoat and umbrella. Water dripped from his chin; dark patches crept across the back of his coat. The official delegation still hadn't moved forward toward the *salon d'honneur*. As he brought out the squash racquet the wet briefcase handle slipped from his hand and the briefcase fell from between his knees and dropped to its side. A bottle of English gin slid out, followed by three clattering tins of vacuum-packed tennis balls. Three Jubba ministers in dress khaki moved back, annoyed at the commotion at their feet. The sweating ministry of information photographer brought down his camera. Talbot stood up, face dripping water, holding the tennis ball tins aloft. "Sorry, easy does it, no harm done. As you were, gentlemen." The photographer lifted his camera a second time. From over his shoulder Talbot caught sight of a pair of familiar dark eyes looking at him with loathing.

"Dip shop still out of gin, I suppose." He recovered his passport, ticket, and baggage stubs. "Still fucked up, is it?" He handed them to Abucar, who went off at a trot to the customs office.

"Got it sorted out now, I think."

Talbot took a cigarette from his worn silver case and tapped it on the lid as he watched Dr. Mohammed Hussein lead his guest into the salon. "It's the heat you forget. Crummy flight, mobbed-up from Nairobi, steerage all the way. The Hail Mary Express. Sorry." He held out the cigarette case.

Peterson declined, embarrassed. Docile, slow, and overweight, he was an ex-Navy mustang who'd joined the foreign service after retirement. Talbot made him nervous. Slim, imperious, often outrageous, never familiar but unfailingly civil, he was an enigma; nothing Talbot did ever seemed wholly credible to him.

On the steps of the protocol lounge the two Cubans were being welcomed by an army colonel, a ranking member of the Jubba revolutionary council. The Iraqi ambassador stood just behind him; the Palestinian representative and his deputy were greeting the Vietnamese.

"Why don't we wait in the shade?" Talbot moved away. "How's the wife?"

"Getting along, I expect." Peterson followed him into the shadows of the terminal steps. A few diplomats stood waiting respectfully, listening to the voices from inside. The Cubans and Vietnamese moved aside. Talbot didn't look at them. A few dust devils sprang up at the far end of the runway, the heat shimmered from an immobile 707, the smell of kerosene drifted from a nearby Aeroflot jet being readied for its seven o'clock departure for Moscow.

Peterson watched, hoping Talbot would be decently silent. In the salon behind them the Aden vice president was talking about socialist solidarity. "Lucky bastards," Talbot said, still studying the Soviet jet. "Must be thirty below in Moscow. Snowing probably. Wouldn't mind that either. Better snow than sand. How about you? Where the hell's Abucar?"

"Shhh," someone called from the shadows inside.

"Shhh what? What's that about?"

"They're having an interview," Peterson said, respectfully lowering his voice. "Radio Jubba."

Ten minutes later Abucar returned with the luggage and they climbed into the rear of the embassy's white carryall.

A few years earlier the ministry of information had erected a series of brightly painted signs on the road from the airport and at strategic locations about the capital. At the time, the Jubba and Arabic legends were indecipherable to Talbot, but their meaning was crudely apparent. In the first a weasel-faced red-white-and-blue-suited Uncle Sam with dollar signs on his stovepipe hat led a group of manacled African and Asian prisoners through a dense tropical landscape. In the second the prisoners had become combatants; in the last a bloodied and maimed Uncle Sam was being led away on hands and knees by a group of victorious green-clad guerrillas bearing the banners of national liberation. During that first drive from the airport two years earlier, Talbot had studied the signs with a fresh and angry eye.

Jubba was one of those impoverished little Third World nations ignored by journalists, diplomatists, and strategists alike until the Soviet Union favored it with its patronage. As Soviet influence increased and Soviet ships, submarines, and aircraft freely used Jubba's facilities on the Indian Ocean, those who'd once dismissed it as a nasty, ill-bred little pauper nation of nomads and camel ports wakened to the menace. Although the national revolutionary council had declared it a Marxist state, in the privacy of its houses, tea shops, gardens, tents, and mosques, it remained a deeply Moslem nation, dominated by centuries-old pastoral and clan traditions. All of this made for a certain schizophrenia in its national life.

Now as he gazed out the window he hardly noticed the signs at all. They were still there, but their colors had faded; some were torn in places; others marked by obscure graffiti, including "Russians Go Home!" also in Jubba, but in a ball-point script too small to be seen by passing Western or Soviet diplomats in speeding vehicles. Talbot's houseboy had once proudly shown him the graffiti by flashlight late at night. The signs no longer seemed stupidly malign but as pathetic as the landscape along the highway. The tarmac was drifted over with sand. Rusty flattened tins and shreds of truck tires lay along the verges. Amid the dunes and scrub stood the rubble of a few private villas begun years earlier before the revolution by local entrepreneurs but still incomplete, their owners in exile in Saudi Arabia or the Persian Gulf. On a hilltop overlooking the road stood the skeleton of the North Korean technical training school whose walls had been erected three years earlier and was still without a roof.

They turned onto the main road toward the capital. Two dark-skinned Abgal nomads up from the south led a pair of creamy-colored young camels along the verges. Heavy Mercedes trucks rumbled by carrying rock fill for the new port. As they jarred over the potholes, a few stones would sometimes tumble free and go bouncing homicidally along the tarmac. Clouds of dust enveloped the carryall as they roared by; a hail of rubble pelted the roof.

They passed into the narrow downtown streets lined with white-washed buildings and shaded by dusty laurel trees. Talbot cranked down the window. A blue bus carrying Russian women back to the sprawling Soviet compound west of the city blocked the turnabout near the mosque, waiting for a donkey-drawn sand cart to move out of the way. A half-dozen small cars and red-and-yellow Fiat taxis sounded their horns.

He lowered his head as they approached the embassy. Located on a narrow crowded street near the port and painted an anemic yellow, it was neither dignified nor imposing, but appropriately subversive, like one of those derelict transient hotels one saw in the slums of Brussels or Antwerp but never had reason to enter. The paint was scaling, the discolored shutters were drawn tightly closed. The only suggestions of a diplomatic presence were the two polished brass plaques flanking the door. Harcourt's official black Chrysler was usually drawn up between the carts, trucks, and small European cars at the curb in front of the door, but was gone at this hour. The embassy closed each day at two. Ambassador Harcourt left at one.

Peterson asked if he wanted to stop.

Talbot said he'd been awake for thirty-six hours. They drove on.

His isolated whitewashed villa with its Moorish arches and orange-tiled roof faced the sea from the far end of the corniche where the tarmac left off and the sand dunes began. Across the macadam road lay the deep white sand beach. The crippled surf stirred listlessly at low tide, broken only by the plash of an erratic wave. The inlet be-

yond was as calm as green glass under the blazing sun, the beach
deserted now in the afternoon heat. To the north of the villa, the
desolation of dunes and rock cliffs began its thousand-mile ascent
toward the Gulf of Aden and the Arabian Peninsula. Behind the
villa to the west lay a rim of broken hills that led into a wasteland
of scrub so harsh and forbidding the frontiers were unmarked, boundaries voided by dust, wind, and hellish heat, crossed only by the pastoral nomads in search of seasonal pasture.

The front courtyard within the low wall was of coarse sand mixed
with oyster shell, tufted with clumps of dune grass. A few scabrous
palm trees and low palmettos grew along the drive. Near the terrace
steps was an iron flagpole, oxidized by the salt air, from which an
American flag stirred listlessly, its stripes gone gray in abandon-
ment, rattling its lanyard tackle against the pole in forlorn tattoo,
mustering the wind-scattered bones of forgotten outposts and pa-
rade grounds in final recall.

Talbot heard it as he climbed out stiffly, pulling off his tie. Two
hundred yards offshore lay the glistening black bone of reef, like a
line of beached whales, where the combers of the Indian Ocean
smashed and thundered in mountainous solitude, the spray lifted to
a sheen of iridescence by the monsoon wind. He stood looking out
to sea, feeling the sweat on his face and back and hearing the desolate
wind-knocked rattle from the flagpole: *Fort Apache, for Christ's
sake.* In the vast swarming heat of the littoral, brain and body seemed
vaporized in a dim, prickly haze.

He was truly back, no escaping that, returned not so much to a
country but a fever, a boiling mirage conjured up by the white-hot
sun and swirling wind from prisms of dust, splintered sea, brine,
dung, sweat, and thorn. Every memory of the past six weeks seemed
only a shimmering facet from the same delirium.

"Nothing much has changed," Peterson said, doggedly climbing
the steps to the small front terrace. His khaki shirt was dark with
perspiration. He pulled his keys from his trouser pocket, looking
back at his driver. "Bring those bags, will you, Abdul Rahman.
Don't know where the servants are. I thought they'd be here."

"Maybe out back." Talbot stopped on the steps to look again at
the discolored American flag hanging limply from the flagstaff.
"What in Christ's name is that flag doing there?"

Peterson saw it, too. "God almighty, she'll have a conniption if she sees it. Pull it down, will you, Abdul." The driver put the bags down on the walk, turned, and called to Mohammed, the day gate guard, who'd raised the flag on Talbot's behalf and stood in his wrinkled khakis watching proudly from the other side of the car. Just six months employed by the embassy and recently elevated from night guard to day guard, he hadn't yet mastered the details of embassy protocol: with the ambassador in residence only his pole might fly the American flag. His ambition was to learn to drive a car and become an embassy driver, after which he would go to Saudi Arabia and find work as a taxi or truck driver at five times his local wages.

"Welcoming me back. Thanks, Mohammed, good show."

"These people got a mind of their own," Peterson said, "worse than any I've ever seen, and I was three years in Lagos."

The villa had been leased for the embassy's deputy chief of mission, but the wife of the former DCM had found it too isolated and it was assigned to Talbot, the embassy political officer. Closed during his six weeks' home leave, it was warm and airless and smelled musty. No one had turned on the air conditioners. The electrician Peterson had sent out two hours earlier hadn't arrived. Sunlight lay on the tile floor and in scattered fragments on the squares of yellow and beige rug. The large high-ceilinged rooms were coldly formal, institutionally furnished with government armchairs, sofas, tables, and lamps. Except for a few watermarks on the coffee tables and depressions on the rugs, there was little sign of his residency in the downstairs rooms. The few pictures on the walls were unremarkable reproductions of familiar African landscapes. Talbot had forgotten how uninteresting they were. Seeing them again, he decided they looked like the sepia wall photographs from some travel agency or airline office. The time had come to do something about that, too.

On the kitchen table stood a few canned goods, soft drinks, and mixers, including bottles of gin and whiskey, sent by Julia Harcourt from her own larder until he could reprovision himself.

"D-Day all over again." He opened the refrigerator. "Why don't we launch a few? Heineken or Amstel?"

But the refrigerator shelves were empty except for a water bottle and a discolored head of lettuce.

"What happened to my beer? I left a month's ration."

"Well, six weeks is a long time, I'd say. Could be the houseboy, maybe."

They went upstairs and along the tiled corridor that traveled the length of the second floor. To the west the corridor was enclosed by a scrolled concrete block sunscreen that looked down on the rear courtyard. The beds were stripped except for the master bedroom. Lined up on the marble sill of the bank of windows facing the sea were six empty gin and vodka bottles.

"Where'd they come from?" Talbot took off his shoes and pants.

"Probably the technical crew that was here, the one Whittington had sweep the house. Musta left them for water bottles." He stooped to turn on the air conditioner.

"Looking for bugs? You mean they stayed here?"

"A couple of days."

"The bastards drank my beer."

On the windowsill was the quasar telescope for spying on the dhows and ships marching along the horizon. When a Soviet vessel steamed into view, he would record the name on the fantail, the date, and the time and send the information to Washington and the Fleet Ocean Surveillance Center, which had supplied the telescope and a similar one on the roof of the embassy. A commendation from the commander in chief, Atlantic Fleet, hung out of sight in the commo room.

He sat down on the bed and took off his socks and garters.

"I'll call the compound," Peterson said, "see what happened to the electrician."

Talbot rejoined him downstairs, wearing boxer underwear shorts, a T-shirt, and shower thongs, and carrying a towel. He inspected his record collection on the bookshelves; the jackets were a little musty, damp to the touch.

"You're right, nothing much has changed," he said as they returned to the drive.

"Never does," Peterson said, looking out over the low wall toward the open sea. "I've got eight months left, and I tell you, my wife's climbing the walls already."

"I thought you were thinking about extending your tour. Didn't the ambassador talk to you about that?"

"Only reason he did was because they didn't have anyone else standing in line. Can't get anyone, that's why. Been here as long as I have, you'd know why. I don't much like living in a walled-up compound."

"It's time to find a house for you."

"Think she'd live in the city, all the surveillance they've got around here? Anyway, something happens, she wants to be near the airport, where she can get out fast. She's got quick feet. Fact is these folks don't want us here, same as the Russians don't, and it's gonna get worse before it gets better."

"I thought she'd be used to it. How's the new squash court coming?"

Peterson's eyes avoided his, lifted again toward the open sea. To the south beyond the billowing spray of the reef, a Soviet trawler and oiler rode at anchor in the roads beyond the breakwater, their rocking superstructures gilded by the afternoon sun above the broken dunes to the west.

"It's not. Had to move the money back to where it belonged. No budget for it."

"I thought you worked all that out."

"Not now I didn't. It's all been changed."

"Who changed it?"

"We got some new people. I guess you know about that."

"So I heard. DeGroot, you mean. What kind of guy is he?"

"I'm not the one to say." Peterson studied his keyring, self-consciously sorting among the keys. "Don't get around the way I used to. Don't forget, seven o'clock. She doesn't like to be kept waiting any more than she used to."

"Is that what she told you?"

"That's what she said when she gave me the invitation, plain as day."

"What's the burr under her saddle these days, anything new?"

"Your guess is as good as mine, I reckon."

Peterson climbed into the carryall, and the driver backed out onto the corniche. Talbot followed, standing just outside the gate in his underwear, searching the road for the small security agent on his blue Vespa who shadowed him about the city. He couldn't find him. Instead a small black Fiat was parked up the beach road twenty meters beyond his own gate. Two men sat in the car. He supposed it was a surveillance car from the Soviet-trained Jubba national security service. Once a Vespa, now a Fiat; he'd moved up a notch or two.

□ □ □

Julia Harcourt sat opposite her husband at the glass-topped table on the outside terrace reading her letter. She hadn't spoken a word since they'd begun lunch. He watched the secretive moons of smoked glass for some hint of her mood. Failing, he moved his luncheon plate aside and sat back.

The African sun lay like salt on the city, parching the color from the orange pantiled roofs and the laurel and palm trees along the corniche. To the west the midday heat shimmered above the scorched tin of the squatters' hovels encroaching on their hilltop. At her back the horizon paled like smoke, blurred and indistinct, as if storm clouds were gathering, pregnant with rain that would never reach the coast. To the south in the shade of the old stone wall below the mosque, a few nomads were sprawled like dogs next to their staffs and milk jugs. A few cars carrying Europeans, white-faced and anguished, were rushing toward the beach clubs, the back seats filled with squalling children. The slim dark faces watching from the verges would be cool and inscrutable.

Odd how a white skin declared its ugliness here. Like mummies, like shriveled corpses, some of the oldest Italians, pickled in the brine of their own corruption; the tithe of colonialism, he supposed—the sweat, blood, and tears of the downtrodden. Here on the terrace there was only silence, broken by the sleepy rustle of the wind through the overhanging boughs.

Were this Lebanon, the Lebanon he remembered from so long ago, not the bloody Lebanon of the morning BBC, on the high mountains to the north a few cusps of snow would lie along the highest peaks. Here, in the distance the Indian Ocean was a vast indigo plain, broken by whitecaps. He stared toward the horizon, perplexed.

Winter in such a season. *Was it a dream? Was it possible?*

He heard the sound of a plane. Far at sea a silver speck hovered, then droned into full silhouette as it veered back toward the coast. It was the weekly Alitalia 707 flight from Rome, Khartoum, and Addis Ababa.

"It's late," he said, rousing himself. "Logan's plane was late, too. Did you hear it? That's one thing, anyway."

"What is?" She didn't look up from the letter. The shadows of the bougainvillaea drifted over her tan shoulders and arms.

"Logan's coming back."

She lifted her head. "You said last night you were going to the airport to meet him."

"I decided not to. The Adeni vice president was coming on the same plane and DeGroot thought it wouldn't be wise."

"What does that have to do with meeting Logan?"

"We don't have diplomatic relations. My presence might have been misconstrued."

"Really? How?"

"We might have had to shake hands." He lifted his wineglass. Lunch had begun with a bottle of pouilly-fuissé, as cold as a mountain brook. Now he was surprised to find the bottle nearly empty. Julia's glass was barely touched. She was still gazing at him.

"Is he a leper? How very stupid."

"It might have been embarrassing."

"It's still stupid. Did DeGroot tell you that?"

"It isn't stupid at all. What he said made sense. Last night I hadn't known the Adeni vice president would be on the plane. I told DeGroot to go."

"Why do you listen to that awful man?"

DeGroot was the newly arrived deputy chief of mission, a preposterous man, he and his wife both, their constant companion a white poodle with limpid black eyes and a red velvet ribbon about its neck who sat up front with the chauffeur during her shopping tours. Named, too, after a character from *The Mikado.* Nothing she did wasn't vulgarly predictable. In the new foreign service, not the one he was born into, one was expected to solve personnel problems *en place,* not pack them up and ship them back to Washington like corked vintage or sea-spoiled draperies.

"With Logan back, we'll soon be back to full staff," he said. "We're also getting a new Agency person, someone named Wingate. I've no idea where he's coming from."

In the light winds a red-sailed coastal dhow plowed a meandering white line against the blue of the outer harbor. Beneath the gray deck awning a few figures stirred, pushing baskets and trunks onto the promenade deck, oblivious of the parching heat and the wretched fecal smells of the Arab harbor.

He'd made a trip by coastal steamer once, to Trabzon, when he'd been a young vice consul in Istanbul.

"Apparently he's coming by ship, which is rather odd," he said sleepily, head still turned away.

"Who's that?"

"Wingate. Next week some time. A direct transfer."

"Who is Wingate?"

"I just told you, Whittington's new man."

"His name is Wingate?"

"Wingate, yes."

"Not another shanty Irishman, I hope." She took a sip of wine.

"Shanty Irishman?"

"Shaughnessy, of course." She sank back again with her letter.

Her thoughts often eluded him, betrayed in judgments as cruel as this one. He lit a cigarette and looked around for Kasim, waiting for coffee. She'd had a tennis match that morning at the court in the UN compound below the villa, but Herr Bochman, the German cultural counselor, had failed to appear. She'd waited fifteen minutes and then left. Poor Bochman. Julia was always slow to forgive. Probably he'd misunderstood. He didn't care much for Bochman, although Lord knows he'd tried, but then Julia's German was better than his. Maybe that was the difference; speaking a foreign language had its civilizing effect, he supposed. In that case maybe he should learn Arabic. He doubted either would help. What was it someone had said about Arabic? That it was a language incapable of dealing with the modern political world?

Politely, he'd agreed. It was Firthdale who said it, the British ambassador; he had absolutely no idea what he was talking about. He'd meant to ask Talbot.

His eyes found the familiar broken stonework on the crest of the hill below them, and he puzzled over it again. Had it been a house, a signal tower? Not a mosque, certainly. Did its mound hide a ruin beneath? Archeology had always interested him. He had gotten his first taste of it in Damascus, where his father was consul general. He might have made it his career. To the south one occasionally came upon a rubble of stones among the acacia trees of the wasteland, as forlorn as the twelfth-century Byzantine churches he remembered from Turkey or the ruins of the Armenian churches north of Trabzon. Here no one knew what they were, no one cared.

She finished her letter and refolded it in its vellum envelope. "Eleanor and Leonard Bryson are going to Madrid," she said, reaching for her wineglass. "He'll be counselor for economic affairs."

So that was it. *"Tiens,"* he said, feeling the shame of envy, as bitter as hemlock. He was fifty-eight, Julia twelve years younger; Bryson was her age, a colleague from her eight years in Paris with the American cultural center. "Economic counselor," he repeated, his windpipe constricted, his eyes brimming with tears. "Madrid, too," he managed finally; "how lucky for them."

"It's what he wanted. She said he was on the list for Mauritius but asked to have his name taken off. Quite sensibly, too, I suppose. One wants to play Napoleon but not at Elba."

Touché, he wanted to say but continued to cough helplessly. She stood up impatiently and nodded toward the shadows of the french doors. Kasim came forward with a bow and began removing the plates. Still gasping, Harcourt watched her go across the terrace. She'd lost weight—too much, he thought. Her dark hair hung in two plaits at her neck tied with white ribbon, like a schoolgirl's. The slim brown legs with their high calves and sleek thighs ended in a small pleated white skirt. The curve of her rump was visible from beneath the swinging folds. Once the cushion of her sex, it now reminded him of the elegant little rear end of the Siamese cat he'd owned in Beirut during his bachelor days. The wretched little Moslems in the hovels behind his garden wall had stoned her to death and flung the dead body back over the wall.

"*Tiens, tiens,*" he said softly, moving his watering eyes away from Kasim to the light flooding from the open sea. *On the list as ambassador to Mauritius, then had his name removed, did he? It's what they always said when they'd been passed over.* A fly touched his cheek and he brought his hand up and found a trickle of sweat crawling from his temple. A second trickle leaked down the hollow of his chest, like a lizard over a damp stone.

He hadn't played decent tennis in years, not since Tunis, where the French attaché had beaten him 6–2, 6–0 and he'd ruptured himself before the third set, a dirty blood worm suddenly there on his groin. They'd once made a handsome couple on the tennis courts; their photograph still hung in the clubhouse, a foreign service inspector had told him. He stared out to sea, lips moving. How long ago was that? Six years? Ten years? *No, impossible.* A squall of black smoke erupted from a Russian trawler as it backed off in the outer harbor, reversing engines. He rose abruptly, touched with vertigo, then limped across the terrace into the cool dining room. Blinded by the shadows, he groped for the bottle and the soda siphon on the sideboard, poured a small brandy-soda, and went back out into the white sunlight to stand at the low wall enclosing the front terrace. Hers was the finest residence in the city, much finer than what awaited the Brysons in Madrid, yet nothing consoled her.

She'd wanted him to take his name off the list, to wait for something more suitable. Morocco would have been suitable, Tunisia, too, both just a few hours away from Paris or Rome, but never East Africa.

They'd argued that evening in Washington after he'd heard his name had gone over to the White House on the ambassadorial appointments list; a rainy evening, they were on their way to a reception, then a concert; they'd taken a taxi, the driver was African. She refused to keep her voice down, the future in ruin:

"Tunis and Rabat will go to an Arabist, Julia. You know that."

"Cyprus, then, or Malta. But not East Africa, not unless it's Kenya. You should insist."

"How can I insist? It's an opportunity I can't pass up. It may not come again."

"I suppose he'll be exhausted after home leave," he said as she returned carrying a tray with the silver coffee service. "Depressed, too. One more year. It usually happens." He kept his back to her and frowned as he stared out to sea.

"Logan, you mean? Not too tired, I hope. I've invited him to the buffet tonight. I hope he won't mind." Still standing, she poured the coffee as he watched the lovely curve of her neck. From Athens he'd written poems to her, pursuing his courtship.

"He'll be very tired."

"Probably."

"But then youth has none of our vices."

"Speak for yourself," she said.

"I meant the fatigue factor."

"I know what you meant."

"He won't disappoint you, I'm sure." A touch of malice there, he regretted, too late.

She didn't answer.

"I wonder if he has any second thoughts?" he asked.

"About what?"

"Extending his tour."

"I should hope not." He heard the quaint echo of Agnes Firthdale, the wife of the British ambassador, whose chauffeur had brought the flowers on the glass-topped table. Julia disliked gardening. She preferred tennis or sailing, more enthusiastically than ever now, something to set her apart from the fair-skinned overweight wives of his colleagues, who sat lethargically under their umbrellas and never strayed into the sun. Now she saw the brandy-soda in his hand and her face showed her disappointment, as cool as the pouilly-fuissé, as the first snows of the High Lebanon. "Really, Lyman, you have a meeting this afternoon."

"The wine was bitter," he protested, like a querulous invalid, "an after-bite. Don't tell me you didn't notice."

"It hardly kept you from emptying the bottle."

"We opened it last night, I think."

"Last night we were at the Pakistani's."

"The night before then. I wonder what he's like, this Wingate."

"I'm sure he's like the others. Why do you need another Agency person?"

"Whittington's understaffed and needs help. So he'll take Shaughnessy's place."

Her eyes lifted suspiciously. "Shaughnessy was foreign service."

"We gave up a State slot for an Agency slot."

"And you agreed? You let Whittington talk you into it? Or

was it DeGroot? Really, Lyman, you let them walk all over you. Who was it? DeGroot or Whittington?"

"I didn't need persuading. It made a certain amount of sense." He sipped his coffee and sat back again, looking out at the Russian trawler. An odd ship, all sorts of radio equipment in its riggings. Should get a photograph, he supposed. He wondered if the Russians were reading their communications. Not that it mattered; like everyone else, they couldn't make heads or tails of it. "With DeGroot here, I doubt that it will make much difference. I suppose I won't have to ask so much of Talbot, either."

"Really? I thought you trusted his judgment."

"I do, but with DeGroot here I won't have to rely on him so much. I wonder what Talbot will think?"

"About what?"

"DeGroot."

"I thought you said you wouldn't have to rely on him so much."

"Logan? I meant substantive matters."

"You once said it was the staff that gave an embassy substance." He considered it for a moment. "It does."

"In that case, you're a two-man post, you and poor Logan." She laughed, but Harcourt, offended, didn't turn.

"Why *poor* Logan. Why is *he* the only one who deserves your sympathy?" He was fond of Logan Talbot but thought him a bit sly. "The fact is he's gotten a little lazy this past year. You really ask too much of him."

Again she laughed. "Lazy? Don't be ridiculous. He's not lazy at all, just overtalented for someplace like this. He belongs in Europe, like you do. Besides, who else is there to depend on?"

"Others would be your friend."

"Please, Lyman. We've been through all this."

"Mrs. DeGroot wants you to accept her."

"I'm not her empress dowager. It's not up to me to accept anyone."

"Accept was the wrong word. Be friends, then."

"I don't accept frightened middle-aged women who think I'm their nanny. She telephoned this morning, a project she wanted to discuss. Discuss *here,* she wanted to come *here,* of all things."

"What kind of project?"

"Painting ostrich eggs with the UN ladies. The ostrich is an endangered species. She didn't seem to know that. She doesn't seem to know anything."

"She's artistic, he told me."

"He would. That's usually the word husbands use, isn't it? She's not artistic at all, just terribly vulgar."

"I feel sorry for her." He felt enervated suddenly. "What do you want me to do?"

"Nothing. I want to be left alone, that's all. I'm not the embassy housemother."

He sat up and moved his chair backward, out of the sun. "I wonder if this Wingate is married. I specifically told Whittington a married man would be better. The social burdens demand it."

"Really, Lyman—"

He roused himself. "It's true."

Whittington's telegram had been garbled in transmission. He wasn't even sure of his first name.

"Why would he be arriving by ship?"

"I haven't the slightest idea. Are you going swimming this afternoon?"

Without a wind it would be hot at the beach cabin, hellishly hot.

"I doubt it, too many jelleyfish." She took a cigarette from the silver urn and lit it, then picked up Eleanor Bryson's letter again. He lifted the brandy-soda toward him, secretly sniffing its dark waters. On the far side of the reef beyond the sand shallows of the inlet, the sea turned bitter green, darker than jade or absinthe. The depths were as cold as the Baltic. He could feel the chill dark breath against his dangling ankles when he'd once summoned the courage to swim out. Logan Talbot had been with him, Talbot and a strange man named Noseworthy, one of Talbot's eccentric drinking friends. Far, far below in the darkness he dared not go he could imagine ghostly amphorae, Greek and Roman timbers, and lichen-encrusted terra-cottas, reclaimed by the sea. But it was the Mediterranean he was imagining, not this vast primitive sea ruled by white sharks, Arab dhows, and Russian trawlers.

Rising, he brought the binoculars from the iron table near the french doors and looked toward the trawler, now at anchor. Beyond the breakwater along the coast the broken rampart of an

old building lifted its rubble from the sea. From a distance it resembled the old Crusader castle at Sidon, which Harcourt sometimes imagined it to be. A fisherman wearing a pair of shorts
squatted on what looked like the mole, patching his nylon nets.

"I don't know why any sensible man would take a ship," he said,
"not in this heat."

Two gulls soared out above the trawler. He lost them against
the sky.

"If he's like the DeGroots, he's probably not sensible at all."

He pretended not to hear. He must be a drinker, he thought,
bringing the glasses down. Of course. Who else took long voyages
these days? Someone from another backwater, coming up from
the south. South lay Nairobi, Dar es Salaam, Mozambique. Inland
lay Kigali, Bangui, Lubumbashi, deep in the tropical darkness.
The Congo, too, where Ray Whittington, the CIA station chief had
served. All south, drained by the great colon of the Nile. He had
once spent three unspeakable days in the Congo during his days
as a foreign service inspector. A wrinkled little black man in tattered shorts had appeared at his bedroom window at the DCM's
residence, bow-and-arrow across his back. He'd thought it some
kind of joke. That wasn't his Africa; his Africa was Rabat, Tunis,
Alexandria. He sipped the brandy-soda, eyes narrowed against the
sun. A slow drinker, very slow. No guests, no intrusions. Not like
the public salon of the 707. In your own cabin most likely, not
care whether you eat or not. Out on deck in the darkness when
you felt like it, sleep like the dead when you didn't. Gin probably.
You could always find gin. Another of Whittington's friends from
the tropical darkness. They had a way about them, didn't they?
He suspected him already, like DeGroot, that preposterous man.

"Probably I should find out more about him," he said.

"Who?"

"Wingate." He returned to his chair. "But then I'm sure DeGroot
can handle him. That's what DCM's are for."

She looked at him disapprovingly. "Really, Lyman. Don't be
such a hypocrite, pretending you don't know. Your former DCM
was a bully and DeGroot is a fool."

"I'm trying to make the best of a very difficult situation."

Poor Julia, friendless and miserable, surrounded by aging dowagers. A tippler, he decided, his eyelids heavy again. That was something, anyway. Already he was a step ahead. Something to bring him to heel quickly, like DeGroot. He hated unpleasantness.

He heard the sound of automobile tires against the gravel and turned sleepily to look across the terrace toward the side gate. His black Chrysler was there, backing carefully into place.

"He's early, isn't he?"

"It's one forty-five," Julia said wearily. "Your appointment is for two."

"Tiens."

His afternoons were usually free, but today the UN resident representative, Nikiforov, the Bulgarian, had called a meeting of chiefs of mission to coordinate drought relief efforts. He looked at his watch. Ten minutes was all he wanted, ten minutes to close his eyes and lift this stupor from his mind. He crossed the terrace and went down the hall, groping for the bathroom door in the shadows. He doused his face in the washbasin, buttoned his collar, and put on his sunglasses. Only then did he inspect his face in the mirror. He was surprised at the supercilious stranger he found there. *Who was this man?* He inspected his teeth. No disguising that. Talbot's loyalty he could count on, but what about Wingate? Like DeGroot, perhaps, but with even more comic ambition. *Going to get rid of the Russians, was he?* He removed his sunglasses, took a tin pillbox from his seersucker pocket and put the pill far back on his tongue, washing it down from the carafe of water on the shelf. Opening his eyes, he again confronted himself in the mirror. Now he was disappointed. Just a plain silly face. He might have been bantering with Najah al-Zeyn, the Syrian ambassador, another of Talbot's absurd friends, smiling at one of his awful jokes. Trying so desperately to learn English, too. He managed a smile. Not half bad, he decided. Julia always said he had a capacity for self-drama, playing out his absurd roles, but which one was this? *As a rule existence hides itself,* he remembered. Sartre, wasn't it? He searched his pockets for his notes for the meeting. Had he left anything confidential behind? One had to be careful. Kasim wasn't to be trusted, Whittington had warned him: on the NSS payroll. The car was waiting—*the life of the spirit is intermittent,* he remembered. Saint-Exupéry this time. No doubt about that. He felt better, vindicated, suddenly released, a swimmer plunging to depths few would dare at his age. Here on the African coast, ambition achieved but existence at a dead end, he had nothing to explore but his own humiliation while his colleagues held royal court in London, Paris, and Vienna, and the Brysons wrote their friends of their ducal villa in Madrid.

Returning down the dark hall, his spirits had lifted; but then the light flooding in from the terrace beyond brought back the sunny silence of Provence and he saw himself as a young man on holiday, paint box in his bicycle kit bag, felt the warm dust of the July afternoon, saw the white mountains in the distance, and the recollection stunned him like a blow. Eyes stricken, he groped blindly through the white light flooding from the doorway and tripped over the small step.

The car was waiting, the door held open. The chauffeur released the brake and the black Chrysler rolled forward, gathering speed down the narrow road as it rolled toward the corniche.

Alone in the back seat, he approved the speed. The hurtling black Chrysler stirred dust and dried dung from the verges, but Harcourt, the wind bathing his face, eyes lifted toward the sea, didn't look back, didn't look to either side, hand gripping tightly the leather strap as he silently searched the herring blue of the horizon for the Italian counselor's sailboat with its red spinnaker.

From the shadowed doorways of the tin hovels huddled in the shade of the old wall at the foot of the hill, dark eyes watched, mothers and wrinkled grandmothers gazing after him through the curtain of chaff, dung, and fine white powder left in his wake. They had a name for him: *the dustmaker, the spoiler of milk.*

□ □ □

"I hear you came back," Julia Harcourt said in the dry exaggerated drawl she affected on the telephone. "Poor boy, why do you disappoint me so? As clever as you are, I thought you'd have managed a compassionate transfer and tricked them into sending you to Paris early."

"I thought about it," Talbot said, standing naked in the upstairs bedroom, dripping water from the shower. Her taunting humor, always double-edged, sometimes left nasty cuts; she had a wicked temper.

"Oh, really. Was London lovely?"

"Raining, I'm afraid. A little chilly. Dismal in fact."

"London dismal?"

"Pneumonia weather all around. Looked deserted, everyone underground, hiding out from the bug. Like the Blitz all over." Through the window he saw a statuesque blond woman in a bathing suit walking along the beach, a child at her heels, and he moved toward the telescope. "Really weird, come to think of it."

"You're lying, of course. How did you find your house? Neat and tidy? Still the same dreadful drapes, the same dismal smells of upholstery cleaner? Poor Mr. Peterson. He tries so hard to make you one of us."

"It looks pretty much the same." The telephone cord wouldn't reach the quasar on the windowsill and the woman passed harmlessly out of view. Turning back, he caught sight of his white buttocks in the mirror, squatted down, moved the receiver to his left hand and groped for his boxer shorts on the floor near the bed. "A few people are missing."

"Who's missing?"

"My cook and houseboy. Otherwise everything's the same."

"I'm sure. Listen, dear, I'm about to take my paperback and drive down to the beach cottage to sit in the sun. There's Amstel in the fridge and a nice breeze blowing. I would like it very much if you'd join me. Is that too much to ask? Are you terribly, terribly tired? If you are, I'll understand."

"No, not too tired." Squatting down again, he moved his right foot, fishing for the elastic waistband with his right toe. "Where's Lyman?"

"He had a meeting at three and then was going to watch a doubles match at the Italian club. Mr. DeGroot has him in tow. Ten minutes, then? See you. Don't dawdle, dear."

He finished his shower, pulled on his swimming trunks and a pair of khaki pants and a tennis shirt, then fetched a basket from the kitchen.

Mohammed was waiting at the gate but was reluctant to leave his post. Talbot had to move him out the gate by the arm. He was from the interior, the son of a nomad from Western Jubbaland, or so he claimed. Talbot had yet to meet a Jubba who hadn't spent his youth as a camel boy, wandering alone with his herds under the stars. The Jubba were romantics at heart, pastoral nomads, warriors, poets, and lovers; now, if one was to believe the national printing press, they were Marxist revolutionaries as well. Not since the Greeks had word and deed been so heroically merged in a ruling aristocracy but never in a race of such incorrigible liars.

Talbot led him along the deserted corniche toward the UN beach club two hundred yards away at the turnabout. A dozen cars were parked at the rear of the club. Most of the UN staff worked only half-days, if they worked at all. He could hear the rattle of bottles from the kitchen. With its dark rooms, wet floors, and its smells of whiskey and beer, it had a slightly dissolute air—well deserved, Talbot thought. Most of the UN staff were layabouts, multiplying like cockroaches in out-of-the-way pestholes like this one. In the absence of a market economy, every facet of state-controlled daily life from public sanitation to infant feeding and port decongestion required a committee of UN or Soviet technical experts; every committee brought two more.

"Disgusting. Yeah, I know. We'll just be a minute." Mohammed balked, refusing to go inside. Talbot left him in the road, unhappily watching the gates of the villa, which he'd left open. Inside at the far end of the bar a few faceless shadows were outlined against the front windows overlooking the sea.

He set the basket atop a stool and slapped out a tattoo at the bar. "Six Amstel, Abdullah. Briskly, if you will."

The small figure bending behind the bar came erect slowly. It wasn't Abdullah but Ali, the sad gray-haired Pakistani club manager. Buying UN beer by job lot across the counter for consumption elsewhere was against club regulations, but Ali was a sympathetic expatriate, hoping for the favor of a job at the embassy. He'd once had his own import-export firm.

"Mr. Talbot. You came back. Welcome. Welcome." His wet spaniel eyes were flushed; his wispy little mustache looked even sadder. Talbot shook his warm hand across the bar. "When did you come? Yesterday? Today?"

"Today. Where's Abdullah?"

"He went to Jidda, Mr. Talbot. No Amstel, sorry. Heinekin, maybe."

"Heinekin's fine. How's the family, Ali?"

"Good, very good, thank you, Mr. Talbot. But not here. Things aren't good here. Do you remember what we talked about, Mr. Talbot? It's worse now."

"What's that, Ali?"

The couple at the end of the bar got up and strolled out the open door to the beach. A dark-haired girl in a bikini remained, sitting alone, her chin on her hand, looking out the side window. Talbot didn't recognize her but from her white shoulders suspected she was a new UN secretary hiding out from the flesh-cating sun. "The commercial assistant's position," Ali said as he searched the cooler for the beer, "at the embassy." Talbot moved to the door as if to study the beach, then looked at her again. He still didn't recognize her. A nice neck and a lovely silhouette. As she sat on the stool, shoulders slumped, the small cups of her undersized halter only loosely engaged a pair of prodigious breasts.

"We talked about it, remember?" Ali said.

"The embassy? You still interested? I'll talk to Shaughnessy, Ali, as soon as I get settled in."

"Good, Mr. Talbot. Thank you."

Talbot paid for the beer, hoisted the basket, and took one last look. She turned boldly to look at him and just as quickly looked away.

Outside again, Talbot passed the basket to Mohammed.

"Just don't drop the damned things, all right? Don't let the goddamned bottom fall out. Just put them in the fridge, neat and tidy."

Mohammed hurried away in his clattering plastic shoes, afraid the guard supervisor might arrive and find the front gate unattended.

Talbot moved on. Fifty yards beyond, the door to the nightclub was open. A lone dark-skinned taxi driver leaned against the fender of his red-and-yellow Fiat chewing a stick. Inside a phonograph was playing. One of the waiters stood in the shadows at the side talking to a young girl. He saw Talbot, smiled, and put his hands over his head. Rotating his hips, he did a lazy cha-cha-cha.

Remarkable memory, these nomads. He and Shaughnessy had

done the town the last night before his leave, beginning at the Lido nightclub. He couldn't remember now where they'd ended up; a smash-and-bash party somewhere in between, then someone had gotten ugly and the police arrived. Talbot had slipped under a table, seen two bottles and a leather riding crop go skating past in a slick of foam, then crawled rapidly out the back door. The sun was bright on his gate when he'd at last driven in, his seersucker knees still damp, glittering with glass crumbs. Shaughnessy had passed out in the back seat. He'd gotten him into bed, then taken a long swim to clear his head and had breakfast with the Harcourts—*Vincit qui se vincit,* as his prep school beer stein proclaimed, the inscription borrowed from the athletic field house. "He conquers who conquers himself."

The Harcourts' was the third cottage in the long line of stucco beach cottages facing the sea. The lattice windows were pushed open in front where the shallow porch was enclosed by a low sea wall. A set of concrete steps led to the beach below. The other porches were deserted in the afternoon heat.

Julia Harcourt lay on a blue lounge chair on the open porch wearing a faded orange bikini, her tanned legs in the sun, her back in the shadows of the cottage wall. She smiled as she sat up, dropped her book aside, and put her oily arms around his neck to press her thin lips against one cheek, then the other.

"You smell just like the YMCA. Peterson must have left you some of his Lifebuoy."

Her breath was warm, her voice very close.

"I found it in the shower. How've you been?"

Awkwardly he leaned over her, her arms around his neck, pulling him down, her face hidden, her warm fingers feeling his bones.

"Bored. I have some Camay I'll send you. You feel a little bedraggled. I think you've lost weight."

"Tired, that's all."

She finally released him and inspected him more formally. "You look starved. Didn't anyone feed you?"

"Not much. Long nights and short days." He dragged a lounge chair from the far side and sank down.

"You're much too thin. Osman! Oh, Osman, he's here."

Her houseboy, who'd been waiting in the shadows of the doorway, appeared on the porch carrying a tray with a bottle of Amstel
and a glass.

"We decided to ambush you, Osman and I."

Painfully he got up again. "Thanks, Osman."

"You've been away, sir."

"Just a few weeks. How've you been?"

"Fine, sir. Everything fine, sir."

"Not a few weeks, a month. Thank you, Osman." She believed
all her Jubba houseboys were government spies. He went inside.

"How was your vacation? Don't tell me everything now, just
whether it was nice or not. Was it nice?"

"Very nice."

"Not even a little bit boring sometimes."

"Vacations are sometimes a little boring."

"Then I'm happy. And now you're glad to come back."

"Straining at the leash."

"Honestly, now."

"Very happy."

"What a predictable liar. Any news, any gossip you can tell me?
What about Kenya? Who's going to be the new ambassador?"

"I don't think anyone knows yet."

"Don't *think?* What does that mean, not to think? Not to know?
Does it mean you didn't ask? That's the first thing he's going to
ask you."

"It's a new administration. Everything's pretty much up in the
air. I didn't hang around."

"Lyman said you'd be in Washington a week. "

"Supposed to. Didn't stay. The new administration's still in transition, sorting things out. Everything was fogged in, no answers
anyplace. Nerd City these days."

"You're not much help." She rested her head against the cushion.
"It must be nice to be so matter-of-fact about it all. Lyman should
have waited. He might have done a little better with the Democrats."

"It wouldn't have made any difference."

"He was so pathetically eager. He deserved so much more."

"He'll do all right."

"Don't pretend. I know what you think. You're a worse cynic than I am."

"Goodness gracious."

She turned, her tanned skin drawn tightly over her high cheekbones. "You are, don't pretend." He saw the warning in her thinly lidded eyes.

"How's he feeling?"

"Very evasive. A little dizziness now and then, but he won't admit anything, not to me at least. I don't blame him. I'd have vertigo, too. They give him a godforsaken embassy in the middle of nowhere and pretend it's a fit finale for thirty years of service. *Le bras d'honneur.*"

"Not the finale. He'll get another post."

"That's not the point. He's aged ten years since he's been here and it's getting worse. I don't know what it is, but I can see it in his face every morning. He's taking pills of some kind." Conscious of her tone, she stopped. "I'm sorry. I shouldn't be talking this way." She leaned forward to pat his hand. "We did miss you."

"He should go to Frankfurt for a physical."

"He won't listen to me. He thinks I'm looking for an excuse to leave. Maybe you can talk to him—not right away, in time. You'll have to be careful about it, very discreet." She sat back again. "Now we have the DeGroots, late of Johannesburg. Or was it Durban? What do you think?"

"I haven't met them."

She lifted her head. "He wasn't at the airport?"

"No. I didn't see him."

"That liar. Remind me to tell Lyman. He said he was going."

"Don't bother, it doesn't matter."

"It certainly does matter. Lyman told him to go. Who met you?"

"Peterson."

"Poor Mr. Peterson, so loyal. Speaking of loyalty, I hate to tell you but your friend Shaughnessy is gone."

"Gone? Gone where?"

"There was an opening in Mozambique, some kind of emergency. The Department asked if Lyman would release him, so he did."

Shaughnessy, the embassy economic officer, had filled in for Talbot while he was on leave; a bachelor, too, they'd shared a few things in common. Julia had never liked him. He was from Worcester, Massachusetts, and had gone to Holy Cross. His father was a policeman.

"Mozambique? Why Shaughnessy?"

"I knew you'd say that. Lyman thought he was a complete disaster sitting in for you. Then because of his Portuguese he had a chance to go to Mozambique and Lyman said he wouldn't stand in the way. DeGroot's been handling your work until Shaughnessy's replacement arrives. He speaks four languages, by the way." She had turned to look at him, her eyes wickedly bright.

"Four languages?" She laughed. He felt foolish. "What's so funny?"

"If you could only see your face."

He reached for the towel. "I'm a little tired, that's all."

"Don't be silly, it's not that. You look so serious, and we're not. I'm not laughing at you. It's just so preposterous and he's so awful, he and his wife both. But all of us are, aren't we? He's what we deserve. He has all these ridiculous ideas. Poor Lyman's completely bewildered. Shaughnessy was no help at all. He doesn't know where to turn. Oh, I'm sorry. I'm dreadful, aren't I? We're such simpletons."

"What kind of ideas?"

"Everything. How to enlarge the embassy, how to get the AID program and the Peace Corps started again, how to get rid of the Russians."

Talbot sat up. "The Russians?"

"The Russians *most* of all."

"That's a crock."

She looked at him in surprise. "You've heard about it?"

"Sure, for a year now. It's rubbish, a crock. Lyman knows that."

"Does he?" Her tone told him the subject no longer interested her. "All I know is he's very persistent, also odd. So is his wife." Carefully she dried her face. "But then we all are. Anyway, it probably did Lyman some good to escape you for a few weeks. You really do make everything so dull at times. Sensible, I'm sure, but so dull. But I won't say anything more. I don't want to prejudice the poor man's case, just to warn you. Things aren't quite the same since you left. So tell me about your vacation."

"It wasn't very interesting."

"Tell me anyway."

The incoming tide battered the foot of the steps beyond the wall as he talked; the salt spray touched their faces.

"New York for five days, how lovely. Then skiing, too. Did you meet anyone interesting?"

"A few people."

"A romance? Look up, dear. Don't hide. A romance?"

"No, no romance."

She sank back again in disappointment. "You are impossible. Your loyalty's pathetic. Lyman thinks you probably regret extending your tour. He feels terribly guilty about it. He blames himself. You really disappointed me. I thought you'd bring more news. Who's going to Rabat?"

"As ambassador? I don't know. I told you, with the new administration it's hard to predict what's going to happen."

"And you don't know about Nairobi either. Lyman should have waited for Nairobi. Nairobi would at least have been civilized. What about Tunis? Who's going to Tunis?"

"I don't keep track. An Arabist, I suppose."

She looked at him reproachfully. "You really didn't talk to anyone, did you?"

"Not really." He finished the beer. "I don't care much for Nairobi."

"There's no comparison and you know it. You can swim if you like. I won't feel hurt. Did you get my invitation? I've asked a few people in for cocktails tonight. Then we're going to show a movie. You did get it, didn't you?"

"Peterson gave it to me."

"Do you know Nicola Seretti? Lyman and I met her at the Abruzzos' farm last month. She had a few ideas for my garden. Would you mind picking her up? It would be so nice. She's staying out at the Rugda Taleh while she's in the city. I told her we'd arrange it. I'll call her and say you're coming. Say about seven?"

"I don't know where my car is. I left it with Shaughnessy."

"Then I'll send you the Chrysler." She sank back again. "She's quite interesting, very un-Italian."

The week before he had left, it had been the Pakistani ambassador's wife when her husband was in Nairobi; the month before that the wife of a Swedish UN technician. He watched the breaking surf, knowing he was truly back on station, a medium-level diplomat exiled to a third-rate post. In professional terms he had no existence at all. In another decade he would be like Harcourt, the Egyptian ambassador or the Norwegian honorary consul, those pitiful men.

"A swim might do you some good," he said after a minute. She never swam in the sea, only in the pool at the compound, but no one would ever know that from the way she rattled on about it.

"Too many jellyfish with the wind the way it is. I wouldn't recommend it." But after a minute she sat up with a sigh. "Go ahead if you must. I'll watch."

He body surfed and swam while she sat atop the wall in her bikini, her long legs crossed, her shoulders erect. Down the beach a gaggle of fat Russian women wth dough-white knees sat deep in the shade of the veranda of their two-story government-furnished beach house. From the shadow of a beach umbrella six beach houses down the wife of the German ambassador fanned herself and watched. A few overweight Russians passed, thickset Bruegel peasants in codpiece bathing suits back from the hunt. They looked up at her curiously.

Talbot watched, too, tired by this time, loafing on his back just beyond the rolling surf, toes to the sun. He knew she enjoyed sitting there on her stone wall. Sometimes, seeing the cords of her neck, the small pouch under her chin, or the lines around her mouth, he felt sorry for her. With her beguiling little smiles, her coaxing little voices, and her sly little hand pats, she cozened everyone into service, sweet Julia, queen of the non-copulative seduction, but loyalty brought only more of the same. She wrinkled up your balls like sun-kissed raisins, fruity enough for Harcourt, he supposed. Beneath the masquerade he sensed only a devouring selfishness that had left her coldly sexless. Love was only its idea, vaster than the sea she so often contemplated but never entered, an immensity she didn't dare: too many lurking threats, too many revolting jellyfish, too many disgusting spermatozoa.

In Paris, Rome, or Tunis, she would be just another selfish diplomatic wife you could tell to fuck off, she and Harcourt both, but not here. At this distance, she seemed happy to be sitting there enjoying her royal realm in this land of myrrh, frankincense, and myth, slim, solitary, and inaccessible, Queen Nefertiti in the Land of Punt, but he knew she wasn't happy. That was another trompe l'oeil confection for the admiring eye, like Grace Bowser's *faux bois* library.

After six weeks of bachelor freedom, he wasn't even sure he liked her very much.

□ □ □

"Ah, Mr. Talbot," a voice sang out as Talbot came into the drive in his wet bathing trunks. A large man stood near his freshly washed and waxed Fiat, which had been returned. In front was the DCM's black Plymouth.

As the gate clanged shut he came sweeping down the drive, one hand extended. "Bernard DeGroot," he said loudly, removing his wide-brimmed coconut hat. "Such a great pleasure. Young Shaughnessy left your automobile in my keeping and I have had my driver return it."

"Thanks. Sorry I wasn't here." The hand was warm and soft, the neck thick and pudgy above rounded shoulders. The voice had a curious theatrical lilt.

"The wait was not long. Such a merciful breeze this time of day." He fanned his face with the hat. He was pop-eyed, like an old turtle, with a wet rosebud mouth and pallid skin. "You've been swimming."

"Swimming, that's right." Talbot's usually sleek blond hair sprouted in goatish tufts from his head; a few snail-like strings of seaweed clung to his legs. On his left shoulder was a reddish welt left by a jellyfish. He'd put on a good show.

"Swimming, yes. The sun is cruel but the sea is kind, as the Ceylonese say. One can almost smell the mangroves."

An inch or two taller than Talbot, he wore khaki shorts, white knee hose, and leather sandals. His body, shaped like a gourd, was narrow in the shoulders, heavy in the hips, and tapered to thin ankles. He was slightly knock-kneed, as if from carrying too much weight, like a large-boned woman. He had the smooth hairless face and arms of a eunuch. It was difficult to guess his age. He might have been in his mid-forties or mid-fifties, plump in the arms and midriff, and henna-haired, sweating from his exertions. His tan safari suit was dark under his arms and across his back.

"The afternoons here can be pleasant. At high noon, however, sad to say, it reminds me of Aden, sad to say because I am no sentimentalist where Arabs are concerned." A handkerchief was at his brow, the ludicrous broad-brimmed Jamaican straw hat still waving in the sullen heat. "Wretched place, Aden. Do you know it?"

"No, can't say I do."

"A coaling station, nothing more. Your houseboy, by the way, is a merry fellow. He led me all about the villa, rapping inarticulately at windows, thinking you asleep. We rapped in vain."

"I was out walking, then took a swim. He's not the houseboy but the night guard. He just came on duty."

"Ah, a gate guard. So I understand now. Ah, yes, quite so—the steady, percipient eyes." He turned to the gate guard, bowed, said something in Arabic, put his hat back on, and turned away, his voice dropping to a whisper. "He is of the Ogaden clan, I believe."

"He's Isaq."

DeGroot blinked, hearing an unpleasant noise. "Isaq?"

"He's Isaq. One of my houseboys is Ogaden. He's also disappeared."

"Disappeared? I see. Yes. I thought he was Ogaden. My wife would have come but has suffered an untimely malaise. Left to themselves, wives are tempted to make an allegory of their complaints, so I mustn't stay."

He drew Talbot away out of hearing of the gate guard. "I have occupied your desk during this last month as well as my own," he whispered, "the ambassador being persuaded that my experience might be put to immediate use. I made some attempt to correct this impression. It has been ten years since I left Hargusha in the north. Public affairs officer. The post is now closed, unfortunately. Have you gin, by the way. Whiskey?" He released Talbot's arm and continued fanning himself vigorously. "I much prefer malt whiskey myself and have brought some to tide you over."

"Thanks. I appreciate that."

"Civilization was built, my grandfather once said, not merely on the division of labor but malt whiskey as well. He was a sea captain." He looked about the terrace. "This is indeed a lovely garden, but shows some neglect. You are still young, not too old to take up gardening. You're not married."

"No, not recently."

"You've been married."

"No."

"You said not recently, implying you'd been married."

"Did I?"

"That was my impression."

"First impressions, my grandfather said, can be misleading."

DeGroot's gaze wandered disapprovingly over Talbot's goatish hair, his white shoulders, and wet face. "I see. You play tennis, I understand."

"Occasionally. I prefer skin sports."

"Skin sports?"

"Swimming is a skin sport."

DeGroot smiled politely and moved on. "I see. You have a salty imagination, a keen sense of the ridiculous, I'm told. I have been warned already. Mrs. Harcourt has warned me. You are her tennis partner, I believe. That is a poinsettia shrub there if I'm not mistaken."

"I'm not sure."

"I think it is poinsettia. We must have a long talk one of these days, the two of us, share impressions, ideas, too, also responsibilities." He paused to finger a polished green leaf. "Poinsettia, yes. I found your cables very robust, very sensible."

"Thanks."

"I'd also expected someone older."

"I lead a double life."

"Indeed." DeGroot strode on across the terrace, looking about, hands behind his back, like the admiral inspecting the quarterdeck.

Talbot wandered after him. "Actually it's a kind of controlled schizophrenia."

"Is it?" DeGroot pointed at a shrub with his hat. "That, too, is poinsettia, I believe."

"I find it helps in shit-holes like this."

"A mango tree, if I'm not mistaken. How majestic the sky this time of day." His head was back, searching the highest limbs of the old tree and the sky beyond. "The sea winds are changing now. If I'm not mistaken, the northeast monsoons are over. That would be the *gu* making its breath felt. Your garden is superbly sheltered, isn't it? Quite lovely here." He lowered his gaze. "I have definite plans by the way. We'll discuss them when I have more time. I find both the ambassador and his wife most sympathetic, don't you?"

"Very much so."

"While at the National War College last year—was it just last year? It seems longer now." His head was back again, searching the sky. Talbot could see the black fillings in his molars. "While at the National War College last year, I did a monograph on the Horn of Africa, having had, as you know, some experience in the region, both here and in Ethiopia." Again he looked at Talbot. His basking blue eyes had various shades of intensity, like water vapor over a shallow sea. "The ambassador has a copy, by the way. So does an old friend at the National Security Council with whom I had lunch in Washington just before my departure. The White House mess. I intended to bring a copy for you to peruse as well, but could not lay my hands on it. I'm sure it will turn up. Customs has also misplaced my piano. You have not served elsewhere in Africa?"

"No, as a matter of fact I haven't."

"The Middle East?"

"No."

"Ahh, I see." Talbot heard the triumph in his voice. "I was two years in Damascus, two years in Amman, where I acquired some smattering of Arabic. More recently I served in Durban and Abidjan. My ancestry is Dutch, as you may have guessed. Talbot. That is English, if I'm not mistaken."

"Originally, I suppose."

"Ah, yes. Originally. This house, I'm told, once belonged to the DCM. It has a Moorish look." He stopped, squinting up at the sunscreen across the second floor.

"Very Moorish."

"His wife, I heard, thought it too isolated. My wife's thoughts as well. She prefers the compound, at least for the present. There's a sense of community there. But this is quite lovely, although a bit large for a bachelor."

"A little large."

"But bachelors prefer their privacy, do they not?" They stood at the side gate, which opened to another walled area, unplanted, where a swimming pool had been planned. The sunlight was dimming already, the evening breeze beginning to move through the tops of the trees.

"I must leave you now. We have been summoned to the residence this evening. Most sympathetic, as I said. Both of them. She has excellent style. You will be there?"

"I'm a little tired, but I'll be there."

"Good. I look forward to our collaboration, as I prefer to call it. You have definite ideas. So do I, as you will learn. I am an activist. You, I understand, take a more quiescent view, as did young Shaughnessy—"

"Shaughnessy?"

"A certain laxness. I have borrowed your cook by the way, but will return him in a few days. I hope you don't mind."

"Not if he doesn't."

The phone was ringing inside.

"He has voiced no objection."

"His English isn't too good."

"So I discovered. We communicate in Arabic. He has proven himself, as has everyone, most eager to oblige."

DeGroot smiled, limply shook Talbot's hand, put on his coconut hat, and went back around the wash cottage to his car. Talbot went inside to answer the phone.

"Logan? I didn't recognize your voice," Julia said. "It sounded odd. Has something happened?"

"I've been talking to a strange man in my garden."

"Really, who?"

"I'm not sure. He said his name was DeGroot."

"So he did come after all."

"Could be."

"What do you think of him?"

"I'm not sure. I think he may be Afrikaner. I think English might be his second language."

"I see. You're lying, of course." Another pause. "I hope you were discreet."

"Very discreet. The bastard stole my cook."

"*Shhhh*. Listen, dear. Mrs. Seretti prefers for some strange reason to come alone. Quite odd. Therefore, I won't send the car. Can you manage to get here on your own?"

"I think so."

"Good. I know you're tired, but do try to look lively, will you? For Lyman's sake."

□ □ □

Soft lights glowed atop the walls of the official residence that sat like a Crusader castle on its hilltop overlooking the sea. The whitewashed walls lifted twelve to fifteen feet above the twisting sand road that climbed from the corniche. Far below an East German freighter and Soviet trawler swayed in the swells, their loops of twinkling lights lifting and falling like the lights of a carousel.

Standing in the soft warm air of the hilltop outside the iron gate, the darkness hiding the surrounding wasteland, Talbot had another sense of the city. Screwing up his eyes as he looked out to sea, he could imagine himself outside a whitewashed village in the Greek islands, on the corniche at Piraeus, or in Barcelona on a mild June night on his way to some discreet liaison at some discreet little restaurant.

He smelled cooking oil and charcoal from one of the tin hovels just below the crest of the hill. Opening his eyes, he saw the shadows of two nomad children against the ridgeline, their eyes hyena-bright in the glow of the wall lights. They disappeared down the slope as secretively as they'd come; drawn by cultural curiosity, he supposed—that or come to forage for tin cans.

On the steps at the end of the front walk Ambassador Harcourt, slim and frail in a blue blazer and ascot, his thin dark hair carefully combed, was greeting the French counselor and his Vietnamese wife in his beautiful French. Talbot waited on the walk below as he described for them the ornately carved front door, newly hung, which Julia had had copied by a local carpenter from the photograph of an Arab door at Zanzibar. "I expect it's something we'll take back with us when we leave," he said as he led them across the foyer toward the front salon where a half-dozen guests were already present.

He turned to see Talbot in the doorway. "Logan," he said fondly, "welcome back. How we've missed you. We must talk, later I hope, after the others have gone. Has Julia told you of our program for the evening?"

The film was *The Treasure of the Sierra Madre,* which DeGroot had obtained through some USIS series and which Julia had heard about. Having borrowed the film, she'd had no choice but to ask the DeGroots.

Drinks were being served. A buffet would be offered in the rear garden before the movie. The Italian ambassador and his wife were arriving. Talbot moved through the crowd, shook a few hands, took a drink from a tray, and slipped toward the front terrace, where he had seen the British ambassador standing alone, gazing gloomily out to sea.

"On holiday, was that it?" Firthdale asked, eyebrows and mustache working. He stood feet apart, whiskey in hand, like a man with a stirrup cup about to mount a horse. His stiff salt-and-pepper hair and spiky mustache gave menace to the face; a vain man but sensitive, too, a man of moods who kept himself apart at cocktail parties and receptions, disdaining them, even his own, preferring that others seek him out.

Talbot patronized him, borrowing books from his very substantial private library, most of it devoted to the travel writings of eccentric nineteenth-century Englishmen wandering the Middle East, few of which he ever finished.

"A few weeks, yes, sir."

"We've a visitor coming in, arriving next week. I wonder if I might send him around to talk to you."

"Yes, sir."

"Good. Basil Dinsmore, the journalist. You know his name, I believe."

"Basil? Yes, sir, we've talked quite a few times." He unconsciously squared his feet, like Firthdale.

"Doing his Indian Ocean survey. I'll send him over if you don't mind."

"Not at all."

"Rather confusing, I'd say. Can't make heads or tails of it, what they're up to. The Russians are playing matchmakers, are they? So preposterous I'm afraid they may just bring it off one way or another."

Firthdale's small staff was exclusively commercial, sent out to promote British goods and services. Unlike him, they preferred amateur theatricals to imperial skullduggery. Since his arrival ten months earlier, Firthdale's one ambition had been to travel the north by Land-Rover and visit the former British Jubbaland whose forts and ruins he knew so well by name but had never seen. His travel requests were repeatedly denied by the Jubba foreign ministry, whose director of protocol, Dr. Mohammed Hussein, disliked Firthdale as much as he did Talbot. At a diplomatic reception, Firthdale had once called Mohammed Hussein a fool and word had gotten back, reportedly carried by the Sudanese ambassador, one of Dr. Hussein's toadies. A century earlier Firthdale might have had him flogged at morning recall and drummed out of the colonial service, but a century earlier Firthdale might also have been a British diplomatist in central Asia dispatching clandestine agents disguised as pepper traders, ivory sellers, or commercial travelers to the Hindu Kush, the Kashmir, or the Punjab to sniff out Tzarist designs. Now he suffered his humiliations in silence, come to the Horn fifty years too late to play the Great Game, reduced to trading cocktail party gossip with his fellow diplomats and spying on Soviet trawlers and oilers on the horizon through his binoculars from his office near the sea. In the suites below, his three-man staff planned new trade initiatives for selling British goods and services, like the window dressers at Harrods.

He was, in short, a serious diplomat surrounded by fools, which made him a prickly quest for Harcourt.

Malfatti, the Italian ambassador, joined them, a small, shriveled black-eyed man, as gray as a shrew. "A bit player, something out of *Volpone*," Harcourt had once written in a memo of conversation; his style was elegantly literary, ornamenting the argument but never advancing it.

"Talking about the Ethiopian problem," Firthdale said.

"Very complicated. Very, very complicated. You've been away?"

"On holiday," Talbot said.

"I understand there's a delegation from the Italian communist party here," said Firthdale, who didn't speak Italian and cared nothing for the opera buffa of Italian politics.

"Not a delegation," Malfatti said politely. "Two members of the Italian parliament, communists, yes. They are meeting with the president tonight, I believe."

"What do you think?"

"I am not hopeful."

"Back at it already," Julia said, joining them.

"Catching up," Talbot said.

"Could I borrow him for a minute?" she asked with a smile and then led him away.

"My wife is a conchologist," Talbot heard someone say loudly from off to the rear as she led him across the back garden. Turning, he saw DeGroot introducing a woman to an Italian couple. She was a small woman with violet-black hair, artificially tinted, a plump face, and small dark eyes pressed like black currants into the white dough of her face, eyes too small and black to have any expression at all.

"That's Mrs. DeGroot. Don't dawdle, and stop gawking. I told you about Nicola Seretti, didn't I? She's done remarkable things in the garden. Have you noticed the difference? They're her plantings. Apparently she knows the woman who owns your villa. I think she may have some ideas for you, too. Would you keep an eye on her. She came alone, in a taxi, poor woman."

Julia was fond of acquiring new friends, but few survived more than a few months or so, when for various reasons they were abandoned, not to be invited again to the residence, Talbot suspected, because they told her nothing new or interesting about herself. As her interest cooled and their patronage became tiresome, she passed them on to others like secondhand clothes.

A slight olive-skinned woman with very short dark hair stood near the side wall of the terrace talking with Harcourt in Italian.

"Mrs. Seretti," Julia said sweetly, "this is Mr. Talbot, whom I've told you about."

She nodded politely, looking up at Talbot with cool critical eyes.

Talbot thought he'd met her at an Italian reception where she'd been heatedly reprimanding Malfatti about something as he'd wandered up. The Italian counselor had tried to introduce him, but she'd been too angry to take notice.

"I believe we've met, at the Italian residence, I think."

She didn't remember. "I'm sorry," she said in English. "I'm very poor remembering people from embassy receptions."

Harcourt brightened. "Good for you. So am I. Among other things, Mrs. Seratti is an agronome."

"I'm hopeful," Julia said to Talbot, "that Mrs. Seretti might do for your garden what she's done for ours."

"My wife cares nothing for gardening," Harcourt said.

"That's not entirely true," Julia said, annoyed.

"And which villa is yours?" Mrs. Seretti asked.

"At the end of the corniche."

"The one I told you about," Julia said.

"The one all by itself. Yes, I know it very well."

"The garden's in terrible shape," Julia said. Talbot didn't recall that she'd ever taken much interest in his garden.

"Mrs. Seratti lives down the coast," Harcourt said. "She manages her late husband's banana plantation. She's given quite a new look to the front plantings."

Julia had turned to look away across the terrace. "I think the Nikiforovs have arrived." She excused herself and led her husband away.

"I understand you've been away," Mrs. Seretti said after a moment. "You've been here long?"

"Two years."

"Two years isn't long."

"I suppose not if you've been here more than that."

"I've been here since 1961," she said, as if it were a rebuke. Remembering the Malfatti episode, Talbot decided she didn't care much for diplomats.

"Have you? Since 1961? That certainly is a long time, isn't it? You live down the coast?"

"Near Merca." She continued to study him. Then, as if disappointed by his caution, she looked away. "This is a lovely villa," she said after a minute. "I hadn't been here for some time. Not until Mrs. Harcourt asked if I'd help with her plantings. You're not a gardener?"

"Afraid not."

"I know the woman who owns your villa, Mrs. Ferrugio. She lives in Milano now, very old. She doesn't come anymore. Most of the original plants came from my farm."

"At my house?"

"In the rear garden, yes." She looked up at him. "Once it was quite lovely."

Again he heard the accusation in her voice. *Gone to seed, has it, all wrack and ruin? Really tough shit, old girl, you should see my wardrobe.* "You should come look at it then," he said with an equerry's ease, polished to perfection during that year at Rome meeting red-eyed congressmen with snapping-turtle dispositions and stupid wives who would blame him for being unable to arrange an immediate audience with the Pope. If a few had been Catholics, not Kansas or Arkansas Methodists, it might have been easier. "You could tell me what's gone wrong."

"How much does the embassy pay for your house?"

"I'm not sure." American extravagance was a frequent subject of gossip in the Italian community. With her shrewd dark eyes and her plain hands, he had a sense of a frugal Italian widow and *rentier.* She was wearing a long inexpensive reddish-orange dress made from a Pakistani wax.

"Probably too much," she said.

"You're from where in Italy?"

"Tuscany. You know Italy?"

"I was in Rome for a few years." She waited expectantly, but Talbot was suddenly conscious of his fatigue, like a dry enervating wind. He must have closed his eyes for a minute. Horses slept on their feet; he wondered if camels did.

"I met a Mr. DeGroot," he heard her saying. She was looking across the terrace and hadn't noticed. "I didn't quite understand his position."

"The tall man over there? He's the deputy chief of mission, the number two."

"He said he was here before, in the north, I understand."

"In Hargusha, the consulate there. It's closed now."

"It's different in the north."

"Very different."

"Have you been to Hargusha?"

"No, sorry, I haven't."

"That's too bad. I think they are beginning to serve." She put her drink aside. "Do you know what the movie is?"

"The Treasure of the Sierra Madre, I believe."

"Oh, yes. Very nice."

"Yes, very nice."

"You know it then?"

"I don't think I've ever seen it."

An awkward silence.

"I saw it first in London," she said, looking away, "years ago, when I was a student there."

"So you went to school in London."

"No, not London. Manchester." She was still looking around.

"Manchester is in the north," Talbot said.

"Do you know England?"

"England? Pretty well." London was cold, rain-swept, far away; he could think of nothing sensible to say about London. Being in its cold streets might wake him up, flogging about in wet shoes; a dip in the sea would be better, clothes and all, sink to the bottom. Sleepily calculating, manners exhausted, he realized he'd been without sleep for forty-five hours. "London is nice," he said, opening his eyes.

"My uncle lived in Manchester."

"Did he?" Talbot said. "Manchester. I don't think I know Manchester." *Who in God's name wanted to?*

"Excuse me," she said, "but I must speak to the Italian ambassador."

He watched as she crossed the terrace to join Ambassador Malfatti. Brightness quickly dimmed from Queen Julia's guests after she abandoned them, their colors fading, like fish dumped out on deck from the sea; then they blamed her colorless stand-ins for their drabness. She did, too; probably thought he was a bloody idiot. He wandered off to the right corner of the garden, pretending to inspect the new plantings. He leaned against the tree there, eyes closed, holding his glass.

He was seated far in the rear and to the right during the movie. The film was scratched and washed out in places; the sound track was a dim cackle, barely comprehensible. He dozed fitfully before he finally fell asleep, thinking himself in the dimly lit cavern of a 747 out over the Atlantic. He awoke to find the movie camera and speakers being packed away, the terrace empty except for Harcourt, the DeGroots, and a Swedish UN administrator whose name he'd forgotten.

"My dear, that was most impolite," Julia said. "Firthdale had something he wanted to say to you and poor Mrs. Seretti went home in a taxi." She turned toward her husband. "The name, by the way, is Seretti, not Seratti."

"Did I say Seratti?"

"You certainly did, didn't he, Logan?"

"Did he?" Talbot said vaguely. "I didn't notice."

"Oh, for God's sake." She turned her back, moving away.

"A memorable evening," DeGroot said, addressing the Swede, although his bright froggy eyes were on Julia, filling her glass from another on the tray Kasim offered just outside the kitchen door. "A film of consummate artistry despite some minor flaws. Banditry in Mexico has not yet been extirpated even in those regions of the country that call themselves civilized."

He looked around for an audience. The Swede had moved away, searching for an ashtray.

"Minor flaws?" Harcourt asked politely, edging closer.

"Scattering gold from ruptured skins would have required a wind of hurricane ferocity."

"Ah, yes," murmured Mrs. DeGroot with a quick intake of breath, her face fixed adoringly on her husband.

"However, the moral was crystalline, wasn't it? Quite superb."

"Moral?" Julia asked irritably. She hadn't spoken to Mrs. DeGroot since the other guests had departed.

"*L'homme propose,*" DeGroot said, raising his glass, "*et Dieu dispose.*"

Harcourt looked embarrassed. "Ah, yes," he said with a long sigh.

"I don't like movies with morals," Julia said. "I'd rather be entertained than instructed. You look terribly sleepy, Logan. Doesn't he look terribly sleepy, Lyman?"

"A brandy, Logan?" Harcourt said.

Talbot caught Julia's warning look. "No, thanks. I'd better be going."

"I wonder," DeGroot said, "that our little diplomatic community doesn't have a theater group."

"The British do," said the Swede. He was a thin middle-aged man with a mouth like a shriveled persimmon; a twitch to his accent made him sound tongue-tied. The only time Talbot ever saw him was at the end of a reception or a party, when he could always be found standing around someplace with the same vacant expression on his face, like a water-filled boot uncovered at low tide, the last peanut in the dish and a cankered one at that. "It is quite good," he said.

"They used to do madrigals," Harcourt said, "but they lost their countertenor."

Kasim came in to say the car had arrived to take the cook and servers home. DeGroot, his wife, and the Swedish administrator departed.

Talbot, watching them go, remembered he'd forgotten to ask the Swede about any new UN staff with virgin white shoulders. Probably he wouldn't have noticed.

"Stay, have a nightcap with us," Julia called, slumping down in an armchair. "It's not even midnight."

"I thought you said I looked sleepy."

"Never mind what I said, just sit down."

He moved between the couch and armchair and sat down, feet stretched out.

"Don't go to sleep, there's something I want to ask you."

"Brandy then," Harcourt said, moving quickly on cue to fetch the bottle.

"Well, what do you think?" Julia asked.

"About what?"

"The DeGroots, obviously."

Talbot gave it a moment's thought. "He has an odd way of speaking."

"I heard he was once a VOA film editor, then an announcer."

"Is that it?"

"I'm not sure. Odd diction, certainly."

Harcourt returned with two brandy snifters and the bottle. "Whom are we talking about?"

"I was asking Logan his impression of DeGroot."

"And what did he say?"

"He said he has an odd way of speaking, which is hardly original."

"I noticed it, too, at first," Harcourt said, pouring out the glasses. "After a while you don't notice. Julia?"

"No, thanks. Where's the Scotch?" Harcourt left to find the Scotch. He returned with a bottle and filled Julia's glass. She said, "What irritates me is he has an opinion on everything."

"Like Hubert Humphrey," Harcourt said. "Like Hubert Humphrey and the ADA. That always infuriated the Republicans. The American businessman, too. Always did."

Harcourt had little interest in American domestic politics; the little he knew he'd learned listening to his younger brother, a Connecticut brass manufacturer who'd thought Richard Nixon the Second Coming.

"Obviously. People who have an opinion on everything understand very little."

Harcourt sat down. "That doesn't follow."

"Only a hypocrite claims an interest in everything," Julia said, "or a dilettante."

"It still doesn't follow," Harcourt said.

"It doesn't matter. Logan knows what I'm talking about."

"As it happens, Hubert Humphrey had strong convictions about quite a few things."

"I'm *not* talking about Hubert Humphrey," Julia said sternly, "and I'm not talking about strong convictions."

"Then what are you talking about?"

"If you don't know, I can't possibly explain it to you."

"Before I forget," said Talbot tactfully, "I have something for

you." He'd left the package of oil and watercolor brushes he'd
bought for Harcourt in London on the front seat of the car.

"For me?" Julia asked.

"For Lyman," Talbot said. "Just a small package. Something you
asked me to pick up for you. Maybe you've forgotten."

"I can't imagine what it could be," Harcourt said. "What do you
suppose it is?"

"I haven't the slightest idea," Julia said. "If it had been me I
would have remembered. Why is it old films always disappoint us
so? Why don't I ever learn? I was very disappointed."

"Everyone enjoyed it," Harcourt said.

"Everyone was bored."

"Sleepy. Too many drinks, maybe," Harcourt said.

"I thought it was very nice," Talbot said.

"How do you know?" Julia said. "You fell asleep."

"I doubt it was intentional," Harcourt said.

"Of course it wasn't intentional. Bad manners are never intentional. I was very disappointed in the evening. In the entire day as
a matter of fact."

"You should have brought her a present," Harcourt said.

"I'm sure he didn't think of us at all while he was on leave."

"I brought her some tennis balls," Talbot said. "What's this I
hear about the new squash court?"

"New squash court?" Harcourt said. "That would be nice,
wouldn't it?" The phone rang. "What new squash court?"

Julia looked at her husband. "Would you get that, please, I'm
too exhausted, my legs are aching."

"Why don't I get it," Talbot said.

"Please sit down," Julia said firmly.

Harcourt disappeared through the doorway. Julia said, "I wanted
to ask you something else but I can't remember now. What was it?"

Talbot tried to look interested. "About DeGroot, maybe."

"No. Oh, yes, I remember." She sat up and pulled her legs under
her, sitting sideways on the sofa. "Would you please explain something to me. I've heard nothing else for days now and it's getting
tiresome."

"Explain what?"

"What everyone's been talking about. At dinner last night, then

again tonight. Agnes Firthdale was talking about Fidel Castro
coming, about the problem with the Russians about Ethiopia. She
seemed au courant, and I felt very stupid. Then they started arguing
about the problem between the Russians and the Jubba government."

"You want the facts or my opinion?"

"The facts. Agnes Firthdale said you're too clever with your
opinions. Far too clever in fact. What do you think she meant?"

"Don't know."

She waited. "You probably offended her in some way."

"Could be."

"You're awfully casual about it."

He shrugged. "Not casual, fatalistic."

"Oh, *really*."

"Only trivial talents are perfect gentlemen. A major talent is
always a bit of a cad."

She sat watching him. "That's ridiculous."

"Could be."

"You're impossible." She reached forward in an impatient gesture to take a cigarette from the inlaid cigarette box. "So tell me
what's happening? What's behind all this cocktail party gossip?"

"Not much, the Russians and the Jubba are having a lovers'
quarrel."

"That's an odd way to put it."

"No, it isn't. If you're really interested, the Jubba think the
Soviets are cheating on them, denying them their Lenin-given historical rights."

"Not too many words, please. Of course I'm interested."

"They're having a falling out."

"You just said that. Why?"

"What Agnes said, Ethiopia. For years the Jubba have been
good socialist soldiers, marching to Moscow's tune. Now with
Ethiopia falling apart next door, the time has come to pay the piper
and Moscow is saying no dice."

"That's mixing your metaphors, isn't it? Pay the piper how?"

"Help them liberate their nomadic grazing lands in Western
Jubbaland, occupied by Ethiopia."

"What exactly do they expect the Russians to do?"

"Help Jubba the way they helped in Angola and Mozambique, give the Jubba National Liberation Front weapons, political support. Free the oppressed Jubba people in Ethiopia from Amharic imperialism."

"That's what Jubba expects?" She was disappointed. "It sounds like a cliché."

"It is. Scientific socialists think in clichés. I'm also simplifying."

"I'm not totally stupid. Don't be condescending." She looked at him. "You don't have to make it too simple, even if you are sleepy. I'm not young Mrs. Kinkaid."

"What's she have to do with it?" Nancy Kinkaid was the wife of the vice consul.

"Nothing. Because she annoys me. She was on the beach parading her children around this afternoon. Did you see her?"

"No. I wasn't trying to make it too simple, I was trying not to make it boring."

"I'm sure." She sipped her drink. "So make it more interesting, please. Why do they expect the Soviets to help? And don't look so bored."

"Because of what I said. The Jubba have been good Marxist soldiers, done their duty, paid their dues to Moscow, supported national liberation abroad. Now they expect the Soviets to help them across the border."

"You sound bored. I want to have it absolutely clear in my own mind. I don't think many people do."

"They don't."

"But you do."

"More or less."

"You're awfully smug."

"I don't feel smug, just tired. Do you really care?"

"That *is* smug. I think that's what Agnes meant, now that I think of it. Too clever in your opinions. Do you think that could be it?"

Harcourt eagerly crossed the room toward them. "What's too clever? Who are we talking about now?"

"I was asking Logan about something Agnes Firthdale tried to explain but couldn't. It doesn't matter. Some other time."

Harcourt sank down on the edge of his chair. "That was the Indian ambassador. I'm afraid he was in his cups."

"He usually is this time of night. What did he want?"

"To invite us to a film showing."

"He sent the invitation, why did he need to call?"

"He wanted to explain. It seems someone from one of his ministries just arrived, so it's not just a film showing."

"How nice," she said sweetly. "I'm not going."

"What were you saying just now, Logan?"

"Julia asked me about Castro and the Russians."

"It was very long and very involved," Julia said. "The next time Agnes mentions it, I'll be ready."

"That's strange, don't you think?" Harcourt said. "Bringing Fidel Castro into it? Bernard seems to think it shows the Russians are grasping at straws."

"Bernard?" Talbot asked.

"DeGroot," Julia said unpleasantly.

"What was Logan explaining?"

"Why the Jubba government is quarreling with the Russians. I'm really too tired to think about it now."

They sat in silence for a few minutes. Harcourt was staring very intently at the bookcases. "Agnes has a very political mind," he said after a minute. "That's the advantage, I suppose, of being born a Hungarian Jew."

Julia put her head back and closed her eyes in an instant of pain. Talbot finished his brandy.

"I think I'd better run along," he said, looking at his watch.

"There's something I meant to ask you," Harcourt said, getting up. "Who's going to Nairobi as ambassador? Any word yet?"

"He doesn't know," Julia said, getting up suddenly. "We've already talked about that. Where have you been all evening?"

"But I've been here," he said, surprised. "Logan and I have hardly had the chance to talk."

"Talk all you like," she said, picking up her glass. "It's late and I'm going to bed."

CHAPTER TWO

The Expatriates

The old well was eighteen kilometers from the border, just a mound of stones at the end of a shallow wadi, but there were no soldiers or drought refugees there, just a few conical tents of the nomads who'd made camp and whose camels and goats grazed in the scrub a hundred meters away.

Dr. George Greevy and Lieutenant Ahmed drove up just as two nomads carried a man with a bloody leg from one of the tents. The nomads, who seemed to know Lieutenant Ahmed, ignored Dr. Greevy in the dusty Soviet-built jeep. They slung the man down near a litter made of poles.

"Good God," Greevy said. The man was either dead or dying. The thin dark legs of a second man were visible inside the camel-skin hut. From the sandals he knew he wasn't a soldier but a nomad. He reached behind the seat for his black medical kit, covered with a fine grit of sand. His loose khaki shirt was dark with sweat even though the day was sunless and densely overcast. A gray belly of hibernal scud rippled off toward the west. The wind had died down, the air was heavy and oppressive; each breath he drew, each muscle he moved brought the sweat swarming to his face and neck. He sat forward and got out stiffly, carrying his bag, a small gray Englishman with a thatch of unruly salt-and-pepper hair, a square face, unshaven for three days, and light blue eyes behind a pair of iron-rimmed spectacles. In the bush, he wore khaki shorts, beige knee hose, and rough leather ankle boots with gum soles, attire his colleagues in the Nairobi UN offices or even his wife in their cool shadowed bungalow in the Nairobi suburbs would have found laughable. He kept his bush clothes hidden in a green metal locker at the UN club in the capital for use during his monthly trips to Jubba.

As he lifted his head he saw Lieutenant Ahmed turn toward him from the tent opening, hand held up in warning. He thought he was asking him to approach warily, as one must do with the nomads, particularly in times of grief. He stopped, hesitated for a decent interval, mopped his face, wiped the dust from his bag, and moved on. His heedlessness brought Ahmed immediately from the tent. "No, wait in the jeep."

"I thought there was something I might do."

"Wait in the jeep, please."

Dr. Greevy obeyed, puzzled at what he wasn't to see. As he plodded back over the harsh rocky pan, he listened to the gabble of voices from inside the tent. He spoke some Jubba, a bit more Arabic, but of these words he understood nothing. Silently he resumed his seat in the dust-covered jeep.

For three days he had been in the bush, looking for evidence of *Trypanosomiasis rhodesiense* and *Plasmodium malariae* among the draw wells and water holes along the Jubba-Ethiopian border. He had also been asked to look into the conditions of the more remote refugee camps whose activities had gone unreported to the UN, which had provisioned the camps since the beginning of the great drought encroaching eastward from the Sahel. The nomads, driven from their scorched grazing lands in Ethiopia, whose government had refused to give them succor, were still appearing in great numbers in Jubba for evacuation and resettlement in the larger camps to the east along the coast. The government was sensitive to inquiries about these more remote camps—the "tertiary camps," the

UN staff in the capital had labeled them in that perfection of bureaucratic classification that reminded him of the Naturhistorisches Museum in Vienna. The drought victims arrived on foot at these camps, were fed, registered, and taken by truck to the larger camps to the east, and finally to locations along the coast where they were taught skills and trades, including fishing, a vocation the nomads despised.

Because most tertiary camps were located in frontier or security zones where army units were also dispersed, Jubba officials refused foreigners permission to inspect them. They also disdained the UN's patronizing advice and its insistence that the rations, medicines, blankets, trucks, and petrol given by international donors be properly certified as having been dispersed as intended and not transferred to the guerrillas of the Western Jubbaland Liberation Front, whose laagers were also concealed along the Ethiopian frontier.

Among foreigners, Dr. Greevy was an exception. Few restrictions limited his solitary travel among the nomads. As a parasitologist and medical adviser for the World Health Organization, he'd roamed this same bush and wasteland since his first visit in 1965, when he'd been the first to identify *Plasmodium ovale* in Western Jubbaland. He had obtained a number of WHO grants for the ministry of health, and scholarships and graduate fellowships for ministry officials for study in England and Scotland.

During this trip he had found only one tertiary camp still in use, that to the north, some twenty kilometers from the Ethiopian frontier. There he had seen what he'd expected to see—inadequate facilities, staff, and medicines and only four young technicians, all recent high school graduates, doing as much as could be expected under the most primitive conditions.

Now as he sat in his jeep waiting for Lieutenant Ahmed, he wondered how the nomads had been injured. Westward across the broken hills and rock-strewn bush veld the rubble was broken by an occasional thorny acacia and sansevieria shrub, by irregular wadis drifted lightly with sand. In the bottom clumps of coarse grass could be found, like the forage just to the south of his jeep, grass from the rains of the season past. The grass had probably brought the nomads here, but from where? They might have hap-

pened on a mine field, he supposed, looking up at the batting of
clouds hanging from the sky like tufts of coarse wool. They reminded him of a yarn mill in the north of England where he'd once
had his practice. The timbers, beams, and roof trusses had been
furred with the gray fleece sent up by the machines; yet there the
operators sat, year after year. A tough, rugged, independent people, the mill hands, like the nomads. He might have been treating
collapsed prostates and arthritic joints in the same small surgery
now, his face as gray as the streets outside, but here he sat instead
looking out beyond the circle of nomadic tents toward their grazing
camels, the air as oppressive as a brick kiln. For him there was
still a kind of miracle in his presence, a kind of providence, like the
fine green grasses that came to the Haud in the north after the first
rains.

The voices inside the tent broke off. He heard the lieutenant's
footsteps approaching but didn't move his head. Far to the west a
brighter band of sky emerged like a glowing ingot from a dark oven
as the sun dropped toward the horizon. The sky was clearing there.
They would have a sunset.

Lieutenant Ahmed started the jeep. They drove in silence over
the hill and down to the track and turned south again along the
hardpan. Dr. Greevy asked no questions. Holding to the wind-
screen, he kept his eyes fastened to the side of the track, hoping to
identify in the flux of rubble and sand some soft, improbable thatch
of mossy vegetation other than the wild henna or sisal, some botani-
cal curiosity that had flowered here in isolation unnoticed all these
years and with the proper development might make these rocky
barrens bloom after all, like the red-and-yellow blossoms of the
sansevieria scrub, year-round forage for camel and cattle. He
seldom looked up. If one looked up, it was all the same; so he
looked down, thinking again of the tents they'd just left. Perhaps
the wounded had strayed across a mine on the Ethiopian side of the
border, perhaps they'd been attacked by a group of *shiftas,* bandits
up from their wasteland in the south from which they foraged into
Kenya as well. Perhaps they'd had a misunderstanding with the
Darawishta, the mobilized police that prowled the interior and kept
the peace between rival nomadic clans as the British Jubbaland

Camel Constabulary had once done in the north, and the Italian Corpo Zaptie had attempted with much less success in the south. Whatever it was, it wasn't his business.

He lifted his eyes as the sun at last reached the horizon, transforming the entire landscape. Even the iron shell of the Russian-built jeep was gilded like the rocks and boulders ahead of them. He was squinting ahead when he saw the sun reflected from the glare of a windshield. Ten minutes later they reached the Darawishta post just beyond the stone obelisk that marked the junction of the two tracks, the westerly of which led to El Goran in Ethiopia. They were two kilometers from the frontier.

Dr. Greevy was surprised to see two Soviet jeeps pulled to the side of the track just north of the red-and-white pole that blocked passage south. On the far side of the barrier were a Jubba army truck and a Toyota with Jubba military plates. Four Soviet military advisers in khaki uniforms leaned over the sides of the lead jeep, where a fifth Russian sat in the front seat fiddling with a portable radio.

Two Darawishta regulars in sand-and-olive camouflaged uniforms leaned against the red-and-white oil drum supporting the barrier, watching the Russians, their automatic rifles slung over their shoulders. Two more stood behind the oil drum on the far side of the track. Inside the guard post, a small blockhouse built of stone and adobe on three sides and galvanized tin on the fourth, covered with a thatched roof, a Darawishta captain held a headset to one ear, listening as he watched the Russians through the open door.

In front of the Toyota, two Jubba army officers leaned against the fender, arms folded. In the bed of the army truck were a dozen men and youths in green khaki, like those just returned from the North Korean training camp. They, too, were looking back over the truck cab toward the Soviet jeep. Some were smiling. They had no weapons.

As Lieutenant Ahmed stopped his jeep at the barrier, one of the Darawishta regulars pushed himself away from the oil drum and stood in front of the jeep, shaking his head, and motioning Ahmed to turn the jeep around. Ahmed waved his hand toward the track ahead. The second Darawishta moved forward, too, unslinging his gun. Greevy watched in silence from his seat, conscious of the guns and the hot dry wind that was now stirring after the heat of the day.

The Russians turned as the Darawishta guard asked Lieutenant Ahmed for his orders. After he was given the identification card from the ministry of health office at Bulet Uen, he handed it back and again told Ahmed to turn the jeep around. He couldn't pass. As the two men argued, a dusty armored personnel carrier came bouncing up the road from the south, carrying an additional six Darawishta troops. In the back of the carrier was a .30-caliber machine gun mounted on a steel firing ring and manned by a slim hatless Jubba youth with a lieutenant's two stars on each shoulder tab.

Ahmed left the jeep to appeal to the Darawishta guard inside the hut. The guard circled the jeep and asked for Greevy's papers. Greevy passed him his ministry of health identification card, a UN laissez-passer, and a letter in Jubba from the minister of health. He glanced at them, laughed, said something to his companion, and handed them back.

The Russian major abruptly climbed from his jeep, pulled on his cotton cap, and approached the red-and-white pole, calling to the two army officers who leaned against the front fenders of the Toyota. He had orders from the headquarters at Bulet Uen, he said in English, from army headquarters. He was proceeding south toward Lugh Ferrani. He demanded the army major let him through.

"Talk to the Darawishta," said the Jubba major, nodding toward the Darawishta captain who'd just left the hut.

The Russian turned and shouted to the Jubba captain, who ignored him, looking instead at Dr. Greevy.

"Who is this man?" he asked Ahmed in Arabic.

Lieutenant Ahmed explained and held out his documentation. The armored carrier had turned off the track and circled to a stop near the shoulder of rubble and stone just in front of the Russian jeep, blocking the track. The Russian major returned to his vehicle and stood conferring with his colleagues. After a minute, he crossed again to the barrier and beckoned the Jubba major.

"Dr. Greevy," the doctor said, giving up his damp packet of documents for the second time. "George Greevy."

"*Dottore?*" the captain repeated, opening the letter. He glanced at it but then lifted his head to look at the Jubba and Soviet majors conferring quietly across the red-and-white barrier. He shouted to the major in Arabic, "If they do not move those jeeps, I will confiscate them, seize them! Tell him that! Those are my orders!" Then he resumed reading the letter. "*Dottore?* What kind of *dottore?*" The wind lifted Dr. Greevy's thatch of hair and pressed against his ears. The sun fell obliquely across the track, no longer so piercing, now a bright metallic haze gilding each stone and boulder along the roadside rubble.

The Russian major returned to his jeep, climbed in, and started the engine. A moment later the second jeep started and the two vehicles circled out over the scrubland and rejoined the track for the trip back to the northeast toward Bulet Uen, the way they had come. The armored carrier rumbled forward very slowly after them. The Jubba lieutenant still leaned against the gun mounting, the .30-caliber barrel tracking the dust lifted by the two vehicles toward the northeast.

"*Jama!*" the Darawishta captain called to the Jubba major. Still carrying the ministry letter, he slipped under the barrier and crossed to the major, holding it out. The major read it, passed it to his companion, and then stood conferring with the police captain. After a minute, they called to Lieutenant Ahmed to join them. Dr. Greevy remained in the jeep, fatigue cramping his joints and settling in that familiar pain at the base of his spine. Still he waited, not looking at the four men who stood talking in front of the Toyota and looking to the west toward the Ethiopian frontier.

At last Lieutenant Ahmed returned to the jeep, climbed behind the wheel, and silently returned Dr. Greevy's documents. The two Jubba army officers got into the Toyota and drove away down the track. The two Darawishta men lifted the red-and-white pole from the supporting oil drums, and Lieutenant Ahmed drove forward very slowly. He continued that way for some time, even after the Toyota had disappeared, but Dr. Greevy asked no questions.

"The old refugee camp near Garba Irir is being used by the Darawishta," Ahmed said finally. "They are keeping some *shiftas* there, some nomads that have caused trouble across the border, attacking the Ethiopian police posts. You know Garba Irir?"

Greevy said he knew it.

"They are keeping them until the ministry decides where to send them. Some will be sent by lorry to the prisons at Jamana or Gelib, but it is not the business of the ministry of health or the UN, not the business of the Russians at Bulet Uen or the Ethiopian police posts. So it is no one's business, not my business, not your business, just the business of the Darawishta. You are a doctor, and since they have no doctors they do what they can."

"I understand," Dr. Greevy said.

Lieutenant Ahmed still drove very slowly. The drifting dust from the Toyota ahead of them had long settled, yet Ahmed didn't increase his speed. The sun had settled below the hills. The batting of clouds overhead was now gray and black, but the seam along the horizon was a fiery red and orange, tinted with purple. The wind still stirred across the barrens, and as the ground rubble was lost to him in the gathering twilight everything about him now seemed the same.

Darkness had fallen as they turned off the track and followed a trail down across a dry streambed and into the long depression formed between two low hills. A final Darawishta roadblock delayed them, but the Jubba guard who flashed his torch through the jeep addressed Lieutenant Ahmed by his rank and name and motioned them forward.

Dr. Greevy wasn't sure what to expect. He supposed the Darawishta was holding a few dissident tribesmen from Western Jubbaland in confinement for their forays into Ethiopia. To keep the peace and prevent an armed clash with the Ethiopian army the Jubba government had long subsidized the Jubba clans whose lands were occupied by Ethiopia, but incidents had increased in recent months: attacks on Ethiopian police posts, on trucks, and even raids on Ethiopian villages. The Ogaden tribesmen of Western Jubbaland had a long history of brigandage, smuggling, and extortion; political opportunists as well, they had recently created their own guerrilla movement, as the Angolans, Mozambicans, and Eritreans had done. Called the Western Jubbaland Liberation Front, its goal was a socialist goal, the liberation of the oppressed Jubba peoples across the border from Ethiopian imperialism. In the capital, the

Soviet ambassador and his cadres, the president's Marxist-Leninist tutors, derided their pathetic pretensions—they were brigands, nothing more, masquerading as a national revolutionary movement.

In the beams of the headlights Dr. Greevy saw a single row of a dozen twenty-man tents, then another row, then a third and a fourth, the outer rows draped with web netting that stretched away toward the circling hills. Vehicles were drawn up in a small motor pool, half hidden under stretched tarpaulins; he smelled gasoline and heard the chug of compressors from the rear, where a larger mess tent stood, the lights strung over the mess tables much too bright to be kerosene pressure lanterns. There he saw a few old men gathered around a table like clan chiefs under a lungi tree, negotiating a problem of grazing or water rights. There was no barbed wire, he saw no *shiftas* in manacles, and the few Darawishta he passed wore only sidearms, not rifles.

A Darawishta carrying a gasoline lantern led them back to a small isolation tent at the rear of the camp where four men lay in confinement on canvas cots, attended by a small young man in a camouflaged khaki uniform. In the light of the lantern, Dr. Greevy had a vague recollection of the young man in the second cot. The attendant spoke his name in passing and Greevy looked at him again. The name seemed familiar. He supposed the youth might have been one of the laboratory technicians he'd helped train in the ministry of health's parasitology division. If so, he had no idea what he was doing in the camp. The young attendant lifted his lantern and moved on, explaining that he'd asked the Darawishta to fetch a doctor because he'd concluded the three men were suffering from the same illness. He didn't know what it was, but he suspected it was communicable. Two of the men were from the same village.

"Which village?" Dr. Greevy asked. The young man, seeing Mahamud Jama's head move, didn't reply. Greevy had seen it, too. "What might the climate be?" He bent to open his kit. "The elevation? Cool, hot, desert, highlands, what?"

"Cool," Major Jama said.

"And this lad?" Greevy said, pulling out his pencil flashlight. "Let's begin with him. Lift the light over here, would you? That's it, right there. Well, let's see now. What do we have? What might it be? Infectious hepatitis, myiasis, cholera, smallpox, onchocerciasis, anthrax—oh, yes, we have, too—schistosomiasis, cerebral malaria. That's it, easy now. Just a look."

The thin figure stirred on the cot as Dr. Greevy's hand moved to the forehead. He lifted one lid, explored the eyeball and socket, then the other, looked up his nostrils, asked him to open his mouth, examined his tongue, then ran his hands under his arms and down his chest. He was shirtless, wearing only a thin pair of cotton shorts; Dr. Greevy unfastened them and asked him to slide them off. He was slow responding until Major Jama spoke, and then he obeyed. The flashlight moved down his hips and probed the genitalia, but Greevy turned to the cot behind him and began to examine the second man.

"Relapsing fever here," he said after inspecting the third man. "I think that's what it is. This one, too. Probably louse-borne. The higher elevations get it, cold and wet, wearing the same clothes through the rainy season. That may be it. See the skin here?" He rubbed his thumb along the sick man's rib cage. "Hasn't been here too long, I'd say. The epidermis is soft, like goat cheese." He turned to the man he'd examined first. "This lad here has syphilis, sorry to say. Hasn't been to Jijiga recently, has he? Some Galla barmaid. But that's what it is, no doubt about it."

"It was an epidemic that worried Major Jama," Ahmed said.

"Oh, yes. I don't doubt it. I don't think he need worry. The water supply is what you have to watch. There was an outbreak of dracontiasis south of here eight years ago, a draw well in a village between Oddur and Uegit. The guinea worm. Very unusual, that was, the first in twenty-five years."

"What would you recommend for the two here?" Major Jama asked.

"These two? I'd take them to Bulet Uen. They can be treated at the clinic there, the sooner the better. This chap, too, poor fellow. Sorry it had to come out like that. I mean it's his business, you see, not mine." He touched the man's cot sympathetically. "Sorry, lad."

"But you're sure the symptoms aren't something . . ." He searched for the word in Arabic, then said something to the lieutenant in Italian.

"Communicable," Dr. Greevy said. "Yes, I'm sure. But mind what I said about your water."

They left the tent. In the darkness outside Dr. Greevy, disoriented, moved off in the wrong direction. As he did, he caught sight of a larger tent he hadn't noticed; its side flaps were drawn up and a half-dozen army officers sat around a long table listening to an old bearded nomad wearing a pistol belt sitting near a military map board. A young Darawishta officer stood to the right of the map board, pointer in his hand, following the contour lines and the sites the old nomad was describing. The old man looked like one of those sly old chiefs from Western Jubbaland who extorted 800 to 1,000 shillings a month from the government as his price for keeping the peace with the Ethiopian army and police posts across the border.

"This way, Doctor," Lieutenant Ahmed quickly called. Greevy turned away.

In a small mess tent to the side of the large mess tent, he and Lieutenant Ahmed drank glasses of sweet hot tea scented with cinnamon and cloves while the meal was brought from the adjacent mess. They were served a kind of pasta and goulash, lumps of tough meat mixed with rice and tinned tomatoes, odd fare for such a remote camp, Greevy thought. They slept in a visitors' tent with a wooden floor.

Dawn broke and he sat up, but the tents were gone, all struck, all vanished now. He was alone in the center of a thorn zariba or camel enclosure, the thin gray light unchanging now, the clouds very low. He was conscious of the wind and the desolation of the wasteland. The nomads had fled, the dream so seamless, so vivid he knew it was true. Here they had come, season after season moving their herds into the pasturage of the Haud and Western Jubbaland as they had done for centuries in their seasonal search for grass and water, unaware of boundaries or political demarcations, aware only that the land was Allah's, like the rain that had brought the grass, a bounty for all belonging to no man but Allah. The idea of someone owning this land and its water and grass was as alien to them as the idea that men might own the sky or the stars, and they moved their animals and tents with the season, as they had always done.

But now they had gone and the grazing lands were empty; the rains had come, but they'd brought nothing, just the heavy sodden cold of the Ethiopian highlands. So they had fled. *From what?*

There was nothing at first, only the wind, the terrible desolation of the wind, but then far in the distance to the north he saw a thin column of black smoke. Just that—just smoke, cold, and wind—no larks, no weaverbirds, no bustards, no Maribou stork, and no ravens. Frightened, he moved out of the zareba and began to follow the track north. But then he saw a long column of men moving along the track toward him, single file. They were small, shrunken, bent like gnomes or dwarfs, some wearing hoods, like medieval monks, all in heavy overcoats, some with lepers' rags about their crusted misshapen feet, some carrying flails, hoes, mattocks, many with rifles. They are coming from the mountains, he thought. These are the people of the mountains, leaving their cold villages in the massif, leaving their oxen, the stone houses, the misshapen fields they tilled for their feudal masters, leaving their poverty, their filth, their superstitious liturgy, the smell of incense and candle smoke in their grotto chapels—the serfs from the mountains, as small as dwarfs, indentured peasants in heavy overcoats, each carrying an implement or a musket, and as the face of the first peasant lifted toward him and withdrew his hood he saw not a man's face at all but the small wizened smoke-blackened face of a bat and then twenty more bats behind him, then thirty, and then the column of smoke wasn't smoke at all but the continuing exodus from the cave high in the mountains, a dark cave, filled with the relics and incense of some mad vestige of Christendom, its brutalized serfs come to claim this veld which the weaverbirds, the francolin, guinea fowl, dik-dik, and bustard had fled, just as the nomads had fled. And as Dr. Greevy finally understood, a small figure lifted his scythe, another his flail, and he saw the tiny eyes blaze from the darkness of the cowl, fierce embers of glowing nullity, like charcoal blown white by the wind, felt the first agonizing bloody blow, then a second, a third, and then nothing.

"*Ka, ka!*" someone called softly. Dr. Greevy sat up, his shirt soaked, terrified, looking toward the entrance of the tent where a Darawishta guard with a hand torch was telling Lieutenant Ahmed to get up. He rolled over and looked at his watch. The sky wasn't leaden, the scud not drifting over the flat-topped hills. The sky was black beyond the tent flap, the moonlight like snow. It was four twenty in the morning. He brought his feet to the floor and took a long deep breath, and as he did the cold dampness of the medieval winter was gone, and he felt instead the warmth of the tent, as smoky, rich, and warm as camel's milk just drawn from the udder, and then with the joy of the dead rejoined the living heard from far out on the veld the shrill retreating bark of a jackal.

They drank hot tea in the small mess. At five they were on the track again. The Soviet jeep had been filled with gasoline from jerry cans, and they left the group of tents in the same darkness in which they arrived.

As the dawn showed in the east and then the light came, warming his face and arms and stirring his blood, Dr. Greevy knew why the Soviet jeep had been turned back and understood what he had seen the previous night. He had seen something remarkable. It brought first a sense of hope, but then as the sun rose in the sky and the terrible heat descended, dense and suffocating, his elation passed. The tainted wind brought the corruption of something lying hidden beyond a hillock where ravens were feeding and high above them buzzards were circling, but then the dust bore it away.

There's going to be a war, he thought in despair, the knowledge as certain as his dream, a bloody, endless, savage war. . . .

□ □ □

On station 240 miles above the Horn of Africa the geosynchronous satellite looked down on a stony projection of reddish-ocher wasteland dotted by microscopic flocculence inland along the high plateaus, like summer cotton in the delta, by canyons of billowing cumulus along the escarpments, and reefs of mackerel cloud shingled out along the deep indigo of the Indian Ocean. In Western Jubbaland the dun-colored scrub was often hidden by clouds during the rainy season but rarely the coastal littoral. The Rhyolite satellite monitored microwave and telemetry transmissions from ground stations far below; the KH-11 satellite sent back telephoto signals and high-resolution film packets ejected at intervals into the atmosphere to be retrieved by American C-130s in the Pacific.

U.S. film analysts could easily identify MIG-21 crates awaiting unloading on the decks of Soviet freighters in Benaadir, the familiar configuration of the Soviet-built missile rework facility at Muzaffar, or the clusters of SAM-2 missile installations around the capital, but not always the fifty-gallon petrol drums being stored at the small settlement west of Dusa Mareb or the concealed guerrilla encampments like the one visited by Dr. Greevy, often hidden by cloud cover, unlike the white-hulled banana boat that now lay at anchor a hundred yards off the beach at Merca, visible from Nicola Seretti's brick villa on the hill overlooking the sea and the beach below, where she stood with Captain Ali Hussein.

"At the hospital I talked to no one," he said, stopping on the shingle to look at his military watch. "No one at all." His dark face was emaciated, his cheeks pitted; his eyes were deeply set behind the thin blade of nose.

"A pity. I don't like hospitals," Nicola said, not at all sure why Hussein had sought her out. To gossip, she supposed.

She had walked down to the beach late that morning to meet the fisherman who'd promised her sea perch, but his small boat hadn't come. Captain Hussein had joined her there, leaving his car behind at her villa. He had been in the military hospital for two weeks, recovering from hepatitis, and had spent the last two days at the government rest house just below Merca. Tomorrow he would report to his unit at Burao. He was as thin as a stick, dressed in freshly laundered military khakis which seemed too large. The blouse stood out from his slight shoulders like a cuirass. His boots were newly polished, the color of oxblood.

They climbed on. She had been to the butcher shop in the village that morning and was wearing flat-heeled leather sandals, treacherous on the spines of volcanic rock. The sky was a metallic blue. Gulls floated on the sea near the banana boat and sailed below the cliffs.

"At Burao before I left there was much talk," he continued ambiguously. "At the hospital Abucar's cousin came to see me. He had heard the talk, too, but no one at the foreign ministry knows. Major Jama's cousin on the revolutionary council says he knows nothing. But at Burao we knew something was happening. If they knew more, some would do something."

"Knew what? What do you think is happening?" She stopped to

rest midway up the rocks above a tidal pool. A dusty gray Fiat was passing along the road.

Hussein stopped, too.

"What the Old Man is planning. He is serious this time. Even the Russians are suspicious. They've reduced the training rations by half, reduced the ammunition allowances, even the petrol. When a tank runs out of petrol, they don't send a tanker with petrol, they send a crane truck. They follow the battalion commanders, always watching." His voice had dropped. "They're suspicious, every week more suspicious. They're right. It will only get worse, then the disaster."

"Disaster?" She stopped again, daring to smile as she glanced up at his cruelly pitted cheeks. He'd been too long recuperating in the hospital. Never known for his physical courage, he'd always been a worrier; his face proclaimed it as quickly as its smell, always tainted with bitter creams and unguents. His Jubba nickname was Skull-face, a name he endured but despised. "What kind of disaster?"

"A war with the Ethiopians."

"A war? You're not serious. War with the Ethiopians? You think there will be a war?"

"Yes, but not just me. That was the talk at Burao before I left."

She'd never taken his tiresome pessimism seriously; his gloom always disguised other grievances: lack of promotion, poor health, his wife's family.

"How many of you feel this way, how many are there? Major Jama, how does he feel?" She brought her sunglasses down. Major Jama was his former commanding officer. An Isaq from the north, he had joined Captain Hussein and other officers from the Mejerteen clan who a year earlier had petitioned the ministry with their complaints, primarily their growing dissatisfaction with a ministry ruled by officers from tribes of inferior rank. They'd been dispersed to separate commands.

"Jama feels the way I do, the way all of us do." He took off his beret and reset it again as they moved along the ledge of volcanic rock.

She didn't believe that either. "What do you plan to do?"

"Warn them, tell them what would happen."

"Warn who? Other officers? These are just rumors, just gossip; things won't change."

"Is that what the Italians say?"

"About what, your disaster? I don't know what the Italians are saying."

"You haven't talked to them?"

"To Ambassador Malfatti, yes, but not about anything like that. Just about the Italian teachers at the university."

"There is trouble?"

"They have grievances, just as you have."

"Everyone has grievances. You are not serious people, you Italians. Do you know the military attaché?"

"No, he just came."

"The old one, Colonel Lattanzi, was a foolish man. What about the English? What are they saying?"

"I see very few of them."

"The Americans are shut away, no one talks to them." He looked back at her, remembering something. "Abucar says you are there sometimes. He heard the NSS say your car was there at the gate for a week."

"I was helping the ambassador's wife with her garden."

She'd been right; he had come to gossip, as he once did with Seretti.

He stopped again, gazing down at the banana boat as he readjusted his beret. It didn't satisfy him and he took it off and reset it. "So you talk to the Americans."

"Yes, but not about serious things."

"What do they talk about?"

"Little things."

"Like the Italian teachers? They complain?"

"Yes, but not the same way."

"They say he is a silly man, that he isn't serious."

"Who?"

"The ambassador. How is he called?"

"Harcourt."

"Is he as foolish as Colonel Lattanzi?"

"I don't really know."

He smoothed his billowing tunic and hitched up his britches.

With his pitifully small stature, his stiffly pressed uniform, a size too large, his cocklike manner, and his pathetic hypochondria, he seemed an absurd figure. "What do they say about the Old Man's difficulty with the Russians?"

"The Americans? I don't know; we've never talked about it."

"They don't ask questions about what is happening?"

"Not really."

This surprised him so much he forgot about his beret. "So they are not curious? Not like you Italians, wanting to know everything, all the gossip."

Like many weak men with an affliction, he prided himself on his bluntness, as if cruelty were a right he'd earned, but his small nervous hands were the hands of a timid boy.

"I don't know them well enough to say that."

Another car passed, this one a dusty black Fiat. She asked if the president was coming to the government rest house for the weekend.

He said he didn't know, watching the car suspiciously, still frowning. Then he remembered another piece of gossip. "Abucar's cousin at the foreign ministry told me there is a new man, a new deputy ambassador, very busy, seeing people, talking to people. How is he called?"

She followed him up the path to the asphalt road, trying to think whom he meant, then stopped for a minute.

"His name is DeGroot," she remembered.

"They say he was here before."

They crossed the road. Curtained by the heat lifting from the asphalt road, the village in the distance was a dusty shimmering haze, only the highest foliage of the old laurels rising above it.

"In the north, in Hargusha," she said.

"A northerner?" He looked at her suspiciously. "Now they send him again? Why? Did he say?"

"I don't know," she said indifferently. "They change constantly, don't they, the local diplomats. Just when you get to know them, they go away. I only met him once. He seems to me an odd man, not at all interesting."

"Who else is there, who else important?"

"No one, no one at all."

"So there is no one serious?"

They began the long climb up the winding road to her house overlooking the sea.

"No one I know. Why are you asking?" She stopped for a minute to rest, looking out to sea, wondering why he was so curious about Malfatti, about the British and Americans. To gossip, yes, but why about diplomats he didn't know and cared nothing about? The deep royal purple was broken by rows of whitecaps moving beyond the reef; the expanse beyond deserted except for the single white-hulled banana boat.

Looking to the south, she thought she saw the fisherman's boat drawn up in the surf near the beach where the East Germans often came. A few stood waist-deep in the sea, holding on to the gunwales, buying *her* perch, she thought irritably.

"Why were you asking me about these diplomats?" she called to him and laughed. "What is it? Do you want me to give them a message?"

Captain Hussein had climbed stoically on and didn't turn.

She caught up with him. "Would you like to talk to Malfatti?"

"No. It would be interesting to know what he says, what he is thinking. I thought you would know."

"Then why not ask him?"

"Don't be foolish. Seretti wasn't foolish. He would have known what to do. The Italian ambassador listened to him."

Angry suddenly, she had no chance to reply. Samina, her housekeeper, was waiting in the shadows outside the rear door, dressed in a bright yellow dress, her lips lightly rouged. She was holding a letter addressed to her son at his military unit in Burao, written out in the uncertain Italian handwriting she was so proud of. Hussein would take it back with him.

She ignored Nicola as she delivered her letter to Captain Hussein. Afterwards she brought a basket of bananas from the kitchen to give to him.

"Where is he now—Federico?" Nicola asked as she walked with Hussein to his car. Federico was her late husband's son, half Italian, half Jubba.

"Umcit," Hussein said vaguely, inspecting the bananas.

"Umcit? Federico's military unit is there?"

He nodded his head and looked back at Samina, smiled and

waved. Nicola waited impatiently, holding the door open. "I thought Federico was at Burao."

"At Umcit," Hussein repeated as he slid behind the wheel. "Not a military unit, with the *shiftas,* bandits, renegades, the Old Man's people. The disaster I told you about, where his war will begin."

Too astonished to reply, she stood holding the open door. On the seat beside Hussein was a pair of driving gloves, which he now put carefully on.

"Why didn't you tell me!" she demanded.

"Why didn't you ask, woman?"

She slammed the door shut viciously. "You're a fool!"

He didn't turn. She watched the car drive away down the hill, and after it disappeared and the sound of the wind and surf had returned she still hadn't moved. Seretti would have been as furious as she had been, but Seretti wouldn't have called him a fool—he would have known what to do. She knew only her own helplessness and it was that which kept her there, unable to return to Samina's kitchen, looking down the empty road.

CHAPTER THREE
Dreams of Empire

Before Talbot's home leave the embassy was an agreeably listless little post, content with its drowsy irrelevance on an isolated stretch of the East African coast. The climate was too torrid for the Protestant work ethic in any case, he was fond of telling the few visitors he got over an afternoon gin-tonic, which was why the Italians had colonized it in the first place. Nations sink to the level of their haplessness, he would add cleverly, warming to his subject, the reason the Russians were there now. The British had shown better judgment in confining their colonial mandate to the cool highlands and mountains of the north, where they'd done better, at least if a decent respect for privacy, habeas corpus, and the traffic code was any example. It was the Italians, on the other hand, who'd taught the local Jubba to drive, the Italian example the Jubba had followed in introducing that parliamentary anarchy that led to the 1969 army coup and the mini-Marxist state that had followed.

Goaded by Nicholas Bashford-Jones, the British commercial officer, he'd repeated these remarks over after-dinner port at the British ambassador's residence a few months earlier. Firthdale had been amused but not Ambassador Malfatti, but it was Firthdale's port Talbot was drinking that night, not Malfatti's. As he said goodbye at the door, Agnes Firthdale had told him rather dryly that the next time he was at the Italian residence, he would have to think of something equally wicked to pay off the debt.

Reconciled to the sleepy ineptitude of the embassy, he had taken less notice of its appearance, never mind that it looked like some decaying Ottoman hotel or seamen's hostel in the back streets of Istanbul or Alexandria; it was adequate enough for a diplomatic mission to a xenophobic little nation of nomads and camel ports. If it wasn't the vibrant nerve center that U.S. NATO at Brussels had been—electric typewriters clattering away, officers and secretaries scurrying about with cables to clear, planes to be met, cars and drivers to be dispatched—it had a certain welcome tranquillity of its own, a tomblike refuge for recovering from late nights and crippling hangovers.

The embassy lobby just inside the massive front door was as unimposing as the building. The first floor beyond was a maze of narrow corridors, jerry-built partitions, and small offices occupied by the local Jubba administrative staff. During the morning hours the rooms smelled of boiled coffee and frying meat from the small unventilated snack bar next to the small dispensary. On the vaulted second floor where the marine guard sat were the communications unit, the CIA suite, and the administrative section.

Harcourt and DeGroot occupied two large offices adjacent to one another in the third-floor executive suite, reached through a single reception room where their two secretaries sat. Harcourt's office faced the sea, DeGroot's overlooked a small alley and mosque. At the other end of the building was the small library and the seldom used embassy conference room. Talbot's small office was just off the secretarial suite in front of DeGroot's. Since his return, however, he found himself spending most of his time in Shaughnessy's slovenly little first-floor office.

Like most ambassadors, Harcourt let his deputy chief of mission handle the embassy's daily administrative detail, and DeGroot had taken charge in imperious fashion.

On Talbot's desk the first morning after his return he found a stack of file folders filled with handwritten notes and incomprehensible statistics brought up from Shaughnessy's office on the first floor. Atop the folders was a neatly typed memo from DeGroot noting that the semi-annual reports on foreign exchange, foreign trade, price indices, and the livestock and banana industries were long overdue:

> I am tasking you, effective today as economic officer, ad interim, to put these reports in order.
>
> B. G. DeGroot

Accustomed to arranging his own schedule as suited his interests, or the lack of them, Talbot was annoyed. At most he drafted three cables a week. The remainder of his time he spent roaming about visiting his counterparts at other embassies, most often the Arabs, whose indolence sometimes staggered his own, visiting with Whittington, the CIA station chief, reflecting idly at his desk, feet up, or reading ponderously, should someone happen by and glance in. *The Economist,* the *International Herald Tribune,* and *Le Monde*—the latter in preparation for his assignment to Paris, scheduled for November—were all kept within grabbing distance on the corner of his typing table. Then, when he was bored out of his skull, he could always fuss with his draft monograph, *The Politics of Poverty,* which was to be the summation of his two years' experience in the Horn of Africa. An editor at the MIT security review had written him asking about any articles-in-progress. The monograph was three months overdue.

DeGroot's rude injunction that he was expected to do the work of both the political and economic sections was disruptive, to say the least: *Who in the hell was going to read all this shit?*

Not Washington, certainly, where no one doubted Jubba's irrelevance. The embassy had no AID mission, no military attachés, no Peace Corps, and an overaged CIA station chief who spent as much time in his Boston whaler on the Indian Ocean as he did his small suite on the second floor of the embassy. As far as the Russians were concerned—and there were 2,500 to 3,000 of them—there was little a CIA station chief could do, as Talbot knew full well. He had once followed Whittington into the men's room at the Giubba Hotel during a diplomatic reception, he at the urinal, Whittington into a

stall; within a few minutes the two urinals on both sides were occupied, so were the two stalls, all in place as the assistant Soviet cultural attaché wandered in to wash his hands, followed by an Italian
journalist and the assistant Iraqi military attaché.

"I wonder," Talbot asked idly at the bar afterwards, "just who in
the hell was trying to dick whom?"

Whittington didn't know, didn't seem to care. The offshore feeding habits of yellowfin tuna and king mackerel interested him more.
Jubba was very much a closed book, a lost cause. Even if he did
have a few local assets, interest was negligible in the Washington intelligence community; the routine military intel could be obtained
more easily and at less risk by technical means, by satellite cameras
and telemetry. If the Soviets were really doing something suspiciously nasty, like building new facilities for their Indian Ocean
nuclear subs at Muzaffar, a U-2 could always be sent over from
Diego Garcia. So Whittington's dilemma was similar to Talbot's
and everyone else's, an excuse for doing little at all.

The communications center, including Whittington's small commo
room with its two-man staff, was often silent for hours on end. Miss
Virgil, the lone State Department communications clerk, spent most
of her time working crossword puzzles or knitting granny-square af-
ghans. She sent out few cables and got back fewer in return. Those
she sent were rarely read at the State Department by anyone except
a junior desk officer in a windowless little office on the fifth floor
who kept a distant eye on Jubba and a few other minor offshore
principalities in the Indian Ocean.

Even Ambassador Harcourt himself seemed content with Benaadir's drowsy isolation. A man of modest ambition, he had no ag-
grandizing needs apart from his unhappy wife's personal comfort.
He was nearing sixty and until his unexpected nomination under a
departing Republican administration had fully expected to be retired. He planned to settle in Italy, Spain, or southern France and
paint landscapes. He'd accepted the post not to rejuvenate a lan-
guishing career but as a final honorarium to add to those other
mementos of thirty years' service that would accompany him into
retirement. He'd spent most of his career in and around the Mediterranean, most recently as a consul general in Italy, a suitable place
for a man with little interest in politics and no political imagination.

In his previous posts, sustained by familiar cultures within civilized frontiers, no imagination had been required. His sole qualification for the assignment was his fluency in Italian, the language preferred by the Italian-educated president. If Washington had its differences with Jubba, as it did, they could at least be intelligently discussed in a civilized language, the message Harcourt gave Talbot the week after his arrival the previous November and the only rationale Talbot had ever heard him claim for his ambassadorship. As far as the Russians were concerned, there was nothing to be learned from the uncommunicative Russian ambassador not available in the pages of *Pravda* or *Izvestia*.

Language and culture aside, Washington's differences with Jubba were so profound that whatever DeGroot's ambition the embassy fiefdom would grow no larger: no more modern or more impressive chancellory, no more officers and staff personnel, no more vehicles. They would be denied because the only raj permitted by the host Jubba government was that of the Soviet Union.

Moreover, if the Jubba government didn't curtail DeGroot's ambition, Washington soon would, Talbot predicted, since it preferred lethargy or even sloth in the most primitive backwaters to the mindless dynamism of the bureaucratic empire builder who brought a bustle that generated more telegrams and posed more questions than a junior desk officer could answer.

When that happened, the attention of country directors and assistant secretaries was drawn from weightier matters, and the ambassador was politely told that in view of the worldwide telegraphic overload, some reduction in cable traffic would be appreciated. In the absence of an earthquake, a tidal wave, or the plague, a timely letter sent by pouch to the desk officer would do nicely, thank you.

DeGroot seemed never to have heard of this higher imperative.

□   □   □

DeGroot had called Shaughnessy lax, Talbot remembered, confronting his sloth from the doorway of Shaughnessy's disorderly office that first morning, but that wasn't quite the word for it. Whatever the pleasure of Shaughnessy's company as a drinking and carousing companion, he had appalling work habits. His little office was hidden away on a narrow back corridor on the first floor. Shaughnessy always kept the door locked when he wasn't at his desk, even from the embassy clean-up crew, not because of the secrecy of his work, but because he did so little of it. The only discipline to his daily life was in synchronizing his goings and comings with those of the ambassador, a trick he'd learned from Talbot. He arrived punctually at the front door precisely three minutes before Harcourt and departed three minutes after, which meant that Shaughnessy, Talbot, and finally Harcourt all marched in late and marched out early in reverse order, as predictably as the changing of the guard. His bookcase was piled with yellowing newspapers, circulars, and an occasional soft drink bottle, like the floor and windowsill nearby. His habits had deteriorated even more since the departure of his overworked Jubba commercial assistant six months earlier.

Searching through Shaughnessy's desk drawers that first morning, looking for his chron file missing from his third-floor office safe, Talbot found hidden away in the bottom drawer with a few desiccated tooth-worked candy bars a dozen or so requests for commercial reports on local firms forwarded from the Commerce Department in Washington, unanswered. Some dated back six months. He didn't know whether DeGroot knew about these or not, but he left them there, buried under the tattered copies of *Playboy* borrowed from the marine house and never returned. In the commercial library in the adjacent room he found three months of unopened book cartons and fifteen heavy envelopes filled with revisions for the *Foreign Affairs* manual economic section, none of which had yet been distributed. Talbot's missing chron file wasn't there either. It contained copies of every telegram, airgram, and memo he'd drafted since he'd arrived at post two years earlier, his own historical archive, his intellectual *Summa,* every political argument he'd written during the past two years honed to Augustan clarity.

Shaughnessy had made use of it during his absence, DeGroot's secretary told him. (She was also his secretary when she deigned give him a few minutes' typing time.) She suspected Shaughnessy probably misfiled it but predicted it would turn up in time, probably in Shaughnessy's airfreight to Mozambique. She laughed as she said this, thinking it funny, but Talbot wasn't amused. Without the file he felt like an amnesiac, his memory of what he'd written during the past twenty-four months slipping away as furtively as those dissolving soap slivers he'd tried to retrieve from under the boards of his shower floor.

DeGroot had made other changes as well. Preferring to live in the penthouse apartment at the walled-in residential compound rather than the isolated beach villa, he'd banned all non-American cars from inside the gates, forbade the washing of diapers in the basement except on Tuesdays and Fridays, and curtailed the number of official cars available to staff members who had arrived without automobiles. He also abolished the embassy film committee which selected the films ordered from Nairobi for the twice-weekly showings at the compound and reserved that decision for Rhinehart, the slow-witted administrative officer, by now under DeGroot's thumb. Then there was the matter of his missing piano, which hadn't yet been found at the port, although the remainder of his limited household shipment had arrived.

The only young children at post were the Kinkaids' and those of the two young communicators who worked for Whittington. His local operations were also affected by the ban on non-American cars from the compound, since they included the car belonging to an admirer of Whittington's secretary, an Arab ambassador, and a CIA-controlled asset who was regularly debriefed in her second-story apartment.

Whether DeGroot was aware of this or not, Talbot didn't know, but Whittington, like Don Kinkaid, had accepted the changes without protest. Harcourt, who still arrived late and departed early, hardly seemed aware of the changes.

In addition to appointing him economic officer, ad interim, to clean up Shaughnessy's mess, DeGroot treated him as he would a staff aide. Five times that first week he was interrupted at his work on the first floor by a call from DeGroot's secretary, instructing him to go to the first floor reception desk to escort visitors to DeGroot's office. They were invariably DeGroot's counterparts from other diplomatic missions, returning his courtesy calls, most often the worst of the lot, men Talbot had never been able to take seriously, just the protocol poodles who thrived on diplomatic ceremony and took to DeGroot like spaniels to a stick.

He had thought DeGroot's administrative overhaul might be finished by now, but no such luck. Returning to his third-floor office late on the second morning, he found Kinkaid, the vice consul, waiting with the marine gunny in his doorway. The two had stopped by on their way from DeGroot's office to tell him that the call-names for the embassy emergency communications net had been changed. There was a radio check that afternoon.

"You're Firefly now," said Kinkaid, "that's what I was told anyway. You'd better make a note of it."

"I prefer Honker," Talbot said.

The marine corps gunny stood next to him in uniform, holding a clipboard. "Yes, sir, all them's been changed."

"As far as I'm concerned, I'm still Honker."

"Sorry, Mr. Talbot," said the gunny, "but I'm afraid you're Firefly now."

"Who's Honker?"

"No one, sir."

"I liked Honker."

"Well, we're just telling you," Kinkaid said. "You might want to write this down. The embassy's Able, the compound is Baker now."

"That doesn't show much imagination, does it?"

Kinkaid shrugged, sucked on his pipe, and said nothing. Tall and lanky with broad shoulders and stiff corn-colored hair, he was never without his pipe, lit or unlit, although he looked barely old enough to shave. He was four years younger than Talbot and had served in Malawi in the Peace Corps and then in Botswana, where he had met his wife. He never wore a jacket or tie to the embassy, but favored brightly colored African shirts, chinos, and open-toed sandals. He was regarded as the embassy's resident expert on African affairs, an agreeable enough arrangement for Talbot, who thought African-studies people one-note primitivists, like anthropologists who taught themselves to play weird archaic instruments cross-legged on their Navajo rugs or musicians who played the timpani, men waiting out their professional lives through long hours of the classical repertoire until their shattering moment of percussion came—a coup or a disaster of some kind that vanished from the headlines as quickly as it was reported. With his gaudy African shirts, Kinkaid looked like a 4-H Clubber from Iowa who'd entered the foreign service after he'd discovered Africa in the Peace Corps, which was more or less what he was. Talbot thought the Peace Corps a treacherous introduction to diplomacy, since it taught that all foreigners were its friends, who through faith, honesty, and good works would finally claim the civilized status of Peace Corps fuglemen like Kinkaid. The missionaries had once had the same creed. Talbot told him so one day in annoyance during a country team meeting; Kinkaid nodded, smiled, and happily reset his pipe, taking it as a compliment.

The only two Black African embassies of any significance were the Nigerian and Kenyan embassies, whose staff Kinkaid sedulously cultivated. The Nigerians were the most slippery—Christian, Moslem, and animist, all in the same skin, loud laughers and loud smilers, fluent in four or five tribal languages, royalists, British-style parliamentarians, anarchists, socialists as well, whatever suited the national moment. Whoever they were, and Talbot didn't know who they were, they were infinitely slyer than Iowa cornhuskers like Kinkaid.

He felt differently about Kinkaid's wife Nancy, a sweet outgoing blond girl he'd danced with too many times at the New Year's dance, a little dizzily for both; he'd had too much to drink and so had she. Until that night, he'd never taken much notice of her. Her husband, busy entertaining the Nigerian couple he'd brought as guests, talking African politics, no doubt, hadn't seemed to mind, although Julia had. "I think that was rather indiscreet of you," she'd told him the following noon at her beach cottage, where he'd gone to sprawl in the sun and sweat out an awful hangover. "She's religious, you know. Her parents were missionaries."

He hadn't known that, wasn't sure what it meant, that he would have cared if he'd known what it meant.

"What happened to Bug House and Turkey Roost?" Talbot asked.

"It's all been changed," the Gunny said. Talbot made no move to reach for his pad and pencil. "What's the residence?"

"Lighthouse."

"I liked Honker. Who changed it?"

"Mr. DeGroot."

"Why'd he change it?"

"He didn't say, just called us up and changed it. So we're just telling you."

"We're getting the new list typed up," Kinkaid said. "He wants everyone standing by this afternoon for a radio check."

"This afternoon I may be busy. What time?"

"We can't say."

"Why not?"

"It won't be a real simulated emergency if everyone knows," the Gunny said.

DeGroot was nickel-and-diming him to death. "If you think I'm going to hang around my radio waiting for a check all afternoon, you're crazy."

"All we're doing is carrying out orders," Kinkaid said. "We'll have the new names typed up and sent around."

As they were leaving, Miss Simpson, Harcourt's secretary, appeared in the door. She was pepper-haired and played golf, a strong-minded foreign service spinster. "Mr. DeGroot asked me to tell you the Iranian chargé is coming at eleven thirty. Would you bring him up?"

"Thanks. I'll be there. There's a radio check this afternoon. Does the ambassador know?"

"I sent him a note."

"You sure you got the time right?"

"Four thirty."

"That's it. You're way ahead of me."

Sweet Miss Simpson, his spy in the enemy camp.

DeGroot didn't mention his injunction directing Talbot to take over economic reporting responsibilities during their *tour d'horizon* that first morning in Ambassador Harcourt's office, a meeting arranged to bring Talbot up to date on the events of the past month. He learned that during his absence Osman Jama, the secretary general of the foreign ministry had finally accepted the ambassador's long-standing invitation to dinner, *en famille,* at the residence.

For as long as Talbot had been at post and even before, the ambassador's sole ambition and the raison d'être for the U.S. diplomatic presence seemed to be to persuade the director general of the foreign ministry to accept the ambassador's dinner invitation. No senior Jubba government official had set foot in an American residence for years. Harcourt's predecessor had failed, as his predecessor had failed, but now, after years of diplomatic isolation and irrelevance, Harcourt had succeeded.

So the director general had come to the residence to dine, accompanied by the Dr. Mohammed Hussein, Ambassador Firthdale's and Talbot's bête noire, the director of protocol at the foreign ministry.

"I think it was an incremental success," said DeGroot, who'd renewed the invitation during his courtesy call at the foreign ministry and who was given credit for reopening the dialogue.

"It's obvious we've suffered too long from a lack of communication," he'd explained in that maddening artificial voice, a little pink-eyed, too, Talbot noticed, watching the handkerchief dab at his nose. He suffered from some air-conditioner-borne allergy. "I've detected among my many friends here a pathetic eagerness to be better understood. A nation striving desperately to clothe, dress, feed, and teach itself needs not only our patience but our understanding. Misery and hunger, as they told the ambassador, know no ideology."

Ambassador Harcourt smiled appreciatively at these warm platitudes, his blue eyes filled with kindness. For Talbot they were symptomatic of everything else that was wrong with a diplomacy that knew nothing about itself except its egregious good will.

It didn't matter that there were 3,000 Soviet military and civilian advisers in country, 1,200 Chinese, a hundred or so North Koreans and Cubans, diplomatic missions from Hanoi and the PLO, fifty or sixty East Germans, most of them intelligence and security officers led by a Colonel Kohler from the GDR ministry of state security, the Ministerium für Staatssicherheit, a handful of Bulgarians and Czechs who'd successfully suborned the various ministries to which they were assigned. It didn't seem to matter either that the country's friendship treaty with the Soviet Union gave the Russians unrestricted access to local ministries, airfields, and the missile rework facility and deep-water port at Muzaffar for its Indian Ocean fleet, while the U.S. couldn't even bring a dinghy into port. All of this might be neutered if the director general of the foreign ministry might somehow deign to accept the ambassador's dinner invitation.

Nor had Harcourt and DeGroot noticed, as Talbot reminded them, that the headlines and editorials in the daily press had remained hysterically the same since the long-awaited dinner: a fresh new wind was sweeping across the Horn of Africa, invigorated by the success of national liberation in Vietnam, where the American imperialists had withdrawn in defeat, and in Mozambique and Angola, which Portuguese colonialism had finally abandoned in humiliation.

DeGroot dismissed this with a silly smile. "No one takes the press seriously," he said to Harcourt, not looking at Talbot at all. "No one. One must look behind the headlines, as I have. Among my many friends I've visited since my arrival, men of patriotic aspiration, I've found a most somber complaint, as I'm sure you have. They long desperately for an alternative to their present dilemma, which has so humiliatingly forced them into the Soviet embrace. These press editorials mean nothing. What is depressingly clear is the historical record. The historical record is what we should keep in mind."

He then explained what, for Talbot, needed no explanation; he had heard it too often from the Jubba government itself: *Don't blame us, blame Washington. You made us what we are.*

"Had it not been for an anachronistic Ethiopian policy pursued so blindly over the past two decades," he continued, "our friends here would be firmly in the Western camp. No society is more egalitarian, more democratic; no peoples have suffered more from Ethiopian or Amharic imperialism. Now they find themselves pariahs, outcasts, tarred by the anti-Soviet brush."

So that first morning DeGroot had clarified the differences between them. He intended to change political relations no less than the administration of the embassy.

Talbot learned that in addition to his courtesy calls he'd met with several of his former Jubba friends at various government agencies, and had even been invited to dinner at the Rugda Taleh, the government hotel compound, where he'd dined with the Jubba UN ambassador and his brother-in-law, an adviser to the presidency. He hadn't informed the ambassador of the dinner invitation beforehand and failed to include Harcourt, who had few opportunities to meet informally with senior Jubba officials. Their presence, he claimed in the memo of conversation he'd submitted the following day, had been arranged without his knowledge. The dinner invitation had come from a Jubba merchant DeGroot had known in Hargusha during his tour there. During their pre-dinner drink in the shadowy Rugda Taleh garden, the two senior officials had wandered by, been invited to join them, and had accepted the host's invitation to continue their discussions over dinner.

Talbot was suspicious. By the end of the second week, after De-Groot informed him by memo that he intended to take over political reporting responsibilities, leaving Talbot free to devote his working hours to the overdue economic reports, he was even more suspicious. It wasn't surprising he'd come to dislike the man so much.

□ □ □

The country team meeting was held on Thursday mornings in the front corner of the ambassador's third-floor office. A large room with white walls and a deep-pile carpet, it might have been sunny except that the shutters were drawn closed, protection against visual or audio surveillance from the four-story building across the way. A grizzled Syrian from Damascus owned the dirty little restaurant on the first floor, patronized by local taxi drivers and assorted idlers in dark glasses who sat over their glasses of tea through the long morning hours, watching the front door of the embassy through the dark windows. They were from the KGB-trained NSS, the National Security Service, keeping their watch on the embassy.

Around the corner toward the sea the PLO had a vegetable market where the *feyedeen* sold surplus vegetables grown on their agricultural farm to the south donated by the government several years earlier after joining the Arab League. To Talbot, who often shopped there, they all looked like three-time losers, mournful-eyed little men in wrinkled green twill sentenced to some remote penal farm but tending their bins of green beans, lettuce, onions, and potatoes with that same gentle devotion of greengrocers everywhere. PLO terrorists were suspected to be among them, three of whom had attempted to bring down an El Al jet at the Nairobi airport with a shoulder-fired SA-7 missile. The North Koreans and Cubans were thought to be training the PLO cadres. Whittington also believed the NSS, with the aid of the KGB and the East Germans, had established a static surveillance post on the third floor of the yellow stucco building across the way.

He now poked a stubby finger through the slats to point to an open window on the third floor of the yellowish-ocher building where, three weeks ago, Technical Unit 3 of the NSS had recently updated its KGB-supplied audiovisual surveillance equipment.

Peering through the shutter, Talbot saw only an Arab woman in a flowered dress shaking a rug from the third-floor balcony. She was the same woman he'd often seen there in the past. He watched her put aside the rug and lean over the balcony, shouting at someone on the street below. From her bellowing voice he supposed she was either heroically crafty or sublimely stupid.

"TU-3? When did you get that?"

Whittington was a portly man in his mid-fifties with wispy orange-gray hair, a round face, and sunburned cheeks with the flush of half-ripe strawberries—a clandestine Santa Claus, Talbot decided one evening as he sat with Shaughnessy in the Anglo-American club bar watching him try to hustle a newly arrived West German police adviser. With his snub nose and drooping reddish-brown mustache, his soft brown eyes seemed to reflect a certain walruslike wisdom. In the past he'd gotten precious little regarding the NSS's organizational structure. That he was now able to identify by number an NSS technical unit under Soviet control seemed a significant breakthrough.

"A lot's been happening. We'll talk about it, feet up one of these afternoons. Stay lean and loose, buddy, like me." He winked, patted his paunch affectionately, and moved to his chair.

Harcourt sat in his usual brown armchair, the morning cable file on his knee, his notes atop it. DeGroot sat to his right, tall and erect in a fawn-colored safari suit, a colored scarf tied around his soft neck. Talbot noticed he was wearing white nylon socks. Opposite him on the brown leather couch sat young Kinkaid, pipe in hand. Next to him was Dr. Melton, the fussy little USIS public affairs officer, then Rhinehart, the bony-faced administrative officer, still smiling at one of DeGroot's jokes. On a chair near the window sat Peterson, who would have nothing to say and would seem to be dozing throughout the meeting. Slightly in front of him sat Whittington.

Seeing them assembled for the first time, Talbot realized many were now growing mustaches or beards, even Dr. Melton, who maintained the U.S. cultural affairs center and library catty-corner from the embassy.

Talbot wondered if he was cultivating a disguise. The dusky-skinned dyspeptic little doctor was a former professor of education from Wilberforce University. His first African post had been at Dar-es Salaam in Tanzania, where he'd gone to embrace the brotherhood. He'd led a strenuous social life at first, a generous host to all and sundry for six months before his hospitality wore thin. His house was robbed three times, first his liquor and foodstuffs consignment, then his kitchen appliances and stereo, and finally his luggage and dog. He'd been set upon twice in the downtown streets, once in broad daylight, by the ex-houseboy he'd reluctantly fired after the police convinced him he was the thieves' accomplice. In Jubba he stayed away from the Nigerians and Kenyans, ordered his suits from London, and lived in mortal fear of kidnapping by the PLO greengrocers. He crept to and from his office each day by a different route, slumped deep in the back seat of his Plymouth sedan. The mustache, like the silvery sideburns, had a lichenlike thinness, too anemic to fool anyone.

Harcourt began the meeting by reading from a cable sent from Washington at the close of business the previous day.

Abdulkadir Abocar, the tireless Jubba ambassador in Washington, had once again met with the assistant secretary for African affairs, repeating his urgent request for a meeting with the secretary. During the meeting Abdulkadir had claimed that as a result of the newly signed Soviet military aid agreement with the socialist regime in neighboring Ethiopia, the president was secretly reassessing his relationship with Moscow. The time had come for Washington to seize the initiative and offer an alternative to his dependence upon Soviet armaments.

Harcourt lifted his eyes toward Talbot. "By any chance did you talk to him while you were in Washington?"

"No, sir. I told the desk officer not to let him know I was in town."

DeGroot stirred vigorously and turned. "You didn't talk to him?"

"No, sorry."

A troubled pause followed by a glance at the ambassador. "I've always found my talks with Ambassador Abdulkadir most instructive."

Talbot didn't. He thought Ambassador Abdulkadir a very crooked tail trying to wag a very treacherous dog. Married to the daughter of the wealthiest merchant in the capital, he'd been subsidized for years by certain Arab states through his business interests in the Persian Gulf, attempting to bring about those internal changes sought by Saudi Arabia, by his wealthy father-in-law, and other exiled entrepreneurs. The president, so it was said, had finally shunted him off to Washington to get rid of him. His original proposal, put to Harcourt soon after his arrival the previous winter, was a plea for a renewal of U.S. economic aid as a first step in loosening the Soviet grip on Jubba. With the election of a new Democratic administration, however, he had slyly shifted tactics, camel trader that he was, and claimed to be under secret presidential instructions to pursue with Washington an alternative to Jubba's military dependence upon the Soviet Union.

Talbot thought the idea absurd. That Washington would willingly arm a devious little pariah nation eager for any pretext to invade its ancient enemy Ethiopia, now weakened by anarchy and rebellion, was preposterous. The American military presence in Ethiopia had once restrained Jubba's ambition, but U.S. military assistance had been withdrawn. The Soviets were filling the vacuum in Ethiopia, and Jubba was growing suspicious: Would Moscow arm Ethiopia as the Americans once had, denying it a historic opportunity to recover its lost territories?

Harcourt looked again at the telegram, eyebrows wagging. "They haven't given him a date for a meeting yet, I take it. Do you know what the delay is?"

"They don't know what to tell him," Talbot said. "The administration hasn't sorted things out yet. They know he's going to ask for military aid and they don't know what to tell him."

"I find that incomprehensible," DeGroot said, "totally incomprehensible."

"It's a tough issue," Talbot said.

"What is?" Harcourt asked. "Abdulkadir's request that we supply Jubba with defensive weapons?"

Harcourt had never served as a Department desk officer in Washington and had only the vaguest idea of how the cumbersome policy machinery worked. At times Talbot had the uneasy feeling he thought the secretary of state personally drafted his instructions—with a goose-quill pen at an escritoire in the Ben Franklin Room, no doubt. Slow and unwieldy during the best of times, the Washington policy apparatus was haplessly inert following the changing of the political guard.

"The arms question. The administration hasn't decided on the policy."

"For Abdulkadir's request for arms?"

"For Third World arms transfers in general."

"And that's what they're waiting for?"

"Right now, yes."

"It's been months now since this internal debate first started," DeGroot said. "It's been raging for months now."

"These are Georgia boys," Talbot said. "They talk slow."

Two months earlier he would have heard an appreciative snigger from Shaughnessy, slouched behind him in his leather chair; now there was only a monotonous silence, broken by the polite rustle of Harcourt's telegrams.

"The Russians are no doubt aware of the Jubba initiative," De-Groot warned, eyelids grimly narrowed as he looked about. "We should be alert to any significant evidence of a change in attitudes." He turned to Rhinehart. "I detected myself an unusual number of Russians departing on the Aeroflot flight two nights ago."

Rhinehart, caught unaware, blinked and turned to Peterson. "Maybe you could ask about it with your contacts there."

Peterson stirred and came awake. "What contacts?"

"Just the usual personnel transfers," Whittington said easily. "Nothing unusual about that."

DeGroot's eyes remained narrowed. "We should nevertheless remain alert."

"Quite so," Harcourt added. "They want us to keep an eye out for anything that might indicate a cooling of Soviet-Jubba relations." He passed on to the next cable and concluded with a few minor matters, including the delay in getting clearances for the diplomatic liquor rations through the ministry of foreign affairs. Then he turned the meeting over to DeGroot.

Dr. Melton complained that one of his visiting lecturers had been refused an entry visa by the Jubba embassy in London. He was to give an illustrated lecture on American graphic arts, a lecture which would be attended, at most, by a few from the diplomatic corps, a dozen or so Italian teachers, and a handful of embassy staff.

"Most unfortunate," DeGroot said, studying his notes. "I'll communicate with the foreign ministry, which is most eager to promote cross-cultural enlightenment. Mr. Whittington, I think you had something."

Whittington told them that for two consecutive nights the previous week anti-government tracts had been thrown from an unmarked car speeding through the midnight streets of the commercial section, attacking the president and the Soviet Union. Two prominent government officials were reported to be under house arrest, both fervent advocates of the country's close ties to the Soviet Union.

"What's happening is that the Soviets want to begin the formation of the political party," Whittington said, "and a lot of folks are against it. It's the same old problem."

Whenever evidence of internal dissension surfaced, Whittington attributed it to the question of the party, an answer Talbot knew to be carelessly expedient. He had discussed the party question dozens of times with the Soviet political counselor, Lev Luttak, who had persuaded him any talk of party formation was premature. The Soviet embassy wasn't pushing it; years of cadre formation still lay ahead. The appearance of the tracts made Whittington's explanation even more dubious. Little or nothing occurred in the midnight streets that the NSS wasn't aware of.

Before he could say as much, DeGroot broke in to explain that the Egyptian and French ambassadors agreed with the interpretation.

Of course they'd agree, Talbot thought, looking at Harcourt, who knew as well why they'd agree. Like the rest of the diplomatic community, the Egyptian and French ambassadors would be eager to credit any rumor that the Soviet ambassador was having as many problems as they were having. The privileges he claimed were those of a Roman proconsul feasting full fig and full steer at the presidential banquet table, while they made a full meal from cocktail party finger food, like Harcourt, and went home hungry.

Harcourt said nothing.

"The Soviets want them to establish the party formally," Whittington was saying, "and a lot of people aren't ready for it."

"The truth is," said DeGroot, eyes lifted to the ceiling, "that there are more people than anyone imagines who believe the country has drawn far too close to the Soviet Union. This is just beginning to be made public. As my ministerial friends tell me, the opposition goes much deeper than most of us suppose. Even I was shocked by the depth of anti-Soviet feeling among my old friends here. That's clearly what these pamphlets are all about."

"Intended for whom?" Talbot asked. "Who was to read the pamphlets."

DeGroot's eyes descended. "Obviously. The people in the street."

"Sure. A car comes flying down Corso Primo Luglio at one o'clock in the morning, throws out a few leaflets, turns up across the Piazza, tosses out a few more, then disappears. Who's going to be on the streets to read them?"

"At six o'clock one morning, I observed an uncommon bustle in the streets—servants, office workers, all trudging to their—"

"This was one o'clock. You think the NSS would let these tracts lie around until six o'clock? Only if they'd printed them. At one o'clock in the morning the only people in the streets are the cops and the NSS."

"Then whom *were* they intended for?" Harcourt asked.

"Probably a government operation. Maybe the Soviets."

Whittington nodded, bemused. "Possible, but that fits with what I said, warning the Sovs not to push the party question."

"Fine, except the Sovs aren't pushing the party question."

"And who told you that?" DeGroot asked, sitting up alertly.

"Lev Luttak, the Russian political counselor."

DeGroot laughed. "Ah, yes. And on what other matters has he

been so forthcoming? The president's unhappiness with the Ethiopian military agreement perhaps, the Muzaffar missile facility, the—"

"He's not the military attaché."

"Not the military attaché? Quite so. And the NSS audiovisual surveillance post in the building opposite, the one Mr. Whittington has so alertly warned us about. Ah, but he's the political counselor, you said. Probably ignorant of such technical matters—"

"We were talking about the tracts," said Talbot, coloring. "That's something I can talk to him about the next time I go see him."

"That would be most unwise," DeGroot said emphatically, "most unwise." He looked at Harcourt, who nodded in agreement.

"Most unwise, yes. I doubt the Soviets would shed much light on this, even if they could."

"And certainly not Mr. Luttak," DeGroot added. "Any meetings with Soviet embassy personnel are to be cleared in advance with the ambassador."

"Quite so," Harcourt echoed weakly, "and certainly not with Luttak, who's been most disagreeable with our Italian and German colleagues." Uncomfortably he began searching his notes for a happier subject with which to conclude the meeting. His eyes brightened as he found one. He asked Whittington about Wingate's arrival.

"Three weeks, more or less," said Whittington, looking apologetically at Talbot. "Sorry, Logan."

"In the meantime," said DeGroot quickly, "Mr. Talbot will continue with his economic reporting responsibilities."

"I assume that's agreeable for the present," Harcourt said, smiling encouragingly. "With an oarsman missing, some will have to pull harder."

The metaphor seemed to please him, so much so he said nothing more. Talbot remembered that Harcourt's brother was coxswain of eights at Yale. That made it all right, he supposed.

▫ ▫ ▫

On the seaward side of the reef, unseen from the beach, Talbot slid into the slick of the incoming surge, the aqualung tank on his back, visor and breathing mask over his face, and dropped into the sea. Accustomed now to the solitude of the mask and the chilling sound of his own breathing—it had frightened him at first, like a man dying, he'd thought as he'd followed his scuba teacher, a rum-sodden Newfoundlander named Noseworthy, during those first descents—he drifted down through the aquamarine light as the mountainous waves boiled overhead, dimming the oblique shafts of sunlight ahead of him like clouds on a green summer meadow. His right hand followed the weighted nylon rope which he'd fastened to the top of the reef with a climbing piton and which trailed off into the darkness. At a calmer depth he left the rope and pushed off from the flank of the reef, gliding out through the dimming emerald-green water, head and eyes moving, his feet trimming the fins as he soared and drifted, searching for the slab of rock he'd discovered thirty feet below the surface, lifting like an anvil from the blackness of the ocean floor below. Here groupers and ugly sea bass shifted in the fading sunlight, docile and sluggish; shoals of small mackerel wheeled in unison in luminous slashes, as white as sunlight. Schools of pencil-slim needlefish, almost translucent, quivered past like flights of arrows along the periphery of his vision. He saw the slab and descended slowly, hovering, circling, drifting, and then alighting on its slippery black face, stopping his drift by seizing the back edge.

Here he sat for a few minutes as goggle-eyed groupers and shoals of fish slowly returned, perched like an alpine climber on his rock. The peaks and black valleys stretched out before him.

For fourteen months he and Noseworthy had been trying to locate the remains of an old Portuguese frigate that had foundered on the rocks in the sixteenth century and had sunk in eighty feet of water just off the reef, this according to an article given Noseworthy by an Italian professor at the university. After exploring almost a thousand yards of reef north of the piton, both had begun to doubt the frigate ever existed but they kept at it—like boys in the backyard digging for China, Julia said. Talbot had invited her; she'd never come, although one night at dinner he heard her talking to someone as if she'd been there.

Poor Noseworthy. A UN fisheries expert assigned to the ministry of fisheries, he'd been ejected from the country following his report suggesting that Soviet fishery research vessels were less interested in surveying Jubba's offshore fish resources in the Indian Ocean than in the placement of certain hydrological devices. He'd discovered one such device while diving in the north off the Harfun peninsula. Soviet nuclear submarines were using the port of Muzaffar for refueling and resupply, and he suspected the devices were for them. Nikiforov, the Bulgarian UN chief, had forwarded the report to the minister, who expelled Noseworthy from the country, denying Talbot his only scuba companion. Now he swam alone, not only stupid but suicidal.

He pushed off finally, moving out to sea as he descended even lower. The iron pressure tightened the flesh of his skull and crushed against his mask and eardrums. Fighting the urge to rise, he descended lower in a long glide, back arched, his feet barely moving as he thrust even deeper, past the fading shafts of sunlight, past the slow drift of sediment and into the shadows of a winter twilight. As visibility decreased, he was more conscious of the rhythm of his breathing and the crushing pressure distorting his mask. He resisted the urge to rise, descending into winter darkness. As the cold current of the ocean floor touched his ankles he leveled off, moved his head and shoulders up, let his legs drift under him, and descended to the seabed. As soon as his fins touched, he drifted back on his heels and, then crouching, let his hands search blindly for what was there—sea litter, muck, nodules, smashed shells, and little more. He kicked up again, looking back to mark the spot of his descent, but could see nothing. Free of the absurd compulsion that had again brought him here—other men played golf, tennis, volleyball, or made love on these torpid afternoons while he was reduced to antics as harebrained as this—he released upwards toward the dim green light, and as he slowly lifted felt the pressure at last free his mask, eyes, ears, and pounding skull. For the next thirty minutes he soared and drifted as he gradually rose to twenty feet below the surface and then began to glide evenly back toward the reef. Once he found its basalt face, he moved laterally, his fear gone, peering into crypts and grottoes where rock lobster, octopi, and eels were sometimes visible. The white nylon rope drifted where he had left it, and with one hand he finally followed it upward into the swarming afternoon sun.

He broke the surface just as an enormous wave lifted behind him, foam dangling from its gaping jaws, crushed kelp slobbering, shining black water grinning far within, the whole insane darkness mucked up from the deepest depths, all mandibles and maw, the Leviathan itself—*Jesus fucking Christ!*—he bobbed under again, terrified, the rope still in his hands. As the boiling white surface dissolved he scrambled onto the safety of the reef before the next comber broke. Turning toward the beach across the lagoon, he saw two plump men in white caps with snorkel tubes dangling from their necks gazing at him stupidly from the shallows of the inner reef where they'd been wading. Each carried a spear gun.

He stripped off the mask, tank, and weight belt and put them in the rubber dinghy on the western side of the reef. He retrieved the nylon rope from the other side of the reef, put on another mask and a snorkel tube, and waded out into open water, pulling the raft behind him.

The two Russians were still looking at him from the shallows thirty feet away. Probably thought he'd been fired from the torpedo tube of some midget NATO submarine manned by munchkins. Incredible the shit the Soviets fed the Jubba military about the U.S. navy: invisible underwater barriers, bat-sized drones with a three-mile audio eavesdropping capability; only a camel herder would believe it. The water of the lagoon was warm and languid after the cold open sea. It was a long tiring swim. He carried the rubber raft up through the dunes and across the tarmac to the iron gate, then made another trip for his tank and mask.

He rinsed his gear under the shower behind the stucco wash house, still a little giddy, and stored it in the back of the garage. He showered and changed into shorts and T-shirt, then picked up the copies of the *International Herald Tribune, Le Monde,* and *The Economist* from the bed and padded barefooted down the long hall and down the staircase from the second floor. He took two bottles of beer from the refrigerator, crossed through the cool dining room, and pushed open the glass door to the back garden. Just outside the door, a dark-haired woman knelt on the flagstones, her back to him, prodding the soil of the flower beds with a trowel.

She heard him and turned. "I didn't mean to disturb you," Nicola Seretti said without rising. "I hope it is all right."

"No, it's fine." He didn't need company, hers least of all. "I didn't hear you come in."

"The gateman said you were sleeping."

"I was in the shower. I've been swimming."

"Have you? Swimming alone? That isn't good, alone."

"Alone? How'd you know I was alone?"

"I saw you on the reef. The guard showed me the first time. Then I came back."

In the harsh sunlight, her short dark hair held tints of auburn, her ankles and calves were those of a younger woman. As her face lifted into the sunlight the lines under the eyes and at the corners of her mouth were magnified.

"How about something to drink?"

She shook her head. "No, thank you."

He put the beer and newspapers on the metal table near his lounge chair and dutifully went back to watch her. "What do you think? Found anything yet?"

"Most of the plants need replacing. It is discouraging after all these years."

"Sorry, maybe I should have paid more attention. You said the owner never comes."

"Not anymore, no. She lives in Milano now, a very old woman. She was last here five years ago. You weren't here then." She slipped the sunglasses down from her forehead and retrieved the straw hat from her shoulders. "Always someone new. Always changing, you diplomats. What one plants, the other digs up. Every few years. Their wives, too. So what can we do?" She pulled off the white cotton gardening gloves, and lifted a clump of dry ugly soil from near the foundation. "The woman who was here before didn't speak Italian. I'm sorry, his name I don't remember. The man who was here before you."

"Mr. Quarles."

"Quarles, yes." She kneeled down again on the flagstones, pointing to a sickly-looking bush. "That is very bad, that one."

Talbot feigned interest, touching the dry stalk. "I hadn't noticed."

"It should have been taken out, that one, too. All three of them. It was a lovely garden once, now it isn't so nice." She scraped away the soil from the roots. "You don't spend much time in the garden?"

"Not working, no, but I sit out here a lot."

"So it seems. The other man's wife was the same way. I didn't talk to her. The gate was always closed." She wiped her temples as she looked out over the garden where the afternoon shadows were lengthening. "She was not so happy, I think, like Mrs. Harcourt. The garden, she didn't care." She shrugged the way the Jubba women did in the marketplace. "So I didn't come in two years. They were very suspicious. Only once, when they were on vacation. But just to look. I don't think it's too late."

"How expensive would it be to put it back in shape?"

"Not expensive if you are the American embassy, but I think the owner will pay. I will write to her if you like, ask her. It is up to you. Something should be done."

"What's the problem?"

"The soil isn't good." She took a few clods of dirt from the bed at her feet and kneeled down to study them, her dark glasses again lifted. "The salt is very bad here, like the old banana plantations in the south. It should be changed, the soil in the beds, all of it."

"Why?"

"Because of the salt." She looked around, discouraged. "I could bring some soil, some new plants. It should have been done, but the ones here before said no. New plants, new soil. But it is for you to say. I have plants I could show you or have them brought."

"Whatever you say. You have a banana plantation, do you?"

"A small one. You could look at the plants at my farm. Then you could choose."

"It's hard for me to travel."

"Hard? Hard in what way?"

"The bastards refuse my requests."

She glanced up, a cool disapproving glance, like that first night in the Harcourts' garden. "The government, yes. Yes, that is difficult." She stood up. "But you should make the request, go see the old cities on the coast. This is your first time here?"

"Where? Jubba?"

"In Africa."

"The first time."

"And the last, too, eh?"

"Probably. You always hope the pits are a one-time stop."

"You don't care for it."

"Not particularly. I don't much like the atmosphere."

The gateman appeared from around the house and told her her car had returned.

"Mrs. Harcourt said you were coming back for another year. If you don't like it, why did you come back?"

"I'm going on to Paris in November, the embassy there."

"So that's why you read *Le Monde,*" she said, looking toward the newspapers on the table, "waiting for Paris and not liking it here."

"More or less. If you think the owner wants the garden put back in shape, that's OK with me. She's not thinking of selling the villa, is she?"

"No, not that I know of."

"Then whatever you say. Are you a big banana producer?"

"Small, very small."

"Do you know anything about the statistics on the banana trade?"

"The banana board. They publish the figures. Why?"

"Just asking. The embassy's doing a report."

"Try the banana board. As far as the garden is concerned, it's a matter of who will pay."

"Either way. I talked to the goddamned banana board. Their statistics are three years old. The new ones are confidential."

"Are they? I haven't seen any recent statistics, but I could ask." She retrieved her bucket and digging tools.

"That'd be a big help," he said. He followed her around the house to the drive. "Where do you buy your cooking oil?"

"What kind?"

"Are there different kinds?"

"Yes, a few. Sesame mostly. Why?"

"I was wondering about prices, whether they're up or down. The figures I've seen don't make sense."

"They often don't. Since it's your garden, it might be better if you chose the plants."

"Maybe I'll ask Mrs. Harcourt. As an Italian, do you have any problem repatriating your profits, any restrictions on your money tranfers back to Rome."

"A few. Why, another report?"

"Yeah. The people at the national bank aren't much help. Do you know any foreign exchange people I could talk to?"

"I do, but they are useless. Why must you ask Mrs. Harcourt about the garden?"

"Maybe she knows what's best."

"She doesn't know."

"Yeah, well she's just had her garden fixed up and I don't want to upstage her. She gets prickly. Who could I call at the banana board?"

"Colonel Yusuf Abdi, but he's in Jidda now. It is your garden, not hers. I'll write to the owner, Mrs. Ferrugio. If I put in new plants, you won't be bothered. Your friends either." Her small Fiat was waiting beyond the front gate, where the gateman had refused it admittance.

"Sorry, he has orders not to let anyone in."

"No, it's all right to be suspicious." She opened the front door, the Jubba driver got out, and she slipped behind the wheel. He went around the car and got in next to her, as stiff as a deaf mute, the plastic bucket on his lap. "That's what he was taught, I think. The people who were here before wanted no one inside. What did you say their name was?"

"Quarles."

"Quarles, yes. They thought I was a Palestinian." She looked up at him. "They were very silly people. You should come look at the plants at the farm, then you can decide. You should travel more. I wouldn't worry about what the foreign ministry tells you."

"You mean ignore the regulations?"

"Of course, the way the Italians do." She turned on the ignition. "Or if you let me know, I could speak to someone in the foreign ministry. If you want to be proper about it."

He heard a quaint little English inflection. "I suppose I could do that. Who would you speak to?"

"Dr. Hussein, the director of protocol. Next time you ask for a travel permit, let me know. I'll speak to him."

He watched the car drive off down the corniche and disappear, irritated by her tone. Why in the hell had he told her he'd ask Julia? Now she probably thought she'd been right the first time, that he was just another one of Julia's embassy lap dogs.

□ □ □

The Sudanese ambassador's residence was a modest villa not far from the airport. In the lantern-lit rear garden under the laurel and flamboyant trees several score guests were gathered, come to greet the members of a Sudanese ministerial delegation. White-coated waiters circulated along the paths with trays of drinks and Middle East pastries and hors d'oeuvres. The visiting Sudanese had moved on to the privacy of the vine-enclosed porch, summoned by their host to meet a ranking member of the revolutionary council.

After two long tiresome conversations with two recently arrived vice consuls, one Libyan, the other from North Yemen, neither of whom had seemed ever to have left his capital before, Talbot had been wandering aimlessly about with a drink, looking for someone of substance to talk to, someone interesting, not those two quidnuncs.

He was standing alone near the rear wall looking for Lev Luttak when he saw Julia sweeping toward him, smiling angelically.

"Darling, you look terribly unhappy; please don't tell me you're unhappy."

When she felt lovely, unhappiness made her sad; when she was miserable, someone would suffer for it; this evening she looked radiant. She wore a long dark dinner dress he'd never seen before, her tan shoulders were bare under the loose shawl. Her dark hair was swept back tightly from her face, which made her long neck seem even more regal.

"I'm not unhappy."

"But you look *so* unhappy. Even your poor suit looks unhappy. Very tired and very unhappy. Hold still." She plucked a piece of lint from his shoulder and smoothed his lapels in place. "Is it so bad for you? Tell me it's not. Lyman's so terribly proud of you."

"Proud of me about what?"

"How you've pitched in. He told me this afternoon. He'd be very sad if he thought you were unhappy." She drew her mouth down in a small pout.

"Where is he by the way? I didn't see him."

"DeGroot took him to the porch to meet someone. Why are you standing back here all alone?"

"I'm not standing. I was on my way to get another drink."

"I've just had the most fascinating conversation with the Egyptian ambassador." She put her arm through his. "Let's go find him. He said you'd been absolutely heroic, getting the economic section on its feet again. Doesn't that make you feel better?"

"Not particularly. How'd he know?"

"Lyman? DeGroot tells him everything. Lyman insists."

"I thought you were talking about the Egyptian ambassador."

"Silly. Lyman and I were talking about *you*." She leaned against him, her arm through his. "It was such a mess with Shaughnessy, and DeGroot has absolute confidence in you. He told us—*absolute* confidence." She lifted his wrist to look at his watch. "We have to go to the Germans' for dinner and I'm afraid we'll be late. It's something that had to be done, isn't it? So doesn't that make you feel better?"

She spoke in that slow exaggerated drawl she adopted when beseeching a favor. Although he was no longer deceived, he sometimes found it irresistible. Her scent, always distinctive, was intoxicating.

"Cleaning up the economic section? I suppose so."

It was important that he sound indifferent, even a little moody; a concession granted too easily spoiled her little game.

"And it's *so* important that we all function together as a family, isn't it? Isn't that what matters?"

"Is that what Lyman said?"

"We had a talk this afternoon with DeGroot, just the three of us."

"Where was this?"

"At the residence. It was *completely* confidential, so please don't mention it."

Sharing a secret—another of her little tricks. Her shoulder was as warm as her hand, which had now found his. He let himself be led on. "I won't. What was it about?"

"We absolutely had to get a few things straight about our representation and household accounts. He was very forthcoming and both of us were very relieved."

"DeGroot was? About the residence account?"

"*Shhhh*. Not another word."

The Harcourts were foolish about money. They spent lavishly, far more than their embassy budget allotment permitted, but the funds were always recovered from somewhere, usually borrowed from another account. The idea that DeGroot might be holding them hostage to their representational or entertainment allowance was an absurdity he hadn't considered.

They stopped to greet the Saudi chargé d'affaires and the mustached Egyptian military attaché, standing near the largest tree in the garden. They lingered for a few minutes, then excused themselves and moved on.

"It was a very frank conversation," Julia said.

"Mrs. DeGroot wasn't there?"

"Don't be nasty." Then, with total disinterest: "I've invited her to tea next week."

On the other side of the tree they found Ambassador Firthdale and d'Aubert, the French ambassador, deep in conversation. Firthdale's back was turned. D'Aubert was whispering intently in his ear. He gave Talbot his classical Gallic stare, all dim and green-scaled, like the gargoyles of Paris. Talbot didn't pause. Julia didn't look at either, although the courtly d'Aubert was a favorite of hers.

"We should consider ourselves a family, don't you think, all of us so very much a family."

As they neared the porch they saw Harcourt coming, and he felt her move away.

"Logan, there you are," he called. "She found you. She said she was going to look. If we don't hurry we're going to be late."

"We were looking for you," Julia said.

"Did you ask him?"

"Not yet. But maybe I won't."

"Ask me what?"

They had been asked to a reception at the embassy residential compound and had promised to stop by but had forgotten they'd been invited to the German residence for dinner. DeGroot was also going elsewhere. Did Talbot plan on going? If so, could he explain, tell everyone how devastated they were?

Talbot said he'd planned to drop by. He walked with them to the car and opened the back door. Julia blew him a kiss from the rear window as they drove away. As he watched their two shadows through the rear window he wondered what had made her so happy that night—her new dress, the anticipation of dinner at the German residence, or the relief of their conversation that afternoon with DeGroot, the embassy beadle, the estate trustee, come to tell the silly weak spendthrift heirs they'd been living beyond their means.

It struck him as all very sad.

How would he have arranged that, leaving Julia feeling so radiant, so euphoric about an embassy family she'd never believed in? New drapes, new rugs, new upholstery for the chairs? A new sofa, a new refrigerator and freezer? She sometimes hinted to her guests that the wife of the previous ambassador had left the residence in shambles, a small lie, since the residence had been completely redecorated just six months before her arrival. Whether she disliked the decor, the colors, or the furnishings wasn't the point. She resented being held prisoner by another woman's taste and style, especially since her own was so unique, so much superior, as indeed he knew it was.

As he was crossing toward the bar at the far end of the garden, he was intercepted by Negussie Belaye, the Ethiopian chargé.

He was a sad dusky-skinned little man Talbot's age, beginning to bald, as shy as a lemur. His brown eyes were slightly protuberant. Talbot had known him since his arrival eighteen months earlier, a second secretary serving his first tour overseas. Now he had been left in charge when the two senior diplomats had been abruptly summoned home by the military regime in Addis Ababa. He was less a chargé than a frightened caretaker in an empty house, so helpless, and so vulnerable that Talbot went out of his way to help him. He'd grown fond of him. The most cruelly isolated of all foreign diplomats, a man the Jubba considered an archenemy, he frequently visited Talbot in his office and occasionally sought the freedom of Talbot's back garden to talk about the week's events in Addis Ababa and Benaadir. Talbot often had difficulty hearing the soft faint voice; even when he could hear him, he had difficulty. Negussie's interpretation of events was often so obscure he could make no sense of it.

His family had suffered because of the Red Terror in Addis. The *kebele* militias from the revolutionary urban dwellers' association had surrounded the houses of two of his cousins and hauled them off to the police station for interrogation. One had been put in prison. His father had lost three of his four houses when urban properties had been nationalized.

Negussie wanted to come see him sometime soon, not at the embassy but at his residence. He had something personal he wanted to discuss.

"Anytime in the evening," Talbot said. "I'm usually there."

"I'll come then. Should I telephone?" Negussie disliked using the telephone.

"No, just drop by."

Someone appeared at Talbot's shoulder. Relieved, Negussie excused himself and hurried off.

"What was the Dormouse saying?" Nicholas Bashford-Jones asked.

"I'm not sure. Where were you? I didn't see you."

"Trying to keep out of sight. You chaps don't own him, do you?"

"Negussie? No, I don't think so."

"Often wondered. I heard you were back. Missed you, I think, the Harcourts. She looked lovely tonight, didn't she? One more year now, is it?"

"Seven months."

Bashford-Jones was the senior commercial officer at the British embassy. He was in his early forties, slim and pale, with light brown hair, long arms, and long white hands. He favored double-breasted pinstripes, brown suede shoes, and pink socks and looked like an interior decorator. He pretended little interest in politics; his gifts were in his voice and his manner, his passion was theater. He wandered languidly through receptions and cocktail parties making witty remarks, drove his bright green Rover too fast and too recklessly through the narrow downtown streets, gave poetry readings, and directed plays, a figure of such limp ambiguity that some of the marines, watching him commence one of his predatory evenings at the Mariner's Cave, thought he was a fairy. So much for marine corps machismo. In his secluded bachelor cottage on a hillside not far from the British residence he gave small intimate dinners, funny parties, held readings, casted plays, and undressed and dressed more women than Bloomingdale's—secretaries, wives, Italian university women, visiting lecturers, overnight airline hostesses, UN nurses—all so charmingly, so delicately, and so painlessly it must have been art or something closely resembling it. Somewhere in the south of England were a divorced wife, no longer beguiled, and two rebellious children who sometimes visited him during their holidays.

"What do you hear from our drunken friend?"

"Shaughnessy? Mozambique."

"Good Lord. Too bad."

"I'm not sure."

"You don't know Maputo. By the way, I tried to ring you the other night. Couldn't get through."

"Ring me about what?"

"A small party, spur of the moment."

"Someone new in town?"

"Briefly. Two girls from Nairobi, entrusted to my keeping by the British Council. Not now, though. Left. Sorry."

"I saw someone new the day I came back."

"This was three days ago."

"Couldn't have been her, then. She was at the UN club."

Near the steps leading to the front of the garden two Jubba officials in business suits were talking to Ambassador Firthdale. They watched him for a while.

"Probably about his bloody trip," Bashford-Jones said finally.

"To the north, you mean?"

"He's mad to go, all he ever talks about." He looked fondly at a dusky-skinned woman Talbot didn't recognize. He studied her for a while and decided she was Egyptian, wearing too much makeup.

"At the UN club, you say?" Bashford-Jones resumed after a moment's reflection. "Could we be more precise?"

"Dark-haired, good figure. Her bikini doesn't hold it. Never seen her before. Prodigious."

Bashford-Jones's smile was instantaneous. "Nikiforov's niece, visiting from Sofia. Twenty-six, I think. Only speaks German, I hear. Other than Bulgarian and Russian. Liked it, did you? I shouldn't if I were you. Only Russians gash Bulgarians."

Firthdale saw Bashford-Jones and beckoned to him.

"Look here, before I forget, you wouldn't be interested in doing theater, would you?"

"Not this season."

"We need a few more chaps for this one. Too much for one man. Think about it, you'd like it. Marvelous spontaneity in our little ensemble."

He wiggled his drink and sauntered away to join his ambassador. Talbot moved on to search for Lev Luttak or some other Russian but none apparently had been invited.

"*Meester* Logan, *Meester* Logan."

Hearing the new Libyan vice consul calling from the shadows of the side lawn, his voice thick with unaccustomed spirits, he moved on rapidly down the walk and out the gate.

□ □ □

The embassy residential compound sat inland away from the sea amid the scrub and thorn of the southern outskirts of the capital. A high wall surrounded the two-hectare plot astride the main high-way leading south to the agricultural regions and banana planta-tions. Inside, a dozen small sand-colored bungalows were arranged around the shell drive under the palm and laurel trees, like those of a Florida roadside motel, circa 1935. A six-story apartment build-ing painted a pale lime green towered above the treetops just inside the front gate. There most of the embassy staff lived, including the DeGroots, who now occupied the top-floor penthouse. An interior wall had been removed and what had once been two apartments, one occupied by a departing secretary, the other by the luckless Peterson, who'd been moved to the floor below, was now one.

Talbot arrived from the Sudanese reception two hours late. The gates were closed and the front parking area outside the high wall was crowded with vehicles, some with diplomatic plates, others with UN or unofficial tags. He made his way up the dark drive past the residential cottages toward the open terrace between the swim-ming pool and the lighted recreation pavilion in the rear, where a few dozen guests still remained, gathered to say farewell to an embassy secretary, departing for reassignment to Madrid. Most were casually dressed.

He had visited the building the previous afternoon, the luncheon guest of the marine guard detachment occupying the second floor. The enclosed staircase, concrete floors, and grimy walls had the

look of a public accommodation, a bus station, YMCA, or a state
university dormitory, reverberating with loud footsteps, loud voices,
loud music, slamming doors, and, he imagined, freshman high jinks
in the middle of the night.

"It's not soundproof, is it?" he'd said during lunch for lack of
anything else to say after a muffled detonation had broken the
oppressive silence that had settled around the table where the off-
duty marines had sat rigidly in dress khakis, ties, and campaign
bars, like plebes at a service academy dinner, listening to Talbot
talk about the treacherous political sands in the Horn. The previous
ambassador had dined with the marines once a month but had suspended his visits after a pre-luncheon dart game when too much
beer had been drunk too quickly and the marines had gotten boisterously familiar. Harcourt had little interest in the marines but
occasionally asked Talbot to talk to them about local and regional
politics, as he had that day. The marines seldom asked questions;
they were there for the same reason Talbot was there, a command
from higher up, and the meals usually concluded in silence.

The reception line had long dispersed as Talbot made his way
across the crowded terrace to find the guest of honor standing off to
one side talking to a short Englishman, recently arrived, whom she
introduced as a British accountant with the UN.

"Mr. Talbot, yes, delighted. Don't think we've met. Just arrived,
have you?"

"Just returned a few weeks ago, yes."

"You're very formal tonight," said the dark-haired secretary,
inspecting Talbot's tie and jacket. "Very formal." She wore a long
loose gown of dark purple, slit at the knee. The Englishman was
wearing a loose, raffish shirt of white Indian cotton, pleated across
the front and open at the collar. A Madras scarf was tied about his
neck.

"The Harcourts plan to drop by later," he said. "They had to go
on to a dinner at the German embassy."

"Did they? I doubted they'd show up."

"I'm sorry I'm late."

"At least you're here."

He said hello to an Australian couple, then an Italian, then a swarthy man who introduced himself as the Pakistani vice consul, who again asked, as he had the last time they'd met, if Talbot played golf. Fifteen minutes later he extricated himself and drifted alone toward the bar just inside the pavilion, conspicuously over-dressed as he moved through a crowd of mustaches, beards, mut-tonchops, safari lounge suits, and a few Aussie bush hats.

He took a gin-tonic from the Jubba barman and carried it back across the terrace to poolside, where he'd seen Peterson lingering near a pair of lounge chairs. By the time he'd found his way through the standing couples, he'd disappeared.

Two middle-aged women sat in the chairs nearby. "Mr. Talbot, how've you been?" one asked. She was a thick-necked woman with straw-colored hair.

"Fine, Mrs. Peterson. How about yourself?"

"Fair to middling. Ask me tomorrow. I'd get up, but I broke my leg." She held up her leg, encased in plaster of paris.

"I'm sorry. How'd that happen?"

"It's a long story."

"I'm Arlene James," said the other woman.

"I know. It's nice to see you."

"We don't see much of you these days," Mrs. Peterson said. "A lot of changes since I last saw you. What do you think of our little place now? Mr. DeGroot meet with your approval?"

"I think so, yes."

"I guess you heard about the diaper problem, the ritzy new penthouse suite."

"I heard something."

"Then there's that crazy piano everyone's looking for. He's had Pete running around like a chicken with his head off."

Talbot took his cigarette case from his inner pocket and held it out. Mrs. Peterson took out a cigarette, looked at the brand name, and then politely put it back. "I always wondered what kind you smoked," she said. They continued to watch as he took one himself, lit it, and looked again toward the crowd. "I seem to see quite a few chin whiskers," he said after a minute.

"Isn't that the truth," Mrs. James said.

"It's the Bill Bagley contest," Mrs. Peterson said, lifting her heavy arm toward a waiter. "Gin, Mohammed Ferguson, except more ice this time." A Jubba waiter in a white coat took her glass and hurried away. "You oughta join in."

"What kind of contest?"

"Something to keep our little community together," said Mrs. James, "an esprit de corps, like the marines have."

"What they call it is 'The Bill Bagley Muttonchop Brigade,' " Mrs. Peterson said. "Don't you think that's a cute name? Ralph at the British embassy thought it up."

The competition was in honor of Bill Bagley, a Yorkshireman from a British telecommunications crew working on an extension of the airport microwave network who'd been expelled from the country. He'd been drunken and rowdy in a downtown bar, insulted the police who'd tried to quiet him, and at eleven the next morning, head bandaged, knuckles scabbed, one eye swollen shut, suntans dark with dried blood—"Oh, you shoulda seen him, he was a mess"—was expelled from the country aboard a Cairo-bound 707, mustache, muttonchops, and all. Expelled perhaps but not dishonored; standing atop the portable steps, he'd turned to his many friends watching from the esplanade, twirled his mustache, tugged at his beard, and raised his fist in defiance.

"Oh, he was a lovely lad, Bill was," drawled a small English voice as a thin dark-haired woman joined them, sinking down on the edge of Mrs. Peterson's lounge chair.

"He made life a lot better for all of us," Mrs. James said, "that's for sure. Not like some I know."

"A bit boisterous, but who wouldn't be?" the Englishwoman said.

"I wouldn't mind that cigarette now, Mr. Talbot," Mrs. Peterson said.

"Oh, is this Mr. Talbot?" the Englishwoman asked. Her light dry laughter tinkled through the silence, like glass falling to a pavement.

Mrs. Peterson introduced them. As Talbot took her tiny hand, a curl of pool water splashed on the flagstones near his feet and the smell of chlorine lifted from the shattered surface. Two shadows swam beneath, as dark as porpoises against the brilliant green illumination of the underwater lights.

"Is it time already?" Mrs. James asked, rising to look at her watch. Behind Talbot, a phonograph had begun and the lights of the terrace had been lowered. "Pete must have left," Mrs. Peterson said. "He always sneaks out when the lights go down. Does his drinking alone, always has, ever since he was in the navy."

"I thought I saw him," Talbot said.

"Oh, he was here all right. So that's the way it worked out, the muttonchop contest, or chin-whisker contest, or whatever you want to say."

"It's a morale thing you could call it," Mrs. James said.

"So all the mustaches and whiskers you see are on account of Bill Bagley," Mrs. Peterson said, "even Pete's, although he says he's not gonna stand up and be judged. What it does is give someone a chance to grow whiskers or a mustache and not feel funny about it. Some people do, you know, even grown-up men you think wouldn't care what people say, just worry themselves sick to death standing up in front of the bathroom mirror with a new mustache. You seen Dr. Melton's sideburns, Mr. Talbot?"

"I believe so."

"That's not even something the cat would lick off." She laughed. "What do you think of Pete's beard? Looks like a blue-eyed Chinaman, don't he? I told him to just let his sideburns grow, but he won't listen to me. Anyway, that's how come they thought up this whisker contest, but it was just an excuse. He's in Dubai now, they say. That'll show them, I expect, the police, the NSS, and everyone else."

"The Kaffirs," said the Englishwoman.

"Show them what we think, that Bill Bagley is still here. You know what they say about all Africans looking alike, don't you? Well, the same thing works the other way. They may have put Bill Bagley on that 707 for Cairo, but twenty more have taken his place. We want those policemen that manhandled Bill to see him everywhere they go. Every place they look, every bar they turn into, he'll be standing there, raising his glass in their faces—"

"Eighteen by last count," Mrs. James said.

"Eighteen then, but remember Mr. Yates got transferred."

"I forgot Mr. Yates. That would have made nineteen."

Talbot had turned to look toward the pavilion. Through the light filtering along the edge of the dance floor he saw a flash of blond hair and a brown neck and brown shoulders, the golden shimmer of California sunshine. A moment later Nancy Kinkaid's face came into silhouette as she bent her head, talking to a woman he didn't recognize.

"Since Bill Bagley was tow-headed," Mrs. James said, "blonds and sandy-haired have a special chance when the judging comes. It's going to be here at poolside. The closest Bill Bagley look-alike gets him half a case of Johnnie Walker Red Label." Talbot's head was turned away, looking again for Nancy Kinkaid, but she'd disappeared. "Oh, Mr. Talbot, yoo hoo—"

He turned. "Sorry."

"I said the winner gets a half-case of Johnnie Walker Red Label. Your glass is empty, Mr. Talbot. You haven't been listening to a thing I said. You know I should be mad at you, but I won't be."

"Really? Why's that?"

"Trying to sweet-talk Pete into extending his tour."

"I'm sorry. I didn't know what your feelings were."

"You don't look it. You don't look sorry; you look sneaky-Pete, you know what I mean?"

Mrs. James laughed in delight. "Oh, my *God.*"

"I always wanted to say that since you first came, I wanted to say that, that you looked sneaky-Pete, Mr. Talbot. When you got off that plane that first time, you looked like you got off at the wrong airport, Pete told me. You should have heard the talk, like you was stuck up, already an ambassador or something, but I didn't think so. Then when you came to the dispensary that day for your shots I knew I was right all along. I speak my mind, Mr. Talbot."

"That's right, you should."

"A lot of people don't, but I do. I speak out, ask Pete. I tell it like it is. If it was me, of course, I wouldn't be sorry, wouldn't be sorry at all."

"Not sorry to leave?"

"Hell, no. Look at us, look at me, look at them, look at this place here, and then tell me I'd be sorry I was leaving." She lifted her leg again, looking at the ugly plaster-of-paris boot. "Look at that mess."

"So you don't mind leaving."

"I sure don't. It's better where you are, out there alone in that

nice house on the beach. I tell the new people not to believe everything they tell you about this place, how bad it is. It's all right, but
you've gotta be a special type."

"Like a camel, say," Mrs. James said.

"No, I didn't say any camel. I'm talking serious now. It takes a
special type, maybe a real bastard. You're not a real bastard, are
you, Mr. Talbot?"

"Not yet."

"I didn't think so." She laughed and held out her glass to a white-
jacketed waiter. "You haven't got a reputation for being a real bastard, just a little stand-offish. You oughta come out here more, have
you some fun. I never see you at the movies. Take Mr. Talbot's,
too."

The Jubba waiter bowed, looking at Talbot. "Oh, Mr. Talbot,
yes. Yes, welcome, Mr. Talbot."

"This is Mohammed Kinkaid," she said.

Talbot nodded and the waiter eagerly took his glass, bowed, and
turned away. "Mohammed Kinkaid?" said the Englishwoman. "How
odd. The other chap was Mohammed Ferguson." Mrs. James reclaimed her chair.

"He works for Mr. Ferguson," Carol Peterson said, "the other for
young Kinkaid, the vice consul. That's how we keep them all straight
when party time comes. They're all Mohammeds."

"If you've seen one Mohammed, you've seen them all," Mrs.
James said.

The two women, now joined by a third, were still talking when
someone turned off the pool lights. Talbot stood in the shadows, and when the three women began talking among themselves
silently moved away. He circulated back through the dark figures
dancing on the open terrace. The Kinkaids had left. He left his glass
on the bar and was threading his way toward the front gate when a
hand gripped his arm. Turning, he saw Whittington at his shoulder.
"I saw you over there, didn't want to get too close. Why don't you
join us for a drink?"

Janice Whittington smiled up at him, a petite gray-haired woman
in a flowered dress. "I suppose you've been awfully busy since you
got back."

"Not too busy."

"Whit says DeGroot has been monopolizing your time."

"Not really. Hi, Lindy."

Standing slightly behind Mrs. Whittington stood Lindy Dowling, a lanky girl with long blond hair a head taller than Whittington, wearing wire-rimmed granny glasses, a white dress, silver bracelets on her tan arms, and leather sandals. She was Whittington's new operations assistant, arrived two weeks before Talbot went on home leave, and serving her first tour overseas.

"Hi. How come you're so late?"

"I had a reception."

"Lindy has a motorbike now," Mrs. Whittington said.

"I know, Lindy told me about it."

"It's very practical," Mrs. Whittington said. "Where are the Harcourts?"

"They're planning to drop by later."

"Yeah," Lindy said with a laugh, "remind me to keep a light in the window."

"How about a drink?" Whittington said. "Lindy?"

"Sure."

"How about it?" he asked Talbot. "Logan, how about it?"

"I wouldn't mind," he said, still looking at Lindy. "Have you been here all night?"

"Seems like it."

"I think it's about time, isn't it?" Mrs. Whittington said, looking at her watch.

"Just a round for the road," her husband said. "How about it?"

"You know what happens—"

"Nothing's going to happen."

"What's going to happen?" Talbot said.

"The hard core takes over," Lindy said with that same peculiar toss of her head. He'd first seen the gesture as Whittington had introduced her the week of her arrival. He'd been busy with his own travel plans at the time. His first impression was of a tall self-conscious girl made uncomfortable by Whittington's flattering introduction. She was a Phi Beta Kappa from Mount Holyoke, Whittington had said; Talbot was struck by her storklike thinness. She reminded him of a Vermont camp counselor he'd known as an adolescent, a slim young girl from Bennington who taught swimming, canoeing, trapshooting, and botany, dissected the sex of toads, skinks, and tadpoles, but hadn't yet discovered her own. At thirteen Talbot had had the romantic notion he might teach her.

"First funny, then stoned, finally catatonic," she was saying. "Then after a little while, not so funny. The worst are the little guys you least expect."

"I'll be right back." Whittington slipped away. His wife looked after him unhappily.

"Why don't we sit down over there," Talbot said, looking toward an empty table near the front gate. He thought he was speaking to Lindy but Mrs. Whittington followed along. Whittington joined them a few minutes later, followed by a waiter.

They sat at the table in the shadows. More guests said their farewells at the nearby gate. The dance floor was deserted except for two couples Talbot didn't know. A few more swimmers had entered the pool. Mrs. Whittington was describing for Lindy the Nairobi game park they'd visited a month earlier. Across the terrace Mrs. James and Mrs. Peterson still sat in their lounge chairs.

"Hey, Lindy, you bring your suit?" called a thin young man, splashing toward them from the pool, his white body dripping water.

Talbot recognized one of the marines; a moment later he saw Talbot and stopped short. "Oops, sorry, sir." He raced back across the terrace to fling himself into the dark pool.

Janice Whittington looked at her husband. "That's how Mrs. Peterson had her leg broken."

"They're on notice," her husband said. "No more nonsense. De-Groot gave them the word."

Lindy looked at Talbot and smiled. She shared his suspicions of DeGroot. Since Talbot had been acting economic officer, DeGroot had struck his name from the CIA daily reading board which circulated each morning through the executive offices. Lindy continued to bring it to him before she delivered it to DeGroot's secretary, even down to Shaughnessy's office on the first floor, technically off limits, since it was outside the vaulted door at the top of the stairs.

A gray-haired man in a wrinkled seersucker suit appeared behind Whittington's chair, smiled apologetically, as if only now identifying his hosts, and gratefully shook hands all around before he wandered on out through the gate.

"What a funny man," Mrs. Whittington said.

"He's the UN ornithologist," Lindy said. "Mr. Dillson specializes in the weaverbird. I forget the Latin name. A very nice man."

"You a bird-watcher?" Talbot asked.

"Sometimes. The extinct species."

A wet volleyball bounced suddenly against the pavilion roof and dribbled back down the incline and onto the terrace. A waiter picked it up, threw it toward the pool, and a moment later it soared backward over the enclosing hedge.

"Don't tell me it's started," Mrs. Whittington said.

They talked for a while before the Whittingtons finally excused themselves. The terrace and pavilion were deserted now. A handful of dark figures thrashed in the pool. Lindy led Talbot around the walk and beyond the hedge, where he stood in the shadows and watched five or six dark figures in swimming trunks playing volleyball by the light of a quarter moon.

"They're all addicts," Lindy said. "Addicts at anything if they've been here long enough."

They returned and circled the pool. Mrs. Peterson and Mrs. James still sat in their pool-side lounge chairs, their voices rising and falling, "Well, you take amphetamines," he heard Carol Peterson saying. "I've seen morphine addiction, and it's not as bad in some ways. I don't know. Look, that's the Big Dipper, isn't that something. So bright tonight, like it didn't know what's going on down here. You'd think you'd get tired of it, the same stars every night, but you never do, do you?—telling you to pack up your cares and worries in the old knit bag, like that old song. You remember that song? 'Pack Up Your Troubles'— What's that?"

"A plane, isn't it?"

"Looks like it, one of those Soviet Antonovs. Awful late to be flying. Up to no good, I'll bet. Do you think he sees our lights? Wouldn't we give him a piece of our mind. One thing though, back in Washington we won't have to wait in the Safeway behind fifteen

Russian women in the butcher shop anymore. They say the Russians get first call at the milk factory, even as fat as they are. Did you ever notice that? What do they think of those nomad babies dying out there in the desert, that's what I'd like to know. Maybe a special flight. What do you suppose he thinks?" She turned, coughed hoarsely, her throat full, and flung her arm out behind her, waving the empty glass. "Mohammed Ferguson!"

"I think he's gone." Mrs. James lifted herself awkwardly from her chaise longue. "I'll get it. After all, you won't have many parties left. I need a freshener, too. It's the least I can do." She took the glass, gathered it against her chest with her own, staggered, straightened, and set off toward the bar, where a lone Jubba bartender was standing, eyes glazed.

"Thanks, not too much ice," Mrs. Peterson called after her.

Talbot's head was back, searching the stars.

"Watch it," he heard Lindy say and he stepped back just in time to avoid the wet thrashing figure who'd just climbed from the pool and was swaying drunkenly in front of him, dangling some wet garment toward Lindy. Behind him in the water a woman was protesting weakly.

"Hubba hubba," he whispered. His eyes rolled back in his skull as he collapsed backwards, as stiff as a board, into the pool.

"Tether the beast at night," Lindy said. "He's one of the oil drilling people. That's his wife. Maybe it's time to go."

"Tether the beast what?"

"What my grandmother used to say. 'Tether the beast at night, by morning he'll know the end of the tether.' Fits this place, doesn't it?"

"I'll have to remember that."

"I can't forget it."

"What extinct species? What were you talking about?"

She smiled, looking away. "Just a dumb joke."

"Like this place. Do you have a ride?"

"I live here," she said, "remember?"

"That's right, you do, but I was thinking of my place."

"That's what you said last time. If there was a way of moving out, I would."

They walked on. "Maybe you could move in with me."

She laughed. "Yeah, I can see her expression now."

"Whose expression?"

She was still smiling: "Whose do you think?"

"Is that what people think?"

"Some people, sure. Something to talk about, that's all."

"That's stupid."

"Maybe. I didn't say I believed it. It's just the way she is."

"So you know her, too."

"A lot of women are that way."

They walked back under the trees toward her building.

"The way we'd work it is you could have the front bedroom, I'd keep the rear," he said. "We could sit up and talk at night, share some of our counterculture secrets."

"I told you, I'm not counterculture, just boringly straight."

"Not now, you mean."

"Always, I mean. I even bore myself."

"That's right, you told me. Maybe that's why I didn't believe you, all this shit I have to listen to."

The smile he'd anticipated came again, the same smile he drew from her while she waited for him to finish the CIA daily reading board in Shaughnessy's first-floor office. That he could be so beguiled by a smile was grim commentary on his infantile erotic life these days, a regression to that junior high school winter as an acolyte when he lived from week to week for the warm embrace of Priscilla Hartung's dark eyes from across the communion rail at St. Mark's. She attended a girls' school, he a boys' school; they never spoke, never met. Then one Sunday he caught her exchanging hot little caresses with his fellow acolyte on the other side of the altar and it was all over. Puerile, maybe, but the pleasure he found in Lindy's smile was the only decent emotion he'd felt since his return.

"Then I'd show you how to scuba, then we could skinny-dip from the beach."

"Sure. Why not?" They walked on. "I'd like to get out and find an apartment someplace," she said after a minute, "but Whit's worried and we haven't worked it out yet. Ask me something serious."

"When is Wingate coming?"

"I don't know, I don't think anyone knows. Are things always this screwed up?"

"Not always." They waited inside for the elevator. He was hoping she might ask him up but she didn't. "Bring your motorbike out sometime," he suggested as the elevator doors began to close. "Any afternoon, I'm always there."

"Thanks, maybe I will."

Disappointed, he went down the rear steps and turned toward his car. As he passed the basement steps, he saw a shadow in the dimly lit basement window and heard the pounding of the washing machine.

Through the window he saw Nancy Kinkaid, still in her white dress, folding clothes atop the dryer. She was smoking a cigarette. A drink was on the edge of the washing machine. Her back to him, her shoulders and hips were swaying. He watched for a moment, thinking he might go down the steps to say hello. Then she turned, did a small step, then a full turn, holding a bath towel. She folded the towel into the basket and then picked up another. She did another full turn, her cheek against the towel, her eyes closed. She was dancing, sweet lovable Nancy Kinkaid dancing all by herself in the basement of the embassy residential compound while she was sneaking her children's laundry into the washer and dryer on a day reserved for embassy singles. He continued to watch through the window. As she dropped the towel and folded it in front of the dryer in full silhouette, something seemed amiss. Her figure had slipped a few feet, down to his belt buckle if they'd been dancing, but they weren't dancing, and that swollen umbilicus wasn't what he remembered pressing its two sharp points against him so firmly on New Year's Eve either. He bent forward. She was pregnant, for Christ's sake. Was that what she was smiling about? That or the diaper regulations? He wondered if she still remembered New Year's Eve. If he went down the steps, what would he say to her? Three months due, five months? What are you going to name it? *It?* What was an *It?* A little blind blob of transparent protoplasm with tadpole eyes, curled up in its watery yolk while she waltzed around the basement?

Feeling ill suddenly, he turned quickly and hurried back to his car. The fresh air cleared his mind. The lonely road back to the city was deserted. She was still a nice girl, spunky, too, but her hayseed husband was making a brood sow out of her, and pregnant women made him nervous.

□ □ □

On the track northwest of Dusa Mareb near the Ethiopian frontier was a ramparted old adobe building in partial ruin. Behind it lay a draw well and two low stone-and-adobe structures, one of which had been converted into a tea shop and restaurant by the old Jubba trader who now sat with Dr. Greevy waiting for the soldiers to return. Darkness had fallen two hours ago.

The army patrol had intercepted Dr. Greevy's UN Toyota just before dusk, claiming he had no authorization to cross their military zone along the frontier. They had confiscated his UN laissez-passer and taken away his Jubba driver for questioning, leaving behind a single soldier who stood with his automatic rifle just inside the door.

Greevy, feeling very gritty and badly needing a shave, had the impression he was under arrest.

The trucks came at night, the old trader was saying, passing along the track in front of the settlement. He stored petrol drums for the trucks striking north into Ethiopia across Western Jubbaland toward Hargusha to reduce their trek north by 400 kilometers. Then, just to the west, the trucks would turn north again, but the Darawishta kept a roadblock ten kilometers away along a draw. The commercial lorry drivers who saw the tire tracks and followed them in the belief that a swift new route had been opened across the wasteland were soon disappointed. They were forced to turn back.

Greevy still wasn't sure what trucks he was talking about.

"Whose tire tracks?" he asked, bending forward. "Smugglers' trucks?"

The old man shook his head. "No, army trucks."

His English had been learned in Hargusha, he told Greevy, but he occasionally lapsed into Italian when the English word was forgotten. He wore a dirty white skullcap and an old tattered cotton shirt. Wrapped around his thin hips was a wine-colored *futa*. His legs were scarred and marked by cicatrices. His narrow grizzled

head reminded Greevy of an old buzzard cock. His face was thin
and wasted, the beak of nose prominent, and his eyes were yellow
in the light of the kerosene lantern on the end of the wooden table
where he set out meals for the drivers who passed, cooked on a
charcoal stove in the sheet metal enclosure just to the rear where
an old woman stirred. Inside the room to one side were a few
wooden racks that held straw pallets where passing drivers and
travelers could sleep. A single Jubba driver was asleep in a lower
bunk. He hadn't stirred since Greevy had entered. A breath of night
wind stirred across the clay floor from the open door.

"And the planes come," he added, looking up at the low ceiling.
He made a slow circling motion with his lifted finger.

"Helicopters?"

He nodded. *"Shiftas."*

"They're using helicopters to look for *shiftas*. At night?"

The old man nodded.

That seemed very improbable, Greevy thought. The old man was
confused. "You're from the west, too?" he said.

"From a long time."

The army would have taken him, too, he continued after a minute, except he was too old now. He would have gone, too, dug up
his old musket and joined them. He remembered when the Italian
Corpo Zaptie had tried to disarm his tribe. He was only a boy at the
time. He remembered when the Ethiopians arrived at Kalafo along
the Wabi Shebele, at Werder, Galadi, and Dudub and had raised
their flag. They had fought them at El Mara pass near El Carre,
where the old fort was. Did he know El Carre?

"Yes, El Carre. You say they would have taken you away? Taken
you away where?"

"To the camps."

"The refugee camps?"

"The army camps."

The old woman stood in the doorway, her hands wet, and called
to the old man. He didn't turn, still slumped at the bench, the glass
of sweet tea in front of him. His head was cocked now and he was
listening.

"She says a truck is coming," he said.

Greevy listened, too, watching the old woman standing in the door, short and plump, her head turned away. He heard nothing. "She is Galla," the old trader added. "She has ears like a fox."

The woman turned, grunted toward the trader, and disappeared. Greevy heard her rattling cooking vessels in the galvanized washtub.

"Listen for a minute," Greevy said. "When you say army camps, what camps do you mean?"

He said something in Jubba.

"Shifta camps?" Greevy asked.

"Army camps," he said.

The Jubba soldier took a few steps across the floor and said something to the old man, whose eyes brightened as he looked at Greevy.

"What did he say?"

"He ask why you come?"

"I was coming back from Hargusha. I was in Djibouti for two weeks, then three weeks in Hargusha. They stopped my Toyota."

"Djibouti?" The old man got up, picked up the glasses, and went through the rear door.

For the first time Greevy heard the sound of the truck. He got up stiffly and went out the door.

The wind was chilly. The truck looked ominous as it bounced over the track, its headlights dim at first. He wasn't certain it was an army vehicle until it stopped and two soldiers got out. The soldier from inside joined them and they stood talking for a while, then moved apart, looking at Greevy, and pointed with their rifle barrels toward the back of the truck.

"Where? Where are we going?"

The old trader appeared in the doorway, spoke to the two soldiers in Arabic, and they began to argue. The truck driver climbed out of the cab and joined them. It was a heated argument that lasted two or three minutes.

"They are taking you to prison," he said.

"Out here? Where out here?"

The trader smiled and repeated what Greevy had said. Another long discussion followed. The driver climbed back into his cab.

The soldiers prodded Greevy forward toward the tailgate, but he stopped and fumbled in his flap pocket. He pulled out his international driver's license, folded a few shilling notes inside, and handed it to the old trader.

"What is this?" he asked, taking the packet.

"Keep it. My name and nationality. In case someone comes looking for me. I want someone to know I was here."

The old man frowned, confused.

Greevy explained that he didn't like being stripped of his papers and put in the back of an army truck by gun-bearing soldiers on some desolate frontier hundreds of miles from the capital.

"He is English," the old man said to the soldiers.

"Keep the license," Greevy said. "Give it to the next truck on its way to Benaadir, with my apologies, and tell them to take it to the British embassy." He turned away. Then, as an afterthought, "Or the UN."

The back of the truck was very cold. The tattered canvas whipped in the wind and he could smell vomit from the dark floor. Taking someone somewhere. More conscripts, more Ogaden tribesmen being taken to camps like the one he'd visited with Lieutenant Ahmed? He stood against the heavy iron tailgate looking back over the track. There were no lights on the horizon. The clouds were broken overhead, sailing against a quarter moon. All very strange. Why now? Had the situation changed that quickly since he'd visited the laager and looked at the sick bay? Was the war imminent?

They stopped once for hot water at a tea shop. He remained in the rear of the truck. Ten minutes after they started again he saw headlights following, bouncing over the tarmac. A few kilometers beyond, the two vehicles had drawn behind them, sounding their horns. As they passed he recognized his UN Toyota following a Russian-made jeep. A few minutes later the truck drew to a stop.

A Jubba lieutenant summoned him from the back of the truck. At his side was Greevy's Jubba driver. He climbed down and they walked forward and stood in the lights of the army truck as the lieutenant questioned him: On whose authority was he traveling the frontier, what villages and settlements had he visited, why had he violated a military zone?

Embarrassed at his appearance and half blinded by the lights of the truck, Greevy tried to answer his questions, but was repeatedly interrupted by his Jubba driver, who came fiercely to his defense. Once a driver with the ministry of public works, he was no more intimidated by the lieutenant and his soldiers than he would be by a government minister or the Old Man himself. In Kenya, Ethiopia, or any other African country, his impudence would have earned him a quick blow from a rifle butt and a pair of leg irons, but not in Jubba, where the lowliest ministry driver sat at the same table as ministers at government canteens or bush tea shops to share their thoughts and offer his own in the old nomadic tradition, fiercely independent but deeply egalitarian, whatever the hierarchic pretense of Jubba's new bureaucratic state.

Turning, the lieutenant signaled to the truck driver to turn down his lights. In the mild amber glow he asked a few more questions and listened patiently as Greevy and his driver explained how they had wandered by mistake into the military zone. He was a small man in an oversized khaki blouse and trousers. On his small hands was a pair of yellow driving gloves. Like Greevy's driver, his name was Hussein.

He gave Greevy back his UN laissez-passer, his international driver's license, and the shillings he'd given the old man at the tea shop.

He was free to go, he told him and then, as an afterthought, added that it might be useful if he reported the incident to the UN office in Benaadir and the British embassy. In that way any unfortunate incidents resulting from unauthorized travel along the frontier might be avoided.

All very odd, Greevy thought afterwards as he listened to his driver rejoice in their escape from an all-night lockup in a felons' prison. Greevy hadn't been in jail in years, not since the Ethiopian captain at Bole had locked him up in the *woreda* jail for twenty-four hours during the cholera epidemic and had confiscated his medical supplies. The Ethiopian administrators had refused succor to the nomad cholera victims. It was then he'd written a long letter to the UN pointing out that if its doctors and medical staff were seriously interested in the welfare of the nomads migrating back and forth across the frontier in search of seasonal pasture, Jubba, not medieval Ethiopia, was the country in which to base their relief efforts.

CHAPTER FOUR
The Impostors

DeGroot had had little to say to Talbot since their *tour d'horizon* in Harcourt's office weeks earlier. Communication was by memo instead—"DeGrootgrams," Lindy called them—short, terse, and insulting. Even so, they were preferable to that braying voice that set Talbot's teeth on edge during the country team meetings. Their few discussions were confined to the overdue economic reports; other than that they seldom saw each other. Even before home leave Talbot rarely visited the embassy residential compound, and now he had even more reason to stay away from the pool and the twice-weekly movie. DeGroot never strayed onto the beach north of the Lido, although Talbot did see him one afternoon in front of the UN club, sunk deep in a canvas folding chair, his plump white knees lifted to the level of his shoulders, his massive bottom filling the canvas like a rain-swollen tarpaulin, hovering a few bare inches above the sand. He was wearing the ridiculous straw hat and his jaws were moving relentlessly to the pounding of the surf. He was with Henry Robinson, a British UN technician who had lived in Kenya for twenty years and still had the mentality of the colonial

133

highlander. The Robinsons were the one couple in the UN mission Dr. Greevy actively disliked.

DeGroot avoided Talbot, avoided him in the outer office, on the stairs, at receptions, and at the Harcourts', where he was a more frequent visitor these days, supervising the improvements to the residence which had been absorbing so much of Harcourt's time as well. The salon and dining rooms had been repainted; money had been found for new bookcases, new valances, new drapes, and newly upholstered furniture with fabrics imported from Italy, new marble counters in the dressing rooms, and a new thatched-roof gazebo in the corner of the back terrace. The refurbishing had seemed to improve or at least silence Julia's opinion of the man.

But if DeGroot kept away, Talbot wasn't spared that grandiloquent voice which drifted through the open door of his third-floor office as DeGroot stood talking to his secretary and Miss Simpson, penetrated up the corridor to Shaughnessy's disorderly little room from the first-floor dispensary as he gossiped with the embassy nurse, or down the stairwell as he passed a few moments with the marine duty guard. The first light sallies emptied his head like a dentist's drill, the creeping barrage hung in his mind like a polluting fog, like the poisons from the smoking industrial dumps of the New Jersey marshlands, scaling his mind with cancerous lichens, smothering the oxygen in his brain like acid rain.

"Being a strict Sabbatarian, I am obliged to forgo this invitation," Talbot heard him tell his secretary one morning as he declined an invitation for brunch at the Nigerian residence. "Sad to say, they live in a sullen nature, brutal and merciless, and have little respect for the private conveyances of the more fortunate," he said consolingly after a few urchins in the pottery market threw stones at her car. "He laughed very heartily and agreed my words would sharpen the point of his thought; the penultimate paragraph will therefore be amended as follows," he explained to Miss Simpson as he dictated the changes in a telegram Harcourt had drafted. "A delightful day. As I drove in, I noticed the foam was cresting the reef with an invigorating effervescence, almost tempting me in, *ha, ha,*" he joked to the embassy nurse one morning as he dropped by for salt tablets for his wife.

Talbot doubted he could swim. How could a man like that swim?

Confront the sea, sure, but only dewlap deep, jaws moving relentlessly—*Behold the Homeric vastness, restless as the coils of empire,
hithering and thithering*—but swim? Never.

He thought his behavior, like his speech and mannerisms, a little
queer. So did Lindy.

"Where in the world did this man come from, anyway?" she
asked him one day, almost in tears. "Why doesn't someone do
something?"

DeGroot had seen her on the stairs that morning carrying the
green-jacketed CIA morning reading board down to Talbot's first-
floor office. He had recognized the green-jacketed file and given her
a priggish lecture on embassy security practices, humiliating her in
front of the marine guard, the gunny, and Miss Virgil, the commo
clerk. He'd followed it up with a terse memo to Whittington delivered twenty minutes later which he asked be placed in her personnel file. Whittington had immediately torn it up, but Lindy
wasn't pacified. Talbot found her at her desk angrily searching
through three old copies of the State Department *Biographic Register* she'd found on Whittington's shelves.

Talbot was more philosophical: "That's not going to tell you anything; give it up. I've already looked."

The *Biographic Register* was precise up to a point. He was born
in Minnesota, where he'd graduated from a small denominational
college. Before he'd transferred to the foreign service, he'd served
with the U.S. Information Service; prior to that he'd been a film
editor and announcer with the Voice of America. There were no
entries for the early 1950s. He'd been in private business in Australia, it seemed, a shipping line and an export-import company.

Whatever his origins, the embassy was too small a theater for
that magniloquent voice, too intimate for his imperious memo-
directives. Differences of opinion should be debated, not ignored,
but DeGroot allowed no debate, permitted no exchange of views,
even in the country team meetings, where his ex cathedra pro-
nouncements went unquestioned except by Talbot. Harcourt didn't
disagree, at least not in public; neither did Whittington, who was
free to ignore them in the privacy of his own back-channel dialogue
with Langley in any case. The others neither knew enough nor
cared enough to dissent.

The challenge was left to Talbot, always ready that first month to suggest DeGroot might be deceived about any imminent improvement in U.S.-Jubba relations or the likelihood the U.S. might be foolish enough to give Jubba defensive weapons. But as the weeks passed his lonely voice had become monotonous, his arguments too familiar to sound anything but tiresome. DeGroot's optimism seemed fresher; his smile was certainly brighter and more buoyant than Talbot's. When Talbot wasn't sounding like an intellectual royalist, disdainful that others didn't understand these political subtleties as he did, a kind of William Buckley out on the jerkwater TV hustings, he sounded like some crackpot heckler at the annual stockholders' meeting, the kind that brought his brown-bag lunch and sat in the back row. "Something of a sorehead," Whittington told him in private one day. "Sorry, Logan. Time to relax and join the team."

DeGroot seemed to be aware of this. One day, to no one's surprise and everyone's relief, he announced he'd had enough of Talbot's kibitzing.

At the country team meeting that morning the two men had again differed on the question of the seditious tracts attacking the president and the Soviet Union which had appeared once more on the downtown streets. DeGroot saw them as an expression of the popular will—*vox populi vulgo,* as he put it—Talbot saw them as an NSS operation.

With a glance at his watch, eyelids fluttering wearily, DeGroot announced they would finish their discussion afterwards in the privacy of his office and moved on to another subject. Standing in front of his desk twenty minutes later, he forbade Talbot to mention the subject again; the matter was closed. Talbot said he didn't consider it closed until they knew what was behind it.

"The subject is closed for purposes of country team discussion," DeGroot interrupted firmly, blinking his half-lidded eyes in that same exaggerated way. "You delayed the end of the meeting by fifteen minutes—"

"I was trying to make a point—"

"Do not raise your voice. If we must disagree, let us do so in silence. Your views are well known by now, but you accomplish nothing by continuing to press your opinion upon matters others, equally well informed, are unanimously agreed upon. Did you notice how lax the ambassador's attention, how lax everyone's attention? No, you did not." He turned away, opened the double windows, and returned to his desk, where he consulted the spiral notebook that he was never without. The pages were tabbed. From his habit of consulting it while someone else was speaking during the country team meetings, Talbot concluded there were pages for every embassy officer and section.

"I, too, suffer the frustration of a romantic," he said after a minute, still consulting his notebook. "I, too, would like to indulge my views at the country team under the spur of some irrepressible private emotion, but I cannot permit it in myself or in others. If, after the silence of some additional reflection, you wish to draft a statement of your views on the matter of the tracts, with the facts to support them, I will be happy to consider it. But for purposes of country team discussion, the matter is closed. You should not again raise it, nor should you engage in acrimonious argument that impacts adversely on everyone's very busy time schedule. Where, by the way, is the banana report?"

He stood brooding over a page in his notebook.

"I'm working on it."

"Ah, indeed, working on it. It has now been exactly four weeks and three days since I communicated my instruction. Mr. Shaughnessy's lassitude, it would seem, has become infectious."

"I've worked hard tracking down the statistics for those reports."

"So it would seem."

"I could also point out that I didn't come back here as economic officer—"

DeGroot looked up triumphantly. "*Ah,* so you didn't. But since you've raised the matter, let us take a moment to clarify it. Your being here is not, as you seem to regard it, a merely personal matter. You are here because you were assigned here and you were assigned here to serve the needs of the embassy. It is not a matter of your personal convenience, although you agreed to extend your tour because it was convenient for you to do so, nothing more. Is that not true? It was certainly not out of any loyalty to the embassy or our heavy responsibilities here that you agreed to return after home leave, as your behavior has made transparently clear.

Your onward assignment, to Paris, I believe, would not become open until November. Had you not remained here for these additional months, the Paris assignment would have gone to someone else. That's correct, I believe. The Paris assignment would have gone to someone else?"

Talbot said nothing; something in DeGroot's manner made him suspicious.

DeGroot watched him impatiently: "Is that correct or not?"

"In a way, yes."

"So it would seem. Good. So now we can be absolutely clear about the reasons for your presence here." Annoyed by the dim call of the muezzin, just beginning from the nearby mosque, he strolled away from the desk and closed the window. "For the time being or at least until the arrival of Shaughnessy's replacement, you are here to serve the needs of the embassy. Those needs are official needs, not private or personal needs. At present and for the foreseeable future, those needs are in the economic section. During this time your inputs on political matters are not needed, will not be solicited, and, because they are so familiar as to have become wearisome, are not welcome, at least at the country team meeting. Do I make myself clear? I see I do."

Again DeGroot looked at his notebook. "If, however, you are so dissatisfied as economic officer, ad interim, that you wish to reconsider your decision to remain until November, I would not object. Another assignment could be found. It would certainly not be in Paris. What other European assignments are presently available, I can't say. None, I would suppose, on such abrupt notice. Fortunately, however, a circular did arrive a few weeks ago soliciting candidates for Zambia. Or was it Botswana?" He returned to his desk and picked up a yellow telegram lying conveniently on his desk blotter.

As he did, Talbot's suspicions were suddenly clarified.

"*Ah* yes, here it is. In July, it seems. Would either interest you? Have your two years in the African hinterlands not persuaded you there is much more to be learned? You're not sure. Perhaps you'd like to consider the matter. Do I make myself clear? I see I do." He was looking beyond Talbot toward the door, where his secretary was just entering. "Ah, here she is, timely in all things great and small, the cable already typed. Thank you, Talbot, I think that will be all."

Talbot left without a word. As soon as DeGroot had picked up the yellow telegram lying so conveniently on his desktop, he'd known the entire scene had been long and carefully rehearsed. The spiral notebook was probably his script. The man didn't have a spontaneous fiber in his body.

□ □ □

In addition to Talbot's other problems, Shaughnessy had named him his check-out officer, responsible for closing out his affairs at the embassy. Going through his accounts, Talbot had come across a note from the admin office billing Shaughnessy for a broken glass tray in his refrigerator, a Turkoman rug, and a yellow porcelain lamp, both missing from his government-furnished apartment. There was another unpaid bill in the file he also wondered about: an invoice from the Italian hospital, unaddressed, for 200 shillings. He had no idea what that was about. Any medical expenses Shaughnessy had incurred at post would be paid by the medical division.

At the GSO office, a small concrete-block building next to the motor pool, the Jubba GSO assistant remembered the admin office billing and showed Talbot the new directive, signed by DeGroot, requiring the administrative section to bill all departing officers for any government-provided furnishings missing from their quarters. He asked to see the inventory of Shaughnessy's furnishings, but the one she found was dated the year before Shaughnessy's arrival at post. There was no record of inventory at the time of Shaughnessy's occupancy.

He'd complained to Rhinehart about the billing. "It doesn't say here whether the refrigerator tray was broken when Shaughnessy moved in or not."

"No, it doesn't."

"It also doesn't say whether the rug and lamp were also missing. It doesn't even say Turkoman, just Turkish."

"No, it doesn't."

"So how do you know Shaughnessy is responsible?"

He didn't. He mutely showed him DeGroot's directive.

After his encounter in DeGroot's office, he refused to pay.

He sent his memo to Peterson, who forwarded it to the admin officer, who passed it to DeGroot. The day following, two new directives appeared, one requiring each officer to open an escrow account in the amount of U.S. $300 upon departure from post. The other named an adjudication board to resolve "matters of financial liability upon an incumbent officer's departing post." Rhinehart, the admin officer, was listed as chairman, Whittington and Kinkaid the two other members.

An annoyed Whittington appeared in Talbot's office late the same morning holding a copy of the memo. "Listen, Logan, I've got enough goddamn work to do without sitting in on another one of DeGroot's goddamn scarecrow committees. Pay up, for Christ's sake. You know Shaughnessy. If Peterson said he broke something, he did. If some stuff's missing, he shipped it out with his airfreight."

"The record doesn't say that."

"Send him a cable then, ask him."

"That'd look like I'm backing down."

Whittington immediately shut the door and sat down in the desk-side chair. "Listen, Logan, stop playing his game. The goddamn guy'll crucify you playing his game. I know his type, like the DCM I had in Lusaka."

"What the hell would you do?"

"Smile dumb and keep your mouth shut, like the rest of us, join the club, then—" He shrugged, smiled ambiguously, and sat back.

"Then what?"

"Then one day nail him to the fucking cross."

At last some encouragement. "How?"

"I dunno. He'll screw up; guys like that always do. Help me out, will you?"

Talbot considered it. "OK. I'll write to Shaughnessy, but you help me out right now."

"What do you need."

"Get that goddamn Wingate here."

Whittington got up. "I've tried, I swear I've tried. Ask Lindy. He's coming, we all know that, but he's taking some accumulated leave en route, more than anyone thought. I think he's in Cairo."

"Can you send him a cable, tell him it's urgent?"

"Sure, why not. I'll try. But listen, I'll get Lindy to call Rhinehart and tell him to forget about the meeting, all right, that you're going to get Shaughnessy to settle up."

"I'll write to him."

"Thanks, buddy. Don't worry, we'll get Wingate here. Just hang loose, like the rest of us."

□ □ □

During Talbot's first year, before he'd let his strings go slack, he would return to his third-floor embassy office every afternoon to work on a cable or airgram, alone except for the marine guard at his desk on the floor below. The silence had suited him then, but by the beginning of the second year it had grown enormous. By the year's end it was deafening. Most of his drafts were never completed, few were ever sent out, and even those rarely brought a response from Washington—letters posted into the void. In his cables he often discovered only poorly disguised epistles to himself, T. Logan Talbot, *Esq.,* Lord of the Sandfleas & Camelflies, essays on alienation or irrelevance, soured by irony, petulance, black humor, and even an occasional lunatic cry from that darker dungeon of absolute isolation far below, the cry of a life passing, wasted, squandered, and now emptying into a kind of madness, like that in Nietzsche's last letters. Discovering this, he would file them away in his private file or throw them in the burn bag. Hard facts were difficult to come by; then as now, his were often questionable, chaff from the diplomatic threshing floor. He was as isolated as the other Western diplomats, unable to make sense of what was happening in the highest councils of government, closed to everyone but the Soviets, with whom he'd been forbidden office-to-office contact.

But with DeGroot handling political reporting, his little essays in solipsism had come to an end. Economic reporting had never come easy for him and he despised it. Political reporting was easier, more colloquial; you could always bullshit your way out of a discursive cul-de-sac, but not with economics: too much math, too many facts and figures, and always a few left over afterwards, a few nuts and bolts lying on the floor that should have fitted somewhere in the whole rickety apparatus but didn't, like the unassembled stereo turntable he'd ordered from Copenhagen that had never worked properly until one of Whittington's technicians rebuilt it for him. Statistics were a nightmare, foreign exchange reports almost as bad. The scribbled notes Shaughnessy left made no sense at all; the figures bootlegged to him by Hafiz Ghanim, an Egyptian friend and adviser at the UN office, were confusing; they contradicted both the official figures and those published by the World Bank. If he'd had any talent for economics, he would have been on Pine Street in Manhattan with Eric Bowser, making his bundle.

He swam in a sea of nonsensical figures that afternoon, haunting his sleep, and awoke from his nap exhausted. The villa was silent, the sun flooded the windows and shadowed the cement arabesque to the west. Mustapha, the cook, and Ali, his new houseboy, had left for the day.

His old houseboy was still missing. Bashford-Jones had learned he was looking for a replacement and had telephoned to recommend someone he'd had to let go.

"Ali's awfully good, actually the best I've ever had, terribly hardworking, terribly honest, but I'm afraid he doesn't like dogs." Bashford-Jones had inherited a Rhodesian Ridgeback named Pepper from his former secretary. "I'm also afraid the feeling's mutual now."

"That's no problem. What else?"

"Children seem to annoy him."

"No problem there. What else?"

A pause. "The odd house guest, too, that seems to upset him."

"Doesn't like dogs or people, is that all?"

"He is that way a bit, not that I mind, you see—"

"Anything else?"

"Well, there you are. Independent, I'd say. I tried to work it out. I might have managed Pepper but not the children or the odd house guest. You see, that is a bit of a nuisance. Would you mind giving him a try?"

Talbot had hired him. He was a dark-skinned Isaq from the north, short and truculent with olive-black eyes and a Bren-gun quickness to his English. No doubt about his independence; he was more accustomed to giving orders than receiving them. More a barracks-room type, he preferred mopping the tile floors to dusting, washing windows, or helping in the kitchen but made the adjustment. Except for a few splayed thumbprints on the deviled eggs, he seemed to do well enough. That first week after he served Talbot at lunch, he hovered nearby with a dish towel, snapping away the flies that settled near the uncovered dishes. Talbot took the hint and bought him two flyswatters from the Italian shop on the Piazza.

Downstairs the kitchen and dining-room floors were still damp from Ali's cleaning up.

He drove back to the embassy. His chron file was still missing. He'd been reassembling it during his afternoons at the embassy, tracing down old telegrams and airgrams in the subject files, then copying them for his own archive; but DeGroot had changed the safe combinations, and his secretary, Miss Penrose, was reorganizing the files. It was very slow work.

DeGroot's arrival had changed everything. He disliked the man so much it troubled him. The wisest thing would be to ignore him the way Whittington did, smile dumb, shit green, and hang loose, Shaughnessy's old rule of thumb, but he couldn't ignore him; he was a fraud and a fool.

Lindy had told him she'd seen him recently prowling about the abandoned thirty-acre tract across the road from the embassy residential compound. There decaying in the blistering sun and parching wind stood the hollow shells of a dozen buildings, the hulks of an incomplete chancellory, residence, staff housing, and administration offices, a forlorn monument to frustrated State Department ambitions in Jubba. Construction had been suspended after the 1969 coup, when the AID mission, the Peace Corps, the military attachés, and those other agencies of a creeping bureaucratic coagulation that spread out from Washington as unconsciously as an oil spill over a distant virgin beach had been abjectly thrown out of the country.

The embassy still owned the land and still maintained the motor pool, the tennis courts and the nine-hole sand trap euphemistically called the embassy golf course, but the Jubba government had forbidden the reconstruction of the remaining ruins.

Lindy, who sometimes jogged along the fenceline, had seen De-

Groot wandering down the overgrown sand roads, not with a sand wedge, like the luckless Pakistani and Kenyan ambassadors, searching for lost balls, but inspecting the collapsing shells of those forgotten residences and lost gardens now overgrown with thorn and cactus, Peterson at his side, the old plat map in hand. She'd asked Peterson later what they'd been up to. Peterson shook his head as if he didn't know. Talbot guessed he was resurrecting the ghosts of that giddy old ambition out there where lizards scurried underfoot and gulls and peregrines soared overhead—which ruin had been designated for the ambassador, which for the AID director and the Defense attaché, and which, of course, for himself.

He understood better why he hadn't taken possession of the DCM's villa. The man was an idiot. Only an ambassador as supine as Harcourt wouldn't have seen that. In Rome or at Brussels he would have been a laughingstock the first time he opened his mouth, but here among layabouts and misfits he'd battened to their ignorance. If he knew so little, they knew even less. Frightened by their own incompetence, they were also silenced by it, like Harcourt, that blissful simpleton, as cheerfully seduced as his banker uncle in Wilmington, nodding agreeably and staying out of the way, hands behind his back as he followed his wife and yet another new architect around the manor house, soon to be dismantled about his very ears—DeGroot redecorating, reorganizing, keeping everyone busy, planning for reestablishing the AID mission, bringing in a Defense attaché after Washington gave Jubba arms and sent the Russians packing; DeGroot sending the sails aloft, recharting the course, and for what? Benaadir wasn't Rome or Brussels; it was a derelict, a rudderless windjammer, manned by misfits and captained by two fools.

His concentration broken, he couldn't get a balky Greenleaf combination lock to open and smashed it savagely against the cabinet. He slammed it a second time, hurt his hand, and heard the voice of the marine guard calling up the stairwell. Quietly he closed up his safe, signed out at the marine desk, and left the embassy in frustration for a late afternoon stroll through the old quarter of the city along the sea.

He followed his usual route. The tea shop on the corner was crowded with dark-skinned Jubba drinking glasses of sweet tea as they listened to the daily BBC broadcast in Jubba from London. He passed quite close to their tables. They ignored him, as did those on the pavement, although many knew him by sight.

He couldn't forgive them for that either: their clannishness, their pride, their arrogance. They were a handsome people, no doubt about that; tall, slender, and sharply featured, except in the south among the riverine agricultural lands where Bantus taken as slaves from East Africa had mixed with the local populations, shortening their bodies, broadening their faces, muddying their features. Traditionally organized into a complex structure of clans and lineages, they were a truly homogeneous people, their polity rarely troubled by those tribal hatreds that so fragmented other African nations.

Ruled by Arab sultanates, by the khedive of Egypt, by Italians and British, now they were in business for themselves, and screwing it up in typically Arab fashion, a Russian satrapy. But nomadic pastoralists still, Dr. Greevy stubbornly insisted, in spirit and livelihood, contemptuous of sedentary life, of farmers, fishermen, artisans, and self-indulged foreigners like himself.

Like Bashford-Jones, Shaughnessy, Whittington, and Lindy, he hadn't one friend among them.

He crossed through the open square next to the Arbah Rukun mosque and continued southeast across the boulevard past the Pakistani barbershop and into a narrow alley between the Italianate facades that led to Hamar Weyne, the quarter of the city dating from the ninth or tenth century. It had changed little since then, a labyrinth of narrow unpaved passageways and tiny dark shops with earth floors where Yemeni, Pakistani, and Arab shopkeepers sold their wares. It was through these narrow cobbled passageways and among these thick-walled houses that Islam had first come to the coast. As he moved slowly through the cool shadowy passageways with their smell of aromatics, spices, and the ancient dust of coral rock, the sea shut away by the ancient walls and only the narrow ribbon of sky overhead, he imagined he might be in Sanaa in the Yemen, in Palmyra in the Syrian desert, or Jerash in Jordan that Harcourt so admired, the afternoon light lifting the texture of buried Roman ruins from the rubble, a link with some ancient Mediterranean civilization that sustained some continuity with the past. But not here; here there was nothing Roman, only indigenous Arab squalor, no continuity at all. At Palmyra or Jerash, Rome or Athens was less than a few hours' flight. Here, even Cairo was six hours distant.

"Benaadir—perla dell Oceano Indiano!" a small voice called from a dark shop in a narrow passageway. Talbot turned. A dusky face watched him from above the half-door of a shop. Talbot had seen the face before but had never stopped. He couldn't have been more than thirteen years old. *"È vero,"* the boy said, rattling a pair of wooden camel bells. *"Italiano?"* He opened the half-door and beckoned. *"Taal,* come. Please."

The dirt floor was two steps below the passageway. The shop was small and dark. On the shelves behind the wooden counter were small parcels of tea, sugar, and rice, a bin of leather sandals, a few rusting cans of Chinese tinned goods, packets of cigarettes, a few piles of brightly colored textiles, and some glass jars of spices and herbs.

On a dusty table in front were a few odds and ends, a sea-turtle shell, a handful of shark teeth, and some cheap tin and glass jewelry. At the back was a small mummified crocodile. Sawdust leaked from its broken tail. From a shelf beneath the counter the boy brought out a package wrapped in scraps of yellowing Arab newspapers. Inside was a nomadic prayer rug made from two soft antelope hides crudely stitched together. It had come from Western Jubbaland. *"È vero,"* he said.

Talbot said it was very unusual and handed it back.

"What for are you looking?" he asked, disappointed. "You come all the time walk by but why for?"

"I'm looking for a hundred-year-old Zanzibar chest," Talbot said indifferently, repeating a scrap of table conversation overheard at the British residence. "Where did you learn Italian?"

He'd learned it in the streets. An Italian had once given him two books. His name was Mohammed Hassan. He didn't look like a Jubba boy; his hair was woolier, his nose blunter and smaller, his face toffee-colored, like the faces of the mixed Bantu peoples of lower Jubba.

Talbot heard a weak voice from the room in the rear. Mohammed Hassan told him to wait and went through the door at the rear. Through the low doorway he saw a small dark figure in *chador* seated in a wooden chair in a small room, her head back against the head rest as he spoke to her, his head bent close to hers. He nodded, looked toward Talbot, nodded again, and got up.

"Come," he called from the low doorway, "she want to see you."

"See me?"

"You, please, yes. She know someone come. Now she want to see."

He followed Mohammed into the low dark room. The old woman, face hidden by the black veil, sat looking at him for a few minutes. Then she rose very slowly, leaning on her cane, and hobbled to a small camphorwood chest. Against the back wall papered with faded pictures from old Arabic magazines was a small Arab rope bed with a straw pallet. The chair she'd been sitting in was a stiff-backed Ottoman chair with a faded red plush seat and plush back. Hanging from one corner was an ancient red shawl with a red fringe. On a small table inlaid with mother-of-pearl was a brass candlestick and a tortoiseshell comb and mirror. On another low table was an ancient gramophone with a flared horn.

He watched as the old woman took something from the chest and turned toward him. Her wrists and hands were very small and very wrinkled but the palms soft as tallow. She held out a string of old amber beads. He saw her head nod as she held them toward him. He took them, and as she moved her head he saw through the slit in the veil a pair of dark discolored eyes gleaming like agate above the glistening red membrane of the lower lids. He saw a tiny skull-like face, not the tallowy skin of an Arab or Hamari woman but the tiny weasel face of an old black woman.

"Very nice," Talbot said uneasily, holding the old amber beads, smooth and worn with age.

Very stiffly she had moved back to her chair and sunk down again. Mohammed said something to her and she replied in a small voice, not in Arabic, Talbot thought, not in Jubba either.

"She says they hers. Ahmed Jama give her."

"Nice, very lovely." He handed them back, but Mohammed shook his head.

"No, look at them, smell them."

He brought them to his face but smelled only the camphorwood of the chest. "Ahmed Jama? Who is he?"

"This his house once, he give to her after he go away to Cairo. Everything he give to her."

"So now she wants to sell them?"

"To you, yes."

Mohammed said something to the old woman, who nodded very slowly, touched her small hand to her skin under the veil as she looked at Talbot, and beckoned Mohammed over. He leaned against the chair, his head bent to hers, listening and nodding. Then he stood up. "Today, yes, tomorrow, no. Today the way she feels, all right. She doesn't open the chest for long time. But today something tell her yes, you will come." He said something else to the old woman. "A voice say yes to her today. Someone would come. Ahmed Jama, he not come."

Talbot didn't know what he was talking about. He still hadn't recognized the language. The amber looked genuine, very old, and very beautiful. He'd seen amber, seen the amber Julia paid ridiculously high prices for and which had never interested him, but nothing quite like this.

"Today she know, she feel something," Mohammed said, touching his chest. "A hurt bad. She sick."

Talbot looked at the old Arabized black woman. The veil was closed again and she was leaning back. He wondered if she needed the money. He supposed she did.

He asked what she wanted for the amber beads. Mohammed questioned the old woman, who hesitated a long time. She finally said something, beckoned to him again, and they talked back and forth a few minutes. Mohammed said she was selling the amber beads because she had felt something, and when she was told things and had made up her mind, nothing could be changed. He mentioned the price. Talbot agreed without argument—it seemed quite cheap—and paid him the shillings. The old woman nodded as Mohammed gave her the bank notes, nodded again, and held out her hand toward Talbot. Her face hidden behind the veil, she took his hands in hers, first one, then the other, both hands holding his, tiny hands, as dry as parchment, her thumbs pressing lightly against his white skin.

"She know," Mohammed said as they went into the front of the shop. "She knew even before she hear talking."

"Did she?" Knew what? he wondered. "Odd."

Mohammed locked the door behind him and led Talbot up the passageway to the Yemeni carpenter's shop. The door was locked. He pounded on the door for a few minutes, and after a minute a small window opened overhead and a yellow-skinned Yemeni woman looked out. *"Ya abiid,* slave boy!" she shouted down. "Go away!" Mohammed didn't move from the door, and she got a pail of dirty water and threatened to throw it down on him.

Mohammed Hassan retreated with Talbot back down the narrow passageway to the locked shop. He told Talbot if he would come again some afternoon before four o'clock, he would show him the Yemeni carpenter's Zanzibar chest.

"I might do that." They stood in the shadows outside the shop. "The old woman inside isn't Hamari, is she?"

No, she wasn't Hamari, not Jubba, not Arab.

"What language was she was speaking?"

"Galla," Mohammed said.

"She's Galla?"

"Galla, like me."

"She's your grandmother, a relative."

"No, she find me. You speak Galla, too?"

Talbot said he didn't think he had ever heard Galla.

"Tomorrow you come?"

"Not tomorrow. Sometime."

Talbot left him there unlocking his shop. *Found him, had she? What had that meant?*

Emerging again from the Hamari souk into the broad sloping sand road that led down to the commercial district full of taxis and donkey carts, he felt his estrangement returning. The evening was coming on now, dusk beginning to fall, the shops closing behind him. The bats were beginning to leave the trees near the old Italian cathedral. He crossed the open square where the buses from the interior left their passengers and went on to the row of tiny shops of the gold souk, looking in the windows. In the shadowy workshops of one he saw a sudden puff of smoke and a blaze of hot coals as gold was being melted down and cast in tiny ingots, as in a medieval forge. In one small window he saw an amber necklace priced at 200 shillings and took the necklace in his pocket out and compared them. The amber in the window was inferior, he decided, as well as three times as expensive.

He walked back to the embassy, still mystified, found his car, and drove out to his villa. The sun was dropping toward the rim of broken hills to the west. The glaring heat of the day that had magnified each stone, shrub, and blade of dune grass was dissolved by a gentler richer light as thick as amber against the beach road and the walls of the old villa. Only the sea seemed defiantly to resist the light, the brinish aquamarine of midday hardened now by violets and dark blues that would grow to basalt at nightfall.

Parked across the road from his gate was a metallic-blue Volkswagen. To the north along the beach a slim figure stood with two small children at the edge of the surf, her back to him, looking out to sea. He stood watching from his open gate, and when she finally turned and stooped to brush the sand from the nearest child's swimming suit, he recognized her. She led the child up the beach and left him there, then turned to the other, but after she'd finished dousing the first child the second was back in the water.

He went out through the open gate and down to the dunes.

Lindy saw him coming and waved, then stood waiting. She was barefooted, wearing a faded blue bikini bottom and a gray Dartmouth T-shirt over her halter.

"Hi," she called. "I thought that was you."

"Hi. It's about time. I saw the Kinkaids' Volkswagen; these must be the Kinkaid kids."

She pushed her damp hair away from her face. "Yeah, Laurie and Carleton. Nancy wasn't feeling so hot."

"I've been looking for you some afternoon."

"I've been a little busy. We're a mess, aren't we? It's why Nancy doesn't bring them to the beach." She called to the boy, on his hands and knees in the sand ten feet away. "Carleton, please come here. We can't go home like that. Now come here."

Carleton, age four, got to his feet, a chocolate-chip cookie in his mouth. His small face and hands were sticky with chocolate; dabs of tar clung to his feet and ankles.

"What's Kinkaid doing?"

"Home, listening to his French tapes. Nancy usually gets them out of the house in the afternoon. Carleton, please. We've got to change clothes. You remember what your mother said?"

Carleton gave her his hand, and she led him back into the ebbing tide to wash his legs and feet.

"I've got a shower in the back." Talbot followed her to the edge of the surf. "It's a helluva lot easier than this. You could rinse them and change clothes there."

"It'd sure help." Her long legs were apart, straddling the little boy, who was dangling by one arm and grinning at Talbot. "Don had a fit last time Nancy came out here—sand all over the seats, tar, too. That's why she doesn't bring them anymore. The tar's terrible."

"We can clean them at the house. I've got some mineral spirits."

"My God, she's sitting down again. Laurie, come on, we've got to go."

Up the beach, Laurie, age three, had squatted down in the retreating water, still eating her cookie.

Talbot carried Laurie and the beach mat, and Lindy took the beach bag and led Carleton by the hand up through the dunes and through the gate. Talbot brought a can of mineral spirits and a rag from the garage and cleaned the bottoms of their feet and then their ankles. Lindy took off her T-shirt, stripped to her bikini, and rinsed them under the freshwater shower behind the wash house.

Carleton and Laurie ran naked around the garden while Lindy finished her shower and changed her clothes in the laundry room. Then she rejoined him in white shorts and a blouse and put white cotton undershorts on the two children.

Talbot offered her a drink and brought two glasses of ginger ale for the children. "They aren't plastic glasses so be careful," she told them. "Don't drop them, because they'll break. All right?" They wandered off to inspect the garden. "They like getting out," she said, watching them from the edge of her chair. "They're such a mess driving home, Nancy thinks it's not worth it. I don't mind. The pool's so tiresome, anyway. Always the same people, the same conversations. Children wear out their welcome."

She seemed more wary, less relaxed than during their talks at the embassy.

"You can use the shower any time."

She sat back smiling. "I'd make a pest of myself it's so nice here. You're lucky."

"Any time. You should get out more. The compound's like the goddamn Y."

"Jogging gets me out. It's hardest for families. Now they've got a new rule about using the washing machines. I keep telling Nancy she should have a house."

"You, too."

"Me, too, sure."

"Do they swim? I never see them."

"Not much. I've tried to get Nancy and Don to come, but he'd rather play golf. He plays with the Kenyan and the Nigerian ambassadors. Twice a week. He thinks that's important."

"What, playing golf?"

"The diplomatic contacts. Then he's got his French tapes every afternoon."

"Why's he studying French?"

"He wants to go to West Africa and that means French."

"Why does he want to go to West Africa?"

"Don't ask me. He just does."

"West Africa's the pits. What does she think?"

"Nancy? It's his career."

"What about you?"

"What, my career?" She laughed. "I don't know. I wonder sometimes what I'm doing here." She turned self-consciously to look over her shoulder for the children.

"It's sure as hell no place for a single woman," he said.

He thought he saw her flush. "Maybe not. It's getting late. I think we'd better go."

"What's the hurry? Where'd the Dartmouth T-shirt come from, by the way?"

"A friend."

"A good friend?"

"More or less." She looked back across the terrace. The children weren't in sight. "I think they must be pretty tired now. Nancy will be worried."

She finished her drink and they found the two children in the adjacent courtyard playing some kind of hopscotch on an old shuffleboard court; it was all she could do to coax them into the car.

"Thanks again," she said as she started the engine. "It really makes it easier."

"Drive your bike out, we'll snorkel."

"Thanks. I'll keep it in mind."

She drove off, her eyes turned away. The sun was gone from the hills, the beach was empty. The sound of her car passed away, and in the steady sigh of the sea and the soft tarnished light of early evening he rediscovered his isolation. He had no reception to attend, no cocktail party, no official dinner. He should have asked her what she was doing that night, where she was going. Why hadn't he? The worm at the core, maybe; call it self-pity, another infantile indulgence. He would spend the evening in solitude, the gate locked, the sea crashing against the beach, the shortwave radio on the table beside him, tuned to the BBC or the Voice of America for some latest communiqué from the richer world of political and historical flux so remote from his own, trying to find his way through volume two of Harcourt's copy of Braudel's *The Mediterranean*. He wondered what she would be doing, why she'd been wearing a Dartmouth T-shirt. She'd told him several times she was straight, boringly straight. He wondered now if she was telling him she belonged to someone else.

□ □ □

The Soviet compound on Viale della Repubblica was surrounded by a high whitewashed wall and entered through two heavy doors fifty feet apart on the boulevard, one leading to the chancellory, another to the protocol office. Talbot told the embassy driver to park down the street under the trees where the sedan wouldn't be so conspicuous should another embassy car happen by and walked quickly back to a steel-clad door and rang the bell in the outer wall. It was two minutes to eleven.

Almost immediately the door was unlocked from inside by the same slim young Russian third secretary who always waited in the inner courtyard to receive him. They nodded, shook hands, and the Russian silently led him back the walk to the protocol entrance and across the foyer to the salon. The Russian gestured toward the claret-colored sofa in front of the draped window, and Talbot thanked him and sat down. Noticing the Russian's new buff-colored suit and raffish oyster-gray shoes, he asked him if he'd just returned from holiday. "Always bad, the sun," he said, screwing up his face. "The sun, you see. Always too hot, yes." He crossed to the window and fiddled with the drapes. "Fine? OK?" He smiled and left.

Talbot waited alone in his usual place. Stiff-backed chairs, also with plush seats, were arranged about the sofa. At his knees was a long low coffee table with an imitation marble top. On the tile floor were machine-made Persian rugs and against the walls glass-fronted cabinets with Soviet consumer goods on display—tins of fruit, small bottles of fruit juice, larger bottles of brandy and vodka, and toylike miniatures of Russian agricultural and industrial equipment. It looked like the seldom-used parlor of some crudely provincial *hotel de ville* high up near the Swiss-Italian border, proud of its local hops, its grappa, its folk festivals, and hand-woven native cloth.

He sat in the sterile silence waiting for Luttak to appear. On his first visit two years earlier, he had entered the chancellory door fifty feet beyond the protocol door by mistake, finding it unlocked and unattended. In the dim foyer beyond, the Russian on duty at the main desk had been too busy to talk to him and too confident of the chancellory's impregnability to give him much notice. Talbot had waited politely, watching a great many people bustling about, all of them Russian—no dark faces in the Soviet embassy. Telephones were ringing, doors were opening and shutting, and Talbot had watched and listened, intrigued, for five minutes or so. He hadn't the slightest idea of what was going on, but there he was, a penetration agent inside the Soviet citadel. He could have planted a bug or a bomb, he told Whittington later, but he didn't. He smoked a cigarette and was just stubbing it out when two burly Russians mistook him for someone else. They listened suspiciously to his polite English, asked the bewildered desk clerk who he was, and were about to throw him out when they were intercepted by a young Soviet diplomat who had recognized Talbot and led him next door to the reception and protocol rooms, where he now waited.

It was ten after eleven when Lev Luttak, the Soviet political counselor, joined him through the door at the rear of the room, followed by a small Russian woman in a black housekeeper's dress. He was in his fifties, a short powerfully built man who walked lightly on the balls of his feet with his chest thrust out, like a gymnast. Above the square muscular face his graying hair was combed straight back from his forehead; the bone of his jaw curved away from the squat powerful neck like a bicep.

Although most Western diplomats considered him elusive and socially primitive, he was usually willing to receive Talbot at his office, always by appointment made several days in advance. He generally agreed to see him when he had a question of his own or when he was curious about some Washington policy announcement but wouldn't see him when he suspected Talbot was trying to run to ground some wildly improbable rumor making the rounds of the diplomatic circuit. Often his secretary would call to abruptly cancel the meeting, never with any reason given. Talbot was seldom discouraged. He would call back a week later to request another appointment. The length of the conversations varied, but they seldom talked for less than an hour.

He was a curious man, crudely intimidating in some ways, crudely irrepressible in others, far less urbane than the Russian diplomats Talbot had known in Europe. His English was as crude as his thick accent, colorful but ungrammatical. His fluency improved at evening cocktail parties after a few drinks, when he could be cruelly funny; but sometimes sitting with Talbot at midmorning in the Soviet protocol office he could be as mute as a dog and just as sad for it. The Arabs thought he drank too much. The other Western diplomats didn't care for him, and the feeling was mutual. He was contemptuous of the Italians and West Germans. He'd never served in Western Europe and apparently had had no previous

contacts with Americans. His only visit to Western Europe had
occurred in the early sixties, when he'd taken part in some sort of
exchange at the London School of Economics. He'd mentioned to
Talbot only one previous assignment, this one along the Pakistani
frontier some years earlier, where he'd learned Pushtu. If he had
ever served a tour outside the Soviet Union, he never mentioned it.
Whittington's people had no record of him and were intrigued.
Whittington had asked him to supply as many biographical details
as he could.

Talbot knew little about him until one evening a few months
after his arrival when they found themselves seated together at a
small dinner at the Czech residence given in honor of the departing
Bulgarian chargé d'affaires. Talbot was seated at a table in a
corner of the side garden with Luttak, a Bulgarian commercial
officer, a Polish adviser assigned to the ministry of mineral resources, and an Italian counselor who'd recently served in Budapest
and disliked it intensely; the ranking Italian diplomat present, he
was obviously displeased at finding himself seated off in the corner
with a Bulgarian, a Pole, and a Russian.

The discussion had turned from his posting to Budapest to the
recent series of strikes in Poznan, where rising prices and food
shortages had driven the workers into the streets.

The Pole was explaining what had gone wrong with the Polish
economy and the measures being taken to improve it. Talbot,
Luttak, and the Bulgarian had listened politely, but the explanation
didn't satisfy the Italian, who continued to interrupt with sarcastic
remarks about the Polish crisis and East European economic difficulties in general.

Eduard, the Polish adviser, had tried to laugh them off, but the
Italian was revenging himself at his improper seating at the Pole's
expense and wouldn't be put off.

"No, no," he'd said, "you say things are improving in Poland.
In what way are they improving? Tell me. Prices are increasing,
there are meat and flour shortages, bread shortages, even coal
shortages—"

"But not all prices are increasing," Eduard protested, face
flushed with embarrassment. "Not all, no. For example, electrical

appliances. Refrigerators—yes, refrigerators. The prices of refrigerators have decreased by thirty-one percent."

In his confusion the little Pole had delivered his head to the block and the Italian laughed as he struck the blow: "Oh, yes. Refrigerators. Yes, that's typical, isn't it? Economic centrism. Good God, man, it's ten degrees below freezing outside, people are hobbling around with frostbite because there isn't any coal, and Gosplan drops the price of refrigerators by thirty-one percent. You call that progress?"

Eduard giggled at his absurdity, reddening even more. Talbot and the Bulgarian laughed, but Luttak wasn't amused. He leaned aggressively across the table, the smoke-gray eyes cold with anger. "Tell me, Italian diplomat. You are diplomat, yes. So tell me, while my Polish and American friends here were helping us, what cellar you and your Italian friends hide in when we kill fascism in Europe, what dirty cellar, eh, Mr. Italian diplomat?"

The Italian politely protested; he'd been too young for military service.

Luttak didn't hesitate. "Too young for military service? Too young? But how can be, too young? Was I too young? No, not too young. Who here too young? At what age is too young to fight fascism, tell us, Mr. Italian diplomat, at what age—seven, eight, fifteen?"

That was the end of the conversation. A few minutes later the Italian got up and left the table.

After that evening Luttak seemed to have enlisted Talbot as a sympathizer in his cause, seeking him out occasionally at cocktail parties and receptions, even approaching him on the beach one afternoon in front of his villa overlooking the sea to offer him two pathetically small redfish he'd speared in the waters just inside the reef, but whose bones were too small, Talbot's cook told him, taking them home for a stew. At the embassy Fourth of July reception that summer, while Nixon was negotiating Salt I in Moscow, they'd toasted détente; and it was during that long disjointed conversation that Luttak, a little in his cups, told Talbot about his years in the Soviet air force, flying American-supplied Bell Airacobras against the Germans in the last years of the war. The Bell Airacobra was a

plane his parents knew, his wife, even his children, the plane that
had more than once saved his life. A granite bas-relief of the Airacobra was chiseled on the Moscow gravestone of Major Bosarov, his
wing commander. The graveyard had been closed to visitors these
many years, but it was there, he'd seen it. A plane like no other.
Designed to give support to armored units, more heavily armored
than the Russian Yak, yes—the 20-mm cannon fired through the
nose, this way; the engine was behind the cockpit, yes, dangerous, very dangerous—and his left hand sought the small of the back
as he explained this technical point—but the armor plating more
than made up for that, as thick as a locomotive boiler, as thick as
Arctic ice, *this* thick—and his blunt fingers measured the distance
as Talbot watched—and so that was why he was here that very
night, toasting Nixon and Brezhnev in the back garden of the ambassador's residence: the Bell Airacobra.

Since that drunken Fourth of July evening at the residence Talbot found Luttak willing to talk to him in a way he wouldn't talk
to an Italian, a Frenchman, or Englishman. The United States was
the only standard against which he was willing to measure his country, an American, like Talbot, the only diplomat worth his attention. But détente had been very much in the air then and times had
changed. Détente's critics had grown; Moscow had shown its military muscle in Africa during the Angolan civil war, and now had
ambitions in Ethiopia, where the U.S. presence had been reduced
and U.S. military assistance withdrawn. Washington watched uneasily as the Soviets filled the Ethiopian vacuum.

Luttak's face was tired and drawn, his eyes a little dimmer, even
his tie and collar were untidy; a very late night, he apologized in
his crude English. He was always slow in finding the right word
but that morning he was painfully thick-tongued and annoyed by it.

He asked Talbot about his home leave, where he had gone, what
the changes had been at the embassy. He would probably be returning to Moscow in July for leave. Two months, he hoped; he would
take his family to Sochi.

After ten minutes Talbot finally turned the conversation to the
tracts thrown from the speeding automobile, attacking the president
and the Soviet Union.

Luttak was silent for a moment. He rarely answered a sensitive question directly but would tell Talbot where to find the answer— in a speech, a press statement, an *Izvestia* editorial, in a commentary over Radio Moscow beamed for Africa, in a local press release or a presidential address. There, if Talbot searched long enough, he might find the answer. In this way Luttak violated no confidences, betrayed no secrets. The answer was usually there for those able to interpret it, but to have the answer, one must first know the question. Few people did. Talking to Luttak was like questioning a medieval scholiast. If you didn't know some of the text, then Luttak's marginal annotations would make no sense. The rule was a simple one: If you went to Luttak with your head and pockets empty, you came away empty. On the other hand if Luttak brushed the question aside, it meant either that the answer was privileged or that the matter was under review and he didn't know the answer.

Frowning wisely, his eyes on the scattered bolts of sunlight against the far wall, he seemed reluctant to discuss the tracts. They weren't important, neither were the arrests of the two government ministers. The talk about formation of the party was nonsense, as he often said. That subject he would discuss and did, for ten minutes or so, explaining the difficulties of cadre formation. Talbot listened and finally returned to the tracts, this time to say he had difficulty taking them seriously except as a government operation of some kind.

"Of course," Luttak said, nodding. "Yes. Because of the opportunists. The men who make trouble, always the same trouble."

Talbot said it had occurred to him the tracts were intended for the Soviet embassy.

"Yes, for us, yes," Luttak said quickly, "but not just for us, for everyone who stands in his way. To tell us if you don't do such a thing, there will be trouble."

"So it's serious then."

"Very serious." He seemed annoyed by something. He started to explain but stopped, started again but for the second time was unable to find the words. In frustration he picked up the package of Winstons from the table, offering Talbot a cigarette. As Talbot took one he impulsively seized his wrist: "What do you think, someone do this?"

"Take my arm you mean?"

"Someone take. Hold like this."

"I'd get mad. Angry."

"A secret message." His grip was like iron. "An ugly message for my ambassador, Kirillan. A communiqué, a paper warning. Like this." His grip tightened.

Talbot understood. "Sent by the government?"

"Who send messages, secret paper messages at two o'clock in the morning, ugly messages? Who think they can hold us like this?"

"The government."

He released Talbot's wrist. "Of course. They hold us. They think we not move."

"What's the president saying about it?"

"The president?" The smile faded. He didn't think Talbot understood. "What can he say? The message, the blackmail messages, say it, it is *him* speaking." He pounded his thick finger against the tabletop. *"Him,* the president."

The small Russian woman in the black dress returned with brandy and glasses. She poured out two small glasses and left. After a minute Luttak said, "He is pretending this propaganda, these tracts, you call them, is come from the peoples, you see."

"The people?"

"From the peoples. What peoples? There are no peoples. Is insulting." He raised his glass. "Drink, please. Is good, this. Better than last time."

They drank. Luttak lit another cigarette. The tracts, he explained, were intended to warn the Russians that unless the Soviet Union stopped opposing Jubba's support for the guerrillas of Western Jubbaland, their puppet president would be overthrown. But the president himself was responsible for the warning and had used the NSS to deliver it. Luttak was angry, angry at the Old Man and angry at Jubba for trying to blackmail the Soviet Union.

"But not everyone on the revolutionary council agrees with supporting the guerrillas," Talbot said. "Who's speaking out?"

"Of course, yes. There was speech. The vice minister, in Burao. The vice minister of interior, Hussein Abdi. Last week. There he gave answer, good answer, best answer. Is right, best, better, what?"

"Best, that's right. Best answer to the tracts, you mean?"

"To everything. A small speech but very important. You hear it? Very good, very good, yes."

"I don't think I heard about it."

"*Oh,* but you must read." He wagged his finger. "Very important, *very* important."

Luttak had given him his answer, had told Talbot where to look and now he turned the discussion to Ethiopia and the bloody events in Addis Ababa. In the past he'd been poorly informed about Ethiopia and rarely ventured an opinion. He mistrusted the Dirgue military regime and seemed bewildered by the situation there.

They had talked for two hours. Luttak walked with him to the front gate. Finding Talbot's car missing, he followed him out to the pavement to wait with him. He was going to the south that weekend, he volunteered, inspecting the sky. For three days. The sunlight was dazzling, the sky empty, a metallic sheen. He was going fishing. One day he would ask Talbot to join him, but not now. Later maybe.

Talbot thanked him and pretended to notice his embassy car parked under the trees down the street. They shook hands a second time.

"Is not a camel," Luttak called merrily as Talbot moved off. "Next time he wait here."

At the embassy he couldn't find the Burao speech in the recent daily bulletins circulated by the ministry of information. He was sorting through back copies in the file room next to the executive suite when he heard DeGroot's fruity voice ascending the stairs:

"The singular idealism of the man, the steadfastness of purpose—"

He couldn't hear Harcourt's mumbled reply.

"No intellectual, certainly, but his thoughts had a pristine clarity."

The two had just returned from a visit to the ministry of sports. He waited until Harcourt's door closed behind them and slipped down the stairs and crossed the street to the USIS library. Sprawled in the cool reading room downstairs were a handful of young Jubba layabouts who'd escaped from the torrid street to browse through tattered copies of *Time* and *Newsweek,* both available from the bookstore opposite the library.

On the second floor he asked Dr. Melton's staff assistant if he thought he could get the full Jubba text from his contacts in the ministry of information.

He got the translation that afternoon, brought by an embassy driver to his villa. In the speech in Burao the vice minister reaffirmed Jubba's adherence to the principles of the socialist road to development as defined by Moscow—support for worldwide socialist solidarity, for national liberation movements, and the defeat of neo-colonialism and imperialism in all of its guises.

It was all pretty dull stuff but meat-and-potatoes for a political officer. When the bits and pieces were added up, the conclusions were unmistakable.

The vice minister was a fervent supporter of the Soviet Union and the Soviet line: socialist solidarity took precedence over support for national liberation movements. Two years earlier the president would have spoken in the same uncompromising way, but he'd been ambiguously silent for weeks. Unwilling to risk an open breach with Moscow, he'd let the phony tracts speak for him, warning the Soviet Union that the people in the streets had delivered their ultimatum: Moscow would have to choose between supporting Jubba and the liberation of Western Jubbaland or supporting international socialist solidarity and the embattled Mengistu regime in Ethiopia.

So Moscow was being threatened. Not quite pristine clarity, but if Talbot read his evidence right, the fact that the speech had been made by a minor pro-Soviet vice minister in distant Burao was evidence enough of how weak Moscow's grip had become and how strong the deviationist passions in the revolutionary council for the invasion of Ethiopia and the liberation of Western Jubbaland.

No wonder poor Luttak looked so weary. He wondered who in the Soviet embassy had written the speech.

□ □ □

The long purple swells were battering the reef, spewing streamers of foam far across the sparkling aquamarine inlet. Shirtless, wearing only shorts and leather sandals, Talbot stood atop the stone wall in the shadows of the north side of the villa, thinking he'd seen a ship far at sea. Under his arm was the *International Herald Tribune*.

Two Russians in white caps were walking along the beach, spear guns over their shoulders, being pestered by a young Jubba boy leading an infant baboon along on a leash.

The Russians weren't interested in buying the baboon, and Talbot watched until they lost their tempers and chased the boy away. A fishing dinghy bobbed in the deep swells west of the reef, hiding the ship he thought he'd seen. Maybe Whittington's Boston whaler, but he couldn't tell.

Move your ass, he thought, unable to find the ship. Upstairs to look through the quasar?

Who cared?

The satisfaction he'd felt in writing up his talk with Lev Luttak had passed; boredom was exhausting him again, all those bottom-feeders stirring and on the rise, like obscene old carp in an abandoned pond, exhausting him like malaria, like those last agonizing weeks before home leave, when he'd felt drugged. A prisoner again, no doubt about it, prisoner in a squalid little Third World dungeon, every morning, every afternoon, every night reinventing reasons to get his mind and muscles stirring. His sex drive was down to about .000002 ohms on the Richter scale, a flea fart. Too much beer, too much gin didn't help.

How would he get his cable into channels? DeGroot had forbidden him official contact with Luttak unless he cleared it with him or Harcourt, and he hadn't. He could lie about it, he supposed, the way Whittington's people did when they attributed some NSA telegraphic intercept from Moscow to some Rumanian diplomatic asset in Brussels. He could claim he bumped into Luttak at a cocktail party, but when? No parties, no receptions for three days. A prisoner in the meantime, no doubt about it, a prisoner of conscience. Maybe he ought to smuggle out a few lines to Amnesty International, get PEN to look into his case, join the International Fellowship of Poets in Prison. A few more rubber truncheons, a few more broken teeth; *all right, you bastards!* What's your ballad for the day?

> The sick were never meant to,
> The dreamers never dared;
> The careless always hoped to,
> The selfish never cared.

>The lordly condescend to,
>   The weak are commandeered;
>The cowardly intend to,
>   The poor are volunteered.

Do what? He'd forgotten. One of his Princeton poems, an Auden imitation published as a senior in a little literary mag Lisa Lerner had worked on during her brief year at Rutgers. Agnes Firthdale had told him at dinner last night she'd once won a gold cup at a Chelsea flower show. He should have told her he'd once had two poems published as a Princeton undergraduate.

He dropped from the wall and went back through the side courtyard and into the garden. He'd made a little money on the stock market since home leave, thanks to Eric Bowser, who'd passed on a few market tips from his firm. What better proof of enterprise, intelligence, pluck, dedication, and virtue than making money, his grandfather had once told him, although gentlemen didn't talk about it quite that way. All those old-fashioned virtues were silently enshrined in their corporate charters, their Harvard law degrees, or their broker's licenses, he'd added cynically the afternoon they'd had a quiet little lunch together, appealing to Talbot's own cynicism in attempting to change his mind about government service. His father had been much less articulate about his decision, and Talbot thought his father had put the old man up to it. Talbot was his only grandson.

Maybe Washington would do better with a corporate charter as well: State Department down 8., CIA up ⅓, NSC steady, Pentagon up 5., like Tootsie Rolls and Squim Surgical, maker of trusses, surgical stockings, absorbent underwear, and inflatable toilet seats. Eric had put him on to both during his few days in New York. Medicare would be a growth industry under Carter, sure; you didn't have to be a Pine Street gaffer to know that. But what about Tootsie Rolls? A nation getting older, fine, but getting younger, too? A nation of geriatric juveniles, like Harcourt, maybe. Like Eric Bowser, too. Louis Quatorze in the *faux bois* library, gilt-edged Tootsie Rolls in the family trust.

But he didn't think that was what his grandfather had had in mind.

Now he had a visitor.

"Am I interrupting anything?" Nicola asked, standing in the rear garden with a pair of potted plants in her arms.

Surprised and annoyed, he shrugged. "Not much." He crossed to the metal umbrella table to fold the copy of the Burao speech and draft cable in the *Herald Tribune*. "I didn't hear your car. Help yourself."

"You're sure?"

"It's OK. What have you got?"

"There's a performance at the National Theater tonight, so I decided to bring these plants. Do you like them?"

"Nice." They were small, green, and waxen-leafed, like boxwood, but most plants looked to him like boxwood.

"I didn't want to leave them in the car overnight. I thought they'd look nice in your two empty pots."

Her Jubba helper brought a wheelbarrow filled with rich dark earth. She looked at her watch, said something to him, and he turned silently and went out the gate. The more Talbot saw of him the more he was convinced he was a deaf mute. A few minutes later he heard her small truck being driven away. She kneeled down and spread out a groundcloth and set the two plants aside. "Are you going?"

"To the National Theater? No."

"You don't go to the performances, like most diplomats, do you?"

"Not much, no." Talbot dragged his wicker chair closer and sat down.

"You don't care for the folk music, the entertainment?"

"What entertainment?" He watched as she removed the first plant from the pot. "Would you pay two hundred shillings to watch the North Korean drum and bugle corps? Neither would I."

"So you don't go."

"Not when I can help it. If the others want to go bark like trained seals in the Moscow circus, like that claque in the audience, that's their business."

"The government notices, of course." Her back was to him as she trimmed the roots from the plant with her snips. Her drooping straw hat hid her neck from him.

"Who cares."

"You don't?" She leaned forward and began to move the earth to the bottom of the vessel. He went back to the table and returned with the *International Herald Tribune*. Eric had recommended two small high-tech stocks, but he hadn't found them listed in the *Trib*'s abbreviated Dow Jones since he'd bought a few shares.

"Probably many ambassadors feel the same way," she said after a minute. "Diplomacy isn't a personal matter, is it? The government here thinks you're antagonistic, that you sympathize with their enemies." Her back was still to him. "They say the Ethiopian comes to see you, the Saudi chargé, the Egyptian counselor. You talk to these people, but you don't go to the performances at the National Theater."

"Maybe they're better company."

"You go see the Russian counselor. Your car is left there in front of the gate for everyone to see. You talk to the Russians and not to them."

He dropped the paper aside. "Who've you been talking to, some NSS type?"

She was busy with the smaller plant. "Someone at the foreign ministry. He says you don't come to the foreign ministry anymore, that only this man DeGroot comes."

"Who at the foreign ministry?"

"Mohammed Hussein, the director of protocol."

"No wonder."

"Why do you say that?"

"Easy, the bastard has it in for me."

"Why?"

"Hard to tell."

"I saw him a few days ago and we were talking." She set the plant in the pot very carefully. "He had just come from a dinner, it was late, and he was disgusted, complaining about something—the Iranians, I think, then the French, then you, then someone else. He has a very difficult position here, very difficult."

"I bleed for him. What are you? His social secretary?"

She began filling the pot with dark soil, tamping it gently around the roots. "You're very critical, aren't you, very contemptuous. I think probably you're very much alike, you and this country, very proud, very easily offended. You think no one is more clever than you, and that's why you dislike each other." She got up slowly and leaned over to massage her thigh. "I shouldn't be doing this." He watched her cross to the wheelbarrow and kneel down. "It is very hot here with no breeze. Yesterday I saw you leaving the front gate with someone, a visitor, I think. Someone from Washington?"

"A British journalist, come to do his semi-annual piece on the Horn." The visitor had been Basil Dinsmore, sent by Ambassador Firthdale. He'd been bewildered by his talk with DeGroot.

"So he came to see you."

"I talked to him."

"What did you talk about?"

"How many Russians, how many Cubans, how many North Koreans? The same Chinese fire drill. Whether this is a Marxist regime or not. How come all the questions?"

"I'm curious. What did you tell him?"

"What I usually say. Everything about this place is a fiction." He got up, thirsty now. "Would you like a drink, some juice maybe?"

She hesitated and looked at her wristwatch. "No, thank you," she decided. "I won't be long. In what way is it fiction?"

"In most ways. Are you sure? How about a beer?"

Again she hesitated. "No, please don't bother. Is that what you think, that everything is a fiction? What, for example?"

"I'll be right back." He went into the house and returned with two cold bottles of beer and two glasses. He handed her a bottle and a glass. She hesitated but finally took them.

"Thank you. You said everything's a fiction."

"It is." He brought another chair near and she sat down. "Everything. Their Marxism, the claim they're scientific socialists, that's a joke, too. Nomads, the rest farmers, traders, small businessmen. Where's the proletariat? There isn't any. Where's the vanguard? There isn't any. Just a few juiced-up intellectuals and a national printing press. They aren't scientific socialists. That's the social text they're studying, the way the Indian kids in Latin America did for the Jesuit fathers. Keeps them down on their knees in the barrios, praying to the Virgin Mary and sweet Jesus. Cheers." He raised his glass and drank.

She didn't move, still watching him thoughtfully.

"What's wrong? That bother you?"

She smiled politely and took a small prim sip from her glass. "So you think the Marxism is a fiction. What else is a fiction?"

"That they're Arab."

"You certainly can't doubt that."

"Ask the Saudis, the Egyptians. They're not Arab, not Arabic-speaking except for a handful. Members of the Arab League, another fiction. Western Jubbaland's one more. That's all this country is, a series of seductive social and historical myths created by a people good at telling lies. Poets and warriors create their own myths, they're good at telling lies."

She cocked her head with the same small smile. "That is very interesting, how you say it."

A little condescending, Talbot thought. "I'm not trying to be cute. You asked me and I told you. What did you do before you became a banana farmer?"

"I was a teacher. What about their Marxism?"

"What did you teach?"

"Political economy."

"Then you know. Third World politicians like the Marxist version of history because it's history on the cheap, like classic comics, like college kids reading Oswald Spengler for the first time."

"Do you mind if I ask you something," she said, "something personal? I don't want you to misunderstand, to be offended, because that is not what I mean."

"Go ahead."

"Do you talk this way, this way you're talking, very contemptuously, do you talk that way to others at your embassy?"

"Sometimes."

"And to other diplomats?"

"Not much. Who's to talk to? I talk to myself."

"And with your ambassador you talk like this?"

"Sometimes. Why? You think I'm all wet?"

"I think the part about the poets and warriors may be true. They are poets, and to be a poet here is to be above everyone else, but poets are also liars, yes. I think that with many Jubba it's the words, the language, the text of Marxism, not the ideas, that makes the president so proud to talk about it in his speeches."

"That's too complicated for me. I'm just a diplomat."

"I'm not making jokes." Her tone was severe. She might have been a prudish teacher reprimanding a smart-ass pupil. "I meant that if you know the Jubba poets, you know words are important here," she said, slowly, "words for their own sake, and so Marx and Lenin are those they can memorize and repeat, and prove themselves, show the people, the foreigners, the Russians, too, that they aren't merely illiterate nomads, as you said." She put her glass on the flagstones and massaged her ankle. "So what about the Russians?"

"The Russian problem is different."

"Whatever you think of the Russians, they've brought a kind of stability, a kind of discipline. That's what their presence has brought."

"Right, so did Mussolini."

"I am not making jokes," she said indignantly, "please be serious. I am not talking about the past."

"Neither am I."

"The discipline isn't one many approve of. Most Westerners don't like it."

"What's to like about it, a ranting little Soviet satellite in East Africa, that's what. They've suddenly got religion, and they're obnoxious about it. OK, it's keeping them occupied, nation building, as the president says, building this phony scientific socialism, not out there on the frontier raiding Ethiopian police posts, stealing cattle, and mining roads."

"So you don't think it's genuine?" She was calm again. She was high-strung, he decided, remembering that night at the Italian residence, her composure skin deep; cerebral maybe, he couldn't tell; prim schoolteachers always sounded cerebral, especially the grass widows, but high-strung, yes, her anger quick, passionate, and unpredictable, like Julia's.

"What the Soviets think they're teaching can't be taught," he said, "not like the Latin alphabet, the way they're trying."

"How do you know that?" she demanded.

He laughed at her anger, so self-righteous it seemed ridiculous. "What do you mean, how do I know that? What is it, a secret only you highbrow Europeans know? You can't teach revolution the way you teach algebra. You can't teach it to Moslem nomads wandering around with their camel herds. You have to suffer something to feel it, and the only thing they're suffering is not having their grazing lands in Ethiopia. There's nothing revolutionary about that. It's been around for centuries, like the Basque problem."

She waited for a moment. "But you agree about the discipline."

"I agree."

"That interests me." She looked away. "Some people don't like to hear that, of course. People in the Italian embassy as well as your own." She lifted her eyes toward the dimming sunlight above the far wall. "But try to imagine what a return to the old parliamentary system would bring. A half-dozen parties, each competing for advantage. What would have the greatest appeal under those conditions? What would happen when the political parties began to argue, when the worst politicians put together a platform to unite the nation? What's the single issue that would most quickly unite this country?"

Another little lecture, he thought as she lifted her arm to point toward the rim of broken hills to the west, where the sun had begun to settle.

"Western Jubbaland," he said. "What I was just talking about."

She brought her arm down. "So we agree about that?"

"I already said I did. Ethiopia that way, Kenya to the south."

"Exactly. That's where the politicians would lead the army, into those pastoral grazing lands claimed by every Jubba you talk to, into a war that would never succeed."

"That's what I said."

"I know that's what you said."

"So what are you arguing with me for?"

"Am I arguing?"

"You sounded like it."

"I was trying to tell you something."

"You were trying to tell me something I already know and you didn't like my telling you I already knew it."

"That's not true."

"And you especially didn't like it since it wasn't the way you wanted it to be told if it'd been taught in your class, OK? So what's the next lesson for the day?"

"You're very insulting."

"Who's insulting? What is it, diplomats aren't supposed to know these things? What do you think we are, a bunch of parlor poodles all wigged out in ribbons and bows?"

She sat looking at him in disappointment. "It wasn't what you said but how you said it. You surprised me, that's all. I wasn't angry at all." The phone was ringing inside.

She got up and looked toward her wheelbarrow.

"You don't much like diplomats, do you?" he called after her.

"No, it isn't that," she said after a moment, nodding toward the house. "Do you have someone to answer?"

"Just me." He got up wearily and went inside. It was Julia. Why had he been so late answering and why did he sound so annoyed? Did he have a visitor? No visitor, he told her; he'd been sleeping. If he'd been sleeping, was it possible he had been invited to the French residence for dinner? He said he hadn't been, thank God. She said she was disappointed to hear that, his own selfish pleasure aside, since the German DCM was in Nairobi and his wife felt awkward going alone. Her voice was very low and very deliberate. She obviously wasn't feeling very lovely.

Neither was Talbot; she hung up on him.

When he returned to the garden five minutes later, he was surprised and a little disappointed to find Nicola gone. He hadn't intended that their talk end on such a sour note and now he regretted that it had.

□ □ □

When Nicola remained overnight in the capital, she sometimes stayed in a guest cottage at the Rugda Taleh, the sprawling state-owned hotel compound on the southwest edge of the city. The two dozen guesthouses lay behind a sheltering wall across the road from the restaurant and garden. It was after ten when the sedan from the banana board returned her from the National Theater. She went back along the walk past the empty swimming pool, through the shadows and onto the small porch. The dim yellow insect light was lit. On an adjacent porch two figures sat in the darkness, smoking and talking. She searched her purse for her key, listening to their Arabic. Their voices died away as they waited for her to go inside. She supposed they were Iraqis or Libyans, part of the two delegations that had arrived that week.

The air conditioners had been left on, but the interior was warm and muggy. She crossed the darkened salon and turned on the light in the bathroom and went into the dark bedroom, still scented by her cologne. She had slipped out of her shoes, removed her blouse, and was unwrapping her long skirt when the telephone rang. It rang four times before she could find her robe and run to the front salon to answer.

Ten minutes later, wearing her garden shoes and a short skirt, she returned past the swimming pool, went through the gate, and crossed the sand road into the rear garden at the Rugda Taleh. The gravel path wound through the shadows under the drooping laurel trees below the elevated terrace. Concealed by the thick shrubbery of the well-planted garden were a few dozen tables scattered at intervals along the winding path. Small groups of men sat, no more than four at each table, smoking, drinking tea, and gossiping softly of politics, as industrious as weaverbirds building their intricate little nests among the trees.

Major Jama was waiting at a green metal table just a few steps west of the ivied wall and gate that led to the parking lot below. A short man sat with him, but she couldn't recognize his face in the shadows. They both rose to greet her; Major Jama towered over them both as he offered her the chair the other man had been sitting in. She sat down and the short man excused himself and hurried away. Major Jama called after him and told him to send the waiter.

"When did you come?" she asked politely after a minute. She felt very uncomfortable.

"This morning." He was wearing a wrinkled khaki tunic open at the neck and wrinkled trousers.

"From Bulet Uen?"

He nodded, looking at two men strolling by. The bars of his mustache bisected his dark face; his hands were folded together as he restlessly tapped one thumbnail against the other, watching the two men until they disappeared. At last he sat forward. "I talked to Captain Hussein two days ago," he said softly. "He told me he talked to you."

"We had a talk, yes. He stopped by one morning."

"He said you were angry."

"I was."

"He said you thought nothing would change."

"That's not what I said."

"What did you say?"

"I said he was a fool."

Jama hesitated, searching her face. "He's been in the hospital."

"He told me."

"Is that what the Italians think, that nothing will change?"

"Change in what way?"

"The war in the west."

His tone shocked her—*the war in the west*—so matter-of-fact, so definite, as if everything had already been decided. "I don't know," she said, caught off guard. "Why are you asking me?"

"Because you talk to them."

"Who? The Italians? Ambassador Malfatti is as much a fool as Hussein. Why does he matter? You certainly have more friends here than I do."

"The wrong friends." He offered her a cigarette, but she declined; her hand would be shaking.

"What about the man who was just here?"

"Osman? He was with me in Cairo. He works with the NSS. Not just the Italians. Hussein told me you have other friends now."

Puzzled, she had to think for a minute before she knew what he meant. "The Americans? The Harcourts?"

"I don't know his name, the ambassador."

"The Harcourts, yes. I wouldn't call them friends."

"Hussein said you talk to them, you see them."

"I was doing some work in their gardens."

"They come to your house at Merca?"

"No, they never come. I've never asked them."

"Why? You don't like them?"

"I don't find them interesting."

"Whether they are interesting or not isn't important. Does the NSS keep a car with you when you do your business?"

Again she was surprised. "I don't know. I'm not conscious of it. I certainly have nothing to hide."

"No, nothing to hide. Like me. Like Hussein. No cars with us either, but we are outside, with the army, talking to the jackals. Hussein has friends at the ministries, but they don't go to the embassies either."

He was from the north but could have been an expatriate, like her. He had studied in London, in Bologna, in Cairo, and at Frunze and the airborne defense college at Ryazan in the U.S.S.R., and mocked them all, even the pretensions of his fellow Isaq clansmen.

He lit the cigarette and sat forward again. "As an old friend, let me ask you a question. Suppose you find something important, very important. A piece of paper, behind you there, on the path." He took a piece of wrinkled paper from his tunic and spread it on the table. "Where is that waiter?" He got up suddenly and disappeared up the path while she waited uncomfortably, still puzzled. He came back with a waiter. "Tea for you?" he asked. "Or soda?"

"I think I'd prefer a whiskey."

"You drink whiskey now? What would Seretti say?" He turned to the waiter. "Two whiskeys, very fast now, run."

He sat down again and spread the paper on the table again. "Today driving from Bulet Uen I was thinking. Suppose you found this on the path there, maybe from my pocket, maybe from the NSS man's pocket. In your room, something left on the table by the Iraqis who are here, something about oil or military supplies. No, not military supplies. Oil deliveries. Not oil, tractors. A warning. A warning to your friends." He looked at her. "You have a friend who sells tractors, don't you? Didn't Seretti have a friend who sold tractors?"

"Rugatto, yes."

"Rugatto. All right, to your friend Rugatto. A contract for tractors. But this is a contract between two of the Old Man's ministers and a Bulgarian tractor company, a secret contract, already signed, with some of the money already deposited in the Old Man's bank account in Zurich. So you tell your friend Rugatto, Don't waste your time trying to sell your Italian tractors. What kind of Italian tractors?"

"Fiat."

"Fiat. Don't waste time trying to sell your Fiat tractors, because a secret contract is already signed and you'll end up with nothing, just more enemies, more people whispering against you." He sank back. "I don't think this is a good example."

"I don't think it is."

"Maybe my idea wasn't a good idea."

"I'd know better if I knew what you're talking about."

"A problem I'm trying to solve in a simple way, a way without trouble."

"Then tell me the problem."

"What I said, the war in the west." He sat forward again but just then the waiter arrived. He put the two whiskeys on the table. "That was not very fast," Jama said. "Do you work for the government? Maybe you have a hole in your shoe." The waiter left. Jama shifted and sat forward, his shoulders hunched toward her. "Let's think about it another way, let's say the information in this paper you found on the path is not about tractors but about the Liberation Front camps, the weapons delivered by the army to these camps, how they would be used. Who at the Italian embassy would find that interesting? Do you know anyone? I am talking about simple things, not complicated for a woman. Who would be interested at the Italian embassy?"

"I don't know." His tone warned her. Was he involved in a conspiracy of some kind? "But then I'm still not sure I know what you're talking about."

"You add, don't you?" he asked brusquely, pushing the bar bill toward her. "Can you add the figures there? You pay your market bills, don't you? What do you do all day at Merca? You pay the restaurant bills? All right. That's what I'm talking about. What's in plain sight."

He sat back, searching the faces of the men sitting at the tables down the path. With a glance over his shoulder toward the restaurant terrace, he pulled his chair closer. "Let's begin again," he said patiently. "You have many friends, diplomats, Western diplomats in every embassy, and in every embassy there are those who are for us, those who're against us, even at the Russian embassy."

"And how do you know that?"

He leaned over the table. "For God's sake, woman, everyone knows that! Are you telling me you don't know that?"

She flushed, feeling very stupid. He was an intelligence officer; of course he'd know that. "That's something I don't know about."

"Then I'm telling you. I know; Hussein's cousin in the foreign ministry knows. Some for, some against. Hussein's cousin knows the names."

Her face was warm. "Then you should ask Hussein's cousin."

"Hussein is a frightened little man, a silly man; you said so yourself. I'm not interested in talking to his cousin. What he knows today a hundred men know tomorrow. I don't talk to frightened little men. I am talking to you, Mrs. Seretti, to an old friend."

"Then what is it you want?"

"To end this talk, to end this foolishness, to finish it." He leaned over and took a slim oilskin case from the seat next to him and brought out a small folded packet, which he opened. "These papers here. If you're interested, look at them, look at what they say."

He held them out and she saw the ministry of defense heading and didn't take them. "I mustn't know your secrets."

"Secrets? What secrets?" He was angry. "My God, woman, every nomad knows, every camel boy, every lorry driver. Take it, look for yourself. It's a list of camps, the officers there, the ration rolls. Say you found it on the table at your room at the Taleh, in a drawer; say your servant brought it. Federico is there; he's at Umcit. Hussein took him Samina's letter."

Her eyes stung suddenly; she felt a prickling in her throat.

"What is it?" he asked. She didn't know what to say. So it was true. *Federico was at Umcit with the guerrillas.* The waiter passed on the gravel path with a tray, stopped, turned around, and went back. "You didn't know Federico was at Umcit?"

She shook her head, avoiding his eyes and looking away. "How many are in the camps now?"

"More than ten thousand. At Ghaleb Uen, fifteen hundred. At Umjat, two thousand. At Uebi Hamar, two thousand. The ration lists are here. This is the problem I'm trying to solve, a very stupid problem."

"The names I don't know." She could have wept.

"Not on the maps, in my head."

"So you think the war is coming."

"Of course, one hundred percent."

She dared look at him again. "How soon?"

"It isn't sure. Not until the rains come. But other things first, the Russians first of all. The Old Man is playing a dangerous game with the Russians, a very dangerous game."

"They know?"

"They know but they aren't sure. Now they are waiting. It is the way the Russians are, to know everything and still not to be sure." He shrugged, lifting his glass. "So they try to know more than everything. In the end a man who tries to know more than everything knows less than nothing. That's the way the Russians are."

It was what Seretti might have said, she thought, watching Jama look over his shoulder. Two men at the next table hidden behind the shrubbery were laughing. "The Russians would never support him if he attacks Ethiopia," she said helplessly, "never."

"Who can say never? What is never? If the Old Man finds other friends, the Egyptians, the Iranians, the Saudis, and the Americans, the Russians won't matter. All of them will come and the Russians will go. So that's the game he is playing with the Russians, a black-mail game, and if the Russians won't help him, they can go, get out, he won't need them."

"But the Egyptians and Americans must know about the camps, about what he's planning to do."

"Do they?" He looked at her scornfully. "Who has told them?"

"I don't know but they have ways—"

"What ways? Who has told them? You, me, Hussein, the spy cameras overhead? Where do the embassy diplomats go, who do they talk to? They go nowhere, they talk to no one. They talk to themselves. What do the satellite spy cameras look at all day? The clouds, all day and all night, just the clouds, and that's why the Old Man has been waiting for the rainy season. Who has said to them in black and white, 'Look, here it is, on these papers—ten thousand in the camps, at Ghaleb Uen, at Umjat, at Uebi Hamar, all waiting for the big rains to come.' Who has said that? No one. So that was what I was thinking about, driving here from Bulet Uen." His voice had dropped again as he shifted forward. "I was thinking about 1969, how the British don't trust the Old Man, not the Italians, not the Americans, but now everyone is talking about how they might give him arms. How can you trust him? You can't. So that's what I was thinking, how to solve this problem in a simple way." He picked up the paper. "Tell me, if you found this list of camps on the path there, who would you give it to at the Italian embassy?"

She thought for a minute. "Giovanni, I suppose."

"I don't know the names anymore, not for two years. Who is Giovanni?"

"The commercial attaché."

"Commercial attaché?" He laughed. "My God, woman, I thought you were clever, like Seretti. What about Malfatti?"

"I don't get on with him."

"What about the British? What is his name, the new one?"

"Firthdale."

"I don't know him."

"The American again, how is he called?"

"Harcourt."

He thought for a minute. "There's another, a small man, older, with gray hair. The CIA man. Osman told me his name but I don't remember. Do you know him?"

"An American?" She frowned. "I can't think of who you mean."

"His office is on the second floor."

"I've never been to the embassy."

He sat back, disappointed. "I thought you knew more diplomats, that you and Malfatti were friends, that every day your car was there at the American ambassador's gate."

"Not now. What about journalists? A friend of mine is coming, Minzonni, from Rome."

"What is he, a socialist, a communist? I'm talking about diplomats, not foreign journalists. No one listens to the foreign press. The Italian communists and socialists are the worst, always making propaganda, like they're doing for the Ethiopians now. My idea is a small idea, between you and me and these papers, not something for journalists." He was looking away down the path.

"I was trying to think of some way to help."

"The journalists can't help, not the journalists you know. It was just an idea, not a good idea." He put the papers back in his oil-skin packet. "Let me think about it some more."

"How long will you be here?"

"Until tomorrow." He stirred restlessly. "Don't say anything to Hussein, not to anyone. Let me think some more."

"I was thinking I could arrange something at my villa, have some diplomats come, someone you could talk to."

"Impossible."

"I suppose so. Are you convinced he intends to attack the Ethiopians?"

"When his own correlation of forces is right, absolutely. One hundred percent."

"I wish I could help," she said after a minute. "It would be a very stupid mistake."

"Stupid, yes, very stupid. I don't know. What can you do? Maybe my idea was stupid, too. These days I don't have many good ideas. I think I must be getting old, like my great-uncle in Sheikh." He looked at the glass in his hand. "He needs English whiskey now to help him remember the old days. That is sad. Tell me about the banana business, about the villa. What did you do with Seretti's rifles, the Beretta?"

"I gave them to Federico," she said after a minute. "I'm keeping them for him." She searched his face. "How is your wife, your children?"

"At Sheikh with my great-uncle."

"You have a son now, Hussein told me."

"A son, yes. Three months old." He looked away across the garden. "I've seen him once, just once. You see how it is, why I must be careful, all of us these days. You, too."

"I will try to help," she said.

"By not saying anything, not talking to anyone, not a word of what I showed you."

"Not a word, I promise. Not until I hear from you."

□ □ □

His talk with Nicola Seretti had been a mistake, a foolish mistake. He shouldn't have telephoned her, even though she believed in the same

things her husband once did, saw the same things he saw, the tribal-
ism, the lies, the fantasies, the corruption, the Marxist-Leninist masquerade, the Old Man's pathetic double-talk, his humiliating little
treks to Moscow or Jidda to sing for his supper. Now he was secretly
pleading for American arms in Washington through Ambassador
Abdulkadir. But his idea of using Mrs. Seretti was too impulsive,
nothing more than a cunning thought during the long drive from
Bulet Uen. Unable to define in his own mind the shadowy line between his responsibilities to his nation and treason, he would be foolish to involve her or anyone else.

Viale Italia was nearly deserted. The asphalt shone like oil under
the arc lamps swaying in the night wind, returned with Jama to
reclaim the city. It was the way he always felt coming back from
the interior. He drove his cousin's Fiat down Viale della Repubblica toward the Giubba Hotel, watching the road behind him.

A few cars were parked in the front lot under the trees. The
bright lobby was deserted. At a phone box in the rear he took the
slip of paper from his pocket with the telephone number left for
him with his cousin's wife and dialed the number.

Major Yefimov answered; it was a moment or two before Jama
recognized his voice.

"I have something for your group," Yefimov said, "something
very important."

"Then come tomorrow," Jama said wearily. Yefimov was once
the Soviet adviser at G-2 headquarters at Bulet Uen; Colonel Mahmoud, Jama's commanding officer, had demanded his removal six
months earlier. He hadn't been replaced.

"We must talk tonight," Yefimov pleaded. "Where are you?"

"At the Giubba."

"Then I will come, please. In thirty minutes."

Jama hung up, looked wearily at his watch, and went upstairs to
the small bar and ordered a whiskey from the bartender. Two officials from the ministry of information were sitting nearby on over-
stuffed lounge chairs drinking tea and talking to a dark-haired
journalist who was taking notes. He couldn't hear his Arabic; from
his dark suit and his wiry black hair he decided he was an Iraqi.
The Iraqis looked like peasants, like farmers, even in military khaki.
As he turned back, he saw a stout European sitting all alone at

a table at the far end of the bar, looking sadly out over the room. He gave Jama a polite smile, which Jama didn't acknowledge.

Suddenly serious again, Basil Dinsmore took a sip from his glass, pondered the notes he'd scribbled following his long talk with Logan Talbot, and made an entry in a small notebook in front of him.

English, Jama decided. He smoked a cigarette as he sipped his whiskey, looked at his watch again, and then wandered back across the lounge, past the stairs, through the deserted dining room where a dinner had been given earlier that night in honor of a visiting Iraqi delegation. He went out onto the rear balcony. From the small nightclub at the rear of the garden, he heard music and leaned against the rail listening.

In the old days the first president of the republic would often stroll over to the Giubba from his small house nearby to sit quietly in the garden below or in the lounge and have tea and talk about matters of state with anyone happening by. On the roads outside the capital his small Fiat could be seen stopped on the verges, empty, the president prostrate on his knees nearby, saying his sundown prayers. Now the Old Man never left his armed cantonment just west of the airport except in a speeding caravan of Fiats and Land-Rovers filled with his military and NSS bodyguard.

He roused himself, looked again at his watch, and went back through the dining room, leaving his empty glass on a table. He'd been awake since four o'clock that morning.

In the lobby a Jubba and an East German were waiting for the elevator, both from Technical Unit 3 of the NSS, responsible for audio surveillance of the hotel's guests and visitors.

He passed by without nodding and went through the lobby to wait in the parking lot. Five minutes later Yefimov drove in. The headlights of his gray Russian sedan lit up a trio of Jubba just leaving their government Fiat, their voices very loud. He recognized Ambassador Abdulrahman, assigned to the presidency, poet and gadfly, publicist to the revolution, secret speculator in rice and sugar on the Old Man's behalf.

"It is better not here," Yefimov said through the window. He was wearing light cotton suntans and a small white cap. "Can you follow?"

"Not the embassy," Jama said.

"No, not the embassy. On the beach."

Jama followed in his Fiat. Yefimov's gray sedan was the only car on the boulevard except for a red-and-yellow taxi in the other lane. The taxi disappeared up a dark street at the Piazza Sayd Omar, and Jama followed Yefimov to the east toward the corniche.

The Russian beach house was an old yellow building facing the sea. The iron gates were open. Jama parked alongside Major Yefimov's gray sedan in the small courtyard as the gates shut behind them.

A group of Russians had been there earlier that evening. Jama could smell the cigarette smoke in the high stairwell. They climbed to the second floor and went through two rooms where the lights were still on; empty glasses sat on the small tables, together with empty Fanta and Coca-Cola bottles. The tile floor was gritty with sand; a few towels lay over the cushioned backs of the bamboo chairs.

Yefimov led him outside onto the second-story porch, screened by latticework on both sides. A few meters below, the surf surged in the retreating tide that left the shore sheeted with silver. He turned on a table lamp, brought two damp chairs near, and sat down. A minute later a tired Russian from the housekeeping and security staff arrived from downstairs.

Yefimov asked him to bring them something to drink; the custodian, a small sleepy Russian who shuffled when he walked, said he didn't know what was downstairs. Yefimov went to look and returned a few minutes later with a half-empty bottle of brandy and two glasses.

Yefimov was small and trim with a round cheerful face; his light blond hair had receded well back from his forehead. He'd learned a little Arabic in Cairo, where he had served as a Soviet adviser to Egyptian military intelligence until Sadat had sent the Soviets home, then spent a year in Aden before coming to Jubba. As Soviet intelligence adviser to the G-2 staff at Bulet Uen he spoke only English but not too well; his brow, cheeks, mouth, and gums did their whimsical little dance to his foolish jokes, but the eyes never changed, too pale under the colorless brows to show any emotion at all. The Jubba intelligence officers at Bulet Uen had nicknamed him *Indoadde*, white eyes; he was an easy man for brown-eyed Arabs like Colonel Mahmoud to mistrust.

Colonel Mahmoud had asked for his recall because he was taking more from the G-2 staff than he was sharing—an eavesdropper, little more. Better maps than those supplied by Yefimov could be obtained through British, American, and Italian commercial sources, better tactical intelligence methods from the Egyptians, better electronic intercepts from their own small commo staff. His suspicions were reinforced by the Egyptian military attaché, who told him Yefimov had the same reputation in Cairo; Egyptian G-2 had banished him to a logistical unit.

Yefimov had never hinted he recognized their suspicions and may not have deserved their mistrust, but whether he did or not, small blue eyes were small blue eyes, Russian, Yemeni, or Circassian, and there was nothing Yefimov could do to change that.

That night Major Yefimov had brought him a gift, like the brandy and vodka he distributed at G-2 headquarters: two intelligence reports collected by the Russian GRU from an unidentified foreign military attaché in Addis Ababa. One claimed the Ethiopian mechanized brigade at Nazareth was being moved south to Harage province opposite the Jubba frontier.

"It came today," Yefimov said.

Jama studied it indifferently. "It should have been passed to Colonel Mahmoud at Bulet Uen."

"You will pass it to him, yes?" Still smiling, Yefimov leaned over and took another paper from his small leather letter case. "Also this."

The second document was a list of Western Jubbaland liberation front cantonments in the north along the Ethiopian frontier identified by their names and coordinates—Ferage, Mursal, even as far south as Umcit.

Jama gave no indication he recognized the names. "Where is this from?"

"From a foreign military attaché in Addis Ababa."

"Where did you get it?"

"It was passed to us. Who passed it I cannot say."

"You don't know?"

"I don't know. But I will say one thing. If this foreign attaché in Addis knows, then the Ethiopians know." He sat back to light a Marlboro. "Of course."

"You think so?"

"Of course."

It was what Yefimov always said: "Of course, yes, of course"— but he had no more sense of the intonation than the Egyptian officers from whom he'd learned it and whose English was equally patronizing. Colonel Mahmoud, who'd lived in England, like Jama, and studied at Sandhurst, had found it insulting.

"But this is not what is most important, not why I wanted to talk," Yefimov was saying as Jama continued to study the two documents. "What I will say is this."

Jama looked up, waiting.

"To know one paper is to know the other," Yefimov said cleverly. He put his small thick hand on the one report. "If this one is right, then this one is right. But we don't know about this source, whether he is right about the Ethiopian brigade at Nazareth, whether he is right about the camps. About some of them, we know, yes. About all of them, no. This military attaché in Addis would interest us. He would interest Colonel Mahmoud, yes?"

Jama nodded, watching the pale blue eyes.

Everyone was playing cunning little games these days—his own foolish game with Mrs. Seretti, the Old Man's pathetic game with the Soviets and the Americans, each pretending not to know what the other knew. Now Major Yefimov with his two intelligence reports. Did Major Yefimov think Jama or Colonel Mahmoud didn't know his game?

"So what is it you want?"

"First we must know whether he is accurate or not accurate, reliable or not reliable. So I am asking you, what do you think?"

Major Jama looked again at the list of guerrilla camps Yefimov was pretending to ask him to authenticate.

"I'll have to talk to Colonel Mahmoud."

"You can't say now?"

"Not one hundred percent, no. I'll have to talk to Colonel Mahmoud."

"Then you will tell me?"

"If we can help and if Colonel Mahmoud wants to see more from your source, yes, we will."

"Of course, yes. Very good."

Yefimov got quickly to his feet. "Ah, Yuri, I did not hear you. This is my friend, Major Jama. We were talking."

A young man, slim and blond-haired, stood in the door looking at them. Behind him was a young Russian woman who saw the two of them there and turned away into the shadows.

Yefimov introduced Yuri Pulyakov. Jama shook his hand. They sat down and drank some more and talked for a while. Pulyakov wasn't a Soviet military adviser. He'd recently arrived. He knew Aden and Rome as well as Addis Ababa; his English was as fluent as Jama's. Jama wasn't certain what his position was at the embassy, except that he was a first secretary. He doubted he was GRU. He seemed more European than Russian.

As he drove out the gate, he was curious as to who was responsible for Major Yefimov's sly little game. Pretending to share information collected from a Soviet GRU asset in Addis Ababa, the Russians were warning them that the Soviet military advisory group knew where the WJLF camps were, knew how many weapons and how many men. They were warning them the Ethiopians had moved their mechanized brigade down to the lowlands and knew also. He doubted the warning would persuade the Old Man to postpone his offensive in the west. Only if he was convinced neither the Soviets nor the Americans would help would he finally see the imbecility of his dream of recovering Western Jubbaland and back down.

□ □ □

Two hundred meters down the beach Talbot and Dr. Greevy sat in a dimly lit corner of the Anglo-American beach club, drinking beer and eating lobster, ignoring the anarchy around them, the only remaining diners at that late hour. The concrete floor was still wet from the crowd that had gathered that afternoon. In the yellow light near the bar four drunken English technicians from the telecommunications crew were playing darts and arguing. They had been drinking since two o'clock that afternoon, were unsteady at five o'clock, and now were raucously near collapse. Already they'd dismissed one of the two waiters on duty. Now the wife of one of the Englishmen, just returned from the ladies' room, jumped to her feet and gathered up her beach bag, insulted. In her absence someone had poured ale on her chair.

"You bastards," she shouted and left.

A bronze-tipped dart shot across the room and quivered into the door frame.

Greevy turned his head sympathetically to watch her go. "Poor woman. Nothing is more vulgar than the most vulgar Englishman." Another dart followed. "You chaps don't always know."

"Know what, the English?"

"The worst in him." One of the Englishmen was standing unsteadily on a chair, taking aim at the Heinekin sign across the room. "Myself, too. There's something of him in all of us, I suppose. Can't help it, you see." He watched the dart fly across the room, clatter against the tin sign, and fall to the floor. The Jubba barman, seeing his chance, slipped along the bar and turned in full flight out the door. "Vulgarity, a kind of mortality. We reek of it." He held out his fingers, which were trembling slightly. They'd both had a great deal to drink that evening, beginning in Talbot's rear garden. "It makes us what we are." Two of the Englishmen were behind the bar replacing the mirror with their dart board. "You find it in our history, our theater. It's antics like that that account for the monarchy." He watched the two Englishmen, bemused. "We may deceive others. We don't deceive ourselves. There's nothing you can tell an Englishman about himself that he doesn't already know. We're neither French nor German in that way, thank heaven." He watched as the strip of hemp carpet was carried to the front of the bar and the distance walked off.

For the past few hours Talbot had listened as Dr. Greevy described his recent journey through the interior. He knew the Jubba nomads as few did; he had drunk their camel's milk, bought their rams for slaughter, studied their stars, and listened to their savage poetry around the campfire, all very romantic, Talbot imagined. Only after he'd visited the doctor's house in the Nairobi suburbs during a four-day visit to Kenya did he better understand Greevy's passion.

The grounds of his detached cottage resembled a garden in the English countryside; the pink-cheeked woman with the musical voice who'd served him tea that sunny Sunday afternoon might have been sitting in an Elizabethan cottage in Suffolk or Surrey. The ceiling was beamed, the deep windows leaded. Mrs. Greevy had her garden and her roses, Dr. Greevy his library with book-lined shelves and its aroma of tobacco and wood ash, its little collection of Jubba milk jugs, woven baskets, and wooden drinking cups. Greevy was a bored suburban wanderer, prowling the bush as other men played golf or tennis. His infatuation with Jubba was genuine, no doubt about it, but more imaginatively than physically erotic, unlike that of the Norwegian honorary consul, an elderly shipping man, now retired, who lived out his sensual fantasies every night doing a geriatric foxtrot at the Lido nightclub or the Mariner's Cave with one of a succession of nubile young concubines who shared his little villa on the Lido road and salted his meals with some obscure herb to prolong his amorous interest and the little subsidy that accompanied it. In a climate of cotton shorts and drenching sunlight, their elixir sometimes crept up on him unexpectedly and left him painfully embarrassed with a semipermanent afternoon erection.

Dr. Greevy wasn't smitten in the same way, but he was smitten. He saw the Jubba as a proud anachronistic remnant, a people bypassed by time, indifferent to the artificial boundaries that couldn't enclose them, their lives bound to the rhythms of the seasons, their animals, the earth, the plants and stars, wandering in a no-man's-land beyond the reach of political and economic law and condemned to remain poor, fierce, proud, and independent, contemptuous not only of the Ethiopians who administered their pastoral lands to the west but also their own government with its printing presses, its national radio, its ministries, and its Marxist-Leninist pretense.

Suburban sentimentalist or not, Greevy had had an interesting trip this time and Talbot envied him. He'd told Talbot he thought he'd seen his missing houseboy during his visit to a WJLF laager.

"What was your houseboy's name again?" he asked.

"Hussein."

"The more I think of it, the more convinced I am he was one of the lads I treated at Umcit, the laager there. Can't be sure but I think he was. Ogadeni, you say."

"Yeah, but he wouldn't have volunteered. The bastards conscripted him."

"Could be. They rounded up quite a few here last month while you were on leave. I think the Swedish hydrologist lost his cook."

"Here in town?"

"So I understand."

"I heard some rumors, that's all. How many would you guess were at Umcit?"

"Hard to say. A few hundred at least."

The nervous waiter brought two kidney pies and scurried away. Four weeks in the bush, Greevy had ordered lavishly; now he regretted it. "I think we'd better hurry." He tucked the napkin in his collar. "Kidney pie?"

"No, thanks, lobster's plenty."

"You're sure? I can't manage both now, can I?"

"I really couldn't."

"You must." Greevy prodded the crusts of both with a fork and passed one across the table to Talbot. "Try this one." He took a bite and wiped his lips. "I saw Bashford-Jones this morning. Thought I'd better tell him what happened."

"What did he say?"

"Not much. They're going to do Shaw, it seems."

"Shaw?"

"His theater group, an August production. Shaw, I think it was. That surprised me, but it shouldn't have. At least that's what Bashford-Jones told me. Looking for recruits."

"About Umcit, you think they're planning something serious?"

"Convinced of it. Very soon. Probably when the rains commence. What's happening with your embassy? It doesn't know?"

"Nothing as specific as that. Basil Dinsmore asked me about the camps and I said I'd look into it. I haven't seen any reporting on it, not since I've been back."

"Odd. Very odd. How's the kidney pie? Where is that waiter with the salad?"

Greevy excused himself to go to the kitchen to find the waiter. In Dr. Greevy's company Talbot knew himself capable of great drinking and conversational feats but absolutely incapable of eating his loathsome kidney pie. He got to his feet and dashed across the room to the open porch on the beach and threw the kidney pie as far as he could toward the breaking waves.

When he returned, carrying the empty plate, the dart-playing Englishmen had disappeared. A beer bottle was still spinning on the bar. He heard their footsteps on the gravel, then a car starting. A minute later a familiar klaxon whined through the streets close by. Greevy returned from the kitchen, walking very fast. "Everyone's gone. I think it's time. Finished already?"

He slid his kidney pie onto a paper napkin and they walked very quickly out the back door and up the darkened beach, putting as much distance as they could between themselves and the Anglo-American club before the police arrived.

On the corniche they continued on foot to the south and entered a small dark passageway between two old buildings leading to a dark courtyard where a few cars were parked. Facing the courtyard were three small cottages rented by the UN staff. On the front veranda of the center cottage a few figures sat talking in the dim light. The cottage belonged to Hafiz Ghanim, an Egyptian economist with the UN.

Dr. Greevy and Talbot joined them. Two more chairs were brought from inside, where a phonograph was playing.

Talbot had spent hours with Hafiz and his wife Fawya on that same porch during the past two years. They were both university-educated Egyptians, as restless in their confinement as Talbot. Hafiz was short and plump-faced, with wiry black hair; Fawya was a slender dark-haired woman in blue jeans, her almond eyes rimmed with kohl-like blue shadow. Usually the same group would gather after a reception or a dinner: Major Mustafa Salim, the Egyptian military attaché, and his wife; Najah al-Zeyn, the Syrian ambassador; and Mansur Azmun, the Iranian chargé d'affaires.

It was Hafiz who asked the question. They had heard Talbot would soon be leaving. Fawya, his wife, insisted it wasn't true, Hafiz had doubted it, too, but Najah al-Zeyn had heard the report from his Jubba contacts.

"Najah doesn't know," Fawya said in her rich Egyptian brogue. "Hafiz and I told him it wasn't true."

"Who told you I was leaving?" Talbot said.

"I didn't say it was true," Najah said, laughing. "I say someone tells me this." He was a former Syrian air force officer and sometime playboy, not a diplomat; he had as much difficulty taking his responsibilities seriously as did the host government, who'd sought his recall. He was stocky, with dark wiry hair, black eyes, and a thin black mustache, the kind of looks Moslem girls in the streets of Beirut or Damascus would have found dashing, but to most Western women seemed effeminately artificial—like an Italian barber or hairdresser, Julia had said.

"Who told you I was leaving?" Talbot asked.

Najah laughed. "Everyone."

"I have heered it, too," Major Salim said.

"Hear what?" Fawya asked.

"That Mr. Logan will be going."

"What is the new one's name?" Najah asked.

"Which one?" Talbot said.

"The long one."

"The tall one, Najah," Fawya said, "not long one."

"The tall one, yes," al-Zeyn said, suddenly serious as Fawya corrected his English. "Tall one, not long."

Hafiz blew out his cheeks and cradled his arms. "Like this. He is fat like a woman." Hafiz worried about his own weight and his increasing baldness.

"DeGroot."

"I think, yes, he is the one."

"He said I was leaving?"

"That everything would be changed," al-Zeyn said. "He was talking with some pairsons at the Rugda Taleh and this is what he is saying." He laughed, looking at Fawya. "Yes, yes, it is true."

"The ambassador, too?" Fawya asked suspiciously. "How? He is just here."

"No, not the ambassador. But that everything else would be changed." Najah al-Zeyn sat forward, taking Talbot's hand in his own lilac-scented fingers. "First, the other ambassador, before Harcourt. He is gone, yes." He delicately separated one finger and held it. "Then the deputy ambassador, the first counselor, what was his name?"

"Quarles," Talbot said.

"Yes." He separated another finger. "Then there was another, the fat one—"

"Shaughnessy."

"Yes. Now who is left. *You.* So they say you will go. Yes. Everyone will be changed." He released Talbot's hand and sat back in triumph, smiling happily.

Dr. Greevy sipped his whiskey and looked on, mildly amused.

"And who is saying this?" Talbot asked.

"DeGroot, the long one. Yes."

"Tall one, Najah," Fawya said.

Najah clicked his tongue regretfully. "Yes. Tall one."

"Fat one," Hafiz said.

It took Talbot twenty minutes to coax the full story from al-Zeyn. He had heard it from someone in the ministry of interior, who had heard it from those Jubba businessmen DeGroot had entertained at the Rugda Taleh. Evidently DeGroot was telling his old friends in Jubba, entre nous, that he and Harcourt had been sent by the Democratic administration in Washington to open a new era in Jubba-U.S. relations, dispatched to replace the old staff who had been indifferent to the changes, some actively opposed. It was a small lie, the kind of lie a weak man might tell to ease his way in a hostile capital, but a lie nevertheless.

"I'm not leaving," Talbot said, "not until November anyway. I think someone probably got the story mixed up."

"That's what I told them," Fawya said.

Talbot could imagine DeGroot's toast at one of his intimate little dinners at the Rugda Taleh: *I bring from Washington a mandate for change,* he would have announced to his hosts as he raised his wineglass, that fraudulent boast modified in his cabled memo to read, *I have come to listen to my many Jubba friends, nothing more.*

He understood better why DeGroot hadn't included Harcourt in those small dinners. He was even more suspicious of his decision to make him economic officer, ad interim, and take over political reporting. Not since he'd returned had he seen any evidence that DeGroot or anyone else was interested in the guerrilla camps in the bush being armed by the Jubba army, like the one Dr. Greevy had visited. DeGroot's reasons seemed obvious enough. Jubba was a country about which most Western diplomats were prepared to believe the very worst, and Talbot was one of the believers.

It was after one o'clock as Talbot said good night and left the front porch. Greevy had already retired to the small transient cottage across the way. Ambassador Najah al-Zeyn left with him, on his way to the Giubba Hotel. He invited Talbot, who politely declined. He'd once been victimized by Najah's post-midnight prowling through the dark streets of the capital.

That evening had begun innocently enough on Hafiz's veranda. A group of Arab journalists had recently visited the capital, invited by the ministry of information to see for themselves that the so-called Soviet missile base at Muzaffar was a figment of the Pentagon's paranoia. The visiting journalists, some from Beirut, others from Damascus and Baghdad, had been taken 600 kilometers up the coast to the small camel port of Muzaffar, shown around the sweltering town and dock facilities, and had seen nothing even remotely resembling the missile facility described by the Pentagon and photographed by a U-2 sent from Diego Garcia, photographs of which had been leaked to the American and European press. In the press conference given at the ministry of information following their return, the spokesman for the Arab journalists claimed the Americans had mistaken the minaret of the Muzaffar mosque for a Soviet missile base. The press conference had provoked a great deal of official mirth; the American spy satellite was soon the butt of every crude joke in the local press as well as much of the diplomatic community.

Hafiz and Najah al-Zeyn were also skeptical of the American claims, as was Major Salim, who had visited Muzaffar and seen nothing even resembling a Soviet missile base. *A missile base at a hot, smelly little camel port like Muzaffar? Where could you hide it?* None of the three was sympathetic to the local government or the Soviet military presence, but all agreed that the Arab journalists were right and the Pentagon wrong. Talbot tried to explain that the whole affair had been poorly handled and had become terribly confused, with Washington itself partly to blame. After a decade of hysterical press, magazine, and TV coverage of Apollo launchings at Cape Kennedy, Washington had made it impossible for a remote people in a country as primitive as Jubba to imagine anything relating to a missile base being any less spectacularly self-evident, like an eclipse of the sun.

The term missile base itself was misleading; what the photographs showed wasn't a missile on its launch pad, but a modest garage-like facility for reworking the smaller Soviet ship-borne missiles. In addition, the Soviet installation wasn't in the port of Muzaffar but some distance away. The Arab journalists visiting Muzaffar had been deliberately misled.

It was nearly two in the morning when Najah, still dubious, proposed to settle the issue. Fawya had gone to bed; Major Salim had left. He suggested they go talk to a second group of Arab journalists who'd visited Muzaffar and were still in the capital as guests of the ministry of information, scattered at various rest houses around the city. They set out in Najah's Mercedes. Talbot wasn't sure where they were going—a lonely stretch of street near the Rugda Taleh first, then a guesthouse up on the hill near the British residence, then another on a narrow street, and finally a high wall with the gates open and a few cars parked inside in front of an old villa.

He was told to wait in the car. Fifteen minutes later Hafiz came to fetch him. At the bar in the front room two Arab journalists sat drinking and talking. Passing back along the dark corridor, Talbot saw through the half-closed door of the first room two more visiting journalists in various states of undress, chewing khat and drinking Coke, attended by a pair of sleek half-dressed Jubba women. Najah was waiting in front of a closed door at the end of the hall. He put his finger to his lips, smiled mysteriously, beckoned Talbot forward, and gently pushed open the door. Inside lay the journalists' host, a stupefied Dr. Mohammed Hussein, the director of protocol at the foreign ministry, lying half undressed on a cushioned divan, his trousers fallen to his ankles. His eyes were half open, a few wet khat leaves hung from his slack mouth. Lying against him was a naked Jubba girl, head against the pillows, her henna-stained fingers sleepily coaxing his limp member back to life.

Dr. Hussein heard al-Zeyn's giggle, sensed the figures in the doorway, blinked, stirred, and grunted. His mouth opened, drooling green camel juice down his chin as he struggled to sit up. Najah and Hafiz fled back down the corridor; Talbot caught up with them in the courtyard, the Mercedes already in motion.

Talbot later learned that Dr. Mohammed Hussein's chauffeur, also waiting in the courtyard, had been able to identify al-Zeyn's Mercedes. It took Dr. Mohammed Hussein a few more days to question the visiting Arab journalists and, probably with the help of the NSS, finally identify Najah's two accomplices.

□ □ □

Julia was attacking furiously. Her mouth was set, the cords of her neck stood out, and her dark plaits were flying. Talbot was terribly hungover. Four times he'd made only a halfhearted effort to retrieve her very fine passing shots, the most recent of which was now dribbling off the back wall.

"Would you please wake up!" she shouted from the net.

"I am awake. You're too good today."

"You're not trying!"

"I am trying."

"Then for God's sake play like it!"

She had bitchy manners on the tennis court. She'd begun slowly that afternoon, missing her first serve. Her second serve was the weakest part of her game, but in his condition he hadn't taken advantage of it. Instead he'd merely kept the ball in play, less painful for his aching head but annoying to Julia, who resented any too obvious concession to her slower speed and weaker power. If he were to move his game up a notch or two and give her the good sound thrashing she deserved, she wouldn't forgive him. Over the months he'd felt his power game deteriorating to the level of her own, as feeble as his intellectual and sexual life these past weeks. So the match was being played on her terms, as always, his own complicity disguised in cunning ways. But now that she was on top of her game, she was even bitchier, suspecting his carelessness too deliberate, a too conspicuous excuse for letting her win.

A match was also in progress on the other court, hidden behind the high concrete block wall. They didn't know who was playing, some kind of lollipop game. "Kangaroo tennis," Talbot called it.

From time to time a green ball would come soaring over the high wall onto their court, breaking her concentration.

It was late in the match. Both were tired, their faces and tennis shirts wet, their feet heavy. Talbot was at the net, wearily retrieving a missed second serve when the latest errant ball came bouncing over the wall onto her end of the court. Julia, tense at the baseline a moment earlier, waiting for Talbot's serve, took it on the second bounce and smashed it viciously toward the far wall—"Get *out* of here, you bastard!"—but lost control of her racquet, and the ball came high and fast over the net, catching Talbot unprepared, just under the left eye. Court and sky exploded in a flash of fire, then swam in crimson; his racquet clattered to the ground.

"Oh, God! I'm sorry."

Dazed, he stood with his hand over his eye, blinking painfully.

She ran around the net. "Let me see."

"It's all right."

"Let me see, please." She brought his hand down slowly, peering up at him.

"I'm fine. Not the eye, just below it."

"Here?" She touched the wet skin. "Does it hurt?"

He brought the eyelid down, flushing away the tears. "No, it's all right now."

"Are you sure?"

"I'm fine."

"Oh, Logan, I'm sorry. I'm so sorry." And suddenly overcome, limp from the competitive fire that had kept her seething for two hours, she leaned against him miserably, her eyes shut. "I didn't mean it. I'm so awful these days, so terrible. *Why,* why, why?"

"It was an accident. I'm OK."

"It wasn't. Why am I so vindictive?"

"I'm all right. You're not vindictive."

"I am."

In reflex he took her shoulders and for a moment they stood in weary embrace, wet, footsore, and exhausted by their unending battle, on the court and off, wet shirt against wet shirt, relieved of any finale except this one. He was conscious of the scent of her shampoo, the strange softness of her skin under his hands, and a growing prickle in his jockstrap; neither was aware of the eyes watching from the doorway to the other court, where DeGroot stood silently in the shadows.

They'd separated and returned to their sides of the court when he entered at last.

Talbot, ready to serve, saw him first, an absurd gourdlike figure with white thighs and too tight shorts; he brought down his racquet. Julia turned, following his eyes.

"Would you *please* keep your balls on your own court!" she shouted.

Talbot smiled at the double entendre; DeGroot politely doffed his white tennis hat with the green visor. "You have a keen competitive stroke," he said.

"And you look ridiculous!"

"Why do I resent that man so?" she asked as they drove back toward the residence through the sunny streets.

"I thought you'd worked everything out."

"We have, but I don't *have* to like him."

The tennis match had left her in an odd mood, and when she was in an odd mood she found other ways to be disagreeable, to punish those she felt responsible. As they drove away in Talbot's Fiat, she mentioned Nicola Seretti. She'd seen her small Fiat truck turning into Talbot's drive with a load of earth brought from Afgoi.

"She overcharged the embassy for the planting she did. Mr. Peterson brought me the bill. It was much more than our agreed price."

"How much more?"

"A thousand shillings. There wasn't enough money budgeted in my groundkeeping account, and I told them not to pay."

"Maybe there was a misunderstanding."

She looked at him, lips drawn thin. "There was no misunderstanding."

"Have you talked to her about it?"

"Certainly not and I don't intend to. She imagined I wouldn't notice, I suppose, that the embassy would just pay without asking me. I think that was very dishonest on her part. I also think she's unreliable."

"In what way?"

"Deceitful. Apparently she had the same problem with the Italian residence."

"Who told you that?"

"Mrs. Firthdale mentioned it. She also told me something about her friends, something very suspicious, so I asked Ray Whittington about her."

She only believed Whittington's confidential briefings when she was looking for confirmation for her social prejudices, like her belief that the Russian-born Madame Nikiforov, the wife of the Bulgarian UN rep, was a KGB agent.

"What did he say?"

"He said she has some very odd ties to the Italian communists. Then to the PCI. What is PCI? That's the communist party, too, isn't it?"

"Right, the Partito Comunista Italiano, the Italian communist party."

"He made them sound as if they were two different things. Are you sure?"

"I'm sure."

"Apparently she entertains them when they come. Her husband was a communist, it seems. Her father-in-law a fascist."

"I thought you liked her," Talbot said.

"I never said I liked her. I said she was interesting at first. I think you'd better find someone else to redo your garden."

Julia wasn't only careless about money but vindictive when reminded of it. She never calculated the cost of her extravagance, but now Peterson had humiliated her by presenting a bill she'd given no thought to. Her desire to have everything about her fine and lovely was now being reckoned in dollars and cents, a reminder of how ugly, grasping, and rapacious were those who indulged her whims and after she'd forgotten billed her for them. Since she refused to admit her extravagance, she imagined she was being taken advantage of, and when she imagined she was being taken advantage of, she turned venomous. She wanted to be loved for herself and herself alone; no one survived her suspicion that she wasn't, that she wasn't admired for her taste, her style, her grace, and compassion, but because she had prestige, power, and embassy money at her disposal. So now Nicola Seretti had entered the circle of conspirators and she was telling Talbot to have nothing more to do with her.

"The owner of the house is paying for it," he said.

"Do you have it in writing?"

"Not yet, no."

"Then the embassy will get some whopping bill we'll refuse to pay. Find someone else."

"What am I supposed to tell her?"

"That it's not convenient, that it's disruptive."

"What does changing the soil in the back garden and putting new plants in have to do with her political opinions?"

"Don't be naive. She has access to your house and garden."

"You mean she's going to bug my palm trees?"

"Don't be ridiculous; you know what I mean. After I talked to Whittington, I remember the strange questions she asked me."

"What kind of questions?"

"Leading questions, questions about politics."

"She's a curious woman, that's all."

"She certainly is."

"I meant inquisitive."

"Too inquisitive."

"I like inquisitive women, they interest me."

She didn't turn. "You really infuriate me sometimes. Now you're just being difficult. I feel very strongly about this. Don't disappoint me."

Harcourt had done a little painting that afternoon, a small seascape from the front bedroom window, but the results hadn't satisfied him and now he had put his brushes away. The sunlight was dimming from the trees and lay in a shrinking yellow flag on the eastern wall of the courtyard, a trapezoid he found himself watching in silent admiration as the square secretly diminished. Colors interested him as much as form, but he had never discovered the truth of texture. The old wall, stuccoed in places, plastered in others, understood it perfectly and gave dignity to the dying day in that incredible patch of pure reflected color. In an hour the sun would be gone, the wall wouldn't exist. *There,* he would tell them, *like that. This is what I brought from Africa.* And it would stand there, like the others, a canvas of perfect color and perfect texture, as large as that shrinking panel he watched from across the court-yard, perfect in every way.

The flagstones were still warm. There was no sound, not even the sound of the wind. But then he heard the car at the gate. He picked up his glass, quickly emptied it, and went to the kitchen to refill the pitcher.

He was standing in the rear garden as they entered, smiling hap-pily and holding a glass. A pitcher of martinis and two glasses stood on the white metal table.

"I've been waiting," he said.

"So I see," Julia said suspiciously. "Why did you make so many? You'll put us on our ear."

"For three. How was the tennis?"

"The usual," Julia said.

"Keenly competitive, I trust."

"Keenly." Talbot said.

Harcourt poured out a glass.

"If you don't mind, I think I'd rather have a beer," Talbot said, "maybe a Bloody Mary."

"Don't be silly," Julia said. "You love Lyman's martinis. Besides the pitcher's almost full."

"There's beer in the new refrigerator," Harcourt remembered.

"He'd much rather have a martini. So would I."

"A martini then," Talbot said.

Harcourt gave them their glasses and then raised his. "To the queen of the court."

"The ogre of the court," Julia said.

"Did she misbehave?" he asked Talbot.

"Terribly," Talbot said. "Shitty, in fact."

"I wasn't, just a little on edge. I don't know what's wrong with me."

"You need cheering up," Harcourt said. "Which reminds me. I want to show you something."

He led them through the kitchen and into the pantry, opened the door of one of the three large freezers, and stood back. Lying inside was the carcass of a large animal.

"What do you think of that?"

"It's hideous," Julia said. "What is it?"

"An antelope. The Italian counselor sent it over. For you, actually. For our anniversary. I thought we'd have a barbecue, American style. Peterson knows the technique."

"Giorgio sent it?" Julia said. "How thoughtful."

"He shot it himself. Magnificent, isn't it? I had to take out the shelf to get it in."

"It's very nice, but our anniversary is months away."

"I think he had the dates mixed up."

"Except we really don't have room, not for two months. Where did you put the other things?"

"In the chest freezer in the garage."

"They can't stay there. Do you have room in your freezer, Logan?"

"I don't have a freezer, just a compartment."

"Well, we don't have enough room here."

"We have four freezers now," Harcourt said.

"We still don't have room. There's an extra freezer at the compound. I think Miss Simpson has one in the basement."

"I'll ask Peterson to find room," Harcourt said. "Magnificent, isn't it?"

"I thought hunting was illegal," Talbot said as they went back to the garden.

"Don't be sly," Julia said.

" 'Tis," Harcourt said, "but he shot it for Julia, a metaphor, you see: *'e quivi caddi, e rimase la mia carne sola*—there I fell and my flesh alone remained.' "

"Who said that?" Julia asked indifferently.

"Dante." He went off to his bookcase to see if he'd gotten the quotation right, but as he stood dizzily in front of the bookcases the pain began again in his left side, clawing up his spine. He moved stiffly across the room, paused to hold himself erect in the doorway, then went down the hallway to the bathroom.

He returned and sat down delicately, listening to their voices in the soft warm air. She had changed and was wearing lipstick, a faint touch of pale pink on her lips that made her sun-darkened face even more angular. Her white peasant's blouse with its loose square neck also had an embroidered girdle of color about the sleeves. She was barefooted, her hair damp from the shower, her sabots kicked aside.

Her voice trailed off. "Are you dozing, Lyman?"

"No, just listening to the two of you."

"The two of us? Good grief, Logan's gone. He's been gone for twenty minutes."

The martini pitcher was empty. He was still watching the wall. The pain had gone and the sunlight had finally begun to fade, dimming to a small feeble square, no longer of consequence. Had he entered the courtyard at that hour, he wouldn't even have noticed it, no one would have noticed it, and the moment had been lost again, swept to the west now, lying on the harbor at Algeciras, at Tangier, at Marseilles, resting there, a slight fragile craft, a trireme it would be, wouldn't it, resting there before it began its long lonely journey across a dark unknown Atlantic.

CHAPTER FIVE

The Beast Untethered

Talbot sat in the rear garden in his damp bathing trunks, comfortably stoned. Beyond the glazed bathroom window on the second floor, Lindy Dowling was taking a shower. She had arrived unexpectedly two hours earlier, bringing her swimming suit and a few ounces of pot given her the evening before by a Seabee from Nairobi come to install some new security equipment. She rarely smoked marijuana, she confessed, and never alone; she needed moral support and a little privacy. Talbot thought the confession long overdue. They had gone swimming, shared a joint, and she had gone upstairs to take a shower while Talbot finished the joint alone.

Warmed by the friendly glow of Kenyan pot and the hot flush of afternoon sun against his skin, he'd considered joining her, but had decided against it. A false step now might spook her permanently. Besides, a joint's forgotten pleasure was one of contemplation, not rashness, the lush enrichment of future possibilities. He consoled himself by thinking of coming visits, coming confessions, future showers, future skin sports.

At last he roused himself and wandered off to the outside shower behind the wash house, fighting to keep possession of the separate parts of his body; his legs, arms, and eyes weren't performing on the same axis. The shower helped, very cold, very disciplined. He was back in the garden drying himself off when he heard the front gate clang open.

It was Whittington. Talbot thought he was looking for Lindy but he wasn't.

"Lindy? No, not Lindy. I wanted to talk to you for a minute, won't take long. I saw her motorbike parked in front. She's here?"

"Upstairs taking a shower."

"How long's she been here?"

"Couple of hours, we've been swimming."

Whittington looked at Talbot's red eyes. "Looks like you got too much sun, too much saltwater."

"We did. Exhausted as hell, both of us. You wanted to talk?"

"Yeah, just for a minute." He sighed unhappily as he sat down.

"How about something to drink, a beer maybe." Talbot got up and limped toward the door.

"Beer's fine, sure. What's wrong with your leg?"

"My leg?"

"The way you're walking."

"Sea urchin, got a spine in my heel."

The kitchen was soberingly cool. He took a bottle from the refrigerator, found a glass, and rejoined Whittington in the garden, limping less noticeably. They sat on lounge chairs in the open sunlight beyond the trees.

"I didn't know Lindy would be here," Whittington said. "Maybe it'd be better I got this over with before she came down."

"What over with?"

"Something private." A cautionary silence. "Nice back here, real quiet. Julia Harcourt asked me to keep it confidential. She told you maybe."

"Told me what?"

"About having a talk about Mrs. Seretti."

"She mentioned it. It doesn't interest me."

"Me either, but it's what she wanted. She's got some oddball friends, here and Italy, too. Ties to the Italian communist party for one thing."

"What kind of ties?"

"Through her husband."

"Her husband's dead."

"His friends." Whittington was gazing with detachment at the glazed bathroom window. "When they come here, they look her up, talk to her."

"That wouldn't be unusual, would it, her husband's old friends?"

"Maybe not, but that's not all. A lot of people think she's a conduit for information, that anything she hears winds up with the NSS."

"An informant?"

"That's the talk. A few years back she got a big loan from the banana board for that plantation of hers, a government loan when she was about to go bust. A little odd, some say."

"Maybe. Where'd you get this? A tracer?"

"In the files."

"Old stuff then. Who from, the Italians?"

"Some. The Rome station, too. Julia Harcourt said she was asking her all kinds of questions, that's why she asked me about her."

"Is that what she said?"

"Yeah, said it made her suspicious." He sat back in the chair and brought his feet up, again looking up at the glazed window. "Does she come out here very often?"

"Not too often. She's redoing my garden but I haven't seen her for a week or so."

"I meant Lindy."

"Lindy? Sometimes. Why?"

"Just asking." Whittington edged his chair closer, his arms on his knees, leaning near. "She doesn't have it easy, a single gal like that. Smart as a tack but not the kind that sets guys off, more the intellectual type, you know what I mean. I've been a little worried about her. She's twenty-six."

Talbot thought he heard awe in his voice.

"Twenty-six? So what? That worries you?"

"A little, sure."

"Why? What is it, her work?"

"Not her work, Christ, no, she's a peach. A little class for a change. People she might be taking up with. I want to keep her in the embassy family right now, not rush things too fast, not yet, anyway."

"Operationally, you mean. Who's she been taking up with?" That idea had never occurred to Talbot.

"No one much, that's the problem."

"Then what are you worrying about?"

"That's the kind you always worry about. Still waters run deep. You had a daughter, you'd know. Is she happy here? Has she talked to you about that?"

"She thinks DeGroot's a shit."

"Who doesn't." Whittington lifted a cigarette from his package of Kents and picked up the lighter from the table. "Gitanes, where in the hell did you get those?"

"Nairobi," Talbot said, discreetly picking them up.

"Used to be my poison. I thought I smelled something funny. That stuff's worse than hemp."

A minute later Lindy joined them, wearing sandals and cut-offs, rubbing her damp blond hair with a towel.

"Hi, what's going on?"

"Nothing much." Whittington smiled at her like a fond Irish uncle. "I didn't know you were here. Logan said you've been swimming."

"We have and I'm wiped out."

"How about another beer?" Talbot said.

"No, thanks, I've had enough." She slumped down in the chair, her long bare legs stuck out. "God, I don't feel like moving, not for a lifetime."

"He didn't take you beyond the reef, did he?" Whittington said, suddenly suspicious, "out there where he and that crazy guy used to swim."

"Noseworthy wasn't crazy."

"The hell he wasn't; he was a nut, both of you out there. Shark bait, both of you."

"We stayed inside the reef," Lindy said.

"Sharks get in there, too," Whittington said. "Don't kid yourself, big bastards, too, eight-footers. Want me to drop you home? I can drop you home if you're tired."

"What do you mean, home?" Talbot said. "For Christ's sake, she lives at the goddamn Y, the DeGroot Hilton. Why don't you get her out of there?"

"Thanks, but I've got my bike," Lindy said.

"I take what I can get," Whittington said. "You think I haven't tried to find her a place?"

"Try some more then," Talbot said, putting his hand on Lindy's knee. "Anyway, she's going to stay. Maybe we'll go to the UN club for dinner."

Lindy smiled. "Barf, barf."

"You've been there?"

"Once, never again."

He moved his hand away. *Jesus Christ.* You tried to educate your ward to a certain level of sophistication, help her manage a joint, give her a little privacy, get her accustomed to using your bathroom shower, encourage a certain individuality, and she rewards you by talking like the goddamned teenagers at the neighborhood drive-in. With just the two of them it had been fine, but with Whittington watching she was someone else, almost a self-parody, a self-conscious young woman embarrassed by Whittington's too obvious concern. A pity; with a little more education she could do better.

"Stay anyway," he said. "We'll go someplace else."

"I can't, really. I've got to go out."

"Out where?" Whittington asked. "Whose dinner's tonight?"

"No place. Just with the Kinkaids to Dr. Melton's for dinner."

"Jesus," Talbot said, "those ding-a-lings?"

She stopped combing her hair. "What's a ding-a-ling?"

"Rinky-dink spelled backward. Call them, say you're wiped out from swimming."

"I really couldn't," she said, continuing to comb her hair. "They're nice people and they've been nice to me, all of them."

Whittington smiled happily and winked at Talbot.

It was eight thirty. Talbot sat alone over his drink at the bar of the UN club, oddly deserted at that hour. Someone, somewhere was

giving a large reception to which he hadn't been invited. Down the
bar two middle-aged Egyptians were arguing with an Englishman
about insurance liability. They were from the UN administrative
staff. He tried not to listen. The voices annoyed him, gnawing away
at his solitude. Voices always annoyed him when he was feeling
sorry for himself. He carried his drink out to the small terrace
where a few couples sat talking quietly, their words carried away by
the soft sea wind.

It was a beautiful night. The canopy of stars was immense. By
day it was the light, the drenching light, colorless in the air, transparent, it coined its objects with edges of gold when it struck under
a sky of the palest blue. Alone, he saw this quite clearly. Now the
stars had come out, immense, cold, clear, attending his solitude.

Where the hell had his friends gone?

He looked around and found himself alone, the nearby chairs
empty. He finished his drink and ambled back through the bar,
empty, too. Maybe he'd go cheer Ali up, tell him he was working
on his problem. He left his glass on a table and steered erratically
back through the passageway toward Ali's small office but heard
angry voices from inside:

"You've been on notice, haven't you?"

"Please, sir, yes, sir."

He heard Ali's pleading little colonial frog-crawl.

"Then there's the matter of the accounts."

"Yes, sir. I know, sir."

Embarrassed, he turned back. The small dining room was about
to close, deserted except for a dark-haired young woman sitting
alone just inside the door, reading from a magazine. As he sat down
at a table in the far corner, he recognized the same mysterious face
he'd seen at the end of the bar the afternoon of his return. His pulse
quickened.

Nikiforov's niece?

He ordered the evening special, a seafood plate, and a carafe of
white wine. The windows above him were open to the sea. On the
floor at both ends of the dining room sat small circulating fans. She
didn't look up, poring over her magazine and chewing rhythmically.
On the plate in front of her were french fries and what was described on the menu as an American hamburger, which was some-

thing between a Polish meatloaf and a refugee-camp soccer ball. It seemed to him she'd gained weight since he'd last seen her. As she picked it up to turn the pages, he spied the cover of a popular German magazine.

A German-speaker, wasn't that what Bashford-Jones had said?

Her dark hair would be fine and fragrant, washed by a scented shampoo. Her nose was long and straight, her hands large and brown. In the V of her white blouse lay two half-girdled white hemispheres below the tan of her throat.

The waiter brought the seafood plate and dropped it in front of him. It wasn't freshly fried but had been kept for the last hour or so in a warming pan. The fillets were soggy with oil. Talbot complained in earnest, mild-mannered, American Express fashion, appealing to the waiter's better instincts, but the waiter didn't seem to understand English and had no better instincts. He shrugged indifferently and turned away. Talbot grabbed the tail of his jacket: *"Nicht so eilig, Freundhchen!"* he demanded. *"Schnell! Actung! Sie verstehen, was ich meine!"*

"Excuse please?"

"I want this goddamn plate immediately removed and replaced, do you understand! *Schnell! Achtung!* Quickly, this instant!"

The waiter picked up the plate and hurried away as Talbot filled his wineglass. The dollar had been weak in Europe recently, the deutsche mark very strong. Surly German voices could be heard bellowing in unison all across the dining rooms of Europe from the Cotswolds to the Dardanelles, including the smoky dining room at the Balkan Hotel in Sofia.

But she hadn't looked up from her magazine.

The fish platter brought by the waiter was no improvement; he didn't complain. He allowed his waiter to refill his wineglass and waited for him to move out of the way. Then before he did, Ali came hurrying in to apologize.

"No, it's all right, Ali, just a little misunderstanding."

"I'm sorry, sir."

"No, it's all right, Ali."

One of the UN club overseers came to join them, watching Ali suspiciously. It was Robinson, the Kenyan highlander, wearing pukka-pukka khaki shorts and knee hose. "You had a complaint about the fish?" No swagger stick under his arm though.

Talbot smiled graciously, looking at the man's pink knees, which seemed to smile back. Then at Ali, squaring his shoulders. "First rate, splendid, Ali."

"The service?"

"Magnificent, Ali, very brisk, very well drilled. My compliments to the chef."

Robinson abruptly marched away; Ali scurried after him.

The Bulgarian girl had gone, leaving an empty plate behind.

He left by the sea terrace and wandered down past the Lido nightclub. He could hear the music from the small dance floor to the rear of the bar. A trio of dark-skinned Jubba girls smiled at him from the shadows.

Lovely.

With Shaughnessy and Bashford-Jones, they might have made an evening of it, but alone was tricky. Find yourself haunches up someplace you shouldn't be, all candlelight and pisspots, getting goosed by an NSS nightstick. Only Shaughnessy seemed to have managed that, but he kept the details of his solo expeditions to himself. He circled the dance floor warily but couldn't find a table and stood near the rear, looking on. The dark floor was crowded with dancers and he didn't recognize anyone. He left and wandered alone along the beach under the stars.

As he turned up toward his villa a black Mercedes came hurtling down the corniche and pulled into his gate.

He began to run, flogging through the sand drifts near the beach road, but the Mercedes was already backing out. Najah al-Zeyn was behind the wheel, Hafiz on the front seat next to him. He shouted but they didn't hear him and sped away, leaving him standing alone in the middle of the road. Probably came to invite him to a small post-reception party in a back garden somewhere. He went inside and called Hafiz's cottage but got no answer. He called Nick Bashford-Jones, but the young woman who answered said he was out. He knew she was lying.

He poured himself a gin and bitters, awful stuff, but he didn't have any vermouth, and went out into the back garden.

"Tether a beast," Lindy had said. Pulling taffy at the Meltons' tonight, was she? What was it, didn't trust him or didn't trust herself? Probably herself. His own manners had been impeccable.

◻ ◻ ◻

Wingate's airfreight had at last arrived, with the man soon to follow, Whittington claimed, but Talbot wasn't convinced. He had finished all but two of the overdue economic airgrams and begun on the new cycle of semi-annual reports. Again he'd tried to reestablish the position of commercial assistant and again had recommended Ali, the embattled Pakistani, but Rhinehart said the funds budgeted for the position had been moved elsewhere for that fiscal year. Talbot suspected DeGroot had transferred them to Harcourt's residence account.

He had planned to raise the matter at the country team meeting that morning—the budgeted commercial assistant position, ten months vacant, Ali's experience as an exporter-importer, the missing funds—but he didn't get the chance. It was all DeGroot's show that day.

In Washington Ambassador Abdulkadir had shifted his offensive from the State Department to the National Security Council, where he'd gotten a more sympathetic hearing. He'd inveigled a meeting with the vice president and even managed to provoke the president's interest.

DeGroot brought its evidence to the country team meeting, a Xeroxed page from a morning presidential brief sent to him by some NSC leaker he'd lunched with at the White House mess. On its margins the former Georgia governor, true populist that he was, had written in his own hand, "Let's see if we can't get Jubba to be our friend."

DeGroot was jubilant; Harcourt, sympathetically stirred, so much so he couldn't do anything but shift his dry bones and smile. *Wouldn't it be a much better world*, the smile seemed to say, *if we were all friends?*

Their two simpering faces were proof enough for Talbot that no one truly knew what was going on, least of all the embassy. When all the rumors and half-truths were traced back to their source, it invariably proved to be the unreliable Ambassador Abdulkadir in Washington, who'd finally made his formal request on behalf of the Jubba president for U.S. arms. Washington knew only as much as he had told the various executive agencies. It was he who'd described for the State Department the long-concluded talks the Jubba president had had in Aden, where he had met with the Ethiopians and Fidel Castro under Soviet auspices. The president had rejected the Soviet mediation effort, he claimed, rejected a proposed regional socialist confederation under which those oppressed nationalities in the old Abyssinian empire now in revolt along its periphery would be granted a certain autonomy—"like those imprisoned minorities in the Soviet Socialist Republics, we assumed," he'd insisted indignantly. So Moscow had failed in its attempt to arrange a *Pax Sovietica* between its two client states in the Horn, he'd claimed, the assurance DeGroot passed on that morning. The way was prepared for the new U.S. initiative in Jubba.

DeGroot didn't mention that in his increasingly infrequent public statements the Jubba president said nothing to suggest he was considering changing alliances, as Ambassador Abdulkadir alleged, didn't mention that he'd repeatedly avoided giving Harcourt an appointment, as requested by the State Department, to discuss his willingness to loosen his ties with the Soviet Union and align himself with the West. Unlike his energetic ambassador in Washington, he'd remained elusively incommunicado, sly old nomad that he was.

In the meantime the Western Jubbaland Liberation Front had grown increasingly daring in its attacks on Ethiopian police posts. In a recent raid it had blown up a section of the Addis–Djibouti railroad. As always, the ministry of foreign affairs and the ministry of information had disassociated the government from these raids. The WJLF was a wholly autonomous national liberation movement, doing what national liberation movements do in fighting imperialism.

DeGroot didn't talk about this either, nor did he mention the airgram Talbot had sent a week earlier, describing the talk he'd had with Lev Luttak during which the Russian had suggested the Jubba president was attempting to extort from the U.S.S.R. military and political support for the liberation of Western Jubbaland—the crudest kind of political blackmail. Their conversation, he claimed, had come during an encounter at a Czech reception. Why should De-Groot mention it? Drafted as a telegram, DeGroot had changed it to an airgram and sent it by pouch. Washington hadn't even acknowledged it.

Numbed by DeGroot's exuberance and Harcourt's beneficent silence, Talbot didn't mention the missing budget funds. He didn't say a word at the meeting and left the embassy soon afterwards—a meeting with a minor official at the National Bank, he told his secretary. Thirty minutes later he was towing his inflatable raft across the shallows toward the reef.

□ □ □

On an afternoon three days later Talbot trudged up from the beach toward the villa barefooted, carrying his sandals. He was followed by Pete Ryan, the visiting journalist from Nairobi, carrying an empty beer bottle in one hand, an empty glass in the other.

The tide was churning in now, the late afternoon light changing. Offshore the reef was partly submerged, a heaving squall line of angry combers blown from a storm hundreds of miles at sea.

Talbot felt a sand burr in his heel and limped the final yard to the corniche curb to sit down.

"It always happens," he said. "God damn this country."

Ryan watched sympathetically as Talbot lifted his heel to his knee. Short, muscular, and overweight, he was sweating in the heat, his face shining with water. "You were crazy to come back."

"I didn't have much choice, not if I wanted Paris. Anyway, the Department wanted a little continuity."

"Harcourt not up to it?"

"I wouldn't say that."

"What about the new man?"

"DeGroot? What about him?"

"Sent out to keep everyone honest?"

"Not that I can tell."

"Something's up, that's for sure. A lot of activity along the border, no doubt about it."

"That's what Dr. Greevy thinks; says there's going to be a war. You should talk to him. He's in Nairobi now."

"What do you think?"

"I think he may be right. On the other hand the same thing's been going on for years. Add to that the old paranoia and you get all these journalists coming up from Nairobi."

"Always simple with you diplomats, isn't it? Can't see the sandstorms for the mosquitoes. It's the little things, sand burrs first, then fleas, then scurvy. It all adds up, always the little things. I once knew a Brit who went mad. Consular agent in São Tomé, I think it was. Couldn't manage it. Most of you people are, you know. It's the isolation."

Talbot got to his feet and limped a few steps. "Are what?"

"Mad. Have to be, someplace like this."

A second black Fiat had joined the other Fiat parked fifty yards down the corniche. Ryan studied it and then looked further south toward the port. "Is that my surveillance or yours?" he asked as they crossed the tarmac to the front gate. It failed to open with its usual clangor.

"Yours probably. Mine's a motor scooter these days." Talbot peered in through the gate. The guard was prostrate on his prayer rug outside the small thatched *tukel*. "Chapel time," he said. He waited, leaning with his back against the gate, looking toward the Fiat. "It's tiresome, all of it. The goddamn monotony most of all, the monotony and the boredom."

"Find yourself a woman. That's the ticket, what I've always said, get your ashes hauled on schedule. What he didn't do. Thought he was above all that."

"What who didn't do?"

"This Brit. That was his problem, what it all came down to, all alone like that. Had a wife in Dorset, I think it was. Big strapping woman. Had her picture taped to the ceiling above his bed. The Chinese water-drop torture. Very dangerous. They took him out in a straitjacket."

Talbot pushed open the gate and they went in.

"What happened?"

"Tried to prong his commo clerk in the wireless room. A Methodist, they said, a strict Sabbatarian. She let out a yell we heard in Lagos. I think it was Lagos."

Talbot looked back at him. "A strict Sabbatarian?"

"So I heard."

"You wouldn't happen to have talked to DeGroot, would you?"

"After I left your office. Accosted me on the stairs. His words, not mine. Odd, I'd say. A wee bit strange. Looks like a breadfruit tree. Maybe mango, come to think of it. A few parrots gibbering in the branches. Maybe colobus monkeys. Want any more?"

"Be my guest."

"Mad as a hatter."

"Thanks. I thought it was me."

" 'A strict Sabbatarian,' he told me. This when he said he couldn't offer me a drink at Sunday brunch. To which he invited me. He gave me a lift back to the hotel. Said something else, too." He paused in the drive to take out his small notebook and leaf through the pages. "Yeah, here it is. 'The current regime has no wish to re-vitalize the congenital germ.' " He put his notebook away.

"What did that mean."

"That Jubba irredentism was dead, no more claims to Western Jubbaland, no more wars with the Ethiopians. Then after they throw the Soviets out, bag and baggage, they'll become decently respectable again, members in good standing of the community of nations, eminently civilized by the Pentagon's defensive weapons. Is the guy real?"

"He's real. What else did he tell you?"

"More of the same, all of it bullshit."

"You should tell the ambassador that."

"What, that it's bullshit? DeGroot's made him a believer, too?"

"More or less."

"Now it makes a little sense."

"What does?"

"Why he was so bloody curious. Wanted to know what I'd talked to you about."

"Screw him. He doesn't trust me."

"Not surprised. What's the problem?"

"My quietism, he calls it. He's an activist, sent out to do things, change perceptions. So he thinks, anyway."

"What's he after?"

They went into the back garden.

"What he told you, onward and upward. His own post someplace. He's just finished the National War College. Did a paper on the Horn, now he thinks he's Bismarck."

"You're kidding."

"He's a phony, an impostor."

"A lot of them are. I'm writing a book, by the way. The effect of exotic tropical climates on classical Nordic types—T. E. Lawrences, State Department Arabists, Afro nuts, the weirdos gone cuckoo. They've all got the same problem."

"What's that?"

"The twenty-four-hour hard-on." He squinted toward the western wall and the golden sunlight splintering on the green leaves. "This is one hell of a place. You know that, don't you? Gin time, isn't it? What time did he say?"

"Six o'clock, I think."

Talbot went inside to get the bottle, ice, and glasses.

"What happened to your heavy-drinking Irish pal?" Ryan asked, pouring from the bottle. "The big raunchy guy."

"Shaughnessy? He's in Mozambique, I think. I haven't heard from him."

"What, find him in some back alley with his pants off? What are the bitters for?"

"The gin. The tonic tastes like lilac water."

The wind stirred through the tops of the trees and fluttered the blossoms on the tulip tree, drawing Ryan's gaze away as he sat down again. The sky was cloudless. "Still sleepy time here, or have things really changed the way DeGroot told me?"

"Changing. No one knows."

"What's Washington want these days? Not what DeGroot wants, I hope."

"Guns for Jubba? No. Still sorting things out. I don't think anyone knows."

"You hear a lot of talk, how we're going to cut a deal with the Old Man to dump the Russians. Not just DeGroot. They say in Nairobi the U.S. and the Europeans are ready to help, that Washington's going to turn the tables on the Sovs for cutting a deal with Ethiopia."

"I think it's too early to tell."

"That's the scuttlebutt in Nairobi. They say the Saudis will finance it. They provide the bucks, Washington the guns. The Saudis think it might work."

"Saudi thinking's never solved anything. For them, thinking is moving a few million in gold and sterling reserves around. In Jidda and Riyadh that passes for political genius, and someone else is always to blame when it doesn't work."

"That's good. Sounds like a cable. Mind if I steal it?"

"Help yourself."

Ryan's head was back, looking at the sky. "What kind of man is he, Harcourt?"

"An old consul general—Italy, Spain, Greece, too. Thessalonica's the bush for him. Malta, too. He'll probably ask you what the Kenyans think of this regime."

"Scared, think the Jubba are true scientific socialists, the real devils. Think they're serious about this bloody ideology they're always ranting about. Nomadic Marxists. I don't blame them."

"For what?"

"Being scared of the Jubba. Steal their cattle in the bush, steal their Mercedeses in the streets, bring here to sell. Steal their women, too, if they weren't so ugly. A very tough people, very sly. The Kenyans aren't like that."

"You give them too much credit. Poor, proud, confused, and underfed. Trying to discover who they are and not doing a very good job of it. Like me. I should have gone into banking, Wall Street maybe."

"Yeah, like me. I'm a diesel mechanic at heart. Also smart, very smart. Very quick."

"Tricky, you mean," Talbot said. "Opportunists."

"Opportunists, too. Pretending to swallow the Marxist line for what it gives them, like the boys in the Salvation Army mess. A few kippers, a spot of tea, a warm bed. They'll sing in chapel every night, any bloody hymnal you give them. Just nomads with their begging bowls, willing to let Moscow dress, feed, and arm them." Ryan smiled, pleased. "How's that?"

"About right. Singing for their supper. Another gin?"

Ryan held out his glass. "Give me the bitters this time. By the way, what happened to your Swedish girl friend?"

"Went home to Mother Stockholm in a snit."

"What about?"

"Thought our little arrangement was permanent."

"No regular these days?"

"In the European sense, no."

"That's what you need, not just a shack-up, a steady sexual income. That doesn't appeal to you?"

"Sure, but I couldn't manage, not without everyone in town knowing."

"What, too risky? Like one of your diplomats I met at the bar at the Hilton, sneaked up from Dar to get fucked."

"*Get* fucked?" Talbot considered it. "Yeah, that sounds like one of ours, taking it on his back." Like Harcourt, he thought, but didn't say it.

Ryan smiled. "You're with the wrong crowd, like I told you before. Wrong crowd, wrong capital."

Talbot got up and added a dollop of gin to his drink. "If you get your interview with the president, he'll know you've been in Ethiopia. If he thinks you sympathize with the regime there, you won't get a word. Tell me about Addis, what it was like when you were there?"

Negussie Belaye, the Ethiopian chargé, had finally come to see him the evening before. He'd been recalled to Addis, and had no idea what to expect when he got there, whether the new regime considered him friend or foe. His two brothers had been arrested; his father's property on Bole Road had been nationalized. He would be searched at the airport. He had brought Talbot his .32 revolver and wanted him to smuggle it to him in Addis through the diplomatic pouch.

"Rotten. Scary. A bad place. The Terror, for one thing. You have to feel it to believe it. I don't like Addis, never have. Goddamn people shot in the streets every night, ten, twenty, thirty. Something about Addis that makes your skin crawl, even before, all that superstition, all that filth. A goddamn feudal empire, locked away in the fourteenth century."

"There are parallels, you know."

"What kind of parallels?"

"Romanov Russia," Talbot said. "It's pretty close."

"I suppose. Sinister, sure. No doubt about it. Rasputins everywhere. The bloody Coptic church, all Rasputins. Maybe you're right."

Ryan lifted his wrist to look at his watch. His eyes were bloodshot from the sun, from the wine with lunch, the beer, and now the gin. "What time did you say?"

"Six or so." Talbot thought he looked unsteady. "Better get ready, then.

"He won't expect a tie, will he?"

"No, come as you are, he said. We'll take him at his word."

Ryan rose, drained his glass, and went inside. Talbot picked up the glasses and followed.

The sunlight still lingered as they drove up the sandy road to the ambassador's residence. Rounding a curve, Talbot dragged two wheels in a sand ditch and discovered for the fifth day in a row he'd had too much to drink.

"It is a bit like a Crusader castle, isn't it?" Ryan said, looking up at the white walls, now bronze in the dimming sunlight. "How long were the Crusaders in Palestine."

"A hundred years, maybe—1170 to 1260, something like that."

"She's a bit of a harridan, I heard, Mrs. Harcourt."

"Not really. But you have to be careful what you say. Sometimes any little thing can set her off."

The iron gate was ajar. They went in, then heard a voice from the small strip of lawn just to the west of the front walk, where a figure in yellow oilskins was being doused with a garden hose.

"—A little to the right . . . that's it. Good. Now let's try a direct assault. Twist the nozzle, that's it. Give us a blast off the port beam, no fine spray. Let's see how it weathers a nor'easter, hard in the face. That's much too hard. Oh, mercy, you've ruined it. I'm soaked through. It's the zipper, caught halfway. No, no, that's enough. Much too hard. Stop it, I say!"

As they watched, unseen, Harcourt emerged from the yellow oilskin cocoon, face dripping water, blue blazer damp. His houseboy dropped the hose and ran back around the house to turn off the water. The box and wrapping paper in which the yellow nylon yachting gear had arrived lay on an iron bench nearby.

"You're early, aren't you," said a cool voice from behind them. Julia stood on the front steps.

"Six, wasn't it?" Talbot said.

"Six thirty, but come in anyway." She turned away irritably. "What on earth are you doing, Lyman?"

He turned toward them, smiling, then smoothed his wet hair in place and came to greet them, carrying the dripping nylon foul-weather gear at arm's length. "A trial run," he said, slightly winded. "What do you think, Logan? Think I'm ready for an afternoon on Firthdale's *Lord Byron?*"

"It looks like it."

"Where on earth did that come from?" Julia said.

"It came this afternoon in the pouch. Harry sent it from Connecticut. Thought I should be doing a bit of blue-water sailing. You must be Peter Ryan." Harcourt held out his hand.

"You can't bring that inside," Julia said. "It's dripping wet."

Harcourt left his foul-weather gear on the front steps and went off to change his shirt and jacket.

Julia led them to the rear garden. "You caught us unprepared," she said, still annoyed. "I didn't know Lyman said six."

"I should have called."

"It would have been better." She looked at Ryan. "My husband sometimes does unusual things; only those who don't know him well misunderstand. His brother in Connecticut also has ridiculous ideas about what this place is like."

"That's usually the case," Ryan said. "Nothing odd about sailing gear. I prefer the saxophone myself."

"Do you? How odd."

"Alone, I mean." He smiled boisterously.

"You've been here before?"

"Quite a few times. Not since your husband's arrival, sorry to say. Visa problems."

"You like it?"

"It's different. How about you?"

"I don't mind it." Julia looked accusingly at Talbot, daring him to refute it. "That's not what others say of me, but it's true. It's a lovely place to be by yourself."

"I was just telling Logan that."

They sat down, but then Ryan got up to offer her a cigarette. The houseboy stood waiting for their orders for drinks but she was silent as she allowed Ryan to light her cigarette. "Have you been drinking?" she asked Talbot.

"A little, why?"

"Your face looks funny."

"Hardly a drop," Ryan said, erect now, moving back to his chair. "You play tennis, I hear."

"A little, yes. Do you?"

"A little."

"That sounds like a challenge."

"I'm not very good," Ryan said.

"Then you should feet at home here. We're all second-raters here, aren't we, Logan?"

Harcourt returned to join them, wearing a fresh blue tennis shirt.

"Mr. Ryan has had visa problems," Julia said. "He also plays tennis."

"Oh, really."

His interest livened considerably when he learned Ryan had served in Beirut. He disappeared for ten minutes as he searched for his collection of Greek and Roman coins. While he showed Ryan his portfolio, Julia asked Talbot to help her with something in the kitchen.

She told the servant to go fetch the glasses and then shut the door behind him, turning to Talbot. "Don't you ever do that again, do you understand me? You're never to bring someone up here in the afternoon unless you've spoken to me first."

Talbot reddened. "I thought you knew."

"I didn't know. How was I to know? I had no idea, and you know perfectly well I didn't. Lyman is sometimes completely unpredictable in the afternoon, and I won't have his privacy invaded by strangers like this, putting him in these terribly awkward situations."

"I don't think Pete thought it was awkward. He's an old friend."

She turned away. "And as sly as you think you are, no doubt. If we're going to continue to be friends, I want that understood."

"It's understood. I won't bring anyone up."

"Don't be petulant. You know perfectly well what I mean." Her back was to him as she took an ice tray from the refrigerator. "We have to protect him, both of us do. You know that. You have to know that. And if I can't depend upon you, who can I depend on?"

"What do you want me to do?"

"You know perfectly well what I want you to do." She broke the ice cubes free in the sink and filled the tray from the crock of filtered water. She brought a loaf of wrapped cheese from the shelf and opened it on the counter. "Nora brought me some cheeses from Nairobi. This is supposed to be Camembert, but the label came off in her bag." She turned and lifted a slice of cheese to his mouth. "Open. Wider, silly. That's it. What do you think? Not bad?"

"Not bad."

"Good. I think I'll tell Kasim to put some out." She went to the door and turned again. "I don't look upset, do I?"

"No, you don't look upset."

"Good. Shall we join them?"

Ryan was strangely silent in the car driving back.

Only when they left the car in Talbot's drive did he say anything: "I think I see the problem. That does make it tough."

"He wasn't in top form," Talbot said.

"I wasn't thinking of him, her. A little problem there. What's she trying to do?"

"Cut off my balls."

"That figures, the old Ottoman way, is it? I think I'd better be getting back to my hotel. The ministry might call. Between eight and ten, they said."

□ □ □

Saturday afternoon Talbot drove south through the undulating heat of the scrubland and into the cultivation of the interriverine floodplain. It was after five o'clock as he turned back along a twisting tarmac road through the rocky white hills toward the sea. As he drove over the final rise, the Indian Ocean lifted majestically before him, an infinity of royal purple and blue slashed with billowing combers scrolling toward shore. As the sea wind purged the heat from the car, he could smell the salt wind and hear the shearing hiss of the spray torn from the whitecaps. At the bottom of the long grade he turned north along a macadam road that followed the sand beach toward the old city that lay in the distance below a sheer stone escarpment rising several hundred feet above the ocean.

A white-hulled banana boat lay at anchor a hundred yards offshore.

The villa was on the bluff overlooking the sea a kilometer south of the town, just as she'd described it. A narrow serpentine road wound up the hill and behind the red brick house where twin turrets had the improbable look of a Victorian railroad station in a small Delaware town. Its isolation made him think of a remote golf club on the Scottish heath. A few raffia and coconut palms were planted along the drive. The vivid green turf surrounding the front terrace was unplanted, even in shrubbery, as if a formal garden had once been planned there but abandoned. Behind the house, lindens, laurel, mango trees, and drooping purple bougainvillaea sheltered the courtyard.

Four cars were parked there, none with diplomatic plates. He heard voices as he approached the slatted door, a shadow appeared in the corridor, and he heard Nicola Seretti: *"Est-ce toi, cher André?"*

"It's me, Talbot."

She opened the door.

"I'm a little late," he said, wondering who André was, "sorry."

"Not at all. Please come in. We just came up from the beach." Her sunglasses were pushed back on her forehead, and her dark hair was still damp. The collar of her white blouse was turned up and her blue skirt splashed with water. "You had no difficulty?"

"No, it was just as you said."

"I'm sorry the Harcourts couldn't come. She sent a message."

"She's sorry, too," he lied. "She sends her regrets."

She led him down the corridor to the front of the house, where a dozen or so guests sat on rattan chairs on a tiled sun porch overlooking the sea. Talbot recognized none of the faces. He was the only one in a coat and tie. Nicola made no attempt to introduce them all, just those whom she'd been sitting with in the sunny corner near the front windows. He shook hands with an Italian doctor and his wife, several Italian teachers from the university, an Italian lawyer on assignment to the ministry of agriculture, and a blond woman whose name he didn't catch and who continued to watch him with intense curiosity from nearby. Like Nicola, they had been swimming from the beach.

His arrival had interrupted a noisy discussion of a party that had taken place the previous night at a nearby Italian-owned farm which had ended in an argument between an Italian diplomat and the host. Now they were in disagreement about who had won the argument.

A tall Jubba woman wearing a white apron over her long yellow dress entered with a tray of drinks and came immediately to Talbot. Nicola spoke to her in Jubba, then Italian; the woman ignored her. She was slender, once beautiful, and still handsome with her smooth dusky skin and her cinnamon eyes, but her voice came as a disappointment, not the voice of a woman but the small shrill voice of a flirtatious adolescent.

In Italian, she described the drinks on the tray—whiskey, juice, gin-tonic, and Cinzano; if he preferred something else, she would fetch it. He took a gin-tonic; she bowed and retired. A few minutes later she was back with an ashtray and a coaster. Nicola again spoke to her—her name was Samina—and she curtsied and disappeared, then returned with a bowl of nuts. Again Nicola called out, reminding her that a few other glasses were empty; but again Samina ignored her, her girlish face turned toward Talbot. After she left, Nicola got up and followed, returning alone a few minutes later with a tray of drinks.

Like most expatriate communities, the Italian colony was a nation unto itself, made up of old colonial settlers who regarded themselves as a squirearchy of sorts, businessmen representing Italian corporate interests, merchants, small traders, underpaid teachers, and fussy diplomats. Rivalries were unending and quarrels constant, especially between the old order and the transient bureaucracy, but the issues were obscure to outsiders, having as much to do with personalities as social jealousies or pretensions. On occasions such as this, disagreements were reviewed, scandals divulged, and new secrets shared, but differences of interpretation inevitably arose, as they did now. Last night's quarrel hotly erupted anew.

Talbot listened indifferently as the ceiling fan beat a soporific tattoo overhead. Few of the names meant anything to him; he confined his contacts to a few diplomats at the Italian embassy and stayed away from the Italian community, a closed little provincial village in which no problem was ever solved, just flogged to death until it disintegrated, like the village washing being pounded around the Piazza fountain, as was happening now.

Seated next to him, Nicola Seretti was embarrassed by the argument and tried to guide the conversation in another direction. As the voice of an Italian teacher lifted angrily in the background, Talbot asked her about the banana plantation.

It had been established by her father-in-law, who'd come to Italian Jubbaland from Tuscany. He had acquired the land and worked the plantation through an adaptation of the traditional Tuscan *mezzadria* compact. He provided the land and the capital and shared the harvest with the local farmers who provided the labor. He had died in the late forties; the plantation had been left to her late husband.

"He lived here as a child," she said, "and after the war, came back. There was nothing in Italy for him. He was never a farmer, only a teacher and journalist."

"You lived here as a girl?"

"No, I came to teach at the normal school in 1961. He was teaching there at the time."

She looked up as a tall thin Italian joined them from the other room. Nicola introduced Carlo Minzonni, a visiting Italian journalist. He was in his early forties. His white shirt was custom tailored, like his worn denim jeans, and unbuttoned halfway down his chest. He had long brown hair and badly needed a shave. Talbot didn't care much for his manner. He reminded him of some minor celebrity, some two-bit rock musician, another overaged junkie from a Mick Jagger look-alike contest.

"You're with the American embassy?" he asked lazily, bringing a chair from nearby. His eyes were a tawny brown, like the eyes of a mulatto.

"With the embassy."

"I was about to show Mr. Talbot some plantings," Nicola said, rising. She led Talbot out the side door. Minzonni put on his sunglasses and followed.

Her garden was behind the drive at the rear of the house. Several outbuildings were nearby. Across the drive under the trees was a small brick guest cottage. Behind the small shrubs was a small banana garden. Under a shed was an old Fiat tractor. Talbot followed her, looking without interest at plants whose names he didn't know and wouldn't remember.

While Nicola was kneeling in front of a scapular-leafed shrub, explaining its characteristics, Minzonni asked if he expected any change in U.S.-Jubba relations.

"I doubt it," Talbot said, bending down to look at the plant. "Your guess is as good as mine. What's it called?" he asked Nicola.

She told him the name, in Italian, then in Latin.

"Those are Mediterranean pinks over there," she said, rising again. "I brought them in on Alitalia."

"I thought you were with the embassy," Minzonni said.

"Maybe that's why I don't know."

"You mean only Washington knows."

"That's a little unusual, isn't it," Talbot said, "bringing them by plane?"

"Not so much. There's a story about de Jussieu, the eighteenth-century French botanist, who carried a tiny cedar from Lebanon back to France in his hat. He shared his water ration with it. The trip took months."

"I don't expect anything," Minzonni said, "not with the Democrats. They are too much in Vietnam's shadow."

Talbot followed Nicola as she moved on and stopped before two plants with gnarled trunks and small polished leaves, like mountain laurel.

"Many are saying there will be changes," Minzonni said, "but they don't know the situation. What do you think? The Democrats, are they still in Vietnam's shadow?"

"Poor Carlo," Nicola said. "He was up very late last night and his poor mind went to sleep with all these words."

"What's wrong with my words?"

"Nothing, except they are always the same words."

She led Talbot on to see her flower garden, which lay beyond a trellis. There were dwarf asters and yellow peonies from France, all lovely, bordered by well-watered English turf.

"Those are my lilies over there, Annunciation lilies. Madonna lilies, I should say. They're described in the Old Testament. In Greek mythology the lily was dedicated to Zeus's wife, Hera. It was the milk from her breast that created the Milky Way, you remember. The lily sprang from those few drops that fell to earth. Lovely, aren't they?"

"Very."

"It wasn't last night," Minzonni said. "This morning, from two until six this morning. I haven't been to sleep."

"There are two beds in the cottage," she said without looking at him, "you can go to sleep now. Carlo and two other Italian journalists met with the president," she added for Talbot. "I suppose you explained everything to him. One of your very concrete, very boring analyses." Then, again to Talbot, "Carlo has just spent a week in Addis."

"He doesn't want to understand," Minzonni said. "It's impossible to tell him anything about Ethiopia."

"Of course," Nicola said, walking on. Talbot followed. "I didn't care much for gardening until I lived in England," she said. "My uncle lived in Manchester. He had very little but he had a garden."

"He thinks he understands," Minzonni said, catching up. "The Americans, too."

"Understands what?" Nicola asked indifferently, bending down to snap off a dead shoot. "This is verbena here."

"He understands the Americans left Vietnam," Minzonni said. "Now they are leaving Ethiopia. So when people talk to him about the Americans, this is what he understands."

"Is that what the president said," Nicola asked, "that the Americans are too much in Vietnam's shadow?"

Minzonni, looking at Talbot, didn't answer. Nicola smiled. "Of course," she said. "His face gives him away, even with his sunglasses."

Behind a screen of poplars was an old stone building. To the side were two more old tractors and a few rusting pieces of farm machinery. They continued back through the drive and stood on the green lawn in front of the house overlooking the sea.

A garden with a loggia had been planned for the front terrace but never completed. Talbot tried to visualize what it might look like.

"I can't quite see it," he said.

"Ugly, very ugly."

Minzonni emptied his glass and looked at Talbot again, at his shoes, his tie and jacket, then his trousers. "How long have you been here?" he asked.

"He has been here too long," Nicola said.

"So you don't think things will change?"

"Hard to say," Talbot said.

"What would you like to think," Minzonni continued, offering Nicola a cigarette. She took one and sat down in the wicker chair just outside the french doors to the sun porch. Through the screen door they could hear the laughter from inside. "You don't care, eh?"

"He would like to think he was someplace else," Nicola said. "So please bring the chairs and stop talking so much."

Minzonni fetched two basket chairs from behind the brick wall at the side.

"You don't talk to journalists?" Minzonni said.

"At the office," Talbot said.

"You don't like questions?"

"What questions?"

"The rumors about the Americans. What do you tell them about the rumors?"

"What rumors?"

"Please shut up, Carlo," Nicola interrupted. "You had your interview last night, not this afternoon."

"Not last night, last night and all morning." Carlo looked at her, then at Talbot, shrugged, and carried his empty glass inside.

"That was not very nice," Nicola said, "but I can't carry on two conversations at once, like the Jubba. It's impossible for me to imagine someone thinking in three or four languages, but many Africans do." They sat in silence, watching the sea bicker in the distance. White gulls wheeled along the cliffs to the south. "You know what he was asking about, don't you?" she said after a minute.

"More or less, and it doesn't interest me."

"We were talking about it before you came—the rumors the Saudis will supply the money and the Americans the arms if the president tells the Russians to go. What do you think?"

"Just a rumor."

"You know the problem, I'm sure. All these years, what the Russians have told them, what they promised them, that their time would come to liberate Western Jubbaland—"

"The Soviets never promised them that."

"No, but it's what they assumed."

She explained what the Jubba had expected from the Russians while he watched the gulls below the cliffs moving against the dark sea, wishing she'd forget about politics. She was high-strung, no doubt about it, but her fragrance was lovely. Above the sensitive little upper lip was a bright beading of silver. She saw he noticed and paused to wipe it away with her finger. Her decolletage was a bit more daring than usual. The first button of her blouse was undone, and he saw the brown curve of her breast, lightly downed. She had seen his glance there earlier but didn't button it. Few Italian women would. He had never seen her in a bikini, but he could imagine her round bottom, her sharp little breasts. He wondered how old she was, thirty-seven, thirty-eight? A nice ripe age, easy in the sack, no expectations, no regrets; he wished he'd come earlier.

At last she paused to ask him a question, but he only shrugged. "You weren't listening at all."

"A little. Just thinking. You made it all sound very sad."

"It is sad. You don't agree?"

"Sure, I agree. I just don't want to get into another argument."

"Then why didn't you say so?"

He stirred himself. "It's obvious, just like what you said last week. They got themselves into this crazy mess with the Soviets, all this lunatic raving about imperialism, all these stupid fantasies about Moscow helping national liberation movements anywhere, any time. Forget the rumors. No one's going to help them go fight Ethiopia. They don't have any alternative to Soviet military support, and they won't help either."

"You forget the United States, you forget NATO."

He laughed, looking at the banana boat. "That's an Arabian nights fantasy. No one with any sense could think the U.S. would give these goddamn people guns with Ethiopia falling apart next door. They're straining at the Soviet leash right now because Moscow won't help them. For anyone else to step in and promise them weapons now would be stupid; it'd be like marching them off to war."

"It's not preposterous at all," she said. "You hear more rumors every day."

"I'm not responsible for what other people think, just tired of listening to them."

She continued to look at him. "You really don't like this country, do you?"

"I think it sucks."

Her lovely eyes opened wide.

He pulled off his tie. "That's an American expression, sorry. It means crummy, rotten."

"You have an odd way of putting things."

"Sometimes. Let's talk about nice things for a change. I liked your plants, your garden, too. I would never have imagined them here, never."

"I'm surprised. I mean that you liked them. I didn't expect you to. You're very opinionated, aren't you?"

"It's the way I keep my sanity in a place like this."

"Does that include your embassy? Also arrogant, if you don't mind my saying."

"No, I don't mind. You already said so. Anyway, your garden is very beautiful. So is the view from here, really lovely."

"Yes, but then you don't have to talk to my garden, do you? The view either."

"True."

"I will say one last thing, do you mind?"

"No, not at all."

"I don't think you admire very much these people you have to talk to. At your embassy, too. I don't think you are very satisfied with these people."

"Present company excepted."

She nodded politely and smiled. "Yes, of course. Thank you."

The tall Jubba woman came out on the terrace carrying a tray,

followed by Minzonni and the blond Italian woman. She looked
at Nicola, then Talbot, and smiled. A gray Mercedes turned off
the coastal road and came up the drive. "Giorgio," Nicola said,
lifting herself from her seat. Minzonni made a sour face, looking
over his shoulder toward the car. The Italian woman sat down and
the Jubba woman held her tray out to Talbot, smiling in that same
strange way.

The other guests came through the french doors to join them.
The Italian doctor brought more chairs from the sun porch but
there were too many for the small square of flagstone and some
sat on the edge of the lawn. A tall barrel-chested Italian named
Giorgio Rugatto appeared from around the side of the house,
dressed in suntans, carrying his car keys. His grayish-white hair
was combed back over the dome of his huge head. He had the
weatherbeaten face of a Sicilian peasant. A few voices called out,
reminding him of his antics the previous night, when he'd had too
much to drink. He grinned in embarrassment, looking at Nicola.
He had just dropped by, seeing the figures on the terrace, but now
he apologized. He didn't realize Nicola had dinner guests.

Nicola said it didn't matter. Rugatto was persuaded to stay. Talbot knew little about him except what he heard from the gossip
around him, that he owned a plantation, sold tractors and agricultural machinery, and had just returned from a hunting trip to
Yugoslavia.

They sat outside until dusk, talking and watching the sea.

At dinner, Talbot sat at Nicola's right, the Italian doctor opposite and the journalist at the far end of the table. Samina, the
servant, had put candles on the table, but they were unlit as they
seated themselves, and they all waited while she lit them. Nicola
looked on impatiently. Samina took a long time lighting the candles, basking in the attention she was given, especially from Rugatto. She'd added a few more golden bracelets and a touch of
rouge to her cheeks. A second Jubba woman from the kitchen,
small and plain in contrast, helped with the serving. With her
teasing smiles and flirtatious banter, Samina was something of a
coquette, Talbot decided, less a servant than a courtesan, ignoring
Nicola's serving instructions, just as she'd ignored her on the sun

porch earlier. She served Rugatto before anyone else, which amused everyone at the table except Nicola.

During dinner, an Italian lawyer on assignment to the ministry of agriculture dominated the conversation at their end of the table. At the far end Minzonni and two Italian teachers from the university were in quiet disagreement about the ethnography of the peoples of the Horn.

Their discussion grew more lively during the second course, when Nicola angrily joined in. The question seemed to be at what date the Jubba people first appeared on the stage of history, whether in the sixteenth century, as Minzonni contended, or much earlier, as the two Italian professors were insisting. They put their ancestry among the nomads of the Arabian Peninsula who'd migrated southward from the Gulf of Aden and by the first millennium B.C. were tending their camels as far south as the savannahs of northern Kenya. Minzonni claimed this was nonsense, that the Jubba people had never been more than a small collection of primitive tribes in the scrub behind Muzaffar up the coast and through intermarriage with other indigenous tribes could hardly be considered a homogeneous peoples or a nation at all.

Nicola was infuriated. "You are absolutely wrong, Carlo!" she cried from her end of the table. "Your Jubba friends would be interested to hear how you ridicule their history, and I will be the first to tell them!"

Minzonni protested weakly: "I am not wrong. I'm just not sentimental about it."

Talbot thought the debate odd, a dead issue, not a living one, a question best left to crusty academicians, linguists, and their dusty monographs, not polite dinner-table conversation. He didn't understand why Nicola was so passionate in her attempts to prove Minzonni wrong.

At Rugatto's urging, the talk turned finally to Yugoslavia, to export problems, foreign currency restrictions, and, inevitably, the old days.

They retired to the front living room for coffee and brandy. On a credenza near the bookshelves Talbot found a small constellation of photographs. One was of the elder Mr. Seretti, her father-in-law, and another of her husband. He was a few years older than Nicola, short, swarthy, and thick-legged. According to Rugatto, who joined him, Seretti was an outdoorsman, like him, a hunter and fisherman. He'd lived alone on the plantation for almost a decade before the marriage. Talbot identified a coquettish figure in the foreground of one of the pictures taken in front of the villa as he listened to Rugatto describe their hunting expeditions together in the south, how Seretti had been a fine bird hunter, how they'd had many a dinner here with the platters laden with grouse and francolin Samina had cooked for the two of them. It was only then that Talbot finally put the odd household together and understood Nicola's difficulties with Samina with her quick teasing eyes and her golden bracelets. The coy old flirt had been her husband's concubine all those lonely bachelor years.

"You found something?" Nicola said curiously, joining him.

"No, nothing. Just browsing around."

She looked at the picture, at him, then put it down indifferently. "No questions of your own now?"

He smiled as if he knew what she knew. "No questions."

The Italian teachers were leaving, and she turned away. After they left, Talbot said goodbye, too.

"It was very nice, but I still don't have any idea about the plants."

"I'll bring a few next time," she said. "I'm very glad you could come. I'm sorry we didn't have more of an opportunity to talk. There were some questions I wanted to ask you."

"Maybe next time."

Nicola said, "Give me a cigarette, Giorgio."

Rugatto handed her a cigarette, then lit it with a gold lighter.

The blue wraparound skirt fell away from her legs above her knees, but she didn't move to cover her thighs.

Minzonni got up and wandered to the window and then returned again. She leaned over to bring an ashtray near.

"Why didn't you come last night," Rugatto asked after a minute. "They said you were coming. They expected you to be there."

"I was tired, I didn't feel like it."

"I didn't know you knew the Americans," Minzonni said.

"Just a few."

"The one who was here, which one is he?" Rugatto asked. "The new one?"

"No, not the new one. He lives in Signora Ferrugio's villa, the one at the end of the corniche. She is afraid they won't renew the lease and wants to redo it, replant the garden."

"She is old, Signora Ferrugio?"

"Seventy-two, I think."

"There is one who has no time for them, they say," Rugatto continued. "They don't like him. The Italian counselor told me. I don't know his name. Maybe he is gone now."

"His name was Quarles."

"This one seems a nice man," Rugatto said, "a nice man, but he doesn't hunt, doesn't fish. Very quiet. He talks politics?"

She shrugged and put her head back. "I met him six weeks ago. We don't talk politics."

"Don't ask her; she was the hostess tonight," Minzonni said. "Donna Seretti. She is very discreet now, Donna Seretti. Remember the vice consul from Bologna, the one who was in love?"

"Which one was that?" Rugatto asked.

"The one waiting to be seduced," Nicola said, her head still back. "He was in love with everything, even the camels. He'd never been away from Europe before, not without his little wife."

"I don't know him," Rugatto said. "Did he fish?"

"The one she seduced," Minzonni said. "I saw him in Rome two months ago."

"I didn't seduce him," she said sleepily. "He seduced himself. What is he doing now?"

"He said his heart was still broken," Minzonni said, "but that with his wife's help he was learning to forget. He's left the foreign ministry."

"Good. I told him he should. He was too young, too naive, afraid of what he thought, especially being away from his little wife." She looked at him coldly. "I don't think he talked to you at all. People like you frightened him. Why did you ask Talbot all those questions? Why did you continue like that?"

"He annoyed me," Minzonni said, "dressed the way he was, following you around like a dog. They know nothing, none of them. As silly as your schoolteachers. Are you driving back tonight?" he asked Rugatto, who looked at his watch.

"In a few minutes," he said.

"Then that ridiculous argument with the professors." Nicola said, angry again. "You don't know what you're talking about. Is that the official line now, the *L'Unita* line, what you were saying?"

Minzonni only shrugged.

"Of course. Which dog are you following these days? Moscow's dog or Berlinguer's dog?"

"Neither."

"Carlo, the peacemaker, the envoy."

She sat up, slipped off her sandals, and brought her legs under her, then rearranged her skirt. "I'm very tired. It's been a long day. I didn't expect so many schoolteachers. You can stay in the guesthouse if Giorgio isn't driving back, but I think I am going to bed, to read awhile."

Rugatto obediently stood up. Carlo toyed with his brandy glass. "Are you coming up tomorrow?" he asked.

"I haven't decided," she said. "When will you finish your interviews?"

"Thursday, I think."

"Could I see what you're writing?"

"If you come tomorrow."

Nicola walked with Rugatto to his car.

"This one, he is not a boy," he said. "You should be careful."

His smile annoyed her. He looked very silly in the moonlight, very stupid and very old. "Which one? I don't know. You are silly, you and Carlo both. We're friends, that's all. He doesn't care and I don't care anymore either. He isn't what people think. Anyway, it's no one's business."

CHAPTER SIX

The Voice of
the Urubamba

*S*haughnessy wasn't in Mozambique at all but in Lisbon, newly assigned to the embassy as economic officer.

His typewritten letter arrived that day. The Mozambique assignment had been broken after the foreign ministry had reduced the size of the U.S. mission in Maputo. After a week at the Department in Washington wandering the halls, he'd met an old friend from personnel and been assigned to Lisbon:

Unbelievable here, dine late every night, then return to my commodious flat overlooking the Avenida de Ceuta and Monsanto Park. There, my maid, a dark-eyed farmer's daughter recently returned from Angola, still prone to occasional tears at the loss of the Portuguese dependencies, has my covers turned down and brandy waiting in the front salon, followed by trampoline calisthenics and a little Go-Go in her bedroom, just to the rear of the walk-in pantry and wine closet, where I comfort her loss of said dependencies with the rediscovery of my own. Med Div said I weathered the African scag like a trooper, no permanent damage to my social member (this from private consultation at a Conn

Ave clinic), which, for a time, I thought might have succumbed to
the pox or dry rot, but here is vigorously reengaged. If I'm sometimes forced to squat-piss in the mornings, it is not from pain but
from sheer post-coital exhaustion.

Exhausting social schedule. There is no aristocracy like the
Portuguese.

Know nothing of said Turkoman rug or yellow lamp or broken
glass tray. My houseboy did tell me one day DeGroot had been
scouting my premises, looking at lamps, rugs, pictures, etc., which
he might sequester to appoint his own Waldorf-Astoria penthouse
above.

Am enclosing a personal check in the amount of $100 which I
ask you to cash and convert into shillings at the embassy cashier.
I would very much appreciate it if you would see to it that a certain Jubba-Italo girl by the name of Faduma Farah receives the
proceeds to give to her dear Aunty to pay for certain medical expenses incurred by the poor old woman recently. She lives in an
old building in Hamar Weyne with her aunt, 2nd floor rear, a blue
door, no address, but am enclosing a map to help you or your
agent find it. Don't dawdle.

My best to the Lord of the Camel Flies and His Marchesa in
terms you deem appropriate (I am still awaiting a copy of my efficiency report which the old fart was still doodling over the day I
left).

Would enjoy hearing how you are managing under the new regime and its sergeant-major, DeGroot, the penultimate asshole
(the ultimate being the klutz that assigned him there). The Jubba
staff and chauffeurs, I discovered the day of my departure, had already given him a nickname, "white eyes." I'm not sure what it
means.

All the best,

> Yr. Obedient Serv.
> Sean

A crude map and a check were included, scribbled out in Shaughnessy's looping script, the carefree scrawl of a fat overgrown kid
whose handwriting had probably changed little since his parochial
school days back in Worcester, where he boasted he once extorted
candy from the neighborhood kids because his father was a cop.

A dizzying crepitation crept into Talbot's head as he stood up;
he felt an emptiness at the pit of his stomach, like a man in a free
fall. He'd gone without breakfast that morning, without dinner the
night before, he now remembered, leaning against the window

casement. The mosque atop the rear building was in shadow. Through the fretwork he saw a few figures kneeling. On the roof-top to the north a woman was hanging laundry over the coping. From the office beyond came the mechanical click of Miss Penrose's electric typewriter; the air conditioner hummed from its window box. DeGroot's door was shut; Harcourt was gone someplace, a *cocktail d'adieu* for some departing ambassador.

In the sand alleyway below his window a young camel was being butchered, long white limbs outstretched in the dust. *Shaughnessy in Lisbon?* He had never envied anyone, he told himself as he watched the camel's dusty white coat being stripped away by the barefoot Jubba straddling him, knife flashing in each hand as he worked his way down the carcass, silver-gray gristle and bloody shank unfolding behind him. Two buckets of blood and offal sat on the ground nearby. A few old men and some children stood watching from the shadows.

He turned away and wandered into the outer office. Miss Penrose was still typing. He stopped for a minute, trying to remember why he'd come upstairs: *Shaughnessy in Lisbon?*

"You lose something?" Miss Penrose asked without looking up. "If you're leaving, don't forget to close your safe."

Seeing the top drawer pulled open, he remembered why he was upstairs. He retrieved the keys from the back of the drawer and climbed to the top of the stairs and unlocked the door. The sun was white on the roof, the mild wind smelled of the sea, of cooking oils from a nearby roof, of gasoline and diesel fumes from the vehicles passing below. He stood looking out to sea and the cool blue horizon and then at the turquoise shallows along the beach toward his villa. He crossed to the small shed, unlocked the door, and shut it behind him. The small shadowy enclosure was suffocatingly hot under the radiating tin. Spiders had built cobwebs in the corners and under the joists; two wasp nests hung just inside the door. He brought the telescope from the corner, uncapped the lens, and opened the small peephole at the top of the frame and fixed the telescope on the bow of the Russian freighter arrived that morning. The lens was dancing crazily up and down. He had to lock the scope in place with the thumbscrews before he could read the Cyrillic letters on the bow. He wrote the name on his sweat-damp pad while two wasps circled overhead, and he slowly scanned the deck for canvas-covered cargo. He moved the telescope out to sea, looking for arriving ships as the sweat fell like raindrops from his face to the dusty floor below. Far in the distance he saw the dipping sail of a coastal dhow, but then the image dissolved in his salt-stung eyes. *Lisbon, for God's sake.* He put the telescope away and locked the shed. On the roof outside he stopped to let the wind blow the heat from his face and arms, scanning the sky, dazzling white and empty, the beach sheeted with silver.

He returned to his office and typed out a six-line cable reporting the ship's presence. Then he went downstairs and cashed Shaughnessy's check.

"Sorry, Logan," Peterson said, intercepting him in the narrow corridor behind the cashier's cage. He looked very hot and very miserable. "Wonder if you could help out. Customs got some papers in Italian, and I don't know what they're talking about."

"What kind of papers?"

"A shipment they're holding."

"Sure, but where's Abucar?"

"Sent him out to the airport. Customs is closing in a half-hour and tomorrow's Friday. The port'll be closed. I got the carryall outside. Could you help? I'd sure appreciate it. We got to hurry if we're going to get there."

He followed Peterson out the door. On the street outside he ran into Nancy Kinkaid. "Jesus, I'm sorry." He stepped aside. "How've you been, I haven't seen you."

"OK, I guess. Oh, God, the heat's miserable." Her face was puffy. Dark moist shadows lay under her eyes, and her blond hair hung in damp strings against her wet forehead. She was wearing a maternity dress.

"Taking care of yourself?"

"Trying to. How about you?" She looked up at him for the first time; the light had fled from all that California sunshine. "Oh, Lord, is this heat ever miserable."

He moved ahead to open the door and she stepped across the threshold like an old woman, one hand on her thigh. Her ankles were swollen, a mottled white and gray.

Peterson was calling him, and he ran to join him in the back seat.

The driver made his way through the crowded streets toward the port, followed by an embassy stake truck.

"What are you expecting from customs?"

"If it's what I think, it's the new duplicating machine for the front office. The one we've been expecting."

"It's been missing?"

"It was shipped out of Genoa three months ago, an Italian ship."

They stopped to let a pair of army trucks pass near the narrow street that led to the port.

"Italians are the worst," Peterson said. "The Italian ships."

Talbot sat looking out the open window at the congestion just outside the gates to the customs area.

"I suppose DeGroot's been on your ass about it," he said, thinking of Shaughnessy's flat overlooking the Avenida de Ceuta and the cool green park below, thinking of the long weekends, the cool high mountains, and the drive north from Spain over the Pyrenees to France, then maybe a few days in Arles or Aix on the way to Paris. A Jubba woman was rudely pulling a squalling child along the foot-worn path next to the road. His mouth was open, his swollen eyes were squeezed shut, and he was bellowing as if heartbroken. Talbot felt a surge of sudden pity. Nancy Kinkaid, too. How the hell did a woman let herself get knocked up three times in five years?

"That and everything else."

"I didn't see an Italian ship in the harbor."

"I figure it must have been lost someplace back in the customs sheds."

The army guards made the stake truck and the carryall wait at the gate. They crossed the hot tarmac and hurried down the steel tracks to a warm little office in the front of a warehouse. A small ebony-skinned Jubba in a white shirt with an open collar creaked forward in his chair to study the pink customs clearances from the ministry of foreign affairs Peterson gave him. He consulted the papers on his desk, shook his head, and handed back the clearance forms. He had long slim fingers that seemed to make a full symphonic score from those few pages of rustling paper.

"He says that's not it," Talbot said, face bristling with sweat. "It's not the duplicating machine."

Peterson sat down on the chair, opened his briefcase, and brought out a file of pink customs releases. The customs clerk looked at the clock on the wall. A blue Japanese fan sat on the floor fluttering the papers on the desk. "You're waiting for all that?" Talbot said.

"Sure am. Must be forty of them. Ask him to give you the shipping manifest so I can know what he's talking about."

Talbot asked for the manifest and the clerk brought a pair of tissue-thin documents from his blue folder. They were typewritten in Italian.

"It's DeGroot's piano," he said, handing Peterson the manifest, "the one he's been bellyaching about. Did you bring the foreign ministry release?"

"I sure hope so. It's here someplace."

After a few minutes searching, he found the pink slip. The clerk compared the two and got to his feet. He led them out of the office and across the concrete floor between crated boxes and container cartons to the rear of the warehouse, where an idle forklift sat. From the dusty rectangular outlines on the floor and the haphazard position of the pallets and crates, one of which had been splintered by the iron prongs of the forklift, that remote corner of the warehouse had just recently been cleared.

"Goddamn, I sure hope that's not his piano," Peterson said, looking at the splintered crate.

"Too small."

The customs clerk moved past it to a boxed crate about the size of an upright piano standing against the galvanized steel wall perforated by nail holes through which the sun shot long shafts of laser light through the shadows.

"That's it, I guess," Peterson said. "Looks all right, wouldn't you say?"

"Looks like it."

The clerk had moved on to a second crate. One corner was smashed in.

"Not so lucky," Talbot said. "What's that?"

"The bench, I reckon." Peterson looked at the customs clearance. "It sure is. I shoulda known."

Talbot pulled away a splintered board. A piano bench sat inside. One leg was bent to the oblique, and the scratched lid was skewed sideways, the hinges sprung.

"He'll have a goddamn fit," Peterson said.

"Better the bench than the piano."

The clerk went to look for the forklift driver. Peterson found a pair of bolt cutters on the forklift and snapped the bands on the bench, then forced back the sides to inspect the damage. Under the sprung lid Talbot found bundles of old piano sheet music, neatly tied, musical scores, and a few faded brown envelopes bound with rubber bands.

While Peterson examined the damage to the crate and wrote out a description on his notepad, Talbot explored the piano bench. In a tattered brown envelope beneath the sheet music marked with the name of a Sydney, Australia, musical supply house he found a few playbills. One was for a production of *Rose Marie,* another *Show Boat.* The featured player in both was a Miss Adele Pearson, recently a showtime performer on the *Queen of Tasmania,* an Australian cruise ship, but now the featured player for the Sydney Operetta Company. She had a small sweet face, vaguely familiar. In another bundle of brown envelopes with the name Geographical Tours Ltd. printed in the upper left-hand corner he found a few color brochures advertising "Lost Islands of the Remote Pacific, the Marquesas, Pitcairn, and the Tuamotus, Birthplace of Ancient Polynesia . . . A Visual Trek through New Guinea, including the Fire-Walkers of Rabaul . . . Touring Inca Peru, from Cuzco to the Gorge of the Urubamba . . . Dyak Villages of Borneo, the Torajas of the Celebes, Ancient Indonesian Hindu-Buddhist Temples . . . Walking with the Maoris of New Zealand, from Lake Te Anau to Milford Sound."

On a publicity still he studied a close-up of a young grease-haired Bernard DeGroot standing at the microphone in a Sydney recording studio, looking very much like a young Robert Trout or Edward R. Murrow from the old CBS radio days. VOA? Evidently not. Geographical Tours Ltd.? So it seemed. "Lost Islands of the Pacific? The Gorge of the Urubamba?"

What the hell was that all about?

He found another brochure, then a third, and as he read through an additional bundle of promotional literature in a tattered gray envelope the fog gradually lifted, slowly at first and then completely as the last lingering vapors were burned away and the entire land-

scape became luminously clear—the sparkling beaches, the long
clean Pacific swells, the corrugated virgin jungles, the sinuous riv-
ers, the snow-slashed Alpine peaks, and soaring above them all on
the rising thermals of the slide projector the elevated voice he knew
so well, the braying sonority of Bernard DeGroot, film editor and
narrator for Geographical Tours Ltd., the omniscient silver-tongued
sound track for GTL's technicolor travelogues, rolling like thunder
from the Himalayas to the Hebrides:

> . . . and so we leave the platiniferous regions of the lower Sepik
> River in New Guinea and travel apace to the gorges of the Yangtze,
> where, immediately visible in the foreground, stand those ancient
> profiles so venerated by the peoples of the empire . . . or fly as
> the condor from the hidden realm of Bora Bora to the sinuous
> vastness of the Urubamba . . .

So there it all was at last.

In the dimly lit port warehouse with the piercing sunlight scattering like bullets all around him Talbot had finally tracked Bernard
DeGroot to his celluloid lair and unmasked the impostor. It was the
voice, of course; it would have had to be the voice, and with the
voice the flat-earth fantasies of that Rand McNally *Weltanschauung*
he so mindlessly decorated in the weekly country team meetings, a
one-dimensional worldview matured not with the VOA, the State
Department or the National War College, but there at the GTL
microphone with his GTL-prepared film script in hand—Bernard
DeGroot, the Lowell Thomas of the technicolor travelogue back in
some distant pre-color TV era.

"What you got there?" Peterson asked. The stake truck was backing in.

"Not much, just some old sheet music."

Smiling, Talbot carefully repacked the envelopes in the bench.

"What's so funny?"

"Nothing. I wasn't laughing."

"I know you weren't laughing. I won't be laughing either he sees
the way they busted up his bench."

"Buy him a chair."

He'd been looking for a few small answers but what he'd found

was King Solomon's mines; what he regretted was not having anyone to share them with.

□ □ □

"You seemed awfully cheerful earlier, I must say," Julia said suspiciously to Talbot from her lounge chair at the beach cottage.

Eyes closed under his white tennis hat, he didn't move. "Did I?"

"You certainly did, didn't he, Lyman?"

"Sorry?" Harcourt turned away from the wall overlooking the
sea. "Did what?"

"Seem awfully cheerful."

"No more so than usual."

"I even heard him whistling while he was changing clothes."

"Maybe it's because Wingate's finally coming," Talbot said.

He'd been invited to lunch with the Harcourts at the beach cottage that Friday afternoon. Julia was exhausted after a hectic week.
The beach was crowded on the Moslem sabbath, much too crowded
for Julia.

"Sit up and talk to me," she said. "We haven't talked for quite a
while."

"About what?"

"Anything. What you've been doing. We haven't seen you."

"Not much." He brought his chair closer.

She was in her bathing suit. One knee was lifted; her eyes were
covered by a white sun mask. "I'm sure you've been up to something; don't be so secretive." Her loose halter had billowed out, un-
covering the delicate rose-tipped fullness of her left breast. Conscious suddenly of the luscious ripeness of that unplucked fruit,
Talbot dragged himself to his feet.

"Just the same old routine. I think I'll go swimming. Do you
want to come?"

"Not just now. Why? Do you see someone." She sat up and
looked out over the beach.

"No, I just think I'll go swimming, cool off."

He stopped at the foot of the steps. "Aren't you going to take off
your hat?" she called.

"What hat?"

"The hat you've got on. You are behaving oddly. Are you sure you don't have your shoes on?"

He tossed the hat back on the porch and walked down the strand and waded out into the sea. There were few swimmers in the open water. He swam toward the reef but after a few dozen strokes decided he didn't have the energy. He paddled about on his back and let the surf carry him back toward shore. Just beyond the breaking waves he sank to the bottom, lay there in a dead man's float for twenty seconds, then drifted back to the surface. When he returned to the porch Julia hadn't moved.

"You are acting strange," she said. "Why didn't you ask Lyman to join you?"

"I had my swim," Harcourt said, leaning against the wall, watching the outgoing tide. Talbot went to join him and they talked about the UN drought-relief effort. Twice Julia called to them, warning them away from the wall, afraid they might attract unwelcome visitors. Then Harcourt had been hailed from the beach by the Indian ambassador and his occasional consort, a British-trained Afghan nurse who worked at the UN dispensary, out for a stroll from the UN club up the beach.

Julia heard the voices and sat up. "Lyman, please, don't bring that awful man up here." Harcourt, still in his bathing trunks, a straw hat on his head and a towel across his shoulders, left his glass behind and dutifully went down the steps to intercept the couple on the strand.

Julia moved her lounge chair, put her sun mask aside, and slipped on sunglasses. She lay back again. "Tell me when they've gone."

"They're walking up the beach now."

"Which direction?"

"Toward the UN club."

On the front veranda of the adjacent beach cottage a few figures were visible.

"Who are you waving to?" Julia asked.

"The DeGroots."

"I know you're lying. They never come to the beach."

"They've got their dog with them."

"I know your little tricks. Who is it?"

"The German second secretary and his wife."

"You would notice her, wouldn't you? You're as bad as Lyman. That's why I hate coming here on Fridays. Come talk to me. You still haven't answered my question."

"What question?"

"What you've been doing with yourself. We haven't seen you. We never finished our little talk about Jubba's problem with the Russians about Ethiopia."

"I thought I explained." He returned to the lounge chair and sat down.

"We didn't finish. You said Jubba helped other socialist countries and now the Russians wouldn't help them liberate Western Jubbaland. That's what you said, isn't it?"

"More or less."

She sat up, tightened her halter, readjusted the straps, and began rubbing cream on her shoulders. "Agnes says Ethiopia is in a very bad way."

"It is."

"Bad how?"

"Everything coming unglued, rebellions in the lowlands, guerrilla wars in the north and south, a power struggle in Addis. Everything that happens to a sick old empire that's falling apart, on its last legs, ready for the rendering plant." He sat watching Harcourt and the couple on the beach. "Like Colonel Lattanzi's horse."

She rubbed her left arm. "Colonel Lattanzi? Who was he?"

"The former Italian military attaché. He left before you and Lyman came. He had this old horse he bought in Afgoi, full of ticks, worms, had rickets, a rotten hoof, everything. He was trying to nurse it back to health, the way the Russians are trying with Ethiopia. Everyone told him to put it out of its misery. So Ethiopia's that way now, dead on its feet, and the wolves are gathering."

"That's terrible. Do you want some?" She held out the tube.

"No, thanks."

"It's still terrible. So what happened?"

"It's not over yet. The Soviets want to get Ethiopia back on its feet, part of the socialist brotherhood; the Jubba want to dismember it—"

"I meant Colonel Lattanzi's horse."

"He took it up the beach and put it out of its misery, a bullet in the head, someone said, then let the surf carry it away. That's what I heard."

"How horrible." He watched her shut her eyes. Since that afternoon with Ryan at the residence, every gesture of hers seemed magnified. He didn't care so much about himself; it was Harcourt he pitied.

"Empires are like that, they end up in a dirty alley someplace, a ditch, a dirty cellar, like the Romanovs."

"That's very cold-blooded, isn't it? Typically Italian, too, I'd say."

"So was Haile Selassie's Ethiopia, cold-blooded, too, a medieval corruption, as rotten as feudal Russia." He watched her face, knowing she didn't give a damn about all this.

"Let's leave out the metaphors. So the Ethiopian empire is falling apart and the Russians and Jubba are in disagreement about what to do."

"More or less. The Russians are telling the Jubba that socialists don't fight each other, and the Jubba are trying to give the Russians ideological lessons according to Lenin. The liberation of the oppressed peoples in Western Jubbaland takes precedence over socialist solidarity. Moscow's telling them they've got it backwards; the Ethiopians aren't their enemies but their socialist brothers."

"It sounds terribly complicated," she said, tugging at her halter as she looked down at herself. She gave another tug. "Speaking of the Italians, what was Mrs. Seretti's truck doing in your drive last Monday?"

"Bringing more dirt from Afgoi."

"Have you talked to Whittington?"

"He came to see me."

She sat perfectly still, not moving, her eyes still closed. After a minute she sat up, tightening the straps of her halter behind her back.

"Would you call Osman for me," she said in that wilted little voice he'd come to recognize—the flowers faded, their beauty fled, winter upon us. Another Quisling in the ranks. "Ask him to bring me a gin-tonic," she added with even more enervation. "Tell him we'll be ready in about five minutes. I think I'll go look for Lyman."

□ □ □

The moon lit up the beach and the long ghostly scroll of breakers. It was after eight. Talbot's gate was closed, the front drapes were drawn, and he was alone, typing a letter to his broker and listening to Eric Clapton on the phonograph in the rear study. He heard a horn honk and the gate clang open. He pushed aside the drapes and saw a car with its lights on just outside the gate. A small figure stood in the glare of the headlights talking to the gate guard.

He opened the door and called to the guard. Hearing his voice, Nicola Seretti came out of the shadows and crossed in front of the headlights and moved to the foot of the steps, wearing a long skirt and a small jacket. The tall gate guard mutely followed her. "I'm sorry," she said. "He told me you'd gone out."

"My fault, not his. I told him to say that, sorry. Come on in."

She staggered as she came up the steps and stopped. "I'm not interrupting anything?"

"No, nothing. Come on in."

"You're alone?"

"All alone."

"I've been to a reception. I thought you might be there."

He held open the door. As she passed inside he was pleasantly aware of her perfume, a breath from another world.

She had brought the letter from the villa's owner in Milan, formally agreeing to pay for the replanting of the rear garden. She sat down on the couch and took out a cigarette as Talbot read the letter. Her short black hair was glossy and shining, as if she'd been to the hairdresser's that day; she was wearing eye shadow.

"So it's all settled," he said. "She'll pay."

"All settled, yes."

"That's very generous of her."

"She can afford to be generous," she said, crossing her legs. Her short jacket was beaded in silver, and a small silver slipper showed from beneath the fold of her long skirt. "She has a very generous lease."

"Still she didn't have to do it. Would you like a drink?"

"I've had a drink already, two, in fact."

"You're ahead of me then. I haven't even started."

"I've had too much, but I'll join you. You were lucky not to be invited. It was an Iraqi reception."

She asked for a Campari-soda, changed her mind and said she preferred whiskey. He turned off the stereo and left her alone and made drinks in the kitchen. When he returned she was looking at the books in the bookcase at the end of the room near the door to the study. She sat down again, put the drink aside, and opened her beaded purse. "You asked me about the banana export figures," she said, bringing out an envelope. "I have some papers here. They may be of some help." She put them on the table. "Don't look at them now. Whether they are accurate or not I don't know."

"Anything helps, thanks. I was about to give up." He'd already completed the banana report, using figures supplied by the Italian embassy.

"Don't thank me. It's nothing if you know where to look. They're very stupid about government figures."

The telephone rang and the sound startled her. "You were expecting someone, a call?" She sat forward and stubbed her cigarette out.

"No, no one."

"I should go."

"Don't go, I'll just be a minute."

He went to the study to answer. She got up and wandered to the bookcase again, then followed him into the study.

It was Julia Harcourt. She wanted to talk to him, that evening if possible. Talbot said he had visitors.

She wasn't pleased. "Give me a call after they've left, I mean if it's not too late."

"I'll do that."

"Will it be too late?"

"I don't know, Julia, I really don't."

"Then try not to make it too late." She hung up.

Nicola stood across the room near the stereo looking at his phonograph records.

"Julia. That was Mrs. Harcourt?"

"Mrs. Harcourt."

"She's expecting you?"

"I told her I couldn't make it."

"It would be better not to disappoint her. She was at the Iraqi reception. I'll be going then."

"I'm not going anyplace. She's in one of her moods."

"One of her moods, yes. You know them then."

"I should by this time. You, too?"

"I've seen her moods, yes, when she's unhappy. Not only with me, with everything. It isn't complicated. She's an unhappy woman, like many here." She took out a record album and looked at the jacket. "The Doors? Who is that?" She put it back. "She is like the wife of an Italian diplomat I knew once who was very selfish about herself. She saw herself growing old here and couldn't agree to it. After a time I couldn't talk to her, couldn't stand to see her. It happens to all women. Soon fifty, soon fifty-five. She doesn't accept it. Mrs. Harcourt." She started to take out an album but hesitated. "I'm sorry. It was very hot at the reception, very hot and very crowded. Could you put more ice in?" She handed him her glass.

He went to the kitchen and filled her glass and when he returned she was still looking at his albums. "Music interests me. I shouldn't be so curious." She took out another album.

"You said Julia's unhappy with you. What's her problem?"

"Nothing, an imaginary problem, a problem in her own mind. Probably, as a man, you know. She feels very young, Mrs. Harcourt, the clothes she wears, her hair. The wives of the other ambassadors don't help. Neither does her husband. He is older, not wiser, just older. Physically, I am speaking. In that he is very old, very foolish, deliberately, I think. You see the games they play. So every day he reminds her, being old, others remind her of being young. Every day she wakes up and doesn't know what to do about it, whether to be old today or young today. So she blames him. Whether she will ever accept it or not, I don't know."

"What? Being old or being young?"

"Both." She didn't turn. "It is plain from everything she does, the silly games they play."

"What games?"

"Little games, very spiteful, the tiny bones they leave each other in the soup. I heard it too much and I was glad to leave. His being older each day, she being younger. I heard them arguing once, about what they would do after this. I was in the back garden. He talked about a house in France, in Spain, in Portugal, where they would go when it was all finished. It was a terrible argument. I'm sorry I heard it."

"He wants to paint."

"Does he?" Her hand moved to the bookcase, as if to steady herself.

"He studied to be a painter once."

"He wants to do nothing," she said disdainfully, "nothing at all, to have his mind free, to wander about his garden, to remember Dante in beautiful Italian, to remember Rimbaud in beautiful French, maybe to put a little color on cloth."

"He's not bad, I mean as a painter."

She looked up, still disdainful. It occurred to him she'd not only had too much to drink but was angry about something. "Painting? What does that mean? At sixty to paint? What is that? Nothing. Painting is a lifetime. It is work, not a dream. Once maybe I wanted to paint, too. It is too late. To drink some more, to dream some more, to drink, dream, and then drink some more, remember some more, to run to his little books in the middle of the afternoon, to take down a book and find the words he thought he remembered. He is a drunken magpie, making a little nest for himself from all the little feathers he finds, all from what others have done." She returned another record to the shelf. "I don't know this music of yours."

"It's popular stuff, most of it. The classical's there on the end. There's some Respighi there. He's pretty well read."

"Respighi I don't like so much. Is he? How do you know?"

"From talking to him. He means well, not a cruel bone in his body, not like some."

"No? Does a jellyfish have cruel bones? No, of course not. I've talked to him, too; I've listened to him. Tonight at the reception I listened to him. It was the same talk we had the first time I talked to him—the first and the second and all the talks after. He still doesn't know my name. Is he always so stupid like that? I think if you put his Dante and Rimbaud and everything else he remembers all together, bound it all together in Moroccan leather, like the little book he showed me one afternoon when I was working in the garden, the book he'd had bound in Barcelona by a bookbinder in the gothic quarter, none of it would make any sense at all."

"What book was that?"

"I don't care what book. If there were something else there, I could understand him, excuse him, but there is nothing. He has no talent I know of. He has no religion; he never goes to church. He has no politics, can make nothing sensible of what he knows. He calls himself a diplomat, but from his talk you would think he were in Siena or Venice. He talks to people as if they had come to take his coat or dust his shoes. Men in his position should not be stupid. It is very annoying when they are. Better to be proud, even arrogant. I don't mind."

"I don't think Harcourt intends it that way."

She'd been deeply hurt by something, he thought, watching her return a Sibelius record album to the shelf.

"Very sentimental, Sibelius. What he intends I don't care. Men in his place have responsibilities. They should not be that way. I've known Italian men like him, men of responsibility and power. That's one reason not to live in Italy, the men are all weak, unless you are a criminal. Because of men like him I live here." She moved along the bookcase. "I feel sorry for her. Everyone is growing old. And he wants his wife there, too, something to be taken out and shown, like his Roman and Greek coins. They meant something I'm sure when he dug them up, but that was twenty years ago. I can't feel sympathy for him, nothing he has ever done has been earned honestly, nothing at all. I surprise you?" She didn't look at him.

"A little, yeah."

"How would you explain it?"

"I don't know."

"Does he still sleep with her? I don't know." She wandered away. "Hearing them talk I have this feeling they don't know each other, their bodies don't know each other. If they did, they wouldn't talk as they do. It's better to be alone. Growing old with a man like that, it would be like being buried alive, buried in all your beautiful clothes. That is how she feels, I'm sure. Are these all the books you have?"

"All I brought with me."

She stood looking at the shelves where several dozen books were neatly arranged. "They are not many." She turned away finally and wandered back to the end of the bookcase and picked up her drink. His records didn't interest her; neither did his books.

"Do you remember the talk we had a few weeks ago, then the other afternoon?" she asked, sitting down again, crossing her legs. "The talk about this country, what might happen."

"I remember."

She picked up *The Economist* and leafed through the pages. "I have a friend, a very good friend. He would like to talk to you as soon as possible."

Talbot wasn't sure he'd heard her correctly. "Talk to me?"

She didn't look up, indifferently turning the pages. "Yes, to you. He's an old friend. He would like to meet you."

"He's with you outside?"

"No, that wasn't possible. He'd like to meet you someplace. To-morrow if possible."

"Tomorrow?"

"Yes. What is the date of this, last week?" She looked at the cover. "I am sorry but he has only a few days here."

"Who is he?"

"He's a friend. I told him I didn't think it was possible, but I said I would try."

"Meet him where?"

She dropped the magazine on the table and sat back with a sigh. "There is another reception. I thought I'd have dinner someplace after. Not the Rugda Taleh, not the Giubba either. The Italian res-taurant. Juliano's, on the rooftop. You know Juliano's. He'd meet us there if possible."

"What time?"

"Between eight and nine. Would that be all right?"

"I think I can manage."

"I'll meet you there at eight." She got up. "That would be better."

"You're not going already?"

"Yes. I must."

"You don't have to go."

She hesitated and sat down again. "All right."

"What's this about?"

"He'll tell you."

"You trust him?"

"It's not a matter of trusting him. Please. I will stay but let's not talk about it."

"About your friend."

"About my friend, yes. Instead if you wanted to play some of your music I will listen. What you were playing when I came in, what was that?"

He played Eric Clapton's *Layla* for her, but she didn't seem interested and talked above the music about how Mrs. Ferrugio had once furnished the house, not the way it was furnished now, which seemed to her very cold, like a hotel suite. She noticed he had no plants in the salon or the study and suggested the names of a few and where they might go. He finally turned off the record player and she asked if she could have some coffee. She followed him out to the kitchen and looked into the cupboards and the pantry while he made a cup of instant coffee. She asked him how many servants he had and why they left so early in the afternoon. On the way back to the study she stopped in the dining room and suggested he might arrange some potted plants there, too. At last she decided it was time to go. He followed her down the steps and stood in the drive as she started the car. She'd left the lights on and for a minute he didn't think it would start, but it did. He watched her drive away in the darkness. She was a very odd woman and he didn't know what to make of her. High-strung, certainly, but also a woman who knew her own mind; maybe a shrewd little actress, too. When he went inside the phone was ringing, but he turned up the phonograph and didn't answer.

□ □ □

The sidewalk tables in front of the corner tea shop were crowded, as many Jubba standing as sitting, all listening to the evening BBC broadcast from London. In the honeyed light of late afternoon the minaret of the Arbah Rukun mosque was washed in gold leaf. Pigeons preened and strutted in the open courtyard under the trees. On the stone wall of the small fountain where a trickle of water splashed, a shirtless young nomad in a red plaid *futa* sat wearily washing his feet. A few humpbacked old men rested on the nearby

benches, talking, their knotted brown hands folded on their canes.
The air was cleansing at that hour, as dustless as the hemisphere of
sky and the soft wind which had blown away the swarming fevers
of the midday sun; the light was luminous, as soft as a feather
against Talbot's skin.

He crossed the street in front of the Italian cathedral, where a
few elderly Italian women in peasant black were hobbling slowly
up the walk, continued south past a few Italian shops and turned
into the cobbled alleyway to Hamar Weyne. The narrow passageways were already in shadow, drifted here and there with the smoke
from indoor braziers. Porters in tattered khaki shorts quilted with
sewing machine patches moved ahead of him, some carrying on
their heads wooden boxes from the port, others with two and three
crates harnessed on their backs in wooden racks, the veins on their
necks and foreheads bulging, faces bent to the ground. They moved
in groups, like donkeys, blind to everything but the earth under
their muscular calves and splayed bare feet. In the entrances to the
passageways Hamari women gathered in twos and threes, mothers
and grandmothers in *chador,* in black veils and black dresses, out
for a breath of afternoon air before returning to their charcoal
cooking fires. From the shadowy grottolike shops came the sound
of transistor radios, the smell of spices, tea, aromatics, herbs, and
bolts of bright new cloth.

The afternoon wind didn't stir in the passageways, which were
always cool except at high noon when the paths were scalding bright
and the shops were closed. He moved on past the small market place
at the heart of the souk. Jubba men peddled plastic shoes from
pushcarts; on the ground nearby Jubba women sold beaded jewelry
and white earthenware on small reed mats spread before them.

He entered a wide sandy road lined with Indian and Pakistani
groceries and spice shops. The passageway Shaughnessy had marked
on his crude map was fifty meters to the south, just below a black
metal sign with a golden cock painted on it. He didn't remember the
sign.

Small trucks with sisal sacks of Tanzanian rice were being unloaded in front of an Indian trader's emporium. Beyond was a tiny
tea shop. Two taxi drivers sat at a table outside under the corrugated roof, drinking tea. A pair of red-and-yellow taxicabs and a

dusty black Fiat were parked in front. A sign hung just below the tea shop, as the map said it would, scaled by the sun, wind, and dust. Talbot, a conspicuous white face amidst the dark-skinned conjunction of the afternoon market, didn't pause to study the dimly plumed figure, which seemed once to have been a rooster. The passageway beyond was in full shadow. Twenty feet inside was the seam of a half-buried water pipe, worn silver by passing feet; nearby was the communal spigot. Around the corner at the end of a high wall built of coral rock was an areaway in front of two very old buildings.

From the wooden balcony of the old building just west of the areaway and opposite the wall a Hamari woman in black looked down at him. He stopped, looked again at the map, and then up at the woman. Behind him he caught a glimpse of one of the Jubba taxi drivers who'd been sitting at the table outside the tea shop and now stood watching him from the turn in the passageway.

The wooden balcony was rickety, but the wooden sunscreen above interested him, an ornate wooden latticework inset with carved petal rosettes and scrolled leaves of the sort rarely found now except in museums.

"Don't dawdle," Shaughnessy had said. *What the hell was that all about?*

He glanced back but the taxi driver had disappeared. He walked on. The house was at the end of the passageway to the right. Beneath the low entrance the stone threshold was scooped like a watering trough by the passage of feet over the centuries. He could smell the cool musk from the small cellar below. A bag of charcoal stood in the shadowy passageway; smoke from a brazier trickled from the doorway that opened into a small courtyard at the end of the corridor. He heard voices, paused, looked up, and began to climb. The wooden staircase was fragile, painted with thick blue marine paint. The risers had pulled away from the old wall and there was no banister. From above he could hear the cooing of pigeons from their dovecotes under the roof. At the top of the steps he stopped, again hearing voices. To the left rear would be Shaughnessy's blue door. The air was scented, not with charcoal but perfume. A radio was playing.

He went along the hall past a closed door and heard a woman's laughter. Ahead of him a young Jubba left a room, still talking to a young Jubba girl wearing a shift. Catching the unmistakable odor of careless hygiene, untidy linen, and bedside washpots as he passed an open door, he realized for the first time where he was.

The blue door at the end of the corridor was open. A small sharp-faced woman with gray hair stood in the doorway, a crutch under one arm, looking toward the young man. Ignoring Talbot, she shouted at him; he turned and they began to argue. In the room behind her a Jubba-Italo half-caste in a white slip sat on a small divan reading a magazine. Near the other end of the divan a Jubba in a white shirt sat in a chair smoking and drinking a glass of tea.

"Italiano?" the woman paused to ask Talbot, putting her hand on his arm without looking up as she continued her argument with the man down the hall. Something about someone he'd brought who'd taken something from one of the girls. The old woman might have been Italian or half Italian. The dark-haired girl inside the room glanced up, looked indifferently at Talbot, and went back to her magazine. She was a half-caste, no doubt about that, the Faduma Farah the shillings in the envelope were intended for, he supposed, and might have asked, but the Jubba man made him wary. He'd stood up to put on sunglasses, looking even more like one of the NSS layabouts from the Syrian restaurant across from the embassy.

"Italiano?" the woman asked with a wrinkled smile, her hand still on his arm. He didn't know how Shaughnessy was involved with this toothless old woman with the crutch, the Jubba-Italo girl, or her suspicious friend with the sunglasses, but the protocol didn't matter. He was in a second-floor whorehouse and wanted no part of it. He brushed her hand away.

"Lassen Sie die Hande von mir, Fräulein."

"Eh?"

"Lassen Sie—Scusi. Turn loose with the hand, old trot, *comprenez?"*

She clutched at his wrist a second time and said something in rude Italian.

"Kennen wir uns? Haven't met, have we? Sorry. *Nein, Fräulein. Auf wiedersehen."*

Politely he disengaged the plucking fingers and turned away. She tottered after him on her crutch, shouting in angry Sicilian. From the room inside, the Jubba man called to her, warning her about something. The crutch thumped twice against the floor as she retreated. An instant later the blue door slammed shut.

At the end of the corridor he turned down the steps and saw halfway down the stairs the taxi driver who'd been watching him earlier. Talbot didn't hesitate: *"Sind Sie verrückt?"* he asked as he brushed past without stopping. *"Stupido, no?"* The taxi driver didn't move, looking after him. He left the front door, walked along the wall, and a few minutes later emerged again into the wide sand road where the truck was being unloaded. The two taxis and Fiat were still parked there; a single taxi driver sitting over his glass of tea looked curiously at Talbot as he went up the road.

He didn't know how the old woman, the young Jubba-Italo prostitute, the Jubba NSS man, and the taxi driver were all involved with each other, but he had his suspicions. The taxi driver probably brought customers to the blue door and worked with the NSS. A few nights he might have brought a drunken Shaughnessy, possibly after one of his never-explained disappearing acts at the Mariner's Cave.

Petty extortion? A noble gesture, or just another loose end from one of Shaughnessy's tawdry love affairs?

Poor profligate Shaughnessy, as crude in love as in work. Shaughnessy gnawing a candy bar and lifting one bun from his office chair to break wind as he talked to Quarles upstairs on the telephone, complaining how overworked he was; Shaughnessy spilling ice cubes from his glass that afternoon at the Harcourts' beach house and putting them in his drink anyway as he continued to mimic some fruity BBC announcer for an indignant Agnes Firthdale, his mouth full of peanut mash; a tipsy Shaughnessy leaning across Nick Bashford-Jones's buffet table that night to ask if he could have sloppy seconds with that tight-assed little crumpet from the British trade mission across the room; Shaughnessy waking Talbot at two o'clock one morning with a forlorn telephone call after his return from another wastrel night at the Mariner's Cave: "I'm tired of dinks, man, let's you and me go to Nairobi, Logan old son, get us some of that real good rose garden pussy."

Shaughnessy, the most primitive of prodigal sons, not in rotting Mozambique but in lovely old Lisbon, for Christ's sake.

He walked back past the pushcarts and through the labyrinth of passageways and down through the shadows to the small shop with the half-door. It was shut now but not locked. He rapped at the door and waited, and after a few minutes it opened and Mohammed Hassan's small worried face was there, looking up.

He gave him the envelope with the shillings inside.

"For her," he said, nodding toward the back room, "for both of you."

The boy took the envelope, saw the thick wad of shillings inside, and looked up; but Talbot had moved away, back toward the commercial district. He turned and waved, as if he understood and it was all right.

She had heard his rapping at the half-door. She lay longer in bed after the sun came up and seldom stirred from her small dark bedroom after her noon nap. The small room smelled of camphor and kerosene, of coffee beans, tallow, Indian soap, the dust of her black garments hanging above the small metal suitcase, and the rose water she touched to her throat and temples before she went out into the streets. She was lying on the same small pallet on the old Arab bed where she'd slept for forty years, an Arabized old black woman from high in the mountains of Bale who'd once been the concubine of Ahmed Jama, the Cairo cotton merchant.

The shutters were drawn, a few pencil-slim strokes of fading sunlight lay across the ticking.

Hearing the rapping at the door in front, she thought of Ahmed Jama again, just as she had two weeks earlier after she'd heard a knocking on the mud wall outside, heard it pass along the window and door frames, and finally the heavy wooden door itself. In the passageway outside Mohammed Hassan had found a hunchbacked old trader from Aden rapping at the old house with the knob of a cane as he described to the young Hamari who was leading him who'd once lived there. The old man wore a dirty turban, black Turkish trousers, and plastic slippers. He was blind, his eyes clotted with cataracts. He was explaining that his old friend Ahmed Jama had left the house to his native wife before he returned to Cairo to his family. Ahmed Jama had once owned four houses in Benaadir but his sons who had inherited the business had sold them all.

That day two weeks earlier Mohammed Hassan had told her the man was from Aden, but he didn't say he'd mentioned Ahmed Jama, whose return she'd been awaiting for fifteen years.

She sat up. After a few minutes Mohammed Hassan brought the envelope thick with shillings. As he took them out she thought Ahmed Jama had finally returned, but he told her no, that it had come from the American, the man to whom she'd sold her amber beads. They were for her, and he would go down to Via Abdulkadir and find a taxi and then take her to the Italian hospital.

□ □ □

Juliano's was an open-air restaurant on the top floor of an old three-story building on a passageway off narrow Via Ahmed Bin Idriss. Talbot parked his car on the empty street in front of the dark Idriss cinema a little after eight o'clock. A flock of "me-watch" boys greeted him as he got out, dirty hands held out for a few shillings to keep an eye on his Fiat. To avoid argument or a fist-fight among them he pointed to the largest youth and gave him a few coins. He went down the street to the passageway and the yellow light over the closed stairwell.

On the open rooftop a dozen red-clothed tables were drawn up under the stars. Spiny green plants sat atop the parapet, which was draped with fishing nets; between them candles smoked in green glass fishing floats. In the rear was a vine-covered arbor and under it a white-clothed table laden with Italian pastries and desserts.

Nicola was already there, sitting alone in the shadows at the third table from the front, looking at a menu.

"A nice view," he said as he joined her. To the north he could see the Piazza and the small cars on the turnabout. "It's Italian-owned, isn't it?"

"Italian-owned, yes."

She handed him her menu. A tall white-coated Jubba waiter wearing a crimson sash came with his pad. She asked for a whiskey, plain, no soda, no water. Talbot ordered a gin and her neat whiskey. The waiter bowed and went away.

"The Italian dishes are very nice," she said as Talbot studied the menu. "The seafood, too."

"Are we to wait for your friend or should we order?"

"I think we should order."

He asked her what she would like and put the menu aside.

"I know this is all very strange," she said, "but it is strange for me, too." Her smile was a little strained, the smile of a nervous hostess giving her first embassy dinner. The rooftop was silent, and their voices carried. Only three tables were occupied, two by Italian couples and the third by a pair of Jubba men.

"Why does he want to talk to me?"

"Just to talk, that's all."

"A friend of yours, you said."

"I've known him a long time. He was a friend of my husband."

"You trust him?"

"I always listen to what he has to say, yes."

That didn't answer the question, but he didn't press her. A warm wind stirred the candle flame in the glass bowl. Her arms were bare under the shawl; the evening wind stirred her short dark hair.

"When I first got here, I got a few strange telephone calls at night," he said, watching a European couple pass the table. They went on to the far corner and sat down. "People wanting to see me, people wanting to talk to me confidentially."

"And did you talk to them?"

"I told them to come to the embassy."

"Did they?"

"They couldn't—couldn't or wouldn't. After a while they stopped calling."

"You have to be careful, of course."

"Sometimes. It's easy for people to misunderstand what I do."

"I'm sure it is."

"On the other hand you don't want to disappoint people."

"I understand that, too."

The waiter brought the drinks. Talbot studied the traffic on the

Piazza and the arc lamps above the roundabout. Beyond he could see the few mysterious yellow lights of the native commune.

"You should not be worried," she said, continuing to watch him.

"I'm not worried."

"You're thinking about something."

"The lights on the hillside. I was thinking I've never been in a Jubba house."

She looked beyond the Piazza. "That's a pity. I don't misunderstand what you do. It seemed to me that you were someone my friend might talk to, someone who would understand."

"You weren't sure of that at first, were you?"

"I'm very slow in making up my mind."

They finished their drinks and the waiter brought the pasta. A few more diners entered, but her guest wasn't among them.

During dinner she asked him why he wanted to go to Paris and where he'd been before. He told her about his previous posts and why he wanted to go back to Europe. His reasons didn't satisfy him but the more he tried to explain them the more fatuous they seemed. He gave up and asked about her own plans. She wasn't sure; she had no plans. She returned to Rome for a month every year, and each time those four weeks persuaded her she belonged here; now she wasn't sure of that, either.

"A foot in both worlds then," he said as the waiter came to take the plates away.

"Both worlds, yes, but more here than there." She looked at her wristwatch.

"You don't think your friend is coming?"

"I'm not sure."

Ten minutes later someone entered the restaurant from the door to Talbot's rear. They were finishing their coffee. She was talking about the difficulties many Italians faced in repatriating their capital to Italy when he saw her glance over his shoulder toward the restaurant entrance, as she had with each new arrival. This time her face brightened as she followed the figure who stopped at their table a moment later. He was a very tall Jubba with short dark hair and heavy mustache, something like a guardsman's mustache, wearing a white shirt and khaki trousers. He greeted Nicola and they talked for a few minutes. She introduced Major Mahamud Jama.

He politely declined her invitation to join them, didn't look at Talbot but stood talking to Nicola. Under his arm was a rolled-up newspaper. As they talked, his head and eyes moved from Nicola to the candle-lit tables around them, to the entrance to the rear, then back again, then back to the tables where the two Jubba men sat. After a few minutes he wandered back to the table under the lattice and stood talking to the waiter. He returned to their table with a slice of pineapple cake. He sat down to eat his cake and ordered a brandy.

A few minutes later he emptied his brandy glass, pushed his plate aside, looked at his aluminum-banded wristwatch, and stood up, leaving his rolled-up newspaper on the table. "I thought Haji Hussein was here. Maybe at the Giubba. Have you seen the article in *Horseed* on foreign landlords?"

"No, I haven't," she said, mildly surprised. *Horseed* was a scurrilous local weekly published in Italian and Arabic, partially subsidized by Iraqi money.

"An interesting article. Some of your Italian landlord friends should read it. Remember what we talked about? Major Dahir Abdi tried to rent a house from an Italian landlord and he set a dog on him." He laughed and glanced at Talbot. "Read it, show it to your friends, the truth about foreign landlords. But he's not Italian, is he?" He smiled again as he looked at Talbot.

"No, he's not Italian."

Watching her face, Talbot thought she seemed confused.

"I didn't think so." He picked up the paper and rolled it up again. "What we talked about before I don't think was a very good idea."

"Then you should have told me two days ago," she said sharply, and Talbot heard again, as he'd heard the night before, the voice of a determined woman with no patience for the irresolution of others.

"Probably I should have. I'm sorry." He tapped the rolled-up paper against one hand, looking around again. "I have to find Haji Hussein. When are you coming again?"

"Next week."

"Next week I'll be in Bulet Uen. I'll talk to you again sometime. Good night." He nodded to Talbot and left.

"What was that all about?"

Nicola, busy with her purse, got to her feet. "Wait, I'll just be a minute."

She hurried out. The waiter came and added the brandy and cake to Talbot's bill.

Ten minutes later she returned, out of breath and carrying her shawl. As she sat down, Talbot saw the copy of *Horseed* half hidden under it. "You looked a little upset," he said.

"I was upset. Now it's all right. Shall we go?"

"Major Jama was the man who wanted to meet you," she said as they walked toward his car. "He's with the armored division at Bulet Uen."

"Why'd he change his mind?"

"He decided it was not a good idea after all. I had to talk to him again to convince him. He didn't like the two men sitting behind us."

"I noticed them, too. Do you know what he wanted to talk about?"

"About the army and Western Jubbaland, I think. Do you know what's happening?"

He unlocked his car. "I have a pretty good idea. Where do you want to go?"

"I'm staying at the Taleh, but not there."

"You know the Mariner's Cave?"

"Of course not, the worst place."

"The Anglo-American—"

"No, the Italian club, in the garden there."

"What about Western Jubbaland?"

As he drove away she unfolded the copy of *Horseed*. Inside was a white envelope and some papers. She leaned forward to study them in the lights of the boulevard.

"He left these for you," she said. "Don't stop, we'll look at them later."

They entered the Italian club through the side garden and found an empty table and chairs near the tennis courts. She said she seldom used the club but kept her membership. She didn't know why, possibly for her old age. She disliked the atmosphere, especially the snobbery, and rarely went to the dining room or the clubrooms inside, but the rear garden was pleasant. She sometimes came in the evening to sit alone in the rear. The tennis court lights were on and a doubles match was in progress. She sat across from him at the white metal umbrella table, studying the papers, turning each page silently. Finally she sat back, satisfied, and handed them to him.

"This is what he wanted to talk about. It's clear."

The four thermofaxed papers were copies of ministry of defense documents. They listed the ration rolls and the tables of organization and equipment for five Western Jubbaland guerrilla units in their laagers along the Ethiopian frontier, the radio frequencies and alternate frequencies through which they received instructions from the ministry of defense communications center. Most interesting of all was a partial list of recent military equipment transfers of trucks, armored personnel carriers, anti-tank guns, and ordnance moved to the guerrilla units and the names of the Jubba army officers assigned command of the guerrilla maneuver battalions. The lists removed any doubt that the Western Jubbaland Liberation Front was a paramilitary arm of the Jubba national army.

"What anyone with any sense figured," Talbot said, "another fiction." He folded the papers inside the blank envelope and handed it back.

"These are for you, please." He took them back and sat looking at them.

"Who's Jama? Why would he give you these?"

A group of people moved from behind the shrubbery and sat down at the next table. He got up and moved to the chair next to her.

"To give them to someone who could help."

"Why?"

"Because he mistrusts the president, dislikes his policies, dislikes the corruption. He is Isaq."

Her tone was brisk and emphatic, all business now, forget the small talk. "He has a grievance?"

"Not a personal grievance, no. He's not ambitious that way, just very proud."

"What's he think of the Russians?"

"As much as he thinks of the Italians, very little."

He watched the foursome on the clay courts, trying to understand what she was up to. It was a very slow game. The lights were dim. Moths and hard-shell beetles rattled against the light reflectors.

"How did he know about me?" He was suddenly depressed.

"We talked once, he asked me if I knew someone. The Italian embassy first, the British, your embassy. Anyone who would help. I didn't know anyone at the time and then after we talked I decided you might listen to him."

A white-coated waiter with a tray came and they ordered soda. "Was I wrong?" she said after he left.

"No, not wrong. It's just a strange way to do business."

"Not so strange if you know Jama. He is always thinking, always, it's the way his mind works."

"But then at Juliano's he changed his mind. You had to talk to him. Why?"

"The two men sitting in the corner."

"NSS people?"

"I don't know. Then that's the way he is, too, the way people are, people who think too much."

A curious answer but as emphatic as the others. "Is that what you think?" he asked, intrigued.

"Of course."

"It'd be better if I knew more about him." The plump Italian woman had finally returned serve. The other three players put their racquets under their arms and clapped. It was a very silly game.

"Major Mahamud Jama, I told you."

"I meant something about his politics, where he was trained, who he's close to."

"You shouldn't be too curious. Not to want to know too much. That's the way the Russians are."

"You know the Russians?"

"A few once, not now, but Jama does. He told me some weeks ago they want to know more than everything and end up knowing less than nothing."

"He said that? He must be an intelligence officer."

She hesitated, surprised. "Yes, I suppose he is."

"You didn't say that."

"I'm saying it now."

"The reason I'm asking about him is that a few people are going to wonder what his motives are. That's the first thing they'll ask. They'll try to discredit him and they'll try to discredit me."

"Then say it was given to me to give to you."

"Then they'll discredit you. They've already tried."

"Me? How? From what Malfatti has said or the one before? Whose lies are they telling now?"

"I don't know, I didn't ask."

"What did they say?"

"That you had ties to the PCI."

She laughed suddenly, her eyes as bright and youthful as a young girl's. "Good, I am very glad. That makes me very happy, what they say. I'll tell Carlo when he comes." She laughed again as she took the glass and soda from the tray. She handed them to Talbot and picked up her own.

"Carlo? You mean Minzonni, the journalist?"

The waiter went away.

"Carlo, yes. He is very serious."

"Why?" It suddenly occurred to him. "Is he from the party?"

"Of course. Didn't you know? He came from Rome for the party, first to Addis, then here. The envoy, the peacemaker. I thought you would have a little dossier, a little book. He won't laugh when I tell him. He takes himself very seriously."

"He thinks we're all idiots, doesn't he?" Talbot watched her face.

"Of course."

"That argument you had with him at your house that evening, did that have something to do with the party?"

"In a way, yes."

"I couldn't follow it."

"It is like something abstract," she said indifferently, "a mathematical game. You must know the rules. He was telling official lies, party lies."

"According to party rules."

"Yes, not just little lies, very big, very dishonest lies."

Someone joined the trio at the next table and Talbot recognized the Italian counselor.

"It won't be easy, all this?" she asked. "Not so easy?"

"No, not too easy, but it doesn't matter. What about you? Why does this matter to you?"

"Why does it matter? Why do you always want to know more, you diplomats? What is there to ask? I am trying to be helpful, to be honest, that is all."

The Italian counselor saw her and came to greet them, Nicola first, then Talbot, who stood up. He wore thick glasses and had a bony head. He seemed to be apologizing about something. He looked a little like a giant grasshopper, Nicola said after he went away, the way Stravinsky had looked when she saw him once in Venice.

"What was that about?" Talbot asked.

"He said he was sorry for what happened last night."

"You had another argument with Malfatti?"

"An argument, yes, a very stupid argument about the money Mrs. Harcourt owes me."

Finally he understood. "For Christ's sake—"

"Not for Christ's sake," she said angrily, "not for Malfatti's sake or these stupid people. For my sake, for my fifteen hundred shillings. At the Iraqi reception I went up to her, I told her I was waiting, that my gardener was waiting, the man with the truck was waiting, that we had bills to pay and I wanted my money. She said I was insulting and would not talk to me. Then Malfatti came and said I was very wrong to do that, to embarrass her like that. Malfatti said that! I don't care. Do you think I care?"

"No, I know you don't care."

"And you don't care either." Her voice was suddenly very loud and the Italians at the next table looked at them.

"I do care, sure. I'll talk to her. But tell me what you started to tell me."

She looked at him blankly. "What did I start to tell you?"

"Why all this matters to you, these papers Major Jama had, everything else."

"Why should I explain? Why do you keep asking? I don't have to explain myself, never. Never to tell things about myself, what I do or why, never, not even with Seretti. In something like this you should never have to explain, just do it. So I did it."

"So don't explain, just tell me why it's so important."

"Because I know. Because my feelings tell me, my intuition, that is all, the way I feel. If they attack Ethiopia, it will all end in nothing. The Russians know this, too, so they will wait, like the jackals, like the jackals in the Serengeti, waiting for the buffalo or the lion to die. They will follow in the distance, waiting. But this is half my country. The Russians, the official Russians, I hate, the Ethiopians, the Amhara, I hate, I despise. So someone must do something, so I decided. Don't ask me anything else. If you feel something is right, do it, not talk about it. No more questions."

She picked up her glass and looked at the quartet on the tennis court, pretending to follow the game.

"Talk about arrogant," Talbot said.

Her chin lifted defiantly as she turned. "About what I believe is right, yes. Yes, I am arrogant. The difference is you are arrogant about everything, everything under the sun, cynical, always cynical, always even with little things, little crazy things you don't care about and aren't important, and that is very stupid."

"*Cynical?* Me? Wait a minute—"

"Yes, it is true. Yes, but no more, no more explaining, please. Finished."

They drank their soda and Nicola signed the chit. They left by the side entrance. She preferred to take a taxi back to the guesthouse. They found one and Talbot put her in it.

"It's important, what we talked about, all of it," she said from the back seat. "You'll make sure the papers are taken care of, the right people see them?"

"I'll make sure."

"Good. And don't worry so much about what people say of me, please."

As the taxi drove away he wondered if the argument with Nicola at the Iraqi reception was what Julia had called him about last night. He drove back to his villa and in the rear study began to type out a draft telegram to Washington, reporting the contents of the ministry of defense documents. Twice the telephone rang but he didn't answer. Probably Julia. If you could only find a way to keep the goddamned women out of it, he thought as he climbed the stairs an hour later, diplomatic life might be a little easier for everyone.

CHAPTER SEVEN

Cuckolds and
Confusion

"He has sullenly opposed any military relationship with Jubba," said DeGroot, vigorously strolling the carpet in front of Harcourt's desk, a copy of Talbot's six-page draft cable in his hand. "Now, at that very moment when Washington has Jubba's request for defensive weapons under active consideration and a decision seems imminent, he presents us with *this* amazing document."

He paused to put on his reading glasses and rustle again through the typed pages as Harcourt and Whittington watched. Harcourt had asked Whittington to join them to discuss Talbot's draft. His sources worried them; he had been curiously vague as to how the ministry of defense documents had come into his hands.

"I am not suspicious by nature," DeGroot continued, "yet when I read these pages detailing a plot of such Machiavellian complexity, what am I to think? Where, I am forced to ask myself, did his information come from?"

He held the cable toward them with a flourish.

"Precisely the question," Harcourt said cautiously from behind his desk.

"Precisely," DeGroot said, resuming his stroll. "On the basis of this elaborately detailed information, he would have us believe the Jubba government has been secretly preparing for war with Ethiopia—"

"One of his points, yes," Harcourt said.

"He would suggest the request for defensive arms is nothing but a ruse devised by a nation about to invade its neighbor."

"So it would seem."

"And eager for that reason to lure U.S. military and political resources to its side in its quarrel with Moscow and Ethiopia." He looked at Whittington, slumped deep in his chair, his cheek against his freckled fist. "Is that not a fair summation of his closing arguments?"

Whittington stirred and vaguely nodded. "I suppose so."

"So the thrust of these ministry of defense documents seems clear, does it not, their purpose to frustrate any military assistance agreement between our two countries. That seems to me the obvious conclusion."

"I would say so, yes," Harcourt said, looking at the final pages of his own copy.

"My incredulity aroused," DeGroot continued, "I sought to give more particular focus to my doubts, to identify the source of these sinister revelations. It was then I recalled that point Talbot has made so often in the past. You will recall it, I'm sure."

"Which point is that?"

"That nothing of consequence happens in this country unless the Soviets are agreeable to it."

Harcourt looked at Whittington. "Is that a fair assessment?"

"More or less, yes. But—"

"If I may." DeGroot lifted a warning finger. "Let me reacquaint you with his argument." He brought a tissue page from the folder he carried under his arm.

"I quote Mr. Talbot: 'In 1969 Moscow benefited from, if not sponsored, the coup which brought down the parliamentary government and resulted in a so-called scientific socialist state based on the Soviet model. In due course the Soviets indoctrinated the military, co-opted the security apparatus and certain ministries, politicized the civil service and the youth, and controlled the media, all of which ultimately created a xenophobic little garrison state which sees itself surrounded on all sides by reactionary enemies led by international imperialism.' "

Harcourt's troubled eyes were on the page in DeGroot's hand; it resembled those copies kept in Talbot's missing chron file.

"I know the argument," said Whittington unhappily.

"What I would suggest to you," DeGroot said, "is that if all this is true, then might not the Soviets themselves be responsible for the ministry of defense documents, and, if so, for the contents and conclusions of Talbot's most remarkable telegram. Sotto voce, of course. Would that not follow?"

No flicker of light dawned in Harcourt's hazy blue eyes. "Sotto voce? I don't quite see what you're saying."

"Then permit me to clarify. Would it not be a particularly adroit maneuver on the part of our duplicitous Soviet colleagues, faced as they are with the president's secret intentions of reducing his ties to Moscow and turning to the West, to cast *doubts* on the president's motives? Would they not attempt to frustrate that plan by maligning the president's purpose?"

Whittington, wearied by DeGroot's tiresome locutions, nodded in assent. "Soviet disinformation, you mean? Could be."

"I see, yes," Harcourt said.

"You may both recall," DeGroot said quickly, "the country team meeting following Talbot's return from leave when you mentioned the tracts dispersed in the middle of the night from a speeding automobile. At the time, he suggested he discuss the matter with Mr. Luttak at the Soviet embassy. Our response at the time was immediate and unequivocal. He was told the matter would not be discussed. You will recall, I'm sure."

Another nod from Harcourt. "I remember, yes."

DeGroot reopened his portfolio. "Whereupon, two weeks later, he drafted a telegram which he submitted to me regarding the matter of the tracts. In it he described a conversation he had with Mr. Luttak on the very same subject." He produced another paper from the folder. "As the subject of the tracts had become of such small moment at the time, I didn't approve the cable immediately but put it aside. I did however inquire as to where the conversation had taken place."

"Why would that matter?" Harcourt asked.

"He was told he was not to go to the Soviet embassy, that he was not to raise this subject with Luttak."

"Oh, yes, of course."

"He assured me he had met Luttak at a reception, a Czech reception, I believe, and that it was Luttak who raised the matter on his own initiative. Being preoccupied with other matters I decided not to pursue the subject. However, at a later date while examining the logs of the motor pool in connection with another problem, that of an embasssy driver inclined to malinger when dispatched on routine errands, I discovered that an embassy car with driver had in fact driven Talbot to the Soviet embassy on the morning of the twenty-third. There it remained for two hours."

A quick rustle of papers as DeGroot consulted his dossier. Harcourt looked on in bewilderment.

"This was a few days prior to the Czech reception mentioned in his draft cable, the twenty-sixth. On the date of his visit to the Soviet embassy, the afternoon of the twenty-third, an embassy car was dispatched from the chancellory to Talbot's residence to deliver the text of a speech made at Burao by a government minister, a speech Talbot was most eager to acquire. This I've learned from the USIS local who procured it for him. This is the text referred to in Talbot's telegram of the twenty-sixth and which he claimed had been brought to his attention *for the first time* by Mr. Luttak three days later."

Triumphantly DeGroot laid the thermofax copies of the motor pool logs and the statement by the USIS local on Harcourt's desk.

"It's all very confusing," Harcourt said.

"Oh, but it needn't be confusing at all. How can this be? How can he pretend Mr. Luttak brought to his attention a speech he'd obtained through USIS three days earlier? Is he prescient, confused, or deviously untruthful?"

Harcourt pretended an interest in the copies; DeGroot, he decided, was a very disingenuous man.

"Let's talk about his cable," suggested Whittington.

"*Ah,* yes, the cable. Quite so. The cable listing equipment and

ordnance transfers to the Western Jubbaland Liberation Front."
He held it out again, shaking the loose pages. "Is it not possible
to imagine that this information whose source Talbot is so unwilling to reveal was provided by the same source, the source Talbot met secretly with at the Soviet embassy on the twenty-third?"

Harcourt looked up in surprise. "Mr. Luttak?"

"Mr. Luttak, yes," DeGroot said with a smile. "Mr. Luttak and
the Soviet embassy."

"Not impossible, no," Whittington said. The same idea had occurred to him. "Or someone else on the Soviets' behalf."

"I see our minds are working in concert," DeGroot said. "Let me
add that when I again questioned Talbot this morning about his
source, he was even more ambiguously vague than during our
earlier conversations. We exchanged words. He refused to discuss
the matter further. His sources were his own, he insisted, his manner suspiciously defensive in the extreme. I sought to contain his
temper. He hurled the draft on my desk and stormed out. I regret
to say that he has made communication between us impossible on
this subject. I can excuse policy disagreements but not misconduct.
Should someone else wish to question him further, then I shall remain mute. But until he has clarified this matter, I cannot in good
conscience permit the telegram to go forward."

Harcourt looked at the telegram DeGroot was placing on his
desk. DeGroot moved to the window.

"I am not one to miscalculate motives," he was saying. "When
someone tells me they wish an alternative to their present misery,
I do not look behind that wish for some diabolical purpose. I assess
what I see and judge accordingly. A nation about to invade its
neighbor? A nation preparing for war?" He moved the heavy drapes
aside. "And what do I see when I look down into the street? I see
a nomad with his milk jug, a natural dignity in his gait; I see a
donkey pulling a sand cart. I see a ten-year-old Fiat taxi broken
down in the street, I hear the klaxon of horns from the roundabout,
drivers anxious to get on about the manifold business of another
peaceful day."

Embarrassed, Harcourt listened; that awful voice, that awful face,
that ridiculous gourdlike figure. Unscrupulous, yes, a monumental
bore, all very true, but still he pitied him.

"When I am told that they wish an alternative to their present humiliation, American armaments to protect their naked frontiers against an Ethiopian army ten times their numbers now being re-equipped by Russian armaments, how can I believe otherwise?"

"You have a point," Harcourt said, wishing to bring the discussion to an end. "I'd like to think about this a little more, maybe talk to Logan about it. Now I'd like to talk to Whit for a minute."

DeGroot smiled forgivingly and left by the side door.

Whittington didn't move.

"What do you think?" Harcourt asked.

"He has a good point. Logan's stuff looks awfully good. Almost too good."

"You think then it's accurate?"

"I hate to say it, but I suspect it just might be."

"For the reasons DeGroot said, a Soviet attempt to frustrate our giving them military assistance?"

"He made an interesting case."

Harcourt reflected for a minute. "Could you pass it through your own channels?"

"I might if I knew more about the source."

"What about the radio frequencies, the communications aspect. Couldn't they be monitored?"

Whittington picked up the telegram and turned to the second page. "We could give it a try, but whether Nairobi could pick them up or not I don't know."

"What about satellite?" He knew very little about that side of it. He'd had the briefing at Langley, and Whittington's people had been awfully kind, but he wasn't quite sure what he was supposed to do with all that very technical information. Feel reassured, he supposed.

Whittington nodded. "It'll take a little time but maybe I can get something out."

"It might be better," Harcourt said with some delicacy, "if you were to keep this between us."

"I will. I'll tell you something, too, just between us."

"Please."

"DeGroot's a very difficult man."

Harcourt nodded. "I'm aware of that."

"It's not that hard for me, I can roll with the punches, but he makes it awfully tough for my commo people and he's got it in for Logan, too. With my people it's all these goddamn rules and regulations he keeps grinding out. This isn't Paris, it's not London."

"I'm aware of that, too, but I don't quite know what to do about it." Harcourt felt only exhaustion.

Fifteen minutes later he called Talbot up from the first floor and told him he was undecided as to what to do with his cable. He would consider it for a few days; then they would discuss it again.

□ □ □

Talbot was still brooding about Harcourt's decision seven hours later, a little unsteadily, too, after a long afternoon drinking alone in his back garden. Now he'd taken refuge with Lindy at a rear table in the shadows of the terrace at the Giubba Hotel. The Egyptian ambassador was giving a reception for the newly arrived Egyptian military attaché.

Harcourt had been nice about it, a little embarrassed, too, unable to look Talbot in the eye as he communicated his decision to reflect upon his cable for a few days. Those were his own ghastly words, "communicate," and "reflect upon." Hollow drum that he was, the poor old bugger was beginning to quiver with DeGroot's incomprehensible noises from next door. But he hadn't hinted that Talbot had lied about his talk with Lev Luttak, as DeGroot had during their ugly exchange in his office, hadn't even mentioned it, in fact. Harcourt had been a gentleman about it, but that had gotten under his skin, too. Always the gentleman, wasn't he, even now as he stood talking with Ambassador d'Aubert in the hotel ballroom under the largest crystal chandelier. Maybe Nicola was right. He wondered where she was. Wore his clothes well, Harcourt did, tonight like any other night, fluent in a few languages, well read, well traveled, a gracious host and obliging conversationalist, wrote lucidly if a little sterilely, but had his opinions, no matter if not a goddamned one of them mattered here.

"Say something," Lindy said, moving her hand in front of his eyes. "Stop thinking about it. Relax for a change."

"I am relaxed."

"You don't act like it."

"I'm not acting, I'm thinking."

"About what?"

"Europe, where I wish to hell I was."

Where Harcourt should be too, consul general in Barcelona, maybe, get his books bound cheap. In Europe he'd managed well enough, living idly on his intellectual and cultural capital, sustained by civilized traditions within civilized frontiers, a man of sensitivity and style, everyone would say, there being so little else to say that wasn't terribly unkind, and he was, as he'd told Nicola, a terribly decent man. His politics, or what he called by that name, weren't politics so much as the indulgence of taste and sensibility, the luxury of the unpolitical. Nothing he'd ever done had required him to think; there were always others who did that sort of thing— overseers, trusts, investment houses, management groups, policy think tanks, the NSC, or some other gentlemen's corporate collective, private sector or public—and when there weren't there were standards of taste and tradition to guide by, as surely as they guided the vulgar American sightseers he and his wife would have so ridiculed as they passed them with their cameras and guidebooks in the narrow streets of Rome, Paris, or Barcelona.

"No one spoke up," he said, rousing himself. "That's what pisses me off. Not even our old buddy Whittington."

"Give him time. You should have told them where the documents came from. I told you Whit said they looked pretty good."

"He didn't tell me that."

"Where'd they come from?"

"An old black woman in Hamar Weyne."

A slight breeze moved through the trees behind them. Harcourt was still in conversation with Ambassador d'Aubert. He wondered what they were talking about.

"It takes something like this to find out how many people you don't know," he heard Lindy say after a minute, chin on her hand as she watched the large crowd milling about inside under the brightly lit chandeliers.

"You know enough," Talbot said. "Don't rush things."

"I just met a few."

"The rest are ding-a-lings."

"You said that before."

"I know I said it before."

"You didn't explain what it meant. Ding-a-lings meaning precisely what?"

"Meaning precisely people who don't talk, just make polite little noises, like Harcourt and d'Aubert."

"Where'd it come from?"

They watched Bashford-Jones leave the dining room, look around the terrace, and move toward them.

"Washington. I was over on the Hill once, visiting a friend, a congressional fellow. We were talking to this congressman, a bell rings, the guy jumps up and goes running off for a vote on the floor. He hits the door, his mouth is already moving, salivating, all juiced up."

She thought for a minute. "Pavlovian."

The Italian military attaché was with d'Aubert and Harcourt: "Three Blind Mice." They signaled Malfatti to join them: now "The Old Woman Who Lived in a Shoe."

Bashford-Jones sauntered up. "Hello, Lindy. Not interrupting anything, am I?"

"Hi. No, nothing. Sit down."

"I can't stay." He put his hand on Talbot's shoulder. "Look here, I hate to be a bore but we're desperate. You must help us. Julia thought you might. Said you were at loose ends."

"Very loose," Lindy said.

"Help how?"

"Our play. The hero walked off; didn't like the costumes. Come read for us, would you? He might just be tempted back if he thought we'd found someone else."

"Not in good voice these days, Nick. Ask Lindy."

Bashford-Jones looked down fondly. "We'd dearly love to have her, but she's not quite what we're looking for. If I'd known, I'd have found a part for her. Sorry. I wouldn't mind having her at all." He put his hand on Lindy's shoulder. "No offense."

"No offense taken." Lindy moved her head away. The hand remained on her shoulder. After a minute the long fingers began to move, independent of anything he was saying, as he lightly caressed her neck and shoulders.

"Just a few readings. You might like it. Do give it some thought, would you? If there were anyone else, I wouldn't ask, but there's no one I can think of. You wouldn't know anyone, would you, Lindy?"

"Not offhand."

"We may have to call the whole bloody thing off."

"I do know someone, come to think of it," Talbot said after a minute, "someone who might be interested."

"Do you? Who?"

"Might need a bit of coaxing, a little shy about it."

"About what."

"His theatrical experience."

"You know someone here who's been in theater?"

"I wouldn't want it to get around. Quite a bit of experience, actually. After that he got into broadcasting. A VOA announcer."

"How fascinating." Bashford-Jones came around Lindy's chair and sat down. "What kind of experience?"

"Gilbert and Sullivan, D'Oyly Carte, Shakespeare, too. He played Osric."

"Oh, Jesus," Lindy said.

"Sorry?"

"He's shy about it, doesn't want it mentioned," Talbot said.

"Oh, I see." Bashford-Jones looked at Lindy. "He is all right, isn't he?"

"Logan? I think he's all right."

"I think he was in the chorus line," Talbot said. "Did some Shaw, Oscar Wilde, led the great Lowell Thomas trek across Antarctica, gave dramatic readings to the penguins—'Queue up, queue up, little gentlemen, standing room only.' I wouldn't mention it, though. A little shy about it."

"I certainly won't." Bashford-Jones looked at Lindy in confusion. "Precisely whom are we talking about?"

"DeGroot."

"The man's been in the theater? You're joking."

"Not in the slightest."

"I can't imagine it."

"Neither can I, but it's true. First thing he asked was about a theater group. Under your hat, OK, but I think he'd go for it. Shaw's right up his alley."

"You are serious."

"Absolutely serious."

"Then I shall certainly talk to him. I think I saw him a few minutes ago." He got up. "Thanks. I'll have a go at it."

Bashford-Jones went away.

"What did you say that for?" Lindy said.

"It was your idea."

"Oh, God, here we go again. It certainly wasn't my idea."

"Osric, isn't that what you said?" Osric had been her name for DeGroot since the second week, when she'd sat in on a country team meeting and listened to one of his more servile court performances, dancing poor Harcourt on.

"That's what I said but it was a joke."

"It's no joke."

"I hope you didn't tell anyone about Osric. Now you're going to get me in trouble again."

"When did I ever get you in trouble?"

"Taking the reading file down to the first floor. Then that time at your house and you left the pot there on the table when Whit dropped by."

"He didn't know. Anyway, Osric was good. Don't be self-conscious about it. Why are you always so self-conscious?"

"I'm not self-conscious? When was I ever self-conscious?"

"You're always self-conscious when you think someone's going to say something, self-conscious about everything, everything except that goddamned Dartmouth T-shirt."

"I'm not, and will you *please* stop talking about that Dartmouth T-shirt. My God, I wish I'd never worn the damned thing."

"You did wear it, that's the whole point."

"I didn't wear it, it was just something I grabbed out of a drawer."

"Women don't just grab something out of a drawer. I happen to know that for a scientific fact. If they're wearing something, there's a reason for it."

"Oh, God." She put her face in her hands.

"Don't be self-conscious." He put his hand on her shoulder re-assuringly. "I'm not going to pry, just ask very quietly, like a gen-tleman. What's he do, anyway? Make birch-bark canoes?"

"I told you once, I've said all I'm going to say."

"It'll be our secret. What about 'Save the Whales'? Am I close?"

"I told you—"

"OK, no more questions. Anyway, you were right about De-Groot. He used to be in theater, studied drama in Sydney, did after-dinner theater on the *Queen of Tasmania* out of Sydney, the MC for the teatime amateur hours when people put on funny hats. His wife played the piano in the first-class lounge. You think I'm joking, don't you?"

"I don't think you're joking, I think you're smashed."

"I may be a little, but I'm not joking. Anyway, if I get you in trouble, I'll get you out again."

"I'll bet."

Julia joined them, looking very elegant in a long rose-colored gown. "May I?" She sat down, crossing her legs to show a slim calf and ankle. "What a nice man Dr. Greevy is. Why is it I haven't met him before?"

"He's shy, only comes out at night, like the bats and the sea turtles. He doesn't live here, only visits. Right, Lindy?"

Julia looked at Lindy, then at Talbot. "Have you been drinking again?"

"Again? What's again? Hasn't everyone?"

"Excuse me," Lindy said, getting up.

"Don't go, Lindy. I'll never find you in this goddamn mob."

"I'll be back. If I'm not, ring a bell. I saw Whit come in." She smiled at Julia and turned away.

"You have been drinking."

"A little." He watched Lindy crossing the terrace, slim and awk-ward suddenly in her white dress as she moved between two groups of Libyans and Yemenis, both a head shorter.

"You look terrible."

He looked back at Julia. Her shoulders were bare but her for-bidden white fruits were modestly sheathed, just a peep of cleavage showing. "Sorry."

"I said you look terrible."

"Do I." He rubbed his face. "I did shave, didn't I? I don't feel terrible."

"Lyman told me you had some sort of disagreement today. He was very upset about it, that it had to happen. He said it was about a telegram. That's a little silly, isn't it, being upset about a telegram?"

"That's probably true."

"All he said was DeGroot took one position, you took another."

"Who?"

"DeGroot."

"Who?"

She looked at him sadly. "You're being very foolish."

"Am I? No more than anyone else. Everyone except Nick, who's casting a play. This is a real play. I mean you sit in the audience and you know it's a play. I mean the people on the stage are impostors, but you look in the playbill and you know who they are. Then you clap afterwards and everyone takes off the costume and you have a party."

"Just the costume?" she said. "I've heard about his odd parties."

"So have I."

"I'm sure you have."

"I've also been to his parties."

"Oh, have you?"

"I have and speaking personally I can say that being at one of his parties is much better than hearing about them or peeping at them through a cocktail party keyhole. If you've been to his parties, you don't have to talk about them. That's true of life in general, isn't it? I mean being there in the flesh, so to speak, you don't have to peek through the keyhole. That's the trouble with embassy life, isn't it? You spend all your life peeping through other people's keyholes. By the way, speaking of parties, peepholes, and impostors, did you know Shaughnessy was in Lisbon?"

"No, I didn't."

"He's in Lisbon, playing a juvenile lead."

"Did you drive?" She opened her purse and took out her cigarettes. "If you did, Lyman and I can take you home. Then we'll get an embassy driver to drive your car. Please don't act like this."

"Lindy's with me. The way I'm acting has nothing to do with

anyone. Did I ever tell you about the talk I had with Mrs. Peterson at the pool and she called me Sneaky Pete? Did I ever tell you about that?"

"No, you didn't, but you're not making any sense at all. I think I'd better get Lindy. You've had too much to drink."

"We've already talked about that. Let's talk about something else."

She sat looking out across the terrace. "You make it very difficult for Lyman."

"That's not my intention, my intentions are decent and honorable. I don't like to see decent and honorable men being victimized by scoundrels."

"I'm sure. He depends upon you much more than you know. DeGroot knows that and is very envious, jealous in fact."

"Who?"

"Would you please stop this."

"I hope I'm not interrupting anything," a voice said. Agnes Firthdale moved to the table, massive and invincible in a gold-and-black gown. Talbot got up and held out a chair. "My dear, you look stunning. Mr. Talbot, we haven't seen you."

"We were just gossiping," Julia said sweetly.

Agnes Firthdale sat down heavily and came bluntly to the point. "Mr. Talbot, I've just had the most extraordinary conversation with Mr. DeGroot. I wonder if you might reassure me regarding a fact of recent local history about which there would seem to be some confusion."

"Who?"

"Mr. DeGroot."

Talbot saw Julia take a small breath. Agnes Firthdale wasn't a woman to be trifled with.

He offered her a cigarette. She put her own brocaded cigarette pack aside and accepted one of his. "I doubt the confusion is yours, Mrs. Firthdale. You are the least confused person in this whole goddamned town. You know who you are, why you are here, and you have a keen nose for impostors. Now then, which particular fraud are we unmasking?"

"I have no idea what you are talking about. May I please continue?"

"It would please the court if you would."

"Court? You've been drinking, I see."

"On the remote American frontier, Mrs. Firthdale, sobriety in the courtroom was the ambition, not the practice."

"No? Why was that?"

"The local saloon was often the venue."

"Of course, yes—"

"As it is with diplomats, cocktail party diplomats. When you go to America, visit Dodge City by all means, Mrs. Firthdale. Have you ever heard of Greywolf in the Yukon Territory? A distant cousin of mine once panned gold there. I think that's where I'm going to retire, Greywolf in the Yukon."

"Are you? Interesting name. Now, if you'll only hear me out and tell me how wrong *that* gentleman was."

Julia listened for a minute then excused herself.

Lindy and Whittington were standing just inside the door with Hafiz Ghanim, Talbot's Egyptian friend.

Julia drew Lindy aside. "He seems to have found his sea legs again," she said, looking toward Talbot still listening to Agnes Firthdale, "but you can never tell. I want to tell you how pleased I am he's taken you under his wing. Lyman and I were both worried about your finding your way, especially since Whittington told us how difficult it was for you. It is hard for someone new, isn't it? I know Logan feels the same. We've often talked about what we could do, the three of us. What a lovely dress." She took her arm. "Have you met Mrs. d'Aubert? Her daughter's visiting her now. I think she's about your age." She stopped. "You do speak French, don't you?"

"Not much, I'm afraid. It's a little rusty. Even worse now that I've started Italian."

"But you'll manage, I'm sure you will."

So she'd let Julia lead her away to stand there like a simpleton as Madame d'Aubert, her daughter, Julia, and Harcourt chattered away in French. After ten minutes she slipped away, her face burning. No one seemed to notice; no one had even seen her go.

"I could understand just about everything they were saying at first," she told Talbot as they walked down the steps and out into the dark garden, "but then my French got mixed up with my Italian and I was nowhere. I felt like an idiot."

"Just the little bones in the soup. Let's go dance; it's nightclub time."

"What bones in the soup?"

"I'll tell you on the dance floor. Come on, before the tables are filled."

"OK, but no funny business tonight, all right?"

"No funny business. How close was 'Save the Whales'? Pretty close or not."

"For the last time, he was just a friend of a friend; that's all he ever was. Now will you please stop asking? *Please.*"

□ □ □

Talbot's cable remained in Harcourt's safe for five days. After mulling over the impasse and consulting with Whittington, Harcourt found a solution to satisfy DeGroot's suspicions and finesse Talbot's refusal to name his source. The cable would be prefixed:

> The following ministry of defense documents have come into the possession of the embassy, which cannot vouch for their authenticity. We note with alarm as well as a great deal of suspicion, however, the allegation of a direct link between the Jubba national army and the Western Jubbaland Liberation Front, which the Jubba government has insisted is a wholly autonomous unit it does not supply and over which it exercises no command or control.

After an additional day spent negotiating changes to the preface to meet DeGroot's objections—"alarm" was dropped, "grave doubts" replaced "suspicion," and a final paragraph was added to describe a Soviet disinformation effort of the previous year, all of which made the whole thing even more murky—the telegram was sent forward.

How anyone in Washington could make heads or tails of this latest product from Harcourt's fudge-and-fuddle factory (with De-Groot now drafting most of the cables, they all seemed equally incomprehensible), Talbot didn't know, but four days later it didn't matter. The State Department telegram arrived announcing Washington had decided to supply Jubba with defensive weapons.

DeGroot was at the UN offices the morning it arrived, and Harcourt, with no one else to share the news with, eagerly summoned Talbot from the first floor.

"It just arrived, just this minute," he whispered, passing the cable to Talbot after he quickly shut the door. "Absolutely incredible— to have come so far in so short a time. Absolutely incredible."

From the passionate flush on his face and his furtiveness in shutting the door, Talbot concluded Harcourt's news was personal, that he'd come into some great good fortune, perhaps the inheritance of his doddering great-uncle who spent his summers in Newport and his winters at the Mill Reef Club in Antigua. He glanced at the cable's subject line, saw the ominous warning, and quickly read the following paragraph. He couldn't believe it. He read it a second time to make sure Miss Virgil or a communicator in Washington hadn't made some grotesque mistake. But there was no mistake. Washington was now willing to arm an already dangerously armed little nation eager for any pretext to invade its disintegrating neighbor to recover its lost territories. Only a lunatic could have made such a decision.

"Surprised? I thought you'd be. Incredible." Harcourt, slightly breathless, eased himself behind his desk, still similing deliriously.

"*Incredible?* Jesus, they're crazy, all of them. They're out of their minds. Why now? Don't they know what the hell's going on?"

Harcourt, disappointed, believed the answer transcendentally self-evident, like all State Department edicts. Of course State knew what was going on. He was more worried about his growing responsibilities. A military survey team would be sent, so would an AID survey mission. The cable instructed him to ask for an appointment with the president for approval to send a U.S. military attaché. He was a little perplexed, however, by the precise meaning of the term "defensive arms." He wasn't a military man. As dubious of Talbot's suggestions as he was bewildered by his reaction, he quickly rang up Whittington to supply the answer. His hand was shaking as he returned the phone to the cradle.

A loud knock came from the door of the adjacent office, and a moment later a jubilant DeGroot joined them. "I have heard from

Miss Virgil in the message center that a most interesting cable has arrived. May I share the welcome news?"

Talbot barely had the courage to turn to look at that simpering face. As he watched DeGroot study the text, he was surprised by his composure. Whittington, too, seemed unimpressed. In answer to Harcourt's question about defensive weapons, he quickly scrawled a large arrow on Harcourt's desk pad. "Which way is that pointing?" He held up the pad.

"North?" Harcourt peered at it, unable to see the point.

Whittington tore off the page and dropped it on Harcourt's desk. "Now which way?"

Again he studied it. "Any way. North, south, east—"

"That's what any military man will tell you."

"And why the expeditious arrival of a military attaché is so necessary," DeGroot said solemnly.

During the days that followed, while Harcourt and DeGroot struggled to interpret the absurdly long lists of Jubba's armament needs being passed to the embassy by the ministry of defense—tanks, TOW anti-tank weapons, aircraft, artillery, hundreds of thousands of small arms—Talbot's incredulity turned to skepticism.

The State Department cables being received every day contained no suggestion that these were the kinds of armaments the U.S. intended to supply. In fact there seemed to be much less to the offer than first met the eye. It certainly wasn't the blank check Harcourt, DeGroot, or the Jubba military assumed, but instead a kind of vague promissory note so ambiguous in its conditions that Talbot couldn't understand why Washington had agreed to it. There was little or no money to fund Jubba's purchases, no willingness on Washington's part to supply major items—no tanks, no aircraft, no anti-tank or even antiaircraft guns—and no suggestion of a formal military assistance agreement. The only military equipment Washington was willing to discuss—discuss but not yet supply—was so pitifully meager and inconsequential that Jubba could have obtained the items more quickly through European commercial sources.

In addition, Jubba's arms needs were to be met in consultation with the British, French, and West Germans, as sure a case of bureaucratic tap dancing as he'd ever heard.

By the time the decision was made public a week later, he'd

grown suspicious. Washington's decision, he decided, was either a carelessly cavalier gesture or a fraudulent one, however seriously Harcourt, DeGroot, and others tried to dignify it. The logic, however, still eluded him. Not until two days after Washington's decision had been made public was it suddenly, ridiculously clear.

He was sitting in his back garden that afternoon waiting for Lindy and studying the wording of the formal announcement in the USIS wireless file. A shaggy young baboon, escaped from a young Jubba boy who'd been trying to sell him on the beach, was sitting high in the laurel tree, the frayed rope leash still hanging from his neck. The boy had returned with the gate guard and some mangoes. Talbot put the wireless file aside as he watched the two finally lure the baboon down. The animal dropped to the flagstones and the boy jumped on the rope leash and the gate guard led the two away.

A minute or two later, as he was looking skyward searching for the vapor trail of a high-flying MIG-21 whose sonic boom had reverberated through the silence a moment before, the answer came suddenly crashing down on him out of the tranquil afternoon blue. Stunned, he sat there dizzily for a few minutes after the shock had passed. *Was he crazy or were they?* No, he wasn't crazy; they were. After the giddiness passed, all of the separate pieces fitted together. He went inside and sat down at his typewriter, appalled he hadn't recognized the truth that first morning in Harcourt's office.

The defensive arms decision was a pathetically hollow gesture, intended not to arm Jubba but to warn Moscow that if it continued to expand its presence in Ethiopia the U.S. was ready to assist Jubba and frustrate the consolidation of Soviet power and influence in the Horn. Jubba itself meant no more to Washington than it had six or twelve months earlier. Jubba's camel ports, its wandering nomads, and the unjust occupation of grazing lands in Ethiopia had nothing to do with the decision, an abstract equation calculated by Washington's geopolitical strategists who at present didn't intend to give Jubba new or improved weapons systems of any kind. The purpose was to tell Moscow that it couldn't continue as the patron of both Jubba and Ethiopia but would have to make a choice. It would either have to restrain its ambitions in its new client state, Ethiopia, or, with the U.S. now willing to replace the Soviets as arms supplier to Jubba, lose its special relationship with its client state here. Moscow couldn't continue to be the sole Superpower benefactor of both these ancient enemies to the exclusion of the U.S., but would have to choose one or the other.

While the decision might have seemed brilliant in the abstract, a cunning piece of statecraft designed by some NSC policy committee to frustrate the growing Soviet influence in the region, it was grotesquely mistaken when brought to life in the sand and thorn of East Africa where two ancient enemies faced each other across a dangerously volatile frontier. The mere promise of U.S. arms would be enough to convince the Jubba president that he could now achieve his old dream of recovering the lost territories: if the Russians continued to refuse to help him, the Americans would.

So Talbot at last understood. Given the congressional mood and the mood of the country—"too much in Vietnam's shadow," Minzonni had said that day at Nicola's villa, quite correctly—Washington's decision was nothing more than a feeble threat sent to Moscow by a cuckolded husband with neither the will nor the resources to back it up:

> If you take my estranged wife as your new mistress, I will take your present mistress as my new wife. Think about this, Muscovite Lover.
>
> /s/ Z. Brzezinski, Outraged Husband and King of
> the Polish Gypsies.

He knew then his long-suppressed telegram or any series of telegrams on the question wouldn't have affected the imbeciles in Washington who'd made the decision. Ignorant of the complexities of Jubba's dangerously pathological little case, their single obsession was the consolidation of Soviet influence in the Horn.

He felt vindicated. Once the policy abstraction was clear in his own mind, he tucked his typewritten notes away in the copy of his forgotten little monograph *The Politics of Bipolarity* in the desk drawer—forgotten, that is, until that moment in the garden twenty minutes earlier. It was an interesting formulation. Having scaled the policy heights, he looked down and wondered, Zeus-like, how it would all play out.

Harcourt didn't quite understand all this. DeGroot pretended not to. Talbot's comments in the country team meeting that Thursday seemed even more gnomic than usual. What did he mean, Washington's decision was intended for Moscow, not Jubba, that its intentions were better fulfilled by the public announcement than its implementation?

Talbot explained that it was little more than a formal diplomatic warning to Moscow. The facts were clear and so was the conclusion: The Soviet-trained and equipped Jubba army was already the best in East Africa; with Ethiopia in disintegration across the border, whom were they arming against?

"The answer's obvious," he said, "no one. Look at the cables. Washington doesn't intend to give Jubba all these weapons they're asking for, they never did."

"Didn't intend to?" DeGroot interjected. "But of course they intend to. The cables have been absolutely clear. We have been instructed to proceed with discussions—"

"Sure, but that's the tactic. 'Instructed to proceed,' which means to talk, not deliver. Washington has no intention of delivering, not now, anyway."

"What then *is* the purpose?" Harcourt asked, unconvinced.

"To warn Moscow that it can't continue to ignore the U.S. in pursuing a *Pax Sovietica* in the Horn. That it either has to cut back its role with its new client state, Ethiopia, or, with us now willing to replace the Soviets in supplying arms to Jubba, lose its client state here."

"A remarkably obscure message, to say the least," DeGroot observed loftily to Harcourt.

"Not obscure at all, not to Moscow. The strategy's obvious. We're warning Moscow it can't continue to be the military and political patron of both these countries. It will have to choose one or the other."

"You've talked to Mr. Luttak?" Harcourt asked, worried.

Good God, Talbot thought, looking to Whittington for support. The CIA station chief was looking on curiously, but if he had any ideas on the subject, they weren't obvious to Talbot. "No, not Luttak. Why should I talk to Luttak? The purpose is obvious, the decision's a political decision pure and simple, intended to warn Moscow that the Soviets aren't the only ones who can arm Jubba, that they're not the only power brokers here in the Horn."

DeGroot laughed. "If I laugh a little too heartily, I hope I may be forgiven." His remarks were again for Harcourt, not Talbot, whom he hadn't addressed directly since their argument over the disputed cable. "Of course it is a political decision. Are not all our decisions, in one way or another, political decisions? Even the sugar on our morning breakfast tables, is it not there because of a political decision, made either on behalf of the cane growers of Louisiana or those of the Philippines?"

That idea had never occurred to Harcourt. Slowly he nodded his assent, remembering the gray sugar sometimes spilled on his breakfast table—Soviet sugar, someone had said. "That's quite true, yes."

"As for Mr. Talbot's suggestions, I can only say that while I am not unfamiliar with the language of realpolitik, I find its locutions as inappropriate to the African veld as I would find, say, the Teutonic melancholy of Wagner, of whom I am also fond, but only as a diversion and then in the solitude of my study. I might also point out that the recent signing of the Soviet-Ethiopian arms agreement means that the Ethiopians will soon be armed far beyond the measure of the Jubba—"

"Will be but aren't now," Talbot said, "but the Ethiopians haven't been responsible for the problems along the border, the Jubba have."

Whatever Harcourt's haplessness as a political analyst, Talbot knew he was too socially acute not to know DeGroot was a fool; why didn't he say something?

"Would some prefer that we wait until Ethiopia is armed far beyond the measure of their bitter enemies, as Talbot characterized them?" DeGroot asked pleasantly. "That to me indicates a certain lack of prescience. I am grateful Washington isn't so shortsighted." He looked at Kinkaid. "You were about to say something?"

Kinkaid, the Africanist, agreed with DeGroot. Washington had held out its hand to an impoverished nation, and the people were responding. A dozen people had stopped him on the street since the decision had been made public to shake his hand.

Harcourt listened with growing gratification. He'd noticed the same reaction as his Chrysler passed up and down the Lido road. He'd even had his chauffeur drive more slowly, the better to let them express their gratitude. He finally moved the meeting on, disappointed in Talbot's cynicism.

"I really hate to see him playing dog-in-the-manger," he said afterwards to DeGroot.

"I'm not surprised, knowing his biases," DeGroot said, sighing sadly. "He has, after two years, a certain career investment in the status quo, as I said."

Changing circumstance had brought the two men closer, not yet confidants but clearly collaborators. The British and French ambassadors were partly responsible for luring Harcourt out of semi-retirement; both Firthdale and d'Aubert preferred to deal with Harcourt rather than DeGroot in carrying out their instructions. Washington was orchestrating the fictitious arms decision and was in close contact with London, Paris, and Bonn; but the British, French, and West German ambassadors also had their minor roles, as did Harcourt. Meetings were held at least twice a week, luncheons were rotated between the various residences, today the French residence, next Tuesday, the West German. For Harcourt, doors were now being opened in the capital that had never been opened before—at the ministry of finance, at the ministry of agriculture, the ministry of fisheries, all of whom had presented hastily drafted agendas for the second AID survey team, soon to arrive.

At the little luncheons at the various residences, one topic of sly conjecture was the behavior of Georgi Kirillan, the Soviet ambassador, conspicuously missing from a few national-day receptions the past week; secretly they enjoyed his distress as he had once enjoyed theirs.

Talbot wasn't privy to these consultations, nor was he invited to the various ministries.

DeGroot had made sure he wasn't lacking for work. He'd given him a list of reporting subjects of great urgency, including the extent of Libyan and Iraqi financing for various local projects, petroleum imports, the effect of Soviet barter arrangements on the Jubban economy. All of these, DeGroot explained in his brief memo, would be of great interest to the AID team in planning its own local projects. This kept him well insulated from the hustle and bustle of the executive offices but not as busy as DeGroot had anticipated.

Lindy told him that morning that his forgotten cable on the Jubba arms transfer to the Liberation Front had paid unexpected dividends. The radio frequencies he'd reported were being monitored from Nairobi and by satellite. The resupply was continuing, additional rations, more ordnance, more regular army officers detached to the WJLF cadres, who were now marauding at will within the Ethiopian frontier. Whittington, for reasons of his own, didn't include the ELINT intercepts on the green-jacketed CIA morning reading board, and this made Talbot suspicious of him as well.

□ □ □

In transit, Hubert Wingate preferred to travel light, semi-incognito as it were, unencumbered by protocol or haberdashery. His battered briefcase held two clean shirts, a necktie, two cameras, three detective novels—two in French, the pages still uncut—a wad of Egyptian bank notes bound by a rubber band, and a bottle of cheap Indian gin with numerous misprints on the silver label. He'd bought it in Port Sudan, the last bottle on the shelf of the dirty little Bengali shop near the port. The misprints should have warned him. Inspecting it suspiciously on deck of the Egyptian ship in the flooding light of the Red Sea, he thought he'd spied a few pepper-like grains in the bottom. At Djibouti, the grains seemed to have taken on legs and locomotion, incubated by the boiling heat of the Red Sea. A day later they'd vanished and he'd acquired a few gastric pains, but gin was gin; he'd filtered the remainder through the finest Irish linen handkerchief, borrowed from Philomena Heflin, a fellow passenger.

He stood now at the rail, wearing a wash-worn poplin shirt with short sleeves, wrinkled gray tropical trousers, and high-topped brown suede shoes. He was in his late thirties but looked older; his porcine face, weathered for two years by the sun and wind of the Chadian wasteland and his recent steamer excursion up the Nile from Abu Simbel, was the color of walnut, like an old plank found on the beach after the winter storms. The untidy brown hair was shaggy on the sides but beginning to thin above the high forehead hidden under the brim of the straw hat, tattered by sun and wind, as dry as winter corn, given to him a year earlier by an Egyptian cotton farmer after his pet baboon had ravaged his old bush hat.

Silently he studied the harsh littoral as the ship moved through the battering sea toward the harbor, searching for the red-tiled roof of the embassy he thought he'd once visited years ago. If he had, he couldn't remember now.

Older ambassadors nearing retirement were the worst by far. Harcourt, he judged, was one of those; so were their wives, a generally disagreeable lot. They looked upon staff as their dragomen. Under diplomatic cover as consul-cum-admin officer, he'd done it all: issued visas, closed caskets, opened small posts in the torrid Middle Eastern or African backwaters, inventoried dirty laundry left in our hotel rooms by expatriate drug freaks or septuagenarian American tourists, notarized the death certificates, found the embalmer, sealed the caskets, and maintained the services for hot water, air conditioning, and liquor for an overindulged American staff.

He saw nothing he recognized along the shore, an icy salt-white glare in the undulating heat. He'd probably been thinking about Tripoli or Tunis. The cigar clamped in the corner of his mouth had long grown sour, and he flung it into the sea. He hoisted the briefcase to the rail and searched for his last package of duty-free Dunhills. A second of dizziness; too much sun brought on vertigo. From the shadows of the passageway the thin-faced Egyptian purser stood watching. On someone's payroll, Wingate decided as he mopped his neck and looked away across the sun-shattered water.

He hadn't shaved that morning, preferring to wait until the last hour before disembarking. Now, hand lifted to wipe the dripping sweat from his jaws, he felt the stubble and remembered his shaving kit still in his cabin. If, in transit, he often seemed the anonymous tourist, during his stops he treated himself in that high style to which, at post, only ambassadors and chiefs of mission were accustomed. In Cairo, he had soaked the dust of the Sahel from his bones in a princely tub in the third-most expensive suite at the Semiramis overlooking the Nile, had dressed for dinner, hired a car and driver, and tipped everyone lavishly upon his departure, but had no regrets about the violation of regulations that made it possible. It was an honest laissez-faire Egyptian pound he was returning to them, liberated from a bankrupt economy. He'd bought the black market pounds with American dollars from an Iranian in the gold souk. His suitcases he had shipped ahead by airfreight with his rifle and Beretta over-and-under twelve-gauge, although he knew from the post report hunting was forbidden.

As he entered the passageway, he met Philomena Heflin and her sister, two British women returning to Kenya from their holiday in Cyprus. Both were carrying small valises for an afternoon ashore.

"I'll get them for you," he volunteered. "Be right with you, ladies."

"I think we can manage," replied the older woman coolly. The memory of the previous night still burned indelibly in those brisk eyes. As she moved past, he flattened himself against the bulkhead to give them room, making sure they didn't touch. Her sister, a statuesque younger woman with blond hair and eyes as pale as blue mist, smiled self-consciously, remembering the previous evening, too, but didn't look at Wingate. She wore a pale flowered dress and leather flats. Lovely name, Philomena. The previous evening they had drunk gin until midnight. After the Greek radio operator had brought his old gramophone out on the cabin deck they'd danced a bit. Wingate had danced her down the passageway to the cabin vacated by the radioman. Philomena was agreeable, but her sister wasn't yet sleeping and had opened her cabin door to find them there, Wingate's knee pressed deeply between her thighs, she riding it, like her sixteen-hand bay gelding at the gymkhana at Nairobi.

He watched their silhouettes against the light flooding from the deck, drawing the younger woman's strong legs in bold outline against the tissue of her skirt. There, where his very knee had been. *Philomena Heflin. Lovely . . .* His groin ached as he turned back along the passageway. Whittington had a young assistant, he recalled. What was her name? Young, someone said, twenty-six or so, first tour. As he entered the small cabin, his companion during the voyage was standing unsteadily near the bunk in his underwear, a flyswatter in his hand as he waited for one of the droning flies stalking him south from Alexandria to settle within reach. One sock was on, loose on his yellow birdlike ankle. He was an elderly French archeologist returning to his duties in the Malagasy Republic after his hospitalization in Paris for jaundice and dysentery.

"Ready to let it loose, are you, Alphonse?" Wingate's words were carelessly slurred, syllables the old Frenchman's fragile academic ear couldn't disentangle. His name wasn't Alphonse. The two had

been waging an off-and-on language war for three days now. Never
gifted in languages, Wingate spoke a little kitchen Arabic, some
Swahili, and a demotic French, vulgarly inlaid with the patois of
the East Asian and African bush. It was a dialect understood by
minor government clerks and officials he cajoled, threatened, and
bribed to assure the continuity of embassy or consulate services,
and among whom, unlike the embassy or consular society he served,
he was often accepted as an equal. But the stubborn old Frenchman
refused to dignify Wingate's barbaric African or Laotian French
and answered instead in pedantic English, learned in London half
a century ago at the school for Oriental studies. Wingate retaliated
with an idiomatic quickness of his own. Someone passing in the corridor might have thought them both mad.

A small man, as intense as a bird, he was still enervated, believ-
ing his fever had returned. During the day he would lie in his bunk
with his books, monographs, and the flyswatter, killing everything
within reach. He blamed the flies for his illness. Two flies copulat-
ing filled him with disgust. He would smash them all the more savagely. By the time the ship reached Djibouti, his consciousness had
shrunk to a pair of cunning fly specks in the watery blue irises. He
seemed unaware of the magenta of the sea, the windless skies overhead, or the bright sunlight on the passenger deck, conscious only
of those magnified surfaces of wood grain, deck seams, paint flakes,
and citrus seeds left by the sticky-handed children of an Arab couple where the breeding, swarming, loathsome flies hovered.

Hearing the anchor chair rattling out of its locker, Wingate left
without saying goodbye.

It was filthy hot. The passengers would be taken ashore by the
lighter that bobbed in a steep violent sea below the final step of the
gangway, rising and falling a full six feet with each lift of the savage swell. The wind had risen.

Too dangerous for the women, Wingate decided.

Canvas fenders were lowered over the side, but the lighter crashed
against the steel plates and backed off, bobbing up and down. A
pair of lines was lowered from the cargo boom to bring up a boatswain's chair from the lighter—well, not quite a boatswain's chair
but an elongated, very decrepit-looking reed basket, its bottom gray
and watermarked. As it reached the deck and the deckhands

steadied it, the few passengers looked on, frightened. No one stepped forward.

Hubert Wingate showed them the way. He dropped his briefcase in first, then climbed aboard fecklessly. The boom lifted, swung him precariously out over the churning sea, then steadied as the hawsers brought the basket under control. The winch rumbled forward, the basket dropped, but the lighter plunged away on the waves. The winch stopped, the basket hovered, the lighter drifted back into position. Wingate released his hold on the rope to signal the deck hands and sneak a look at Philomena Heflin, eager for an encouraging smile. She was braced against the wind, legs apart. *And smiling, too. Beautiful figure, lovely name, Philomena.* As the basket shifted and spun, his knees, braced against the side of the basket, gave way and he was suddenly weightless. The winch recovered the slack, the basket jerked skyward, Wingate dropped seaward. The rotted fibers in the bottom opened like a trapdoor, and he fell like a stone the final fifteen feet to the lighter, crumpled to the midship planking with a harsh grunt, and fell backwards into the bilge, his head just missing the engine. His briefcase joined him an instant later and spilled open across his unconscious figure, splashing cameras, detective novels, and a brisk flutter of Egyptian bank notes to the slopping bilge. The tattered straw hat was carried away by the sea.

□ □ □

Talbot lifted his head from the thundering sea near the reef and went under again, the rope still in his hands. At that moment he saw a nude sea nymph undulating seductively toward him through his watery glass. As the seething white foam slid away he scrambled onto the safety of the reef before the next comber broke, and as he did a slim hand steadied him. Lindy crouched on the reef wearing a white bikini he'd never seen before. The metamorphosis surprised him; either she'd put on weight or his binocular vision hadn't recovered from the magnification of the sea.

"Thank God. We've been looking all over for you."

He was out of breath. "What are you doing out here?"

"Whit sent me. The foreign ministry called. The president's coming back from Jidda a day early, three o'clock at the airport." Her left hand and arm modestly shielded the top of her halter.

"Where's the ambassador?"

"Down at Afgoi. DeGroot's with him. We can't reach them. Don't get mad. Whit said I'd better find you, so I did."

He stripped off the mask, tank, and weight belt and put them in the rubber dinghy on the western side of the reef.

"Why the hell didn't Whittington go?"

"He can't. He's at the embassy trying to get a charter flight to Nairobi for Wingate."

He turned. "He's here? Wingate's here?"

"His ship came about one. He's at the Italian hospital. He fell, broke his leg and collarbone, maybe a concussion."

He stood looking at her. "Wingate gets off the ship and breaks his goddamn leg. I don't believe it."

"He didn't get off, he fell off."

"Fell off? I still don't believe it." He retrieved the nylon rope from the other side of the reef, put on another mask and a snorkel tube, and waded out into open water, pulling the raft behind him. "How the hell can you fall off a ship and not just drown?"

"He fell through the basket and into the lighter. Are you going to swim or row?"

"Swim. It's quicker. What was he doing in a basket?"

"Getting off the ship. It's almost three now. Don't swim too fast." She waded after him. After the sea the water felt as warm as bouillon. It was a long swim, and the last twenty yards she was ahead of him. She lay stretched out on the sand as he carried the rubber raft up through the dunes and across the tarmac to the iron gate. A few minutes later she followed with his tank and mask. "That's awfully stupid," she said, "swimming alone like that."

"Why didn't you come like I asked? Did you bring a car?"

"It's on the way. I'd already made plans, I told you."

As they went up the drive, the guard handed Talbot an envelope. He stuffed it in his waistband. Her motorbike leaned against the wall where she'd left it.

"What was that?"

"I don't know, an invitation to a hanging. I've got to change."

He quickly rinsed the equipment under the shower behind the stucco wash house and stored it in the back of the garage and ran upstairs. It was five minutes to three. He slipped on his wristwatch, grabbed shorts and a shirt from the drawer and a coat from the closet, glanced under it to make sure the trousers were there, all neat and tidy, picked up his shoes, and ran back downstairs barefooted. The gate was opening for the embassy sedan, just arriving.

"Hop in, we'll just make it."

"*Me?* I'm not even dressed."

"Neither am I. Hold these." He gave her his clothes and shoes, took back the shirt, and opened the door. "Where are your clothes?"

"The Meltons'. We were sunbathing in the garden."

"You and Dr. Melton? Jesus, I'd never have thought it."

"With *her,* dummy, just the two of us."

But as they reached the turnoff to the Melton villa on the Lido road, they heard the drone of the plane. The driver pointed out to sea, and Talbot told him to drive on.

"Let me out, I can't go out there like this."

"We don't have time, you can stay in the car. Here, take my sunglasses; they'll help. Now hide behind the coat while I change, like a good little girl."

They sped on to the airport as Talbot struggled out of his damp trunks. "Just keep looking out the window, all right? That's it." He put on his shorts and then pulled the trousers from the hanger. "That's a nice bathing suit. How come I haven't seen it?" He rolled back to put on his pants.

"It's a long and embarrassing story."

"I won't be if you're not. What happened?"

"I wore it in Bermuda once and there were some English guys on the beach and I swore I'd never wear it again."

"What kind of English guys? Rockers?" He looked down suddenly. "Jesus Christ, this isn't right."

"What?"

He sat up. "These are the wrong goddamn pants."

"How can you tell?"

"They don't fit. They're my old white ducks, the ones without any cuffs, about two yards too short."

"No one's going to notice."

"What do you mean no one's going to notice? I look like Buster Keaton. Where the hell are my socks?"

He sat up, looking under him for his socks, the car careened around the corner onto the airport road and he fell against her and lay there, face nuzzling her damp hair: "You're really irresistible today, Miss Bermuda; but as your mother used to say, Is this the time or the place?"

"Stop horsing around." She twisted away. "People are looking."

Two black Fiats sped past filled with Jubba officials.

"What people? Where the hell are my socks?"

He couldn't find his socks; neither could she. He slipped on his loafers.

The diplomatic cars had already arrived, lined up near the protocol gate as they sped in. On the tarmac inside, the chiefs of mission were milling around in the scorching sun. At the head of the line in front of the Jubba ministers stood a dozen schoolgirls from one of the communes, all dressed in tan skirts and white blouses, all carrying flowers for the president. Two tall Jubba women in long dresses stood near them. The chief of protocol hadn't begun to arrange the queue according to diplomatic rank. Talbot would be assigned the rear, next to the PLO rep and possibly the Vietnamese from Hanoi.

"This is like a bad dream, I can't go out there."

She slumped down in her seat, sliding below the window. "How do you think I feel sitting in the back seat in a wet bikini I should have thrown away years ago."

"You look great; there's nothing wrong with that bikini. All you need's a pair of high heels."

"I should never have worn it. I was *so* stupid."

A few chauffeurs waiting at the fence were watching them. Two passing diplomats looked in the car.

"Who cares. Anyway you've got on sunglasses. I have to walk out there in a pair of baggy white pants and strollers like a goddamn Fire Island clamdigger. I'll get propositioned. I need my sunglasses back."

She took a firm hold on them. "Like hell you do."

Talbot leaned over the front seat. "Kasim, be a sport and lend me your sunglasses."

The driver passed back his wire-rimmed sunglasses.

"Why don't we just leave? So what if no one's here from the embassy?" The 707 was touching down.

"Can't. Dr. Mohammed Hussein's watching us, the bastard. You wouldn't want to get out of the car and wave to him, would you? Cuddle against the fence, wiggle a little. He'll go ballistic, right out of his goddamn underwear. Relax, don't be so self-conscious. Speaking of underwear, did I ever tell you my story about the good doctor?"

"No."

"Remind me to." He slipped on a dark blue linen jacket, but no tie, and combed his hair with Kasim's comb. He waited until the last possible moment.

"Fuck it. If I can't pull this one off my name isn't Fred C. Dobbs or whatever the hell his name is. Did you ever see *The Treasure of the Sierra Madre?* Neither did I."

The door slammed and he was gone.

She waited for a few minutes until he was far away from the car and lifted herself slowly to watch him stroll through the protocol gate. He made his way past the young schoolgirls with their flowers and along the back of the receiving line, shook a few hands, stopped to talk to someone, then to someone else, laughed at something, and then wandered off to stand at the end of the line, the last of the sixteen diplomats who'd come that day, all summoned as unexpectedly as he had been. Firthdale and d'Aubert wore coats and ties, the Russian was dressed in a sport shirt. The Indian and Pakistani ambassadors were more casually dressed. Watching him in the blue jacket, white ducks and sunglasses, she didn't see anything unusual in the way he was dressed. She thought he brought it off pretty well, even after the president stopped to shake his hand, his brown ankles naked as Talbot's above the worn sandals he wore.

As the queue broke up and the diplomats said their farewells, she saw a few Jubba officials from the protocol office looking her way and she felt naked again and slid far down in her seat. She didn't see Dr. Mohammed Hussein's assistant stop Talbot and speak to him, didn't see Talbot wave him away, then wave him away a second time, didn't see the two tall Jubba women march their schoolchildren away in the other direction, avoiding the protocol gate.

Talbot had taken off his coat by the time he reached the car and once inside draped it protectively over her shoulders. She pulled it around her, but only as they were back on the airport road did she finally sit up.

"Thank God that's over. Did anyone say anything?"

"About me? No, a few funny looks, that's all."

"It looked like it went pretty well."

"Well enough. I shouldn't have dragged you out here. I'm sorry."

"I don't mind now. It's over. I feel OK now."

"If anyone asks, I'll explain, OK? Let me do the talking, all right? You were just doing what Whit told you to do, what I asked you to do, OK?"

She looked at him. "What's there to explain?"

"Nothing, that's the point. But just in case. Why don't we stop at the Meltons' house and pick up your clothes, then we'll get dressed and go someplace, have dinner."

She was still watching him. "C'mon now, something did happen, didn't it?"

"Something that hasn't anything to do with you. What about tonight?"

She was still suspicious. "I guess so, sure, if you'd like to."

Dr. Mohammed Hussein's formal complaint, telephoned by his assistant from the office of protocol at five that afternoon, concerned not only Talbot's appearance but the semi-nude young woman waiting in the back of the embassy car whose appearance and conduct, like Talbot's, had insulted the dignity of the presidency, the officials of the revolutionary council, the ministry of foreign affairs, the diplomatic corps, and the Jubba children and womanhood assembled on the tarmac that afternoon.

Harcourt received the call at the residence. DeGroot was still there. An official apology was demanded. Harcourt, very upset, immediately telephoned Talbot to learn what had happened. He listened a little incredulously to his story and, questions of protocol being infinitely simpler than policy abstractions, instructed him to draft an apology.

"Would you *please* tell me what's going on?" Lindy pleaded as Talbot hung up the phone. "Something happened. I know it did."

"I will, just give me a few minutes. Our evening's still on, but first I've got to type something out. Would you call the duty officer and have the duty secretary brought in?"

"What is it? I can type it."

"OK, but don't say anything, just type. I'll explain later."

He dictated and she typed, puzzled at first, then angry, finally resigned. "It's *so* stupid," she said as she rolled the draft from the carriage, "so utterly stupid. I knew you'd get me in trouble, I just knew it."

"You're not in any trouble; just relax. You're in the clear. Don't worry."

Pleased by the decisiveness of his decision, Harcourt met Talbot at the front door and was gratified by the propriety of his dress—white shirt, tie and jacket, polished banker's brogans. Lindy waited anxiously in the embassy car. Talbot listened silently while Harcourt and DeGroot fussed over the draft. After the final wording was agreed upon, he continued to the embassy, where Lindy typed it as an embassy note, delivered in two copies.

The embassy car drove them to the foreign ministry on the airport road. Again Lindy waited in the car. Except for the security guards and the night watchmen and Dr. Mohammed Hussein's office on the second floor, the building was empty. It was six thirty. He carried the note to the second floor, where Dr. Mohammed Hussein was waiting, up the long double staircase with the red carpet, but even after he'd finished his climb and was walking down the red-carpeted corridor, he was still miraculously ascendent, rising beyond the roof and the tiny black sedan waiting in the drive, over the airport road, and there at the far end the little white Crusader castle where Harcourt and DeGroot were waiting, rising over the port and the shrinking Soviet freighters lying at anchor like toy boats—still ascendent as he sat waiting in the silent perfumed anteroom of Dr. Mohammed Hussein's office for fifty-five minutes, his mind soaring in pure sunlight now, high above the earth-entangled purple twilight gathering beyond the window, and where at some final oxygen-free altitude he seemed to drift as weightless as during those dark soundings beyond the reef, tumbling buoyantly along the curve of the earth toward the western horizon and the not-yet-extinguished sun whose queer but unmistakable smile told him that what had happened that day was no longer of the slightest consequence to him, no more than his past had been or what might happen tomorrow or next week or next month might be. None of it any longer mattered.

When Dr. Mohammed Hussein's aide came and said his presence was no longer required, it was all so utterly and absurdly insignificant he could even bow graciously and flatter him with an obsequious smile.

"It was most unfortunate," DeGroot said from his armchair in the Harcourts' living room, still nursing his whiskey. "It clearly showed his contempt for our host."

"At the very least it was thoughtless," Harcourt said.

"Thoughtless, yes, but that itself clearly betrays his opinion. He is one of those young men who find Europe more congenial, you see. I remember his remarks the first time we met. Miss Dowling, I'm sure, was an innocent victim, as he said."

"I'm sure she was." After a minute Harcourt added, "I'm a little worried about him."

"Myself as well. I've noticed a certain lethargy, a certain loss of mental energy. He's been slow in his completion of the economic reports."

"Then there's the drinking, too."

"The drinking, yes. So I've heard."

Julia sat listening, pretending to read a book as she sat on the couch. She'd come in from the study thinking DeGroot gone, but there he sat, still sipping the whiskey her husband had given him twenty minutes earlier. Lyman would want a refill, she was sure, but wouldn't say so if that meant replenishing DeGroot's glass. She had refilled her own glass, but, in punishment, had said nothing to Lyman or his guest. His self-restraint surprised her. She wondered which would yield first, his wanting a drink or his hope that De-Groot would leave.

"A third year here is often difficult," DeGroot said. "I suggested to him a month ago that if he felt as he did perhaps he should consider another post."

"Did you?"

"He didn't mention it to you? To you, perhaps?" He looked at Julia, legs crossed, swinging one plump calf back and forth.

She looked up. "Sorry."

He repeated the question.

"He hasn't said anything to me, not at all." But then, deciding to break the impasse, she added, "But I would be very very disappointed if circumstance forced him to leave. Excuse me, but I think I'd better tell Kasim about dinner."

She picked up her drink and left the room.

"Kasim is his name?" DeGroot asked, watching her through the door.

"Yes, Kasim."

DeGroot studied the lights in the harbor through the french doors. "I've heard he's very much the noctambulist, young Talbot."

"Excuse me?"

"A prowler of the night. Like his late departed friend Mr. Shaughnessy. Deviously lustful, I'm told. Shaughnessy, I mean. Mr. Talbot's affairs are none of my own. I'm now persuaded Shaughnessy was much the weaker of the two."

Harcourt said nothing.

"This is very fine malt whiskey. Civilization, my grandfather once said, was built not only upon the division of labor but malt whiskey as well."

"Did he now?" Harcourt said, exhausted by his pretense. "I think I'll have another," he said, rising. "Would you join me?"

"Delighted," DeGroot said, holding out his glass.

Julia was waiting in the kitchen, leaning against the counter as Harcourt came in shamefaced.

"I was wondering who would yield first," she said contemptuously, watching Harcourt fill the two glasses. "I see you did. It serves you right, you coward, serves both of you right. I think sometimes you deserve each other."

"That's unfair," he cried instantly, "totally unfair." His shaking hand spilled the whiskey.

"Is it? Then do something about it. Do something before you both drive me out of my mind."

She went out into the rear garden, slamming the door behind her.

◻ ◻ ◻

They had dinner at Juliano's and then returned to Talbot's villa and sat in the back garden drinking and sharing a joint as they listened to Jackson Browne on the phonograph through the open windows in the study. It was an almost windless night. After the horn sounded at the front gate and Talbot ambled off to see who it was and send them away, Lindy quickly lit the two insect candles and got the aerosol bug can from the kitchen to douse the smoky air near the two lounge chairs. By the time Talbot led a tired and confused Whittington back along the passageway she was in her chair again, nonchalantly smoking a Winston.

Whittington, just come from talking to Harcourt and DeGroot, was bewildered and hurt. Talbot's thoughtlessness had embarrassed him, damaged the station, but worst of all brought Lindy a notoriety she'd be unable to live down. It might even have compromised her future effectiveness just at a time when he was thinking of giving her operational responsibilities. Harcourt had been very upset, DeGroot, too. They'd had a long talk, the three of them, as to what to do.

"How to 'mitigate' the repercussions, like DeGroot said," Whittington rumbled on. "It really worries me."

"That's rubbish," Talbot said, "just bullshit."

Whittington creaked forward in his chair. "Listen, Logan, you may not give a damn, but it's Lindy I'm thinking about, Lindy and the embassy—"

"No, you're not. Those goddamned idiots up there don't know what happened, you don't either."

"I know what they told me." Whittington looked at Lindy and then back at Talbot. "You mean there's more? So what didn't you tell them? C'mon, spill it—all of it."

Talbot described the incident from beginning to end and explained his problem with Dr. Mohammed Hussein. You had to look behind the event to understand, and no one except him knew the whole story. Harcourt didn't know the whole story and even if he tried to explain wouldn't have understood; his featherweight keel didn't drag that far down. All he was worried about was the reaction at the foreign ministry; but the foreign ministry or, more specifically, Dr. Mohammed Hussein, had wanted nothing more than to humiliate him. So Talbot had obliged, had delivered the note personally, just as Dr. Hussein had insisted; the note had been accepted, and so the matter was closed—at least until Dr. Mohammed Hussein saw his chance to blindside him again.

"OK, but what about Lindy?"

"What about Lindy? Nothing about Lindy, zilch."

Her name hadn't been mentioned. No one except Harcourt and DeGroot even knew who she was. At the airport the assistant from the protocol office at the foreign ministry had thought she was some blond Swedish woman from the UN, just as he'd told Talbot on the tarmac—a young woman he'd known Talbot was once friendly with.

"What blond Swedish woman?" Whittington asked.

"It doesn't matter. She's gone now. The guy doesn't know anything; he's just another frightened little foreign ministry frog crawler who doesn't jump until Dr. Mohammed Hussein gooses him, and at the airport Hussein did. Hussein doesn't have a clue who Lindy is either. He's been reading some out-of-date shit from NSS surveillance about me and a blond Swedish girl and it all happened last year. One of the diplomats in the receiving line made the same mistake."

"You're sure about that?"

"Sure I'm sure. You're dead wrong if you think Lindy was compromised."

Lindy was a little disappointed when she heard Talbot say this but she said nothing.

In conclusion Talbot said Whittington might as well blame the whole thing on that idiot Wingate, since it was because of his accident on the ship that Talbot had been summoned to the airport in the first place.

"Yeah, I'm sorry about Wingate, I really am." He looked at Lindy, then at Talbot. "Is all this on the level?"

"Sure it's on the level. What's wrong with Wingate?"

He didn't have a concussion, just a few broken bones; Peterson had chartered a Cessna and they were flying him to Nairobi in the morning.

After a drink, Whittington left, mildly reassured. Twenty minutes later the phone rang. Talbot didn't answer it. Ten minutes later it rang again and he still didn't answer it. Lindy, thinking it might ring again, said she thought she'd better go. Talbot persuaded her to take a walk on the beach.

They left the front gate and walked through the dunes to the strand, stood there a few minutes, and strolled on to the north. The tide was out, and she took off her sandals as they drifted down the glistening slope of sand, looking up at the stars. A long line of ghostly breakers curled against the reef. They walked north again.

"You're all right, aren't you?" she said.

"I'm OK."

"You're weaving a little."

"I'm looking at the stars."

"Not still stoned, I hope."

"I never get stoned. Have you ever seen me stoned?"

"No, I guess not. Fast talkers never get stoned."

They walked in silence. "Are you chilly?" he asked.

"No, it's nice. The wind is warm." She continued walking, her arms held out to feel the wind moving from the south. He took her right arm.

"You're chilly. Your skin. I can feel it."

He slipped his fingers down her arm and took her cold hand in his and stopped, chafing it between his own, and then took the other hand and held them both together.

"Your hands are warm." She looked up at the sky, her head back. There was no moon, no light, just the distant lights of the UN beach club, forgotten now, like the faint running lights of the ships beyond the breakwater. They turned away, her hand in his as they moved toward the north where no lights were, just the desolation of the dunes and the rocks where a few grottoes lay. Still holding his hand, she led him down into the surf and waded, her arm extended. "It's cooler than I thought, but nice."

"Don't get cold," he said.

"Why?"

"I don't want to go back. Here, let me take those."

"I can carry them."

He took her shoes under his arm, and she moved back up the beach again toward him and then her footsteps began to slow and she finally stopped. "The cliffs are ahead," she said.

"There's no one there."

She turned and looked back, both hands gathering her hair behind her neck. She took his hand again and they stood together looking back. They had outwalked the lights, the telephone in the study, the black Fiats, the anxious gateman, the music from the Lido nightclub, and now stood alone gazing back at the lights of the corniche.

"You ready to go back?" she said.

"Not yet. How about you?"

"It's up to you."

"Let's lie down and count the stars. That's what our counselor used to have us do in camp at night, shut the little bastards up."

"You're still weaving."

"I always do that when I navigate by the stars."

"I don't see where you put all that stuff."

"It's out of my system. I'm cold stone sober."

He turned and she let him lead her up the beach until they found a stretch of firm warm sand above the reach of the waves and below the dune grass and the cockleburs. He pulled off his shirt and spread it out. She sat down and lay back and they looked up at the stars. After a few minutes she said, "You know what my roommate said once?"

"I don't want to hear about roommates."

" 'I think I'm very much more aware of the universe than the universe is aware of me.' "

"That doesn't interest me."

"That's what she said once when we were lying out like this. You know, September, your freshman year when everyone's trying to figure everyone else out, maybe impress a little. She was from Cleveland, a philosophy major. Then she switched to journalism and transferred to Columbia."

"Who cares?"

"I was just telling you."

"She didn't know much about the universe. The night has a thousand eyes. A couple of them are watching you right now."

"Are they? She was really full of it. So are you."

"No, I'm not." He reached over. "Here's a little space walker, come down to introduce himself." He walked his fingers up her midriff and began to unbutton her white blouse.

"Sneaky little fellow, isn't he? You finished counting already?"

"Ten minutes ago."

"How serious are you?"

"You asked me that last week. Dead serious. I've always been serious, from that first day."

He kissed her and opened her blouse and she took his hand. "You tried that once, remember?"

"That was on the dance floor, doesn't count." He kissed her again and then a second time and after a few minutes she didn't move his hand away, her face still against his as he finally took off her blouse and her bra, their lips, tongues, and hands still busy, hers as much as his, and five minutes later they were both undressed, both naked, both wet and slippery as frogs, and finally with no place left to explore he slipped his fingers up her damp thighs, but they closed, the muscles taut; but then as the moments passed she relaxed and came alive again, her skin vibrant, every membrane flushed and trembling, her eyes closed, holding him so tightly, so pathetically he could barely breathe or move, but move he did and entered her as massively as a flood tide after weeks of dizzy failure.

He felt her gently shaking him and he awoke and sat up.

"I fell asleep," he said stupidly, looking around.

"Did you? I didn't." She was lying on his shirt, hands under her head, wearing briefs and a bra.

He looked at his watch. It was after one o'clock. "Do you know what time it is?" He began to dress.

"More or less."

"What were you doing?"

"Nothing, just lying here."

"Not counting the stars, I hope."

"No, why?"

"Dangerous stuff. Empties your mind like the goddamn brine tank in the morgue. Why I didn't go to med school." He sat up again groggily, still looking around. "A woman shouldn't do that."

"What, look at the stars?"

"Bad for her psyche, all that cosmic plasma swimming around, the shit your eyeballs are made of, your goddamn blood turns to frosty pudding, all that hydrogen gas." He leaned over her again. "Didn't you know that?"

Her eyes were wide open. "I didn't notice you were so dead."

"Me? I was scared shitless."

"What, lying on your back?"

"Lying on your back, hiding out in your storm cellar, all creatures great and small. I'm a burrower at heart."

She pushed him away and sat up. "I thought you were serious." She pulled on her skirt.

"I was serious. Didn't you think I was serious?"

"Then maybe, not now." She finished dressing. "You didn't even say anything. You're weird sometimes."

"I'm not weird, I'm a diplomat, a professional nerd. I thought everyone knew that." He helped her up and they walked together down the long dark beach. "What did you want me to say?" She didn't answer, and he didn't let go of her hand until they crossed the tarmac to the front gate.

"My mouth's dry," she said. "I need something to drink before I go."

"Go where? You're not going anyplace."

"Sure I am."

"You can't drive that motorbike back now; it's after one o'clock. You're going to stay here."

"Where, in the guest bedroom?"

"Not in the guest bedroom, for Christ's sake. What's wrong?"

"Nothing's wrong. I won't have any problems driving back. If you're so worried, I can call an embassy car."

"I don't understand you."

"Good, maybe that makes us even."

"You're not going to drive that goddamned motorbike back. I forbid it; it's against the house rules. *Verboten!* Lock the gate,

Mohammed! Lock it up! *Schnell! Achtung!*" The gate guard looked at him, confused, still holding the gates open. Talbot went down the drive and closed them himself.

"Are you teaching him German or something?" She let him take her arm and lead her up the steps.

"Stress. I've got a recessive little Nazi gene running around loose somewhere."

"You are weird."

"That's sorority talk. I don't listen to sorority talk."

They went upstairs. "I'll have to get up awfully early. Whit said the plane leaves at six. Do you have an alarm clock?"

"Only dairy farmers and mailmen have alarm clocks."

She stopped in the hall. "I'm serious, Logan."

"So am I. Out of the sack at five for my three-mile run. Even fix your breakfast for you, how's that?"

"I'll bet. I think you're still stoned."

She took a shower, and when she finished, the bedroom was dark. She groped her way to the bed and joined him under the sheet, still warm from the shower, and for a few minutes it was all right again.

"Thought I was sleeping again, didn't you?" he said, bringing her against him.

"I wasn't sure."

They lay there for a few minutes. "What did you mean, weird? You want me to play you the mandolin in the moonlight, something like that?"

"I don't want you to play anything, just be yourself. I wasn't sure whether you were serious or not. I'm still not."

"Those are parts of a woman's mind I don't know anything about."

"How come?"

"They're not the friendly parts."

"I should have figured. And don't care, either."

He lifted himself. "I didn't say that. Did I say that?"

She pushed him down again. "Why is it you always think you can get away with so much?"

"Me?"

"You. You always think you can, you and no one else. Why do you?"

"Is that what you think?" She lay against him silently. "Listen, let me explain something, all right? We'll begin at the beginning. It's important and I want you to understand. OK? Are you listening?"

"No—"

"When I was at camp, aged thirteen, I had this girl counselor. No, not that camp, another camp. No, it began before that. Six, I would say. Maybe seven. I guess it was seven. I had this Irish governess, maybe twenty-two or twenty-three—"

"Please be quiet."

"I'm trying to explain. Twenty-three, maybe. Not a governess but she worked for my grandparents. Sometimes on weekends when my parents were away she took care of me. She liked to give me sponge baths and rubdowns afterwards—alcohol, witch hazel, wintergreen sometimes. Talk about infantile sexuality. You ever had a squirt of wintergreen on your little spigot, age seven? I mean that makes a stand-up man of you pretty goddamned fast, makes a burrower of you the rest of your life—"

Her arm was lifted and she'd put her fingers over his mouth. "No more talking, please. You'll talk yourself right out of my life."

CHAPTER EIGHT
The Imaginary War

A little after midnight under a quarter moon dimmed by a veil of transparent clouds the armed laagers at Umcit, Ghaleb Uen, and Uebi Hamar were stirring. Lanterns moved back and forth in the darkness, trucks arrived, were loaded with dark smoky men, and moved out. By two o'clock the columns began their journey, dust lifting in the desert wind as they moved toward the Ethiopian frontier, past the old adobe buildings at Dusa Mareb, where the grizzled Jubba trader and the Galla woman, wakened by the rumbling of armored personnel carriers and trucks, watched sleepily from the doorway of the dark tea shop.

"*Ilah mahaddi,*" he called to the two Jubba drivers who'd been asleep in the racks in the rear. "Thanks to God."

The Ethiopian police posts inside the frontier had been silently disarmed just after midnight by infiltrators from the Western Jubbaland Liberation Front on forage these past weeks, striking from the north. They stood silently on the track as the Soviet-made T-34 tanks rumbled northward, followed by BTR-152 armored personnel carriers and trucks filled with regulars, riflemen with automatic weapons, each carrying 400 rounds, grenadiers with BM-21 rocket launchers, machine-gun squads with belt-linked 7.62 ammo, radio-men, and behind them the mortarmen.

A few old tribal chieftains, in confinement on the coast all these years, had been brought up in the trucks and disembarked at the police posts, some with knives in their belts, some carrying old carbines.

Detached from Colonel Mahmoud's G-2 staff at Bulet Uen, Major Jama stood in the darkness near his waiting Land-Rover watching as they embraced the tattered WSLF guerrillas. Muddled old hypocrites, he thought, old courtesans brought out of retirement for this farce in the occupied territories. They were passing out small flags of the sort schoolchildren carried. In his own pistol case was an old Colt revolver given him six weeks earlier by his great-uncle, Mohammed Ghalib Mahmoud, almost eighty and dying at Sheikh. He had given it to Jama and told him that when the Old Man's war began he wanted the revolver to be fired in Western Jubbaland, in the Haud where his camels and his father's camels and his grandfather's before him had foraged in the wet-weather grazing grounds. Jama had said the Old Man was bluffing, what had happened could never be changed. From his sickbed his uncle had given the revolver to Jama's five-year-old son and told him to bury it then, far out in the veld with the bones of the *toumals* who fed on carcasses and unclean meat, that his father had lost his faith.

At the police post one battalion was detached from the brigade moving northwards toward Kebre Dehar and sent to the south to seize the small airstrip under construction near Idole, twenty kilometers inside the border. Jama followed in his army Land-Rover. With him were Lieutenant Samantar, his deputy; a radioman; a rifleman; and a driver. The WJLF guerrillas were already in place along the perimeter of the airfield as the regular troops arrived. Two light-weapons companies dispersed just to the north of the landing field and at dawn commenced the attack. Phosphorous-white tracer fire lit up the dark humps of stone and adobe barracks where the Ethiopians were billeted. Fusillades of automatic weapons fire smashed away doors and windows. Dry grasses near the verges of the field caught fire, and a wooden roof began to burn.

Hearing the gunfire and watching the white tracer filaments arcing across the airfield, Jama turned anxiously and searched the oyster-gray skies to the west for Ethiopian aircraft, summoned from Gode or Kebre Dehar. Asleep in their small barracks and separated from their weapons, the Ethiopians quickly surrendered. A white shirt fluttered through the smoke from the front door of the first barracks; the guns fell silent as the Ethiopians filed out of the buildings, hands raised. Three Ethiopians lay dead inside the first barracks, two in the second. The flames from the burning roof died away, but the dry eucalyptus poles continued to smolder as the prisoners were marched across the airfield. Two frightened cooks hiding in the small mess fifty meters to the rear took to their heels out across the scrub, but they were unarmed and no one followed. A rusty road patrol and a small grader, both painted olive drab, were the only pieces of construction equipment; no aircraft were on the field or in the corrugated sheet-metal hangar. In the barracks armory they found a few dozen American-made M-1 rifles, as dirty as the barracks. The filthy building smelled like the Italian-built felons' prison at Bulah.

Eighteen Ethiopian prisoners were taken, all from an engineering battalion based at Kebre Dehar, 200 kilometers to the northwest. They were laborers, frightened little men with thick callused hands, some in uniform, some in their underwear. They stood in single file, elbows raised, hands locked behind their heads as they were searched one by one and allowed to squat in the growing sunlight on the patch of sand between the Nissen hut that served as a headquarters building and the temporary barracks. They looked on mutely as the Ethiopian flag was lowered from the rusty pole and the flag of Western Jubbaland replaced it. The silence of the ceremony was broken only by the sound of the wind, which had now returned, whispering through the dry grass and across the roof channels of the nearby Nissen hut. Watching and listening, Jama felt no elation, no joy, only uneasiness at a ritual so pathetically meaningless in that vast wind-haunted wasteland. The constant, tireless, invisible voice seemed to be mocking them even now, like the distant cries of the jackals that had followed him as a boy as he'd accompanied his uncle's herds out of the Haud.

The Ethiopians had a single Land-Rover and no trucks. In the back of the corrugated headquarters building was a radio room with a generator-operated radio. Lieutenant Samantar searched for radio codebooks, navigational maps, and message logs from Kebre Dehar. He found nothing, just a few message pads scrawled with Amharic. Under the new egalitarian socialist regime in Addis, the engineering unit was commanded jointly by a lieutenant and a sergeant. The lieutenant was an Amhara, the sergeant a Galla. Jama interrogated them separately in the dusty little office.

A demolition team arrived by truck, prepared to blow up the landing strip, but Jama persuaded the sergeant to drag the disabled construction equipment into place instead, blocking the runway. The WJLF unit that had attacked the airfield had moved on to the small dusty village a few kilometers to the south. He listened uneasily to the desultory gunfire from the south as he interrogated the lieutenant. The engineering group had arrived three weeks ago to enlarge the airstrip, but the equipment that had been promised hadn't arrived. They had no petrol and had received no messages for two weeks. They'd had no warning of the attack. No aircraft were stationed at the field. An operational order from Debre Zeit forbade overnighting at the field because of WJLF raids.

Major Jama asked to talk to the radio operator, but the WJLF corporal returned to report he was missing.

A little before noon Jama and his group left the airfield and drove south. It was July, the season of the *hagaa* and the southwest monsoons. The spring rains that had brought blossoms to the acacias, the crimson flamboyants, and wild petunias of·Western Jubbaland had passed. The vegetation was burned over and barren; dust was everywhere. They drove into a sun-scorched village, a clutter of adobe and low stone buildings along an eroded sand road. A single tabid acacia tree stood in a narrow baked yard in front of the office of the Ethiopian *woreda,* the local administrator. Two dead men in gray police khakis lay in the road just outside the gate. The handful of Ethiopians who lived in the village had been taken prisoner by the WJLF company and now squatted in the small yard, hands on their heads, being watched by the local Jubba, many of whom were carrying old muskets and stabbing knives. A Jubba elder in a plaid skirt, carrying a walking stick and an old Egyptian rifle, pointed out the radio operator from the airfield who was seated with the prisoners.

A plane came over, high to the north. They turned and watched as it continued to the southwest. A WJLF rifleman saw a young Ethiopian teacher smiling and prodded him to his feet with his automatic rifle. Stuck in his trouser band was a small dirty paperback. The rifleman searched him, took his identity card and the book, and handed them to Lieutenant Samantar. Jama questioned the frightened radio operator, who repeated the story told by the lieutenant and the sergeant. He'd spent the night here in the village, as he sometimes did after he closed down his receiver. They'd received no messages for weeks.

Samantar gave Jama the teacher's identity card and his book, an English translation of Lenin, and Jama asked the teacher why he'd been sent here. The village had no school. He said he'd been sent after graduation from the university in Addis, but the authorities there hadn't told him there was no school. So what did he do? Very little. What was there to do?

A troublemaker, Jama decided, a political hothead exiled to the lowlands where, apart from the police and the army, no civil administration had ever existed. He gave him back his identity card and book and the teacher sat down. Another prisoner immediately stood up, claimed he was a UN official, and demanded to be released. Two young Jubba women watching with the crowd gathered in the road shouted at him. One, suckling an infant, bent to find something to throw; the other took a stick given her by a cattle boy and leaned over the fence trying to reach him. A smiling WJLF sergeant interceded, but within a few minutes she was joined by a dozen other women, all shouting at the WJLF lieutenant. He summoned the Jubba elder. As the discussion continued, Jama pushed his way through the crowd, passed the bodies of the two dead policemen, and wandered away down the dusty street. He saw no goats, no chickens, and no camels, no livestock at all. He passed only two cars, one a gray Toyota Landcruiser with UN markings. He crossed the road to look in the doorways of a few dark shops. Behind the counter of the tea shop belonging to the Ethiopian he saw a small dark woman rinsing glasses in a basin on the counter.

The stone floor was dirty and smelled of tallow and sour milk. He asked her if she had any beer.

She silently nodded and brought a warm bottle of Ethiopian beer from behind the counter.

"You're Ethiopian?"

Another nod.

"Why aren't you with the others?"

She continued rinsing her tea glasses. Would her life be any different now, he wondered, tasting the warm beer. "I don't have Ethiopian money, just shillings."

She was still busy with her glasses. To the victors belonged the spoils, he remembered. She had no breasts, no body, her legs as thin as a pullet; her bony face was as bitter as a dried root. He left the shillings on the counter and went out into the hot street, filling his mouth with beer. He washed it about and spat it out, looking at the rust-stained label. The beer was from an Italian brewery in Asmara. He left it on the window ledge and walked back up the road. In the yard in front of the administrator's house a dog was sniffing at the corpse of one of the Ethiopian policemen. The young Ethiopian teacher had again provoked the WJLF sergeant; his wrists were tied and staked to the ground. The Jubba from the village were still arguing with the young WJLF officer about the prisoners. Jama interrupted to tell him the dead policemen should be buried and sent his radio operator back to the Land-Rover to radio Bulet Uen. He went on through the dusty yard, past the prisoners, to inspect the administrator's office. It was as filthy as the small office at the airstrip. When he returned outside the WJLF lieutenant was being led by a group of Jubba women to the public health clinic across the road. Lieutenant Samantar and the Jubba elder were already there, being hectored by another crowd of Jubba at the front door. There were three rooms to the clinic. In the first were a few chairs, in the second a desk, an examination table, and a small gas-operated refrigerator. It held nothing—no serums, no vaccines, no needles, nothing except a few warm bottles of Fanta. Lieutenant Samantar smashed the locked door to the storeroom and inside they found boxes of bandages, smallpox and cholera kits, hypodermics, and dried milk, all stamped with UN markings. In the third room was a dirty bed, a Japanese fan, and a transistor radio. Standing under a lean-to in the rear was a Landcruiser with UN markings.

The WJLF lieutenant crossed the road and asked the Ethiopian administrator for the name of the regional health officer. He pointed to the pop-eyed Ethiopian in dirty trousers and a white shirt who sat a few feet away, the same little man who'd demanded to be released.

The lieutenant asked for his UN documents.

He explained that he wasn't a UN employee but represented the UN. The Ethiopian administrator interrupted to say all UN programs in the region were administered through the local government. The Jubba elder told the WJLF lieutenant the government in Addis didn't allow the UN teams to come, not even during the cholera epidemic.

"That is your office across the street?" The lieutenant pointed to it. The Jubba crowd watching from the road had grown larger.

Jama's radio operator returned to say they were to continue to the north. The sun was merciless, and what little shade lay in the yard was occupied by the Ethiopian prisoners. The lieutenant told his men to move the prisoners into the sunlight, looked again at the pop-eyed Ethiopian health officer, glanced at his watch, and beckoned to Jama.

"This isn't my work," he said. "I'm to go south. Do I shoot him, shoot all of them?"

Jama suggested he take the Ethiopian health officer with him, interrogate him, then turn him over to WJLF in the next village where he wasn't known.

They talked for a few minutes, and the lieutenant told his sergeant to put the public health official in Jama's Land-Rover. The Jubba elder protested; the women waiting beyond the gate moved to intercept him.

"Take the administrator, take the teacher!" the elder cried, "but leave him with us." Jama explained that the public health officer traveled southern Harage province and had information about the tracks, about wells and water. He would need the Ethiopian for a few hours and afterwards would bring him back.

They left the village in the hazy afternoon sunshine and followed the track north toward Shilabo. The Ethiopian sat between Lieutenant Samantar and the radioman. His name was Ato Kebede. He was from Debre Markos high in the massif north of Addis and had been in Harar for three years. He knew nothing about draw wells or cisterns.

The landscape was stunted and dry, the heat boiled above the scrub and the stunted acacias. Searching his pocket for his sunglasses, Jama couldn't find them and wondered if they'd fallen from his pocket at the airfield. The Land-Rover was stifling with the windows open and the fiercely sweating Ethiopian smelling of spiced food made it worse. As each kilometer passed Major Jama expected to hear gunfire, see the muzzle flashes of rocket launchers, smoke boiling from tanks, the geysers of dust and black smoke from the Ethiopian F-15s hammering at the mechanized column, but ahead there was nothing except silence and heat. It was like a mirage; nothing had changed.

It was two thirty when he told the driver to stop.

He got out of the Land-Rover, walked a few meters ahead, turned, looked back to the south, and then west toward the cool distant mountains of Bale, hidden in the heat and haze.

He walked back to the Land-Rover. "Take off your shoes," he told Ato Kebede through the window.

The Ethiopian looked at him, then at the driver, then at Lieutenant Samantar. Silently he bent over and took off his shoes.

"Now get out."

The radioman got out, then Ato Kebede, then Lieutenant Samantar. The rifleman pushed back the rear door and stiffly climbed out, his long legs creaking.

Major Jama stood pointing across the undulating heat of the scrubland toward the west and then toward the massif.

"Do you know where you are? Debre Markos is that way, to the northwest."

"I know, yes."

"Now go. Walk."

"Walk?" He looked up in disbelief.

"Go!"

Moving painfully in his stocking feet he took a dozen steps away from the Land-Rover and stopped. He looked to the west and then back at their faces. He hobbled on, leaned down to take a thorn from the sole of his foot, limped a dozen steps and stopped to look back miserably. "It would be better if you shot me."

"We're not going to shoot you."

He crept on, limping even more. High to the west bustards and vultures were soaring, and he turned again. "I know the country."

"Then go." Jama pointed west.

"To Imi, then Goba." He looked away again. "Maybe only to Goba."

"To Goba then. Go to Goba. Find Goba."

"Then Addis."

"Find the hyenas!" the rifleman shouted. "Go find them!"

"Do you think my father didn't teach me to walk," he cried, "even without shoes?"

"Then walk without shoes!"

"Go!" Lieutenant Samantar shouted. "Go!"

He turned away, hobbled a few painful steps, and turned. "One day I will walk back, all of us!" he cried. "All of us will walk back, even without shoes." He spat but then heard the ugly sound of the breech of a Kalashnikov being cracked closed. Frightened by what he'd done, he began to cry.

Jama watched hopelessly, unmoved.

The doubt had lurked in his mind since he'd heard the first gunshots and looked to the west searching for Ethiopian planes, when he had watched the flag being raised, when he had convinced the demolition chief not to use his explosives, when he saw the smiling Ethiopian teacher and the ugly woman in the *tej bait*. Dreams were silent and theirs was a dream; tracers and demolition charges would bring planes, mechanized divisions from Nazareth to wake them, to once again bring down on their heads the misery of the past.

His great-uncle was right; he had no faith. History had passed them by, there was no justice in their birthright. They fed themselves with fantasy. It was too late, all a dream, all impossible. The little play flags would be passed out, the flowers brought by the village girls, the flags would flutter from a hundred poles, and after it was all over, the flowers would be wilted, thrown into the ditches with the corpses and dead dogs, the flags lowered to be trampled into the dust, the Ethiopian *balabats* would return, the administrators, all of them, worse than ever, those faceless thousands like the pathetic little civil servant from Debre Markos who now stood weeping miserably in the afternoon sun but who one day would return to search out those women in the yard that morning who'd taunted and humiliated him.

"Shoot him," Lieutenant Samantar cried.

The rifleman looked at Jama. "He's a civilian," Jama said. "Is the first man you shoot to be a civilian?"

"He has no shoes," the radioman said. "Let him walk."

"Did you see the women, the medicines in his clinic?" Lieutenant Samantar cried. "Shoot him!"

They stood in the swarming heat listening to the click of the metal roof of the Land-Rover.

"I think he should walk," the driver said after a minute. "Let him walk without his shoes." He turned and went back to the vehicle and started the engine.

"I'll do it." Lieutenant Samantar seized the automatic rifle from the rifleman, pointed it toward the Ethiopian, and with a nod motioned him out across the hot pan.

The others walked back to the Land-Rover and sat waiting.

The shot came a minute later. Still they waited. Two more shots followed, and after a few minutes Lieutenant Samantar joined them. Jama heard the angry rattle of the cartridge canister after he slammed the door and told the driver to move on. He emptied the breech and gave the rifleman back his weapon.

They had been too long at peace, Jama thought as they drove forward in silence. All except young Lieutenant Samantar, born in Western Jubbaland in a village just to the northeast, where his uncles and cousins still lived—hotheaded young Lieutenant Samantar, so long at war with his clansmen's oppressors, with history and justice, so long at war with himself, now come as a lion to reclaim his birthright.

□ □ □

A dozen kilometers to the north they passed a gutted Ethiopian truck overturned on the side of the road, still smoldering. A lump of ash sat in the blackened cab, perforated by automatic weapons fire, recognizable only by the bones of one hand fused with the door panel. Lieutenant Samantar scraped at the door to find the marking. He thought the truck was from the Ethiopian ministry of highways, carrying drums of petrol and asphalt to the south. They walked out on the scorching roadbed away from the Land-Rover, stretching their legs. Jama searched the horizon to the north for some sign of the mechanized column that had moved out that morning ahead of them. Far in the distance he thought he saw a faint puff of smoke. His eyes stung with sweat; he'd wiped them on his sleeve and the puff vanished. As they were walking back to the Land-Rover his radioman stopped and pointed off to the west.

A column of dust lifted in the distance, moving toward them across the pan.

Jama retreated slowly, trying to calculate its distance and direction. The others climbed into the Land-Rover. He heard Lieutenant Samantar calling to him. The Land-Rover moved forward and Lieutenant Samantar called to him again.

Ethiopian armor, a column from a mechanized brigade? Sent from Nazareth, the one Major Yefimov had warned them about?

Still he waited, and then the cloud of dust veered sharply, lifted higher, and was gone, dissolved by a shear of wind like the one that had lifted it from the rocky wasteland.

He heard the laughter from the Land-Rover as the dust devil disappeared. His father would have known in an instant, his great-uncle, too; but he had been as uneasy as Lieutenant Samantar.

They droned forward in silence across the immensity of scrub. His eyes ached. Samantar passed out raisins and then lukewarm tea from the thermos.

The mechanized column had vanished, blown away by the shearing wind—men, tanks, personnel carriers, trucks, all swallowed up by the devouring heat, like fat on a griddle: men, machines, iron, and bone—*a dream still?*

Two kilometers beyond, the driver slowed and Lieutenant Samantar leaned forward and passed Jama a map, pointing to a small irregular line enclosing a well marking. A sand track led off the broken tarmac toward the small low cluster of buildings lying on a small rocky escarpment less than 300 meters from the road.

They drove across the wadi and up the trail to the turnabout in

front of a mud-walled building. A burned-out Volkswagen Beetle
lay on its side nearby. The warm wind stirred the dust and fluttered
the papers scattered across the stone threshold. Along one side
of the building was a low balcony with flaking railings. The door
was open. Lying a few steps inside was the body of a man in under-
pants, arms and legs flung out, his chest blown away, his jaw missing. Green and blue flies swarmed over the cavity like hiving bees.
The walls behind him were pocked with automatic rifle fire. On
the floor were a few dozen 7.62 cartridge casings. A few meters
away was a circle of whitewashed stones and in the center a small
flagpole from which hung the forlorn flag of Western Jubbaland.

Behind the building to the east was the well, a low depression
in the earth covered with thick green scum and smelling of goat
dung. As Jama bent down he heard the sound of a goat from behind the low stone wall. He stood up and moved up the slope. Two
frightened Jubba children were hiding behind the wall, each holding
the leg of a small brown-and-white goat. One child stayed with the
goat and the other led him to the collapsed stone house just to the
north of the main building. An old Jubba and his wife were hiding
in the corner under a roof tin.

They came out very slowly, very mistrustfully, looking queerly
at Jama's uniform, then at the radioman, at Lieutenant Samantar,
and at the rifleman. Weakened by their long cramped wait, they
sat on the ledge of the porch as the old man described what had
happened. The WJLF guerrillas had come before dawn, had killed
the Ethiopian policeman and the Ethiopian administrator, had
raised the flag, and disappeared to the north. After they left, tanks
and trucks passed on the road, pursuing the guerrillas, they thought,
and they'd remained hidden, expecting the Ethiopians to return
and find the bodies inside. They'd be shot. They were waiting for
darkness, when they would flee to the east. The old man pointed
to the flag and asked if Jama would take him and his wife and two
grandchildren with him.

Jama said the tanks and trucks they'd heard were from Jubba,
not Ethiopia. The old man's eyes, bright a moment earlier, dimmed
in disbelief as he studied Jama's collar insignia. Jama asked how
many Ethiopians had been attached to the post. The old man held
up four fingers and looked at the hulk of the burned Volkswagen.

Two Ethiopians had arrived very late the night before in their Volkswagen and been sleeping inside the administration building during the attack. The guerrillas had burned their car after the two men had escaped out a back window. The older child spoke up and pointed down the path to an abandoned stone building at the end of the settlement whose roof was gone. She thought she'd heard voices from there.

Lieutenant Samantar and the rifleman walked across the turnabout to look at the Volkswagen's tags. The old man asked if Jama was certain they weren't Ethiopian tanks. Jama nodded, listening to the old man's wife telling his young radioman how she had been at Ramallah when the Ethiopians had poisoned the draw wells and her brother's goats had died.

She turned, remembering something, and slipped from the shadows of the porch to call to someone.

They heard the clattering of tin; fifty feet away a piece of galvanized tin was being pushed aside. A dark hand waved to them, then another; a young man and his wife had been hiding in a wet-weather cistern.

Lieutenant Samantar said the Volkswagen had an Ethiopian official government plate. He and the rifleman unslung their weapons, and Jama and the radioman followed them back toward the stone building. They heard the two Ethiopians talking quietly even before they entered. They were sitting in the shadows of the stone wall, knees raised. They looked up silently, studied their faces, their uniforms, and their guns. Neither spoke. Both were dressed in dark trousers and white shirts.

From the doorway the villagers watched silently as Lieutenant Samantar asked if they had any weapons.

No, they had no weapons. Why would they have weapons? They were teachers from the agricultural college at Alamayu near Harar.

Major Jama asked to see their Ethiopian identity cards and driver's licenses. They said their papers were in the Volkswagen. Lieutenant Samantar told them to stand up and asked what they were doing here. On their way to an experimental farm to the south, one explained. Jama wasn't sure who they were. They weren't frightened but had the inscrutability of Amharic civil servants who'd been temporarily inconvenienced. They might have been two *bala-*

bats who'd had a flat tire while out on the track and were waiting for their driver to fetch someone to repair it.

Lieutenant Samantar circled them, studying their belts, their clothes, and their shoes. One had a package of cigarettes in his pocket, American-made Winstons. He asked them if they were Amharas; both said they were Gallas. He had them hold out their hands and turned and beckoned to Jama, who looked at their fingers and their palms. The hands of the short man were rough and callused, and those of the taller man small and well cared for. Jama smelled stale *tej,* the honey mead Ethiopians were so fond of. Asked what they taught at the agricultural college, the tall one said he taught agriculture. What kind of agriculture? Just agriculture, what the farmers could grow here in the lowlands. He could give no better answer than that, neither could the shorter one, and Jama doubted either was a teacher.

Lieutenant Samantar and the rifleman marched them back to the administration building, hands behind their heads. Jama followed with the old man and his wife and asked if they had weapons. The old man had a rifle, wrapped in sacking, and buried in the bush not far away but he had no ammunition. Jama promised to bring him a rifle and ammunition on his way back to Bulet Uen. He told them the Ethiopians wouldn't be coming back, but in a few days the WJLF front would send a few men to be stationed at the post.

Standing near the Land-Rover with his two prisoners, Lieutenant Samantar suddenly dug his rifle barrel into the stomach of the short Ethiopian, then slashed him across the back of the head as he dropped to his knees. He fell forward, legs quivering, and Samantar switched his rifle to single shot and jammed the muzzle savagely into the side of the standing Ethiopian. Jama didn't know what had happened. The two Ethiopians had been talking in Amharic, despite Samantar's warning; perhaps one had smiled, had looked at his companion in a sly way Lieutenant Samantar didn't like, but whatever the gesture he knew young Samantar was even more sensitive than he to any suggestion their presence that afternoon was merely a few hours' occupation by a handful of marauding WJLF guerrillas who would disappear back across the border with the coming of darkness.

Still worried about the Ethiopians returning, the old man asked about the bodies inside. Samantar suggested the two Ethiopians bury them, but Jama decided it would take too long. He had the two Ethiopians retrieve the bodies from inside and drag them down the sand track as the Land-Rover followed. When they reached the track the two Ethiopians stopped to rest. Lieutenant Samantar ordered them to keep moving. A kilometer beyond, Samantar pointed out across the scrub from the Land-Rover. There, a hundred meters off the road, the bodies were left on an outcropping of rock.

Lieutenant Samantar told them to take off their shoes. He flung them away and ordered them onto the front fenders, the shorter man to the right fender, where the rifleman watched him with his muzzle out the window, the taller man to the left.

They passed through two WJLF roadblocks, saw four burned-out trucks, and two small companies of WJLF regulars strung out along the road. An hour later they reached Kubwale, a large village with two dusty streets and a dozen mud and stone buildings, pink in the deepening afternoon sun. As they entered the village a few Jubba boys jogged alongside the Land-Rover pointing at the two Ethiopians. Two sand-colored MIG-21s from Bulet Uen thundered low across the barrens to the east, the first Jubba planes they'd seen that day. A company of WJLF regulars was bivouacked along the wadi just below the village. Nearby a rabble of Ethiopian soldiers squatted inside a thorn camel enclosure, knees drawn up, hands behind their necks. As Jama's Land-Rover drove up, two long-legged Jubba youths had joined the small boys running alongside the Land-Rover, calling one of the Ethiopians by name. Before Lieutenant Samantar could leave the Land-Rover they'd dragged him from the fender. Two WJLF front regulars intervened and helped Samantar recover the Ethiopian prisoners.

The Jubba youths claimed the two men were from the Ethiopian security police sent to the local peasants' association from the central revolutionary investigation department in Addis, looking for counterrevolutionaries and members of the WJLF and Oromo liberation fronts. Jama asked who else could identify them. Two of the boys were sent off to find someone who'd been released that morning from the *woreda* prison administered by the peasants' association.

Jama left Lieutenant Samantar with the two prisoners and drove on to talk to the WJLF commander whose troops had liberated the village. He found him with another WJLF officer leaning against a small Deux Chevaux near the market studying an old map spread out on the hood. His dark face was so powdered with white dust he looked like an albino. A glass of tea stood on the roof of the old car. They shook hands and talked for a while but every few minutes were interrupted by someone coming to shake hands, to bring flowers or glasses of tea. An old Ethiopian, very stiff and very lame, moving heavily on his cane, was brought up to the lieutenant by a middle-aged Ethiopian woman who held his arm. In a loud voice he identified himself as a Galla, bowed, stood erect with dignity, took the officer's hand, bowed again, and in the same loud shouting voice thanked them for their merciful liberation. He'd been one of the prisoners released that afternoon from the *woreda* prison, his woman companion explained, touching her finger to her ear. He'd been tortured at the prison and was almost deaf. Arrested during the Red Terror, he had been a prisoner for fourteen months. Bending over, his right hand passing behind his legs, he explained how interrogators had tied his big toes together, shackled his wrists under his knees, and passed a bar between knees and hands. Then he'd been hung up like a drawn goat to be flogged with a rhinoceros-hide whip.

The WJLF commander shook his head sadly as he accepted another bouquet of petunias from a young woman.

The woman who accompanied the old man looked at Jama. He didn't know what he was to confess to, she said piteously. It was all a mistake. How could a man his age—he was sixty-five—be a counterrevolutionary? He was a Galla but so was Colonel Mengistu. Wasn't that true?

Jama said he thought it was. A group of older Jubba women came up and began talking excitedly to the two WJLF officers.

The old man turned to Jama. "There was no light!" he shouted. "I had no candle at night, no *shama!*"

Jama nodded, sadly shaking his head.

"Even in Haile Selassie's prisons you could buy a candle!" he cried. "I bought many candles there, five birrs', six birrs' worth of candles, all out of my own pocket!"

Jama nodded. "So you were in Haile Selassie's prison, too."

"What?

"You were in Haile Selassie's prison?"

"What did he say?"

The woman shouted in his ear and Jama moved away. The old man took a firm grip on his cane, the woman still holding his arm, and hobbled indignantly after him.

"The darkest, the worst! Many times! But for smuggling, never for politics! Now everything is politics. Who is your father? From what village?"

"From Hargusha."

Jama and his radioman wandered on. Young women in bright market-day dresses flocked along the road, some with flowers, and he found himself envying the young WJLF guerrillas. In the marketplace goats had been slaughtered, and the fire glowed even brighter in the lengthening shadows. Jama walked on. The buildings and banks of the wadi were rose-colored, and along the far side stood a half-dozen dusty camels. He was studying them, looking at their size and conformation, when he heard gunshots in the distance and turned, looking east. As he and his radioman were returning to the Land-Rover, a passing boy told them the shots had come from the *woreda* prison. He waited, listening, but heard nothing more. The group of villagers gathered around their vehicle repeated some of the rumors: the mechanized brigade that had moved out that morning from Tugwajala had taken Jijiga and was on the outskirts of Harar. Their own mechanized brigade was far ahead of them, still moving north.

With night coming on, Jama decided they would pass the night there. Standing against the Land-Rover and watching the crowds moving by, he had no desire to be anyplace else.

Lieutenant Samantar returned, followed by two young village women who stood discreetly aside, both holding flowers. The young man had been right. The two Ethiopians were interrogators from the security police in Addis, on their way south. The tall one was the interrogator, the fat one the flogger. They'd been shot. He asked Jama if he wanted to see the *woreda* prison where they interrogated their prisoners.

Jama shook his head. "No, not the prison. Enough for one day."

He watched Lieutenant Samantar move away with the two girls and join the crowd moving along the dusty road. What he saw here was real enough, he decided, leaning against the Land-Rover, and this was what he wanted to remember.

□   □   □

The reception that night was at the Italian ambassador's residence, an ornate villa in the heart of the city. It was a little after seven as Talbot and Lindy arrived, made their way through the open doors of the residence, through the large rooms, and down the steps into the rear garden. There among the frangipani, the flamboyant trees, and the flower gardens a hundred or so guests were gathered, come to greet the members of a small Italian delegation from the ministry of foreign trade in Rome.

The visiting Italians were dispersed out along the walks beyond the front steps. Talbot stopped to greet the Saudi chargé d'affaires and the new Egyptian military attaché. He lingered for a few minutes as they talked about the latest news from the Ethiopian front.

The shattered Ethiopian army in the south was either encircled or in retreat, its remnants streaming north and northwest toward the highlands. Although most military analysts knew Ethiopia was desperately short of ammunition, equipment, and spare parts, its army besieged by guerrillas the length of its frontiers and thinly spread from Eritrea in the north to the Kenyan border, none anticipated the swiftness of the collapse. The Soviet military resupply to its socialist foundling in Addis was still just a trickle. In the south entire units were cut off, without ammunition, rations, or water. From those with a battery-operated radio, the daily appeals for support grew grimmer and weaker:

Where is the help headquarters promised, where are the planes from Debre Zeit, the armor that was being sent? pleaded an intercept Talbot read that morning at the embassy sent by an unidentified Ethiopian company lost somewhere in the scag between Werder and Kebre Dehar. *We are surrounded by two dozen* shiftas *left behind by the guerrillas. They could kill us but they do not shoot their ammunition,* another weak voice radioed from further to the south, overheard in Amharic by the monitoring American satellite, eavesdropping on the ugly little war. *We have fifteen rounds among us and they wait. Our grave will be the bellies of the jackals.*

The intercepts were dispatched to the computer banks of the National Security Agency at Fort Meade, translated by NSA linguists, fed back by Agency channels to the commo room at the embassy, and from there circulated on Whittington's daily reading board. Talbot had read a half-dozen such messages that morning, like those from the day before, giving U.S. military eavesdroppers from Kenya and NATO Brussels to the Pentagon a much surer sense of the Ethiopian collapse than was available to Jubba or Addis officials or the two Arabs Talbot was now listening to.

Neither the Saudi nor the Egyptian was certain how devastating the Ethiopian losses were, but Talbot said nothing.

Neither did he mention those other U.S. intercepts gathered by satellite or the NSA monitoring crew that had arrived from Nairobi and was secluded in the vaulted second-floor commo room, listening to those clandestine Jubba military channels Talbot had reported in his disputed telegram. The intercepts made it clear the Jubba national army was as much on Ethiopian soil across the border as the WJLF.

The official pretense was maintained, however, as the Jubba government insisted its army wasn't involved, just the WJLF, fighting a war of national liberation in occupied Western Jubbaland as had the MPLA in Angola, FRELIMO in Mozambique, the FLN in Algeria, and the Viet Cong. The Jubba government clung to its pretense, and the WJLF to its Marxist-Leninist figleaf, both confident their cause would soon be recognized by the leadership of the world socialist community in Moscow, which had helped the cause of national liberation in Angola, Mozambique, and Vietnam, but had contemptuously failed to endorse the WJLF offensive.

Learning nothing he hadn't heard on the BBC at six o'clock, Talbot excused himself and moved on. Lindy was still talking to Hafiz and Fawya. He searched the side of the garden, looking for Nick Bashford-Jones, thinking he'd seen him there a few minutes earlier, but he'd disappeared. Instead he discovered Nicola Seretti standing alone on the path near the gazebo, looking out over the garden. It was the first time he'd seen her in three weeks and he felt the pleasure of a clandestine intimacy, of shared secrets in common.

He called to her, but she didn't look in his direction. She'd told him once she was shortsighted.

He moved toward her. "Hey," he called just as she seemed about to move away, "it's me, Talbot."

She turned and recognized him. "I'm sorry. I didn't see you."

"How've you been? Haven't seen you for some time."

"Fine, thank you. And you?"

"Getting along."

"How is the garden?"

"Nice now, much better. You haven't finished yet, have you?"

"Not completely, no."

"I've sort of been expecting you. I've missed you." She gave him a polite smile and nodded. With her dark eyelashes so unlike Lindy's, her figure so different, too, and now in an unfamiliar long green dress she seemed suddenly a stranger. He was disappointed. "You seem to have a fondness for back walls," he said after a minute.

She looked up at him puzzled. "Excuse me?"

"At the Harcourts' that first evening, you were also at the back wall."

"Was I?"

"That was the night I fell asleep during the movie."

"You did, didn't you?"

"Were you planning on coming by again?"

"I was, but I've been busy."

Lindy joined them, out of breath. "Sorry, I got tied up."

Talbot introduced them.

Nicola was unusually formal. She spoke only a few words to Lindy and these in Italian. "I was on the Lido road the other day," she resumed, speaking to Talbot, still in Italian. "I passed the gate but I didn't stop. You were busy, I think."

"What time was it?"

"In the afternoon. Four, I believe. Four or five."

"I wish I'd known. Why didn't you just go on in and wait?"

"No, you are very busy, I'm sure. I saw you swimming another time, too, out near the reef."

"Could be. We're out there almost every day. How's the major?"

"The major?"

From her face he knew he'd made a mistake. Their secrets were now best forgotten, her expression told him, but he blundered on. "I meant to explain about that," he said, "it's a little complicated but I'd like to explain."

"There is nothing to explain, please."

"There's something to explain."

"Please, we won't talk about it."

"I'd still like to explain, maybe the next time you come by." She nodded, a quick, impatient nod, then looked toward a heavyset Italian Talbot had noticed standing near an iron bench smiling at her. Behind him near the steps leading up to the front of the garden stood three Jubba officials in business suits. "Excuse me," she said. "I see an old friend. We'll talk sometime."

Talbot watched her go.

"That's the woman everyone's so suspicious of?" Lindy said.

"That's the one."

"I thought she spoke English."

"She does."

"Not too friendly, I'd say. She does seem a little mysterious, doesn't she?"

"Not when you know her."

"I don't think she wants much to know me. C'mon, let's go. I think Fawya and Hafiz have already left. I told them twenty minutes."

He watched Nicola join the Italian and the Jubbas and a fourth man in military uniform. He followed Lindy up the stairs, turned and looked back. Nicola wasn't looking at him at all but was laughing, and that annoyed him a little. What could she share with those popinjays?

He and Lindy spent an hour on the veranda at Hafiz's cottage, drinking and talking. It was the third time he'd taken her there. She enjoyed their company, but Talbot, with her nightly companionship to look forward to, had grown weary of their tiresome stories, even though they now had a little war to divert them.

Najah al-Zeyn, the Syrian ambassador, had brought an Italian woman, a teacher of some kind, very plump, very full-figured— Rubenesque, Lindy would say later, anticipating his own description. Talbot had never met her. He listened to Hafiz and Ambassador al-Zeyn talk about the Arab role in resupplying the WJLF. The Egyptian military attaché repeated a few stories Talbot had heard at the Italian reception and then asked Talbot about U.S. military aid for Jubba. Why hadn't it arrived?

Talbot gave the question more dignity than it deserved and described in his limpest State Department drawl how the Jubba arms lists were still being refined by Washington's experts.

Lindy abruptly turned away from her polite little conversation with Fawya and al-Zeyn's new Italian mistress to look at him queerly. Washington, of course, hadn't supplied Jubba with a single musket, not a single cartridge, and had no intention of doing so, despite the hysterically long lists of military equipment still being sent by the Jubba ministry of defense to the embassy. The latest list that had arrived two days earlier had included 200 jeep-mounted 106-mm recoilless rifles, 50 Bell Huey Cobra helicopters, and 8,000 TOW missiles. The military equipment was still under discussion, the fiddle-faddle Talbot had predicted weeks earlier.

Neither did Talbot tell them the president had declined Harcourt's request for a U.S. military attaché nor remind them that in none of his interviews or his infrequent radio speeches did the Old Man suggest he would continue to be anything other than a loyal friend of the U.S.S.R. To Talbot, who'd always suspected his appeal for U.S. military help was a kind of blackmail designed to force Moscow to give him more arms, this meant he was waiting for Moscow to cease its arms shipments to Ethiopia and renew its resupply to Jubba, rumored to have been suspended. The Soviets and their military advisers were still very much present in the capital, but much more a passive presence now, watching and waiting in Jubba as in Ethiopia, not knowing quite what to do about the ugly war between their two client states.

An hour later al-Zeyn and his Italian companion left, and Lindy and Talbot followed. "They're not very well informed, are they?" she said as they drove back to his villa.

"Nothing a KH-11 satellite wouldn't cure."

"Sometimes I had to bite my lip, listening to what they were saying."

"Good training for the clandestine life."

She turned to look at him in the headlights of a passing car. "That's not what I meant. They're my friends. How can you have friends and not share with them?"

"You can't; that's why Whit has his Boston whaler."

"You're really not much help. If you can't tell them what you know, you don't have to lie to them."

"I wasn't lying to them, I was giving them the official line."

"Which is a lie, and you know it."

"Good God, I thought you took the Agency junior officers' course down at the farm. Didn't they teach you how to lie with a nice sweet face. That was what they hired, you know—not your Mount Holyoke degree, not your brains, just that sweet lovely face. Don't you know that?"

"I don't think I knew anything then; it wasn't the same. I certainly didn't know then what I know now."

"You can thank your professor for that," Talbot said, turning through the open gates.

"God, here we go again. You take credit for everything, don't you? You think no woman anywhere in the whole wide world ever had an open mind until *you* came along."

He held her door open as she climbed out. "Did I ever say that? Do you ever hear me say that?"

"You didn't have to say it."

"It's not that you're not romantic," she said as she slipped a record from its jacket twenty minutes later. "That's not all I meant. You just aren't that way, so OK, I accept that."

"What's being romantic have to do with it?" Talbot said, pulling off his tie.

"I just sometimes wonder what you're thinking. I'm not talking about your official life; I'm up to my ears in that. I'm talking about your personal life. You don't tell me; you don't say anything."

"What do I have to say? Every night begin with a little romantic prologue when you drive in the front gate."

"I didn't mean romantic that way." She put the record on the turntable. "That's another thing, me always coming here."

"I thought you liked it here."

"I love it, but I hate sneaking around."

"You're not sneaking around."

"I feel like it." She glided along the floor, arms lifted, moving to the music, and then dropped lightly onto the end of the sofa. She'd been sitting on his lap before the last record had ended but now sat on the end of the sofa, where she'd sat for the first ten minutes or so. She was the most morbidly sensitive girl he'd ever known; every word, every sigh, every gesture altered the distance between them, and now that he'd said something casually thoughtless while she was changing the record, she was sitting again at the end of the couch.

Being with her was sometimes like turkey hunting in Pennsylvania; just when you thought the sly old gobbler was within range, you'd hear his mating call from across the mountain. She must be clairvoyant, he decided. She sure as hell no longer had any reason to be shy.

"When you say romantic," he said, "what you mean is something else."

"It's how a person feels, I suppose. Some people are demonstrative, some aren't. Just sleeping with someone isn't enough, not always." She dropped her head on her arm. "I can't believe I'm talking this way; I can't believe it." Determined to be more dignified, she got up solemnly and crossed the room to rummage in her leather purse hanging from the back of the chair where she'd left it. Looking for one of those goddamned mentholated cigarettes, he supposed, the ones she never finished.

"I mean do you want a preamble every night, every time you come in the door or we get into bed? Some sweet little doodad to hang in your ear, some kind of passkey? Like driving on the Jersey turnpike, and you come to the toll gate and throw two quarters in the basket for the toll lady: 'I love you, baby, open your gate.' 'Sure, honey, drive on through.' Is that it?"

She put her head in her hands. "That's awful."

"Some people do."

"I know some people do."

"What if I asked you to wear your bikini when we sit here, put on a pair of high heels, and strut around. How'd you like that?"

"Logan, that's not what I mean."

"Do you want me to grow a mustache and wear hair oil and silk suits and whisper in your ear, like al-Zeyn?"

She winced: *"Please,* don't say any more. Just be the way you are; that's fine. I'm sorry I even brought it up."

"Then come sit here where you were."

She stood up and smiled, moved in a half-turn, then a full turn, and sank down on his lap. A few minutes later he reached over and turned off the light.

After a while they would put on the slower music, roll up the scatter rugs, and turn off all the lights, the dark salon illuminated by the glow of the lamps on the wall outside. He would kick off his shoes first, she would follow, then his shirt, then her blouse, then his trousers, her skirt, and so on, their clothes kicked aside until only warm skin separated them moving together as romantically as he could make it without freaking out or blowing a head gasket. Why she needed a nightly preamble, some vow of undying love and devotion in addition, was a little perplexing. Must be her youth and inexperience, gilding his lily a little, to say the least.

□ □ □

The old Italian-built compound where the WJLF had its offices and held its press conferences was some three blocks southeast of the Piazza. Talbot had often passed it but had never been inside the high walls until that morning he drove in, uninvited, finding himself in the vicinity near the hour of a scheduled press conference.

The century-old stucco building was roofed in tile and surrounded by deep latticed porches. It had a colonial look to it—the decaying plaster and peeling paint, the cool tile floors, the slatted doors, the high ceilings with their slowly rotating fans, the exposed plumbing pipes scabbed with hides of thick paint, and the lingering smells of bat shit leaking from the ceiling cavities on the porch. Once the headquarters for the Italian police and the camel constabulary, it had been given to the WJLF gratis a few years earlier by the government. Parked in the treeless sand courtyard were a few dusty Land-Rovers and Fiats.

The press conference commenced at ten, and Talbot was fifteen minutes early. On the latticed veranda a few khaki-clad figures lounged in bamboo chairs, drinking tea. The Tass correspondent, wearing his familiar gray Nehru jacket, stood inside near the door with a swarthy Cuban and an East German second secretary. Nearby a few WJLF officials in spotless khakis were talking jubilantly to a pair of Italian journalists who were taking notes. Unchallenged by the WJLF cadremen wandering about, he strolled on across the porch, through the foyer, and into the large two-story whitewashed hall where the press conference would be held. A small balcony surrounded two sides. At the far end was a stone chimney, the fireplace concealed by a wooden platform and lectern. The WJLF flag hung across the left wall.

He could imagine the old Italian camel constabulary lounging about here, reading, drinking grog, or playing billiards, waited on by white-liveried Jubba servants, like Julia's houseboys. He wondered if Ambassador Firthdale had it on his itinerary. He'd have to recommend it. You could smell the wood smoke on the air, even now, see the old colonial ghosts gathered here, as thick-skulled as Nicola's friend Rugatto. Not quite all ghosts either. Ten feet in front of the small elevated platform sat the emaciated Vietnamese who'd been his seat companion on the flight from Nairobi so many months ago, alone in a folding chair in the first row. His legs were crossed, his small gray head floated in a nasty fog of cigarette smoke as he read the newspaper folded on his knee. Behind him were a few Germans and Scandinavians, including two photographers. Further along sat a couple of Nairobi-based British journalists and behind them was a tall woman with jaggedly cut dark hair and a bony androgynous face who looked French. The other journalists were more difficult to place; there were a dozen or so Arabs. One entire row was occupied by civil servants from the Jubba ministry of information. All alone at the end of the sixth row of chairs sat Basil Dinsmore.

Talbot strolled down the aisle to say hello. Dinsmore got to his feet in surprise, a bit flustered, as always. He was gray-haired with ruddy cheeks, bright blue eyes, and an elegant gray mustache which made him look rather like a foreign office diplomat.

"Didn't expect to see you here, I must say," Dinsmore said quietly, still flushed.

"Shouldn't be." Talbot put his finger to his lips and they walked back along the aisle to the door. "Wasn't invited; just decided to drop in. I don't know whether they want me here or not."

"That could be embarrassing, couldn't it? I just got in yesterday and someone brought me an invitation this morning." He searched his pocket to find it, one of those pointless, frantic little gestures Dinsmore seemed always to be occupied with. Talbot said not to bother. Dinsmore remembered something else. "Before I forget, I wanted to talk to you about something. Firthdale said you were leaving. Not right away, I hope."

"A few months."

"Good, then we'll have a chance to talk. I'll ring you if you don't mind, after I know a little better what my schedule is, what the deuce is going on. The Ethiopians seem to be having the worst of it, don't they?"

"Pretty much."

"I'd have telephoned, but I seem to be entirely in the hands of the ministry of information."

A WJLF official moved them aside to open the double doors. Those standing outside began to file in.

"Not surprised," Talbot said. "We all are, one way or the other. Call me. Better still, stop by for a drink."

"I will indeed."

Dinsmore went back to claim his seat. Talbot waited outside. On a table next to the open slatted door he found a few mimeographed WJLF information sheets and tracts. There was also a cheaply printed, brightly colored map of Western Jubbaland, whose boundaries, he now saw, reached far into the Ethiopian heartland itself, much further than he had ever heard anyone claim. The northern and western limits of that blue swatch of Ethiopia marked on the map as WJLF territory had never been considered Jubba's pastoral grazing lands.

To the victor belonged the spoils, he remembered, looking again at the map. Ethiopia had once played the same game; an imperial power long before Jubba was freed from British and Italian colonialism, its present boundaries in the north and south had been expanded largely as a result of Allied victories in East Africa during World War II, including those disputed territories the Jubba were now repossessing, never under effective Abyssinian administration. Since those boundaries had been accepted internationally long before Jubba achieved nationhood, justice hadn't been its birthright in 1960. Now the WJLF was redressing the wrong and adding a little territorial booty as well, Abyssinian style.

The WJLF director of information opened the press conference from the lectern at the front of the hall by reading a series of congratulatory telegrams sent the WJLF by local workers' and peasants' committees for its triumph against the imperialist enemy. The door was unattended, and Talbot slipped in and took a seat in the last row. The information director, he discovered, was a tall thin Jubba in a gray suit who suspiciously resembled one of the civil servants from the ministry of information. He introduced a grizzled old Galla chief who mumbled a few unintelligible remarks in his native tongue which were interpreted by the information chief at greater length and in more vivid detail describing the social deprivation of the oppressed classes in the liberated territories and the certainty of the coming victories. The old chief seemed to lose his place in his text and stood in bewilderment until a young press attaché arrived to tell him he was finished. The young man led him from the rostrum, assisted by a young woman in a red beret, crisp khakis, and military boots. A map board on a tripod was brought out and a WJLF brigade commander, also in clean starched khakis, described the WJLF advances made during the past twenty-four hours. He claimed he'd recently returned from Harage province.

Listening in the back row, Talbot wasn't so much surprised by the ideological purity of all this as stupefied by it. The brigade commander was followed by the Jubba woman who'd helped the old chief from the rostrum. She described the heroic role of the Jubba women in mobilizing themselves in the formerly occupied territories; cadre formation, she assured the journalists, was already under way in the liberated regions. She then read a number of telegraphed greetings from revolutionary women's groups in Mozambique, Angola, Guinea-Bissau, Vietnam, and here in Jubba.

As the names droned on and the press corps became increasingly restless, Talbot wondered how much longer she would continue.

He was no longer stupefied but embarrassed for her, solemnly spewing out this nonsense for an audience of foreign journalists who knew far better than she how the game was played, men who'd been to Angola, to Mozambique, perhaps Prague, Pankow, or even Hanoi and who knew how these telegrams were drafted. Who was she kidding? Didn't they realize they were being made fools of? Where in Christ's name were those nomads he'd come to hear and Dr. Greevy had talked about—that heroic individualism, those lonely warriors with their fierce pride and their savage poetry.

The feminist revolutionary was followed by a WJLF doctor educated in East Germany who had brought with him a group of enlarged photographs mounted on poster board. They showed pictures of WJLF clinics and tent hospitals in the liberated homeland. The photographs were imperfect, grainy, a little fuzzy. The journalists had to stand to see them.

The doctor was describing the leg wounds of an old WJLF warrior who lay on a surgical table somewhere north of Werder. A pressure lamp was at his head. The doctor seemed to forget the old warrior and began to talk about the treachery that had ceded Jubba's pastoral grazing lands to Ethiopia. He described an Ethiopian empire in decay, torn asunder by revolutionary fervor, and finally returned his pointer to the wounded figure on the poster board, in whom that revolutionary spirit was now embodied—"*This old man,*" he cried, tapping the poster board emphatically, describing the correlation of historical forces that had made his war of national liberation inevitable.

Talbot was on his feet with the others, wanting to learn more, to see more—the blood on the table, the wound that had opened the dark leg to the bone, every grain of dust, every drop of sweat, wanting to hear from the lantern-lit table the nakedness of a human voice, lost to him all these weeks.

A Dutch journalist in the second row interrupted the doctor to ask if the old warrior was indeed typical of the WJLF cadres. Was he, in fact, the embodiment of the WJLF cause and that zeitgeist he'd mentioned earlier? Or was he not, as his nomadic clothing seemed to suggest, simply someone swept up in the fighting.

Zeitgeist? Talbot looked across the room at that pale Nordic face. The historical thread now, was it, the zeitgeist? Oh, Christ, yes. We've all been to school, haven't we? We all know the zeitgeist, don't we? It runs right through that old man's asshole, through the other rifleman's asshole, just to his left, through all the others we don't see, through the Dutchman's, through the doctor's, standing there and now explaining in his ministry of information–approved brief that the old man was a WJLF cadreman, much honored for his longtime struggle against the Ethiopian imperialists. He called to an aide to supply the skeptical Dutchman with his name and unit and proposed he seek him out and talk to him during the forthcoming WJLF-sponsored visit to the occupied territories.

Talbot sat down, swallowed up in the standing crowd.

Who were these goddamn people?

They were the same people who sat around the Politburo meetings in the Kremlin deciding whether or not spring would come to Prague this year, the same diplomats who in a few hours would be sitting down to lunch in Washington, London, Paris, and Bonn and pretending to orchestrate the Western arms effort—Brits on the violins, French on the bassoons, Germans on the percussions, the Italians, should they truly want some of the action, maybe on the piccolo—how to give Jubba guns without giving them guns. They were the same NSC academicians who sat in the rococo nineteenth-century nooks and crannies of the old Executive Office Building in Washington and scrawled their little geopolitical calculus sets on the blackboard, deciding that if they couldn't do big grandiose nineteenth-century things like sending the fleet into the Black Sea to blockade Sevastopol or bomb East Berlin back to Reichstag rubble, they could still do small stupid ones, like promising Jubba defensive weapons.

He told himself he'd never doubted what would happen if Jubba received the assurance of American weapons. Did that mean that if they won, these same people would be sitting in Dire Dawa or Harar giving this same press conference, these same people in their starched khakis and play-soldier boots, giving play-book instruction.

He got up and left. A young Jubba official in a business suit and tinted glasses intercepted him outside the door to say the press conference wasn't over. Talbot said it didn't matter. The man followed him and shrilly demanded to see his press credentials.

"Do translations, do you?" Talbot said, not pausing. "Try *Hau ab!* That's German for Happy New Year and fuck you, too."

He jogged down the steps and away toward his car.

"Fucky you, too, new year Jaale!"

The man's footsteps scrambled across the gravel behind him, but Talbot was in his car and backing up before he caught up. He dodged aside nimbly, whipped out a notebook, and quickstepped after Talbot's Fiat, out the gate and into the center of the street to stand ostentatiously copying down the diplomatic plate number. Looking in the rearview mirror, Talbot saw the man's coattails lift as his NSS shadow breezed by on his blue Vespa, a near miss, but the official recovered, dusted himself off, and returned inside, a fitting end to another piece of government-sponsored theater; not a WJLF guerrilla after all, just another lounge lizard from the ministry of information.

□ □ □

DeGroot sent off two daily "sitrep" cables to Washington, communiqués from the front, as it were, describing the victories of the WJLF as it advanced steadily northward into Ethiopia. He also included observations on the mood of the capital—"atmospherics," as he called his impressionistic little social column. One was sent at the opening of business each morning, the other at the close. Both were a pastiche of gossip, rumor, and hearsay he'd picked up during his rounds of diplomatic receptions and cocktail parties the night before and which he spent much of the following morning chasing down at coffee sessions with his colleagues in the other embassies. The Pakistani ambassador was the source of much of his gossip, as was the Iranian chargé d'affaires, who shared some of his dubious Savak reporting. Harcourt also contributed a few nutmeats to the salad, eagerly solicited by DeGroot for his potluck buffet.

The principal subject of speculation was the Soviets. Were they still straddling the fence or were they reducing their numbers, beginning to move out personnel, as the Iranian claimed, preparing to come to the assistance of their Marxist swaddling in Ethiopia. Had the Soviet ambassador delivered an ultimatum to the president demanding the withdrawal of Jubba armies from Ethiopian territory?

No one seemed to know.

The Soviet embassy was strangely silent. Kirillan had once agreed to meet with Harcourt, the appointment arranged by DeGroot, but it was abruptly cancelled at the last minute and never rescheduled. The Soviet embassy refused to return DeGroot's calls.

If DeGroot's cables did nothing to clarify Soviet intentions, they were colorful in their other details—the names of obscure villages, queer landmarks, precise longitudes and latitudes, and often erroneous military terminology. His information from the front was drawn from the unreliable WJLF daily bulletin, from the unreliable daily press, from American journalists who came to visit and compare notes, and the unreliable confidential briefings given him by the Egyptian military attaché.

Talbot thought him overreporting the military action. His cables were often confusing, even contradictory from one day to the next. Passing Harcourt on the stairs one afternoon, he stopped to suggest the embassy distance itself a little more from the war and stop issuing euphoric daily communiqués.

Surprised, Harcourt lifted his eyerbows, paused on the steps to reflect for a moment, and then admitted he didn't understand.

"I think maybe it's a little embarrassing," Talbot said, "embarrassing for State and the NSC both to be reminded twice daily of the smashing success of the Jubba military offensive and the stupidity of their decision to promise Jubba arms."

"But that decision wasn't intended to start a war."

"But it did, and that's the point. State and the NSC must be feeling pretty silly now, so why remind them of it twice a day? Better to let them learn what they can by digging through the *Washington Post* and the *New York Times*."

Harcourt paused again as he digested this. "You mean Washington might be having second thoughts?" he asked, troubled.

"That seems to me very likely."

Harcourt moved on absentmindedly down the stairs, Talbot at his heels. "DeGroot's reporting is going to blow up in our faces if we don't watch it. You ought to think about that."

They stood at the Chrysler on the pavement outside.

"Don't you think that would be a little disingenuous?" Harcourt asked, but then, reminded of something even more bewildering, added, "But I thought you were opposed to the whole idea of giving them arms. Weren't you opposed?"

"Sure, but that was weeks ago. It's too late now. Things are bad enough as it is. They'd be even worse if Washington decided it had made a mistake."

Harcourt said he would raise the matter with DeGroot.

If he did, he wasn't successful. The daily communiqués from the front continued. Talbot was resigned at this point. He didn't point out what else was abvious in DeGroot's military dispatches, that they were drafted by a man who knew nothing of military tactics, who was confused and often mistaken about weaponry and nomenclature, who had never served in the military, and whose expertise, in war as in peace, was bombastically topographical.

"I think we need a map room, a situation room," DeGroot announced that morning at the country team meeting, taking his place a few minutes late. He was still winded from his long climb from the first floor and was holding a handful of notes taken during his early morning breakfast with the Egyptian military attaché. In his other hand was a much-worn Michelin road map, his Baedeker to the war, and now heavily marked up with grease pencil.

"A map room?" Harcourt said brightly.

They waited as DeGroot shuffled through his papers, unfolded the tattered map, looked at it, examined his notes, and then put both aside. "A control room, a center for following military developments. It is very difficult lacking a proper loci for all this information. I think the conference room would be best."

"The conference room might do," Harcourt said, "but what did you have in mind?"

"Some alterations would be required: map boards, two telephones, a cipher lock on the door, window screens."

He had evidently given the matter a great deal of thought.

"More of a crisis center," Kinkaid suggested.

"A crisis center exactly," DeGroot said. "It would be of great utility. Our greatest need is maps. Who is map officer?"

"Is there such a thing?" Harcourt said.

They looked at Rhinehart. "I'll have to see" he mumbled. "Don't remember offhand." He turned to Peterson.

"Not me, I don't think," Peterson said, stirring awake.

"It's my impression the political officer is usually map officer," DeGroot reminded him. "Map procurement officer, I think the term is."

Peterson, Rhinehart and Harcourt looked at Talbot as DeGroot struggled with his disintegrating Michelin map.

Talbot, slumped in his chair, sat up slowly. "Not me either. I'm economic officer. I think I'm economic officer."

"We will not quibble over titles," DeGroot said, bending his nose closer to his map. "Michelin, it seems, is lacking a few crucial place names, but in a region of the world not known for its cuisine, perhaps that is understandable. Has anyone ever heard of Wadi Shimeli?"

So Talbot spent the morning and early afternoon ferreting out maps, old maps, new maps, anything that might give the newly designated third-floor map room the feel and texture of a crisis center. Peterson put two carpenters to work at the GSO compound. Corkboard couldn't be found; plywood wouldn't do. In the end Peterson had a carpet cut up and glued it face-down to plywood sheets enclosed in wooden frames. The fiber backing made an adequate map board, sufficient to hold thumbtacks and small brads. Heavy drapes were hung over the windows, a cipher lock was mortised in the door. Having a crisis center also required a name on the door, and so a plastic bar with the words OPERATIONS CENTER was screwed to the door panel.

"Quite handsome," Harcourt decided, brought by DeGroot and his secretary to inspect it. "I'm sure that will please the inspectors next month." DeGroot beamed. Talbot, standing nearby, saw the two men in wrinkled suntans, stars on their collars, Ike and Patton at Omaha beach.

Talbot swam alone late that afternoon, a lazy swim just beyond the surf, bobbing and drifting, his mind not in the sea at all but on Lindy, who was in Nairobi, sent unexpectedly the previous day by Whittington to take part in some Agency-sponsored regional workshop. He missed her company, missed her in his steam-hung bathroom afterwards, missed her warm tint of pinks, tans, and whites against the gray glass shower door as he brought towels and then joined her inside. She would be gone two weeks, the worst time for her to be gone. He wondered if the workshop was a preface to some kind of operational role Whittington had planned for her, leaving her with less time in the afternoons and evenings.

Sitting alone in his back garden after his shower and swim, he decided he'd missed his generation after all, not the Pentagon sit-ins or the protest marches, but the Pine and Wall Street frontier where the real revolution was under way. Since his home leave he'd made $4,200 in the stock market, all as a result of that confidential little pink internal forecast sheet Eric Bowser had bootlegged to him. Doodling on the margin of the *Tribune,* he calculated that if he'd begun his investments ten years earlier, he would have netted $255,000. If he'd studied the market with the same energy he'd given to issuing visas or parading lame-duck congressmen about Rome to have their photos taken around the fountains of Rome, drafting cables in Bonn, Brussels, and The Hague, he would have doubled even that. His thesis at the NATO Defense College in Rome, *The Politics of Bipolarity,* had probably cost him a cool one hundred K. Add to that his graduate and undergraduate courses at Princeton, his thesis on A. J. P. Taylor, and he'd dropped another quarter of a million.

All in all, maybe half a million, he decided, opening a new bottle of Boodle's gin, sent by Pete Ryan in Nairobi via the *Time* correspondent. No wonder Eric Bowser and his Manhattan, Greenwich, and Westchester friends didn't know where the hell Jubba was.

□ □ □

There were ruins of mud-walled houses now, twisted hulks of trucks and personnel carriers blackened by fire, even an occasional tank carcass. At night the sky to the north flamed purple and rose where the remnants of the Ethiopian army, encircled at Kebre Dehar, were being annihilated. To the east pulses of light flickered silently along the horizon like thunderstorms on the savannahs. The Ethiopians at Werder were cut off. The blackened skeletons of vehicles along the road or in the adjacent scrub had been overtaken in full flight;

trucks were sometimes abandoned, petrol still in the tanks, the poorly armed soldiers scattered like francolin and sand grouse to the dry durra grass and thorn.

The Ethiopian prisoners brought to Major Jama daily under the shade of the tarpaulin slung from the Land-Rover roof were frightened, confused, hungry men, unprepared and poorly armed.

So many rumors were astir, fed by the delirium of the victories that had come so quickly and at so little cost. It was the slower, clumsier war of attrition that might yet come that most worried Jama, as it did everyone. They would win quickly or not at all— Kebre Dehar, Jijiga, Harar, Dire Dawa, cutting the rail line, then across to sever the Assab road, cutting the Ethiopian heartland from the sea.

Behind them jackdaw and bustards soared, above them the vultures, drifting and veering lazily on the afternoon thermals. Ahead of them they saw nothing but the flash of guns at night and the smoke on the horizon, dispersing as they advanced. The front was moving northward but more slowly. Jijiga had already been taken, so had Harar, a Galla livestock trader told him on the road. The same evening the courier from Bulet Uen brought word that both Jijiga and Harar were still held by the Ethiopians.

Assault headquarters at Bulet Uen had planned on seizing the Ethiopian armories at Werder and Kebre Dehar—M-1 and M-16 rifles, ordnance, small arms, anti-tank weapons, all to be turned over to the WJLF front, now armed with a hodgepodge of weapons—but the ammunition there had been drawn down in recent months, and the Ethiopians were as short on munitions and petrol as the Jubba armies. Disciplined, well-trained troops were also in short supply. Illiterate serfs from the peasant militias had been recruited in the highlands and trucked down to the lowlands.

In the lengthening shadows of the broken wall that afternoon the wounded still lay on reed mats, on dry fronds, on old sacking, some on the dusty earth. Only a few were on litters. They had been assembled there in the rear that morning to wait for the trucks that had been promised, but now at four o'clock in the afternoon the trucks still hadn't come. Most had suffered shrapnel wounds, some superficial head wounds, none thought to be serious. The critically wounded had been evacuated by truck ten kilometers to the south, where they would be flown by helicopter to the military hospitals in Jubba. Their temporary blood-soaked dressings had dried a rusty brown; they were hungry, tired, and restless. The flies bothered them, so did the waiting. Once soldiers, now they were evacuees, made veterans by their wounds, looking forward to their convalescence across the border. After hours of waiting, their vacant minds had already left the war and soared with the bustards and hawks high on the wind; but now, at four o'clock in the afternoon, here they sat, cramped, hurting, hobbled in the dust, aware of their small miseries, conscious again in the vacuum of the present, not the future, beginning to feel the crippling ache of their wounds, to taste fear again. Who would rouse their hearts a second time?

Far in the distance Jama heard the thunder of a howitzer. He looked up, waiting for the shriek of the shell, but it didn't come; and he continued filling his canteen from the damp rubberized water bag hanging like an udder at the back of the medical unit enclosure. On the olive drab lockers marked with both the red cross and the red crescent were bottles of orange disinfectant, salt tablets, rolls of cotton bandage, gauze, and scissors. The water was warm and brackish; as he tasted it he wondered where it had come from.

He drank again, watching the two dusky-skinned young women in bright red scarves and yellow-and-red dresses he'd noticed as he walked up standing shyly watching the medical corpsmen rebandaging the wounded. One was leading a goat with a salt sack tied over its udder. The tallest of the two girls finally led the goat forward and asked the medical orderly if they would like some goat's milk. The orderly looked over his shoulder at the dirty goat and shook his head. She said the milk was good and wouldn't give fever. He didn't reply and moved on to the next man, dragging his medical kit after him. After a minute she asked a WJLF soldier whose arm the orderly had been rebandaging if he was going to the hospital in Jubba. He nodded, sat forward to reposition his shoulder, and asked her why she had asked. She said if he was to be taken to the hospital, he wouldn't need his rifle; she would give it to her young brother.

The WJLF corporal smiled and moved his hand up his bandaged

thigh. He had no rifle, only the sword of love. He rubbed his crotch and said she was welcome to that. The wounded soldiers laughed, a soft low sound, no more than a light rustle of wind moving through the trees, and then it was gone. He watched the two young women slowly moving away down the track with their goat.

It was the same question the villagers always asked when his Land-Rover stopped, not the young men or the old men, most of whom had weapons, but the others, young girls, young boys, old women: Could they leave a rifle, an old musket, a pistol? The same old doubts, generations old now, older than the flowers, the little artificial flags. Despite the singing, the slaughtered goats, the glasses of sweet tea, they had their doubts. They were here when they came, they would remain behind in their mud-walled houses and their misery when they left.

He turned and went back down the path through the bracken and chalk boulders. The dry wind lifted and fell, constant in his ears, lifting the fine powdery dust to his mouth and nostrils. Artillery shells sometimes fell on either side of the road, lobbed from the Ethiopian batteries dug in south of Harar, fell so unexpectedly and so harmlessly that those passing now ignored them. His cheeks and lips were chapped, his knuckles were cracked, his dirty khakis smelled of smoke and charcoal. Unaware of his smoky face and beard until Lieutenant Samantar had reminded him, he had shaved that morning before he'd interrogated the first group of Ethiopian prisoners, trying to restore a little dignity to his office before all that peasant rabble. Lieutenant Samantar, ashamed of Jama's appearance, had brought him his own razor and said he'd begun to look as much a scarecrow as the Ethiopian prisoners.

A new group now waited near the Land-Rover, seated on the ground, hands behind their heads, all facing south. Even freshly shaven that day, Jama felt no less weary than they looked, exhausted men with frightened, haunted faces.

They were stragglers for the most part, wandering up from their shattered units to the south, the sons of peasants and farmers from high on the Ethiopian escarpments and overtaken on their retreat by WJLF units or by liberated villagers themselves, men whose fathers or uncles tilled their stony hillsides of millet and teff with oxen and wooden plows, Christians all of them, men Colonel Mengistu's bloody Bolshevik revolution in Addis Ababa might transform after thirty years of collective farms and industrialization into steel puddlers, mechanics, good sturdy thick-legged Ethiopian muzhiks, not these shriveled gray corpses.

On a spiny ridge a few hundred yards from the road a MIG-21 had crashed, its fuselage pleated and twisted, its wings and cowling scattered nearby. It was one of their own MIG's from the squadron at Bulet Uen. The plated white underbelly, turned toward the road, looked queerly pathetic, like the bleached shell of a sea turtle washed up on the rocks, gutted by the gulls. Already the villagers were beginning to strip away the aluminum panels to make utensils, pots and pans, perhaps even jewelry.

A WJLF sergeant had told him an Ethiopian F-15 had surprised it over Kebre Dehar and had shot it down. A local herdsman whose thorn-enclosed zariba was just to the south said the pilot had escaped. They had seen a few Ethiopian F-15s streaking south just below the overcast to the west but fewer of their own planes. The Soviets, it was rumored, had refused to supply spare parts for Jubba's MIG's. The American military equipment, on whose assurance the Old Man had decided to launch his war, confident that the Soviets would ultimately support him, not the Ethiopians, hadn't arrived.

As he ducked into the shade of the tarpaulin, he asked the WJLF rifleman to bring him the senior prisoner in the group. He returned a few minutes later with a sergeant by the name of Getachew with a hollow face, discolored eyes, and yellow teeth. Jama knew he couldn't answer the questions G-2 at Bulet Uen was asking. He already knew what he would say. The answers they were seeking lay to the north, among the Ethiopians dug in at Harar or Jijiga, where Soviet and Cuban advisers were rumored to have been seen. Were Soviet and Cuban advisers present there? Were Aden pilots flying the Soviet MIG's that had appeared unexpectedly in support of the Ethiopian armor?

Jama saw a chain hanging from the prisoner's dark neck, nodded, and asked to see what was hanging from it.

Among the prisoners Jama interrogated that morning was an old

man from a peasant militia. He was wearing a medallion around his
neck, not a cross, but an old silver coin hanging from a dirty cord.
It was a 1780 Vienna thaler with the head of Maria Theresa. For
over a century the same thaler had circulated as specie in the Abyssinian highlands, and now this peasant was wearing it around his
filthy neck. Jama had asked him the name of the woman on the
thaler. The old man said she was the Virgin Mary. So there you
were, the whole 2,500-year farce in a nutshell: Maria Theresa was
the Virgin Mary, this illiterate Abyssinian peasant was descended
from King Solomon and the Queen of Sheba, like Haile Selassie
himself. The Old Man back in the capital was the spiritual grandson of *Jaale* Marx and *Jaale* Lenin, like *Jaale* Mengistu in Addis;
and Jama was the direct descendant, eighteen generations removed,
of Shcikh Ishaq bin Amed of the Quarish tribe of Mecca.

Getachew brought from his khaki shirt not a thaler but a small
silver cross made from old coin silver. So the sergeant wasn't a
superstitious peasant but a professional soldier from Gojam, high
in the mountains. His eyes were feverish, and in his terrible exhaustion he smelled like raw fish; but his shoulders were back, his
head erect as he summoned some last shred of self-respect for his
interrogation. His father had been a farmer, but he was a soldier,
not a recruit from the peasant militia. He had fought in the north
against the Eritreans, had been wounded by a land mine, and after
his recovery had been transferred to Werder in the south.

Jama looked at the cross again and asked him if he was a Christian. The sergeant nodded. Jama then asked the other question: If
he was indeed a Christian, what had Haile Selassie done for him or
his father. To put it another way, what had 2,000 years of Abyssinian Christianity done for his fathers and their fathers before
them?

The sergeant hadn't understood the question and Jama slowly
repeated it. The sergeant seized the small silver cross and clutched
it so tightly the greenish-black chain dug into his neck. So there he
sat, no longer a professional soldier from Gojam but the superstitious son of a superstitious father and his father before him, vas-
sals of a corrupt Ethiopian emperor who kept his serfs hobbled in
medieval filth and degradation, unable even to comprehend the

question. Like his shrunken belly, his shriveled mind couldn't digest it. He thought Major Jama was asking him to denounce his Christianity. If he'd repeated the question a third time, Jama didn't doubt he would have strangled himself with his chain.

"Your religion is your own," Jama said. "It is your business."

His own, certainly. Belonging to no one else. Like his patriotism, it was only the filth of his poverty and ignorance, clinging to him like dung to a donkey. Who would cleanse them of that, Colonel Mengistu in Addis?

"What about the government in Addis, is that Christian?" Jama asked. The sergeant nodded. Jama asked him how recently he had been in Addis.

He'd visited Addis ten months ago.

He asked him if he knew that the prisoners kept by the Ethiopian security at the old Addis prison, Alem Baqagn, built by Menelik II, weren't allowed to bring the Bible with them.

No, he didn't know that.

Did he know what the security police did to its prisoners at Alem Baqagn? Did he know that the dungeons there were so dark, brutal, and medieval that even the Italian fascists had closed them during their occupation? Did he know the first thing Haile Selassie did after his return in 1941 was reopen them? Did he know the prisoners of Mengistu's Red Terror were kept there?

No, he didn't know these things; he didn't know anything except the cross of Christianity hanging from his neck like a talisman. Jama asked him the name of his unit in the north and whether it was still deployed there, then sent him away to the little thorn enclosure a few meters to the west. A small group of local Jubba and Galla stood watching with their automatic weapons. A few old women, old men, children, and young girls had joined them, bringing them tea.

Late that afternoon they drove north again and stopped fifteen kilometers beyond at the roadblock and decided to pass the night nearby. Lieutenant Samantar knew the nearby village and went off to visit it. As they were rolling out their bedrolls near the Land-Rover he returned with an egg and an old musket with a splintered stock an old woman there had asked him to repair.

Looking at it more closely with a small torch, Jama saw that the bolt was useless, that it had a broken firing pin, the reason someone had thrown it away; but Lieutenant Samantar sat there in front of the dying coals late into the night trying to repair it.

CHAPTER NINE

A Fashionable
Little Capital

The ugly little war in the Ethiopian wasteland had become an international event, and everyone at the embassy was very much into it—DeGroot with his daily communiqués from the front; Harcourt with his consultations at the French, British, and West German embassies; and Julia as social doyenne. Foreign correspondents, magazine writers, and TV camera crews were arriving almost daily to report the bizarre little war. The sweltering seaside capital had become more fashionable than Nairobi, a front page feature in the *New York Times,* the *International Herald Tribune, Le Monde, The Times* of London, as well as weekly summaries in *Time* and *Newsweek;* and Julia was determined to stay very much at the center of things. She arranged luncheons, dinners, and cocktail parties, decided whom she wanted to entertain and who would be left to DeGroot and Dr. Melton, the public affairs officer, officially charged with press relations at the embassy. Dr. Melton telephoned her daily to announce the new arrivals, most of whom gave advance warning to the USIS press officers in Nairobi or Rome; whether any well-known TV personalities were with the CBS and NBC film crews; the hotels where they were staying; and any other social notes arriving almost daily by cable.

"I *much* prefer it to Nairobi," Talbot heard her tell the *Newsweek* correspondent that afternoon as they sat at the white metal umbrella table at the beach cottage. His name was Gelman and he'd arrived the previous day, sent from Rome. It was his first visit, and to Talbot as they shook hands he seemed as if he were still seated off somewhere in the high ozone of Alitalia cabin class, not yet adjusted to the wilting heat, his new time zone, or those bewildering hors d'oeuvres of local culture Julia was now stuffing him with. Andrews, the *New York Times* correspondent from Nairobi, was also there, a man Talbot's age, but this was his second trip and he was now beginning to find his way around. A tall Frenchwoman had also been invited, she for the first time, but she had been in town for several weeks or so and looked to Talbot like someone who would never have any difficulty finding her way around. Her name was Vallon; she was thirtyish, with dark jaggedly cut hair and a long bony face that seemed ugly at first but then as he grew accustomed to it seemed to have a certain stark Gallic appeal. She was from Agence France-Presse, based in Belgrade. Julia had attempted to discover whether they had any mutual friends in Paris but hadn't had much luck. She'd given up after Miss Vallon, guessing her purpose, said her father was a Marseilles policeman. Her face was familiar, and only later, long after they were introduced, did Talbot remember she'd been at the WJLF press conference that morning.

The other woman was a Mrs. Lawrence, one of Julia's old friends. She had once been a freelance writer of some kind but was now married to a successful American businessman in Paris, which made her even more a dilettante. She was fiftyish, with blondish-gray hair and a deep throbbing voice which shadowed Julia's thoughts like an echo. She was there for a few days visiting Julia while her husband was in Nairobi, hoping she might do a story.

"You can walk anywhere at any time," Julia was saying, "day or night. And the streets are *so* clean."

"That's certainly not true of Nairobi from what little I saw," Gelman said, daintily touching his handkerchief to his forehead.

"Nairobi is *so* dirty," Julia drawled, *"so* sprawling."

"Oh, darling, it certainly is," Mrs. Lawrence said. "It's so awful."

"And so dangerous."

While Julia was extolling the virtues of living in a well-disciplined little Marxist garrison state as compared with the hazards of slum-ridden laissez-faire Nairobi, where her French cheeses and French wines came from but where all those market thieves and *pangas* lurked, a few Jubba beach peddlers with their fiber baskets had begun to flock along the enclosing wall. The porches of the other beach houses were empty that afternoon, the broad white beach deserted except for a few waders in front of the UN beach club. All the riffraff were drawn there to Julia's wall. On other days, with Julia alone and sulking on the front porch, she would have had her houseboy scatter them like roosting starlings, but today, with so many guests present, they were another dash of local color. Inside the cottage Harcourt nursed a gin-tonic as he stood talking with young Andrews, the *New York Times* correspondent. DeGroot and his wife stood listening. Harcourt wore his bathing trunks under his cotton beach robe; Andrews also had on trunks. Both appeared to be waiting for someone to show the way into the sea, a sparkling milky aquamarine at very low tide.

"They're so fiercely independent, the people here," Julia said, on the porch. "Quite unlike the Bantu peoples . . ."

Talbot had brought his trunks but hadn't changed yet. His invitation to lunch had arrived at the last minute, delivered at mid-morning by Harcourt's secretary.

Julia was calling everyone out to look at the vendors' wares. She even introduced her guests to a few beach peddler friends whose names her houseboy knew, and invited everyone to inspect the baskets.

The others were lured out of the shadows inside. Even Adele De-Groot, that mysterious little woman with the tinted black hair, small black eyes, and little white parrot beak of a nose dabbed with sun-tan cream ventured out cautiously, not saying a word. In all her months at the embassy, Talbot had never spoken more than a dozen words to her, although he had sometimes heard her piano and her soft sweet voice drifting down through Lindy's open window from the penthouse above. She was wearing a colorful Indian or Chinese kimono. From the gold-threaded hem emerged two very small feet in brocaded slippers.

Talbot finished his Amstel and went to the dressing room to change. Miss Vallon, bored with the conversation on the porch, had preceded him and emerged from the dressing room wearing a black two-piece bathing suit on her gaunt frame.

"I was about to suggest you take them out to the reef," Julia said, seeing Andrews, Miss Vallon, and Talbot standing at the top of the steps. "You'll love it out there. It is *so incredible.*"

As they waded out into the sea, Miss Vallon said with a shiver she had no intention of swimming that far. Andrews felt the same. Talbot told them there was an atoll of rocks just a hundred yards out and led them through the small crippled surf and out into the open water. They swam out to a formation of volcanic rock and coral just a few inches below the retreating tide and rested.

"You were at the WJLF press conference last week," Talbot said as they sat on the coral and drifted back and forth, unseated by the waves. "I remember you there."

Recovering her seat, Miss Vallon said she didn't remember him but did recall the press conference. "Very bad," she said, making a sour face, "very bad."

Talbot nodded. "Very bad. All that shit. *Toute la chirie philosophique, toute la drouille du Marxism.*"

She laughed in surprise. *"Exactement."*

"I missed it," Andrews said. "You're one of the old-timers, someone told me. How long have you been here?"

"Too long, two and a half years."

"Vous n'êtes pas ramolli maintenant?" she asked drolly, nodding toward the distant beach. "You're not soft-headed now, like the others?"

"Mais je me camoufle. I'm in camouflage, hiding out."

"La vie clandestine," she said and laughed again.

Julia was annoyed that they'd returned so late. In their absence she'd had a chance to think about it, Talbot supposed—the three of them so far away and seeming to be enjoying themselves while she was stuck with entertaining the very wilted Mr. Gelman. She was also disappointed they hadn't waited for Mrs. Lawrence to put on her suit and join them.

The buffet lunch was held inside. Gelman was persuaded to take off his tie, and after everyone served himself Julia arranged the seating on the cushioned bamboo chairs scattered informally around the front room. Once they were all in place, she discovered she'd forgotten Mrs. DeGroot, standing alone in the door to the dining area. Talbot got up to give her his seat, but Julia insisted she wanted him to sit *there,* noplace else. Talbot said he'd sit there but in the meantime Mrs. DeGroot could have his chair and he would find a stool. This didn't please Julia, who told him to sit down and called to her houseboy for another chair. Talbot shrugged helplessly, looking at Mrs. DeGroot, who smiled weakly in return, and in that instant those eyes once too small and dark to have any expression at all suddenly told him everything he needed to know: She was terrified of Julia Harcourt.

It was warm inside. Having first arranged the seating, Julia now orchestrated the conversation. It wasn't easy for her, especially since her husband, sleepy with too much gin before lunch and now too much wine, gave her so little help. She had put DeGroot next to her to keep him quiet, and very quiet he was. The conversation she had decided upon, unlike the menu, wasn't very successful. Andrews, Miss Vallon, and Gelman, slowly coming awake, were interested in the war and the politics behind it, subjects she knew little about. They might be diverted for a time by her recollections of journalists and magazine fashion editors she'd known in Rome and Paris, by her familiarity with local culture and custom, but their political curiosity couldn't be denied. Confronted inevitably with the topics her visitors had come to explore but whose details she knew little or nothing about—the war, the WJLF, the Marxism of the Jubba, or the ugly revolution under way in Ethiopia—she retreated as she always did to her other favorite subjects, the rugged beauty of the littoral, the magnificence of the Indian Ocean, the majesty of the sky, whether in the early morning, in the late afternoon, or at night, as well as the natural and unaffected dignity of the people. Her guests should relax while they were here, relax and drink it all in as deeply as she had.

So to their restless curiosity she offered nothing more than the kind of consoling pantheism she fled to when out of her depth, that seamless organism of land, sea and sky and all living creatures therein, appreciation for which made even more sordid particularistic little subjects like war, misery, and politics, made them utterly insignificant, the cruel consequences of cruel leaders. Never mind that the sea frightened her; never mind either that she was terrified of flying, thunderstorms, or the unexpected tidal wave, of native crowds in the market or in Hamar Weyne and carried a can of Mace in her shopping basket even when flanked by her chauffeur, houseboy, and cook; never mind either that she disliked gardening and lived in harmony with nature only so long as it didn't sting, bite, soil, or bilk her. These reveries were just Julia's way of faking it, and Talbot, like Harcourt, had heard her fake it so long and so often that neither of them was really listening to her bullshit at all, as DeGroot and Mrs. Lawrence seemed to be, smiling rapturously at her pathetic nonsense. In describing these wonders—the magnificence of the sea, the vast sky, the stark beauty of the littoral, the stars at night, the luminous wafer of the full moon—her voice had taken on that soft beguiling little-girl quality Talbot recognized so well, Julia now deceiving herself as well as others, a child lost in a dark fairy-tale forest, crooning herself to sleep.

She was answering one of Gelman's polite inquiries about the goals of the WJLF freedom fighters, but had stood the question on its head and was describing the nobility of nomadic traditions and the pastoral way of life when Miss Vallon's harsh laughter interrupted her. Talbot, brooding now about Lindy in faraway Nairobi, woke with a start.

"Toute la chirie philosophique, toute la drouille da la nature," Miss Vallon was saying, looking mockingly at Talbot as she repeated what he'd said to her on the rocks.

Irritated, Julia stopped. After a moment of silent censure for the benefit of the others, she politely asked if, after less than two weeks in the country, the Frenchwoman's opinion differed. To Talbot's surprise, Miss Vallon said it did and repeated in French and then in English his comment about the WJLF press conference, namely that what she was hearing was just the same sack of philosophical shit dished out by Westerners who knew nothing of nomadic life, like the quasi-Marxists at the WJLF press conference.

Julia was shocked. So were DeGroot and Mrs. Lawrence, but Miss Vallon handled it all very well. There had been nothing personal in her comment. As it happened, she'd traveled among the nomads in the Maghreb, the Tuareg tribes of Morocco and Algeria, and knew a little about them, not a great deal but enough to know their lives weren't quite so idyllic as many Europeans thought them to be. The same was true, she was now sure, of the Jubba.

Her tone reassured Julia. She asked her a few polite questions and was rescued by her husband, who had a few of his own; Morocco had always fascinated him. Listening, Talbot wondered if Harcourt now had ambassadorial ambitions for Morocco. The exchange didn't last long. By then Julia's domination of the conversation had begun to take its toll. The journalists were anxious to get on with their afternoon schedules. The luncheon broke up very quickly, much to Julia's disappointment.

The DeGroots left. As Talbot got up to leave, Julia asked him to stay behind for a minute. Harcourt was seeing the last of the guests to the embassy cars sent to take them back to their hotels.

"It didn't go very well, did it?" she asked, standing alone at the wall.

"It went well enough."

"They seemed anxious to leave, everyone seemed anxious to leave, even you. Do I bore them that much?"

She turned to look at him and at that moment he felt a terrible, hopeless sympathy for her, hopeless because his sympathy went deeper than the words he couldn't find and that wouldn't reassure her anyway but could only be expressed in a more intimate way that would surely shock her husband and probably terrify her.

"No, you didn't bore them."

"You gave me no help, no help at all."

"Why do you go on like that?" he asked, but at that moment Mrs. Lawrence joined them from the shadows of the cottage.

"That was lovely," she said, "perfectly lovely."

"I'm glad everyone seemed to enjoy it."

With Mrs. Lawrence listening, she then told Talbot she had thought it might be nice for him to pick up Miss Vallon and bring her to the small dinner she was giving, but after some additional thought, she had decided Miss Vallon could very much take care of herself.

□ □ □

"What did you expect at the press conference?" Nicola asked re-proachfully as they strolled along the beach the following afternoon. "You said it was all a fiction. So why did you go?"

She was annoyed about something—maybe him. She'd appeared unexpectedly at his gate a little after four. She'd brought no plants and had on her market clothes, a dark blue skirt, a white blouse, and no makeup. She looked rather plain. She'd been too restless to sit in the back garden. It reminded her of the work still to be done, and she didn't want to think of that. She suggested they take a walk. Like Talbot, she seemed very much at loose ends.

"I thought some WJLF guerrillas might have been there."

"Why should they be there?" Her head was down. "Only the propagandists were there. You're sometimes naive, in spite of every-thing you know, not like Ambassador Malfatti, but naive. What would any WJLF guerrillas say at an official press conference?"

"I don't know. That's why I went."

"Do you think they could say what they feel? No, any more than you could if you had a press conference. Mr. Talbot of the American embassy will now speak to us." She smiled and put her hand on his shoulder. "Stop a minute." She lifted one foot to take off her sandal, then took off the other. Holding them in one hand against her dark skirt, she walked down the slope of wet sand. A few ghost crabs streaked away to hide themselves in the retreating surge. To the east a line of clouds hung low in the horizon, darker in the slanting afternoon light.

The port was empty of Soviet ships. Only a rusty freighter of Panamanian registry was in the roads, unloading sugar from In-donesia. The rumors were the Soviets had suspended all military shipments.

The wind moved her skirt open at her knees and she reached down to rebutton it. Her knees were knobby, not smooth at all like Lindy's, which were as sleek as glass.

"It's pretty depressing, the whole thing."

"If that's depressing, you can imagine what it's like for the Ethio-pians." She walked on. "It's very bad, I hear. Are the radio bulle-tins true?"

"More or less. I thought you hated the Ethiopians."

"I do, the Amhara, yes. But not like this."

She continued more slowly, her head down, studying the sand. "And as far as your embassy is concerned," she said, "it didn't matter, the papers Major Jama gave you. It didn't matter at all. Why?"

"I tried. It was Washington, not us."

"Why Washington?"

"They made the decision for their own reasons."

"What reasons? To give them weapons they don't need? How stupid."

"That wasn't the reason. Besides, we haven't given them any weapons. To send a message to the Russians."

She stopped, looking up. "I don't understand."

"To warn the Russians, tell them to stop thinking they were the only power in the region, that the U.S. could play the power game, too."

"Explain better. I still don't understand."

He told her the arms offer was a tactic, nothing more, intended to warn the Soviets that if they continued to arm the Ethiopians, the U.S. was prepared to arm Jubba. The tactic was part of Washington's grand strategy these days, designed to force the Soviets to restrain their political ambitions here on the Third World frontier.

"The Russians"—she sighed—"always the Russians. That is what is wrong with your embassies—always the Russians, no one else. What did Ambassador Harcourt say?"

"About what?"

"The papers from the ministry of defense."

"He was suspicious, thought they may have come from Lev Luttak at the Soviet embassy."

She stopped, annoyed. "He said that?"

"It was DeGroot's idea."

"What did you say?"

"Nothing, just that it came from someone I trusted."

She moved on. "You didn't say who."

"No."

That seemed to disappoint her. "You should have told everything."

"Why?"

"Because it is the truth. You don't help stupid people by telling them lies, by pretending. It only makes them more stupid. I couldn't do what you do. I would tell them what I thought, exactly how stupid they are." She moved down the slick sand a few steps and stooped to pick something up from the retreating surge. She studied it, wiped it on her skirt, studied it again, and handed it to him. "It's nice, isn't it?" Her voice had changed, the anger was gone; he heard only pleasure.

He looked at it. It was a small opalescent valve from a chambered nautilus. "A pearl."

"It is not." Quickly she took it back. "From the nautilus. Like a white opal." She gave it back. "Don't throw it. Keep it. Remember finding it."

She stopped again, looking out to sea. "You have a lovely beach. You will miss it when you go. In Paris there's a very ugly *piscine* on the Seine. You can walk there from your apartment in your beach robe, walk down the dirty sidewalks and cross the dirty streets, and then swim. It will be very nice for you. As you walk you can think of this."

"The Seine's nice; so is Paris."

"There is nothing in France like this, not even in the south. There are no beaches like this in the world, not even in the Seychelles."

"Is that what keeps you here?"

"Don't be stupid."

"Silly, not stupid. There are other English words besides stupid."

Three squat muscular figures approached wearing bathing trunks and white rubber caps, striding vigorously just along the edge of the wet sand. Nicola saw them and moved toward the sea, not looking at them. After the Russians passed she rejoined him.

"I didn't mean you were stupid, not at all. You're too clever for them, even for me, I think. Where is the valve?"

"I still have it."

"Let me see." He opened his hand. "Keep it, put it in your pocket at the house, in your swimming trunks. Then at the little piscine take it out and look at it, show it to your little French girls. On a gray day it will not seem so bright, neither will they."

"I will. Listen, I'm thinking of having some people to lunch, maybe next week. I was wondering if you would come."

"What people?" She looked at the Russians, saw one of them look back, and immediately turned away.

"Some journalists from Nairobi, friends from the embassy—"

"The Harcourts, no," she said angrily. "No, I will not come. Still she owes me more than a thousand shillings, still she refuses to pay, refuses even to talk about it. Does she think I'm rich, that I have money?"

"Not the Harcourts. I wasn't thinking about them. When will you be in town?"

"For now and the next few weeks, I think. I don't know. I'm staying at the Abruzzos' apartment. They're in Rome."

"So you'll come."

"I don't know, I won't promise. I don't want to meet strange people, strangers. It is better to be with people you know these days, people who don't just talk, people who understand."

They walked on.

"I think the president has made it impossible with the Russians, has burned his bridges," she said after a minute, "that it is all finished. That is what they are saying. What do you think?"

"I doubt it. That wasn't part of the plan."

"What plan?"

"The race against time. The president's betting he can bring on the collapse of Ethiopia before the Soviets or anyone else can save it."

She thought for a moment. "Yes, that could be. Yes, possibly. And after that?"

"My crystal ball clouds up there. Whatever it is, it's a bloody mess that's going to get worse."

"Is it?"

"Sure, worse every week."

"But I think that's what you like, bloody messes. I think you're not a diplomat at all, you're an anarchist, a Trotskyite. As soon as everything is officially settled, you want to smash it." She looked up at him, amused. "You are a political agnostic, I think: Everything can be taught but nothing learned."

"Is that what I am?" He was vaguely pleased.

"I think so. 'Politics is anger,' Seretti used to say. 'Politics is anger, so don't talk to me of words. Get out of my house.' " She clenched her small fist.

"Seretti?"

"My husband."

It was the first time she'd mentioned his name since their talk at her villa months earlier. *Seretti?* Odd way to talk about a dead man—like a body washed up on a beach: *Here lies Seretti, FNU, who took a concubine on the Benaadir Coast.*

The villa was cool and empty when they returned. She was thirsty and drank a glass of soda water in the kitchen. She noticed a worn Russian grammar and phrase book lying on the counter and picked it up curiously.

"Are you studying Russian?"

"It belongs to my cook. He thinks knowing Russian might help him get milk from the Russian milk factory."

She stood turning the pages, then raised her eyes and looked at him shyly. "I was not truthful the other night at the Italians'," she said in a soft voice. "I made a small lie."

"What kind of lie?"

"Maybe your guard told you. I came several times, four times, maybe five. Each time you were swimming out near the reef. So after a while I didn't come."

"But today you did."

"Today I did, yes." Her face, still lifted, seemed even more uncertain. "Maybe it was not right, my coming, maybe you had other things to do."

"Don't say that. I'm glad you came."

She still seemed unconvinced, a woman who needed consoling. What more could he tell her? He took her shoulders reassuringly, remembering that night in the Italian club garden, and brought her against him. "Relax, I'm glad you came." She came easily and didn't move as he touched his mouth to her forehead, found the fragrance of her hair, then her cheek. Her skin was cool from the sea wind, and he moved his face down her neck and a minute later was tasting the salt on her lips, very full lips, very soft; and what followed wasn't the consolation of friendship but the forgetfulness of instinct as his right knee moved deeper into the fork and his mouth browsed on, probing for more, but then he felt her stiffen.

Politely she brought his arms down, unstraddled his thigh, and released him with a soft kiss on the cheek.

"You're very sweet," she said, not offended, "but I'm very tired today, very tired. I must leave, yes, I must. I promised to go to the Italian hospital to see someone, and then some people are coming, very silly people and I must think in the bathtub what I am going to say." She turned and looked at him, still holding his hand as she moved away, and he had no choice but to limp after her. "The way you do, too, when you go to your embassy reception, always making your words ready for someone standing alone at the back wall. Come, walk with me, please—and don't look so sad. We will have other afternoons."

□ □ □

They had circled far to the west by vehicle and turned east on foot, walking along a herdsmen's path through the low barren hills. The ancient city of Harar was to the east and slightly south. The two WJLF scouts had gone ahead and were waiting as Major Jama and Lieutenant Samantar came up and unslung their weapons. A child appeared in the dark doorway of the low-walled house, her face as purple as a dusty plum in the fading light of the afternoon sun. Jama could smell charcoal. A few wisps of smoke trickled from a brazier. Against a small mound of stones a dozen meters below the house, two WJLF riflemen lay prone watching the track that wound at the foot of the low hills. Above them just inside the thorn enclosure a radioman sat on the ground next to the portable field radio, his legs stretched out in front of him, arms folded, his eyes shut. In the shadows of the mud-walled house, a small plump man lay sleeping, his head covered with a white kaffiyeh. His black robe and white gown were patched with brown dust; on his feet was a pair of gold-tooled leather sandals.

Shell craters and the deeper pits dug by 500-pound aircraft bombs lay along the track to the east toward Harar. The blackened skeleton of a truck blocked the track just below. At the bend to the east lay a gutted T-34 tank, its 85-mm gun splintered like a cane stalk from an explosive charge. A few charred corpses lay scattered on the far hillside, crisscrossed by goat paths, like the path that led them there.

The radioman opened his eyes, recognized Lieutenant Samantar, nodded, and went back to sleep. Lieutenant Samantar and Jama sat down to wait for the coming of darkness, watching the silent track below. The Ethiopians were dug in along the defensive perimeter east and south of Harar 5,000 meters to the north behind the low hills, where a heavy weapons group was deployed. The other eight men from the reconnaissance patrol joined them one by one, and after fifteen minutes fourteen now waited, including eight WJLF riflemen with AK-47s, two grenadiers with grenade launchers, two scouts with knives and light Soviet carbines. Each carried four grenades but no rations and little water. Two grenadiers also carried Claymore mines taken from the Ethiopian stores at Werder.

Lieutenant Samantar brought out his creased map and lay back studying it. The plump stranger awoke finally, got to his knees, spread his robe on the patch of dirt, and began his evening prayers. After he had finished, he sat down again and adjusted his kaffiyeh, his back against the mud-walled house, talking softly to himself. Watching him, Jama thought he might be a fair-skinned Harari, separated from his native city; he was olive-skinned and unshaven, his cheeks covered by a scraggly growth of gray beard. Locks of stiff gray hair hung from the front of his kaffiyeh. After a few minutes Jama heard the soft pure melody of classical Arabic on the afternoon wind.

He crawled forward and sat down beside Samantar, who was still studying the map, and asked about the stranger. A Saudi trader found wandering on the road, Samantar said softly. A reconnaissance patrol had brought him here, thinking him a holy man, a sheikh. He'd refused to retreat any further. Samantar returned to his map; Jama crawled away and slumped down again. He listened to the trader's low whispered voice for a little longer and finally called to him. "What wouldst thou here, uncle?"

The trader turned, his dark eyes bright with surprise. "What song is this? Dost thou sing to me, brother?"

"Aye. What wouldst thou here, uncle?"

Misery and misfortune had brought him here, a stranger in a

hostile and heathen country. Jama asked if he was from Jidda in
Saudi Arabia, and he nodded and moved closer. "Aye. Thou art a
man of good understanding."

"Who will attend thee home to Jidda?"

"I knowest not."

"No? Art thou not among brothers."

His eyes widened incredulously. "Brothers? I bear witness that
there is no god but God alone and I bear witness that Mohammed
is the Messenger of God, but I knowest not these brothers." He
looked at the riflemen watching him silently. "Hast thou no fear
of the wolf, the wild dog?" he whispered, crawling nearer. "Guard
thee thy weapon, thy knife."

"A stranger is a guest of Allah."

"Open thy eyes. Knowest thou where thou art? Amongst the
Sudan, the heathen black folk, the lawless Bedew."

"These are my brothers."

He was very shocked, his voice a whisper. "How are they thy
brothers? They do not speak as thee. Hear the noises they make."

"I hearest. Why art thou here?"

His name was Ali Salim al-Mas'ud, a Saudi merchant lost in
a hostile land he knew nothing about apart from its spices, aromatics, hides, and coffee. Except for a single visit to Cairo, where
he'd spent only two days before he returned home, confused and
frightened, and two visits to Sanaa, he'd never been abroad and
vowed never to go again. He and his brother were Saudi coffee and
spice importers from Jidda. They'd bought a large shipment of
robusta coffee from an Ethiopian coffee trader in Dire Dawa, but
learned too late the shipment was an illegal one, not approved
by the government coffee board, smuggled by camel train through
the mountains of Bale. The coffee was impounded. A merchant of
modest means, he couldn't afford the loss. Like a fool he was lured
to Dire Dawa by the Ethiopian trader's promise of full recovery of
his merchandise. When he arrived, the Ethiopian persuaded him
he could negotiate the release of the coffee with certain Ethiopian
coffee and customs officials. He'd agreed to deposit a certain sum
to an account in Barclay's Bank in Jidda, ostensibly for the care
and upkeep of the Juma mosque in Harar, but in fact for the
Ethiopian coffee and customs officials who would release the cof-

fee. But before the transfer could be completed, the Saudi and the Ethiopian were caught up in the war; the Ethiopian trader's vehicle was intercepted by WJLF guerrillas foraging between Harar and Dire Dawa. He and his Arabic-speaking interpreter were shot, their Land-Rover taken. Ali Salim al-Mas'ud, found terrified in the back seat, was thought to be a holy man and was set free to return to Harar. Two days later a WJLF patrol found him again, wandering the roads, discovered he was a Saudi, and brought him back with them. He refused to go any further south, where the wild Bedew foraged. He was waiting for the fighting to stop. Then he would go to Dire Dawa and take the train to Djibouti.

"God is my witness, the Ethiopian Kebede Tamrat, for that was his name, defrauded me and my brother and then defrauded us again. He conveyed me to Harar to see the mosque, this to satisfy my brother, whereupon we were set upon by Bedew on the road, and Kebede Tamrat was taken and murdered on the side of the road, and that done, the Bedew came to me. I answered as I am answering now, 'The Lord strengthen thee, how great is Moham-med,' and the heathen said to me, 'What language do you speak?' and I sayeth to them, 'What language does thou hear? Is it not Arabic? I speak what language ye hear. What all these other noises are, I know not.' Then after many days the Bedew come again and said in a noise very foreign to me, 'Come, we will take you,' and so here I came and here I wait, where thou hast found me. For pity, canst thou not help me?"

"I will help thee. I will take thee south after our business is finished."

"South?"

"To the south is the only way, then by truck to Benaadir in Jubba."

Ali Salim's frightened eyes turned away. "Through the waste-land? The Jubba there are *bahaim, kuffar,* heathen beasts, are they not?"

"Who tells thee this?"

"In Jidda, it is known. God knoweth. Who grazes his herds in the wilderness of the Jubba? Only thieves, lawbreakers, lunatic folk. No one will help thee there. They will cut thy throat, murder thee miserably. Dost thou not know that in their savage land no man fears to kill a stranger? They have no dates, no sweet water, only salt wells. Does thy head ache? It aches from the poisoned wells, the unlawful meat. They fly now, everywhere, like the wind, but the Ethiopians will have them again, as birds in a cage." He beckoned Jama closer and said in a very low voice, "Why dost thou wander with these wild Bedew yonder? A punishment will fall upon thee."

"I am Jubba, uncle."

"Thou are not. Jubba? How canst thou be Jubba?"

"From the Isaq Jubba."

"Aye, but from the oasis folk."

"From the wild Bedew, from the lawless folk. But I will help thee. How canst I not help thee? Was not my father twenty times removed Sheikh Ishaq bin Amed of the Quarish tribe of Mecca, the brother of your brother, twenty times removed?"

The Saudi watched him for a minute. "Peace be with thee, cousin. The Lord strengthen thee. I will pray that thou be spared. Should I wait in this place for thee?"

"Ay, uncle."

He crawled back and sat with his back to the mud-walled house, looking silently at the setting sun. Ten minutes later he called Jama over, pointing to the west.

"How name thou yonder peaks of mountains. Where the coffee grows?"

"No, not there. Far away, the other side. Why dost thou ask?"

"I would tell my brother I saw the mountains where the Ethiopian coffee grows."

He sat looking off into the setting sun, fingering his beads, his lips still moving silently as darkness came and they began to move out, the two scouts first, then the others.

□ □ □

Broken clouds drifted overhead against a faint three-quarter moon. They crossed the road one at a time and moved off along the flank of the hill, strung out at intervals behind the lead rifleman, and followed a dry streambed overgrown along the banks by sharply spined acacia. Jama had difficulty seeing the grenadier ahead of him, who moved without a sound. Lieutenant Samantar had placed him to the rear, just ahead of the last rifleman. Traveling with little water and no rations had seemed sensible, but fifteen minutes after they'd left the observation post his throat and nostrils were filled with dust. Occasionally the rifleman behind him closed on his heels to touch him on the shoulder to move him ahead. Then he'd prodded him twice in succession as Jama had stopped, bent over, trying to stifle a cough in his dry throat. He handed Jama a short length of stalk he'd cut from the bank and split at the ends, like a length of sorghum. He put the end in his mouth and tasted a strange aromatic sap in the pulp. He felt the rifleman touch his shoulder again, draw his hand down his throat, and shake his head. He chewed the pulp without swallowing and after a few minutes spat it into his hand. His throat had cleared and his thirst was gone. He stuck the remainder of the stalk in his belt.

The rifleman behind him knew these things, knew the secrets of the wasteland, whose vast sky and endless horizon made all wisdom infinitely small—sap from a dry stalk, the medicine of an herb, acacia, or sisal, how to sharpen a tool from a tiny francolin bone, the meaning of a spoor or the roots of wild grasses where rain had fallen three seasons past, the hidden warnings of the wind and clouds. If Jama had been taught them as a boy, tending his great-uncle's herds, he'd forgotten them now. He had gone to London and Rome, where these things weren't important, gone to Cairo, Moscow, and Jidda, where he'd known traders like Ali Salim al-Mas'ud.

A punishment will fall upon thee, he had said. A strange little man, he and his brother, his uncles and cousins, all of them the same, sitting and gossiping in their dark little alleyway shops, traders in coffee, spices, hides, sugar, rice, tallow, butter, salt, camels, dates, electric fans, refrigerators, and air conditioners, as their fathers and their fathers before them, men whose trading and credit world extended from the Philippines to London and New York, but who in their private lives moved no further than their teahouses, their mosques, the public gardens, and their houses or their brothers' houses, and no further, knowing nothing of the great beyond, of liquefied gases or electromagnetism, unable even to disassemble the Japanese electric fans and air conditioners that had made their new fortunes, had never seen the factories of Tokyo or the coffee trees of Kaffa, but let the Koreans build their streets and sewers, the Jubba drive their taxis, the Americans build their planes, the Palestinians staff their banks, sheltered in a frightened feudal kingdom as small as Ali Salim's, men whose fears of the great colossi beyond made them even more deeply conservative, clinging to the splintered wreckage of a world everywhere else smashed, in chaos, sin, or in folly, but which anciently rooted there at home under the shade of that great dead tree that was Mecca seemed wholly intact.

A punishment will fall upon thee. What had frightened him in Cairo? What, indeed? The swarming streets, the ribbons of lights, the wild throbbing music, the eroticism in the women's faces, that great promiscuous chaos that lay at the outer edge of the universe.

And then there was Jama's great-uncle, as devout as Ali Salim but English-educated, like Colonel Mahmoud at Bulet Uen, his uncle with a fondness for English gin, English tea, English phonograph records of military marching bands, the drums and pipes of the Scottish Highlanders, and *The Illustrated London Gazette* in his summer house at Sheikh, remembering the names of his former British commanding officers who would never remember him, as he pretended when he'd come to visit Jama at the tutorial college in London, never show him their gardens in Suffolk or Kent. It was the semi-Anglicized, semi-Arab, semi-nomadic world in which Jama had grown to manhood.

What kind of madness was that?

"Who grazes his herds in the wilderness of the Jubba?" Ali Salim had asked in a classical Arabic unchanged in ten centuries. Here in the wasteland the wild Bedew kept a secret country of their own, more fertile than the Nile Delta, as rich as the Koran, but not like those sheltered interior courtyards of Jidda, Cairo, and Damascus, not in Ommiad tile, in the mosaic of floors, walls, and fountains, not in ivory, silk, or marble, but in a greenness Ali Salim would never see and never know, the infinite memory of their language and their poetry, that measureless well from which every man might drink, even the most savage of those who so terrified Ali Salim.

The first rifleman had stopped and now the others. Jama crouched down, his face and neck wet. He found the stalk in his belt and began to chew it. A mild rustling evening wind had sprung up, moving through the acacia.

The two scouts had gone ahead to disarm the two Ethiopian rifle positions along the wadi. They didn't move at night, not from their isolated police posts along the frontier or their garrison towns deep in the south, where night belonged to the hyena, the jackal, the lion, but most of all to the *shiftas;* a cultural truth as well, known to the nomads—secret, conspiratorial men, these Amhara of the mountains, these feudal princes of the massif surrounded by those ancient enemies they'd subjugated, the Galla, the Tigre, the Eritreans, the Afars, the Borana, the Shankalla to the south. To be an Amhara was to be a conspirator, the law of survival in Haile Selassie's empire and now Mengistu's. Nothing betrayed it better than their soft sly native tongue, which left every truth half hidden, every lie half revealed. Suspicious men were frightened men; frightened men rarely ventured out at night here in the lowlands.

The wind died away, then came again. He watched the clouds floating near the three-quarter moon. They waited, crouched in place; after ten minutes they began to move forward again, past the Ethiopian gun positions where the two bodies lay hidden, their throats cut, and Jama could smell the breath of spiced meat and sour coffee. The dry wadi ended in a seam climbing to the low plateau. At the top was a track, to the east lay the mortar batteries, to the west a sandstone outcropping. Where the ground lifted to the north were two artillery batteries protected by earth embankments.

Lieutenant Samantar sent two riflemen on each flank. The others waited in the wadi. After twenty minutes they heard voices and men talking as they walked along the track between the forward mortar positions and the artillery battery to the rear. After they passed, one of the scouts carrying a Claymore mine moved as silently as a cat up the seam and disappeared onto the track. A minute passed, then another. At a signal from Lieutenant Samantar, two grenadiers moved away to the east and two to the west.

They waited.

Ten minutes later the scout returned from the track, but Jama didn't see him, didn't hear him until he dropped among them. The other scout handed him a scrap of green towel he carried on his belt, and the scout sat with his face pressed into it, his shoulders heaving.

Twenty minutes later they heard more voices passing above, and as they faded in the distance the other scout moved his weapon to the rifleman, patted it once, moved up the slope, a pistol and knife in his belt, and disappeared onto the track.

Jama watched Lieutenant Samantar, who kneeled unmoving in the acacia shrubs, head lifted toward the track, a rifleman next to him, head lifted. The wind came again, and they heard the voices return, this time from the artillery battery. Lieutenant Samantar passed the detonator to the rifleman, lifted his AK-47 silently, and crawled forward to the end of the wadi.

Jama took a deep breath, still kneeling at the rear, holding his weapon, his legs painfully cramped. He heard voices drift closer on the track above, soft quiet voices, dreamlike, as far from the war as he seemed, then heard a shot, heard someone cry out in pain, heard a second shot, then a third.

From the east came the two explosions as the grenadiers fired their grenades at the mortar batteries. The artillery batteries came to life—sudden cries, men shouting in the darkness behind their battlements. Feet came sliding down the slope and through the scree as the scout carried his prisoner down the slope. He dropped into the streambed, and the other scout immediately bound the Ethiopian's mouth with the towel, lashed it in place with a leather belt, and they retreated back up the wadi, dragging their prisoner with them. Lieutenant Samantar waited, crouched among the rocks with the detonator. As the squad of Ethiopians trotted along the track above toward the besieged mortar position, he detonated the Claymore mine and the track erupted in a geyser of fire, phosphorous-white on Jama's retina, then dissolved in yellow and crimson flares. Bodies were ripped sideways, flung across the track and down the slope. The two riflemen on each flank began firing at the bloody figures crawling away to the east and west. The reverberations from the exploding Claymore were still echoing in Jama's ears as the two grenadiers to the west fired their grenade launchers at the artillery battery. The Ethiopians were in panic; more cries, more shouts mixed with the screams of the wounded. The four flanking riflemen withdrew one by one to follow Samantar back to the wadi. The grenadiers from the east were already waiting at the entrance to the wadi near the burned-out tank. A few minutes later the other grenadiers joined them. They jogged rapidly across the track and up the slope to the observer post below the mud-walled house.

While they rested, Major Jama questioned the prisoner, an Ethiopian lieutenant who was wounded in the right arm. One scout held a knife to his throat. He had arrived a week earlier, and Jama suspected he might know something about the role of the Soviet advisers who'd been sent from Addis Ababa to aid the Ethiopians. The Cubans had already entered the battle on the side of the Ethiopians near Harar. Jama told them to untie his hands and let him bandage his arm. He woke Ali Salim, who was sleeping outside the small house. They moved out quickly and filed down through the barren hills, taking their prisoner with them.

◻ ◻ ◻

They had rested once and now were walking again, the low hills and the mud-walled house far behind them. The sky was still dark.

Ali Salim's tireless voice came again: "How name thee that veil of stars yonder, Jama? Do these Bedew know the stars by names or numbers?"

"By names, uncle."

"Would it not be better were the moon to shine in good grace?"

"Aye, uncle, the moon. And after the moon the sun in good grace."

"The sun, cousin?"

"Aye, the sun." Jama's voice moved as mechanically as his heavy feet. "Aye, the sun, the rain, and the green grasses, and the young folk and the old folk all, all cometh, the living and the dead, all in good grace, uncle, and this be called Paradise."

Ali Salim lapsed into silence. After a minute, Jama heard him say very softly, as he had after his evening prayers, "I would thank thee, moon, for shining now, to show me this path." Then, more loudly: "Be it a goat path or hyena path our feet are traveling, Jama? Who is coming behind? If enemies be coming from behind, shouldst we not walk more quickly? If there be no one, shouldst we not sit down and rest again? Art thou not weary of walking? What think thee, cousin Jama? Dost thou know what thoughts their minds take in the darkness. They follow one to the other as silent as wolves. Steal not, kill not, covet not. They knowest the law, do they not?"

"Aye. They keep the law. They are weary."

"So what think they? Do they think to outwalk the night? What man outwalks the night?"

"A foolish man, uncle."

"Wait. I saw that stone move there ahead, did I not? Dost it walk with us? Didst thou not see that stone moving, Jama, walking with thee?"

"It is one of us, uncle."

Ali Salim had stopped. The WJLF scout walking behind him prodded him on. After a few minutes of silence, Jama heard the voice again. "Who is this smiler and jabber walking behind? Does this shadow have no voice? I would have water but have none. What is this herb he passed to me. Will its juice make thee mad?"

"It is for thirst, uncle."

"Whose thirst? It is well chewed already. Dost thou chew one?"

"Aye, uncle."

"Tell me, do the oasis folk know the fig, the citron lemon, large but not so sweet as the small but better for thirst? This great-uncle of thine, does he do his living only by the copulation of camels? Hearest me, Jama? Where art thou?"

"Here." Jama waited. "Aye. Soon we will stop."

"Not goats? What be that light there? Has a star fallen?"

Jama looked to the north. A red flare fell slowly to earth.

"No, uncle. For the guns. My great-uncle trades goats, too, goats to Jidda and Yemen." He began walking again.

"From Jidda buy we not camels of the Jubba, goats, hides, and bananas? Not salt. The salt cometh from the Danikil Bedew, the savage black Bedew who go naked as frogs. Hast thou seen them, Jama?"

"Aye."

"Wouldst thou dare walk there as thou walk here, Jama? Amongst those who worship idols and know not the law."

"No, uncle, I would not walk with the Danikil Bedew."

They continued walking to the south, turning at last onto the flat pan and then back along the tarmac to the brigade command post that lay under the webbed netting spread over the rocks and acacias. In the first gray light, far in the distance to the northwest, they heard the sounds of guns begin again.

As the light lifted, Ali Salim's fears eased. He'd stopped to say his morning prayers. As he continued walking and the morning grew brighter he saw the khaki uniforms of the two scouts, stained with blood, and the Ethiopian prisoner with the bloody shoulder. He'd had nothing to say. He waited in the shadows of the command post, looking about in bewilderment.

The Ethiopian lieutenant said he had seen a few foreigners in the rear but didn't know their nationality. He'd seen them at a distance. They were dressed in khaki and were driven about in a colonel's Land-Rover.

The colonel decided to have the lieutenant sent to the rear. Jama found the truck that had brought up rations that morning and talked to the driver, asking him if he would take Ali Salim to the rear with him and find a place for him on a truck going on to Bulet Uen. But Ali Salim, after inspecting the truck, the driver, and the woman corporal dressed in khaki twill, decided he would wait here and rest.

"What is her folly?" he asked indignantly as he followed Jama back to his own Land-Rover. "Who commands her, this woman who would be a man? Wherefore laugh? Is this not a blasphemy, cousin Jama?"

As they were sitting in the shade of the Land-Rover drinking tea and eating ration biscuits, Jama tried to explain to Ali Salim how he would arrange his transportation back to Bulet Uen. But then Ali Salim got up, moved his position slightly, and sat down again.

"Speak not so openly, cousin Jama," he said softly. "The Bedew yonder looks at thee like a thief. What dost thou have he covets?"

It occurred to him that Ali Salim was carrying a great deal of money in his hidden money belt, as most Saudi traders did, and he got up again and went to look for an Arabic-speaking driver who would take him back to Jubba as soon as possible.

□ □ □

The sun was low on the western hills as they returned from their walk along the beach. The afternoon light was in flux, quick and painful in their eyes, bright on the columns of raffia palms, as soft as honey against the whitewashed walls of the villa, carving dark hollows in the rubble of oyster shell inside the wall.

The gate guard was saying his evening prayers as they reached the front gate and they waited.

Talbot turned, looking back out to sea. The wreck lay in eighty to a hundred feet of water, he told her, pointing out where he'd been swimming that day—a hundred meters beyond the reef some-where, maybe less—a Portuguese frigate sunk during a storm in 1695.

"So that's what you've been doing out there," she said with a for-giving smile, her words uttered with that same tolerant, ladylike voice he'd heard for the past hour. She'd been to the hospital again that afternoon, she'd told him, but hadn't explained why. Whatever the reason, her visit had left her distant, detached, even a little sad.

They climbed the steps and went into the front salon, refresh-ingly cool at that time of day.

"Time for the news, isn't it?" Talbot said cheerfully, trying to awaken some flicker of liveliness. He turned on the Grundig short-wave radio and searched through the static for the BBC from Lon-don. The prospect of the latest news from the Ethiopian front didn't seem to interest her. She sat nearby, idly looking at the front page of the *International Herald Tribune*.

"The reception isn't very good this time of day," she said indif-ferently.

He turned it off. "How about a drink then, gin maybe?"

She was still looking at the paper. "I don't know. What time is it?"

"A little after five, early yet."

"Probably I should go." She didn't look up.

"Not yet. Gin'll pick you up, make you feel better."

"Will it?"

"It's an anti-depressant, what fueled the Industrial Revolution, what kept the Brits so long in Africa. Without it, they'd have gone bust a hundred years ago."

She seemed to smile. "Maybe a little one then."

Encouraged, he went down the steps and across the dining room to the kitchen. The tile floors were still damp from Ali's afternoon mopdown. He'd come late that day, obliged to appear at the police station early that morning as a result of some altercation with a local taxi driver, and hadn't left until almost four.

He made two gin-tonics and was quickstepping back to the salon before she could change her mind when he slipped suddenly. The ceiling reeled dizzily overhead, two surges of gin-flavored tonic splashed across his shirt, and the two flung glasses splintered to the floor somewhere behind him. He lay on his back on the damp floor. He tried to lift his head, felt a numbing pain in his hip and elbow, and lay back again. *"Jesus Christ!"*

She came quickly down the steps and kneeled beside him. "Are you all right? What happened?"

"I slipped on this goddamn floor."

"Did you hit your head? No, please. Lie still."

He lay still for a minute as she hovered over him. "I'm all right." He sat up, wincing. "Not my head, my elbow."

"This one?"

"This one. It's all right. Two jiggers' worth of gin all over my shirt. I don't give a damn about the tonic."

"It could have been very bad."

She helped him get to his feet. "My ankle feels funny, too." She steadied him as they went up the steps.

"You could have broken it."

"I think it's all right now."

"Your shirt is wet, your face. Hold still."

She took a handkerchief from her purse and dabbed at his chin, then his neck. Stirred by the scent of the handkerchief and the dark lifted eyes, he took her by the waist. She didn't seem surprised—hands still lifted, like a woman waiting for a partner on a dance floor—and let him set his mouth to hers. "You weren't hurt at all," she said as their faces separated a few inches.

"Sure I was; my elbow's killing me."

She didn't seem anxious to move away, and he kissed her again, not certain it might not end there as quickly as it had in the kitchen two afternoons earlier, but it didn't; and very shortly they'd moved to the couch, where they lay for several minutes. Her mouth, lips, and tongue were soft, gentle, and forgiving, yielding more and more.

One hand had already unbuttoned her blouse, the other was far up her thighs under her blue skirt, and it was then she struggled to free herself. The room was still filled with dimming afternoon light, the drapes were open. Lifting their heads they could see a few figures walking along the beach.

"Please," she asked softly, "not like this, not here."

She had on too many clothes, she said, and that made it awkward. He took her by the hand and they went upstairs to his bedroom. He pulled the drapes closed while she sat on the side of the bed undressing, and then he joined her under the sheet. In his first embrace of that small nude body he felt a certain awkwardness. Her lips and tongue weren't quite as spontaneous as they'd been earlier. She was now a woman who knew very well what she wanted and how she wanted it. For all his ardor she didn't seem quite ready to surrender to his passion or her own, all of which left him after ten minutes feeling like a traveling salesman in a strange hotel room—not his bed, not his house, not a woman he truly knew, not himself either, not quite, despite the guilt he'd felt at identifying Lindy's soft sweet scent hovering on the air. But inevitably, after what seemed to him like hours, he felt a final coaxing embrace and heard a long contented sigh which told him it may have been worthwhile. For the moment at least nothing else was required of him and so he fell asleep.

They had both fallen asleep. He had awakened to a sudden clangor at the gate and gone to the dark window, but whoever it was had gone away.

"From sixteen until twenty-one or -two, I lived a kind of rebellion," he was now saying, massaging one ankle lifted to his naked knee, half covered by the sheet, "intellectual rebellion, rebellion against everything, a real adolescent bastard."

He didn't know why he was telling her all this. He was depressed and his elbow ached. His lovemaking, he now told himself, had been merely mechanical. He'd learned nothing new except that the passion she was capable of when arguing with Malfatti or with others, even with him, didn't so fiercely possess her in bed, where her sensibilities were cool and withdrawn. They should have stayed on the couch, broad daylight or not, where her lovemaking might have been as spontaneous as his pratfall. Something was bothering her, something he hadn't reached, but then what had he expected? Women had a hundred reasons for making love, never the simple one he'd once believed in. Maybe that was why he was sharing something more of himself, that old unexcavated Talbot, the young romantic who bought secondhand books withdrawn from the Firestone Library at Princeton, the shucked-off Talbot, stone cold dead in the mausoleum of academia, who no longer interested him, now half bored, half dead, half lecherous, half crazy in the diplomatic Wild West.

He moved his hand down her soft shoulder and along the slope of her hips. Maybe a second success would be better.

Turned on her side, she said nothing, head on her two hands, the way a child would lie listening to a bedtime story, looking out across the shadows of the room toward the window. Her eyes felt very bright, very luminous, able to summon forms and figures from the shadows, the way she'd felt listening to her Tuscan grandmother's stories. She'd wakened with a rawness in her throat and found the air conditioner on. She had been sympathetic and let herself be seduced, she told herself. It had seemed much the simpler thing to do, more from fatigue than anything else, she pretended. Darkness had come and she didn't know what time it was. Seven, seven thirty? No later, she hoped. She would leave, have dinner someplace, set her mind on other things, and resume her life as if it had never happened. His youth had always frightened her a little, so boundless, so improvident, so reckless, and never more than that afternoon as they'd walked on the beach. Now she felt very sore, rubbed raw, and the wound still seared. His passion had hurt her, then exhausted her. Conscious of what she had given in return, and which now seemed too little, she felt humiliated.

"No one could tell me anything," Talbot was saying. "The only people who made sense were the writers I'd discovered, nothing else."

"Which writers?" *Didn't he ever tire?*

He tried to turn her over, but she moved his hand away. Exhausted and wounded, she didn't want to talk, only to listen, to move everything as far from her as possible. Now that she felt even older, he was a stranger, the distance between them absolute.

"American, European. Silone, Malraux, Hermann Broch, Koestler, Orwell. Poets, too, a pretty mixed bag. Not the Beats."

"And so what was the result?" She moved the sheet aside and crossed the bedroom and turned off the air conditioner.

"Are you cold?" He looked up, hoping to catch in full figure that small body she so shyly hid from him.

"No. I wanted to hear the sea."

She pushed open the door onto the balcony and let the warmer breath of night air in. Another woman had been in this room recently, been there many times, and she wanted to banish her scent. In this little bedroom with the air conditioner always on, he couldn't distinguish one season from the other, his young mistress either, she told herself vindictively, the northeast monsoons from southeast, the *jilal* from the *hagaa,* when the sea air was soft and warm, as it was that night. She turned back to the bed and thought about turning on the light, showing him how tired her body looked, how ugly and shrunken he'd made her feel, but she didn't. She climbed back onto the bed, remembering as she brought the sheet up how Seretti told her she made him feel so many years ago.

"Nothing, a kind of alienation. I was just anti, anti-everything." His hand moved along her arm and down her side.

"I mean what did you do with it, this alienation? In Europe, poetry and politics are often mixed." Her body still burned terribly. She wanted to leave, to think her own thoughts, to let her wounds heal, to share nothing with others.

"Nothing, just kept it inside. Then I decided I'd get a doctorate in European history and screwed that up, too."

"How?" Again she drew his hand away.

"Screwing around, like I am now."

"You didn't share all this with others?"

"No, I just played the game."

"And not to share it with others, that made it all right? How, by feeling superior?"

"Maybe." *Superior?* Why in the hell did she still think that? "I was pretty much an odd man out."

"Why? Because you weren't a good poet?" She sat up, letting the sheet fall away from her breasts. They hadn't aged as the rest of her and she took some pride in that. "In Italy it is like that, of course.

You go to university as an adolescent, you suffer, and then you write poetry. Very odd, very avant-garde poetry. Only you can understand it."

"I didn't write much poetry. I didn't have the talent."

"And so you did other things, you were politically active?"

"Not really. The worst summer when I really hit rock bottom I got a job on a fishing boat in Nova Scotia instead."

"How old were you?"

"Nineteen."

"So now you're a diplomat," she said matter-of-factly. "A Trotskyite and an anarchist inside, but outside a diplomat and now everything is settled."

"Not now. I don't have the ambition for it anymore. I don't have any plans, not really. None and it doesn't matter."

"Why did you come here?"

"I was still playing the game. I suppose I still am."

She could hear the sound of the sea and listened as she silently took his wrist and looked at the luminous dial of his watch.

"It's seven forty," she said, rising. "I must go."

"Go where?"

"Drive back."

"You said you weren't driving back, that you were using someone's house."

"I can't stay here."

"We'll have dinner someplace."

"I have to shower."

She dragged the sheet from the bed, covered herself, retrieved her scattered clothes from the chair, and went into the bathroom and closed the door.

After she dressed she went downstairs to wait. Standing at the glass doors watching the waves break against the beach, she thought she might leave. She turned quickly back across the room, found her purse, picked it up, and stood there listening. He was still in the shower. A moment passed, then another. She sighed, put her purse down, found the shortwave radio, and listened to the eight o'clock BBC from London and the bulletins reporting the war in Ethiopia. He joined her a few minutes later, carrying his coat, too late to hear the bulletins.

She couldn't make up her mind. She didn't want to go to Juliano's or the Palestinian restaurant, not the UN club, never, not the Anglo-American club, which was even worse. They left the front gate in his Fiat, and it was only as he was halfway down the Lido road that she thought of the Italian club.

But standing outside the rear garden looking at the crowded tables, she recognized a few Italian friends, saw Ambassador Malfatti and a few from the Italian embassy staff, and thought she might have made a mistake.

"I don't think you'll like this," she said. "I never come here. Maybe we should go to the Giubba Hotel instead." An Italian journalist from Rome was sitting at the table next to the Malfattis, a man she knew and disliked. The low terrace above the garden was crowded with diners.

"Whatever you say."

"It wasn't a very good idea."

"It's up to you."

But then the waiter arrived and she yielded again, turning, eyes lowered as she followed him across the terrace, past tables where a few heads had lifted. As they did, she discovered a certain exhilaration in their curiosity, her triumph mirrored in the small shrewd eyes of Mrs. Malfatti, in Julia Harcourt's bitter astonishment, in the abstract notice of their two husbands, and the sad wise look of Giorgio Rugatto. But then she looked neither to the right nor left as she moved toward the far corner. Whether Talbot stopped to say something to them, she didn't notice, and it didn't matter. He had too much youth, too much energy. Nothing they might think or say in their own pettiness would diminish him as it might her, and she had shared both.

"I was wrong. It is sometimes nice here, isn't it?" she said as they sat down, she facing the terrace, he with his back to the other tables. "Coming alone I don't like, no." She didn't acknowledge the glances that came her way, even from Rugatto.

Seeing the others, Talbot knew he'd made a mistake and would have preferred to be someplace else, out of his temporary cul-de-sac, but it didn't matter much. His elbow still hurt. Sitting at the Mariner's Cave might have been preferable, as much as he'd grown to despise the place, but not with Nicola, who deserved better. He should have taken leave and gone to Nairobi with Lindy.

She asked him about his plans for Paris and whether he yet had a flat. She said again what she'd said two days earlier, that he would miss the sea, the beach, the narrow passageways of Hamer Weyne, his diving excursions off the reef for a ship he'd never find.

It seemed to Talbot an oddly secondhand conversation, a patchwork stitched together from their many talks, the woman across from him as detached as she'd been on the beach and later in bed. He wasn't sure what he was to make of it.

"I wanted to tell you something," she said with a small smile. "This afternoon when you mentioned it I remembered, but then I forgot. It's about the Portuguese ship. Do you mind my saying something about it?"

Had she ever asked his permission to express an opinion? Hell, no. Why was she asking now?

"No, not at all. What is it?"

She told him there was no Portuguese ship off the reef. The Italian professor, the one who said he saw a map, he wasn't serious. Just an old man, seventy-five, seventy-six, she thought, an old gossip who collected old maps and loved to talk about them. He'd told many Italians many stories about maps and Portuguese ships, but none was true.

"I'm sorry," she said. "But everyone knows."

"Who cares? It doesn't bother me what these goddamn people say."

"You're sure?" She put her hand on his. "Please, it's better I told you, isn't it? Not someone else, some Italian here."

"I don't talk to those people." He was conscious of her small warm hand on his, and it made him uncomfortable. "Whether I ever believed there was a ship or not isn't important. Maybe I didn't, Noseworthy either. Anyway it wasn't the ship so much, just the diving down, floating off somewhere. The fish, too. It's all that together, that and the compulsion to go down, find out where the bottom is, even when it sometimes scares the shit out of me."

"The truth is you're bored, you're bored and you have too much energy. How old are you?"

"Thirty-two."

"You see? Thirty-two is young still."

"Young for what?"

She thought for a moment and said thirty-two was still young enough for anything; forty-one wasn't.

"I thought you once said you were forty."

"I did," she said, "but now you know forty, then forty-one doesn't seem so much older, does it?"

□ □ □

The WJLF office of information had sponsored a tour of the liberated areas of Western Jubbaland, inviting several dozen journalists and diplomats to take part. They'd been driven in convoy across the border into Ethiopian territory and visited a few liberated villages where the Jubba populations had all been carefully prepared and carefully rehearsed, provided with small flags, flowers, and the other narcissi-like symbols of their emancipation to welcome the visitors.

Talbot had been told of the trip by Miss Vallon, the Agence France correspondent, who'd telephoned and suggested he might like to sneak along. But a State Department cable had forbidden embassy personnel from taking part in any excursions into WJLF-controlled areas, even as observers, since their presence might imply U.S. recognition of WJLF sovereignty in the illegally seized Ethiopian territory. The official U.S. position, repeated daily by the Department press spokesman since the Jubba invasion, called for the immediate withdrawal of WJLF and Jubba troops and a peaceful settlement to the territorial dispute.

At a diplomatic reception, Lev Luttak of the Soviet embassy told Talbot this was blatantly hypocritical, since it was the U.S. offer of arms that had tempted the Jubba military to begin the long-awaited campaign to recover the occupied territories. Moscow, he reminded him, had strenuously opposed the invasion and had never supported the pseudo-Marxists of the WJLF or any other national liberation movement in Ethiopia.

Despite the State Department instruction, DeGroot announced he intended to take part in the WJLF-sponsored trip, but insisted he intended to travel with the WJLF caravan only to the border and no further.

"Should we deny to ourselves what is freely available to our journalist colleagues?" he said at the country team meeting before his departure. "I will remain at the border and from there observe what I can with my binoculars."

He was gone two days. Following his return, it was obvious he had gone a great deal further and seen considerably more than might be visible to someone standing giddily atop some solitary frontier obelisk, reeling from the heat and dust, binoculars in hand.

They met in the refurbished situation room the morning following his return, assembled to learn firsthand from an experienced American diplomatic observer what was going on in the occupied territories. Freshly shaven, dressed in suntans, brown shoes, and the customary white nylon socks, his pearlike face saddled with sunburn, DeGroot sat in the brown leather chair next to Harcourt, both feet on the floor, his notes on his plump knee.

Whittington began the debriefing by asking DeGroot how it was he didn't leave the convoy at the frontier, as he'd told everyone he intended to do. His tone was skeptical, even disapproving. The same question bothered Talbot. Like Whittington, he would have liked nothing better than to visit the occupied territories and at last hear those naked human voices so long denied him.

"As it happened," DeGroot said solemnly, "the border village where I was to be sheltered had been demolished by Ethiopian aircraft the previous day. It was most unfortunate, an entire village laid waste."

Like Talbot, Whittington glanced at Harcourt to see whether the ambassador was satisfied. He apparently was.

"A pity," Harcourt murmured, "most unfortunate."

DeGroot smiled gratefully. "I immediately made it clear to my WJLF hosts, of course, that my presence must henceforth be considered force majeure, the accepted diplomatic practice in such circumstances. This they clearly understood. Reassured but most disappointed, I had no choice but to continue my journey with the invited correspondents."

Talbot had to smile. How could anyone seriously believe this rubbish? Did DeGroot really believe he could get away with it?

Harcourt, politely bemused, scribbled something idly on his yellow legal pad.

"Quite so," he said abstractedly, not anxious to embarrass his DCM and aide-de-camp in front of the embassy groundlings. "What can you describe for us? We'd be very interested."

"The reason, of course, for our little assembly this morning," DeGroot said with a froggy smile. "Let me begin." He consulted his notes, spreading them out on his spiral book. "Most interesting indeed. My first sight of a liberated village was a most memorable one. Its brightness still sparkles. I saw before me in the sun-baked streets a colorful Kiplingesque scene, a motley of dress and costume, old men, old women, young girls with bouquets, all richly dressed and smiling, a virtual *folklorique à plaisir* after the presumed fashion of pastoral village life in some idyllic time." He seemed to have lost his place in his script and paused to turn a page over. "It was so festive I had to consciously remind myself of the suffering that stirred just below this happy surface."

Talbot's smile still hovered, painfully obvious; DeGroot didn't look up, searching for a misplaced page.

"How did you find the WJLF cadre people?" Kinkaid asked.

DeGroot, missing page in hand, paused to reply from memory, eyes on the ceiling. "The WJLF leader we talked to, a captain, I believe, was somber, religious-minded in outlook, I would say, very well informed, but no intellectual. I engaged him in some moments of private conversation, as did other of the journalists. His khakis were less well laundered than his lieutenant's, who was inclined, I would say, to dandiness. After the first day I came to recognize a weakness for grain alcohol."

He consulted the misplaced page.

"Did you actually go to the front?" Talbot asked, still smiling despite himself.

DeGroot chose not to look at him. "I was about to mention my particular guide. He was, if I am not mistaken, a fellow of the Ogaden tribe, a man of solemn aspect and sinewy purpose, not robust, but long of stride and lean of figure. I did see the front, yes, or what passed for the front, it being so hazy in the distance one could not tell. But also being among a nomadic people and escorted by a guerrilla organization in which perjury is not considered a crime, I could not know for sure." He smiled at his locution. "What was there to see?" He consulted his notes. " 'Behold the battle-ground,' our lieutenant said to us, his arm sweeping out over desolate scrubland, sun-baked and barren, over petrified wadis held captive by time, sand-patched and verdureless beneath a melancholy sky."

"So you're telling us you saw no military action," Whittington interrupted. Harcourt's veiled gaze traveled after DeGroot's lifted arm, which remained suspended, the dramatic flourish incomplete.

"By chance we did, albeit brief." He brought his arm down, disappointed. "I had left the party to explore a curious crater nearby and had taken no more than a dozen steps from the vehicle when a recurrent seismic murmur distracted my attention. Following the finger of my guide I beheld a pair of silver shapes streaking from some hidden apogee above the brow of clouds. Quickly they plunged, like shrieking falcon, talons flexed. Threads of fire streaked from their pinions. A cacophony of detonations pierced the air as their bombs tumbled to earth, raising fountains of dust and fire." He turned to Harcourt, who stirred himself in uneasy anticipation as DeGroot ad-libbed from memory: "These were the F-15s, I was told by my guide, flown by the Ethiopians who had destroyed the very village from which I was to make my observations."

"I see, hmmm."

"What about casualties," Kinkaid inquired, "the wounded?"

"Field hospitals? Yes." DeGroot shuffled through a few pages and found the one he was looking for. "We visited one field hospital, a most sombering experience. Once inside, I distanced myself from my comrades, wishing not to intrude further on the somber silence of the surgical table, where an operation was under way. There on a litter nearby I saw a mere youth, clad in bloody raiment. He seemed sensible of my presence, for after a moment, he opened his swollen eyelids. His soiled hands lifted and waved weakly. Ascertaining that he was seeking assistance. I went to search for the orderly, who was then assisting a doctor, an Englishman, I was told. The medic came to look at him, a chap from the Red Crescent, I believe. He gave him water and I saw a small smile of gratitude form itself on his black lips. But at that moment, alas, his head slipped aside. I saw no further speculation in his gaze."

After a moment's silence, during which Harcourt continued looking at DeGroot uneasily, Dr. Melton asked about the accommodations provided by the WJLF.

DeGroot smiled gratefully. "Ah, yes, the accommodations. A most interesting question. The first night we arrived after dark and were housed in some discomfiture in an ancient mud-walled house once belonging, I was told, to the Ethiopian administrator for the region, not *balabat,* as one of the journalists claimed, *balabat* being more a generic than a particular Amharic nomination. The walls were quite filthy, as were the crude toilet facilities, being merely a septic hole in the floor of a small closet, primitive even by the most primitive African standards. Or Arab, for that matter, as those who've traveled overland from Damascus to Baghdad might recall. The meal, I should say, was quite primitive, fowl of some kind, whether native or imported I do not know. We slept on the floor. I had no more settled down to sleep when I was awakened by the cry of a jackal off in the barrens, the jackal, I am told, being quite common to the region, as is the hyena, and, until recent years, the lion. Ostrich are also found there but lesser in recent years, owing to the depredations of the herdsmen who rob them of their eggs, as those of us familiar with the wares of the beach peddlers know so well. I roused myself early from my pallet, wishing to explore our immediate surroundings in some privacy, free of the meddlesome intrusion of our host. I looked from the door disappointed, thinking morning still far off, but to my pleasure dawn was breaking already, over cold gray hills, over wadis and flint-strewn ridges of a sullen mist encumbered—"

"How was the food?" Dr. Melton asked. Talbot, sitting next to the door, suddenly got up and bolted from the room, closing the door quickly behind him.

"Ah, the food, yes . . ."

Harcourt sat staring at DeGroot, Talbot's departure unnoticed, Dr. Melton's question unheard, DeGroot's words droning on as Harcourt's spine, neck, and forehead prickled with some dreadful, humiliating, undiagnosed fever his body had too long suppressed.

Slowly, very slowly, like light percolating through the darkest of darkness to finally illuminate that tiniest of crypts where he kept his most painful secrets, his wife's desperate unhappiness, his own abject weakness, it occurred to him the man was insane.

CHAPTER TEN

History's Orphan

At ten o'clock that morning DeGroot was hastily summoned from the map room by Harcourt's secretary, Whittington from his second-floor suite, Kinkaid from the first-floor visa office, where he was busy signing visas for a six-man Jubba military delegation on its way to Washington to discuss yet another ministry of defense arms list.

No one could find Talbot.

He was on the roof looking out to sea, telescope adjusted to the distant figure leaning over the wheelhouse railing of a derelict Soviet freighter that had appeared in port that morning, the first in two weeks. The figure appeared to be a woman, but at 3,000 yards it was difficult to tell. The four beefy Russians leaning against the railing on the deck below had stripped off their shirts and were enjoying the morning sun. The more modest figure above was wearing a white shirt and eating something. A banana, possibly.

He'd discovered the figure while waiting for the battering seas to move the lonely freighter a few more yards so he could make out the final letters of the Cyrillic name on the rusty stern. No deck cargo was visible, no wooden crates under tarpaulins, of the kind that once carried MIG fuselages or Oryx missiles. With its orange-and-copper-streaked plates riding so high in the water and its punt-like instability on its hawsers and anchor chain, Talbot suspected it was empty. If so, it was additional evidence that the Soviet Union had suspended all military shipments to Jubba, even munitions and spare parts, as a Jubba vice minister at the ministry of defense had told Harcourt. Lev Luttak had hinted as much to Talbot at an evening reception four days earlier.

The freighter finally swung around a few meters and he copied the missing letters on his pad. He took a final look at the figure against the railing and saw her lean forward, looking at one of the men on the deck below who was waving his shirt at her. She made a seductive gesture, hands at her blouse buttons, the sailors below boisterously waved their shirts, and Talbot concluded she was indeed a woman. Satisfied, he capped the telescope, locked up the shed, and walked across the hot roof to look down into the narrow street still in shadow below.

Harcourt's car was there at the curb; so was DeGroot's. The wind carried the smell of frying oil from the rooftop just to the north, where an Arab woman was roasting corn cakes over an open brazier. Crossing the street toward the USIS library he saw Lindy, returned from Nairobi three days earlier, walking easily between cars, tossing her head in the same easy familiar way as she nodded to the taxi driver who'd stopped to let her pass. At the pit of his stomach he felt again the devastating loss, the stupidity of what he'd done, the folly of his cul-de-sac. He loved her, he told himself, and love was the only opportunity he had left, the only way he could reclaim anything, and now something once part of him was gone, an arm, a leg, two legs, and there they were, his legs belonging to another person entirely, walking across the street below in that long easy stride, not even aware of his existence.

He'd asked Whittington to tell him as soon as he knew the date and flight number of her return from Nairobi, but Whittington hadn't and had met her himself. Not until they met on the embassy stairs the following morning did he know she was back. She'd been cool, even abrupt, and he'd known something was wrong. He didn't know how she knew about Nicola or who had told her, but she knew, maybe from Whittington, who'd come to his villa one afternoon while Nicola was there, maybe from the Kinkaids', whom he and Nicola had passed once on the beach at dusk, out for a walk with their children. She no longer brought the CIA reading board to his first-floor cubicle but sent Whittington's secretary instead. She wouldn't return his calls, wouldn't see him, wouldn't give him a chance to explain at all.

If he loved her why hadn't he been able to tell her that? God knows he'd told her everything else. Maybe it was the loss he felt, the loss more than her, maybe it was the pain he needed, more genuine than anything else these days, more deep, more real.

In front of the Syrian restaurant a small gray-haired surveillance man from the NSS was leaning against his blue Vespa smoking a cigarette. Talbot looked north along the wide stretch of beach toward his villa, crystalline clear in the morning air, and crossed back toward the stairwell to be swallowed up by the oppressive shadows of his first-floor office.

He went back down the corridor to return the telescope shed key to the safe in the executive suite. Harcourt's door was shut.

"They've been looking everywhere for you," Miss Simpson said distastefully without looking up, as if he reeked with infidelity. She was no longer his spy in the enemy camp but a defector. The same unspoken censure seemed to be in everyone's eyes these days, even Whittington's—the embassy mongrel returning to the kennel in the wee morning hours, bringing the smell of his bitch's heat back with him. He supposed it was all over the embassy by now. Whittington had had nothing to say to him for a week. He wondered if Lindy was giving him the cold shoulder because she was operational now. If Whittington still believed Nicola was an NSS or CPI informant, maybe he'd told Lindy she'd bugged his bedroom. That would keep the operational types away, wouldn't it?

"You'd better go in. Everyone's there."

"What about?" He hadn't been invited to their strategy councils these past weeks; he had little interest in them now.

"Something important. A cable just came in."

"I've got to make a phone call first."

At a country team meeting a month earlier, young Kinkaid had suggested that they might benefit by a more open and frank discussion of policy matters. DeGroot, warned by Harcourt's smiling assent, had agreed. His tactic at the country team was now to invite discussion on subjects raised by incoming cables, the contents of which only he and Harcourt had seen. Few were quick enough to organize their thoughts in the time it took for DeGroot, notes already in hand, to define the subject and express the consensus.

He went downstairs to the commo room, rang the bell, and waited. A few minutes later Miss Virgil, the Department commo clerk, answered his ring. She knew immediately why he'd come.

"They've got it upstairs," she said.

"I know, but I want to see your copy."

"There wasn't a garble, was there?"

"I don't think so. I just want to check."

He followed her back to her desk and she opened the folder and handed him her copy.

One glance at the telegram's subject line was enough.

The Department would inform the Jubba ambassador that day that the U.S. was withdrawing its offer of defensive arms. The action had been taken in response to the Jubba invasion of Ethiopia.

"Those goddamn idiots."

"That bad, huh?" Miss Virgil said. "I knew someone was all shook up."

Having reaped the whirlwind, Washington's fussy little geopolitical academicians had beat a hasty retreat, leaving the bloody mess across the Ethiopian frontier for the diplomatic bucket and broom brigade from the State Department to clean up. The Department was calling upon all parties to end the conflict and find a political solution to their differences.

The telegram was still being discussed as Talbot joined the group in Harcourt's office and found a chair near the window.

DeGroot and Harcourt were quietly discussing some obscure point of etiquette which Talbot, in his present mood, couldn't identify. Kinkaid sat sucking reflectively on his cold pipe. Whittington was busily scribbling notes to himself. Rhinehart was moving his right ankle back and forth as he studied his new Hush Puppies,

arrived from Sears the day before in the sea pouch. Peterson was
gazing sleepily out the window. During the interlude Dr. Melton
was editing his USIS wireless file notes for his noon news sheet.

As the conversation resumed and Talbot managed to quiet the
angry throbbing in his ears, it was apparent neither Harcourt nor
DeGroot was upset at the decision. On the contrary, as DeGroot
was explaining, the withdrawal was eminently reasonable under the
circumstances. Jubba forces had violated the sovereign territory of
Ethiopia. If as yet no deliveries of U.S. arms had been agreed upon,
much less delivered, from the point of jurisprudence the U.S. was
not associated with the Jubba offensive.

Talbot had expected disappointment, anger, even outrage, but
not this.

"Jurisprudence!" he said hotly. "What jurisprudence? They
wouldn't have gone into Ethiopia without our offer of arms. Don't
you people understand that yet?" He had been incensed originally
because the offer should never have been made, because it was a
dishonorable one, never intended to arm Jubba in ways the Jubba
government imagined. Now he was outraged because they could sit
there as they did, swallowing all this nonsense without a murmur
of protest while all those bodies rotted out there in the sun and
more joined them every hour. "Don't you understand what's going
on! What's it take to wake you up?"

DeGroot looked at him in amazement. Harcourt's blue eyes
darted toward him. He caught himself and lifted his hand in warning. "Please—"

Whittington, Rhinehart, and Dr. Melton continued to stare at
him.

"Should armaments be delivered," DeGroot continued, his voice
rising in anticipation of any further outburst, "this obviously would
no longer be the case, and the U.S. would be associating itself with
that aggression. On the other hand a negotiated political solution
everyone deeply desires. With the WJLF now holding large sectors
of Ethiopian territory, a timely political solution might now be
negotiated."

"That's absolute bullshit," Talbot said loudly.

DeGroot turned crimson.

"Just a minute, please," Harcourt said, ears reddening too. "What is it you want to say, Logan?"

"What's obvious. If a political solution had been possible, it would have been negotiated months ago by the only ones who have any leverage with Jubba or Ethiopia, the Russians, and God knows they tried—"

"The Russians?" DeGroot said immediately. "Are we to—"

"Just shut up a minute. The Russians, like it or not. Only the Soviets have any leverage over both sides, they supply the military hardware, here and in Addis. But they weren't able to do a bloody thing, nothing, even though they wanted a political settlement worse than anyone. So you've got a war going now because there was no political solution, none the Russians could find, and they had more money on the table than anyone. If we think we're going to pull one off now with no leverage, no table stakes at all, just kibitzing from the sidelines, we're still kidding ourselves."

"You're that convinced," Harcourt said quickly, seeing DeGroot impatient to interrupt.

"Absolutely convinced. The only political solution right now is a Jubba withdrawal."

"You are recommending a return to the status quo ante," De-Groot said, pretending amazement. "A Jubba withdrawal?"

"That's the only solution."

"That's not a solution but a surrender."

Again Harcourt interrupted, this time to prevent an outburst from Talbot. He agreed that this might be true, but yet one had to try. It was the only honorable way to end the entire unfortunate affair.

Talbot knew then that they still didn't understand. For them, that decision had been an honorable one from the very beginning, made for an honorable purpose, the defense of Jubba's borders against aggression. Now it was being withdrawn for honorable reasons which gentlemen also understood: Jubba had betrayed American trust.

Harcourt asked DeGroot to continue, and he did, attempting to claim some of the credit, saying he wouldn't be surprised if his cable of two days ago, alerting Washington to the fact that the

Soviet Union had suspended arms shipments and spare parts to
Jubba might not have prompted the Department to do likewise, in
the interests, as he put it, of "superpower symmetry." The dispute
was to be raised in consultations at the UN, beginning that day.

So there it was. The U.S. had thrown in its empty hand and was
turning the whole mess over to the UN crowd, the Security Council
and General Assembly ding-a-lings. *Point of order, point of order!
Would the honorable representative from the People's Republic
kindly keep his feet on the floor and refrain from pounding his*
panga *on the microphone! Thank you.*

Talbot had started to rise, ears pounding again, but hesitated as
Kinkaid volunteered a few comments on how the Africans would
view the matter. The Organization of African Unity in Addis would
also play a role in negotiating an end to the war, this according to
the State Department cable—

Oh, yeah, sure, Talbot remembered, by all means, the African
specialists, like Kinkaid—they'd be involved, too, wouldn't they,
being chauffeured through the tropical sun at Lagos, Nairobi,
Dakar, and Kinshasa on their way to ask for foreign ministry support for a political solution, Kinkaid and men like him, the worst
of the lot, the most obeisant African tribe of all, the diplomatic
tribe, the Bene Oui Oui, prostrate before the reigning African
royalty: *"Oui, Monsieur le President, oui, oui. Bien sur, Monsieur
le President, oui, oui, oui—oui oui oui . . ."*

As the minutes passed and Kinkaid droned on, the pounding in
Talbot's ears grew steadily louder. He was standing up for yet a
third time when a knock came at the door interrupting him. It was
Miss Simpson. Harcourt was wanted in the commo room, the green
phone from Washington. The meeting was over.

□ □ □

In his first-floor office he telephoned Lindy and said he had to talk
to her that afternoon. She said she was busy and hung up. He sat
there a few minutes, the phone still in his hand. When he couldn't
stand it any longer he got up and left. He stood for a minute on the
sweltering sidewalk in front of the embassy, not knowing where he
was going. High overhead something was tumbling far to the north,

a cosmic glint. Another dizzy truth smashing down out of the empyrean? Leave a crater probably, right there in his skull. He waited, eyes lifted. A satellite, silver-skinned? Venus's moon, a MIG? Couldn't tell.

"What?"

An embassy chauffeur was plucking at his elbow, asking if he was waiting for a car. He shook his head and turned south. *What a fucking mess.* Small cars were passing; a horse cart pulling a kerosene tank was stopped nearby. A car pulled around it and someone waved and he heard the sonic boom from the MIG-21. A hundred meters down the street he stopped at the civilian bookshop and looked in the window piled with dusty books from the foreign languages publishing house in Moscow. All those goddamn books, acres of them. A few dead cockroaches lay among the Lenin and Mikhail Sholokhov. *Virgin Soil Upturned*, volume 2.

Something was wrong, terribly, pathologically wrong. Nothing satisfied him, not the wrong decisions, not the right ones. He'd opposed Washington's original decision, now he was opposed to its withdrawal. Why? Everything was tainted by the same self-righteousness, corrupted by the same hypocrisy, poisoned by the same delirium. Either way, right or wrong, wrong or right, up and down. Got it wrong? Make it right; a few lines in a cable would do.

It was him, he was out of step now, completely out of step and each day lagging further and further behind, marching to a different drummer—not different either, a bloody lunatic pounding in his ears, not lagging either, the blind staggers out in the scag, pith helmet gone, like Ralph Richardson in *The Four Feathers*. Sooner or later the hyenas would catch up. He'd have to change his ways, fall in, get back in lockstep for the long march to the top. No more drinking, no more late nights, no more evasions, no more screwing around.

It wasn't too late. At thirty-two, still a promising young officer, what his efficiency reports had been saying for years now; a bit fucked up now but no permanent damage, brain still functioning, reflexes a little ragged, a little paranoid, but nothing a few years in Paris wouldn't cure, get back to basics, then two years in the Foggy Bottom Jacuzzi, float away all that grime, scrub him down to the quick: cheerful, ambitious, quick on his feet again, loyal to his superiors, unfailingly discreet, what they used to say; clever enough never to allow his personal feelings to overrule his sense of duty, whether in handling junketing senators, prickly assistant secretaries of state, or some ambassador's neurotic wife, quivering to be stroked but never laid.

Washington was safe and sound, home territory, where every cliché was cut in Roman granite. It wasn't there or the civilized European metropolises that idiot strategies or bully pulpit jingoism was betrayed for what it was but out here in the hinterlands in places with unpronounceable names whose reality no one could authenticate except its voiceless bush rabble, its landless nomads or peons, fighting their hallucinatory wars, just like he was.

He moved on down the sidewalk.

Not a man of strong or eccentric passions, not a zealot, not excessively imaginative or adventuresome either, so his reviewing officers wrote year after year, a man to be depended upon, someone you could always count on to do the right thing, reliable like most ambitious graduate fellows, bright young lads who'd mastered every text in the syllabbi and were persuasive in advancing the ideas of their intellectual mentors, in convincing the dullards of the soundness of accepted doctrine, the abstractions of those map-board strategists who invoke the usual reasons for distant wars others are sent to die in.

So what? At thirty-two, Mozart was dead, Einstein immortal, Malraux making history in the Orient, Orson Welles a credible genius, Eric Bowser on his way to his first million. Those well-intended bureaucratic clichés he'd invested ten years in shackled him like leg irons, told him no more about himself than his passport photo.

He crossed through the courtyard of the Arbah Rukun mosque and through the small garden.

If he wasn't careful, he'd always be thirty-two, zapped by some lunatic flash of light on the East African littoral, curled up like the little charcoal lap dogs of Pompeii.

He'd almost told Harcourt and DeGroot both to shove it, almost walked out, not once but three times. Close, very close; a trickle of sweat crept down his collar.

There goes poor Logan Talbot, they would whisper, their voices following him like a fog through the basement of the State Department cafeteria as he shuffled to some dim corner table with his skim milk and tapioca, down from his dusty little scholar's carrel in INR:

Who?

Talbot, T. Logan, Esquire. Poor chap, blotted his copy book at Benaadir, tried to tell the ambassador and DCM to fuck off but went spastic, they say. Poor chap, brought him out in a straitjacket. Worst case of the Sycophanic Stress Syndrome the medical people have ever seen. Brought on semi-paralysis, bent over that way permanently, hands dangling that way, mouth dribbling, still trying to get out the words. Don't know how he manages to hang on. No, I wouldn't do that, don't call to him now, better not, might wake him up, he'll pee down his leg. . . .

Maybe he'd always be thirty-two, maybe thirty-two was destiny.

Sly? Sneaky Pete? Priggish but dependable, that's what they should be saying. There goes Talbot, T. Logan, *Esq.*, the functional diplomat, the professional nerd, an ambassador now, there he goes, off for his foreign ministry debut, up on his hind legs already. . . .

He crossed the street and went into the Pakistani barbershop. The first chair was empty. His usual barber was gone somewhere. The ticked apron hung folded across the brown leather back, the empty seat in full sunlight. Queer silence, too, hardly a sound. In the second chair a new barber stood, back to him, stropping a razor. In the chair was an elderly Italian, eyes closed, lather rimming his ears.

The barber moved behind the chair and drew the razor down the cheekbone, a little unsteadily, Talbot thought. Hands shaking a bit, too. He turned, moving to the other side, and Talbot recognized him. He'd lost weight, his face was a little gaunt, but it was Ali, late of the UN beach club, now shearing frazzled heads in his cousin's barbershop.

"Hello, Ali. Didn't know you were working here."

"Hello, Mr. Talbot. How are you?"

"Fine, Ali. How have you been."

"Not too well, Mr. Talbot."

Talbot watched the trembling razor stripping away the lather from the Italian's ear, thought he saw a homicidal flicker in Ali's cinnamon eyes, and stepped back. Maybe that was why the old Italian had his eyes closed. Awfully warm today, the little shop.

"Sorry to hear that. Your cousin not around?"

"At the bank, Mr. Talbot. But I'll be finished in a minute."

Talbot sneaked a look through the portiere that hid the rear room. Not someone trussed up back there, by any chance, all bound and gagged? "I think I'll come back this afternoon, Ali," he suggested cheerfully, his paranoia complete. "You'll be here, will you?"

It wasn't professional opportunity that brought him to the Benaadir coast but Ali's karma. Sent him out to get his goddamn throat cut in a Pakistani barbershop, that's what.

"After four, Mr. Talbot."

"Righto. After four then, Ali." He paused at the door. "How's the family?"

"My wife is sick, Mr. Talbot."

"Sorry. Still trying, Ali. My best to the wife."

Ali didn't answer and Talbot left.

Still trying, sure. It wasn't enough.

□ □ □

Harcourt summoned Talbot from the first floor that morning, telephoning himself. Could he come right up?

Talbot dutifully emptied his coffee cup, pulled his tie in place, and retrieved his jacket from the back of the chair. He wondered what he wanted to talk about—not his indiscretions, he hoped. The two men had hardly exchanged a word since Talbot's outburst three days earlier. Harcourt had given him a wide berth on the stairs, pretending to be absorbed with other matters.

Harcourt's door was closed and he slumped down in the brown armchair near Miss Simpson's desk to wait. She looked up from the vellum envelopes she was addressing. *Well?*

"Well what?"

"He's *waiting*. Good heavens, what does one have to do? Didn't he tell you that?"

"He said to come up."

Miss Simpson's social status had risen somewhat since she'd begun appearing regularly at Julia's soirées, Talbot's had sunk into obscurity since his banishment following his night with Nicola at the Italian club.

He rapped at the door, opened it, and found Harcourt alone, sitting in the distant twilight behind his desk, writing on his yellow legal pad. He nodded with a faint smile as he got up.

"Any news from the front?" he asked brightly as he crossed the room to the sofa and the constellation of chairs where the country team had once met. He opened the drapes and then the venetian blinds, flooding the deep carpet and the leather chairs with morning sunlight.

"Not good, I'm afraid." Talbot sat down, puzzled.

"DeGroot was waiting for me this morning when I came in. His usual morning brief. I'm afraid I wasn't paying a great deal of attention. I'd like to hear what you think."

"Me?"

"About what's happening. I have his cable on my desk. I wanted the advantage of a second opinion. We're in a bloody mess, aren't we?"

"A bit of a mess I'd say."

"I have a tick list here I drew up last night," he said, looking at his yellow pad. "I'd be interested in what you think. It seems any expectation Jubba might have of a quick decisive victory over Ethiopia is gone. Or so Firthdale, d'Aubert, and I agreed last night. What do you think?"

Talbot, still confused, agreed. The Russians had stopped all military supplies. With Washington's withdrawal of its offer of defensive arms and no source of resupply or spare parts for Jubba's crippled tanks, artillery, and aircraft, and with ammunition reserves running dangerously low, the Jubba armies had dug in, unwilling to gamble their limited assets on a new offensive. Their assaults on Harar and Dire Dawa had failed. Now they were buying time while Jubba agents traveled the Continent to purchase what they could from international arms dealers, not enough to resupply and support a modern mechanized army in the field, only the individual weapons of maiming and killing for the jackals' long and bloody guerrilla war.

"Then the president's trip to Moscow," Harcourt resumed, looking at his pad. "A failure, everyone says. Is there any reason to think differently?"

"No, that was a failure, too, I hear."

In desperation the president had gone to Moscow to plead the cause of national liberation according to Lenin and appeal to Brezhnev to help, or, failing that, to persuade him not to help the Ethiopians. "The reports are Brezhnev had refused to see him," Talbot said. "He met instead with Suslov, the old reptilian party ideologue from the Stalinist days, who told him national liberation wasn't the issue: Get his goddamn armies out of Ethiopia."

"Luttak told you that?" Harcourt interrupted.

"No, sir. The Czechs heard it from the Soviets, who passed it to the Yugoslavs. I was talking last night to Berislav Minic, the number two."

"I don't think I know Minic. The tall one or the short one?"

"Tall and heavyset."

"His wife plays volleyball, I think."

Oh, shit, here we go again. "I'm not sure."

"I think Julia said she did. Ethiopia? The situation there is pretty bad, too, it seems."

He handed Talbot a cable received from the embassy in Addis that morning. Ethiopia was little better off—short of ammunition and spare parts for its U.S. equipment. The Soviet military resupply was only a trickle, its weaponry unfamiliar to the U.S.-trained Ethiopian army and air force.

"They can take the short-term losses," Talbot said, handing the cable back. But the empire was vast, as vulnerable as it was in the lowlands, impregnable in its mountain heartland. But with a population ten times Jubba's, it could better survive a long war of attrition than its smaller neighbor.

"You have kept up, haven't you?" Harcourt said agreeably, getting up to retrieve DeGroot's morning communiqué from his desk. He passed it to Talbot and returned to his chair. "I thought we also might have a little talk about something else, a private talk, just the two of us if you don't mind. Like we used to have."

"Yes, sir," Talbot said, his heart sinking.

"I've been a little worried recently and I'm not quite sure what I should do about it."

"If it's about that morning the telegram came in, I'm sorry. I was on a pretty short fuse that morning—"

"No, not that." He shook his head, glanced at his pad, and looked off toward the window. "Something else. It's difficult to know quite where to begin, especially after all this time. I thought I'd begin with you, since you've been here the longest. To tell you the truth, I'm not sure quite how to ask." He hesitated, thought for a minute, and studied his yellow pad. "The truth is I'm not satisfied with the way some things at the embassy are being handled."

"The economic work, you mean."

"No, not that particularly, other things. Little things. I'm not even sure they've occurred to anyone else. That's what makes it so difficult, you see." His gaze had again moved to the window; he might have been talking to himself. "Have you noticed anything a bit unusual, a bit odd, leaving aside personalities for the moment."

"Odd? About the embassy? A few things, I suppose."

"You don't want to make too much of an issue of it, not yet anyway, since there may be a perfectly logical explanation. I ask you this in all confidence. You have, or I think you have, a sense of these things, the way Julia has. I mean despite everything else. Did you ever find your missing chron file, by the way?"

"No, sir, I didn't."

"When it comes right down to it, you're never quite sure of these things, the little things, I mean. Things that might not occur to anyone else." He sighed.

"You mean wondering whether it's you or something else."

"Yes, that you may be trying to find an excuse in the little things. I'm not making myself clear, am I? No. You see certain things, small things, and it's very difficult to translate them into words, to give them meaning without sounding foolish. Some things can only be captured in certain ways, you see, light, for example." He was looking at the bars of white light on the drapes. "The way the light comes in the afternoon, the way it hangs in the air. On the terrace, on the wall there in the back garden. You can capture that with a brush, a trick of the texture, the eye, the hand, but you can't de-

scribe it to others. The same is true of those small moments when
you realize something might be dreadfully wrong but in a way, in a
small way, that's, well, almost untranslatable." His voice trailed
off wistfully. "At the same time it's no good trying to explain them
to someone else unless they've seen and felt them in the same way."

Talbot didn't know what he was trying to say.

"So let me ask you this. You've noticed certain little things, I'm
sure, little characteristics, little mannerisms?"

But Talbot could only meet his embarrassed eyes with his own
embarrassed bewilderment.

"Naturally," Harcourt added delicately, eyes downcast, "I'm re-
ferring to Mr. DeGroot."

"DeGroot?"

"Mr. DeGroot, yes."

At last, a flicker of light. "I think so. I think everyone has."

"Things that go a little beyond, shall we say, what is acceptable
behavior?"

The words floated off, as dreamy as smoke. "I hadn't thought of
that so much," Talbot said.

"But very odd."

"Very odd, sure."

"Lying is not acceptable behavior, is it?"

"No, it's not."

Harcourt nodded and made a notation on his pad. "I want you to
think some more about this and we'll talk again. In the meantime,
I want you to resume your old political reporting responsibilities.
I'm particularly interested in what the Soviets are thinking. That
interests you, I'm sure."

"Yes, it does."

"I don't quite understand what they're doing."

"I'm not sure anyone does."

If Washington had abandoned the political wars to the UN, not
yet the Soviets, who kept their military mission in Jubba, but still
straddling the fence. From his brief talks with Luttak at a few receptions and national-day parties, he had the feeling Luttak was
drifting, the Soviet embassy was drifting, the way Washington was,
as confused as everyone else, and just as unimaginative as to what
they might do about it.

"I thought you might take the problem in hand. There's been a vacuum. We have this cable in from Addis. I think you should go talk to your friend Mr. Luttak. Ambassador Kirillan is incommunicado these days. Would you do that?"

"Right away."

"Good." Harcourt got up.

Talbot hesitated. "Does DeGroot know about this."

"I've told him, yes. We had a talk this morning. I told him what I'd planned on doing."

He rapped at the adjoining door, opened it, and asked DeGroot to step in. He entered a moment later, standing with unusual formality just inside the door. He gave Talbot a smile, as distantly cordial as that first afternoon in his rear garden.

"I've told Logan he's to take over political reporting again," Harcourt said as he continued on toward his desk, "just as we discussed."

"Ah, yes," DeGroot said, still smiling enthusiastically. "Very good."

"In the meantime, he's going to call on Luttak."

"Most appropriate, as we agreed."

"Good. That's all."

"Excellent."

DeGroot nodded brightly and immediately withdrew by the side door, shutting it softly behind him.

"One more thing," Harcourt said, picking up the green CIA reading board from his desk. "Do you know what Whittington and his people are up to? An unmarked 707 came in three nights ago, carrying munitions. It had an American crew." He looked expectantly at Talbot.

"I heard some talk, that's all."

Planes passed almost nightly over Talbot's villa, bringing in weapons from Europe, many bought in Hungary and Czechoslovakia, he'd heard, both supporters of Moscow's line. The planes were wet-leased by small firms in Liechtenstein and Luxembourg and in some cases flown by U.S. pilots.

"Ambassador Firthdale asked me about it. Bashford-Jones was evidently at the airport talking to the British telecommunications crew. He saw the two Americans in a stairwell looking for the local weather office. Would you see what you could find out?" he handed Talbot the CIA reading board. "Also have Miss Simpson return this to Lindy."

DeGroot was waiting for Talbot in the outer office, cable in hand.

"Here is the cable from Addis, my copy, as you see," he explained, arm thrust out. "I have made a few notations, which you might study before meeting with Luttak. I have heard Ambassador Kirillan has been recalled; this you might explore—"

"Fine." Talbot took the cable.

"The matter of the Cuban brigade in Ethiopia as well—"

"Sure."

"The question of what the president discussed at Moscow is also a matter of urgency, as I've noted here. I shall put my car at your disposal when the *entretien* is arranged," he called down the hall after Talbot. "We should also convene a meeting with Kinkaid for the transfer of economic responsibilities. As I have explained the situation to him, he is most eager."

"Good. Thanks. Any time's fine with me."

"Perhaps a luncheon, *chez moi*. I shall consult my bride." DeGroot nodded, beaming, and turned back toward his office.

Talbot stopped on the stairs to look through the CIA reading board, some of it material for the ambassador only. He found little that was new.

The military stalemate had made for strange bedfellows. The Israelis helped the Soviet-backed Ethiopian socialists, secretly supplying spare parts for the U.S.-made F-15 aircraft. A Cuban mechanized brigade brought from Angola was fighting alongside the Ethiopians near Harar; Soviet-trained Arab pilots from Aden were rumored to be flying MIG-17s in support of the Cuban-manned Ethiopian armor. In Jubba, the Egyptians aided the Jubba army with arms and spare parts taken from the old Soviet-supplied military stocks; so did Peking's puritanical Chinese communists and the profligate Iranian royalists, most of the purchases financed with Saudi money.

It was all very confusing, a crazy little war now run completely amok.

"Oh, it's you," Lindy said listlessly, opening the door after Talbot had rung the bell on the vaulted door. "Whit's not here, sorry."

"Harcourt wanted me to give you this. Can I talk to you for a minute."

"There's really nothing to talk about."

"Business talk."

She let him in and he asked her about the unmarked 707 bringing munitions.

"I don't think Whit knows anything about it," she said, taking back the file, "but if Nick saw them it must be true."

"Is that right?" He remembered seeing Lindy in Nick's bottle-green Rover as they flashed by on the Lido road. "Pretty convincing these days, is he? You didn't used to be so crazy about him."

She colored. "He's dependable, that's all."

"What's that mean?"

"Just that. He always has been, just in case you haven't known."

"Haven't known what?"

"Never mind. If you don't know, it's none of your business anyway."

"What is there to know? You mean what you two have been sharing these days?"

"I didn't mean that at all," she said. "He's head of station for MI6, that's all I meant, and we haven't shared anything!"

Jesus, Shaughnessy's old ploy, hinting he was CIA. He couldn't believe it, even Nick now. "He's giving you a line, for Christ's sake. Don't tell me you fell for that old bullshit. That's what all those overaged British commercial types tell their local girl friends."

"I didn't fall for anything and he's never even mentioned it. No one has. I found out at Langley before I came out. I was having lunch with someone after a briefing and he was name-dropping and let it slip. He knew Nick in Amman, Jordan. I think he was declared there. You'd better not say anything. I shouldn't even have told you. I should never have told you anything, never!"

"He's not the kind of company you should be keeping."

"Thanks, I'll remember that." Her face was flushed as she turned away. "I could give you a little advice, too. Now if you're finished, I've got work to do."

"Why are you so goddamned mad?"

"I'm not mad, just wiser."

"Wise about what? You can at least tell me that. Who've you been talking to?"

"It doesn't matter."

"It does matter. Just give me a chance to explain. At least talk to me, and let's get it out in the open. It's about Nicola Seretti, isn't it?"

Again she flushed, angrily sitting down at her desk, her eyes turned away. "It's about nothing. There's nothing to get out in the open. I prefer things just as they are."

"That wasn't the way it was when you left. What changed your mind all of a sudden?"

"Nothing."

"Something did."

"Just leave me alone."

"Where's Whittington? It was Whittington, wasn't it? I want to talk to that old bastard."

"He's not here."

"Where is he?"

"I'm not going to tell you. And if you dare say a word to him, I'll never speak to you again."

"Then he did talk to you."

"No, he didn't! Now get out! You're ruining everything for me, you already have."

"What did he tell you, that I was a corrupting influence? What is it, your professional life you're worried about? Your goddamn career? Is that what he told you?"

But she couldn't look at him, her shoulders turned away.

Whittington's secretary came in from the commo room carrying a sheaf of NSA intercepts. "What on earth is going on?"

"Nothing's going on." He didn't turn. "I'm sorry then, I really am. But it might have helped if I'd known, if we'd have talked just a little. That's all I asked."

He left. Not until he was on the first floor did he remember his office was on the third floor now, but by then it made little difference.

□ □ □

Talbot parked his Fiat outside the Soviet chancellory a little before eleven. The sun was dazzling on the high whitewashed walls, recently repainted after a late-night visitor had scrawled graffiti along part of the wall. Seen by a Russian security man, he'd taken to his heels and dashed what remained of his blue paint across the far end of the wall. Now a few Jubba, including two nomads just in from the bush, hands dangling from the staffs carried across their shoulders, stood idly at the glass-fronted bulletin board outside the main entrance, puzzling over the photographs of the most recent Soviet space launch.

The English-speaking third secretary admitted him and led him to the reception room. Luttak arrived with unusual promptness a few minutes later. He was followed by a slim smooth-faced Russian with blond hair, wearing a tan suit and a yellow linen tie.

Luttak, as tired as he'd seemed when they'd met recently at diplomatic receptions, introduced Yuri Pulyakov, a first secretary who would be taking over for him while he was in Moscow on leave. Pulyakov's English was much better than his, he said with a sheepish smile, so they would have much to talk about; he would listen.

They sat down and Luttak said his leave would begin in October. When would Talbot be leaving for Paris?

"A month or so."

"So you won't stay?" Pulyakov asked, surprised. Well groomed and well dressed, he was a generation removed from Luttak. His English was almost without accent.

"No, it's almost over for me."

Luttak nodded sadly. "For all of us, maybe."

The little Russian woman in a black nylon dress and white apron brought coffee. Pulyakov put his cup aside and asked for tea instead. After she left he offered Talbot an American Winston and told him he was lucky to be assigned in Paris. He said he knew Paris. Talbot nodded, noticing his French or German shoes, and asked how long he'd been in Jubba. Six months, he said, consulting his digital watch—yes, six months and four days, he added with more precision. Talbot asked about his previous posts, and his memory grew a little vaguer. He said he'd been at the foreign ministry in Moscow and let it go at that.

Luttak began by asking Talbot about the U.S. decision to withhold arms from Jubba. Did Talbot think the decision might be reversed?

"No, I don't think so."

"For us, the same," Luttak said. "Nothing. To give Jubba nothing, no spare parts, nothing until their army goes out from Ethiopia, I told you, yes?"

"You told me, yes."

Pulyakov, sitting back now, his long legs crossed, said he thought it constructive the two superpowers had agreed on a common policy in the Horn of Africa. A bit of a dandy, Talbot decided, regretting Pulyakov was there. Two Russians were always more difficult to talk to than one, their troikas even worse—like talking to a local party committee plenum. Probably he'd come to observe the ground rules for their little tête-à-têtes, but in his presence Luttak would volunteer even less than usual. Talbot reminded him the Soviet Union was supplying arms to Ethiopia. Or had they stopped?

"No, not stop," Luttak said.

Pulyakov quickly came to his assistance. The amounts were modest, wholly defensive in nature, intended only to enable the Ethiopians to defend their sovereignty against the Jubba invasion.

Luttak sourly drank his coffee, listening to Pulyakov. The sunlight fell thickly through the gauze curtains, lying in trapezoids on the wine-colored Persian carpets and the terrazzo floor. Luttak's cautious silence told Talbot it wouldn't be much of a conversation. His visits here were coming to an end, he remembered sadly.

He asked him what Brezhnev had told the Jubba president in Moscow. Luttak said he hadn't seen Brezhnev, just as the press had reported. He'd talked to Podgorny and Suslov, who told him to remove his troops from Ethiopia, as the press had reported.

It was all very formal, very stiff. Talbot searched for something to break the impasse.

"What about a political settlement? Can Moscow work that out?"

Luttak shrugged slowly, brooded a bit, fussed with his cigarette in the ashtray, and finally said he was pessimistic. The Jubba army refused to withdraw.

Pulyakov, eager to respond but forced to wait until Luttak had found the right words, leaned forward to embellish the point.

His English was impressive, no doubt about it, Talbot thought.

Luttak may have envied his fluency but wouldn't have recognized what Talbot mistrusted, that superciliousness that often crept in with Russians so superbly confident of their English. Since Talbot spoke no Russian, his reaction was in part psychological, he'd once decided, an envious inference. Luttak's English, like Ambassador Kirillan's, was often primitive and gave the native English speaker the illusion of a certain intellectual superiority. But he'd grown so accustomed to Luttak's English he preferred it to Pulyakov's. Whatever Luttak's secretiveness, his crudeness was that of a man struggling honestly to express himself, the quality missing in Pulyakov. Luttak, even when he was quoting from Soviet orthodoxy, made its clichés sound earned; Pulyakov's orthodoxy was too facile to seem anything except devious. Luttak may have been no less dishonest than Pulyakov, but Pulyakov's English made him sound more devious. He seemed the perfection of the Soviet career diplomat achieved, all uncertainties banished, all truths as certain as they were clever. Sitting there smoking his American cigarettes in his French jacket and English tie, Pulyakov seemed the efficient machine-tooled product of a primitive inefficient society—only for export, of course. Who could afford bourgeois luxuries like Pulyakov at home, certainly not the muzhiks crowding Moscow's new bureaucratic and industrial slums, five to a room and no place for Pulyakov's dancing feet.

He wondered if his old man had been a diplomat.

Searching his pocket for a handkerchief, he brought out a crumpled pack of Lindy's mentholated cigarettes, carried for her one night and forgotten. The scent of her purse and her hair lingered there still, and for a minute he wasn't there in the Soviet chancellory at all but sitting with her in his back garden.

Pulyakov was saying that for the moment no political solution was possible. Neither Jubba nor Ethiopia was willing to concede; that being the case, their differences wouldn't be settled politically but militarily.

Talbot agreed with a nod, recovering lost ground. "Very well put."

Pulyakov nodded appreciatively. In the long run, he continued, Ethiopia's larger army, larger population, greater size, and far greater resources would turn the tide. That being the case, Jubba had only to recognize this and withdraw.

Luttak nodded with Talbot in glum agreement.

"But they don't understand this, they refuse, you can tell them nothing," Pulyakov said, encouraged.

"Why?" Talbot asked disingenuously. "I thought they were scientific socialists."

"Please," Pulyakov said with a smile, taking out another cigarette. "We are serious men, aren't we? Of course. So we must be serious."

Talbot put a little backspin to the question and grinned like a party hack. "You mean they're *not* scientific socialists?"

Luttak wouldn't have taken the bait but Pulyakov did.

"Scientific socialists? These people?" He laughed. "But you know what they are. We all do."

Saw the joke, did you? Talbot lit Pulyakov's cigarette. *Thought you might, old sport.* They might have been three bounders sharing some wicked gentleman's pun at the Royal Automobile Club in London, where the foreign office lads lunched. Pulyakov was a windbag, a ballroom butterfly in dancing pumps. Talbot hadn't met a Russian quite like him since Sergey Sinitsyn in Brussels, who got drunk with him one foggy Sunday afternoon in one of those little cafés not far from the Metropole Hotel where everyone dances, even with the girls from the brothel around the corner that Sinitsyn didn't know was there. Two weeks later poor Sergey was reassigned to Sofia.

"Just nomads, are they?" Talbot said. *I like your tie, by the way? Mayfair or Oxford Street off-the-rack?*

"Exactly. Nomads, you see," Pulyakov said. Moslem nomads. Not scientific socialists at all, never had been. The Jubba government wasn't communist obviously, not even socialist, not technically, never.

For all his awkwardness, Luttak had never misled him. Those questions he couldn't answer or refused to answer he simply turned aside. But Pulyakov's English was so sure, so certain, it danced him on, even if he sometimes splashed through those same old Muscovy mud puddles where Luttak often swam—there are some English words no Russian can ever master, not even after twenty years in Washington—his fluency capering him along like the Bolshoi, drawing out the line beautifully, spinning out his counterfeit verbal specie the way DeGroot did, those neat little word arrangements of Soviet doctrine all arranged so carefully together, like frozen cod fillets wrapped in cellophane, a dozen to a package, no more, no less, take two dozen or go hungry . . .

Very much divorced from reality, the Jubba junta was, Pulyakov was saying, objectively speaking, of course. Their speeches, their edicts, nothing to them at all—

"Just a national printing press."

"I would say so, yes."

Talbot asked him about Ethiopia, and Pulyakov smiled like a true believer. "Different, completely different," he said, and then explained why. Talbot listened as Pulyakov described the revolution in Ethiopia, Mother Ethiopia, where the revolution had been two thousand years in the womb, two millenniums of political evolution bringing on the revolution—two millenniums? Did the military junta here think they could teach their revolution in six years, sixty, a hundred? Nomadic Jubba and Mother Ethiopia. How could one compare the two? Jubba, what was Jubba? A shriveled incubus, a backward little Moslem nation that hadn't appeared on the stage of history until the sixteenth century and then as an insignificant little tribe in the hilly wastelands behind Muzaffar, a tiny anomaly, not a nation, which had never truly existed until 1960. How could anyone compare Jubba with the ancient nation across the border, two millenniums in the making, once called Abyssinia, now Ethiopia, where a true revolution was under way.

As Talbot listened he was no longer sitting in Lev Luttak's protocol room but was seated in the shadows of the candle-lit dinner table in Nicola's villa above the sea, hearing the voice of Carlo Minzonni as he gave instruction to the two Italian professors about Jubba's past, the same words, the same argument. Odd how past and present were mixed, how history was circular sometimes, unrecognized until it passed you the second time—Nicola a stranger then, Lindy, too—and how terribly it all made sense now, too late. How blind he'd been then, how foolish, how smug, how stupid.

So objectively speaking, it was clear, Pulyakov concluded mercifully. Jubba didn't matter, was unimportant. Ethiopia's strength would tell—Abyssinia and Addis Ababa, the true center of those manifold peoples populating the Horn of Africa.

"So they've been deceiving themselves, the Jubba," Talbot said, beginning to tire of it, "and it wasn't their scientific socialism, that wasn't what deceived them."

He sat back, looking at Lev Luttak, wanting to go.

Poor Jubba, history's orphan. How could you escape Marxist predestination? You couldn't, no more than Calvin's. Find another faith? Like the Palestinians, the Armenians, the Basques? Car bombs, a little *plastique,* Beretta .22 automatics, short range; nothing, of course, that would ever rewrite the history books.

Luttak, silent the past thirty minutes, frowned even more deeply.

"Sorry," Pulyakov said quickly. "Deceived? I don't follow."

"It wasn't scientific socialism that deceived them, it was history."

Pulyakov reflected, lips compressed, satisfied at the history lesson so completely mastered, but reluctant to concede its final conclusions to his pupil.

"Objectively speaking, I would say yes, of course, history." Nodding vigorously, he looked again at his digital watch. Discovering how quickly the time had flown, he got to his feet.

It was one o'clock when Talbot finally left the chancellory, head reeling, face flushed by brandy.

The official Soviet line for full support for the Ethiopian revolution had long been in place, the intellectual scaffolding long erected by the party theorists back in Moscow, just like the party congress, everything prepared weeks in advance: the bunting in place, the halls repainted, the speeches all written, the press releases prepared, everything ready, the dialectic so well rhearsed that even an Italian communist hack like Minzonni had known what would be said. But if the political decision had already been made by the party theorists in Moscow, why not the military decision? If the Ethiopian revolution was all that mattered in the Horn, why was only a trickle of Soviet military equipment reaching Ethiopia, why were the Soviet military group and 2,500 advisers still in Jubba?

That made no sense at all. He still didn't know the answer.

□ □ □

Talbot's afternoons were his own again—no more invitations to Julia's beach cottage lunches, no more swims with Lindy. He was back in his Third World dungeon, his only companion these days his stereo or Grundig, his typewriter, an occasional journalist visitor, or, more often, that calm clear voice that now called to him as he sat in his lounge chair in the rear garden.

"*There* you are."

He got up. "Here I am."

"I telephoned first," Nicola said, coming across the flagstones from the rear passageway to give him a quick kiss on the cheek. "No one answered. Then the embassy said no, you weren't there. You'd left. You've been working? Working or swimming?"

She seemed in a hurry and was wearing high heels and a dark blue silk dress, as if she might have just come from an afternoon bridge party.

"Working. Trying to, anyway."

"I wanted to bring these two plants for your dining room." She turned and called to someone, and a moment later a short Jubba in a gray chauffeur's jacket discreetly left the shadows of the passageway where he'd been waiting, holding two potted plants.

Talbot had never seen him before. He went to take the two pots. The Jubba driver bowed, nodded, brushed his coat and went back around the house.

"Who's he?"

"The Abruzzos' driver. That one's heavy, be careful. You're alone?"

"All alone."

He moved a pot to his knee, opened the door from the terrace into the dining room, and followed her in. She shut the door behind him. "I hope I'm not interrupting."

"No, you're not interrupting. Where do you want me to put these?"

"Next to the steps to the living room would be nice." She crossed the room and stopped at the foot of the five steps leading to the living room. "Here, I think. I was thinking the other afternoon they would be nice here. They'll get much larger, of course. A friend gave them to me. This is gloxinia, this one, this is caladium. She had them repotted this afternoon."

She had a beautiful memory for plants, but she never talked of their afternoons and evenings together. He lowered both plants to the floor. "They're very nice."

"This one's rather uncommon, this gloxinia." She bent down to move it closer to the railing, then picked up the smaller one and carried it to the credenza. "This one is a little more delicate. It has pink blossoms, very lovely. I couldn't resist. Do you like it?"

"They look nice. Just like you. Smell nice, too."

He took her waist as she stood up, but she slipped aside. "Not now, please. You'll make me all wrinkled. Someone is waiting in the car. Tonight would be better. I came to ask you."

"Who's in the car?"

"A friend. Are you always lonely in the afternoons this way?" She opened her purse.

"It's not just being lonely. What about tonight?"

"We'll have dinner. You look very sad. I feel very sad myself. This morning I was thinking to myself, What will happen to you? All morning like that, so I decided to telephone, to tell you we would do something. Please, not now." She held his arms and kissed him lightly on the cheek, then she took her handkerchief from her purse and wiped off the lipstick. "You must behave; not every afternoon this way."

"What about tonight?"

"Nine o'clock. You know the Abruzzo apartment?"

"Near the Piazza, the tall building where I picked you up the other night."

"Yes. Nine o'clock then."

"They're back from Rome?"

"No, just the two of us. I must go. She is waiting. Would you like to meet her? Please, come. She would like it, I think." She took his hand. "Behave now. They are her plants. I tried to bring her to show her the garden, but she said no. She is very shy. Please."

He went out to meet the woman waiting in the back seat of the Fiat. She was the middle-aged blond woman Talbot had seen before at Nicola's house that day at Merca, the one who'd kept looking at him curiously. He said hello and the woman smiled and nodded. Nicola kissed him on the cheek. "Nine, then, nine o'clock. Earlier if you like."

"Earlier."

"Eight then, eight thirty."

The Jubba driver drove them away and they both waved from the back seat.

He had been feeling lonely and now he felt even worse, the burrower trapped in his burrow, digging even deeper.

He returned to the rear garden and gathered his papers and pad together and went inside. Basil Dinsmore was back in the capital and had left a message for him at the embassy that morning. He called the Giubba Hotel and asked for room 404, but there was no answer. The operator didn't come back on the line and he had to hang up and call again to leave a message, but the voice that answered wasn't a woman's voice and didn't sound like a Jubba and he hung up without giving his name.

The apartment was on the fourth floor. A small balcony off the living room overlooked the Piazza. In the hallway leading to the living room were recessed niches, glass-fronted, and lit by hidden lights behind the velvet-draped pedestals. On display were three *jambiyas,* ancient silver-sheathed ceremonial daggers from the Yemen, silver jewelry, wooden cups, and a piece of very old Azanian woodwork taken from an old window along the coast. Mrs. Abruzzo was a collector. On the malachite coffee table was a bowl of ostrich eggs and a glass-lined sea turtle shell.

Nicola made a small dinner and Talbot stood with his drink in the kitchen as she prepared it. She had sent the Abruzzos' cook and houseboy home. They got underfoot, she told him, always in the way. When she was in the kitchen, she wanted no one else around. At her farm it was different in the kitchen, terrible sometimes, always the arguments with Samina. They exhausted her. Samina was still a child, she would always be a child, what Seretti had made her. Living with her was like living with a retarded child.

"I am talking too much," she said finally. "Tell me what you have been doing, something nice."

He told her that he'd finally understood what Minzonni, the Italian journalist, and the two Italian professors had been arguing about that evening at her house so many months ago.

"Moscow's official line," he said. "Minzonni was putting it out weeks ago."

She glanced up. "I know, I told you."

"I didn't understand completely, not at the time. I heard something similar from someone at the Soviet embassy a few days ago."

She returned to the cutting board, her small hands moving very quickly. "Then you weren't surprised."

"I think I was, despite everything."

"What did they say?"

He repeated what Pulyakov had told him. Jubba was little more than a cluster of obscure nomadic tribes from the back-country scrub that hadn't appeared on the historical stage until the sixteenth century. Its scientific socialism was a farce, the military disguised as revolutionaries, the avant-garde of a proletariat that didn't exist. Nothing the Soviets had been able to do, not their years of cadre formation, their attempts to politicize the civil service, the schools, or the military, not their weekly tutorials at the presidential compound with their Russian films and Leninist primers had in any way altered the Islamic, clan, and pastoral traditions of Jubban society. The whole thing had been a dismal failure and they knew it. Now they'd given up in disgust.

They sat at the small dining-room table with the candles between them.

She nodded. "Yes, it's true. But it was always a failure, always. They've always known that."

"But pretended not to?"

"What else could they do? They had their opportunity here. Were they to deny it, admit all those lies? But you forget, the president was using them just as they were using him. One day he thought they would help him take back Western Jubbaland. Did they talk about Ethiopia, your Russian friends?"

"Sure, they had to. They wouldn't have talked the way they did about Jubba if it weren't for Ethiopia. It's Ethiopia that makes their failure here so obvious, why they've given up. Ethiopia's their true Marxist-Leninist swaddling, the real political center of this vast conglomeration of the peoples of the Horn, ancient, corrupt, long-suffering Ethiopia—"

"The same lies," she interrupted impatiently. "I don't want to hear any more. About the Russians or Minzonni, either, that toad."

"I thought he was your friend."

"No, never a friend. Seretti's friend, not mine, and only those last years when he was sick. He's a toad, *crapaud*. We should practice your French, talk instead about what is going to happen to you."

"Why do you dislike Ethiopia so much?"

"Because of what it is, what they are. Racists, ugly, very ugly, not civilized at all, like the Greek Orthodox monks or the Armenians you see in Jerusalem. All those evil smelly medieval monks carrying the keys to the Holy Sepulchre."

"So you don't believe what Minzonni or the Russians are saying is true?"

"Only words, stupid words that make it easy to pretend it's true. I don't want to hear. There is nothing I can do now, and so it's finished as far as I am concerned, all finished. My personal life is all that matters now, my life and my friends. I can do nothing to change anything else. Don't ask me questions." She got up and went to get the salad. "What is going to happen to you?" she said as she sat down again. "I think about that. I worry, very much worry."

"I'll be leaving, that's all."

"After you go I am talking about. In Paris. In Paris they are all like Malfatti except more clever. The diplomats I am talking about. It is not where you should be. They will make you like him, like your ambassador. Or they will find a pretty wife for you that will make you like him and then all finished, your sentimental education, all over."

"Where do you think I should be?"

"I don't know, I haven't decided yet." She got up and picked up her plate. "Are you finished?"

He helped her clear the table and rinse the dishes in the sink. She made coffee and they went into the living room. On the table in front of the window were vases filled with flowers and potted plants wrapped in tissue or foil.

"Why all the flowers? She gardens, too—Mrs. Abruzzo?"

"No, she doesn't garden. She doesn't know how. All she knows is how to shop and have a Jubba goldsmith make these things for her.

Those are from Federico's room at the hospital." Her voice had changed, very tender for a minute as she rearranged two of the plants. "I brought them today after Federico left."

"Who's Federico?"

"Seretti's son. He was wounded at Werder during the fighting." She sat down on the couch. "Now he's resting at Merca with his mother."

"So you've been visiting him at the hospital."

"Federico and someone else I know, yes."

She had a cordial with her coffee, and Talbot turned off the table lamp and sank back against the cushions, listening to the cars on the boulevard below.

"What I don't understand is why the Soviets are still here," he said after a minute. "If what all the party hacks are saying is true, why are they still mucking around here. Why hasn't the Soviet military thrown its full weight with the Ethiopians."

Her head was back and her eyes were shut. "A coup, I think."

"No, that's not it."

"Why? Not all the army supported the war. The Russians are thinking the time will come when everyone grows tired of the war and then, finished. So they wait." She opened her eyes and turned. "You don't think so?"

"No."

"You can't trust them, never."

"The Russians? No, but that's not it."

"So what is it then?"

"I don't know."

"Your mind is always working, only not tonight, please." She shifted closer and moved her hand along the back of his neck. "Close your eyes, put your head back."

"I'll go to sleep."

He took her arm and brought her even closer. Her neck and shoulders were cool. He pulled the blouse from her waistband and started to undress her, but she pulled his hands away. She slipped out of her shoes and got up and turned out the other lamp and led him in her stocking feet across the scattered carpets to the small hall and the bedroom beyond.

"This is the guest room," she said as she shut the door. The lamp on the table next to the bed was on and the covers were neatly turned down. On the other table was a vase of peonies, the same color as those on the dining-room table. She went into the bathroom, and he turned off the lamp and undressed in the darkness on the far side of the bed. He was under the sheets when the bathroom door opened. She was wearing an almost sheer white night slip that reached her hips and for a moment before she turned off the bathroom light her figure was very lovely. He lifted the sheet and she joined him, very warm and very fragrant, her shoulders and breasts sleek with talcum.

She was tender and affectionate. After a few minutes she let him undress her, like a shy schoolgirl, but his first contact with her warm naked body was as strange and awkward as it had been those other times. He wanted to see her face but couldn't, wanted to hear her voice, but she had nothing to say. She was less inhibited in the darkness, anxious to begin things right but very ladylike, too. There was passion in her lips and mouth but kept under control. The gentle breathing in his ear was that of a brisk walk, nothing more voracious than that as she moved him, manipulated him silently with the same small busy fingers that trimmed the roots and crumbled the soil, now planting him, very delicately at first, very firmly at last, very definite as to how these things were done, the way intellectuals are, whether in making a martini or trimming a bonsai tree, silent still, except for the businesslike urgency of her breath, and so he let her have her way, as he had in the garden. As the moments passed she seemed to have no more identity than he. Not quite love, he decided, this masque of silence in which they were so strenuously engaged. She was very sweet and he was very fond of her, but it had been foolish of him to pretend there was anything more to it than that. Some truths were better left unexplored, but what had been done was done, and there he was, trying to make the most of them. He made love to her, but her abstract passion had cooled his own, separated him. In the darkness somewhere he heard a cat scratching in a cat box and hadn't realized the Abruzzos had a cat, but then the trigger of her release summoned his own. As it did he heard her sigh with lonely pleasure, like the sound of the sea breaking on a distant beach, and in the aftermath read on the darkness of his mind the epitaph that had been hovering there for some time: *Here lies*

T. Logan Talbot, Esq., planted affectionately, firmly, and deeply for all eternity here on the Benaadir coast by his Gardener, Teacher, & Mistress.

□ □ □

The tide was rolling in under a pale moon. The long silver-tipped breakers smashed far up the beach to dissolve in snow fields of churning white lather, visible to Talbot as he climbed his front steps, still pondering the same unanswered question about the Soviet military's intentions. A few taxis waited in front of the Lido night-club. He could hear the faint distant music, broken by the rumble of the waves and the mild night wind. The Lido road was deserted. The UN and Anglo-American clubs were closed, the brooms of the night sweepers would be knocking their way past the tables and bar stools.

He turned on the light in the study and found the telephone number for the Giubba Hotel. The operator put his call through to Basil Dinsmore's room but before Dinsmore answered he heard his voice on the line, talking to someone, then a woman's voice, and as he listened realized the conversation was taking place in Basil Dinsmore's room.

"Hello, 404 here," Dinsmore said, picking up the receiver.

"Basil, this is Logan Talbot."

"Logan, yes, I've been trying to reach you."

"I know. You've got two people with you. I don't know who the woman is but I thought I heard Nick Bashford-Jones. Not being indiscreet, I hope."

A startled silence. "Nick. Yes, yes he is here, with a friend, as a matter of fact. How the deuce did you know that?"

"By what you're holding in your hand. The line was open before you picked it up, which means there's a live mike in the receiver, OK? Enough said. Could you call me in the morning. Or drop by here, then we can talk."

"By all means, yes. Not tomorrow, the day after if you don't mind. And thanks, too. I'd forgotten, yes. Stupid of me."

"Tell Nick hello."

"I will, thanks again."

Basil Dinsmore put the phone down and turned to Nick Bashford Jones and his companion, a secretary from the British embassy. "That was Logan. I'm afraid we haven't been alone. Before we get even more indiscreet in what we say, I propose we adjourn to the nightclub if you don't mind. I'll explain there."

Four floors below, the brightly lit lobby was empty. A trio of late drinkers sat in the second-floor bar, including two tired American journalists, buying drinks for a ministry of information press officer whose long disjunctive history of Jubba-Ethio relations since the time of Menelik had begun to tire them. They were more intrigued by his tireless narrative energy.

On the third floor a Brussels arms broker who had arrived that afternoon to conclude the sale of 100 jeep-mounted 106-mm recoilless rifles and 75,000 rounds of ammunition waited for his call from the ministry of defense scheduling his appointment the following morning. In a small basement room an East German technician wearing a headset replugged the lead which a few minutes earlier had been inserted in the room 404 tap, turned off the tape recorder, and waited sleepily to monitor the call, his elbows on his knees, tapping his foot to the distant sound of the radio from the third-floor room.

On the dark Viale della Repubblica outside a red-and-yellow taxi passed and behind it a speeding gray Moska. A thousand meters further along the Moska turned in at the gate of the Soviet chancellory. Standing at a window on the second floor of the chancellory watching the garden below stood a man who might have answered Talbot's last unanswered question. He was dressed in light military cotton, a large impassive man, heavy in the shoulders and neck, with thick hands, stiff gray hair, and bushy eyebrows. Better than anyone else his presence explained why the Soviet military group and its 2,500 advisers were still in Jubba long after the party swallows had migrated north-northwest to Addis Ababa.

Seeing his Moska enter the compound, he let the drape fall and returned to the shadows in the far corner and sat down. He rarely came to the Soviet chancellory. He was there that night because Ambassador Kirillan, busy at his desk across the room, was awaiting a summons to the presidency. General Lobatoff wanted to make certain he was aware of any last-minute instructions Kirillan re-

ceived from Moscow. Ambassador Kirillan was very much aware
of his presence; his uneasiness was apparent in his voice, in his gestures, in the light banter with his staff assistant and his secretary
bringing to his desk reminders of those discursive points to be made
in his talk with the president should the telephone call come.

Kirillan was a man of medium height, with wavy chestnut hair, a
long nose, narrow chin, and quick green eyes, not handsome but not
repellently dour either, like General Lobatoff. He smiled easily, a
kind of leporine smile, the Western ambassadors thought, offered
too quickly and too often to be sincere. Since he saw the president
so often, he was thought to know everything that was happening in
the councils of government or in Soviet installations scattered about
the country, but this wasn't true. Nevertheless the smile was resented by his Western colleagues, like the dry quips and light banter
offered at cocktail parties and diplomatic receptions, which offended
their dignity and suggested nothing deeper to him than the usual
Soviet arrogance and superciliousness.

They seldom called on him in his office in the Soviet chancellory
on the Viale della Repubblica; he rarely called upon them. It had
never occurred to them that there was as much uncertainty to his
role as to theirs, that he disliked many of the host government officials as much as they did, that he felt his little humiliations at the
presidency as painfully as they felt theirs, the veiled threats, the
absurd demands, the hypocritical Marxist-Leninist pretense. Could
a British high commissioner ever seriously dignify the pretenses of
some Micronesian potentate who had never read the King James
version of the Bible or the Book of Common Prayer and who only
spoke, say, pidgin English? That was Kirillan's problem as well. It
had also never occurred to them that as the ranking Soviet diplomat
in the country, he wasn't also the dominating Soviet presence but
was instead very much in the shadow of someone else, a man few
people had seen and fewer knew about, not the GRU or KGB
rezident, but someone as simple and uncomplicated in his thinking
as General Lobatoff, the ranking Soviet military adviser, now waiting silently in the far corner of Kirillan's office. He wasn't a gadfly,
not a sycophant, a Kremlin butterfly dancing about in the latest
breeches and pumps of political fashion, like Yuri Pulyakov, who at
that moment was bringing Kirillan a typed page, and whose silly

figure General Lobatoff's eye now settled on disapprovingly. He was a military officer and a deeply conservative one. He had taught at the Frunze Military Academy in Moscow, received the Order of Lenin, was fond of gardening and flowers. He had been married to his wife for thirty-two years.

The silence that shrouded the Soviet embassy those months since the Jubba invasion of Ethiopia and the accompanying paralysis—it was a historical anomaly, preposterous, actually; one Soviet client state invading another—was due to the deliberations of men as basic in their thinking as a Spartan, a Prussian, or a General Lobatoff. For such men and others like him at the ministry of defense in Moscow, a nation doesn't give up present certainties for future promises, doesn't immediately give up horse cavalry for tanks or tanks for aircraft or aircraft for missiles—not right away. Least of all does it give up military or strategic properties it presently enjoys—Jubba's deep-water ports on the Indian Ocean, Jubba's airfields and communications facilities—for the sake of visionary assets in the hostile environment of a nation in anarchy like Ethiopia. Whatever the first light breezes or seductive zephyrs whistled up by the courtiers of political fashion in Moscow it doesn't dismantle its walls and take to its ships as the Athenians did, but, Spartan-like, stays rooted to its native earth. Political sophists might, political swallows as well, like Pulyakov, but not military thinkers. General Lobatoff cared not a fig for their sophistries, for the abstractions of socialist solidarity, and that two centuries of feudal oppression that had prepared that vast derelict kingdom in the Abyssinian highlands for its revolution, like France in 1789, like Russia's peasants in 1917, among whom General Lobatoff had his roots.

So he sat now in Kirillan's office, heavy, stolid, impassive, sunk in thought, gazing out through the lamplight toward Kirillan's desk, watching him as alertly as a hawk watches a hare—if Kirillan had done his work effectively, there would have been no Jubba invasion—sitting there as he had for the last thirty minutes, watching the door open and shut, waiting for any cable that might suggest that the ministry of defense in Moscow no longer agreed with him.

Kirillan, very much conscious of General Lobatoff's opinion and conscious even more of that growing glacier of silence separating them, called to ask if he wanted coffee, brandy perhaps. He declined. Kirillan, anticipating his answer, called to his side and asked him to fetch him a small glass of brandy.

At one fifteen the call came from the presidency. Kirillan stood up and gathered his papers. To Lobatoff's relief, there had been no change in Kirillan's instructions. He was to tell the president what he had been told so many times before, that he was to remove his troops from Ethiopia. Only then would they again take up the matter of some kind of political settlement.

General Lobatoff joined his aide in the anteroom and went down to his gray Moska satisfied. But just to make sure, he stood there for a long time watching Kirillan's car carry him out of sight.

Talbot, still sleepless in the second-floor darkness of his villa, listened to the sound of the sea through the open windows. It was two o'clock and he was no longer thinking of his unanswered question but how he'd gotten himself into his mess with Lindy and how he would get himself out of it.

□ □ □

Harcourt had again summoned Talbot, this time to the residence. The telephone call had come just after lunch as he was getting ready to take a solitary swim. He'd called Lindy's apartment to ask if she wanted to join him but she'd said no.

"Then just come talk to me," he'd pleaded, "not talk, just listen. That's all I ask. I've got to explain—"

"You don't have to explain."

"I do, I've got to. I didn't know I was screwing things up for you. Why don't I come pick you up, come right now. Or we can talk there."

She'd seemed to hesitate. "I can't today."

"Tonight then, tomorrow, any time. I'm going nuts like this. Just say when."

"Tomorrow maybe. I'll let you know."

"What time? Two? Three? When?"

"I'll let you know. I've got to go, sorry."

A little better but not much. He was on his way upstairs to change clothes when Harcourt's call came.

Pete Ryan was staying with him, but he had gone to the WJLF press conference and then on to lunch with the Egyptian military attaché. He was leaving the following morning for a two-day excursion into the occupied territories.

Julia was on the rear terrace when Talbot arrived, arranging the tables for her buffet that evening. She'd been expecting him and led him with barely a word to the rear study, where Harcourt was waiting. She didn't join them as she usually did. Talbot supposed she knew why he'd been summoned.

Harcourt was wearing his tie from the office, but it was pulled loose and he'd shed his coat. His briefcase was open on the table next to the cherry secretary. He was agitated about something. On the desk was a yellow airgram he'd been studying. He asked Talbot to sit down. He had something important he wanted to discuss with him.

"It's about DeGroot," he said distastefully, "as I'm sure you've guessed by now."

Talbot sat down. Harcourt began pacing the floor. "I hate unpleasantness, I always have. I was willing to overlook his idiosyncrasies, willing to go along with almost everything from the first day—his preposterous manners, that insufferable voice, even the way he looked. He seemed to know something about the area. I didn't, of course, as you know, so I was grateful for that. He was well organized in the little things, no doubt about it, but there's much more to it than that, I'm afraid, much more." He turned impatiently. "For heaven's sake, Logan, you of all people know that, you sensed the same thing from the very beginning, that first day when he brought your car back."

Talbot didn't remember he'd discussed with him that first day in the back garden with DeGroot. "He may be a little odd, sure—"

"Odd? *Odd?*" Harcourt give a pitiful laugh. "Odd! Logan, the man's unbalanced, I'm convinced of it, the man's totally unbalanced!" He sat down suddenly, eyes swimming with indignation. "The man's unbalanced, a complete fraud, Logan. We have to face up."

"Unbalanced? That's pretty strong, isn't it? Unbalanced in what way?"

"That preposterous story he told." He jumped up again. "That ridiculous story about waiting at the border, observing from there. He was lying, the man was lying! There was no village destroyed by Ethiopian aircraft. Miss Vallon described the whole trip to me just last week at the d'Auberts'. Then this trip report. My God, these are the ramblings of a lunatic!" He turned to the desk and snatched up the airgram. "Have you seen his report? I'm convinced of it, the man's unhinged. Read this. It's beyond belief! You'd think he was out bird-watching on the Scottish heather."

Talbot took the five-page airgram and sat back. It was the report of DeGroot's trip to the occupied territories, typed in final draft in the form of an airgram to the Department. He'd given it to Harcourt to sign as he'd left the embassy that afternoon.

"Is this what convinced you?"

"I'd had my suspicions before. This was the last straw. All the little things, months and months of them. Then this, that preposterous story about having to remain with the Land-Rover caravan because a border village had been destroyed. That was a lie, in direct violation of State Department instructions. It's grounds for sending him home, for asking for his recall."

"Throwing him out?"

"Absolutely. Without a doubt. The man has no judgment at all, none. He's a menace to the mission, to me, to everyone. I'd heard stories before. Firthdale told me months ago that DeGroot was hinting he'd been sent here to personally oversee a new era in U.S.-Jubba relations. I didn't tell Julia this before, not until this, when it all came out. She knew, too, as it turned out."

"Julia did?"

"Agnes Firthdale told her, told her months ago. Not just hinting he'd been sent out to change things, telling everyone outright. *Months* ago. What a fool I've been. I saw the same thing. Now the inspectors are coming; the date's been set. The cable came in last night."

"Julia's read this report?"

"At lunch. Every word. In addition to what Agnes told her she's always suspected something bizarre about him, something very odd, just as you did. And then there's the matter of your chron file. DeGroot has it, he's had it all this time."

"Has he?" It no longer seemed important. He looked at the airgram. Typed out there in even more baroque fashion were those pompous tropes DeGroot had read from his notes that morning, that absurd fustian that had finally driven him out the door, unable to keep a straight face, reeling down the hall, sides aching in horrible laughter.

"It's pretty bad stuff, I admit, pretty awful, but it's the way he is. It doesn't mean he's unbalanced. Have you talked to him about this?"

"Not yet, no." Harcourt looked up in surprise. "Why?"

"You haven't said anything to him?"

"No. I mean yes, we had a talk after I decided he could no longer be trusted with political reporting responsibilities. I was a little curt with him, yes. That was last week, when I told you to go talk to Luttak. But about sending him back, no. I just got this airgram as I was leaving today."

"So he knows you're dissatisfied."

"I think he does, yes."

"Does he know you're thinking of sending him home?"

"No, but he will. I've made up my mind. I'll send him back, ask for his recall. He violated a Department instruction and did it deliberately, knowing full well the consequences."

Talbot looked at the second page, then the concluding paragraphs. "Do you know what his background is?" he asked, putting the airgram aside.

"No, and it doesn't interest me."

"No? Then there's nothing I can say."

"Nothing you can say? What do you mean, nothing you can say? You disagree?"

"I think maybe I do."

"For God's sake, Logan, the man has lied, he's willfully violated an instruction. What he did might have had very serious policy implications. He's blatantly misrepresented himself and his purpose in being here, he's embarrassed me and the post, he's embarrassed Julia with these ridiculous stories about my being merely the caretaker, about his being the guiding presence, I think he said. 'Guiding presence' was what Agnes told Julia he'd said. The man's a shameless liar, he's made me the laughingstock—"

"Then tell him."

"Tell him! I certainly intend to tell him. I'll demand his recall. I'll call Washington today on the green phone." He jumped up again, looking at his watch. "What time do you have? What's the time difference, six hours, isn't it? I'll call the assistant secretary—"

"I think you'd better wait."

"Wait? For what? In three weeks the inspectors will be here."

"Is that what Julia wants, too. DeGroot sent home?"

"Immediately. On the next plane."

"You need a better reason than that, strong and convincing reasons."

"I have seven months of reasons, *seven* awful months!"

"Then write them out, one by one, from the beginning. You can't do it in a phone call. You have to think about it some more. If you decide to throw him out, you have to figure that at his age his career is finished. Yours isn't going to look so hot either."

Harcourt sat down again in dismay. *"Mine!"*

"Yours, sorry. That's the way it is."

"Why mine? You can't think I've encouraged all this? You can't possibly believe that."

"It's what Washington believes, not me. He was your DCM. You solve these problems on the spot, not ship them back to Washington after it's too late. If I were in your shoes, I'd talk to him, tell him exactly how you feel and have it out."

"I intend to when I tell him—"

"I think you should have a talk with him first, confront him with all this, hear him out, and after you've thought about it some more, decide."

Harcourt was too disappointed to say a word. He sat looking at Talbot from the straight-backed chair, hands on his knees. "I really don't understand," he said miserably. "I don't."

"I just think you should talk to him, that's all."

"I'm disappointed." He took back the airgram, got up, and returned it to the desk. "I don't mind telling you I'm disappointed. That's not what I expected, not at all what I expected. It's impossible to sweep this under the rug, and I certainly don't intend to." He turned to look at Talbot, as if he'd just thought of something. "Is there something you know that I don't. Is that it? Must be. You'll be here tonight, won't you?"

"Tonight? I don't think I was invited. Anyway, Ryan's here, staying at my place."

"Then you'll both come. I'll tell Julia I've asked you. Come early. We'll talk about it again, but my instincts tell me the sooner he's told the better. Please, nothing to Julia about our talk, not yet, anyway."

Talbot drove back to his villa, sorry he hadn't told Harcourt more. So DeGroot was unbalanced, was he? Mad as a hatter, was he? Out bird-watching on the Scottish heather, was he? Just where the hell did Harcourt think he'd been all that time? Antigua? The Mill Reef Club? At the Cosmos club maybe, like his Wilmington banker uncle, all those nine o'clock arrivals and twelve o'clock departures. What about those dizzy afternoons on the terrace? Off in cuckoo-land, chasing after those bright little lymph blossoms that swam across his gin-pickled corneas just before sundown, butterfly net in hand, then back to the library to press them in buckram. Nicola would have told him, quicker than anyone: Sure, they were mad, all of them.

He parked his car in the drive and went back through the passageway to the rear garden.

Pete Ryan was sitting in his shorts, his portable typewriter on the table in front of him, typing out a piece. "Where you been?" he asked. "Some Italian woman was here, thought I was a trespasser. Something up?"

"Not much. What'd she say?"

"Said she'd call you, that she was going someplace for a few days."

"Merca?"

"Sounds like it. Something like that."

"That's down the coast. How about a swim?"

"Can't, sorry. Maybe later. Just got the word from the Egyptian."

"What word?"

"They're going to throw the Sovs out, bag and baggage, break relations."

"The Egyptian said that? When's the break coming?"

"Within the next three days."

"Maybe I'll send a cable. You wouldn't mind. I'll attribute it to you."

"Not yet." Ryan looked at his watch. "Tomorrow morning it's all yours. In the meantime go take your swim and forget it."

Talbot went upstairs to change. That was par for the course, too. The biggest scoop of his two and a half years in the country and Pete Ryan, his visitor from Nairobi, got to break it before he did.

□ □ □

Julia had invited a few early guests to her buffet that evening, a few sympathetic Americans, she'd said. Talbot, arriving with Pete Ryan, knew something was wrong as soon as she met them in the foyer to lead them inside. The ambassador was subdued, talking in the salon with Lindy and Andrews from the *New York Times*. Julia had arranged for Andrews to bring Lindy. If Talbot's invitation hadn't come at the last minute he might have thought the arrangement another of Julia's carefully planned little humiliations. Lindy nodded to him coolly and looked away. Miss Vallon was also there, come early by mistake, having misunderstood her telephoned invitation.

Talbot guessed Julia and Harcourt had argued about something and she was still upset. She tried to put the best face on her displeasure, but her carefully planned little prelude went very awkwardly. Harcourt, sulking, gave her very little help. Then they'd quarreled about the canapés and the mood rapidly deteriorated as she began taking her revenge.

Talking to Andrews, she said there were a few people in the local diplomatic community who had no business being there—crude, unreliable, and in some cases totally treacherous. Yet here they were, remaining because others were too cowardly to do anything about it.

"But I won't name names," she continued, ignoring Andrews's polite bewilderment, "except for those everyone knows by now. Mrs. Nikiforov for example, that hideous woman. Or Nikiforov either. The Bulgarians are what they are, no one can change them, just like the Russians. The locals quite despise them."

In the sudden silence she sensed disapproval. "Logan knows exactly what I mean," she added quickly. "If anyone does, he certainly does. I hadn't realized he was so fond of our *dear* Mr. De-Groot."

Andrews looked at him, half smiling, still mystified. Lindy, sitting next to Julia on the couch, flushed and searched for her cigarettes.

"Which locals?" Talbot asked from the footstool, knowing at last what she and Lyman had argued about. She was furious Harcourt was wavering about sending DeGroot home. She blamed him. His eyes were bloodshot from the sea; he had lost a mask while snorkeling and had spent a futile twenty minutes searching for it. "You mean the houseboys?"

"He's just being difficult," Julia said. "Mrs. Nikiforov is very close to the KGB *rezident*. Everyone knows that. Just as everyone knows about Mrs. Seretti, that awful Italian woman who infiltrates local diplomatic life on behalf of a certain foreign intelligence agency. Need I say more?"

"You needn't say more," Talbot said. "I think everyone understands."

"I'm sure they do." Then, to Andrews again, "He's still being difficult. He has a talent for being difficult."

"I'm not being difficult," Talbot said.

"You *are* being difficult," she said sharply. "We live in a fishbowl, you see, Mr. Andrews," she added pleasantly. "We have to be careful. Some of us aren't. You know, I'm sure, don't you, Mr. Ryan? You've visited here so often."

"I think I might," Ryan said vaguely.

"I'm not being difficult," Talbot said. "You just don't want to know."

"You *are,*" Julia said angrily.

"I'm not. It's just another case of your not knowing what you're talking about."

Julia turned as if struck. Lindy looked at her in surprise, half smiling. Andrews's confusion hovered awkwardly on his lips. Harcourt, already standing, walked slowly to the bookcase.

"And I suppose you do?" she said, two spots of color flaring on her cold cheeks.

"I know what I know. I don't pretend to know what I don't know."

"Pretend to know what you don't know?" She laughed falsely. "How can that be, pretend to know what you don't know? How awkwardly put. Can that be our political officer speaking?" She laughed again, but her voice betrayed her. "No wonder everything is so impossibly confused. What can he possibly mean, do you think? Pretend to know what you don't know. Lyman, is that possible?"

Harcourt looked miserably at the bookcases. "I don't think we need make an issue of it."

"I'm not making an issue of it, I'm simply asking you what you think he meant."

"What I think is that accusations and gossip have their place but not in a fishbowl."

"I think the ambassador is right," Lindy said quickly, sliding from the couch. "I think I'll get a refill. How about you, Andy?"

Andrews got up quickly. "I think I would." He held out his glass but just as quickly retrieved it. "What am I doing? I'll come along."

"I wouldn't mind a little freshener myself," Ryan said, rising.

"The Scotch is under the bar," Julia called in a brittle voice, "the new bottle."

No one turned. "Why don't I show you," Harcourt offered graciously to Lindy.

"*Moi aussi,*" Miss Vallon said laconically. "*Tu l'as dans le cul,* you've had it in the ass," she muttered to Talbot as she passed, making an unfeminine gesture.

He didn't move, still sitting on the footstool. He knew Julia deserved it, but he felt terribly sorry for her, sorry for Harcourt, sorry for all of them. She was still on the couch, legs folded under her, her fingers drawn across her forehead, her eyes turned toward the french doors and the lights of the port. She continued to stroke her forehead and he saw the white of her knuckles.

"I'd like to say I'm sorry but I'm not." She ignored him, continuing to massage her forehead. "You deserved it. You say some goddamn silly things sometime and you were saying them just now."

"You pushed me to the edge," she said, her voice tremulous, her eyes moist, "you and Lyman both, both of you, right to the edge."

"You don't have to carry the whole load."

"You don't know what you're talking about. You enjoy it. I know you both enjoy it."

"That's bullshit. It's not worth all this, nothing is. Not worth arguing about, not worth making a fool of yourself about."

"You enjoy it."

"I don't enjoy it."

"You *do* enjoy it. If you say another word I'll never speak to you again. I'll go in the other room and never come out again, not as long as you're here, as long as anyone's here."

"Go ahead. If I didn't care I wouldn't be sitting here; if it didn't hurt seeing you make a fool of yourself I wouldn't be sitting here."

"You're such a deceiver, such a terrible fraud."

"Sometimes maybe. Like you. Like everyone sometimes."

"You enjoy it, I don't."

"You work at it, I don't. Anyway, I'm serious sometimes."

"I've always known you were sly, but I never knew you could be so terribly vindictive, so ugly."

"Talk about ugly. What you were saying was ugly, and you make yourself ugly when you say those things."

"That's so trite." She drew her fingers lightly across her eyelids. "No one understands, no one. No one knows what I've been through. No one—"

"I do. I've always known."

"You don't, never, no one has."

"I have, Lyman has."

"You haven't."

He moved to the blue wingback chair next to her. "Poor Julia. Now you're feeling sorry for yourself."

"That's ridiculous and you know it. You know only what you want to know."

"That was my line."

"It's true."

"Then you should have laughed me off, told me to buzz off, then talked about something else, the way you always can. You can charm a bug out of a bottle when you want to, and by the time the others got here, everyone would have forgotten. Anyway if I didn't care about you, it wouldn't matter. If it weren't for you, I'd have left a long time ago. I wouldn't even have come back here for another goddamn ten months. Everything else was just a substitute. So when you say those silly things, things you don't believe, it hurts, and I want to tell you to shut up, just like I did."

"You wanted to humiliate me and you did."

"I didn't, never."

"You did." She looked at her trembling fingers. "What do you mean, everything else was just a substitute?"

"Just what I said."

"That's not true. It wasn't me, it was Paris."

"No, it wasn't, but I'm not going to argue. You have too many little tricks. Some I didn't mind, I even looked forward to them. It was nice sometimes just sitting and talking, just the two of us. But all that bullshit in between got awfully tiresome. I mean it's really terrible stuff and you know it."

"You came back here because of Paris, nothing else." She touched her lids and brought her hand down.

"That's not true either, but it's too late now anyway. But I didn't mind, even taking all that shit from DeGroot, cleaning up Shaughnessy's mess. Something would always happen to make it worthwhile, playing tennis or doing something else. Something like that comes along and you don't mind so much, like the time at the Sudanese ambassador's."

"What time?" She sat watching him, her hands limp in her lap.

"The time you said I looked unhappy and then we talked and I went on to the embassy compound and talked with Peterson's wife at the pool and she called me Sneaky Pete."

"I don't remember."

"It was the night you had on the new dress and were going to the Germans' for dinner and I'd never seen the dress at all."

"You didn't notice at all. It wasn't new, not really. I'd taken in the waist a little, that was all."

"It looked new, anyway I thought it was new."

"At least I don't think it was new." The houseboy came in and stood in front of the table awkwardly and Julia beckoned to him and took a glass, still looking at Talbot. "He's not ready yet, Kasim. Come back in a few minutes. I'm not sure I remember the night."

"It was the night you talked about the embassy family and said I looked unhappy."

"You did look unhappy."

"Maybe a little. Then we walked across the back garden, and Firthdale and d'Aubert were hiding behind the tree."

"I remember d'Aubert hiding, yes."

"So that was nice. And I was wondering to myself whether you were happy because of the new dress or the dinner at the German embassy—"

"The residence, not the embassy."

"Residence, that's right, or because you'd finally sat down with DeGroot and gotten things straight about your representational accounts, and that really pissed me off, DeGroot sitting up here with you two like some kind of small beer collection agent, but then I finally decided it was because of the dress."

"Why'd you think of that? It certainly didn't look new, did it? Maybe I'm not thinking of the same dress. I'm just not sure, I suppose, but I remember the night."

"That's a fib."

"It's not a fib. I remember perfectly."

"A woman always remembers the first night she wore a new dress."

"Does she? How do you know that?"

"From the things they say."

"What do they say?"

"When you take them home and they say, 'Well, all right, if you really want to, but be careful of my new dress.' "

She smiled. "You're very wicked."

"But not just that, from how they look."

"And how do they look?"

"Like you looked that night. Whether the dress was new or not didn't matter. Because of you everything else was new, even me, I even felt new."

"It was new, come to think of it. Was that how I looked?"

"That was how you looked, how you looked and felt."

"How do you know I felt that way?"

"From your face."

Harcourt, hovering cautiously in the doorway to the terrace, had heard their voices and ventured further, followed by the others.

"Did I? I seem to remember you were very sweet that night. I wasn't sure why."

Harcourt heard the front gates clanging. "I think the Firthdales are here."

She looked up. "Bring them in, please. Now that I think of it, I do remember I was annoyed with d'Aubert hiding behind the tree. Sit down everyone, please."

Lindy and Andrews sat down.

"You didn't show it," Talbot said.

"But I don't always," she said, smiling at Miss Vallon, "even if you do pretend to read my mind sometimes. Miss Vallon, please. Won't you join us? He's such a *blagueur, mon petit coquin.*"

The Firthdales came in, and Talbot got up and yielded his chair.

"My dear, you look absolutely radiant," she said as Julia stood up to embrace her.

"We were just reminiscing," Julia said gracefully. "Have you met my other guests. Miss Vallon, Miss Dowling, Mr. Andrews?"

"Ah, Talbot. What's the latest communiqué from the front?" Firthdale asked.

"I'm not sure, to tell the truth."

"Not sure," Agnes Firthdale called. "Not sure. He's not sure?" She turned in mock astonishment to look at Julia. "The poor man must be smitten."

"I think he is," Julia said. The others came—Dr. Melton and his wife and two American correspondents, the French and Italian counselors and their wives. Tables were set on the terrace for those who preferred to sit there. It was to be terribly informal, Julia told everyone. Some sat on lounge chairs, others on the steps, and afterwards most of the guests stayed until after midnight. Everyone agreed afterwards it had been a lovely evening.

Talbot and Ryan left just after Lindy, Andrews, and Miss Vallon. The three were still standing beyond the gate in front of Andrews's rented car when Talbot and Ryan strolled up. Andrews said they were thinking of going on to the Giubba nightclub for a nightcap; he wondered if they'd like to join them.

"Sounds like a good idea," Ryan said.

"What about my place," Talbot said. "We can sit in the back garden."

"No, thanks," Lindy said.

He'd tried to talk to her all evening about her promise to go swimming, but she'd avoided him. "What's wrong with my place?"

"Everything. I really couldn't believe it, that shit you were giving her afterwards."

"What's that have to do with my place?"

"Everything. Who do you think you are, anyway? Always on the make, that's who, the same old preppy. I really couldn't believe it. No one could. What were you apologizing for? She doesn't know what she's talking about, she never has."

"She got herself out on a limb, that's all. She was right on the edge—"

"Yeah, sure. Better her than anyone else I know. Talk about Osrics."

"Come on, now," Ryan said, "let's forget it."

"You just don't understand," Lindy said, turning away. "Are we going to the Giubba or not?"

"*Please*," Miss Vallon said, sagging. "My shoes hurt, please."

"Screw it," Talbot said, watching Lindy and Miss Vallon get into Andrews's car. After a minute Ryan decided to join them. Talbot drove back to his villa alone.

He didn't go to bed but turned on the phonograph and poured a gin and bitters, awful stuff—what he promised himself he wouldn't do.

Thought he was a preppy now, did she?

It was Whittington, her goddamn Irish uncle, he was the one who'd talked to her. Amazing how many CIA old pros turned out to be altar-boy Catholics after all—Seton Hall, Notre Dame, St. John's, Holy Cross—taking their holy orders out to the Third World frontier. Whittington, an old Marquette man from the Midwest, once worked for a Milwaukee newspaper. Thought all Ivy Leaguers' balls were silver plated, kept ready in a hand-tooled English leather billiard case, like dueling pistols. *Watch your wives, daughters, and secretaries, men! Cocks up! Talbot the Dirk is loose!*

Shaughnessy, too, now in widowed old Lisbon, mourning her lost husbands and sons.

Marquette, explorer of the Mississippi, wasn't he? Père Marquette. A Jesuit, like LaSalle once, got his bones dug up and carried back in a birchbark canoe.

He opened the front door and stood on the porch looking at the silver-sheeted beach, the black and silver sea, the luminous fissured moon, almost veined, as mysteriously tremulous as a sea turtle egg. Why mysterious? It rang like a gong when a meteorite struck.

Still a mess. The metal tackle rattled against the rusting flagpole in the sea wind, still summoning all those old parade-ground ghosts.

Fort Apache once but not anymore. Fort Crèvecoeur now, where that winter LaSalle arrived too late and found it pillaged, burned, and abandoned by the handful of rabble he'd left behind, Frenchmen gone mad in the wilderness of the Illinois and Iroquois, one of whom had scrawled a last message on a burned piece of plank left behind: *Nous sommes tous sauvages—1680.*

What would his message be, left behind here in the country of the Jubba, 1976? He stood for a minute listening to the sound of the lanyard and the slow wash of the sea, and then emptied his glass over the railing and went inside. It was after two and he was drifting off to sleep when he heard the front gates clang open and the sound of a car. A few minutes later Ryan's jangling voice lifted through the darkness as he made his way up the steps to the guest room down the hall:

> "My ex-wife was a superior soul,
>   a superior soul was she.
> Cut out to play a superior role
>   in the goddamn bourgeoisie."

Talbot heard him stumble and climbed out of bed, turned on the hall light, and went to remind him of his trip the following morning.

Ryan hadn't forgotten. He stood in the hall in front of the guest bedroom blinking in the painful light as he pulled off his tie and then his shirt. "How you put up with all this crud I don't know. Never could understand it, can't now."

"Which crud?"

"All of it. Like tonight. Come with us tomorrow. See the territories, talk to the people out there, not all these goddamn people here."

"Sure, get my ass thrown out good."

"Better now than later. Don't kid yourself. Don't wait until it's too late, like those people up there in the *palazzo* on the hill. Never again up there for me, never. You're on the wrong side of the field, Logan, old son, wrong team, wrong uniform, wrong coach. Wake me at seven, would you?"

"Sure, seven. How was the nightclub?"

"Civilized, a very civilized little group ours was."

"What'd you do, dance, talk, what?"

"Talked, danced, drank. Sensible talk for a change. You should have come."

"I wish I had. Seven, see you then."

□ □ □

Giorgio Rugatto kept a tent among the sand dunes along the coast thirty kilometers south of the capital. Nicola invited Talbot to join them that Sunday. Rugatto would have invited him himself, she said when she called, but hadn't been able to reach him. She and a few others were leaving early. Talbot decided to meet her there.

He drove out to the motor pool to pick up an embassy Land-Rover. On the airport road he trailed two blue Soviet buses ferrying Soviet military advisers to the airport for evacuation by Aeroflot to Aden. The exodus had been continuing for five days now.

Ryan had been right. Following an all-day and all-night session of the ruling revolutionary council, Jubba denounced its friendship treaty with the Soviet Union, denied it use of its ports, airfields, and communication facilities, and expelled all Soviet military and technical advisers from the country. The Soviet embassy was reduced to a skeleton staff, no larger than the U.S. embassy staff the day of Talbot's arrival so many months ago.

He left the paved road and continued south along the sandy

coastal track parallel to the sea. He arrived a little before noon and found Rugatto's blue canvas tent sheltered in the lee of the barren dunes along the sea half a kilometer from the track. The sun was merciless. Rugatto's Land-Rover, a second Land-Rover, and a Toyota were already there, parked on the sand a few meters from the dunes overlooking the blue tent. In the glaring sun outside, a Jubba cook was tending a charcoal fire in a brazier. A second cook was putting small game birds wrapped in grape leaves on spits. The tent was large, thirty by fifteen meters, the flaps had been rolled up, and in the diffuse blue light inside seven or eight of Rugatto's guests sat on canvas chairs on the tarpaulin floor covering, smoking, drinking, and talking.

Nicola, wearing a bikini that showed too much of her figure to be flattering, greeted him with a kiss on the cheek. Rugatto, also in a bathing suit, shook his hand and asked him what he wanted to drink. A bottle of German Krombacher pilsner was passed from the ice chest as Nicola introduced him to a middle-aged Italian couple. He imported cottonseed-processing machinery; as they stood talking, Talbot discovered how little he knew about cottonseed processing and how little more he wanted to know. After a few minutes they invited him to sit down, joining another Italian who was an adviser to the ministry of fisheries. Nicola excused herself to help Rugatto's Jubba servant find something in the Land-Rover.

Talbot was disappointed to find so many guests. Among them were two Italians he'd met that day at Nicola's villa. He recognized the Italian commercial attaché from the embassy. Seated in the hazy blue far corner was the blond Italian woman who'd brought Nicola to his villa that afternoon. He spoke to her and nodded and she gave him a discreet smile. The others he'd never seen before. Some were in bathing suits, like Nicola, but no one had been swimming or seemed interested in swimming.

The tent lay in the lee of the dunes to the east and west and he couldn't see the sea, the sky, or feel the salt wind. The interior was hot, the canvas at his feet gritty with sand. The conversation he overheard was similar to the talk he'd heard that first afternoon at Nicola's villa, talk that hadn't interested him then and didn't interest him now. After Rugatto left the tent to help Nicola find whatever was needed from the Land-Rover, he learned from a conversa-

tion between the cottonseed man's wife and the fisheries adviser that
Nicola's bastard stepson Federico Seretti was convalescing at Nicola's
villa with his mother, Samina, the sly old swindler who coveted
Nicola's banana plantation, and that Seretti's old friend Rugatto
had left the carabinieri after the Italian officers were dismissed,
lived on his farm to the south growing bananas, and made a little
money selling Fiat and Bulgarian tractors. He was also a widower;
the heavyset Italian woman in a bathing suit in the far corner helping prepare the lobster ravioli had once been his mistress. From the
talk he concluded they didn't think Seretti a very good husband,
Rugatto particularly bright, or his ex-mistress particularly attractive.

He finished his beer and thought he might go for a swim. He
asked if anyone was interested in swimming, and a man nearby told
him it was too hot. Rugatto, he learned, had spent the night here
and swam each day just after dawn, the best time for swimming.

Their inertia annoyed him, the conversation annoyed him, the
hot airless blue tent annoyed him. Rugatto didn't annoy him, he
liked his honest stupidity, but the way he looked at Nicola annoyed
him, just as the size of Nicola's bikini annoyed him, showing too
much of the cleavage of her breasts and buttocks. He got up to get
some air but once outside decided he'd go swimming. He climbed
the dune and with his strollers full of sand went back to his Land-
Rover and changed into his bathing trunks. Leaving the Land-Rover,
he saw an orange Volkswagen jeep bouncing through the ruts toward the Land-Rovers. Two more Italians got out and waved to
him; the man was carrying a picnic basket. He'd never seen them
before. They disappeared into the tent.

He went through the dunes and down onto the beach and swam
for fifteen minutes. The bottom wasn't firm but mucked up, and
clots of tar from ships blowing their bilges were strewn along the
strand; he wondered why Rugatto had put his tent here, who his
present mistress was, and if he'd ever slept with Nicola. In the Italian *circus maximus,* like that of the small tent he'd left behind, such
small truths mattered. He swam north and waded back onto the
beach, climbed the scalding dunes, and crossed the ridge to the
promontory of volcanic rock fifty meters above the sea. The wind
was steady, pressing against his ears and hot skin. An enormous sea
turtle lifted on the incoming waves and wallowed in the churning

sea lashing against the rocks below. The volcanic rock about him was littered with smashed crustaceans, bleaching crab shells and fish bones brought by the gulls. He smelled the sea's timeless rot, as caustic as blood, not the silent submarine sea beyond the reef where he dove, hidden now below the splintered surfaces and the windrows of white combers stretching away endlessly, but the old reptilian sea, the ancient of ancients, an infinite heaving nothingness that burned, scraped, blistered, and devoured. He saw her brick house poised above it, looking out over this same murderous metallic blue, the polite green grass, the hum of insects under the laurels, the garden beyond, floating like a mirage on a carpet of brilliant English green turf, all of it a dream. How much would remain after she was gone?

The sea turtle was still floating below, bobbing among rafts of kelp.

He went back to the tent. The salt had dried on his skin and Rugatto apologized for not having a freshwater shower. He knew Americans were accustomed to this kind of camping luxury and was planning to order one. "Here, let me show you." He proudly brought a tattered catalogue from a locker. It was from a New York sporting goods house. Rugatto pointed out what interested him—an inflatable catamaran, a foot-powered self-propelled pedal boat, a cordless electric kettle. Here, this was interesting; he showed him a solar-powered ventilated pith helmet. The catalogue was passed around and a few laughed at the frivolity of the fun-loving Americans.

Lunch was served. He took a plate from the folding buffet table, was given a serving of lobster ravioli, a small partridge or francolin wrapped in buttered grape leaves, and a glass of white Bordeaux. As he sat there eating, it took a few minutes for the conversation to make any sense to him. As it did he realized they were talking about the old Italian professor at the university, now back in Bologna, the one who'd told Noseworthy about the Portuguese frigate.

He looked up and saw Rugatto smiling at him. "So you swim from the reef, looking for the ship," he said.

A few laughed.

"He is the one?" an Italian woman asked.

"He is the one," Rugatto said.

The woman asked him about it, what it was like, and they all looked at him, smiling sympathetically.

"I think that is very romantic," an older woman said. "Maybe there is a ship."

"Maybe it's not a ship he's looking for," Rugatto said slyly.

"What would he be looking for?"

Rugatto smiled, looking overhead, waving his fingers in a lazy spiral. "What do the satellites look for?"

"At the bottom of the sea?" a man scoffed.

"That's where the carabinieri would look," someone said. They laughed and Rugatto reddened but wasn't offended. He shot wild boar in Yugoslavia; they kept tiny finches in their terrace cages.

"He is young and he has this energy, you see," said a middle-aged Italian. "Isn't that it? Don't you have this energy?"

"Yes, he is young," the woman said, "but also he is looking for this Portuguese ship. He is looking seriously."

"But his house is there across the beach," another said, "so it is easy, maybe not so serious. Whose house is it?"

"Ferrugio's house," the cottonseed man said. "With the garden in the back, the one Nicola is making all right."

"Did Seretti have such energy?" the woman asked.

"Sometimes," Nicola said, looking up from her plate. She seemed to reflect as her mouth moved. "Intellectual energy, yes. Too much. Physical energy, no, not so much." She took a small bone from her mouth and dropped it aside.

"Ask Samina, she would say the same?" Rugatto asked, making a stupid joke.

"At the end, yes, she knew," said Nicola indifferently.

"So you are going to Paris soon?" the wife of the cottonseed man asked.

"In a week or so," Talbot said.

"You will have a flat in Paris," she asked, "or a house?"

"A flat," he said, wondering what the hell else Nicola had told them while he'd been swimming and they'd sat here talking, the way they talked about Rugatto after he'd gone to the Land-Rover. He saw the Italian seed-processing man's wife and the commercial officer looking at him in a friendly way as they ate their fowl, a way that had nothing to do with machinery, his goatish hair, or his prickling shoulders. He knew by the time the story of their affair began making its way through the diplomatic community, the question would be who had seduced whom. There was nothing he could say by then, nothing he could do except sit there eating and drinking his Bordeaux, as he already was, nothing he could change in any way. They were there and so was he, T. Logan Talbot, *Esq.*, shot on the wing like one of Rugatto's game birds, now plucked, eviscerated, cooked, masticated, and sucked clean, nothing left for their devouring curiosity except his skeleton of indigestible bones, large and small, piled up like those small francolin bones being collected on a platter by Rugatto's Jubba cook.

Everyone took a walk after lunch along the beach but after ten minutes found it too hot, and after they turned back Talbot continued along the same rocks he'd climbed after his swim.

"Why did you leave?"

He turned at the sound of Nicola's voice. "Nothing. I'm tired of sitting, that's all."

"It's something else. You were upset. I saw it."

"No, I wasn't, not upset." He was again conscious of her absurdly small bathing suit. "It's just too much."

"It's what they said? What is it?"

"I don't know."

"Then tell me. Too much what?"

"Everything. It used to be simple; everything used to be simple. Talking to you used to be simple. This country used to be simple." He turned back to the sea. "There were some sea turtles down there."

He pointed below, but the turtles had sounded and now there was nothing except the angry surge of the sea, tilting murderously in its impoundment of pool between the rocks, the waves smashing ten feet high against the canyon. "I feel like diving," he said. She had already turned away and was impatiently retracing her steps back across the volcanic outcropping. He watched her go, moving carefully across the rock until her feet found the hot sand of the dunes. She began to run, the way a woman runs, not a jog but in short bursts. He was conscious of how small she was, how she painted her toenails, how her hips were too broad. He was conscious of a hundred defects except for her voice and her eyes, the smell of her skin, and her anger, but her anger was gone and she was at loose ends again, drifting back into her little fishpond flotilla of Italian friends. It would take a revolution to bring her alive in the way she'd been that first month, when so much had seemed so important.

Now she was powerless again, powerless, reconciled, and withdrawn to her own femininity, a woman in that uncertain bloom of Indian summer, as much a puzzle to herself as to him possibly, unsure of what she was or what she wanted. But maybe it was simpler than that; maybe he was just the last chocolate éclair before she slimmed down, the last double martini on an autumn afternoon in Manhattan before she collected herself for the commuter train back to Connecticut, and went home to her husband and children to dry out. He watched her stop at the top of the dune, hesitate, and then try to slide down, one leg out, the other flexed, but she got no more than a few feet and came to a halt. Not athletic either, just cerebral, self-willed, lonely, proud, sometimes cold, wanting her lovers polite and domesticated, not demanding too much of her energies, so that those other lonely feminine preoccupations wouldn't suffer. What else she was he would never know.

She waited there until he came to join her. Slowly she scooted down on her bottom and sat nearby. "We can go swimming," she said. "Then take a walk." She adjusted her straps. "What is it? My bathing suit? My friends? What is it?"

"It's nothing. I'm fine."

"No, it is something else. We must be honest, please. If it is not me, it must be someone else."

"I'm not sure."

"It is someone else. What is it?"

"We're just kidding ourselves, that's all."

She didn't seem surprised and sat silently for a minute moving her fingers through the hot sand. "Yes, in some ways, but for me it isn't the same. Not the same as it is for you."

"What is it for you?"

"For me, I know what I want. So I can be satisfied. For you, you want too much, you are always restless because then you always want more. So I think that is what you feel." She hesitated, scrolling the sand with her fingers. "It isn't bad to feel that way and that is the way I felt once but not now." She lifted her eyes for the first time. "Now I am only what you see, just me, just like this, just what is left, no more."

"That's a lot."

"No, not a lot. Then you were lonely, too."

"Pretty much. But it wasn't just being lonely."

"No, but that was part of it. Don't mistake it for something else."

"What about you, you weren't lonely, too?"

"A little, yes. But in a different way."

"I suppose it's been that way for you."

She looked up quickly. "Since Seretti died? No. No, I was more lonely when he was alive. Yes, it's true. You don't know what that means, do you?"

"I'm not sure, no."

"When you give yourself to someone, give everything, everything, all there is, and then find you have nothing for yourself, that it is all taken. That is being lonely."

He watched her face. "I don't understand, not completely."

"Someday you will."

"Does it always end like this?"

She shrugged. "It's not like a play, like a book; it doesn't have an ending. It just stops, the pages stop, and that's all. You look for the missing pages, but there is nothing."

"Not in this ending—"

"You forget, I am older than you, so I know. It is different for me."

"That doesn't have anything to do with it."

"It does a little, yes. But it is an excuse, too. Fooling ourselves, yes, but that is nice sometimes, to fool yourself, even to pretend." She got up impatiently, brushing the sand from her hips. "But no more talk, no more explaining. Today we'll pretend some more, and tomorrow, who knows? I don't know the future, neither do you. If nothing else we'll always be friends. You'll come see me in Rome when I'm there, and maybe other things." She pulled him away. "Please, let's swim, not talk. No more talking. In a few weeks when you are in Paris, we'll remember the day we went swimming here, not what we said. Please, for me."

As Talbot drove by the embassy through the gathering dusk, he saw Whittington's car parked just behind Harcourt's, unusual for a Sunday evening. DeGroot's car was also there. He parked across the street and went in.

He found them in the commo room on the second floor reading a flood of cables and NSA intercepts. The Soviet military resupply for Ethiopia had at last begun, plane after plane arriving at Addis Ababa filled with Soviet military equipment and more on the way, overflight requests already filed with Iran, Turkey, and a half-dozen other Middle Eastern countries.

So there was Talbot's answer.

The political scaffolding had long been in place, the Marxist bunting, the heroic portraits of Lenin and Brezhnev, but on an empty stage in a deserted theater. Now the Soviet military was packing the house, throwing its full weight behind the production, giving it bone and muscle. The Soviet Union, that colossus of military might and ideological dynamism, paralyzed for months by doubt, confusion, and indecision, was now on the march, determined that the revolution so long vaunted by its ideological butterflies and their hired intellectual hacks like Minzonni not fail.

Talbot had never quite so despised Moscow's hypocrisy or its murderous pretense as much as he did at that moment, standing there in the embassy commo room watching that flood of teletype copy chattering out on the crypto machines. The Jubba army, once Soviet-armed and Soviet-trained, was now to be abandoned naked in the Ethiopian wasteland with no dependable source of military equipment or resupply. Moscow, in the meantime, was making sure its newest harlot in Ethiopia lacked for nothing.

□ □ □

"Sorry I'm late," Basil Dinsmore said, standing in the fierce sunlight of Talbot's drive where a car from the British embassy had left him. He was as immaculate as ever, his gray hair damply combed, but his suit was a little limp from the heat, his tan tropical jacket dark under the arms and across his back. The British ambassador's residence, where he had lunched, was on a hillside in the city, bowered and colonnaded; the rear terrace where he'd dawdled over too many glasses of wine shadowed with cool green light. Now in the flooding light from the open sea he discovered again the drowning immensity of the littoral. He blinked painfully as he searched his pockets for his sunglasses. "Still as isolated as ever. Can't escape it out here, can you?"

"I've stopped trying," Talbot said. "How've you been?"

"Far too busy, hardly a moment to myself. Not even enough to quite know what's going on." He glanced out to sea. "I think if I were posted here this is where I'd prefer to be. Marvelous out here." He turned back. "Firthdale was a bit wound up, I'm afraid. Agnes, too. Thanks for the other night, by the way. Silly of me, not remembering where I was."

"Nothing compromised, I hope."

"A few of Nick's bad jokes."

They walked along the drive and through the passageway. Dinsmore stopped for a minute to look about the garden.

"When I think of my visits here, this is what I think of. I must have described this garden to my wife a dozen times. I think you've done something new."

"It's been replanted. That's all new over there. Nice now, much better. Something to drink? Soda?"

Lying open on the flagstones were two suitcases brought from an upstairs closet to air in the afternoon sunshine.

"Soda, yes, please. The sun's left me a bit dry. I'll be off to Cairo in the morning, my last trip for a while, I'm afraid. You'll be leaving when, next week?"

"Two weeks."

"Paris, Agnes Firthdale said. Quite a change. I'll have to give you my new address in London."

"You're being reassigned?"

"I'm to become foreign editor," he said with a modest smile. "Bit of a change for me. Next February. About time, too, I'd say."

"I didn't know. Congratulations."

"Well, thank you. My wife's pleased. I'm not sure yet." He sat down and took out his notebook, laid it aside, then took out another. "A bit of a problem right now though, finding someone to take over. Resident in Cairo, but more likely Beirut, which seems to have quieted down again. Never easy is it, finding the right man. Wouldn't interest you, would it?"

Talbot thought he was joking. "What, Cairo? It might if my Arabic was a little better. I'll be right back."

He went in to get the soda and returned a minute later.

"Thank you," Dinsmore said, taking the glass. "Not necessarily Cairo, Beirut's more likely. Your French is quite good, Agnes told me. She isn't an easy woman to impress. Do you know the Lebanon?"

"I've never been there."

"But you'd never been here before either, had you?" He returned to his notebook. "I'd like to take stock for a minute, share a few impressions, see what you make of it. Not the official view, mind you, I've had enough of that, but how you see it."

He asked the same questions Talbot had been pondering the past several days, ever since the first cables had come in describing the massive Soviet air- and sea-lift to Ethiopia. Talbot told him what he had inferred from his talk with Pulyakov and others. Moscow had found in Ethiopia a genuine revolution, not a masquerade. The different aspects of its revolution—the feudal peasantry who organized in its support, Ethiopia's ancient civilization, the non-African, non-Moslem aspects of its feudal past, the use of terror to eliminate counterrevolutionaries—had proven too seductive for the Soviets to resist. That revolution had also shown how fraudulent was Jubba's own. The Soviets had rejected Jubba's appeal for support in liberating Western Jubbaland as nothing more than the same crude old Jubba nationalism disguised in Marxist-Leninist terms, and cast their lot with the Ethiopians.

As he talked, Talbot seemed to be a man apart, the voice belonging to someone else. Gone were the antics, the asides, the improvisations. Hearing his own voice, he paused from time to time, aware of something he couldn't identify. The light overhead was the same, the hemisphere of sky. A slight wind stirred the palm trees. Somewhere along the sea a plane was droning toward the airport.

What was different? he wondered.

Why had Moscow waited so long in coming to Ethiopia's support? He heard Dinsmore's voice again, repeating the question.

"Sorry." Talbot said he wasn't sure. He suspected the more conservative Soviet thinkers, like conservatives everywhere, preferred the safer course, to hold on to what they had in Jubba rather than gamble on costly and uncertain future assets in an Ethiopia being torn apart by anarchy and rebellion. But now the choice had been made for them. Jubba had thrown the Russians out, and the Soviet military was determined to make the political choice the correct one by the sheer weight of military arms.

Jubba's troops still retained their Ethiopian territories, Dinsmore reminded him. What would happen now? What kind of political settlement did he think likely?

Talbot remembered what he had said to Harcourt and DeGroot that morning at the embassy.

"I don't think a political settlement possible," he said. Jubba would ultimately be forced to withdraw its troops, the advice Washington was now giving the president in response to his appeals for advice.

"Now the Jubba military are talking about an Ethiopian invasion," Dinsmore said. "Soviet 'hegemonism,' they call it."

"Crying wolf now, sure."

He doubted the Ethiopians or the Soviet Union would do anything so foolish. Their position was legally and diplomatically correct: Moscow was helping Ethiopia defend its sovereign territory against external aggression, and they would soon win the military victory within the Ethiopian border.

Hearing himself again, feeling himself sitting so slack in his chair, his arms along the sides, his feet lifted to the small metal table, his body settled in that heavy gravity of discourse, he knew what was so different. His voice bored him. He was talking like someone for whom the long voyage was over, Hakluyt back from the antipodes, LaSalle back from the country of the Illinois, a man for whom the lesson had been mastered, the doubts and ambiguities banished, nothing left to be discovered. Two and a half years of his life all indexed, he sitting there like his professor of Slavic history in his untidy little office at Princeton, not quite a Yuri Pulyakov, the ballroom butterfly, but worse, a canting pedagogue.

"You were about to say something," Dinsmore said anxiously.

"No, just wool-gathering. What was the last question again?"

Their conversation began at two. It was almost four when Dinsmore put his notebook aside.

"I was serious about what I mentioned earlier," he said, "quite serious. I am looking for someone for Cairo and Beirut. Perhaps I'm being a bit selfish, presumptuous, too. But last year when I was here I heard Ambassador Firthdale say to someone at dinner that you couldn't be very satisfied here. Agnes told me the same thing."

"I don't remember ever talking to them."

"I don't think it was anything you said. In any case I mention it now because those were my thoughts as well. Think about it. I'll be leaving Cairo in January. Possibly we can get together in Paris sometime between now and then, have lunch, talk about it further."

"Maybe we can do that."

"I have no quarrel with the diplomatic life, mind you. But one has to balance out the whole life, not just the half of it."

They were on their way back to Talbot's car when the phone rang. It was Julia, asking him to bring some beer with him when he arrived at five o'clock for cocktails with two visiting U.S. congressmen. She seemed to be in short supply.

He drove Dinsmore to the Giubba Hotel.

"Give it some thought," Dinsmore said as he got out. "I'll be returning to London in February. If I don't manage to get to Paris, drop me a line. Better still, ring me; we'll talk some more. Thanks, very useful, very, I must say. Have a good trip."

It would always begin as it ended, on a terrace or in a salon somewhere, holding a drink and talking to someone about matters you cared little or nothing about, or listening to someone talk about something he or she knew nothing about, as Talbot was doing now, listening to the U.S. air force officer and the congressional staff member who were accompanying the two congressmen on their visit to Jubba. The two congressmen would have a late evening meeting with the president, during which he would appeal to them for help in persuading the administration to suspend its arms embargo and deliver the armaments he needed to repel the coming Soviet-backed Ethiopian invasion of northern Jubba.

The congressional staffer was talking about the Soviet Union in Pentagonese—an aggressive interventionalist predator with a swift global force projection capability for asserting military power in the Third World—Angola first, now in Ethiopia. The air force officer agreed, but not Kinkaid, who was fervently defending the administration's position that superpower rivalries in Africa and the Third World should be treated in their own political and socioeconomic context—namely, in finding African solutions to African problems, the quaint little voice of another Bene Oui Oui.

Listening silently, Talbot found he preferred the lofty voice of DeGroot, lifting from nearby, as he described for the benefit of Congressman Simpson the individualistic nature of the Jubba nomad.

But after a few minutes he wandered away from Kinkaid, moved past DeGroot, stood for a minute looking toward Harcourt talking to the other congressman, remembered who should have been here but wasn't, and went on into the kitchen. He heard Julia calling to him from nearby, but he didn't stop. He left his drink on the table and went out the back door.

□ □ □

The golden afternoon light was swarming high in the trees, stirred by the mild southwest wind. Talbot saw Lindy sitting alone on the side of the pool in her bikini, dangling her legs in the water. Except for her, the pavilion and the concrete walks were deserted.

She looked up as he came through the rear gate and watched as he crossed the walk and into the pool enclosure.

"Hi," he called. "What are you doing?"

"Relaxing. What brings you out here? A little overdressed, aren't you?"

"Maybe that's my lot in life, being overdressed. I was looking for you."

"Me?" She recoiled in feigned surprise, hand flat across her chest. "My God, it must be my new Fiat, my new bathing suit. I thought you'd be at the ambassador's."

"I was. I left."

"Who'd you insult this time?"

"No one. I wanted to talk to you and you weren't there." He sank down on the warm concrete beside her. Her arms, face, and shoulders were as brown as mahogany. He could smell suntan lotion. Her light hair, parted in the middle, was streaked with the sun. She wore two long plaits down her shoulders. "I got tired of waiting. You said last week on the phone you'd come swimming, that you'd let me know."

"Did I?"

"That's what I remember. Then I didn't hear. There are some things I wanted to explain. They're a dead load and they're pulling me under. I'm tired of carrying them around."

"You don't have to explain; there's nothing to explain."

"Yes there is, there's always something left over—hash, my mother used to call it. What are you hiding out here for? How come you didn't go to the ambassador's?"

"I didn't feel like it and I'm not hiding out."

"You were invited; I saw your name on the list."

"What are you, her truant officer? I told you, I didn't feel like it. I'm tired of having my life arranged, and I don't want any part of it. So I came here."

"So what have you been doing here?"

"Nothing. I was trying to decide whether to go in again or just go home and take a shower, but it's so nice now I hated to leave."

"It's nice this time of day." He looked around. "Like the municipal pool they closed down because of typhoid."

"I knew you'd say something like that. You always do, always knocking something."

"So what else is new."

"Nothing. You should have seen it twenty minutes ago. All the kids were here. They have to be out by six. Then it's only adults. In between is the best time, like now. That's when I usually come down. Why am I talking like this? Tell me why I'm talking like this? I don't have anything to apologize for."

"You're not apologizing, I am. There's something I've got to talk about. You don't have to do anything except listen."

Two women were approaching through the trees, towels over their shoulders.

"If it's about that night at the Harcourts', don't. It's been on my mind, too, that and everything else, but I've been so mixed up I didn't want to think about it."

"That's not it. It's about some idiot things I did while you were in Nairobi."

"I don't want to hear."

"Neither do I. I didn't know how I felt about you until you came back. I mean I knew how I felt but I didn't say. I don't know why I didn't, tell you, I mean, even before you went to Nairobi—for God's sake." He sat back, leaning on his hands, squinting across the pool. "Maybe I ought to start over again."

She leaned over and took a leaf from the surface. "You sound as mixed up as I was."

"I'm not mixed up. I know how I feel, about you, I'm talking about, not anyone else, just you—"

"Don't say any more."

"I've got to. How I feel about you is all that matters, nothing else, just you. When I'm not with you I'm not much of anything and I do stupid things. I guess I've blown it again."

They sat in silence for a minute.

"You haven't blown it," she said finally. "I wanted to talk to you. I did, but not at the embassy. I had this feeling everyone was watching, everyone was waiting, and I just couldn't stand it. I was serious about going swimming that day you telephoned. I was. You don't have to believe me, but I was. But then we had that stupid argument outside the Harcourts' the same night and I just couldn't understand. Then I thought how ridiculous it all was, all of it, just so preposterous, all of it, everything. I thought maybe you might have misunderstood. Anyway, I felt pretty bad."

"Bad about what?"

"What I said to you at the Harcourts' that night. I shouldn't have." She moved her feet in the water, her head still turned away.

"Maybe you were right."

She shook her head. "No, I wasn't, not really. I didn't understand, not until I started thinking about it."

"Forget about it. It doesn't matter."

"No, I want to say it. I didn't understand at first. I thought you were just rolling over again, the way everyone does, that's what infuriated me. Then afterwards Pete Ryan and I were talking about it at the Giubba. Did he tell you?"

"No, we didn't talk about it."

"I think he understood right away. Anyway, we talked, mostly about Julia Harcourt. She's like my sister's tropical fish. You have to be careful, water temperature, tank, plants, pebbles, everything. If you aren't, they die. They don't know how fragile they are, but there's nothing you can do about it. So you keep changing the water, aerate it, do everything, and they just hang there in their warm little stupid world." She put her face in her hands. "God, that sounds awful the way I said it."

"*Yoo hoo,* Mr. Talbot. What are you doing here?"

Mrs. Peterson stood across the pool wearing a flowered bathing suit. Talbot stood up. "Just visiting, Mrs. Peterson. How've you been?"

"Just fine and dandy. How about yourself? How come you're all dressed up?"

"Just coming from someplace."

"Must have been a cocktail party." The cast was gone from her leg. "You gonna count the laps for us, Lindy?" Mrs. James joined her from the dressing room wearing a black bathing suit. "Where'd that other one go to?"

"He's getting dressed, I made sure of that. Hello, Mr. Talbot. What brings you out here. You all set to leave?"

"Just about, Mrs. James. How've you been?"

"Can't complain."

"You sure?" Mrs. Peterson said. "He's sneaking around here someplace, that's for sure. Go on home, Sonny!" she shouted toward the deserted walk that led to the dressing rooms, "your supper's waiting!"

Talbot didn't see anyone.

Lindy looked up at him. "So I decided that's what you were doing."

He sat down again. "I don't know what I was doing, trying to help her pull herself together, I suppose."

"I was furious, I really was."

"She's not the happiest woman in the world. There's nothing anyone can do about that."

"She doesn't matter anymore. I don't want to talk about her. Am I crazy or what?"

"About what?"

"This place." She brought her feet out of the water and turned, sitting Yoga-like, her calves dripping water.

"It's a little screwed up, that's all. Not this place, me, everything maybe."

"It's not just you. Then Pete told me something else, something that made me wonder even more. He said you were in the wrong profession, the wrong business. Did he tell you?"

"We talked a little, yeah."

"He thinks you should be doing what he's doing. He says he thinks you're crazy getting yourself stuck this way." She hugged her knees. "When he said that, all of a sudden everything began to make sense; it all began to fit. I began to think about myself, too, what I was doing here."

"I've been wondering about that, too."

"Maybe it began to make sense because I felt a little trapped in the same way. It's not always this way, is it?"

"Not in the beginning."

"That's what I asked Whit, whether this was the way it was. He said no, but he's retiring, so what does he care."

"He cares. He just keeps his mouth shut, the way I should."

She had turned to watch Mrs. Peterson lowering herself into the pool from the steps at the far end. The skirts of her bathing suit billowed out on the water. Her chin was raised as she dog-paddled a few strokes. She stood up, breast deep in water.

"Are you doing anything tonight?" Talbot asked. "That's another reason I came out."

"Not anything special, no, but I don't want to start the whole thing again, I don't."

"You don't have to start anything."

"Just getting the chill out," Mrs. Peterson called. "I'm not any Esther Williams, Mr. Talbot, in case you're wondering. You coming to the movie tonight?"

"I don't think so."

"You're leaving pretty soon, Pete told me. Time sure does fly, doesn't it?"

After a minute Lindy said, "I told Nancy Kinkaid I'd go to the movies with her. Is something else wrong?"

"Something else? No, why?"

"You just look so funny. Not funny, strange."

Mrs. James had joined Mrs. Peterson. "It's cold today, isn't it? I swear." She stood with her shoulders hunched, shivering.

"Shouldn't be, what all those kids paddling around left behind. I wouldn't swallow any. You bring your suit, Mr. Talbot?"

"No, sorry. I wish I had."

"Pete tells me you swim in the ocean, said he saw you once. Well, I tell you, this pool isn't big enough for me and them sharks both. This is plenty for me." She turned to look toward the bathhouse. "You know he's over there, sure as I'm standing here. Go on home, Sonny! Pool's closed!" She turned over on her back and floated a few feet. "Nice and quiet, most peaceful time of day, Mr. Talbot. Lookit those clouds floating there, all pink like. That's what I'm gonna miss, times like this. You going to float some more or are you ready?" she called to Mrs. James.

"Lord, I've been ready."

"We'll do six. No, seven. We'll do seven." She beckoned to Arlene James, and the two women waded through the water to the far edge and dropped their heads down below the wall. "We'll do seven," she shouted.

"All right, seven," Arlene James cried.

"Ready, set, go!" Mrs. Peterson shouted, and a moment later a small wet figure streaked from the corner of the bathhouse and sailed out over the water in a spindly cannonball. The two women wallowed triumphantly toward him. "Now we got you good, you little devil," Mrs. Peterson cried. "Didn't I tell you we'd get you, come playing tricks on us." She grabbed one leg, Mrs. James the other and they hauled him thrashing and choking to the shallow end. "No more tricks, go on home to your supper, for sure now."

She gave the ten-year-old boy a small pat on the seat. He climbed out and sped off through the trees.

"I don't mind so much when there's just one," Mrs. Peterson said, rolling over on her back. "I'll bet you did tricks like that when you were little, didn't you, Mr. Talbot? I'll bet you did."

"What ever happened to Esther Williams anyway," Mrs. James asked, pulling up her suit.

"Lord knows," Mrs. Peterson said. "If we had TV it'd be different. Now you see a movie here and you can't tell whether any of 'em in it's dead or alive. If we had TV we might even find out about that war they're having. Never did make any sense to me. What about it, Mr. Talbot? What's happening over there? Who's winning?"

"I'm afraid no one's winning, Mrs. Peterson."

"Like Vietnam all over, only thank God it's not our boys. They sure sent those Russians packing, sure cleaned them out fast, didn't they? I heard they're all over there in Ethiopia now, every last one of them. It sure is a mixed-up world, isn't it Mr. Talbot?"

"I'd say so."

"We got an AID mission and military people coming in now, but I guess you heard that," she called as Talbot and Lindy walked back along the pavement.

"When you say you're thinking about what Pete said," Lindy asked as they went through the gate, "what do you mean?"

"I don't know. I've just had it. I'm tired of it, all of it. I'll go on to Paris, but I don't know what I'm going to do."

"You're talking about your career?"

"I think so. It's all up in the air, I don't know what I'm going to do. I haven't talked to anyone. Do you have to go to the movies?"

"No, I don't have to. You'd better wait before you do anything you'll regret. Once you get to Paris, you'll change. I know you will."

"No I won't. We could go to Juliano's, maybe the Palestinian restaurant."

"I don't want to start anything again."

"I'm not trying to start anything. I want to see you, talk to you. I don't have much time left and neither do you."

She stopped. "Me?"

"You. You're going to Paris with me." He walked on, but she was still standing on the gravel path. He looked back. "You think I'm kidding?"

She was smiling, then laughing. "You must be crashing on something. *Me?*" Her head was back. "Oh, God, you're as crazy as Whit thinks you are."

"So it was Whittington."

"Who cares. He doesn't know beans. That's really marvelous, me trotting off to Paris after you."

"I didn't say after me, I said with me."

"You are unbelievable, you really are. Absolutely unbelievable. I'll go tell Nancy. You want to come up while I change." She stopped. "No funny business either."

"No funny business."

They went up in the elevator, rising through the sound of the marine house phonograph and the voice of a country and Western singer. She started laughing again but then bit her lip as they chugged higher, on into the cooler silence of the third floor. Her apartment had changed a little since he'd last been there, a new sofa and new lamps. As she drew the drapes against the late afternoon sun they heard the sound of the piano from above and the distant voice of Adele DeGroot.

"That poor woman," Lindy said with feeling. "I heard they may be leaving."

She stopped to listen. She was singing a Mozart aria. "I'll bet you had something to do with that, too," she said.

He didn't say anything.

"That's what I figured."

A minute later she went into the bedroom to change and he heard the lock click from the inside.

□   □   □

Talbot's replacement as political officer was a man named Middleton, who'd arrived three days earlier with his wife and ten-year-old son. He was forty-one, rather small, with a somber, worried face, his stiff dark hair already streaked with gray, his voice as flat and unmarked as the Nebraska prairies. He'd come from Dakar.

Talbot was giving a small lunch for him and his wife. Bashford-Jones was there, Dr. Greevy, Lindy, even the Kinkaids, God forbid, but that was Lindy's idea. Middleton seemed slightly bewildered sitting there with his honest worried face, the face of an amnesiac, trying to puzzle out where he was, precisely what he was doing there, his mind still grappling with the intricacies of Senegalese politics.

"Tomorrow Harar, after that Dire Dawa," Dr. Greevy was saying with a wry smile, glancing at Talbot. "You still don't believe it, do you, don't believe they'll bring it off?"

Sitting as host at the head of the long polished mahogany table, Talbot only smiled. He'd decided to say nothing reckless that day, to give the Middletons a taste of that decorous diplomatic life they had to look forward to. He had the uncomfortable feeling both were Methodists, that they lived a serene domestic life, slept in the same room with their ten-year-old son on holidays, and all prayed together on their knees. He was also acutely conscious of Lindy's slim face just down the table to his left. Beyond the bank of windows to his left the sea ran bright and quick in the early afternoon sun.

"He's very cynical about it," Lindy said, glancing at him.

"About everything," Kinkaid added as Dr. Greevy helped himself to another bowl of gazpacho. Ali, the houseboy, doubling as server that day, had expected the offer to be declined and the fish platter brought. Now that it hadn't, he abruptly took the ladle from Greevy's hand and served him instead to hurry things along. The cook was waiting in the kitchen with the fish platter.

"You're not so cynical, I take it," said Bashford-Jones, leaning back, his long hands pressed against his frilly white tennis shirt. The invitations had said informal but Middleton had arrived in a coat and tie.

"Heavens no," Nancy Kinkaid said proudly of her husband, "he's anything but cynical."

Kinkaid smiled appreciatively. Bashford-Jones politely returned the smile and looked again at Dr. Greevy, for whom the question had been intended.

"Not yet," Greevy said. "I'm still hopeful, as a matter of fact. It was inevitable, you know, the war." He carefully wiped away a few drops left by Ali on the table.

"You knew it was coming?" Middleton asked, surprised.

"I think everyone did," Dr. Greevy said.

"The president always said the same thing, didn't he?" Bashford-Jones said. "I mean the war being inevitable. With Ethiopia in utter chaos, it was now or never for Jubba, 'correlation of forces,' strike when the iron is hot, that Marxist catechism he's so fond of citing. Evidently this was what he was telling the Russians up until he threw them out."

"Not just the Marxism," Lindy said. "Ethiopia was collapsing, and you didn't have to be a Marxist to know if they didn't take back their territories now they never would. Even an idiot like me can see that."

Again she looked at Talbot.

"What I mean was the Marxist pretense," Bashford-Jones said.

Middleton turned expectantly from Bashford-Jones to Lindy. His wife was gazing out the window at the beach. Noticing her, Nancy Kinkaid leaned over and said in a soft voice, "You said you swam in Dakar?"

"Is it just a pretense?" Lindy asked.

"Without a doubt," Bashford-Jones said. "Not Marxists at all, just nomadic wolves in sheep's clothing, wouldn't you say, Logan? I mean you're the institutional skeptic."

But Talbot just shrugged.

"Was a skeptic, looks like a true believer now," Bashford-Jones said. "Disgusting what a little success will do. I propose you be barred from the club."

"There's a club?" Middleton asked.

Excellent gooseberries, Talbot thought, looking at Middleton's square Methodist face. But for the kidney pie, try the Anglo-American, just a discus throw from the beach.

"The skeptics' club," Bashford-Jones said, "although we've never really given it a name, actually." He looked out the side windows and into the bright sunlight of the garden. "I should think it's a bit late now, everyone going. A bit sad, actually. Just believers left."

Dr. Greevy finished his soup and put his spoon down. Ali immediately whisked his bowl away.

"I suppose the war was more or less inevitable," Greevy said, glancing shyly at Middleton, whose blank face seemed riveted to his, "but historical inevitability wasn't Marx's invention. I don't really know Marx. I was thinking of the Peloponnesian wars."

"Dear me," Bashford-Jones said with a sigh.

"In what sense?" Lindy asked.

"The precise sense," Greevy said, "The way Thucydides described it. It struck me driving back from the border that what Jubba did in launching its attack was in some ways as daring as what the Athenians did."

Dr. Greevy had been inside Ethiopia helping set up the field hospitals.

"In what way?" Lindy said.

"I never managed to get all the way through Thucydides," Kinkaid admitted as he fondled his cold pipe.

"Book One, very simply detailed there, the Spartans and the Athenians," Greevy said. Bashford-Jones's eyes wandered in boredom to the ceiling. "It was one of those silly thoughts that come to you when traveling, especially a long trip you've made so many times. Don't take me too seriously."

"I don't quite follow," Lindy said.

"Quite simple, actually," Greevy said. "Since independence in 1960 Jubba has been a nation whose pastoral lands have been under foreign occupation." He hesitated, his gaze drawn away as the cook brought the fish platter and began to serve. "To that extent you might say its destiny these past years has been unfulfilled, yet to be discovered."

Lindy nodded her head. "Yes."

"So since 1960 it's lived in the present, yes, but in the future as well, dreaming of the day when it could recover its lost territories. That's what occurred to me."

"Yes, of course," Lindy said.

"I hadn't thought of it that way," Kinkaid said, furrowing his brow.

"Women evidently know these things," Bashford-Jones said.

"I think they do," Lindy said without looking at him.

"I don't disagree," Bashford-Jones said. "It's a very romantic notion."

"Not necessarily romantic," Lindy said without turning. "You didn't finish, Doctor."

Greevy nodded. "So I remembered what Thucydides said, that a nation with an existence yet to be discovered lives not only in the present but in the future as well."

"My wife's views exactly," Bashford-Jones said with another sigh. "She would have preferred I find my future with her father in the City."

"Not just a feminine notion," Lindy said quickly and then flushed. Bashford-Jones smiled with pleasure.

" 'Sayeth the milk maid to the young squire,' " he said to Talbot. "Marvelous."

Kinkaid and Middleton were both looking at Bashford-Jones. Middleton studied the long fingers, long hands, and the queer shirt.

"But don't take me too literally, please," Greevy said, embarrassed. "I've been thinking of the parallel since the day I got word they'd struck across the border. Now I'm afraid I feel very awkward."

"You have our absolute attention," Bashford-Jones said.

"Please," Lindy said.

"I *don't* like saltwater so much," Mrs. Middleton was saying in a half-whisper to Nancy Kinkaid.

"Well, when the Athenians took to their ships and abandoned their city to the barbarians, they left the present and past behind. In a word they destroyed in a symbolic act the grip of security. They staked their lives for the sake of a future that had an existence, as Thucydides tells us, only in desperate hope."

"Only in desperate hope indeed," Bashford-Jones interjected. "The poor buggers are going to get crushed out there with the weapons the Soviets are pouring in."

A momentary pause. "Or, as the Corinthians warned," Dr. Greevy continued, "for an empire that was still part in contemplation. That's all I meant."

"That's marvelous," Lindy said, smiling, "that's really marvelous."

"I shall have to go back to my Corinthians," Bashford-Jones said. "Some stagestruck bit of crumpet setting off for Hollywood, would that do?" He swirled his wineglass around and drank.

Middleton studied the long hair and long hands. The man, he decided, looked like an interior decorator.

"Yes, I suppose so," Dr. Greevy said, momentarily confused. He fussed with his silverware.

"Continue, please," Lindy said.

"Yes. Well, since destiny for the Athenians was yet to be fully discovered, they might go wherever history would take them, unlike the Spartans. With no gift for abstraction, the Spartans thought first of their soil and their houses, the Athenians looked beyond to the sea and a city. You see, don't you?" He was looking at Lindy.

Talbot nodded, too, but despite the appeal of Greevy's idea it occurred to him they were all talking absolute rubbish, civilized, clever rubbish, but rubbish nevertheless, as foolishly as the local press and local radio, as the Jubba gathered around the radios at the tea shops. It was all over.

"That's lovely," Lindy said after a moment of silence. "I wouldn't have thought to make the comparison."

"I wasn't actually comparing," Greevy said modestly, "and it was just one of those thoughts that come to you on a trip, the rocking motion, I suppose."

"The Spartans won, as I recall," Bashford-Jones said.

"Which doesn't detract from everything else," Lindy said. Bashford-Jones looked at her sun-streaked hair and her slim face, smiling again.

"Now, of course, Jubba has very much burned its bridges with the Russians," Kinkaid said.

"Which wasn't part of the plan," Lindy said.

"So you know the plan, do you?" Bashford-Jones said. "Thank God someone does."

"What plan?" Kinkaid asked.

"Ask Logan." Lindy looked at Talbot, but he turned away toward the door, trying to interpret Ali's hand signals.

"The plan," he replied, "is to have coffee in the garden."

As they rose, Kinkaid said to Middleton, "Too late for the Russians, but not for us."

Julia watched from the porch of the beach cottage as the odd caravan trudged into view, wondering what on earth was going on. She recognized Bashford-Jones first, wearing a silly white tennis hat, walking with Nancy Kinkaid, who was heavily pregnant. Mr. Middleton followed alone, trudging doggedly through the sand in a dark suit, like a man who'd had a flat tire somewhere in the middle of the desert. Behind was Kinkaid, his pipe in his mouth, flanked by Mrs. Middleton in a flowered blue dress. They were listening to a short little man wearing knee-length hose and shorts, his hands moving expansively as he described something. Now he had Kinkaid's arm and was flexing it back and forth, as if he had suffered an arm injury. She recognized Dr. Greevy. A dozen paces behind walked Talbot and Lindy.

"Why didn't you say something?" Lindy was saying. "You just sat there."

"You told me I was always knocking something."

"But I didn't mean you had to be inscrutable."

"Was I being inscrutable?"

"Middleton's inscrutable. You don't have to be like that, do you? That's not what I meant."

"I thought you'd be pleased. I internalized the debate."

"OK, but I want to hear. So tell me what you were thinking."

Julia's guests were still there on the front porch—Dr. Melton, his wife, and two journalists from Nairobi. Dr. Melton's pathetic voice came again as he described the dangers of urban Dar es Salaam, and she knew the journalists were bored. Next time she would have to think of a different arrangement, but her resources were running dangerously low, like her wine cupboard.

□   □   □

No Soviet ships on the horizon now, so the quasar telescope would go back to the navy and the Fleet Ocean Surveillance Center. The pictures weren't his and would stay. The books would be packed up, the record player, too. Or maybe he should sell it. The Egyptian administrative counselor would buy anything available, a note on the embassy bulletin board reminded him. And then there were the new people coming in, eager for those items that make a house a home—AID officers, already four in place; the people from the Defense attaché's office; maybe even Middleton, the new political officer who'd been shadowing him day and night the past week, his official double. Two days earlier the Firthdales had given a small lunch for him, and there he'd sat with his amnesiac's face; the night before he'd been at the Ghanims', still trying to puzzle out where he was and what the hell he was doing there.

"It's so sad," Lindy said, opening another drawer in the study cabinet. "It is, don't deny it."

"I'm not denying it."

It was late on Friday morning. On the beach in front of Talbot's villa a few Europeans and Jubba were walking, silhouetted against a milky aquamarine sea, out for a stroll on the Moslem sabbath.

"I think part of you is glad, even if you say you aren't."

"Part of me is, part of me isn't."

She sorted through some old *Economists*, the pages marked by rusting paper clips. "I hate being left behind. I hate it, all these same damn people here."

"Join the new AID prayer group. That'll take care of Saturday nights."

"Shut up."

"Fridays you can go to the DeGroots' new reading circle. 'Bring a book that gives you pleasure, share your pleasure with your friends.' Isn't that what your invitation said?"

"Stop rubbing it in. What do you want to do with these old magazines?"

DeGroot would remain on. Julia, Harcourt, and Talbot had had a long discussion about DeGroot at the residence. Talbot had finally convinced them they'd be making a mistake requesting his recall. Since Julia's career ambitions extended far beyond Jubba—Morocco would do nicely, Tunisia, too, maybe even the Holy See, but they were royal purple Episcopalians, not Catholics—she wasn't anxious to see her husband blot his copybook, as Talbot persuaded her he would should he send DeGroot packing. Julia had been quick to understand but not Harcourt, who remained unconvinced during that first hour.

Whatever DeGroot's gaucheries, Talbot had argued—Harcourt's words, not his—U.S.-Jubba relations had changed dramatically under Harcourt's able stewardship. With his reputation enhanced, why risk giving the talent spotters back at State second thoughts? Personnel problems were best solved *en place,* as Harcourt so often reminded him. In addition, if DeGroot's deracinated prose in that godawful trip report suggested he was a mental case or, more seriously, drew the attention of the foreign service inspectors to his violation of Department orders, then shred it, burn it before they arrived; no one would be the wiser. Last but not least, if DeGroot was crazy, his lunacy at least had a pastoral sweetness to it that drew no blood. You couldn't say the same thing of those barbarisms inflicted daily by the USIS wireless file or any other of those lunatic speeches and drum rolls from imperial capitals so far from the flesh-and-blood historical countryside. He'd read Julia and Lyman a paragraph from the morning USIS reading file to document his case: "Unfortunately, in nuclear competition the contest between the two superpowers is increasingly turning into a qualitative race whose outcome cannot yield meaningful superiority. There is no over-trumping total annihilation."

What could Harcourt make of that? Would he like its author, some weird NSC Dr. Strangelove like that sitting in on his country team meetings? How about Schopenhauer? Or Henry James? Or the lead writer on the New York *Daily News?*

Gently Julia put her hand on her husband's as they sat together on the couch. "Lyman, you couldn't stand someone like that, you're much too sensitive," she'd said, and Harcourt had nodded in sad surrender. He would shred the incriminating trip report, have a long frank talk with DeGroot, and they would begin again.

Talbot left unsaid what else was on his mind, namely that fools flourish best among fools; that Harcourt's supreme incompetence had contributed to a war that should never have taken place and might not have had he done his job; that at either Rome or Bonn, chancellory executives like Harcourt & DeGroot, the Abbott & Costello of the East African scrub, would be out on their ass in the stage door alley in twenty-four hours.

But then, talking to Lindy later that same evening, she persuaded him he couldn't really blame Harcourt for that either, since like the rest of them he was nothing more than a first-class passenger in a closed train, passing over an unfamiliar track and pulled along by engines he hadn't stoked, didn't understand, and over which he had no control.

"Anyway, no one has much to be proud of, even you," she'd said. "You know what Marx said, don't you? Every time the train of history rounds a curve, the intellectuals fall off."

"I didn't say I was an intellectual."

"I'm just telling you. If you knew so much more than they did, why didn't you do something?"

"I tried, for Christ's sake. Do you think I didn't try?"

"Don't be so defensive."

"I'm not being defensive. How come you're so intellectual all of a sudden."

"I'm talking to you unofficially. I'm not paid to be intellectual."

So Talbot's better judgment, or rather Julia's ambitions for her husband, had prevailed. The DeGroots would stay. Talbot's villa would go to the DeGroots, who finally had decided that conditions were suitable for reclaiming the old DCM residence.

Lindy hated the idea of that, too.

"What in the world is this?" she asked, taking something from the back of the drawer.

"Let's see."

It was the Colt revolver Negussie had left him, wrapped in chamois cloth.

"I'd forgotten all about that." He took it and opened the magazine. "Negussie brought it one night. He was going back to Addis and didn't know whether he was going to be reassigned or arrested like his two brothers. He thought he might need it, so he wanted me to see if I could get it to him in the diplomatic pouch. That's a helluva thing, isn't it? After twenty-five years of U.S. military assistance to Ethiopia, that's what it comes down to, an Ethiopian diplomat coming to your house at ten at night and asking you if you can get a goddamn gun to him through the diplomatic pouch."

"What are you going to do with it?"

"I don't know, maybe ask Whit to ship it in."

"He can't. Or won't."

There was so much he wouldn't and couldn't leave to Middleton, busy that morning in his third-floor office, reading silently through old cables and airgrams. So much would vanish when he left, kept alive only in memory: the night Negussie had come, the nights with Greevy drinking at the Anglo-American or UN club, with Bashford-Jones scouting the cocktail party singles, with Lev Luttak or Ryan in the back garden, or that evening on the embassy roof with a CBS news cameraman taking pictures of the U-2 shots of the Soviet missile facility at Muzaffar after he'd convinced them the Jubba ministry of information escort officers had tricked them during their twelve-hour visit to the old camel port.

All these things were unrecoverable, and Talbot felt their loss as sadly but as inevitably as the loss of a career he sensed was finally coming to an end.

Lindy disagreed. "Paris will change you; it'll change everything," she'd said the night before, lying there in the burglar's silence of the second floor. "I know it will."

"You're wrong."

"I'm not wrong. Right now you can't separate yourself from your life here. When you get to Paris, you'll be able to, to do what you've done in the past. So I seem to be part of that now. In six months, no. You'll be the way you were before."

"That's not true."

"It is true, you'll see."

"What if you're wrong. What do I do to convince you?"

She hadn't answered, as silent as the night before when he'd again told her he loved her. He didn't know whether she didn't believe him or didn't dare to.

"Which records are you keeping?" she now asked, sitting on the floor of the study.

"I haven't thought about it. Not many, just a few. Take what you want."

She began sorting through his records, arranging them in two piles.

"I'm not really leaving you behind," he said. "Anyway it's not too late to get your ticket."

"Let's see what happens first."

"That's still not an answer."

"It's the best I can do right now, and I don't think you should expect anything more. You don't deserve any more."

"No? How can you be so hot and cold like this? One night it's all right and the next morning you're not so sure."

"Am I any different from the way you are?"

"Yeah, because what's over for me is over. I can't see me going and you staying here."

"We'll see how you feel when you get to Paris."

"I know how I'll feel when I get to Paris. I know how I feel right now, just like I told you last night."

"That doesn't help much, not for our predicament."

"So you admit it's a predicament."

"Of course it's a predicament."

He looked at the records she was putting in a cardboard carton. "Are those the ones you're keeping?"

"I think so."

"Which ones are they?"

"Just these, the best ones." She looked up and saw him watching her. "Oh, no, you don't." She got up suddenly, holding the box of records. "You can't see."

"Come on, show me."

"You rat, always snooping around, trying to embarrass me. You're not going to see."

Quickly she carried the records outside and locked them in her new Fiat.

"So what are we going to listen to tonight?" he asked when she came back.

"Something else for a change," she said, "something that doesn't remind me."

"Something new tonight," he said after a minute. "OK, but I get to keep those."

"You're such a big talker." She sat down cross-legged on the floor. "I wish I could be there when you waltz into the embassy in Paris that first day. I'd really love to be there. It'd be worth the price of a round-trip ticket."

"So come on with me, pack it up."

"Here he is folks!" she called. "Mr. Logan Talbot, the Big Noise from Benaadir, Jubba! Let's hear it!" She clapped her hands, put her two fingers to her lips and blew an ear-piercing whistle that volleyed off the plaster walls like a rifle shot. Talbot looked down, astonished. *Where in God's name had she learned to whistle like that?* Now she was boisterously clapping her hands. "Hey, hey, hey! Everyone! Let's hear it for the Big Noise!"

She whistled again, another shattering blast, rocked over and collapsed on her back, lying there smiling, looking at the ceiling. "Oh, God, would that ever be funny."

"Everything's funny to you these days, isn't it?" He dropped on her, holding her down. "Think I'm some camel-burr hayseed now, do you? I thought you said I was a preppy."

Her eyes were open, luminous flakes of green and agate, as mysterious as the sea in their tiny whirlpool contractions around the dark iris. She didn't answer. Then, just as silently, she lifted her fingers to his lips.

"No, not a hayseed. It just hurts so much I don't know whether to laugh or cry."

"So you've got to come with me. That's it—"

"We'll see what happens. That's all I can promise."

□   □   □

Mrs. DeGroot, lying on the sofa in a Chinese kimono, waited nervously for her husband to complete his description of the events of the afternoon. Lying next to her on the cushions was a small white poodle, sprawled uncomfortably on a few carefully chosen books from her library.

"After an intimate discussion at the chancellory defining our new working relationship, we adjourned to the club." He carefully removed his fawn-colored jacket, gave it a flourish, and draped it neatly on the back of a nearby chair. "A small kiss first." Bending over, he pressed his lips to her forehead.

"The *club?*"

"*Mmmm.* So sweet. The Italian club." Standing again, shoulders back, heels together, his onion-shaped figure erect, like a matador, he began to turn back his shirt sleeves. "There we watched the tennis match, having learned that Colonel Mohammed Hersi would be among the spectators and was expecting us there, not at his office. I introduced him to the ambassador after the match. They had never met."

"*Never?*"

"Never, sad to say. I attempted to conceal my surprise at this. The tennis match was unappealing. Both combatants were singularly docile, satisfied merely to keep the ball in play." He paused, one bare arm raised, the other dangling, feet together, then danced across the carpet, a fencer with a foil. "*Advancez!*" With a final extended lunge, he thrust the foil home.

"*Bravo! Bravo!*" She came erect, clapping softly.

He bowed from the waist. "*Merci, madame.* After the match, we had an aperitif in the bar, discussing the briefing for our new military attaché. The conversation was congenial. Perhaps we could arrange a lunch—not here, of course—perhaps at the Giubba Hotel. I must, of course, consult the ambassador."

"Oh, yes."

"But I was encouraged, communication having been established.

Afterwards I returned to the residence and then proceeded to Talbot's villa."

"Mr. Talbot, yes." She sat up anxiously.

"The packers had been there—Peterson communicated this to me immediately after their arrival—and he was not alone. He had not heard my engine. Miss Dowling was there."

A gasp. *"Oh, dear."*

"In the briefest of swimsuits, most compromising, their position. Thus." Head back, eyes closed, he flung his arms out, kissing the air.

"Oh."

"I had no intention of spying."

"Nevertheless."

"Nevertheless, I found myself there at the passageway but advanced no further. He had, however, detected my presence."

"However?"

"However, he seemed not in the slightest discomfited and we had a most agreeable talk while Miss Dowling, a percipient young woman, as you know, went inside for refreshment."

"Did you tell him?"

"Indeed I did. I said I was most grateful for his exertions in my support and regretted we had not had a meeting of minds earlier."

"How lovely."

"I complimented him on his garden, and he explained that my comment upon our first meeting that it showed some neglect had some profound influence. Most gratifying."

"Of course."

"Miss Dowling returned with drinks, and we discussed recreation. They both, it seems, prefer skin sports."

Her eyes opened wide. *"Skin sports?"*

"Forgive me, a most innocent idiom. Swimming is a skin sport. I extended our invitation for cocktails, and he most graciously accepted and then inquired after your health. So it is done, it is resolved, and how is our little headache?"

"Sad. Buttercup has it." She stroked the small white poodle lying at her side.

"Oh, dear. Poor Buttercup. What to drink?"

"Gin, please."

"Another kiss first. *Mmmmmm.* So sweet. Wintergreen?"

"Cloves."

"Ah *ha*. I took the occasion also to invite Miss Dowling, having the distinct impression there is much between them. So small their secret, it shall be ours. She is, I understand, out of favor with Mrs. Harcourt, not surprising for a young woman of spirit. Gin it will be."

He marched across the room, but as he passed the piano he paused to strike a few chords.

Turning, he sang, " 'Sweet honey flows from petals pressed, bright silver from the dew.' Remember?"

"Ah, yes!"

Joining him, she sang, " 'Sweet silence swells a life caressed . . .' "

" 'Caressed—' "

" 'With memories of you.' "

The chords faded away. "Ahh. In love."

"Indeed."

He moved to her side, gave her a reassuring kiss on her pale cheek, then moved briskly to the kitchen to prepare two gins.

CHAPTER ELEVEN

Outward Bound

Talbot was off at last, a strangely alien landscape spinning away dizzily as his 707 finally lifted from the tarmac that sweltering afternoon, two hours late, not even leaving behind a small gaggle of well-wishers at the protocol fence. Those few who had come to see him off had returned to their official and private lives almost two hours earlier, all except Lindy leaning sadly against the gate, her lonely new Fiat parked behind her. Julia had given him a warm kiss on the cheek and promised she'd be in touch. Lindy would wait alone for another hour, the others back in their apartments, their villas, or on their terraces overlooking the sea by then. The 707 climbed quickly over the Indian Ocean, so quickly he was denied even that last glimpse of her Fiat meandering away beetle-like somewhere along the airport road, that lonely villa lying at the end of the corniche, and the bone-white city along the sea.

They avoided Ethiopian airspace and flew up the Red Sea. Off the starboard wing was Aden, where Rimbaud had come before setting out for Abyssinia and Harar; to the north was Hadramaut, where in 1934 Malraux had come to search for Mareb and the tomb of the Queen of Sheba; behind him was Benaadir, where he had come to seek his diplomatic fortune. There had been a war, a nasty, ugly little war, but he had seen nothing, witnessed nothing, heard nothing of its naked human voices, living a comfortable secondhand life shut away in the embassy keep or his isolated villa overlooking the sea.

But watching Yemen's blue-veined flint mountains sliding away far below, all he could think of was Lindy waiting there all alone at the fence, already desperately homesick. Those few insane lines from a Neil Young lyric they'd listened to the night before returned, his frightened mind spinning them like a hamster on a treadmill:

> I feel like going back,
> Back where there's nowhere to stay.

The emergency door next to his seat wouldn't close properly, but a Pakistani flight steward carrying a jar of olives who looked like he didn't know much about faulty door gaskets or passengers getting whiplashed out of jet airplanes at 32,000 feet assured him there was no danger. It was dark when they circled Cairo, a lava of yellow and white light streaking away from a white-hot crater along the Nile. He had missed his flight to Rome and stayed at a small modern transit hotel not far from the airport. He might have been in Rome, Brussels, or even Newark.

He was back at the airport at nine and at ten thirty was seated on the Alitalia 707. At eleven thirty they were all ordered off the plane—some kind of mechanical problem. He had expected the quiet interlude of an orderly transition, his mind free for self-indulgent recollection, anything but this.

It was hot, very hot; the sun, now blinding him, had taken away the details of the airfield like an overexposed negative, leaching away the outline of the distant buildings of the Egyptian air base which wavered just above the horizon like a mirage blown by the desert wind. The heat lay on his mind like a fever. It was a few minutes before twelve, and the passengers now stood in random groups inside the departure enclosure where the attendant had led them, frustrated, impatient, and silent. A hundred yards away the

Alitalia 707, two hours and twenty minutes late, still sat on the
tarmac in the sunlight, growing hotter, uglier, more inert, with the
mechanics, looking dumber and more primitive as the moments
passed, Neanderthals, in fact, squatting on their ladders and hy-
draulic lift under the port wing with their ball-peen hammers. *What
could you fix on a Boeing 707 with a six-pound hammer?* The panels had been removed, and they were huddled around what looked
like the turbine blades. Behind them, the ugly black smoke of the
exhaust had streaked the wing pods. At first when the passengers
had been led from the cabin, they'd been animated as they returned
to the terminal. Just a short delay, the cabin steward said. There
were jokes, smiles, even laughter. But now there was little talk except for the three Americans—military types, Talbot suspected,
like the advance DOD team that had come to Jubba the week before he left. They now leaned against the wire fence. They had been
solemn and intimidating behind their sunglasses at first, large men
among strangers, ignoring even the dozen or so elderly and middle-
aged American tourists among the passengers; but now they were
reverting, playing grab-ass GI games.

He envied the tourists their patience. He had none; he had forgotten who he was. At long last the announcement came that they
were to reboard the aircraft.

The interior was hot and airless. The pilot apologized for the
delay. Then minutes later the plane lifted off. Some were waiting
for the seat belt sign to go off, others for the first view of the Mediterranean, some wanted drinks, and a few minutes later the voice
of the pilot again came on and again apologized for the delay while
below the silent brown shadow of Africa drifted out of sight unseen under their wings.

In and out, up and down, moved here and there by travel and
booking agents, ticket clerks, lounge attendants, airport loudspeak-
ers, flight boards, and cabin stewards, they would soon be served
cocktails and lunch but now, politely respondent to the soft pulses
of light and sound overhead—*No Smoking, Smoking, Place Seats in
an Upright Position, Fasten Seat Belts*—they were all prisoners of a
kind, some docilely infantile, like the row of middle-aged tourists
in front of him, their freedom surrendered long before, sitting bliss-
fully unaware at 27,000 feet of the abyss below, like Harcourt, who,

if he'd been aboard, would be sitting someplace up in first class wondering when the flick would come on.

In his emptiness he disliked them for that, too, for what Harcourt and Julia had done, trapping him in their own foolish, ignorant, unconscious lives.

The Rome airport was even worse.

He missed his flight to Paris and after a long and unsuccessful argument with the Alitalia ticket clerk who refused to change his ticket to Air France reconciled himself to spending the night in Rome.

His hotel in downtown Rome was a typical airline transit hotel. He wandered the streets for a few hours, puzzled at all those white faces. He didn't sleep well in a strange-smelling room with strange-smelling sheets. The following morning as he sat waiting in the airport-bound bus for passengers from another hotel near the Via Venti Settembre to board, he watched an old Italian hoisting rubbish cans to the back of a truck. As he banged the trash cans back to the pavement, he seemed conscious of the sleepy tourists watching through the windows; his performance improved. He winked at a pair of Englishwomen two seats ahead of him. Talbot seemed to hear their voices:

There he is, that awful man! Making that terrible racket every morning! Look at him! Disgusting! Is he turning this way? Merciful heavens, his trousers are falling off! Turn away! Don't look! Is he saying something?

As he watched the old man through the window, Rome seemed to him very gray, very dirty, belonging to another century entirely. All except the old man, who seemed to him very happy. Other Italians might work in banks or for the foreign ministry, might take tourists about in their old Chevrolets, take street photographs or sell lemon ices, or when their beards went gray and they looked like men to be trusted, would peddle contraband cigarettes from Naples outside the train station, and then when there was nothing else they would work on the garbage trucks, like this old man was doing, but at night they would smell of her shampoo and her skin, and every night would be a night to remember, every night of every week of every year, and whatever men did or became to possess her wouldn't matter.

Lindy, Talbot heard him say as the bus rumbled away. *Her name is Lindy.*

It was the light he remembered, the drenching light; colorless in the air, transparent, it defined itself in defining the earth, lying on the beach road, on the beach, on the white wall, on the oyster rubble of his front garden. On the way out to Fiumicino he saw in the distance a gray mass, like the heaving hulk of some giant beached skate, or the tailings from some industrial plant discharge, but then as its mass grew realized that it was Rome's Mediterranean they were passing.

It was three o'clock in the afternoon when he arrived in Paris. No one was there to meet him; he took a taxi to a little hotel on the Left Bank. All those puzzling white faces on the street still, all those cars. They drove through the blur of traffic and the stink of exhaust fumes, past cobbled alleys, carved doors, stone archways, and into a shadowy courtyard that stood at the center of that intricate matrix of medieval past and civilized present where a pair of orphaned chestnut trees shivered naked under a patch of gray sky. As he climbed the steps to the third floor, the frightened little hamster was spinning even more wildly in his cage:

> I feel like going back,
> Back where there's nowhere to stay.

□ □ □

Paris was gray and wintry, or so it seemed, although it was autumn. At the embassy those first few days he heard a chorus of DeGroot-like voices, saw himself surrounded by a collection of DeGroot-like faces, and wondered if he would be able to get through the first week. He'd promised Lindy he'd give himself six months. He talked to her twice a week on the phone the first month and persuaded her to reduce his sentence to four months. The next week he hoped to reduce it to three. He felt out of place with his threadbare suits and his ragged collars. His Indian Ocean suntan drew the curiosity of a few embassy secretaries, who would smile sweetly at a distance and afterwards, someone told him confidentially, ask who he was. Some dimwit from the security staff, following the usual security briefing, asked if he used a sun lamp. Talbot told him he had a weekend villa at Saint-Tropez.

The political counselor was off to a meeting in Brussels. The acting political counselor was named Farraday, a thin-faced anemic man who squinted when he smiled and spoke in a very low voice with the calm precision of a university professor. After twenty minutes' conversation Talbot discovered he'd never been south of Corsica. He had made a career of French internal politics, beginning fifteen years ago; he was serving his third tour in Paris. Talbot would be working in external politics, he informed him with a queer little smile—Africa, the Third World, that sort of thing. He was given a small little office smelling of honeyed tobacco smoke from his predecessor's pipe and a brunette secretary he shared with two other political officers, one working on Soviet and Eastern European affairs. His predecessor had left him a list of a dozen contacts, among them a first secretary from the Ethiopian embassy who was thinking of defecting.

The faces took longer to get accustomed to—white faces everywhere, young faces, exhausted middle-aged faces, old leprous faces eroded by the corrosions of the Metropole, like the bridges along the Seine. Crowds pursued him, gave him no peace, flocking after him along the streets, trying to run him down in the senseless traffic, joining him in the tiniest of restaurants, swallowing him up on the deafening metro platforms. He found an apartment on the fifth floor of an ancient sixteenth-century building on a small cul-de-sac off Boulevard Saint-Germain near Rue de Rennes. One night he awoke to a strange noise pounding on the dormers. It grew ominously louder, and then he heard the smashing of debris against the panes, the roar of caissons in the narrow streets below, and thought, Good Christ, it's happened again! and bolted out of bed. *Under attack, an air raid, Paris under enemy occupation!* but it was only the rain, a savage flooding November rain that swept through the narrow street below like the sheets of monsoon-driven surf pounding against the reef, and he stood a long time at the window watching his first autumn rainstorm in three years. The second week of December it grew very cold and he bought an electric heater for his monastic little flat, a more comfortable bed, and a few pieces of secondhand furniture. Although Lindy's telephone voice reassured him, she grew dimmer in memory. One Saturday on the metro staring into the dark window and the ghosts of those faces crowding the aisles above him he made a conscious effort to summon her and found he'd forgotten her face. For a few agonizing minutes he was a corpse, a man without memory, hurtling underground in the company of a few hundred gray cadavers destined for some subterranean catastrophe, there to be buried together in their lacerated steel shell. The man sitting next to him smelled of coal smoke and maggoty cheese. He got up and left the train at the next stop, although it wasn't his destination; the chilly air revived him, and after a few minutes her memory miraculously returned. Thereafter he always kept her picture with him and taped a second one to the bathroom wall near his swivel-armed shaving mirror. During their next telephone conversation, he persuaded her to come to Paris in late March on R&R. It seemed a very abstract reassurance.

The Christmas holidays helped. There were Christmas parties, the embassy Christmas party of course, and at a small dinner at the political counselor's apartment the woman sitting next to him who'd come from another party put her hand on his left knee. He didn't know her name and even if he'd known told himself he wouldn't have been interested.

Being driven across the Pont Neuf three days after Christmas, returning from a small party in the Marais, the lights along the Seine brought back a few lines from a poem by Howard Baker he hadn't remembered in years, not since Princeton, he supposed.

> Henry the Fourth rides in bronze,
> His shoulders curved and pensive, thrust
> Enormously into electric
> Blazonments of a Christmas trust.

That was reassuring, too. What better the advantages of a few forgotten Princeton humanities courses than being summoned from memory crossing the Pont Neuf on a cold December night? Not to illuminate those dark unlit corners of your life, but rather to sprig out certain certainties already possessed, a little parsley collar for one of life's little lamb chops, a little greenery on the mantel at

Yuletide. What better a Yuletide celebration than lovely old Paris, spread out like a gift along the Seine.

By the end of his first five weeks he had adjusted well to the rhythms of embassy life, just as Lindy had predicted. With the money he'd put aside for their March holiday, he bought two new suits, new shirts and underwear, and recovered himself anew, T. Logan Talbot, *Esq.*, living once again within civilized frontiers among well-established traditions of culture, protocol, precedence, and drafting style. Nothing like the prophylaxis of clearing your telegram through the embassy corridors to rid yourself of all those little mental quirks brought from the African camel shag. Like a dose of grandmother's salts, a Bavarian mineral spring.

Possibly she'd been right, he decided. Jubba had been very much an aberration after all, as Paris now told him, and if that was the case, then possibly his emotional life as well. Perhaps he wasn't being fair to her, he argued in judicious, exculpatory masculine fashion, unfair to easy, forgiving, understanding Lindy. Perhaps he wasn't being fair to himself. He understood better how weak were the certainties of the past one gray morning in January as he met with his French counterpart at the Quai d'Orsay to talk about Chad, Zaire, and Jubba, the latter being rather far down on the current list of priorities. The young Frenchwoman who sat in on their conversation was very attractive.

Jubba, what a strange situation, the Frenchman said with a queer smile. "A *jacquerie,* wasn't it, that little war?"

During the first weeks he would smile ambiguously when someone mentioned Jubba and the little war still stalemated in the Ethiopian lowlands, as if in secret possession of some sad shabby little truth of the law of nations. That morning at the Quai, wearing his new English tweeds, conscious of the warmth of the Frenchwoman's admiring eyes, he agreed it was. "A *jacquerie,* indeed." Her name was Simone Saunier.

The Defense attaché at the embassy was also interested in his familiarity with the war but not in its ambiguities. He asked Talbot to give a briefing for a few official visitors from U.S. military commands in Europe. In the beginning the briefing hadn't been easy; too much information to digest in so short a time. His preamble also disturbed them.

He began his little talk by telling them something about those shabby little truths that lay behind that remote little war in Ethiopia, which weren't quite what they seemed—Washington's folly on the one hand, Moscow's hapless passivity on the other. But the third time he gave the briefing, he'd dropped his preface and reduced it to the twenty-minute flat-earth view the Defense attaché preferred, talking less of Washington's folly and more of Moscow's interventionist policy and its growing global force projection capability in the Third World, supported by Cuban proxy forces.

Although some inner voice warned him that this wasn't quite the case, it seemed simpler that way. The Defense attaché was pleased, the political section was pleased, the military visitors were pleased, and Talbot obliged as docilely as those fast food French countermen in the embassy cafeteria.

But then one week in early February he flew to NATO Brussels for a meeting and as he was driven in through the gates saw a handful of bundled protesters holding placards, a rag-tag army of Walloons, Danes, Dutch, and Germans shivering in the cold. He had no idea what the protests were about. His escort officer wasn't sure. He was curious, but he was inside the car and they were outside. That made him uneasy. As he was driven out again they were still there.

A similar demonstration was taking place at Frankfurt during his two-day visit there. When he returned to Paris he found the embassy watched by an unusually heavy French police cordon. Just precautionary, he was told on Monday morning. The business of the political section went on as usual. He got a sweet letter from Julia giving him the names and telephone numbers of some of her Parisian friends he should look up. She planned to visit France alone in May and asked him to set aside some time for her, perhaps even a week. Possibly he could take leave and they could drive south to Aix and Arles.

He threw the letter away.

□ □ □

He'd spent an uneventful day at the embassy, had left early, and was on his way to look at some furniture being sold by a Quai diplomat being assigned to Brazzaville. He was a little early and was dawdling. He had stopped on the Rue du Faubourg Saint-Honoré, looking in a shopwindow when the explosion came. The pavement crawled forward beneath his feet like a railroad coach leaving a station. A tremor stirred the plate-glass window, a second oscillation rippled through the straining glass like a breaking wave. He moved backwards into the sudden vacuum of the Paris afternoon. The handful of shoppers on the narrow side street had stopped, heads turned with his to the west, searching the rooftops for the source of the blast.

An old woman holding two shopping bags turned on the pavement a few feet, circling in confusion, looking east and then south and then east again, her arms drooping from the weight of her packages.

Her terrified eyes met his. "I don't know," he said uneasily. "I don't know what it is."

A few young shop boys sprinted past. People had begun to leave the shops, searching the street and the sky. A hundred yards away he saw a few figures running and he moved with them. As he turned the corner he saw smoke belching from a shattered hulk that lay half on the sidewalk and half on the curb a hundred yards away. A curtain of boiling white smoke lifted from a small shop whose glass windows, doors, and marquee had been blown away, like the plate-glass windows of the restaurant next door.

"What was it? Whose shop?" he heard a man ask an old woman being helped away by two men. Her face was streaked with ash and blood. She was crying. He couldn't hear her answer. One of the men carrying her fell; she fell, too. He stopped to help her, feeling the glass under his soles. A middle-aged man helped her up. When she saw the bomb crater that lay astride the curb, still smoking, she began to scream. Scattered along its periphery was the twisted vertebrae of what had once been a car chassis. The stench of something like carbolic poisoned the air. The iron engine block lay thirty meters down the pavement, still smoking. The Frenchman led the woman along the sidewalk away from the crater, supporting her with one arm, and then two women standing in the doorway of a small grocery recognized her and hurried to carry her inside. From the restaurant next door the injured were

straggling out, dazed, some with bloody faces. Behind him automobile horns had begun to clamor at the snarled intersection, immobilized by the blockage in the streets ahead and by the scores of
the curious streaming across the intersection and down the narrow street to the north. Looking up, he saw the dust still drifting
around him.

He heard the pulsing klaxon of the police and hospital vehicles
behind him. "The bastards," he heard a Frenchman say, "the
bloody bastards," and turned to see an old man leaning heavily on
his cane, a small schnauzer between his legs. He watched as they
arrived, drawn up in the center of the street, followed by the cadre
of policemen in helmets and plexiglass visors as they finally broke
through the crowd to clear the street in front of the demolished
shops. Two medics in white jackets knelt in the center of the street,
bent over a dark low mound of smoking rags from which a bright
stump of something projected, painted in vivid red acrylic. As he
stood facing the improvised police cordon, surrounded by smoking
rags, twisted fragments of chassis, and broken glass, a policeman
shouted at him to get behind the cordon.

He moved across the street and into the crowd. He heard someone say the demolished shop was a bookstore with a small Syrian
emigré newspaper office upstairs; others that the target had been
the restaurant next door. He turned down the sidewalk, looking
overhead. A pension door had been left open. He climbed a dark
staircase to the third floor, where a painter's dropcloth lay in the
hall. Looking up, he saw that the trapdoor to the roof had been
thrown back, and he climbed on. Two painters in white coveralls
were standing at the edge of the roof looking down. Talbot joined
them. In front of the demolished building front where he had led
the old woman away lay three body bags. As a policeman came
forward with a foam fire extinguisher to examine a lump of smoking
cloth, he turned back and called one of the medics, who came to
inspect it. He shook his head, and then turned back to the curb.

"*J'ai eu la trouille,*" one of the painters said. "That scared the
shit out of me."

"They're nuts," the other said. "All of them."

"This guy, too. *Te toque, non?*"

"A little," he said, "you, too, right?"

They were standing on the roof turned toward him, two harle-
quin figures on the parapets; behind them was the smoke of a
terrorist's bomb and the roofs of Paris.

One of history's orphans running amok, he supposed, another
impotent child of injustice firing off another salvo in his secret hundred years' war. He moved closer to the edge, still looking down.
What emigré paper? Whose car was that below?

Two policemen were moving a few onlookers off the roof of
the building across the way. Another policeman was clearing the
roof of a building just to the south. A helicopter clattered near,
hovered, as if about to land, lifted again suddenly and dipped
away over the canyon of streets to the south. Another helicopter
appeared, this one a two-man chopper with a plexiglass bubble
canopy, lifting from somewhere below. Talbot watched as it settled
slowly on a roof across the way.

He wondered if they were tracking someone.

"What the hell's going on?" asked one of the painters.

A short Frenchman jumped from the helicopter and joined the
two policemen on the roof as the helicopter lifted again and clattered away. The roofs to the south and north were clear, and so
was the roof across the way where the three men stood against the
skyline pointing at Talbot and the two painters. The short Frenchman was waving his arms.

Looked like a fascist type, an old Barbouze, Talbot thought,
watching his frantic gestures. Yeah, well, the action's down there,
Alphonse, not up here. But on the street below a few policemen
were looking up.

"Get off the roof he's telling us," one of the painters said.
"Let's go."

"Screw him," said the other painter.

They waited a few minutes and by then the policemen on the
building to the south were shouting at them. The two painters returned to the trapdoor, and Talbot soon followed, disappointed he
wouldn't see the conclusion of whatever was going on. The painters
descended ahead of him on the narrow stairs, and by the time Talbot reached the second floor he could hear their protesting voices
from below. He stopped, listened for a minute, heard the questions
from the French policemen who'd intercepted them, and realized

their laggardly departure from the rooftop constituted a misde-
meanor of some kind.

He readjusted his tie, took out his wallet, found his official identification intact, and began his dignified descent.

It was all very embarrassing. What made his case more difficult
was that he, unlike the two painters, was unknown to the building's
concierge, whom the police had summoned. A foreigner with a foreign passport which he didn't have in his possession? An official
from the ministry of interior was summoned and was quickly satisfied. He kept Talbot's identification and led him through the police cordon and back to his car, parked behind a police car near
the center of the street.

Talbot waited while he made a final telephone call from the
front seat. A dozen steps away three French demolition experts in
coveralls were measuring the crater with a tape while another
was explaining to two French officials how the bomb had been
rigged.

Hexogen was responsible, Talbot heard him say as he wandered
closer, not dynamite; probably a hexogen collar wrapped around
a butane cylinder. Hexogen delivered the same explosive charge as
three times as much dynamite.

"What are they measuring there?" Talbot asked, nodding toward
the crater.

They were calculating the amount of the charge. There was a
formula, derived from the diameter, the depth, and the density of
the soil underneath.

"Must have been a big charge," said one of the French officials,
turning. "Look at that fucking car."

"What car?" Talbot said. "That's the engine block."

He looked at Talbot, then at the demolition man. "As bad as
last week on Rue Copernic?"

"Worse, much worse."

The ministry of interior official left his car and joined them. He
gave Talbot back his identification and said he could leave.

"What happened on Rue Copernic?" Talbot wondered. The five
Frenchmen looked at him more closely.

"Who is this man?" the demolition expert asked.

"A diplomat," said the ministry of interior man. "You can leave now."

"Diplomat? What kind of diplomat?"

"I'm on my way," Talbot said.

He crossed the street and went through the police cordon and stood there for a few minutes looking back. It was awful, bloody awful. He didn't go on to the apartment to look at the furniture. He walked over to the Champs Elysées and wandered morosely down toward the Arc de Triomphe, not seeing the passing faces at all but aware of them, his mind out of register, everything out of register as his feet moved him on. He would stop from time to time, looking skyward, conscious of the knowledge that any one of ten thousand clerks could do what he was doing, whether this year or the next, and that he had been right and Lindy was wrong.

He put in a call to her that night, but the French overseas operator said the circuits were busy. He told her to keep trying. Twenty minutes later the phone rang but it was the embassy regional security officer, calling to ask what had happened that afternoon. He'd had a call from his ministry of interior liaison. Farraday from the political section also called and Talbot explained a second time. A little morosely, Farraday suggested he write a memo for the record.

It was ten o'clock when the French overseas operator finally got the call through. Lindy had been out.

"Where in the world have you been?"

Her voice was very distant, very far away. "At the embassy."

"At this time of night? What's going on?"

"I can't hear you."

"I said what's going on?"

"I can't talk about it, not over the phone." Her voice faded out. "Oh, God, I feel so rotten," he heard her say. "Is that why you called?"

"What why I called? Is it something personal?"

"No. Haven't you been reading the cables?"

"Not since this morning. I had to talk to you. Listen, you've got to come, as soon as possible."

"When? Now?"

"Now, tomorrow, this weekend."

"I can't, not this weekend. It's just impossible. There's too much going on."

"What the hell's going on?"

"I can't say over the phone."

"What about next week? Can you come then?"

"I'll try, yes."

"Promise?"

"Promise. You didn't do anything stupid, did you?"

"No, nothing. You promise?"

A long pause. "All right, I promise. Can you call me tomorrow, after I talk to Whit. About eight o'clock local time. Can you?"

"Eight o'clock, OK."

"Eight o'clock. Oh, Logan, it's so rotten, all of it, just so futile. I can't say any more. Tomorrow then, eight o'clock."

The French operator was again on the line and a moment later the connection was broken.

At the embassy the following morning the surveillance system seemed to have been augmented by additional TV cameras cocked outside and inside the main entrance. Beyond was a magic little doorway through which visitors passed before they were received at the reception desk. With its pressure threshold, electronic sensors, shrew's ears, and x-ray eyes that dissolved flesh to bone, it made the embassy seem a privileged private world, like the safety deposit vault at the Bowsers' Manhattan bank, secure from the anarchy of the lobby above or the Manhattan streets outside, but that morning Talbot was a little uneasy. The magic doorway, the TV surveillance cameras, and the hard-eyed guards absolved only the pure in heart, of whom there were many. He wasn't certain he was still among them.

As he went upstairs he sensed another's gait in his, another's breath tight in his chest, and then heard a strange voice in his ear, urging him to flee. For an instant he sensed that demonic little shadow who sometimes dogged his footsteps, not the Jubba NSS man on his blue Vespa, but that other Talbot who'd broken free of his confinement at eleven o'clock at night over the back wall to commence his maniacal disco dance at the Lido nightclub or the Mariner's Cave.

So he felt trapped, the same feeling he'd once had on an El Al flight from New York to Rome. Following that flight he'd concluded that for all their sophistication, the Israelis had a somewhat benign view of human nature that they could apply that kind of crushing pressure to a weak, self-indulgent, often hopelessly guilt-ridden passenger living far beyond his biological and financial means to be suddenly awakened to his existential predicament 30,000 feet above his natal earth in El Al cabin class on an overdrawn American Express credit card, as he'd been that stormy night. He was flying on a government-purchased ticket, had no money in his pocket except $1,000 borrowed from the State Department credit union. His guilt had left him no appetite, but he was eating and drinking, and all this was being monitored by two pairs of cold questioning eyes seated just to his rear. The wonder wasn't that El Al flights were secure from hijacking, but that a few planes weren't occasionally lost by a kind of spontaneous combustion in which hundreds of split and multiple personalities were detonated out of their seats at the same instant—Rye, New York, accountants; Manhattan secretaries; Bronxville auto accessory salesmen; Wilmington, Delaware, diplomats; Queens diamond cutters—all exploding out of their skins like flares from a jet-age Roman candle in an infinity of Jungian, Freudian, Adlerian, and post-Freudian trajectories leaving only that burnt-out metallic pod behind, the way the planet would be emptied one day, just a fiery little parabola lighting up a once exclusive little franchise in a secluded corner of the galaxy.

At the morning meeting of the political section the bomb incident wasn't mentioned; neither was his brief detention by the Paris police.

That was odd, too. Surely they knew about it.

The silence began to unnerve him. The tidy little conference room began to suffocate him. Certainly the political counselor knew of the little incident; Farraday must have told him. But as the moments passed and nothing was said, he understood and could imagine the nation-state of the future living this way. Its governments would be inside, in a room as small as this, secure against the barbarians outside, whose sullen silence concealed a million grievances, hundreds of secret causes, scores of would-be martyrs, and as many lunatics; the bureaucrats in here, the barbarians out there in the streets waiting to ambush a prime minister, a speaker of the house, a minister of defense, or some young diplomat who'd failed to prevent a war that should never have happened and had returned from the bush with all sorts of lunatic rubbish in his head.

The counselor at the British embassy had given a small dinner party the night before. Everyone, the political counselor said, had had a jolly time.

A jolly time?

Talbot studied his face. Nothing there, only jollity. He studied the faces of his colleagues. Nothing there either. They didn't care, they didn't know. They stayed inside too much, like the Parisian shop girls or the tea-tray stackers at Lyons or the clerks at Sears, State, or the Pentagon, all day inside, day after day, year after year, like these men, like himself these past months, all dispersed to that same bland molecular evenness, like gas filling a vacuum. Of course they didn't know. They all had room-temperature IQs, that was what they had, all sitting here, all of them without the slightest clue as to what was going on in the streets outside, all those futile, secret hundred years' wars under way. They didn't know either that if they didn't wake up soon they were going to end up sitting in a little country about the size of a goddamn broom closet, like this conference room.

Suddenly they were all looking at him.

"Did you say something?" the political counselor asked with polite impatience. He didn't like being interrupted.

"Did I?"

"I thought you said something."

Had he said something? What the hell had he said?

"I don't think I said anything."

"I had the distinct impression you did."

The meeting resumed.

My God, were his secrets out? Had someone broken his code, wired his internalized debate, leaked his secrets? Some double agent sitting in his English tweeds?

The political counselor was still looking at him as the meeting broke up and he reassembled his telegrams.

Farraday stopped him outside the door. "What was it you said? If you have something to say, better wait till he gets to you."

"What do you mean, say something? I didn't open my goddamn mouth."

Farraday reddened. "I distinctly heard you."

"Heard me nothing. What the hell am I, a Pentecostal?" Farraday turned and hurried away, Talbot at his heel. "Do I speak in strange tongues. Do I babble in Aramaic, in ancient Greek. Tell me, do I? What language then, what the hell did I say?"

The others, now filing past, looked politely the other way, as if they hadn't heard.

He left the embassy thirty minutes later, forgetting to look for the cables that might tell him why Lindy had been so upset the night before.

He telephoned her that night. It was eight thirty when he finally got the call through. She was waiting.

"I'm in even bigger trouble now," he told her, "real big trouble. Someone's spilling the beans about me. Did you talk to Whit?"

"Yes, I talked to him."

"What did he say?"

"He said what I thought he'd say, that you were crazy."

"He said *that?*"

"So what? I knew he'd say that. I'm coming next Wednesday. So don't do anything stupid until I get there. What do you mean, spilling the beans?"

He couldn't believe it.

"Next *Wednesday?*"

"Why? Something wrong with Wednesdays all of a sudden?"

He still couldn't believe it. "Wednesday's great, perfect. What time, what flight? Listen, stay away from Cairo, don't transit Cairo, OK? Rome either."

"I have to transit Rome."

"If you have to fly Pakistani Air, then sit on the aisle, not next to the window."

"I'm flying Alitalia. Listen to me. You didn't do anything stupid, did you?"

"Maybe. No. I don't know. Not yet anyway. Wednesday. I can't believe it."

"Neither can I, but I'll be there."

The same night he called Basil Dinsmore in London. Basil asked him if he could confirm the rumors he'd heard that day at the foreign office, that the Jubba army had begun its withdrawal from Ethiopia.

◻ ◻ ◻

Not since 1540 when a Jubba army had set out from the coast to conquer the Ethiopian massif had they come this far, but they would go no further. Neither would Major Jama. The secret orders had already come, sent by messenger from Bulet Uen, known to only a few senior field officers. They were withdrawing from the occupied territories, returning back across the frontier.

He stood studying Harar through his binoculars, leaning against the stone outcropping. The road was silent, the brassy sky filled with puffs of white and black smoke above the city far in the distance on its medieval hilltop, an ancient walled city surrounded by gardens and orchards. The trees were splintered now. Within the walls was a labyrinth of narrow passageways, twisting cobbled streets, and stone houses crusted with the smoke and soot of the centuries— Ottoman, Islamic, Christian—just a faint shimmering speck on his lens in the morning heat.

He thought he could see the Senga gate on the southeast corner. He would have liked to see more, the seams in the old stone, a face or two. A Russian face, Yefimov's smiling face and dead blue eyes, General Lubatoff's square face with its lynxlike eyebrows. An intelligence report claimed he was now in Addis Ababa, head of the new Soviet military mission.

For months the war had been static along this front as the Cuban-manned tanks held the Jubba armor in check while far to the rear the Ethiopian army was being massively resupplied by the Soviet sea- and air-lift. In time the Ethiopian offensive would come, but they would be gone by then, withdrawn to the safety of Jubba's borders, leaving behind what retreating armies always left behind.

It was the waiting that had been so dangerous, those long lulls when the days passed and nothing happened and the mind was empty, the way this day had been. Now the waiting was over. He would be among the first to leave.

He raised the binoculars for a final time. He would have liked to wander down through its passageways, find a shop, drink a bottle of English ale, cool but uniced, like the ale his great-uncle kept at Sheikh. Stroll the streets, visit the old Jubba quarter, as they called it, the European and French tourists with their cameras and their little handkerchief hats knotted at each corner.

He would tell his children of those months he spent here. He hadn't spoken to his wife and children since July; they were at Sheikh with his great-uncle. Not speaking to a woman or to a child except as strangers denied something in him, something incomplete, a roughness in his voice, his feelings, his mind. Maybe one day after the war was forgotten he would take them to Harar and point out from the Senga gate that distant hillside white with dust where he had once stood with his binoculars.

He turned and went back down the rocky trail. Thirty meters behind him in the draw the T-35 tank sat under the shade of the netting, immobilized, its track off. Now it sat there, its metal shell giving off the heat of the morning; another lay a hundred meters away.

An Ethiopian shell exploded suddenly in a field far to the north of the road, the fountain of white and brown dust lifted, settled back to earth, and drifted off silently to the east-southeast. What would the Old Man do now? He had gambled everything on a war neither the Russians nor the Americans would support, and now he had no alternative except to withdraw in defeat, his armories empty.

"Enough?" his driver said as he came down the trail.

"Enough."

His radioman and rifleman were gone, sent back a week earlier. Lieutenant Samantar came out of the shadows on the far side and climbed into the Land-Rover, as silent as when he'd first seen the withdrawal order. He had refused to join Jama as he took his last look at Harar. For him the order to withdraw had been a personal betrayal, a surrender to injustice, the denial of his birthright here in Western Jubbaland. The two men had hardly exchanged a word since the news came.

They drove off in silence toward the south.

That evening after dark they stopped and made camp near a small village where a WJLF company was bivouacked. His driver, an Abgal from the coast whose tribe grazed its herds not far from the Indian Ocean, talked about what he would do when he returned to Benaadir. Lieutenant Samantar listened silently, his back turned, his hands over his knees as he looked out over the scrub toward the western mountains hidden in darkness. The driver continued to talk, and Samantar abruptly picked up his sleeping roll and walked away out on the scrub.

He didn't return. Jama stretched out under the night sky.

What would his great-uncle say? What would he ask him?

He fell asleep thinking of what might have been done differently, but he didn't sleep well and when the driver woke him in the thin gray light he felt as though he hadn't slept at all.

They drove all that day.

The sky was a dome of blue ice. Red dust hovered in the distance; bomb craters mounded the verges of the road like anthills, and in the distance acacias, slabs of rock like a mirage as they passed. It was late afternoon when they approached the village where they'd spent that first night so many months ago and the old Galla smuggler had shown him his scars from the local prison. The day was cloudless, the sun deep in the western sky, gilding the broken walls in pink and amber, bright still in their eyes. They shuttled silently through the rubble, bombed that morning by two Ethiopian F-15s that had chased the Jubba MIGs from the skies, past the broken alleyways, the demolished buildings, the wrecked hulk of a car, the twisted tin roofing, the smoking rags of someone's abandoned suitcase, cart, or barrow.

At a checkpoint between narrow streets, the Land-Rover had to stop again, delayed by a truck blocking the street where the villagers and the WJLF soldiers were still searching for bodies. Waiting again for the escort, he saw the sun lying in a bright yellow flag upon an old wall, half Roman, half Byzantine, it seemed, half modern, too, where new plaster had begun, painted blue, but the old wall gave the sun texture, relieved it there, gave it dignity, gave it repose for a final time that day, magnifying the dried red stroke that had passed down its surface, like the stroke of a thick horsehair brush, and where at the foot of the wall, just touched by the sunlight, was the broken body of the woman who had made it, lifted now by a WJLF soldier, her knee and thin smooth thigh visible. He moved his gaze higher, his brimming eyes fixed only on the wall and its ancient surfaces, on the sun that seemed to rest there lightly for a moment, like an old man resting at the side of the road, drawing breath before he rose and resumed his long dusty pilgrimage.

He didn't move his eyes from the old wall. Every stone, every seam and fissure, every scar of its surface seemed alive, seemed to tremble with energy, like living tissue, a living membrane, like the sun and the sky itself.

"Jama," Lieutenant Samantar called, "we're ready."

Unable to move, unable to separate himself from the wall, he stood for another minute rooted to the spot. Only when Samantar called a second time did he finally return to the Land-Rover. They drove out on the tarmac to the west.

Ahead of them a short little man was making his way along the side of the road. A tall Jubba woman in a long dark dress held a parasol over his head, and behind her followed a few Jubba elders and a half-dozen children carrying their wooden learning tablets on which nomadic children copied verses from the Koran in charcoal dust.

As they drew abreast of the small roadside procession, Jama told his driver to slow.

What wouldst thou here, uncle, wandering with these wild Bedew? he remembered, thinking of Ali Salim al-Mas'ud, the Saudi trader whom Jama sent back so many months ago. He was back in Jidda now, he supposed, back in his small dark shop, gossiping with his brother about that great promiscuous world beyond the rim of mountains. The man trudging along the road was a local sheikh. He declined Jama's offer of a ride but seemed to recognize Lieutenant Samantar, who talked to him for a few minutes.

They continued south, and that evening just after sundown as the last transparent gray light hovered still in the air, they pulled off the track and into the circle in front of the old administration building where they'd found the old man and his wife hiding the first day of the offensive.

A few of the stone houses had been rebuilt, and the tin emblem of the WJLF hung above the gallery. A Russian jeep was in the drive. The glow from the kerosene lanterns lit up the windows; inside a pair of Jubba ordnance officers were talking quietly to the three WJLF guerrillas who manned the post. They looked up as Jama entered and got to their feet, but the three WJLF cadremen remained seated. They seemed suspicious, even hostile. Brothers in victory, one nation, one tribe, now they were strangers again, separate Jubba tribes with separate birthrights, separate ambitions. Lieutenant Samantar knew one of the Jubba officers, a fellow Ogaden tribesman from Western Jubbaland. He drew him aside and they talked while Jama and his radioman returned to the Land-Rover.

A few minutes later the two Jubba officers left. Lieutenant Samantar remained inside. Jama and his driver ate cold rations, sitting with their backs against the stone building and looking out over the scrubland as the last light died away to the west.

Lieutenant Samantar finally joined them. The WJLF guerrillas inside knew about the withdrawal orders. The two ordnance officers had told them.

"They blame the army then," Jama said, not surprised.

"The Old Man, the army, everyone."

He broke a hard biscuit apart, looked at it, and then threw it away. "What do they think they're going to do?"

"Stay," Samantar said.

"With what?"

"What they had before."

"Who were the two ordnance officers?"

"Friends," Samantar said, "officers who feel the same way."

"Troublemakers," the driver said.

After they finished the rations, the driver took the kettle and made tea over the fire. Lieutenant Samantar returned inside. Jama and his driver sat listening to the noises of the night. "I don't like this place," the driver said.

"Do you want to drive on?"

"No. But we should leave early, long before sunup."

Jama had fallen sleep when someone touched his shoulder. He sat up and found Lieutenant Samantar kneeling next to his bedroll.

He told Jama to move his bedroll further out in the bush.

"I'm telling you as a friend, not an officer. If you stay here there will be trouble. They don't want trouble, not with you. They have a right to feel the way they do. You admit that."

"They have a right, but being right doesn't matter. What do they want?"

"But they have a right, just as I have a right."

"I admit they have a right. What do they want?"

"The Land-Rover and the radio."

"That's foolish. Did you tell them?"

"What could I tell them?"

"You, too, then. Where will you go?"

"To the south."

Samantar turned and shook the shoulder of the Abgal driver. Jama got up stiffly, rolled up his pallet, and walked out into the scrub to the east. A few minutes later he heard the Abgal driver calling to him. He waited and then they both walked further out into the darkness.

"They're thieves," the driver said. "The Ogaden people have always been thieves."

Brothers in victory, enemies in defeat, Jama thought. "Samantar isn't a thief," he said.

They walked on. At last they found a place that satisfied the driver and spread out their bedrolls.

"He'll be a deserter," the driver said.

"Many deserters," Jama said. A handful here, a few there, continuing their ugly futile war, not a war of armies but of bitter, desperate, and impotent men who killed the innocent to show the strong how just their cause.

Now Lieutenant Samantar had joined them. Come as a lion, now he was gone with the jackals. There was nothing Jama could do.

He finally fell asleep but awoke several times, heard nothing except the slow steady breathing of the Abgal driver, and fell asleep again. But then in the morning mist he seemed to hear something, the soft shuffle of moving feet, a faint whistle, the flourish of drums, and then the sound of the pipes as they came in double column out of the dawn shadows, the white plumes, the green tartan and red, the dance of their kilts, came as they had so many times, the strong-legged troopers of the British Army of the Nile, Enfields flat against their shoulders, arms swinging, marching against the Italians at Bizerte, where his great-uncle had fought, at Tobruk, in Ethiopia; and behind them, too, came the loping stride of the British camel constabulary, brought back from boyhood and the tales of his great-uncle in front of the wood fire at Sheikh, gray men now, grayer and leaner, but come at last, and he rolled to his side painfully, moving out of their way, pointing off to the north, and then the sounds retreated and the pipes dissolved, like the dust devil on the track to Kebre Dehar that day and there on the track were the silhouettes of the camels moving by, come from the west, on their way now back toward the frontier and the pastures that would soon be green again.

He sat for a long time watching the darkness lift in the direction they'd disappeared.

The driver finally woke up and they walked across the pan and climbed the knoll to the administration building, but the Land-Rover was gone, the rooms inside empty. Lieutenant Samantar was gone, too, and the low stones and adobe houses to the rear were empty. The little play flags were gone, the flowers scattered, but the flag of Western Jubbaland still hung from the old pole in front. A dream, all of it, and how quickly it had passed. There was no sound except the sound of the wind, and they walked past the flagpole and down the path, across the wadi and up to the track, hoping a truck would come along as they commenced their long trek eastward toward the frontier.

□ □ □

It was late April and the monsoon winds were moving toward the southwest. The Harcourts sat waiting for their six o'clock cocktail guests to arrive, sitting on the outside terrace overlooking the sea. An American destroyer sat snugly at anchor in the harbor.

"The new economic officer seems quite agreeable," Harcourt said. "Did post-graduate work at Columbia, very well informed."

"His wife seems a little young," Julia said, searching through the letters arrived that afternoon by pouch from Nairobi. "She called today."

"Did she?"

"Very young, very sweet. Is this all the mail you brought, just these two letters?"

"Just two. One's from Mrs. Lawrence in Paris."

She tore it open impatiently. "This wasn't the one I was looking for. Why didn't you open it? It's addressed to both of us."

"I can't read her handwriting. Thought I'd let you have the honor."

She read it as Kasim brought him mineral water and a vodka-lime for Julia. Harcourt was watching a gray embassy car on the Lido road below, wondering whom it was bringing when he heard her small breath of surprise. "Logan Talbot's resigned."

He turned, shocked. *"Logan* has? When?"

She shook her head and read on. "He's left the service; he's resigned and left the service."

"Resigned? I can't imagine it. Are you sure?"

"Of course I'm sure. It's right here."

"Logan? What on earth will he do?"

"She said he never returned her phone calls and she dropped in to see him at the embassy. They told her he'd resigned and left the service."

"Good Lord."

She turned the letter over. "Nothing about what he'll do, nothing at all."

"Did she ask?"

"Of course she asked. No one seemed to know, just that he'd left, went back to Washington to settle things, then was going to return to Europe for a while."

"I can't imagine."

She put the letter aside. "Did he say anything before he left?"

"No, nothing to me. Did he say anything to you?"

"No, nothing." She sat looking out over the ocean, her mouth a thin bitter line. "Not a word."

"I can't imagine," Harcourt said in bewilderment.

She picked up her glass impatiently. "Did you invite the Whittingtons tonight? Did you? He *must* know; I'm sure he does."

"Know what."

"Lindy Dowling, of course. She didn't come back."

"Lindy?"

"Of course, Lindy. Taking leave, then coming back to pack up. Now it all makes sense." She turned vindictively. "Why are you always the last one to know?"

"The last one to know what? I thought you didn't want the Whittingtons tonight."

"I said they were tiresome, not that I didn't want them. Don't you ever listen?"

"That's not what I remember. I didn't invite them."

"You should have. I'm sure they must have known, both of them."

"Must have known what?" he demanded. She ignored him. "Maybe something happened in Paris," he said, "something unexpected. Maybe Morgan Guaranty offered him a place?"

"*Unexpected?* My God, you don't think it wasn't planned, do you? You don't think anything he did he didn't plan, do you? He may have fooled you, but he certainly didn't fool me, ever."

"Logan? You're wrong."

"I'm not wrong. I feel cheated, I really feel cheated, not telling us."

"Not telling us what?"

"Going off with Lindy Dowling, doing whatever they're doing. She set her cap for him from the first, don't think she didn't."

"That's what he did?" He sat back in surprise. "That's marvelous. She didn't belong with Whittington's people, never did. That's marvelous. I'm happy for him, I am. Say what you like but I am, both of them. Are you sure?"

She looked at him accusingly. "Why on earth should you be happy for them?"

"Why shouldn't I be? I was fond of him and so were you. And nothing you can say will spoil it. Nothing." He got up, hearing the sound of a car. "I am, very much."

"That's idiotic."

"Maybe so. But I am."

He moved across the terrace, buoyant suddenly, something surging through his body, swelling his heart, lifting his tired legs, so stirred he had to stop for a minute, eyes fixed on the splash of luminous sunlight across the far wall. Then he moved on to greet his guests, remembering a warm summer day like this during his undergraduate holiday in Provence, a younger Harcourt pushing his bike up the hill to Cézanne's old studio behind the ivy wall in Arles. I am, he remembered, absolutely happy for them, grateful and happy both, for both of them.

□ □ □

At Algeciras on the Spanish coast, night was coming on and the yellow lamps hidden along the perimeter of the terrace under green leaf and vine began to flicker on. A few couples stirred out through the colonnade and stood along the terrace wall, some already dressed for dinner. They moved along the wall, then drifted on to the small tables at the far end of the terrace where a young American couple sat alone.

On a cushioned chair near the wall an elderly man, very frail in a white linen suit, watched them, listened to their secret voices, to her laughter most of all.

"You are," Lindy said, "you're such a big talker. I'll never learn Arabic, not in Beirut or anyplace else, not in a million years."

"I'll teach you. Your mentor in all things, great and small."

"Oh, God. I've heard that line before."

An eighty-year-old American diplomat, retired twenty-five years now from his last posting to Madrid, sat docilely upright with his middle-aged daughters and sons-in-law but not listening to them at all. In the harbor a freighter rode at anchor and beyond it the white-hulled Greek passenger ship, outward bound for Genoa the following morning.

The young American couple had arrived the same day as the tour group and that afternoon had driven their rented car out into the countryside and returned just before dusk, past the apricot-colored houses, through the empty streets, past the shuttered shops and the patches of sun-shattered water showing between the flaking buildings to the old seaside hotel. In the drive in front, a dozen British and American tourists were leaving a dusty minibus. Some were carrying cameras, others, British Airways flight bags; their shoes were dusty, their faces shrimp-pink in the sunlight. On the top step of the old veranda a waiter directed them toward the trellised garden where tea was waiting, an hour late, and where the elderly man sat in a chair deep in the shadows, crisp in his afternoon seersuckers, their young voices summoning him away then as they did now.

Now they sat at the next table, away from the exhausted middle-aged and elderly tourists.

"With an apartment on the corniche, maybe there's a beach nearby," Talbot said.

"Dinsmore said the best beaches are to the south," Lindy said, "near Khalde."

"Where the hell's Khalde?" He unfolded his map again.

They were bound for Beirut. A year, he'd heard him say; they would give themselves a year. After that he didn't know. Back to Maine, like her uncle, build boats, go to Pine Street, have a house in Southampton. They would be outward bound at eight the next morning, off to Cyprus and then Lebanon.

He watched her open her purse. "My God, I left the traveler's checks upstairs."

"I'll get them. Where?"

"In my jacket pocket, the tan suede."

The waiter came and she ordered for both of them and he came back with the traveler's checks.

"Why don't we try something different tonight," Lindy said. "Walk to the little restaurant where we had lunch the first day."

"The one with the cats on the floor?"

"I forgot about the cats. Pine Street isn't realistic. If it doesn't work out or things begin to blow up, we could go to China. I could teach English in the provinces, like a friend of mine from college is doing. Or to Maine. I really wouldn't mind."

"Things aren't going to blow up. Beirut's as quiet as Bar Harbor these days. What about Alaska?"

"What about Alaska?"

"Buy a glacier."

"Oh, sure. Then what?"

"Big bucks. Barge it to Saudi Arabia, sell it for drinking water, a Dixie cup at a time."

"Sure, get the Kool-Aid concession, too. Make a cool million. What kind of salary has Dinsmore promised, by the way. You haven't talked about that."

"Enough to make it interesting. What, by the way, are your own employable skills?"

"I waited tables one summer at Yellowstone, bartended, too. Anyway, I'll find something, something serious. We are going to be serious, aren't we?"

"I think we're trying, aren't we?"

"I think so. I hope so—"

He heard their voices and listened, the sea wind stirring his fine white hair. He had loved an Austrian girl in Vienna once, fifty years ago, or was it longer? He saw her face, her long lashes, her high forehead, her long light hair—through snow, through autumn streets, the cobbled arc-lit corners where they walked, the orange-lit cafés where they'd danced. Fifty years now?

His daughters spoke to him, but he didn't hear, watching the young American couple slowly get up, move to the sea wall for a minute, look out toward the ship, and then stroll on.

"Daddy, *please*. Are you going to order or not?"

Through rain, through summer green, through sifting snow—he would always remember. But then they were out of hearing, the two of them; he wouldn't hear, would know no more, ever again; and then they were gone; the colonnade was suddenly empty, desolately, terribly empty, as sealed as the tomb of memory.

About the Author

W. T. Tyler is the pseudonym of a former foreign service officer with the Department of State. He spent most of his career abroad and was living in Somalia at the onset of the Ethio-Somali war of 1977–78, which forms the background of this novel. He left the diplomatic service in 1980 and now lives in Fauquier County, Virginia. This is his fifth novel.